DREAD KNIGHT

Dread Knight
The Kallattian Saga
Volume Four

Andrew D Meredith

Games Afoot, LLC

Copyright © 2024 by Andrew D Meredith

All rights reserved. No part of this book may be reproduced in any manner whatsoever without written permission except in the case of brief quotations embodied in critical articles and reviews.

First Edition, 2024

Books by Andrew D Meredith

NEEDLE AND LEAF SERIES

THRICE

FOUR-SCORED

FIFE AND DRUM (*UPCOMING*)

SWEAR BY THE SIXTH (*UPCOMING*)

THE KALLATTIAN SAGA

DEATHLESS BEAST

BONE SHROUD

GLOVES OF EONS

DREAD KNIGHT

SIDEWAYS TALES

QUAINT CREATURES: MAGICAL & MUNDANE

*To Dean and Sue,
Your growing legacy both here and in the life to come
continues to be an example to the younger generations.
Thank you for your continual support
and spiritual guidance.*

Forward

The *Kallattian Saga* is a story of separate threads running in various directions, bringing similar decisions to vastly different characters, with wildly different results. Shared experience (in this case, the trauma of that night in the Rose Convent at the end of *Bone Shroud*) does not, however, lead to similar reactions.

That was my hope: to explore the results of those involved and those surrounding them.

I wasn't expecting to explore Aurín Mateau's fate starting in *Gloves of Eons*, and now in *Dread Knight*, but here we are. I love resolution, but I also enjoy providing long-form explorations of different lengths—like different instruments in an orchestral composition coming together under a shared spotlight.

I hope that your time here in Kallattai is a thoughtful one, a relaxing journey, and an exciting adventure. The road ahead is sprinkled with plenty of the things you've come to expect: from legendary stories to dangerous foes. Yet we might end where you least expect...

To the long road ahead and straight!

—*Andrew D Meredith*

Eastern Ganthic

DREAD KNIGHT

ANDREW D MEREDITH

SUMMARY OF EVENTS THUS FAR

After the event at the Rose Convent, Hanen Clouw came into possession of the boneshroud. Escaping the city of Mahn Fulhar and the new occupying religious faction, the Praetors of the Chalice, he and his sister made their way to the city of Haven, capital of Limae. There, Paladins fallen from the faith worked to establish a new order, unifying the dark tools of skyfall metal their sect had developed. Hanen took possession of one of the gauntlets of skyfall, and later, the second, giving him command of the metal. In the culmination of events, he used the gauntlets and a bleeding wound in his shoulder to fully repair the boneshroud, and found a means of destroying skyfall coins. In doing so, he infected a portion of the city with an unknown dream sickness, turning those affected into revenants. At the same time, the city had little time to prepare for the siege brought upon Haven by the Praetors of the Chalice when Ophedia del Ishé brought news of their advancing armies. The city of Haven is now besieged by a tyrannical church bent on dominating any who fall under their influence.

Meanwhile, Katiam Borreau recently returned from the realm of dream to find the Rotha, the seed pod she had been cultivating, was a thinking, speaking creature. Charged with taking it east to find others like it, she and Astrid Glass journeyed into Boroni and then to the city of Waglÿsaor, where the Paladin Pater Zoumerik put the entire city under a stringently enforced code of conduct as penance. Butting heads with the acting Prima Pater Nichal Guess, and Champion of Grissone Jined Brazstein, it was revealed that Zoumerik was a heretic. In a confrontation, Zoumerik was killed, and the Paladins and Paladames continued east, leaving a small handful of Paladins, under the leadership of Dane Marric, to pick up the pieces of the city, and form a truly penitential sect of the church of Grissone.

Lastly, Seriah Yaledít, Monk of Nifara, was made the unassuming messenger of dark gods. In guilt, she fled her order and ended up in Haven, struggling to find purpose, and seeking help from heretic Paladins to take away the feelings of remorse and shame—numbing her mind with skyfall bells. In the Revenant event, she almost became one herself. Instead, she was rescued by the goddess she thought she had betrayed, and was brought back to the land of the living, now with the ability to see the effects of the Dream Realm all around her, even when awake.

PART 1

THE AERIE CITADEL

THE SLAB

THE REVENANT QUARTER

HAVEN CITY

PROLOGUE

The key clattered as it found its home and the lock turned over. The door opened, and the short silhouette of the Pater Minoris filled the entryway, torchlight haloing him as he considered the occupant within.

A chair was offered and he sat, not daring to take another step into the dark space. "It was a rather warm night. Were you quite comfortable, Loth?"

The man sitting on the bed said nothing.

"Nearly two weeks and not a word. It is not like you. I had hoped we might discourse."

Again, no response.

"You've eaten heartily. So I can only assume your choice not to interact a personal one. Very well. I shall continue to provide you what comfort is only proper and kind. But unless you heed my words, unless you accept the opportunities I offer—to return to the faith of Grissone—I fear you shall remain in this room until your life passes away, and you begin a much longer durance in Noccitan."

The older Paladin rose and a guard took away the chair.

"Let us prepare for the evening prayer," the Pater Minoris said.

"Yes, Pater Averin," the guard responded.

The door closed, and Eralt Loth remained unmoved.

Moments passed and he breathed deeply of the darkness.

The bells of the Green Bastion sounded and the susurrus of

others shuffled along the halls. He patiently waited for the sounds to dwindle and darkness to be joined by silence. The temperate air was neither cool nor warm. He took hold of the robe at its hem and lifted. His chest bared to the tepid air felt nothing. He nodded to himself and gave into the nothingness that pressed in around him.

A sound came to him through the nothingness—a whisper once unheeded.

Lights danced before his eyes, formed by his own imagination.
Dream.
The voice hissed the words into and through him. They were not there, and yet, he felt them each night.

Lights behind his eyelids began to coalesce into singular moving forms. They ceased moving and before him, the vision solidified. The grass, once towering trees, gnawed at the soles of his feet. The odd capricör-like creatures with the crescent moon-shaped horns on their heads stood a ways off. The purple skies overhead bore darkening clouds, darker to the horizon.
Seek.
He began his walk. On other nights the desert far off on the horizon could never be reached, distant as it was, his feet weighed down by his frustration. This time, it took him only a few short steps. The sand that stretched out before him was endless. He felt something in his hand. Wood. He still sat upon his bed in his cell.
Let go.
He released his grip on the edge of the bed and it disappeared. The entirety of the desert tilted, and he stood not on a great expanse, but on the edge of a conical sand pit, hundreds of feet to the bottom. The sands shifted and his footing slipped. He attempted to backpedal into the grass of the meadow he had so long desired to leave, but it was not there. Behind him, only purple sand under a stormy sky.

The sands shifted again under his feet and he turned to look back down the bowl as something massive began to rise up out of the shimmering violet. At first, it was a white dome, with a series of holes set about it like an anti-crown. Then emerged two larger, menacing sockets where eyes might once have been, an elongated and inhuman nasal cavity, and finally the teeth of a skull, with larger canines smiling wickedly. If he hadn't known any better, he'd have called it a wyloth skull, and yet there was something distinctly human about it. It rose from the sand, one hundred feet tall. The empty eyes bore into his soul. Then, it opened its jaws, teeth rattling as it spoke.

Finally.

"It was you who called to me?"

Yes.

"Who are you? What are you?"

Direct.

"There is no point in mincing words. If you're a god, then little I say will save me. If you are something else, then we need not dance around one another."

Elsewhere.

"No riddles. What are you?"

Empty.

"Can you provide a means to escape? I've been unjustly imprisoned. Dreaming of another world will not move me from my cell."

Remove me.

"You'll have to give me more than that."

The giant maw opened, rasped, and the sands began to move and shift, falling out from underneath him.

"Stop this! Stop!"

The shifting sand continued to fall away, and suddenly he was sliding down the slope, the blackness of the maw open wide. Loth put his feet out before him, and stopped himself on the teeth, purple sand pouring into the mouth, trying to wash him down the colossal gullet.

Fall.

"No! You'll not consume me!"

The teeth above him lowered down, threatening to sever him in two.

"Oh gods," he said, and leapt down into the darkness. The rasping voice surrounded him in a taunting laugh.

He fell for days, or moments, he did not know. No wind moved with his passing, merely oblivion. He flailed his arms, righted himself, and stood. He had not fallen. He was on a floor.

Someone walked past the door with a torch, providing some light. No bed. No cell. Somewhere else.

His eyes adjusted to the light from the distant torch on a wall outside the room. Approaching the door and reaching for it, his hand met not wood, but the steel of a vault.

Next to a stack of candles by the door he found a tinderbox. He crouched down and struck flint to steel until the tinder took, and lit a candle.

The light revealed the bastion vault. Somehow he had moved from his cell and down the hall, through stone room after stone room, and had arrived in the vault that held the bastion's most valued treasures.

He rummaged around, considering the long-forgotten riches and damaged books intended for repair. Near the door, not far from the supply of candles, a newer item sat that had not been there when the Pater Minoris had shown him the vault upon his arrival. It beckoned his attention.

The burlap sack was in itself inconspicuous. He took the edges and pulled them back to reveal a series of holes punched into a forehead above two vacant eyes.

"The skull from Dream?" he muttered.

Take.

Loth startled, pulled back his hand. He reached out to touch it again, his fingers tracing the holes there.

Take.

It did not surprise him this time. "And do what?"

Make whole.

"If I can escape this new prison," he said. He took up the skull in his hands. It did not feel any different than any other thing in his arms.

Through Dream.

He settled down to the ground, his hand resting on a plinth as he lowered himself. His fingers traced a small satchel of coins—his coins—made of skyfall metal. Averin had taken them from his cell when he was put under arrest. He took hold of the satchel and tied it to his belt, then crossed his legs as he sat on the floor of the vault. The skull lay in his lap as he pinched the candle out, plunging the place into darkness once more.

The hissing of the skull washed over him in a sibilance that drowned out the world.

When he opened his eyes, the sky was purple, and the flat sand beneath him a lighter hue of the same. The skull looked up at him with a wicked smile.

Go.

"Where?"

To me.

From the skull, a thin gray line like the thread of a zvolder's web led out across the expanse. He began the long march across the desert, to unite the inhuman skull with itself.

He was no longer in a cell. No longer a prisoner for actions others took against him unjustly. He was in another world, and he was free.

I

TOLLING BELLS

Breathe unto the hills a prayer,

To the lofty heights rise the requests of the downtrodden,

For an answer shall come upon the winds—

The steadfastness of the pantheon be upon you.

—MORRIG 29:3

The calm of the room and the distance from the purple lights were a solace, even with the grating and constant jingling of the two small bells, suspended on hoops and hung from the blind that covered Seriah's eyes. She ran a hand over her head. It had been too long since a barber had touched her. The rough stubble poked and prodded at her fingertips, and rubbed at the blind on the sides of her head.

The door opened with a wretched creaking, and the heavy, haphazard footsteps of Pater Minoris Pellian Noss entered. He was not a bumbling man, but often the distracted scholar. There was intentionality to how he moved, but it never held any rhythm.

"Holy Nefer," he said in the tight voice of an educated man.

"Why am I being treated as prisoner?"

"What do you mean, Nefer Yaledít?"

"It has been three days," she said, "and your men have done nothing but toss me scraps of food like an ynfald, refusing to answer any of my questions."

"I'm afraid that was on my own orders," he said, dragging out a chair across from her. He did not sit. "Something happened three days ago. I preferred that you stayed in ignorance until I had answers, rather than endanger you."

"What happened?"

"We still do not know. Some...cloud of evil exploded across a quarter of the city. Those that breathed in small portions of the dust appear to be infected with an otherworldly purple light in their eyes. We can make nothing of it."

She had breathed in the dust herself. And died. That violet flame had rushed down her throat, scorching her lungs and mind. Had not her goddess been there...

"Why are you here now?" Seriah asked.

"To apologize for the inconvenience. I brought you to this city. I took you to the citadel to begin proceedings with the Chalicians, and now we've a plague running rampant in the streets and a siege not only unbroken, but pressing at the walls."

"Then they have chosen war?" Seriah asked.

"So it would seem."

"What is the next course of action?"

"Over the past three days I've been in several negotiation sessions with the Black Sentinels. They have offered protection to my fellow Paladins and myself, in response to the siege. But we need a ruling made, in order to make it official."

"I'm only a monk. Not even one of rank."

"That does not mean you bear no authority. We will go into more detail at the citadel, but I do need you to come with me."

"So you apologize, but really, you just need me."

"Nefer Yaledít, why the change of tone?"

"I am certain there is little left for me to fear and I am seeing the world in a clarity that I did not have before."

"Then the bells upon your blind must be working."

Seriah rose. "Shall we go to the citadel?"

"We can go over more of the legal precedence first."

"I'd rather not wait anymore. I should like to hear all sides of the argument at the citadel unprompted."

"I...alright," Noss said. "I'll have the sleipnirs prepared and we'll leave."

Noss left, closing the door behind him.

"Something has changed in her," she heard him mutter on the other side of the door. "Has she acted differently while I was away?"

"No more than asking to speak to you at each meal. She stopped doing that last night."

"And what of the night of the incident?"

"When we returned to the inn, she was completely alone, sitting in her room in silence."

"Very well," Noss said. "See the sleipnirs prepared. We leave within the hour. I'm going to go find food."

Seriah reached through a torn seam of her pillow, taking out the bits of cloth stashed there, and carefully pushed them into the small bells by her ears, muting the ringing that had been plaguing her mind. Then she took up her staff leaning on the wall; the rings jangled where they hung from the single standing ring atop the staff, but they did not have the same effect on her mind as the bells by her ears had done. She turned toward the purple lights off in the distance. They were unmoving, with small wobbles and quivers, still far away, and no threat to her or those around her.

She walked to the door and tapped on it.

"Nefer?" the man without said.

"I am ready to leave."

The door opened. "Pater Noss is not ready."

"He requests I sit in judgment. As judge in the matter, I leave when I decide. And I wish to go to the citadel now."

He hemmed and hawed and then called to another Paladin. "Please inform the Pater that the Nifaran is going to the inn's stable."

No longer in fear of Coldness and his brother, the energy she felt within her gave her an otherworldly bravery.

The scent of sleipnir assaulted Seriah's nose as she entered the stable. She could hear the six hooves of the animals stamping about as other Paladins brushed and saddled them.

A few moments later, Noss barreled into the space, tearing noisily at a piece of bread.

"I had hoped to finish a meal before we left," he said tersely around his bite.

"And it was my hope to not be kept prisoner by a member of a fellow order. I should like to go to the citadel. I'll feel safer there, anyway."

"Then you do not mean to return to this inn?"

"I mean to discuss the best way to resolve this conflict, and then leave the city."

As they began their trek, Seriah gripped the edge of her saddle, her sleipnir following the one before it. No one accosted them. The lack of clinking and clanking led her to believe the Paladins did not wear their regalia, although they did have to slow as they reached a rations line—the assembled crowd grumbling of besiegers to the south. She found herself looking toward the south often, keeping an eye on the purple lights she could still see collected there, even through her blinds.

They cleared the crowd and continued north, the smell of refuse assaulting her along with the sound of bricks grinding against one another.

"What is that noise?" she asked.

"It looks like workers reinforcing a drain," someone said.

"It was discussed in one of the meetings I attended these past few days," Noss said. "When I told the council of the secret entrance by which we entered the city, they began the work, discovering along the way several less palatable means to enter, including this point here. They've been working to stopper them up, without risking a backup of refuse."

"If there is one way, then there is another," another Paladin said.

"What do you mean, Primus?"

"We were led in by two storytellers. If a simple sagasmith can find a way into the city, there are bound to be more."

"They were no mere storytellers," Seriah muttered to herself.

The sounds of the worksite faded as they came to a rise in the city, their mounts stepping up every few paces.

"We enter by way of the front gates this time?" she asked.

"We're now welcomed members of the council," Noss said. "There is no reason to lurk about."

"Then why did we not stay within the citadel itself?"

"Sometimes the safest place to stay is in secrecy."

"But now we ride in broad daylight."

"The time for secrecy has ended."

The ground leveled out and they moved across the courtyard, the clip-clip clop of their six-legged mounts echoing off the walls loudly. Doors before them boomed open, and they moved into the even louder inner courtyard.

Another set of doors opened as Paladins around her dismounted, then helped her down onto the cobbles.

A hand pressed her back and nudged her forward, then let off. She felt her way in, allowing the cool of the interior to envelop her.

The warmth of torches on the walls caressed her at intervals. As they came to a break, she was urged to the right and down a smaller corridor. The final door opened, and the musty scent of a library surrounded her.

"Where is everyone?" Noss asked.

"They were called away," someone said. Her voice was quiet, but confident.

"Not you, Commander Domic?"

"I chose not to go with them. I knew what they were about, and did not need to further enter into that secret. Also, I did not want them to know I knew."

"Rather forward of you to admit that to me," Noss said.

Seriah heard the clink of glass, and the woman spoke from directly next to Seriah.

"Holy Nefer," the woman said. "I've a glass of wine for you. Won't you come and sit?"

Seriah felt her way to a chair and took it. Noss sat next to her, Domic on the other side.

"I admit this to you," Domic said, touching the glass to Seriah's hand and speaking past her, "as I wish you to know what I am about, and where I intend to fit into this new Order of yours."

"Commander Domic, without the other commanders here, it may be best to wait."

"There is no reason to wait," she said. "You haven't."

"What do you mean?"

"You made an offer to the Black Sentinels to join this new Order of yours, offering the opportunity to the commanders to join first. And yet, the first Black Sentinel you offered a role was not even a captain. You intend to make Sentinel Aurín Mateau an Axe before anyone else."

"You're well informed."

"That is my speciality," she said. "As a small, slight woman, I cannot afford to remain uninformed."

"You are right. I did offer it first to Mateau. He approached me, in fact, and I used him to retrieve something. I might have used you, if you were easier to find. I think that Mateau will serve us all well to inspire others to join up."

"The other commanders may not like him becoming one first."

"But not yourself?"

"I've other ambitions."

"Well, the offer stood open. That someone other than a

commander approached me first is of no consequence. The commanders will join, or leave."

"They've already made their decisions, even if they will not state which way they stand. They're all playing a game of Edi-Fożz."

"But no one will make the first move," Noss said.

"Not true," Domic said. "I have."

"Oh, truly?"

"Why else are we sitting here?"

"I think you ought to explain what we're talking about," Seriah said. "If I'm to be involved in this."

"I offered to tell you at the inn," Noss said, an edge of irritation in his voice. "But in short, I am looking to form a new Order, with some specialized tools that have been developed. We have invited the Black Sentinels to join."

"A new Order outside of the Hammer?" Seriah asked.

"With Pariantür abandoning their holdings in the west, there are those of us who do not wish to leave, and do not plan to give the holdings over to the Chalicians."

"Then the meeting I attended was pretense."

"It was meant to open up negotiations," Noss said. "But it was pretense for the Chalicians, too. They never intended to enter the city peacefully. Thus, we ally with the Black Sentinels, to ensure the city is safe."

"From the Chalicians?"

"From the baronets who would sell this city out."

"And," Domic added, "those Sentinel commanders who would use this opportunity to gain additional power."

"A new Order would stand stronger," Noss said. "It will prevent them from just disappearing."

"Why am I here?" Seriah interrupted.

"What do you mean?" Noss asked.

"You've been dragging me around, affording yourself my presence to legitimize your choices. But you intend to do as you wish anyway. What need do you have of me?"

"I desire for you to see the truths in what I teach," Noss said, "to understand our goals and aims. Then, as others come with their questions, you will understand and perhaps explain it to them."

"Then you wish for me to be a legitimization to other monks and orders?"

"Let me ask you this," Noss responded. "Why do the Chalicians hate the Paladins, the Black Sentinels, and the Nifarans?"

"Because we question their rule?"

"Close," Noss said. "I believe it is for the same reason that they persecute the Crysalas: because they act in opposition to the Chalician's actions. They do not allow many Black Sentinels to operate in Œron because of the liberty they represent. But the Nifarans? They do not allow them to work their justice within their nation for that very reason: you represent justice and fairness. And the Chalicians are anything but."

"If they do not allow the Sentinels to work in their lands," Domic said, "they'll surely not work with us if they take a seat in this council."

"Authority, and the right to that authority, will always reign supreme in the mind of a Chalician."

"The leader of the Chalician force, the Catechist, Provost Abrau, seemed to indicate that if he held a seat on the council, he would acknowledge our status," Domic said.

"But only by his grace. If and when he is moved elsewhere, and the authority commission of this city is bought by some other member of their clergy, it will mean nothing. If the baronets are offered a chance to take control, then the Black Sentinels and Paladins will be ousted."

"I do not yet think the baronets know your plans," Domic said. "But I do know what they have planned for themselves."

"Oh?"

"They're hoping to sell the paladinial seats to the Chalicians."

"I don't blame them," Noss said. "Now, what role do you hope to play in all of this?"

"I've made it clear now that intelligence is what I deal in," Domic said, the small woman placing her hand firmly on the table. "I am considered by the others to be the weakest in terms of authority."

"And yet," Noss interrupted, "I've seen the inn you operate from. It would be better called a manor."

"You should see my country estate to the south," Domic said.

"You've done all that by knowledge and intelligence alone?"

"I was a street urchin. Searn offered me a chance back in the day, and I took it."

Seriah's ears burned at Searn's name.

"Well then," Noss said. "I take it you are offering to be the first commander to take up the axe?"

"Yes, and the last."

"What do you mean?"

"I want to be made an Axe in secret. Then, as the others begin to take up the role, the announcement of my joining will tilt the scales. Should there be an adverse reaction by the other commanders, then I shall remain in secret, as an agent of the Axe."

"An interesting proposition," Noss said. "I'd question, though, whether you wouldn't truly be planning to stick a knife in our backs."

"A risk you'll have to take. It's safe to say, without Limaean rule, that I have no power or place in the world. I like my houses too much to move elsewhere and reestablish myself."

"Very well. Then before someone else happens upon us, let's plan to conduct the ceremony in secret."

"I'll come and visit you at the inn," Domic said. "You can make me the Order's Black Knife."

"Good title," Noss said as Commander Domic rose.

A door across the room opened and shut.

"She is gone now," Noss said.

"Domic moves with such silence," Seriah said.

"An admirable trait in a spy."

"You're very comfortable interacting with someone of her trade."

"A side effect of my interactions with the countries our fortress sat between."

"Between Temblin and Hraldor, you mean?"

"I've housed ambassadors and spies in equal numbers, and prevented just as many deaths under my own watch. A spy would much rather lower a knife to throat in threat than actually draw the thin red line."

"What is your true aim?" Seriah asked.

"What do you mean?"

"The Hammer abandons its holdings, and you, a Paladin not from the west, but from the fortress of Piedala, closer to Pariantür than here, marches out to seize this citadel and make a new name for yourself."

"It does appear that way, doesn't it?"

"You've been quick to share with me the goals and aims of the bells and tools at your disposal, not seeming to fear my judgment. Nor do you seem ambitious. I need to know why you do all this."

"I am ambitious," Noss said. "Not for worldly power—but for knowledge. I have so much I wish to learn. And thus, I do what I can to secure knowledge and prevent its destruction, if only to push it out to a time in which I can study it."

"And if you die?"

"I have made arrangements."

"For others to take up that banner."

Noss did not reply.

"Why Limae?" Seriah asked. "Why the country butted up against the western nations?"

"Limae is central to the entire continent. It is a very defensible nation. That's why the Chalicians want it, as we're higher than other nations. You can't just march on Limae and Haven. None but Limaeans have the tenacity to fight in the mountain air. If Limae can be convinced to defend itself, for the sake of its continual freedom, it proves a point."

"That is?"

"That humanity is strong. And it is the world of Kallattai that should fear it, not the other way around."

This time it was Seriah who remained quiet.

"You've known fear," Noss said. "It was why you were so quick to adopt our bells."

"You do not know the fear I have faced."

"I know you were witness to the death of your Archimandrite."

"How do you know this?"

"Word spreads. I was in the city at that time, as well."

"Yet that was not the most fearful thing I faced while there." Seriah's breathing increased to a manic pace. "Nor was it being met at the judgment tree by Coldness and his Brother."

"Coldness?"

"That was when I was made to deliver a message to my own goddess by those two."

"Who is Coldness?"

"What kind of scholar are you? That you do not know the names of the Cursed gods? That you cannot recognize with your own eyes when they travel with us, and stay in our very inn, under your nose?"

"What do you mean?" Noss asked.

"You invited them into our company. You let them stay. Your bells may have kept them from harming me, but what did I matter to them? I had already done their bidding. Who can know what secrets you gave them? Or by what means they now have you under their bond of promise?"

"Cease your rambling, woman, and tell me plainly what you mean!" Noss shouted.

Seriah leaned back in her chair, and sighed. "Pater Noss, you have no doubt been inexorably tied to my fate. You delivered me to that Judgment Tree, where I first met Nair and Kash, then you delivered me to this city, and those same two storytellers showed us the way in. They may not be here now, but if you have made any deals with those two, then you have sold your soul to the Deceiver and his brother, the Mad Gift-Giver."

"You lie," Noss hissed.

"In this, I cannot lie. I have been chosen, not once, but twice."

"They were mere storytellers."

"They were not. And now, through their machinations, we're stuck in this city, with the ghosts of war haunting the streets."

"I...made no deals," Noss muttered to himself. "I made them no promises, save vapid hospitalities."

"And in that?" Seriah said, smirking. "You are caught in their web, as I was. Am."

"Where is the timid, quiet monk who came to the city with me?" Noss retorted.

"Tired. Tired of being pulled around by my nose. I wish to leave this city and return to Birin, to face those I fled."

"Such a change..."

"I have faced death. Others and my own. And I have been pulled back from the brink by saint, sinner, and deity."

"I believe you," Noss said. "If we're in this prison together, perhaps we can escape together."

"You will not escape the deceits. Not so long as you continue on the path you tread."

"Silence, monk," Noss said. He banged on the table and the side door opened. Someone approached.

"I have decided to change our plans," Noss told the person. "Return the Holy Nefer to the inn. We'll keep one of our number to watch over her, but she'll not stay at the citadel. See a sleipnir prepared."

The person left.

"Can't stand the sight of me?" Seriah asked.

"If I decide that you may return to the safety of the citadel I'll give the word. For now, you'll stay at that awful inn."

Seriah rose from her seat and followed the clinks of another Paladin from the room. She turned back to Noss as she reached the door. "The prison you are in at the citadel will be far worse."

2

Blind Flight

Trust thine ears and touch, to discern lies and unveil wickedness.

—NIFARAN TREATISE 456:89

The din of carousing at the tavern across the street would have kept Seriah awake if she had been trying to sleep. If she had not left the tiny bells on the side table by the bed. If her heart wasn't racing.

A short while ago the entire tavern had roared with men and women trying not to think of the occupying force outside the walls. Now a single table of the most dedicated drinkers laughed at one another, ignoring the aggressive tankard polishing from the barkeeper.

Across the back of her door, Seriah's staff acted as a jam, the rings atop covered with a travel cloak, bound tightly with a leather strap. Her cowl was stuffed into her satchel, which lay across her chest. She had complained to the Paladin escorting her back to the inn that she had been cold at night, and he had given her several dank sleipnir blankets. She'd folded them neatly, hoping they'd help mask her appearance when she made her move.

The sound of the innkeeper seeing the men to the door finally floated across the street. Seriah stood from her bed and shuffled to the wall, placing her ear against it. The Paladin in the next room was snoring loudly.

She lifted the staff from the door and pulled back slowly. To her relief it did not creak.

Wrapping one blanket around her head and shoulder she pulled her satchel over her frame to tie it against her. She took up her staff, the rings muffled in the cloak and straps. She moved on woolen socks down the hall, but she froze as a floorboard under her creaked at her passing. The sound of the other Paladin's uninterrupted snoring gave her the courage to continue and she took a wider step over the board, matched her pace with his snoring, and came to the landing at the top of the stairs.

She hugged the wall as she descended. The embers in the main room's hearth popped, but gave little warmth. The heavy bar across the door to the stable pivoted on a swivel. She lifted one end and opened the door. As she pushed her way through, the bar almost swung back and slammed, but she caught it, and took out her small knife and touched it to the bar, sliding the knife down as the door closed, lowering the bar in place. Instead of dropping with a loud wooden thud, it fell from the knife with a small clap.

She breathed a sigh of relief and turned to the stables. Two sleipnirs snorted in their stalls as she passed to the side door. It was lashed with a strong leather strap which she had little trouble unbinding, opening the door to the cold, mountain fresh, night air. She hung the strap on a hook by the door, as though it had been forgotten by the innkeeper, and then pulled the blanket once more up and over her head, far enough down to hide that she had the blinder over her eyes.

The late night streets were quiet. She traced the turns they had taken to get to the citadel and took deep breaths, trying to follow her nose. The whiff of sewage played on the breeze and she knew she was headed in the right direction.

A small commotion rose from an alley nearby—whispered voices shushed one another.

She continued walking confidently forward.

She felt someone exit the alley and approach her, carefully, but not threateningly. Her grip tightened on her staff.

"Pardon," the woman approaching said politely. "What are you doing out this late at night?"

She stopped and turned to face her.

"Why do you ask?" Seriah replied.

"There is a curfew, enforced by the worst of men, and you carry yourself as someone blind. Do you know it is night?"

"I have Day Blind," Seriah lied.

"Then come with us. We'll keep you safe."

"Who are you? And how can I know you're to be trusted?"

"By the Rose and Thorn," the woman said.

Seriah sighed a relief. "You are Crysalas?"

"Yes."

Seriah smiled and moved to go with her. She stopped.

"Prove it to me," she said.

The woman paused. "You are wise to ask that. What proof I can offer is that we seek to protect, and we make arrangements for women, should the Chalicians enter the city."

"What of the Chalicians?"

"They persecute the Crysalas. We'll not have anyone under their thumb that does not welcome them."

"I thank you for the offer," Seriah said. "But I will have to decline. Not because I do not believe you, but because I have my own means to escape persecution."

"A blind woman with a way out of the city?"

"I believe so."

"Please, wait here," the woman said, and ran off. A few moments later, she returned.

"This is the woman," she said.

"She knows of a way out?" an older voice said. Seriah recognized it. They had been forced to the ground alongside one another before Searn VeTurres. It was the voice of the Prima Pater, Dorian Mür.

"She says she does," the woman said.

"What way is it?" another familiar voice asked. Rallia Clouw. "We've twenty men and woman all seeking a means out."

"Odd that you have no plan," Seriah replied.

"We know of one possible way," Rallia said.

"It will work," Dorian retorted.

"This woman, blind as she is, does not trust me yet enough," the first woman said.

"I do now," Seriah said, pulling back the blanket from her head.

Rallia gasped.

"Well…" Dorian said. "What providence."

"How are you here?" Rallia asked. "Last I heard, you and the monks had fled Mahn Fulhar, without a word to the Black Sentinels."

"It is safe to say we no longer trusted your organization after what Searn did."

"And yet," Dorian said, "you're here, in a city run by the Moteans."

"Another reason to leave," Seriah said.

"By what means?"

"When I came into this city, it was after the gates were barred," Seriah said. "Those who accompanied me took us in through a secret way. It was revealed to the city leaders, who blocked it up, but uncovered additional routes into and out of the city. There is one not far from here, the mortar is likely still fresh. I go there to leave."

"If you will allow, I'd like to go with you, with the refugees we're helping escape the city," Dorian said. "Rallia, let us see our friends away."

Rallia and the other woman walked away to the side alley.

"How is it you are here in Limae?" Seriah muttered to Dorian.

"It was a long road, but this is where I am," Dorian replied.

"Are you leaving the city as well?"

"I am not, but we could not refuse help to those in need. Especially when a member of the Crysalas spotted me on the street."

"Then you are in hiding," Seriah said.

"I am dead, Seriah," Dorian said. "At least, that is what most of the world thinks."

"I wonder if I am, too," Seriah muttered to herself.

"I'm sorry?" Dorian replied.

"Never mind," she said dismissively. "I'd like to see this city behind me."

Dorian took her arm as they began walking down the street.

"Where will you go after this?" Dorian said. "Perhaps back to Birin? To tell your leadership what has transpired?"

"I don't even understand all that has transpired."

"I'm still piecing that together myself," Dorian said. "Rallia and I were up near the citadel when an explosion covered a quarter of the city in a dark cloud."

The thought of that night sent a shiver down her spine as they turned toward the Revenant Quarter. She could see pricks of purple light visible through her blinder where Revenants stood or shambled in their half sleep.

"Are you alright?" Dorian asked.

"No."

"But you don't wish to talk of it."

"I don't."

They walked along in a now very awkward silence. The stench of sewage grew.

"Over there," Seriah said.

"Where?"

"Follow the smell," she said. "That is where they were working, to shore up a defense."

"Then we'll move people out through that," he said.

"Who are you helping escape?"

"Women and elderly Œronzi who can offer little help in a siege, with no desire to be once again under Œronzi rule."

"I don't blame them."

"Where are we going?" Rallia asked as she approached.

"Down through there," Dorian said.

"I'll scout ahead," she said, walking past them.

"You trust her?" Seriah asked.

"Should I not?"

"The Clouws served under Searn. How do we know they do not share his goals and visions?"

"They've proven themselves to me, and our goals align."

"Searn was a liar. What leads you to believe they are not?"

"Gut instinct," Dorian said, "tells me that they have a part to play. In Rallia especially, I see my childhood friend, who it turns out, is their great-grandfather. I'll not betray that feeling."

They stood in silence for a long while.

"Ah!" Dorian said. "Rallia is coming up out of the hole now."

The patter of Rallia's boots rushed toward her.

"Run!" she hissed as she took hold of Seriah's arm and began pulling her away.

"What's happening?" Seriah asked.

"Soldiers down there coming into the city," Rallia huffed. "The hole is already being used by invaders."

"They were hot on your heels!" Dorian shouted.

The sound of boots behind them resounded in the square.

Dorian pulled them into the alley.

"How far to the inn?" Dorian asked.

"Four or five corners," Rallia said. "But the others?"

"Sounds like we need to send a signal."

The old man next to her began muttering a prayer.

"If I tell you to run," Rallia said quietly from her side, "do what you can."

"What's happening now?"

"Twenty Œronzi soldiers came up through the construction, with a Praetor of the Chalice leading them."

"No one from the city knows," Seriah said, a panic rising in her voice. "They'll silence anyone they find."

"No they won't," Dorian said under his breath. "Both of you, close your eyes, and Rallia, be prepared to act with me."

"I don't need to close my..." Seriah said as a brilliant flash she could see even from beneath her eye blind lit everything. Rallia's silhouette stood out in stark contrast. As soon as the flash subsided, Rallia rushed away into the street. The sounds of conflict reverberated off the brick walls. Men cried out, lamenting their sudden blindness as Rallia and Dorian descended upon them.

A new silence fell.

Seriah gasped as someone took her hand.

"Come on," Rallia said. "Let's get somewhere safe."

"Where are we going?" Seriah asked.

"Depends on the day," Rallia laughed. "Dorian and I have a couple of small abandoned homes we've been able to hole up in. We'll keep you safe."

3

Crossroads

I am told of the man who passed through your congregation and was shown no bed, nor given bread. By what means is this? And by what reason? The wrath of the Anka is upon your own head if you do not make amends.

—HAMULEON 24

Twelve sleipnirs bearing six Paladins and five Paladames crested the forested hill, bringing into view the Garrou tidal plain. The Garroulon River ran from south to north and into the tidal delta to the west of the city, rising from the opposing hill a full day's ride away. With the tide out, hordes of people moved across the sand, scouring the beach. To the far south, a flotilla of boats sat beached near a smaller town, though by no means all that small. The forest they rode through stretched north a ways, but its edge could be seen long before the northern scablands took over and stretched to the horizon. Over the tops of the trees a newer watchtower stood halfway down to the floor of the valley. A single guard gave a wave and Jined waved back.

Primus Jined Brazstein's heavy eyebrows and thrice-broken nose might have caused many to think his face bore a passive glower. As all Paladins of the Hammer, his head was shaved, and he wore his full regalia, from the plates strapped across his legs under a leather skirt, to the plate across his chest and arms, and most importantly the signature tower gorget that rose from his shoulders, all but covering his chin. Across his armored chest black cordons hung, with three vow beads nestled together, one for each vow he had taken upon himself: chastity, poverty, and most recently, prayer.

From his belt, twenty-two links ran, terminating at the end of the haft of his two-headed hammer, which for the time-being sat across his lap.

Jined adjusted his rein-hold atop a black six-legged sleipnir purchased from a farmer just past the Bortali dunes. The farmer had insisted that the huge stallion had been born and raised a plow-sleipnir, but Jined had found it took orders normally reserved for Northern Scape nobility. It had side-stepped a log with a parade-like prance, and once, when a small drækis crossed his path, it had calmly reared back on its four hind legs without so much as a panicked whiney.

He leaned forward, running his gloved hands through the majestic animal's white-gray mane, another indication of higher breeding than the farmer let on, and patted his neck as it pulled back its massive head with pride.

"What do you think, Tyv?" Jined asked the animal as Prima Pater Nichal Guess pulled his sleipnir up next to Jined.

Nichal's sleipnir, a smaller stallion, although still the largest of the sleipnirs they had brought from Waglÿsaor, swung his head at the cold-blooded destrier.

Like Jined, Nichal's pale skin had been slightly burned red from passing through the dunes to the west.

"Did the watchtower notice us, Jined?" Nichal asked. He bore a permanent look of worry upon his face. The worry lines had grown deeper over the winter and budding spring—an attestation to the new role he had taken on.

"They did," Jined said. "They don't give any indication of trouble."

Another figure came up out of the hatch in the top of the tower. The first guard pointed to the two of them. The second figure wore the trappings of a silver-armored Paladame.

"A sister," Nichal said.

"Shall we send Astrid ahead then, to prepare and make introductions?"

"Yes, and Silas."

"Silas has proven valuable as your Seneschal," Jined said.

"He has. Though he has much to learn, and bears a great deal of stress."

"He probably gets that from you," Jined said with a smile.

"Is it showing?"

"Nichal," Jined said, "I've never not known you to bear the weight of the world upon your shoulders."

Nichal gave a weak smile back. "It is a sad thing, how few of us are left. The entourage had what, thirty Paladins when we journeyed from Pariantür?"

"That sounds about right."

"Now we number eleven. Only six of us left from Pariantür."

"We've made new friends along the way."

"Didus seems to do well in our company," Nichal said. "At times he reminds me of Killian Glass."

"He may not be as cheerful as Killian was," Jined said, "but I know what you mean. Pater Koel is a very passionate person. He and the twins get along well."

"And you?"

"Me, what?"

"Do you get along with him?"

"I do, though I often have trouble not deferring to him as a Pater Minoris."

"I'm a Pater Segundus. You have no difficulty being familiar with me, rank or not."

"You are Prima Pater, Nichal. Until the day you are not, you ought to remember that."

"Oh, I know."

"I'm comfortable with you, due to how long we've served alongside one another. Even before this journey."

"It's funny," Nichal said.

"What is?"

"Not a year and a half ago, I was berating you after you'd gotten into another fight."

"With Brother Hivvello?"

"Yes. He had broken your nose over some silly thing, and yet he had lost that fight, bruised all over. I forget what started it."

"He had been mocking my nose, almost daily, for over a month. So I broke my nose on his. What is funny about that?"

"The game turned. You are the one berating me now, for not acting my station."

"Hardly berating you," Jined said. "Just...encouraging you to do so."

"The same thing, Jined," Nichal said.

The rest of the entourage caught up with the two of them,

starting in on the final switchback to the top of the rise.

The twins took the lead, Cävian holding aloft the Standard of Grissone, with sculpted book and four wings of the Anka, bright gold and shining in the sun. His brother Loïc rode just behind him. Cävian made a joke with one hand to Loïc, who responded with a silent laugh. They both bore the sun-dark skin of Seterans, and sat under the Vow of Silence.

After them rode the Paladames. Astrid Glass led the women, wearing her full regalia on display: her silver armor over white garments was embossed with rose motifs. The fine chain hanging across her arms and shirt was framed by plates in the shape of leaves. Upon her blonde head she wore a silver diadem of leaves with a rosebloom in the center.

Behind her rode the short and curvy, raven-haired Katiam Borreau, her pale face off-set by a brown traveling cloak pulled about her. Next to her was the dark-skinned botanist, Esenath Chloïse, a stern woman with shaven head, bearing brown garments rather than white.

Next came two younger girls. Onelie Clemmbäkker plucked at a small bowl-backed instrument. She was every bit a seventeen-year-old girl of the Northern Scapes, unaware of her surroundings, and yet, watching all of the others with the wary eye of someone trying to fit in. Beside her rode the now-veiled and hooded Maeda Salna, who responded to the epithet "Little Maeda." She had been badly burned in the incident at the Saor and so covered her entire body, refusing to show any of her face. She rode stoically, ignoring the constant chatter and humming of the young girl next to her. On a lead walked the pack-sleipnir just behind them.

Lastly, Pater Didus Koel and Brother Silas Merun took up their positions as rearguard. Merun hung on Koel's every word. Both had been victims of the Motean uprising the winter before: Silas Merun, a captive at the bastion of St. Nonn, and Pater Koel under the gauntlet's oppression, his mind enslaved by heretics before being freed by Jined.

All came to a stop alongside Jined and Nichal.

"It appears the watchtower below has a Paladame in residence," Nichal said to Astrid. "She was summoned by the watch and our position pointed out."

"I'll ride ahead, then," Astrid said, "and make arrangements for the stay."

"If they'll have us, that would be good."

Astrid did not hesitate, but urged her mount down the hill.

"She does remind me of Mother Smith at times."

"She's less stern," Jined said. "There is still a pent-up joy beneath the surface, locked away after her brother died."

Nichal laughed. "That's true. Smith has most likely never smiled. Not that I've ever seen, anyway. And I'd certainly never ask her to. She'd probably tear my arm off for the suggestion."

After a long while, two sleipnirs rode up the hill, Astrid atop one, and a red-headed Paladame on the other. As they came nearer, Jined recognized the second as a Paladame who'd ridden with them during most of their journey in his home country of Boroni.

"Prima Pater Guess," Astrid said as they pulled up short, "I'd like to reintroduce you to Sister Toire Siobh, both Paladame and Shieldmaiden, as well as daughter of Rhi Barra of Bronue Jinre."

Nichal lowered his head slowly in respect.

"I offer my sorrow for the loss of your previous Prima Pater," Toire said. She had a thick Bronuan brogue, but it was tempered with the clear speech of a court-trained lady.

"With heavy heart, we journey eastward," Nichal said. "Are their arrangements to be made for us at the tower?"

"That will entirely depend on the decision you make, after we've shared the news with you," Astrid said.

"What news?" Nichal asked.

"King Vorso has become even more paranoid over the winter," Astrid said. "He's not accepting many into his city. Toire is here because news travels quickly, and this entourage has not traveled unnoticed."

"I rode out from Garrou myself, to see what you were about, and to escort those I could back to the city," Toire said.

"We'd appreciate the escort," Nichal said.

Astrid winced.

"What is it, Sister Glass?"

"Toire can only take the Crysalas. I lied to the tower guards and said that you Paladins were escorting us from Waglÿsaor, and then returning the way you came. They were readying riders to send to Garrou to warn the king of your arrival, and guards were preparing to detain you if you came down to the tower."

"Detain?"

Toire held up a calming hand. "Let me be brief."

Nichal indicated for her to continue.

"Over the winter, Vorso cut off ties with most other countries, save my own father. Something changed a month ago, however. My father sailed from our city of Œndin, to the city north of here, Igahli, and was stopped there by the Bortali forces. He's been there ever since. Garrou now refuses any and all. I alone was granted permission, as ambassador from my father. Vorso fears my father rides under pretense, and will commit to war on Garrou. Add to that, a new ship is said to have arrived in Igahli not a week ago, coming from Mahn Fulhar, bearing members of the Œronzi church. The Chalicians had come to Œndin, and upon hearing my father was in Igahli, they proceeded there to speak to him. The last note I received from my father was that the head of the delegate, Provost Zehan Otem, was trying to convert him to the faith, and he had no desire to capitulate."

"Is there a worry that he will?" Nichal asked.

"Not from me. The Chalicians are known for their persecution of the Crysalas churches. My dead grandmother would rise from her grave and haunt my father if he betrayed the Crysalas."

"Very well. If we're not welcome in Garrou, where are we to go? We're not returning to Waglÿsaor."

"I aim to escort the sisters under your care to Garrou, and from there we can make arrangements to have them safely moved eastward," Toire said. "I will endeavor to convince the king to be amenable, to you and my father. Perhaps you might proceed north, to Igahli, meet with my father, and help him rebuff the Chalicians."

"I'd hate to think what might happen should this Provost Otem arrive in Garrou," Jined said.

"I'd like to know what's happened in Mahndür since we left," Nichal said. He turned back to Toire. "Very well, Sister Siobh. Swear to the safety of the sisters and escort them to the safety therein. I will ride north to aid your father."

Toire gave a bow. "We'll look for you and my father from the walls of Garrou."

Can she be trusted? Loïc signed in the hand language of the Paladins of the Vow of Silence.

Astrid took her hands from her reins. *She can. Her father has been an advocate for resolving the burgeoning war with peace and trade.*

But will the Crysalas be safe in Garrou? Jined added.

No less safe than on the road, Astrid signed.

Try not to stay there long, Jined signed. *No more than a week.*
Unless we're needed there, Astrid signed back.

Toire had turned away from Nichal, and Astrid joined her as they gathered the women to speak in hushed tones. In response, Nichal dismounted, and guided his sleipnir aside, indicating for the other Paladins to do the same.

"It looks like Garrou remains unwelcoming," Nichal said. "So we'll be staying out of doors again tonight, and then riding north."

"Astrid indicated that she trusts the Shieldmaiden," Jined said. "So we need not worry about the Crysalas."

"Still, I'd like to get north, assess the situation, and then proceed southeast," Nichal said.

"Then we can ride on Wings of Faith and make haste," Jined said.

"I'd appreciate a night of rest before we do so," Didus said.

But the evening is young, Cävian signed. *We could make our way down through these woods on foot, reach the bottom, and possibly ride hard all night. We could see Igahli by morning.*

"What do you think, Jined?" Nichal asked.

"I'd like to rest as much as anyone else, but I also know of a nice inn just south of Igahli. We could make for there and get rest before entering the city."

"I do like the sound of a comfortable inn," Didus said.

"That settles it for me," Nichal determined. "Let's ride."

If we can find our way through this forest, Loïc said.

The Crysalas made their way down the road and out of view as the Paladins led their sleipnirs through the forest growth.

The sky darkened overhead, and Silas and Loïc lit torches.

"Such an uncared-for forest of old growth," Didus said.

"More the reason we should get past this," Jined said. "I don't like that we need torches. We're begging for trouble."

"Afraid we'll light the place aflame?"

"Drawing bad attention to us."

"You think the watchtower is out here watching us?"

"Or worse," Jined said. "There is no knowing if there are vül out here, or Üterk."

"Vül I understand, but Üterk?" Koel asked.

"If this is one of their forests, then we're trespassing. Even if it's not, they may give us trouble. Add to that, while we rode east, the Sisters confided to me that the Saor is said to be important to the Üterk. That a Paladin tore it down, heretic or not, probably doesn't sit well with them."

"The ground is leveling out," Didus said.

Silas's torch could be seen farther out in the grass past the edge of the woods. Loïc and Cävian joined him.

I'm going to range ahead, Loïc signed as they came near enough to see him in the torchlight.

"No need," Jined said. "I recognize where we are now."

He pointed north to a rocky outcropping, lit by the setting red moon, Norlok, on one side, and on the other the rising white Umay.

"The road from Igahli circles south around those rocks on the way to Garrou. We were only a few hundred yards from the road the whole time."

The six Paladins mounted up, and crossed the field at an easy pace. A small stream ran alongside the road, and they let the sleipnirs pause to drink.

"How long is the ride from here to Igahli?" Nichal asked. "If you were traveling without prayer."

"I made the trip a couple of times as a young man. It was generally a three to four days' easy ride."

"A hundred miles then."

"Do you think Jurgon has made it to the College?" Silas asked.

"I doubt he's made it to the south end of Bortali yet," Jined said. "Especially with all of those children in his care."

"I bet they're a sight to see," Nichal chuckled.

They've been on our minds, Cävian signed. *Aren't those woods to the south dangerous?*

We've been praying for their safety, constantly, Loïc added.

"Most woods in Bortali are dangerous," Jined said.

"Then as we pray our way north," Nichal said. "Let us all turn our hearts to Jurgon and the Mooneyes traveling with him."

They urged their mounts back up on the road and spread out across it with Cävian holding the Standard of Grissone in the lead position. He and his brother began signing, and the other four joined in prayer audibly as they sped up to a gallop.

"Grissone-Anka lift us up.
   Our faith lies in you.
  Give us your wings.
    We shall fly.
    We shall fly.
    We shall fly."

On and on they repeated those words. Jined took solace in them as the wind whipped around them, carving away at the hundred miles. The sleipnirs gave no indication of tiring as the silver moon reached the top of the sky, and the eastern horizon bloomed with light.

Nichal pressed his mount to the lead and motioned for them all to slow to a canter. Loïc and Cävian continued their motions with their hands, and they all came to a stop as they crested a hill and the sea breeze came upon them from every side.

Igahli sat upon a peninsula perhaps ten miles across, featureless and flat. A few bushes grew here or there and from their viewpoint, the five lighthouses stationed on its shores could be seen, although, in the fading night, their flames could not. Farmsteads with shaggy sleipnirs and even shaggier capricör dotted the landscape. At the north end, the city of Igahli sat as a high-walled fortress.

"Mostly livestock then?" Nichal asked.

"The breeding of the sleipnirs is sought by those farther north, across the Lupinfang," Jined said. "Their main trade is in hardy capricör wool, and the few root vegetables that grow here. The wind prevents much more than that."

"Is it always this windy then?" Didus asked.

"Always," Jined said.

I can't even imagine, Loïc signed. *It would get on my nerves.*

"It gets on the nerves of those that live here, too," Jined said.

"Where is this inn you spoke of?" Nichal asked.

"I'll lead the way."

They rode well into the morning at a normal pace and soon came to a crossroads. To the west and east the first two lighthouses could be seen, with the sea lying just beyond both. The Stone Cask Inn was a sprawling affair, dug down into the earth with no second story. Jined dismounted and led Tyv to the stable doors and knocked.

A boy peered out, his eyes starting at seeing the six Paladins. He opened the door wide, and they each dismounted and entered. A ramp took them down to the earthen floor, and each sleipnir was given its own stall. Another boy was summoned from the kitchens to help, and along with the Paladins they unsaddled, brushed, and made their mounts comfortable.

The boys showed them to a room with a large bed for Nichal and several stacked beds along the wall. As one of the boys built up the fire, the other led them into the common room, which bore a low ceiling with rafters Jined almost knocked his head against. Behind the bar, large stoneware vessels, rather than barrels, sat off the ground on a brick shelf. The proprietor was a stern-looking man with furrowed eyebrows. His wife wore a heavy, voluminous woolen shawl over her head and down to her heels. She looked up at their entrance and came out from behind the bar to give a low curtsy.

"Many greetings, Holy Paladins," she said.

"Hello Aelasaev," Jined said.

"Do I know…" she said, looking up at Jined. She started back a step, her hand going to her chest. "By Aben, Crysania, and the saints—Jined?! Beneven! Look who it is!"

The man behind the bar scowled for a moment and then his face broke into a wrinkled smile. He suddenly leapt over the bar.

Jined and Beneven stared at each other for a long moment, then threw themselves into an embrace.

Aelasaev had her hands clasped together, but then could no longer contain herself and wrapped her arms about him, joining the hug with a joyous cry. The others stood around, watching the moment awkwardly. Finally, Aelasaev pushed Jined out to arm's length.

"It's been ten years, Jined! We heard a rumor you'd died!"

"Not entirely untrue," Jined said. "Ben, did Aela finally get you to settle down?"

"I still watch the lighthouse once a week, so my father can go into town."

"You're both in charge of the inn now?"

"My parents left to join family in the Isles a few years ago."

"And those two boys who helped us settle our mounts—are they yours?"

"Torbal and Duvlas, yes."

"It is so good to see the two of you," Jined said, with a broad smile plastered across his face.

"Jined?" Didus said.

"Ah!" Jined said, turning. "Aelasaev and Beneven, I would like to introduce to you the Prima Pater of the Paladins of the Hammer, Nichal Guess."

The two innkeepers gasped and dropped to the ground.

"No need for that," Nichal said, motioning for them to stand.

"To what do we owe this honor?" Beneven asked.

"We're journeying to Igahli, to speak to someone."

"The Rhi of Bronue Jinre is currently visiting his sister, married to the Duke of Igahli," Aelasaev said.

Jined nodded.

"Well," Beneven said, "please make yourself comfortable, and we'll see you well-fed."

"It has been a very long road," Didus added. "That sounds wonderful."

Nichal gave the two of them a respectful nod and proceeded toward the large hearth as Beneven rushed ahead to begin feeding the embers. Jined took a seat next to Nichal.

"How do you know them?"

"They've long lived here, and my father often visited the area when negotiating with the lords of Ighali," Jined said.

"Then you stayed here?"

"My father always prefers to stay at local inns, to spread out his influence. Aelasaev's parents, Bronuans from the Isles, built this inn. Beneven was son of the nearby lighthouse keeper. I've always known they would get married."

Beneven approached with both boys in tow, all with stoneware tankards in their hands. The ale was a frothy, grainy drink—more bread than beer. It was refreshing, and Jined sat back and sighed.

"Drink as heartily as you would like," Beneven said. "I'm off to nearby friends to see if he has a capricör worthy of a fine meal."

"Thank you, Beneven," Jined said.

Beneven smiled. "It is so good to see you, Jined."

"And you, Ben," he replied.

4

A Shared Meal

Suffer not the indignity of a haughty man. The lye upon his tongue makes its own bitter soap in his mouth.

—SACRED WORD OF MINU THE GENTLE 4:78

The city of Igahli sat as low to the ground as the Stone Cask Inn, hugging the shallow bowl that led down to the shore. The streets were narrow and set even lower, while the constant wind whistled overhead. The city walls acted as the main thoroughfare, circling the city, and rising toward the keep, built out and away from those walls. The piers down at the water housed mostly fishing boats, but several larger vessels had been docked for repairs, and out on the water, several Bortalian war vessels sat at anchor.

Igahli Keep was made of gray stone, and rather than rising up from the gate, dropped down below the rim.

Nichal Guess rode up to the gate with Cävian and Jined at his sides. The guards that had admitted them to the city had marched ahead and disappeared into the keep. Before Jined had the chance to announce Nichal, the doors boomed open and a Bortalian soldier stood in the entryway. Across his green uniform he wore a tartan tabard of reds and purples. His beard and hair were a rich auburn, and his boots were black and well-cared for.

"Greetings, Prima Pater, I am Duke Rogvan," the man said. "I welcome you to my city. Please, follow me to our stables."

Nichal urged his sleipnir across the stone walkway. "The

kindest greeting we've ever received in Bortali."

"The Igahlians are a different people. Almost more Bronuan than Bortalian."

"Like Clehm?"

"More so," Jined said. "Clehm in Boroni adopts more northern Bronuan traditions, which in turn has more Nasunian traditions. Those all harken back to the old traditions of the north."

Nichal dismounted and gave a curt bow to the duke. "I did not expect to be greeted personally by a duke."

"I make a habit of greeting all my guests," Rogvan said. "You also come at quite the opportune time."

"Oh?" Nichal reponded.

The duke took hold of Nichal's reins and they walked across an inner courtyard to the stables. "I have received several important guests over this past week. Your arrival could not have been more perfect as we're in the middle of a very interesting discussion. Bringing you up to speed and getting your opinion will be rather helpful."

"I look forward to hearing more," Nichal said.

"Are you refreshed? Do you need refreshment?"

"We stayed the evening at the Stone Cask Inn all of yesterday before coming."

"A comfortable establishment, indeed. I'll explain more later, but I believe it would be in your best interest if you stayed there, despite the ride to and from the city. I do not deny you my hospitality without reason."

"Intriguing, to say the least," Nichal said. "We shall endeavor not to be a burden."

"You are not! Please do not misunderstand me. Let us go to my study."

They moved into the dark hallways of the keep and down flights of stairs to a drafty study with several chairs around a roaring fire attempting to fight back the chill.

The duke indicated toward the chairs and the six Paladins took them. The duke acted the host himself and drew ladles of white beer similar to what the inn had served, brought over in large-mouthed bowls.

Having served his guests, he took his place in a chair across from Nichal.

"I would love to hear of your travels and know you better, but in all urgency, it is important I speak with you before we're interrupted, because we will be interrupted."

Nichal took a sip and waved a hand for him to proceed.

"In short, I have two other important guests. My wife's brother, the Rhi of Bronue Jinre, came to visit just ahead of the other—Provost Zehan Otem, come from Mahn Fulhar. I'll tell you this: they do not get along at all. It doesn't help that when Otem journeyed first to Œndin he was turned away by Barra there."

"I have not met this Praetor of the Chalice," Nichal said.

"He is second to the head of the order, as I understand it. He converted Mahn Fulhar to his sect over the winter. He's now circling the Lupinfang, with a mission to do the same everywhere."

"Did he stop in Boroni?" Jined asked.

"I do not think so. He comes here with the sole purpose of continuing on to Garrou. I do not like it one bit."

"You are not of a mind to join his cause?"

"My wife is Bronuan—sister to the Rhi, as I mentioned. The Isles of Bronue Jinre are, as you likely know, quite loyal to the older faiths of both Aben and Crysania, what with the Shieldmaidens having such a presence. They do not take kindly to sects that preach the subjugation of anyone, most particularly women. They keep the laws and records in the warp and weft of their wool."

"And Rhi Barra," Nichal said, "he is here to see you do not buckle?"

Rogvan shook his head. "That is no fear. He is here to support me and to enable me to negotiate with our king in Garrou, on his behalf."

"He'll not be continuing on to Garrou then?"

"If he runs on ahead of every stop this Otem makes, I do not doubt that it will cause the Chalicians to go to war against his Isles. He cannot police the inner workings of the nations around the Lupinfang, but he can shore up his own friendships."

"Very well. Then what do you hope my appearance will attain?" Nichal asked.

"A show of solidarity from the Grissoni Church here may help. I understand that there are things happening in Waglÿsaor, and I should like to know the news."

"It would be best not to bring up Waglÿsaor in your negotiations," Nichal said. "We have left the city under the care of two Paladins who mean to reform the city. That will be done best in isolation. If Otem turns his gaze there, a fire might be reignited."

"Very well. And what of Boroni? Do they intend to war with Bortali?"

"Only if Bortali will go to war with them."

"The commanders want it, that much is certain, but not all dukes of Bortali agree."

"That is good to hear. Are there any Paladins in the city?"

"One of your own: the Pursar, Dikun Polun. He came here after he was denied entry to Garrou, and has been a benefit to my household."

"Dikun is here?" Nichal asked with a broad smile.

"He and several provisioners stay at a nearby inn while Otem is in town."

"He is a dangerous man? Otem, I mean?" Nichal asked.

The duke nodded. "In Œron he is known as the Enquêteur. He is an intense individual."

Nichal pursed his lips in thought.

"But," Rogvan said with a sly smile, "it's very entertaining to watch Barra and Otem go at each other. Barra is easily angered, but he also enjoys pressing Otem as far as he can."

"I shall endeavor to enter into the conversations peacefully then."

"Oh, I don't think you should," Rogvan said wryly.

A knock came at the door and a servant entered, whispering in the duke's ear.

"It appears that the Provost has returned," he said to Nichal, "and he knows of your arrival, as well. Shall we go and greet him?"

"And Rhi Barra?" Nichal asked.

He rose. "If you'll give me some time to precede you, I'll send word for you and your company.

Nichal nodded and the duke left.

"What do we hope to accomplish here?" Nichal asked.

"Just knowing that all of Bortali is not set on war is more than enough," Jined said.

"What do you think of the Chalicians?"

"I had the displeasure of hosting a delegation of them at my fortress in Birin several years ago," Koel said. "We're all about to receive a lesson in frustration."

"Loïc and Silas, can you both act as secretaries, and record anything you think worth noting? Cavian, stand with them at attention. Jined and Koel, if seats are offered, please join me."

The door opened and a servant entered. "If you'll follow me, we'll make our way to the great hall."

Journeying through the keep, they came to a small vestibule before a solid oak door. The servant gave a rap on the door with the metal ring hanging there.

The muffled announcement for the Prima Pater boomed as it opened.

Several curved tables sat around a massive open hearth of flaming coals, with breaks between the tables for servants keeping each group separate. Thirty high-backed chairs stood mostly empty. While there was no designated head, Duke Rogvan stood from the table at the far end. Behind him, a dais with his colors sat empty. Next to him, a woman with flaming red hair, loose and cascading down over her shoulders did not rise, but rested her hands over a full and pregnant belly. She smiled demurely.

At the table to Rogvan's left, a hulking man with bushy red hair and beard wearing a tartan of dark and light greens over a deep blue doublet held a tankard in his hand. Next to him, a young man who looked much like Toire Siobh stood with his arms crossed.

To the duke's right, a single man sat at his own table. He wore a form-fitting silvered breastplate, and over that, a gray tabard coat verging on white, across which hung a regal blue sash. His gray, nearly white hair had been plastered evenly to both sides of his head. He had a sharp nose and sharper eyes. His lips were rigid and unemotional. He, too, did not rise, but tapped his fingers on the table. Behind him, a complement of twenty Praetors of the Chalice stood, with arrowhead-shaped spears and broad-topped, almost cup-shaped helmets.

"Please, Prima Pater," the duke said, indicating the table next to the Rhi of Bronue Jinre. "Will you join us?"

Nichal nodded, and walked to the table indicated. Jined and Pater Koel came to stand on either side of him, but stood at attention, not taking their seats.

"Thank you for allowing us to join you today," Nichal said. "May I introduce to you Pater Minoris Didus Koel from Birin, and Primus Jined Brazstein, Thrice-Vowed."

The Praetor at the table glanced only at his host, averting his eyes from Nichal derisively.

"Hale and well met," Duke Rogvan said. He indicated to a servant, who rushed forward with a silver tankard. "I would first like to introduce you to the Rhi of Bronue Jinre, Barra Siobh, with him, his son, the prince Lachtnor Siobh."

Both men gave a respectful bow to Nichal, who returned it.

Rogvan turned to the Praetor. "This is…"

"Provost Zehan Otem," the Praetor announced. "Second to the Praetor Praeposit Anhouil Chétain, sent on mission to the countries upon the Lupinfang by the Benefactor, Missioner Abithu Omrab, Highest in the Path of Aben."

"I am fortunate to make your…" Nichal began before Otem interrupted him.

"I am not through," he said sternly. In response, the Praetors along the wall smacked the butts of their spears on the flagstone in unison. "That I was not first introduced, as the highest authority in this room, was insult enough. I'll not be interrupted again."

Jined clenched his fists. Nichal nudged Jined, and made a single motion he had often used in the field. *Calm. Sit.*

Jined and Koel took the seats next to Nichal.

"I have been sent to establish our authority in the void left by the abandonment of the holdings of the Hammer."

"We did not voluntarily…" Nichal interrupted.

The Praetors once again rapped their spears on the ground.

"The void left by the Hammer," Otem proceeded, "is being quickly filled, so as not to allow men and women to abandon the path set forth by the Book of the True Path. Mahndür has now fully adopted the rule. Varea, Redot, and, I have no doubt that by now even Limae, sit comfortably under our influence. Once Bortali has agreed to it, the rest of the Lupinfang will follow."

"You did not mention Grisden, nor Morraine," Nichal said.

"Insignificant countries do not bear so heavy a burden, as they do not present stumbling blocks to our faith."

"It would appear you have the intention of bringing all nations under the Chalice," Duke Rogvan said.

"Have I not been clear that this is our intention?"

"To what purpose?" Nichal asked.

"I would think it obvious: to unite humanity, to see everyone in our care to Lomïn. Is that not clear?"

"In principle," Nichal said, "but in practice it…"

The spears cracked again.

"Our guidance is god-ordained. Questioning it is tantamount to apostasy. I'll not allow it to take root. We have been provided proof—visions, new scriptures, even miracles. There can be no denying our authority is ordained."

"You keep stating the undeniability..."

"Be quiet!" Otem raised his voice. The spears cracked.

Nichal stood from his seat.

"The Sanctioned Letter of Chétain states," Otem said, raising his voice, "translated to a vulgar tongue:

"'All find their Path ordained by their fate and sanctioned or cursed by their actions. All who heed not the light offered shall remain in darkness and their blindness leads them unto the thorns. All who refuse recognition of the Lomïn-ordained authority show only their rebellious nature. Heed these words. Drink this cup. Follow this light and by your actions may you bring about your sanctity.'"

He stopped and stared at Nichal, eyes bulging with intense hatred.

"Well?"

"Well what?" Nichal asked, lifting his chin. His mouth was a thin line.

"Do you heed me?"

"Now you deign to let me speak?"

"To heed or heed not."

"The Gospel of St. Ikhail, chapter 23, says in vers..."

"I am not here to listen to your false gospels."

"You're not here to listen to anyone!" Nichal roared.

"I give no ear to one so lost in utter darkness," Otem hissed.

"I will no longer be silenced by your diatribe," Nichal said.

"I am the highest authority in this room!" Otem shouted, standing.

"You have no authority that supersedes mine. I am Prima Pater! The Order of the Hammer bears as much authority as any nation, and runs back in tradition further than any currently reigning monarch!"

"Your status is a falsehood," Otem shouted. "Your former Prima Pater still lives. You are an actor."

"And you are a despot, bent not on guiding people to any good and lovely path, but to bring them under your iron fist, to force feed them drink from your own poisoned chalice!"

The Praetors on the wall all took a single step forward. Otem did not wave them off.

The two holy leaders began shouting at and over one another. Jined lost track of the insults hurled at the other amidst the scriptures quoted, and the shouts in angry Œronzi tongue. Jined glanced over at Koel, preparing to stand up and join Nichal, but Koel shook his head.

It went on for several minutes before, through the racket of their argument, a rhythmic banging pierced the din. Jined glanced to their host and Rhi Barra, who both slammed their empty tankards down, stern looks in their eyes, as they watched the two holy men give in to their anger. Jined took up his own and joined the beat. Nichal glanced to his side and saw them doing this, then shut his mouth, his face going red in anger and embarrassment. He put both hands down on the table, breathing deeply and violently. The cups continued to rap. Otem continued to preach, looking up into the air, and avoiding looking at anything that might prevent him from stopping.

Nichal dropped to his chair, took a drink, and leaned to Jined.

"Alright, Jined. Bring order."

Jined nodded.

"Grissone and Anka, give me voice," he muttered. "Enough!" he hissed in no more than a whisper.

A wind shuddered across the room. Otem was knocked off his feet and into his chair. The Praetors behind him took a bracing step backward. Otem opened his mouth to speak, but for all his roaring blunder it was as silent as a whisper. His face reddened in rage. Jined looked to the duke, who opened his mouth to speak, and the same happened to him.

Jined scanned the room.

Loïc motioned, *Invoke an accord*.

Jined nodded and turned back to the room. "As I am the only one with voice, I bring this meeting to order—though we've not even passed the introduction of the parties—and invoke an accords, following the Bronuan Skaldic Traditions of old."

Both the duke and Rhi nodded profusely, while Otem scowled.

"I am, by divine miracle, allowed to gift you your voice once again. You'll not raise your voice, but follow the tradition, or be cast from the congregation, and deemed defeated."

Otem clamped his mouth shut and crossed his arms.

"Rhi Barra of Bronue Jinre, please lay out rules of the Tradition."

Barra rose from his seat, clearing his throat. His voice had returned to him and he smiled.

"The Skaldic Tradition is an old one. We can trace it back to the rules and laws that humanity held even while under the enslavement by the hrelgrens, twenty-two centuries ago. We were not given the ability to rule while under their authority, but they could not take from us our music. Words spoken to music were deemed merely poetry. Words delivered this way held no value to hrelgrens, but were, in secret, binding to all humans that held them to be true. Thus, we must call for a musician. Each party shall be given the opportunity to state their business, and the other an opposition. There shall be no raised voices or discord, but only discourse."

"Will you agree to this?" Jined asked Nichal.

Nichal nodded.

"And you, Provost?"

Otem gave a curt nod.

"Does your court have a minstrel?" Rhi Barra asked the duke.

Rogven shook his head. "He is away to the east."

"Loïc and Cävian," Jined said, turning to the twins. "Did you ride with your instruments this morning?"

They both nodded, and marched out of the room.

"When they return," Rhi Barra said, "the proceedings will go as such: They will play their music. While they play, Prima Pater, having been on the receiving end from our other guest's previous diatribe, shall be allowed to choose whether he speaks first, or whether you grant that to Provost Otem."

"I shall allow Provost Otem the first volley."

Otem smiled smugly.

The twins returned to the room.

Cävian held in his hands a bowl-bodied mandolin; his brother followed with a three-staved lute and bow. The duke indicated to the seats on the dais, where he no doubt normally sat in authority.

They both obliged and took seats, quickly tuning their instruments.

They glanced at one another, and without signing a single word, began to play.

Loïc drew out a long note to start, the lute held vertically on one knee. The sympathetic notes droned on and provided a backbone for Cävian, who began plucking away and then flourishing with strums.

The duke turned back to the table, a quaint smile playing across his face. "Provost Otem, you may begin."

Otem stood. "Duke Rogvan, Rhi Barra, Paladins," he started. "I am a reasonable man. Sent for that very reason—to bring reason to those without it. The Praetors of the Chalice are not made up of volunteers and criminals, as other Orders are, but chosen from the most intelligent children and raised with exposure to truth, rather than coming to it later. And so through this, the Praetors exemplify authenticity, better providing us the means to recognize counterfeit truths.

"The True Path, the way by which we conduct our lives, is proven to be the surest way into the Green, Green Kingdoms. Thus it is, that we have been charged to bring the True Path to the world by whatever means necessary. Œron has been the longest on the Path, following the tenets set before them, and earning the camaraderie the True Path provides. Living in community with the other travelers, they are better suited to follow those tenets, and ensure continued endurance.

"There are those that would draw attention to the split and fractious sects within the Abecinian Church, which focused on the varied symbology of Aben: The Path, the Light, the Arrow, the Chalice. Our Order marries all under a single doctrine. The Path is for all. The Light illuminates it. The Arrow prods and protects. The Chalice is the reward to those that remain true. It is never too late to take to the Path, but it can be too late to find it.

"As we have in Redot, in Varea, in Mahndür, I invite you to the True Path, under our tutelage. You shall not regret the sweet drink of simple refreshment it provides your soul, knowing you have chosen truth over lies. Should you refrain, there lies before you a road of thorns. For to the shadows, the light is a biting thing. You shall find yourself beset on all sides, scurrying in the shadows as vermin do, ever fearful of the light—the dread knowledge of your destination, the even deeper, darker shadows of Noccitan your just reward."

Otem took his seat and the twins resolved the song. They gave each other another glance. This time Cävian started the song, plucking out the opening refrain of the Hymn of Porumarias. Loïc joined in and overlaid another tune, a hymn Nichal had often, while on patrol around Pariantür, hummed to himself: Ikhail's Glad Tidings, a celebratory song that spoke of good food, good company, and peace.

"It is well met," Nichal began, "to finally come to the understanding of just what it is your Order stands for. The resolution of four distinct facets of the Church of Aben provides the perspective I have long wondered at in my own study of your scriptures. Seeing this now causes me to then question just what the various factions have been doing all of these long centuries, awaiting the True Path to reveal itself, and why it has been so long until it was revealed? What has Aben been doing all this time?"

Otem opened his mouth to interrupt, but the duke raised a hand. The Praetor crossed his arms and sat back.

"It is common knowledge amongst the peoples of man that Grissone, their Creator, left them to their devices when they turned from his faith. If you'll recall, he did so after a conversation with his own father, Aben. It was agreed that it would not be a parting of ways, but would provide instead a choice for each man, woman, and child. Those that sought out Grissone and believed in him would be brought into the Faith, by their faith, and through that Faith, refine themselves. Aben, on the other hand, called specific individuals, by way of the Watcher-Messengers he sent. Through their teachings, priests arose, known metaphorically as The Gateways, offering, at easy reach, ways for anyone to immediately join the path set for them and draw themselves along its eddies. As the poet, Juren Leifsen penned:

> *The Long Road ahead and straight,*
> *Its eddies as the sea,*
> *The curves wind like wind and wave,*
> *The lands a tapestry,*
> *Take now your life, be free.*

"It may not be scripture he spoke, but he summed up the Abecinian doctrines. That the Path is meant to guide, not to pay for the destination. A road may be traveled, but it does not change the traveler if the traveler does not look up—it rather only tires them.

"It seems to me that the Chalicians promote a religion of actions. Those actions are the only means by which to access the Green, Green Kingdoms. And yet, to gain that chalice and drink deeply of it, one need only be placed upon the Path, specifically into their own Order, that only those that have been placed shall partake. The rest are only second-class citizens to these kingdoms. Curious. For all these long centuries, Lomïn has been called the Kingdom of Aben. That now new knowledge is given, of there being multiple kingdoms, implies there are other kings, as there are on Kallattai.

"Our own faith resolves to invite any that would wish to change their faulty path for one that exemplifies actions, and offers to share the heavy load of guilt and regret, so that when one stands before the Judge in Noccitan, humility halos each as they beg for his mercy. The Chalicians would have one stand proud before Wyv, and expect their personal shining light to blind him to their dirty rags. As though a god with three eyes could not see the truth."

The song changed and Nichal took his seat. Otem stood.

"What need do I have of rebuttal? The Paladins of the Hammer state they are unclean and in need of faith and carrying one another along the road to destruction. They abandon their holdings and return to their isolation, as their god once did, leaving humanity to their own devices. That we, as Gateways to the Path, seek to offer a way onto the Path should be self-evident in its truth. If not for your own condemned and abandoned souls, then for those of your children. If you have no hope, then provide hope for those to come."

He sat abruptly and the twins were forced to end their song with a crash.

"Prima Pater," the duke said, "as you allowed the Praetor to go first, you are now granted permission to offer resolution."

Nichal stood and Loïc set out a low, sad note. Nichal gave him a nod of approval and turned to Otem.

"As occurred with Aben and Grissone, the Paladins of the Hammer leave behind the west, not because we abandon, but because we have been asked to leave. The actions of others within our Order condemn themselves, but force us to do what is right, returning to Pariantür.

"As it has always been, Pariantür welcomes any and all who would seek the Refining Faith, which does not justify, but rather, provides a pasture of rest and healing. If the Abecinians offer an alternative path, you can, as their own scriptures say, examine the teachings against those of old. For no word from the Pantheon contradicts, but sustains. Consider for yourselves the words spoken. It appears to guide, but instead only condemns. That this shackles you for the sake of the children is an empty threat of fear. Faith in Grissone offers a difficult climb up a mountain to a promised vista. We shall not consider you outside our fellowship should you choose to stay—but we then encourage you to a faithful life of protection for the downtrodden and helpless.

"Again, we shall not cast aside your friendship for doing so. The service to the goodness of others, not for personal gain, but to ensure their continual survival, bears more weight in the three eyes of the Judge than lip service and coinage to a man who has never stepped foot alongside his fellow man. As short-lived as this visit is, I choose now to leave, for my resolution is that you must choose your own path."

"With that, you admit defeat, and hang your head in shame!" Otem said, rising and pointing an admonishing finger at him.

Nichal stopped in his tracks. He did not turn around. "'To dwell among the unreasonable is to drink a bitter tea and call it honeyed ale,' Hamuleon 89."

"Unreasonable?" Otem roared. "'Let they who speak the truth never allow the words of the foolish to taint thy reason,' from Words of the Watchers."

Rhi Barra rose from his chair and crossed the room to Nichal's side. "Will you return to the table and break bread with us?"

"I'll not remain another moment in the presence of a man who condemns yet offers no words of decency or respect."

"I'll come to your inn. I wish still to speak with you."

Nichal gave a curt nod and left, without another backward glance.

5

THE RISING THREAT

They bore upon the company maws of gnashing teeth. And on their hands they wore finely crafted gauntlets of metal and stone. They were a desecration. And their bestial rage knew no fetter nor bound.

—QUATRODOX BOOK 4, 35:7

Loïc and Cävian sat nearest the hearth with Silas between them, Loïc's three-staved lute upon his knee, and the bow in his other hand. Loïc was grimacing as the younger Paladin pressed the bow across the strings with a screech. Silas had his tongue sticking out in concentration and hid it away as Loïc took hold of his hand again, guiding it along the strings. It was an improvement, but not much.

Cävian leaned back with his own instrument across his chest, negligently toying with the strings while he silently chuckled at the two of them.

The sound of sleipnirs on the cobbles outside the inn alerted innkeeper Beneven, who moved to the door and then let out a sharp whistle. His two boys appeared and followed their father out. A few moments later, Beneven's wife appeared behind the bar. She indicated to Jined that he approach.

"What is it, Aelasaev?" Jined asked.

"Your Prima Pater is about to receive guests. I don't see him."

"I'll get him," Jined said. "May I ask who?"

"The Rhi of Bronue Jinre."

Jined tapped the bar. "Thank you, Aelasaev."

She gave a nod and began drawing ales.

Jined turned to the side door, walked down the hall, and found Didus standing guard outside Nichal's room.

"What is it?" Didus asked. "Nichal is praying."

"Rhi Barra of Bronue Jinre has arrived," Jined said.

The murmurings of prayer that had been heard a moment before ceased as Nichal came to the door and opened it before either of them had even attempted to knock.

"Barra is here?" he asked.

Jined nodded.

"Didus, please get my cape," he said. Didus entered the room as Nichal ran his fingers up the chain of his hammer, mouthing the Twenty-Two. The Pater Minoris attached the red slashed cape to the grommets on the back of Nichal's gorget mantle.

Nichal finished and nodded to Jined. "Lead the way."

Jined turned. The music in the common room ceased as they came out and around the corner.

Rhi Barra sat by the fire, which was being fed logs by one of the boys. Behind the Rhi stood two guards who had a relaxed air about them, long war bows hung over their frames. Nearby stood an older man in a brown robe—Dikun Polun, the Paladin purser.

Rhi Barra stood and gave a bow to Nichal, who returned it with a salute.

"Prima Pater," Barra said, "will you join me?"

Nichal nodded and approached. Before he sat he finally noted Dikun, and stopped in his track.

"Polun!" he said as he threw his arms around the old man, who returned the hug.

Dikun was stiff but gave a quaint smile. "Prima Pater," Dikun said.

"It is so good to see you. Please, come and sit."

Dikun nodded.

Barra gave a wave to the innkeepers, and motioned to one of his guards, who took up a purse of coins and moved to pay the husband and wife.

"Drinks and food for all," Rhi Barra said. "As well as for our host and hostess. We've a celebration to drink to."

"A celebration?" Nichal said, indicating everyone take a seat with them. Jined sat to his right.

The Rhi smiled, took the cup offered to him, and lifted it, awaiting everyone else to do the same. As Nichal took up his,

Barra lifted his higher.

"To the Prima Pater Nichal Guess, who has emerged victorious, having vanquished Zehan Otem's pride!"

Didus Koel blurted out a laugh, and both Loïc and Cävian's free hands shot to their mouths to stifle their own.

"What do you mean?" Nichal asked.

"He ranted for an hour after you left, and gave not a moment for either my brother-in-law nor myself space to speak."

"It appeared that was normal for him."

"Not in such an uncontrollable rage, though. You made him very angry. Angrier than he was at me when I did not allow his ship to dock anywhere on my isles."

"Then that is true?"

"He tried coming to my port at Œndin, then after three days of being denied, tried going up the coast to Killark-Sloane, but I had already sent messengers to every port to deny him. When I then beat him here by a day, he was livid."

"He believed you here to undermine him."

"I think that was apparent, yes," Barra said.

"May I ask why you wish to bear such animosity?"

"I journeyed to Redot in my youth. There I watched a group of Praetors march through the city, preaching and shoving their way through. Their interactions, the way they treated everyone as lower than themselves, was deplorable. It ruined my journey for me. My hostility slowly grew toward the entirety of the Abecinian church. The previous High Priest from Mahn Fulhar visited me when I was crowned the Rhi of Bronue Jinre. He turned my point of view on its head."

"How so?"

"By showing me a different, kinder way than what the Chalicians preach. By showing me consideration and compassion. Yet the Chalicians remain unchanged, which is no surprise. That High Priest Klent Rigal in Mahn Fulhar has joined them, I do not doubt causes the previous High Priest, Ernüst Veybal, to roll his bones."

"Unfortunately," Nichal said, "I do not think Klent Rigal has merely joined them. I think that while he states he is the highest authority, he's in for a ruder awakening himself."

"How so?"

"Otem has stated Benefactor Missioner Abithu Omrab is highest along the Path of Aben."

"He has said so often," Barra said. "What of it?"

"Implying that the Benefactor Missioner is highest, implies that Klent Rigal is below him."

"Ah. I see," Rhi Barra said. "Well, regardless of all this, I do not wish to dwell too long on the subject. I bring tidings from Duke Rogvan. He wishes you to know that he shares many of my sentiments. Igahli bears many similarities to my country. We wish to pledge our fealty to you and your church."

"Fealty?"

"Alright, perhaps not fealty. We're not going to oust Abecinians, if that is your worry. I wish you to know that Bronue Jinre is a safe haven, from this day forward, for any who would escape the persecution of others. Indeed, the Shieldmaidens keep a public edifice. My own daughter is a ranking member of their organization."

"A woman I've had the opportunity to meet on a few occasions."

"She is in Garrou now," Barra said.

"She met us along the road," Nichal said, "and indicated we ought to come here."

"Is what Provost Otem said true? Are you leaving the west?"

"We are," Nichal said.

"Why? Why abandon us?"

"We do not abandon. We journey back to Pariantür to put our house in order. There are those within our order that seek to tear us apart. I mean to get to the heart of the matter and reemerge stronger."

"What of all your holdings?"

"We will worry about that when we return. They are only mortal assets. I am of the Vow of Poverty. I do not hold possessions in high regard."

"Why not strengthen your stance from my country? We offer you a haven there."

"I thank you for that kind offer," Nichal said. "Perhaps one day I will come and visit. It will not be until I know that our Order is whole. Until then, await our messengers. Even before that, I think you can expect a message from our brothers in Waglÿsaor."

Barra took a drink, cocking an eyebrow in curiosity.

"There was a catastrophic event, in which we confronted a member of our order who turned against us. Through his machinations, he set fire to and destroyed the Saor."

"That seems quite unlikely. It's indestructible."

"Well it fell, and upon him no less. I've left the Fortress of St. Rämmon in the care of two men: Beltran Cautese and Dane Marric. Beltran is a scholar and diplomat. While Dane is at times forceful, he has a desire to pursue the true faith. If the two of them lead alongside one another, I think they will be a stone amidst the rivers of change the Chalicians try to bring about."

"I will send ambassadors to meet with them."

"If you've any Paladins of the Hammer who have remained, have them all make a journey there. Beltran will apprise them of the situation, and provide them the chance to choose."

"Where do you go now?"

"We will journey to Garrou and after that, we'll begin our trek home."

"Let us feast this day, and you can leave tomorrow," Barra offered.

Nichal looked around at the Paladins with him and nodded. "Loïc and Cävian, can we have some music?"

The road from Igahli led into shallow hills hugging the coast. The trees were sparse and as windswept as the short grass that clung to rocky outcroppings. The bushes grew denser alongside the valley-like road, running between two hills.

"Do you smell that?" Didus asked, riding alongside Jined.

"Smell what? My nose has been broken enough times, I don't have much of that sense anymore."

"I smell smoke."

"Could be a homestead."

"This is different."

Loïc pulled his sleipnir up short and held a hand up. *I smell it, too.*

With how strong it is, and with this much wind, it's not likely a home, Cävian responded.

Didus guided his mount up the hill toward the coast, and stopped, unmoving.

"What is it?" Nichal called.

Didus did not respond.

"Everyone?" Jined said, and led the way.

As they came to the top, a pall of smoke rushed up over the hill and stung Jined's eyes. Down below, a small fishing village burned. A handful of boats hovered out at sea, eyeing the village and those milling about the town square: ten hulking figures reveling in their destruction.

"Vül," Jined muttered.

"Ten that I can see," Nichal replied.

And no doubt a few more besides, Loïc signed.

"Do we ride at them or move on?" Didus asked.

"If they are attacking a coastal city," Nichal said, "I have no doubt they are moving up the coast."

"They've seen us," Jined said.

"They can't be more than beasts," young Silas said.

"They are not merely beasts," Didus said. "I've not faced them myself, but they are more brutal than the T'Akai are cruel."

"At least they aren't led by Gold-Eater this time," Nichal said.

"Gold-Eater?" Silas asked.

"A vül made of all the gold he consumed. Dorian and Jined faced him. I think he broke your arm, didn't he, Brazstein?"

Jined touched his arm as a ghost pain flashed up its length.

The ten vül gathered at the edge of the square and moved with a chaotic purpose.

"Quarter mile up the hill?" Nichal asked.

The twins nodded.

"Assemble the counter charge," Nichal said.

"I will lead the center," Jined said.

"I've never fought," Silas said, a hint of panic on the edge of his voice.

"Then stay behind we five," Didus said, "and watch our backs."

"But I've never fought!"

Jined reached over and put a hand on Silas's sleipnir's mane. "Have faith, brother."

They turned back to the vül now at the bottom of the hill and loping up it. Three other vül had come out of side streets to join the first ten.

They were various shades, the colors of human hair. One of them was motley, with white across his body, and large black and brown spots covering much of him. A few of them held large broadswords. Others bore axes. The motley vül wore a pair of clawed gauntlets.

They had large, slavering maws, but their noses were more like that of a sleipnir, though flat to their skulls. At a distance they each appeared disheveled, but if one had the time to inspect them, it would be noted they were rather over-decorated, with tuffs of hair bound in metal rings. Many had well-worked leather. While the epitome of madness and chaos, the vül at the same time exemplified their god's original purpose as crafter.

"What are we waiting for?" Silas asked.

"They run uphill," Nichal said. "We're waiting for them to near another hundred yards. They'll have worked themselves up, but they're going to be very tired."

"Nichal will give no signal," Jined said. "So be ready for any moment."

Loïc was making motions with his hands. Jined felt a warm glow wash over him.

"Grissone and Anka," Jined began to pray, "guide and protect. Offer Silas the courage he never knew he had. Let our hammers fall, and our laughter rejoice at our victory."

Silas suddenly burst out in uncontrolled laughter and the tension was released. Nichal kicked his sleipnir into motion and as one, the five Paladins out front took off down the long slope. Tyv's muscles pulsed and flexed with a cold and resolute drive, while the other sleipnirs chomped at the bit, whinnying as Silas continued to laugh.

Then, the young man began to sing a hymn:

Hear O enemies, to Grissone I sing,
    Brothers heed, to the Anka I call.
I shall sing of valor. Of glory. Of honor.
    I raise a hymn of Faith and Hope.

The wave of blood flowed down that hill,
    And our god rode before us,
        Protecting hammer in his hands.
The enemies stood against us,
    And far above, the glint of glory shone.
        And all was silent as hammers ceased.

As they closed the distance, one vül leapt forward and through the air, heading straight for Didus. Jined swung across and his hammer snapped the vül's head to the side. It fell as deadweight to the earth. Didus pulled his sleipnir up short, his mount rearing as another vül came up under it. The sleipnir's two front hooves pawed down on the monster, battering it with blows. Jined's mount suddenly leapt, using the slope to gain air. He came down on top of a vül who dropped its own sword in surprise. Jined took hold of Tyv's mane and swung left and right as vül tried to take advantage of his sudden stop, clawing their way up the animal. Nichal arrived and brought down swift and violent force upon one vül. Didus, on the other side, rapidly pummeled another.

The twins had faced no opposition and pressed on down the hill toward a slower vül. They came upon it in a pincher, their hammers underswung, and simultaneously took the creature in the jaw. They did not stop, but continued toward the three vül near the bottom of the hill, drawing out bows and crossbows, and barking orders to one another.

Four remained at the top of the hill, surrounded now by Jined, Nichal, Didus, and Silas, who didn't seem aware of his surroundings at all as he continued to sing his hymn. The vül with the clawed gauntlets barked something at two of them who threw themselves at Jined and took hold of Tyv's reins and Jined's saddle. The second vül took hold of Jined and pulled him down off his seat.

"Grissone drive them off of me," he muttered.

The two of them were flung down at the foot of Nichal's sleipnir. The sleipnir began to paw at one of them, as Nichal turned it round and pointed his hammer at the motley vül leader.

Arrows began falling overhead. Loïc and Cävian were just closing the distance to the archers, and looked like they would make quick work of them.

"Face me!" the vül barked.

"Call your pack off," Nichal retorted.

The vül gave a command and they each sunk their heads low in submission, then stood. Jined picked himself up off the ground.

"You will fight me?" the vül asked tentatively. "Not him?" The creature pointed to Jined.

"I will," Nichal said.

"I will not fight him," the vül said. "He killed Gold-Eater."

"I said I will fight you," Nichal said.

"On foot," the vül said.

Jined looked around. Didus held the throat of a vül, unconscious with a bloodied maw. The twins, unaware of the standstill were killing the final vül below. The leader had only the two remaining vül with him.

Nichal dismounted. "What are the conditions?"

"Conditions?" the vül replied.

"What should happen if I defeat you?"

"Why should I care. I will be dead."

"If I defeat you, those that live shall be granted their lives."

The vül laughed. "If I defeat you, then you all surrender, to be slaves and playthings of my pack. Our new pack-leader is not a gentle vülkin."

Nichal looked to Jined, who nodded.

"Give us room," Nichal said, handing his reins to Jined. "And I shall say my own prayers. It is only fair."

"He will not fight fair," Jined said.

"But we will stand by our words."

"Do you remember when you were challenged by that T'Akai?"

"The one covered in bony growths and spikes?" Nichal laughed. Jined nodded.

"The thing is, I trust the T'Akai to fight honorably."

Nichal turned back to the vül, who was muttering to his pack mates. The two other vül laughed to themselves and stepped to the side. Didus had recovered his sleipnir, and stood next to Silas, who had remained in his saddle. He looked about him, shock across his face as he realized where he was.

The vül eyed the Paladins across from him, and checked the straps of his gauntlets.

Nichal held up his hammer in both hands. "Tell me when you are ready."

The vül sneered. "Your confidence is foolishness."

The vül rushed forward with no further warning. Nichal dropped back a step, the head of his hammer dropping to the side, and continuing in an arc, back around, up and over. The vül threw his hands up and caught the hammer haft, then shoved with his entire body, trying to throw Nichal back. Nichal stepped to the side and took hold of the loose fur on the back of the vül's neck and yanked. The vül took a stumbling step to the side and lost his hold on Nichal's hammer.

The Prima Pater stomped down on the vül's exposed foot, and rushed with his shoulder, pushing him off balance. The vül took three long stumbling steps and fell to a knee, right as Nichal brought his hammer down again.

The vül rolled out of the way, came to his feet, and leapt onto Nichal, shoving him to the ground and straddling him.

The vül began savagely punching down on Nichal, denting his gorget, and pushing the metal dangerously close to the man's face.

"Off!" Nichal shouted.

Jined could see a wave explode from Nichal's mouth and the vül was thrown back ten feet. Nichal scrambled to his feet and dove on top of the vül, hammer raised. The vül once more caught the hammer haft. Nichal shoved it down onto the vül, pressing against the creature's throat.

"Yield," Nichal roared.

"No!" the vül croaked. "Attack!"

The other two vül did not hesitate, but leapt into action, diving atop Nichal, tearing at his armor and trying to pull him off.

There was a single moment where everything stopped. Jined saw the twins riding up the hill toward them, the Standard of Grissone raised high in Cävian's hand. Nichal had a look of determination upon his face. In an instant, light pulsed from Nichal's hammer. The two vül atop him were thrown up into the air, fifty feet, and the vül beneath him shoved down into the hard earth with as much force.

The twins flew through their midst and toward the remaining two. They struck them down as they tried to stand.

Nichal leapt to his feet, unaffected by the pulse of light.

The vül at his feet looked as though a boulder had been dropped upon him. He did not move again.

"We would have stayed true to our word," Nichal said, "and let them live."

"They know nothing but fear and terror and deceit," Didus said. "They live a sad existence."

"Apparently," Jined said, "the local pack has a new leader."

"All the more reason to get to Garrou and warn the king," Nichal said.

"And the village?" Didus asked.

"We'll check for survivors, and then burn the bodies of the vül here at the top of this hill."

The smell of the vül pyre still clung to him two days later as they crossed the valley floor to the gates of Garrou. Two young men, of the ten survivors at the small village, had joined them, while the others had stayed to bury the dead. It had been a morose ride in silence. As they neared the gates, they boomed open, and twenty armored knights rode out, carrying city pennants. At their head rode the city mayor. The same that had met with the Prima Pater the year before.

The knights across from them pulled up in a long line, the Mayor atop his sleipnir only a few strides ahead.

"We bring news," Nichal said.

"State your name and business," the Mayor said.

"I am the Prima Pater Nichal Guess."

The Mayor laughed. "You are no Prima Pater. He was here only last year. Add to that, we received message that you might be arriving. You are a fallen Paladin. You bring upon us destruction."

"We have only brought destruction upon the vül that attacked the village of Estmol. These young men are but two of ten survivors. We sundered thirteen vül. They indicate more vül on their way."

"And to the accusation?" the Mayor asked.

"I am Prima Pater, selected as such by Dorian Mür. We carry with us the Standard of Grissone, and at my side stands a champion of Grissone, Jined Brazstein."

"A Boronii name. You are granted no access to our city. Begone."

They gave no further word, but turned and rode back into the city, the gate booming closed behind him.

6

WARDENS OF THE AXE

The metal is workable, my lord. By deep flame and cold blood, it is workable!

—LETTER FROM UNKNOWN WRITER TO PATER GLADEN

Ophedia knocked on the open doorframe. Over her Black Sentinel cloak hung her long raven hair, with hints of red that showed up in the direct sun. Under the cloak, she wore a dark vest over a loose white blouse. With the thick wooden soles of her boots, she stood an inch taller than Aurín, who looked up and gave a weak smile.

"Oh good," Aurín Mateau said. "I'm glad it's you. Come help me."

He had an odd contraption sitting across his desk, and laid the back of his left wrist down over it. His pencil-thin mustache twitched as he considered the piece before him. His hair was parted down the middle and plastered flat to his head.

"What are you doing?" Ophedia asked.

"Help me strap this on. It's impossible to do with one hand."

She sighed, stepped over, and reached for the buckles.

"Be careful though," he hissed. "The tips are very, very sharp."

Where his fingers went sat five sharp-looking talons. She nodded, then moved around them to set the buckles to rights. In the center of his palm sat a flat disc of metal.

"There," she said, and stepped back. "Now what is it?"

"Something I found."

Ophedia rolled her eyes. "Stop being cryptic. The commanders sent for you. You need to come with me."

"They'll wait," Aurín said. "Watch."

He stood, a broad smile across his lips. He held out his left hand, and flexed. The talons were not long, but impressive none-the-less.

"Are those skyfall?" she asked.

Aurín nodded. "You know why the commanders are summoning me? Why I'm here preparing?"

"They're making you a member of the new Order."

"The first," Aurín said. "None of them made the first move. So I did. Noss asked for my help. I climbed that tall tower at the top of the citadel. I found axes. Orbs. This talon. Noss doesn't actually know I have this. Nor what I'm wearing. Nor what sits hidden under my bed right now."

"What's under the bed?" Ophedia asked.

"I'll show you later. But first, take a look at this," he said, tapping the armor across his chest and legs.

"So?" Ophedia said.

"Tap it," he said, puffing out his chest.

She did. "That's not leather."

"It is not. It's boot-blackened skyfall armor."

"Another thing Noss doesn't know about?"

Aurín smiled.

"You don't think he'll take offense?"

"I don't much care anymore," Aurín said. "It'll protect me. That's all I'm really after."

"What do you mean?"

"I feel like I've been pulled around by my nose these past few years. More so when Searn dragged us all north. I'm taking matters into my own hands. Well...my own talon," he chuckled.

He moved the Sentinel cloak on the bed, revealing a bleached white griffin skull.

"Where did you get that?" Ophedia asked.

"Same place." He threw the cloak over his shoulders and took up the skull and pushed it under the bed.

"You're not going to wear that skull on your shoulder?"

Aurín gave her an impressed look. "That's a great idea!"

Ophedia rolled her eyes.

"I'm ready," he said.

DREAD KNIGHT

Ophedia opened the door, leading the way.

"So, you climbed that old tower, and just found the talon and armor?"

"They were in pretty bad shape," he replied. "I hired a leather worker to help me put them back together."

"What if Noss takes the armor from you? What if he wants it for himself?"

"Honestly, if he really wants it, then he'd be showing his hand."

"You're willing to risk your life?"

"I've had my life threatened without knowing it was. So I might as well do it by choice now. Watch me rise through the ranks, Ophedia. Nothing is holding me back now."

"I kind of like this new and confident Aurín," Ophedia said.

"I do, too," he replied with an excited, quavering voice.

They came to a main hallway and walked past guttering torches to the main entryway of the citadel. By the door, two Paladins stood. Pater Minoris Pellian Noss approached from a side hall.

"I was starting to wonder," Noss said.

"I am here, and I am ready," Aurín said, standing a little taller.

"Ophedia, you can take the side door down that hall and out into the courtyard to witness with the others."

She stepped out through one door, then through a second into the wind-blasted flagstone yard. The space outside the main doors sat as a wide platform, descending several sets of stairs to the main cobbles. The Sentinel commanders stood at attention, a few yards between each of them, and each with one or two Sentinels as bodyguards, save for the lone Commander Domic, ever by herself.

Behind the commanders, a row of Paladins stood at attention, black cloaks hanging from their frames.

Ophedia came and stood next to Commander Bolla Elbay.

"And?" Elbay asked. She had graying hair that in the past might have matched Ophedia's auburn-highlighted black hair. She had only the other day acknowledged that she was Ophedia's mother. Ophedia felt as though Elbay was constantly staring at her now. It made Ophedia uncomfortable.

"As you surmised," Ophedia said.

"The other commanders are quite angry."

"And you?"

"Someone had to step up first. That it was a Sentinel who isn't even a captain yet is upsetting, but not surprising. We are an order of ambitious men and women."

"It is a new side of Aurín," Ophedia admitted.

"He's going to get himself killed," Elbay said.

"I think he knows that," Ophedia said.

"If that is so, then the other commanders may try and help hurry that along."

"Are you one of those commanders?"

"I will do what is best for the Sentinels. If that means he must be spent as a currency in the coming conflict, I will not hesitate."

The doors opened and Pater Noss stepped out into the daylight. He walked to the top of the stairs and stopped.

"Friends and allies, commanders and brothers, I greet you."

He held his hands down toward them, palms up.

"As we have agreed upon, upon this day we gather to form a new Order, the Order of the Axe."

He took from his back a large axe forged of skyfall metal. In the gray-skied day it was dull and lifeless. It bore a long s-curve edge set on a long handle.

"Together we shall stand united—an Order not of staunch protection as a dam upon which the river breaks. Rather a keen edge, set to sever those that would sunder. To cleave in twain those that would bend all to their wills. For we are an order of equals. An order of undaunted liberty."

He held the axe out toward the Paladins in the rear.

"Brothers. You are here because you follow me. You are here because we have plumbed the scholarship of the worlds. No longer shall I be your Pater Minoris. No longer will you bow in subservience, but only in honor. Thus—" He reached to the cordons across his chest and tore them off. "I am no longer Pater, but Dean Pellian Noss, Princep of this citadel. Doff your gorgets, and join me as Wardens of the Axe."

As one, they unclipped the gorgets that sat upon their shoulders and let them fall with a clatter on the flagstone. They marched around the commanders and came to stand on the steps. From behind their backs, from beneath their cloaks, they took out axes made of skyfall.

"Cast aside your hammers. You shall be leaders of Wardens."

They unhooked their hammers and let them fall.

"Those who held rank of Primus or higher, take up the rank of Magister below me. All of Dean or Magister rank shall be a part of the Guardian Tier."

Three of the armored Wardens took out orbs of skyfall and

DREAD KNIGHT

lifted them high.

"Next, we invite others to join our order. Any who would call themselves Sentinels, and might claim a rank of captain can become a Warden of equal rank, taking up an axe. Who would be the first?"

Ophedia watched Commander Deggar open his mouth to speak when another voice rang out.

"I will take up the axe!"

Noss turned, giving no notice to Deggar. Aurín marched forward from the doors to stand next to Princep Noss. He cut a fine stance, with his sentinel cloak over his left arm, his right hand set upon the axes at his belt.

"Who are you?" Pellian asked formally.

"Aurín Mateau, Sentinel. I wish to join the Wardens."

"We welcome the willing," Noss said as he held out his skyfall axe. "Swear upon this blade."

Aurín nodded and placed his right hand upon the top.

"What do you offer?" Noss asked.

"Ambition and protection."

"What will you protect?"

"The rights of others," Aurín recited.

"How shall you do this?"

"I shall tread upon the despot and subjugator."

"By what means?"

"By the axe, and..." Aurín said with hesitance in his voice. Then, he unfurled his cloak and held up the taloned gauntlet. "And by my talon."

The look of surprise on Noss's face was genuine. He gave a suspicious glance around him, and his eyes locked with Ophedia for a second. He clamped his mouth shut and turned back to Aurín.

"Then we welcome you to the Wardens. No longer a Sentinel, but a Vigilant tier Warden. Bring pride to our order, donning a new name, the Talon. Make proud your leaders, and rise above your rank."

Aurín gave a flourishing bow and another Warden stepped forward, handing him an axe. Aurín took it and stepped to the side.

Then Noss looked at the commanders and leveled his axe at them. "Will you join us? We offer you commanders a status as a Magister in the Guardian tier. Join us. Take up axe and orb."

Commander Deggar and Commander Forenor stepped forward without further prompting. Deggar leapt up the stairs and stood before Noss. Forenor took longer to reach the top, his gold chains and fur-lined cloak trailing behind him. Noss took out an orb.

"Place your hand upon this," he said to Deggar. The man slapped his hand upon it, and took Noss's prompting to repeat much of what Aurín had said.

"Will you act with the order's best interests?" Noss asked.

"Why should I not," Deggar announced.

Elbay scoffed next to Ophedia.

"Then take up this orb. Take it and march forth to the wall. For upon this day, the southern wall shall be under your authority."

Deggar took up the orb and turned, raising it high. Elbay and Domic both took a step back, wary of his erratic movements.

The commander stepped to the side, a stupid smile plastered across his face.

Noss repeated the actions with Commander Forenor. He was much more regal, but he looked down upon the others with clear superiority and disdain.

"Take up your orb," Noss said. "The western wall is yours."

"Will you join these ranks?" Noss asked, looking down the stairs to Vore, Hardin, Elbay, and Domic. None of them moved.

Noss smiled. "No offense is taken nor made. Our invite is an open door. Six commanders. I would see four, if not all of you, join. When you have, know that Sentinel and Warden shall become one. The marriage of our orders shall bring about a lasting power. Together we can rebuff the Chalicians who come to take this city from us. Tell every Sentinel in the city that they can take up the role. We shall craft for them crossbolts of skyfall when they join. It is time we lifted the oppression outside the walls."

Noss descended the stairs as the Wardens left to enter the citadel. He walked up to Elbay and Domic. Commander Vore and Hardin had already turned to leave the citadel and enter the city.

"I had hoped to have one or both of you join," Noss said. "To be the first women to join the order."

"I will join if and when I deem it necessary," Bolla Elbay said. "It will not be as a token, but because it benefits the Sentinels."

"Your loyalty is admirable," Noss said. "I do not ask you to abandon the Sentinels. I ask you to help me take Searn's vision to heights he only dreamed of."

He turned to Ophedia. "What does Searn's daughter think?"

Ophedia scowled. "Of what?"

"Will you join us? Searn would be proud to know you had."

"You may have known my father," she said, "but you do not know me. I didn't know he was my father until the day he killed himself."

Noss gave a nod. "Accept this then, as a gift. In remembrance of your father."

He held out a leather tube. Ophedia took it tentatively and opened the top, turning out the quiver. The tips of the bolts were made of skyfall.

"Whether you join or not," Noss said, "they are yours." He turned back to Elbay and Domic. "Consider joining us. Please?"

The other two women gave a nod and pulled back. "We will consider," Domic said.

Ophedia turned to walk with them.

"I will not join if it is only to die," Bolla said.

"What do you mean?" Domic asked.

"Forenor and Deggar were quick to join, and he was just as quick to assign them the walls. They will not last the week."

"You think he did so for that reason?" Domic asked.

"I think he expected them to fall on their own swords. Their hubris will run them through, willingly or not."

"What about you, del Ishé?" Domic asked. "Your friend was first to join. Will you join alongside him?"

"I do not know," Ophedia said. "I won't do it merely for my father's sake. He may have been my father, but I am still an orphan at heart. I need no parent to carry me."

Bolla gave her a glance bearing a melange of sadness and pride.

"Well, consider those bolts he gave you," Domic said. "I'd be interested in knowing if they work better than others."

"Give a warning to your friend," Elbay added, "if you're able. I am suspicious this whole thing isn't just meant to take over the Sentinels and remove the Commander Council."

"I will," Ophedia said.

"What about Hardin and Vore?" Elbay asked Domic.

"I believe Hardin will leave the city. He feels he is losing control. He had hoped to become the High Commander. Vore may try to go with him, but Hardin won't accept him. He doesn't trust him."

"Who does?" Elbay said.

Domic laughed. "Well, I'm off to business."

"Are you ever not on business?"

Domic shrugged and walked away.

"I think she has already decided to join the Wardens," Bolla said.

"But you haven't?" Ophedia asked.

"I doubt I'll have much choice in the end. I think I'll hold out for a time."

"I may do the same."

"You get that from me," Bolla said.

Ophedia stopped in her tracks. They both stood at the entrance of the citadel courtyard, the city spread out before them. To the south and west the armies of the Chalicians camped in looming dread.

"I understand that you're trying to relate to me," Ophedia said. "While I can't thank you enough for all you've already done, I need you to understand me clearly. You may have birthed me, but you are not my mother. We can be friends. Colleagues. Wardens even, if that is what we both choose, but you are not my mother. It is too late for that."

"I didn't expect you..." Bolla said before Ophedia interrupted her again.

"Let me finish."

Bolla closed her mouth and nodded.

"You made a decision, and we both bear the consequences of that. I was not raised by any holy order, even if the Crysalas and Nifarans tried. I was not raised by Searn. He only found me a year ago. I was not raised by any caring old lady, adopting me off the streets. I wasn't even raised by the rough streets. No one raised me. I raised and made myself. I adopted the mannerisms that I have chosen to take on. I make my own decisions, sometimes arbitrarily just to be the one who chooses. My path is my own. I'll not ever, ever do something that I did not think through, as erratic as my behavior might seem. So I'd ask you to give me the space I need. Treat me professionally, but do not treat me as a daughter, because I am not your daughter."

Bolla stood in silence, lips pursed, as she eyed the woman next to her. She turned back to the city.

"I almost left the city the night you helped that Mahndürian over the wall," Bolla said. "I would leave, and never look back. I would let you thrive outside of my shadow, if you're even in my shadow. I'm starting to wonder if I'm in yours."

Ophedia shook her head. "You're a commander. You could leave and go with Hardin. He'd probably welcome it. You could also make a name for yourself in the Wardens, too. Searn is gone. He no longer has a shadow to cast."

Bolla placed a hand on Ophedia's shoulder.

"Daughter or not," she said, "I'm proud of you. For making something with your life when I left you with nothing."

"You gave me determination."

Bolla nodded.

"And these stunning curves," Ophedia added with a laugh.

"Enjoy them while you can," Bolla replied with a laugh as rich as Ophedia's.

7

Indigo

There is a place that I can go,

    Where no wing finds the air.

But mind is free to rise and sing,

    In dream I do go there.

—O, PURPLE LAND BY TASHARI

POETESS KELICA MONDURI

Where those at the citadel gave off the air of suspicion, the city below lived under a cloud of fear. The news of the opportunity to join the Wardens was spreading, but few had taken up the skyfall. While she had not made the commitment, Ophedia carried her crossbow openly once she found that other Sentinels gave her a wider berth when she did so. The chants from the Chalician army along the western wall droned on incessantly. In response, some inns tried to drown out the hymns with ribald music and ongoing parties, but even these had grown lackluster.

When she passed the center of the city and entered the southern half, though, a different air pervaded. The absolute silence was oppressive. Blockades had been thrown up to keep parts of the city completely locked away, where all had fallen to the developing new plague.

Some called them Revenants, like the myths of those that had risen from the dead during the Protectorate Wars, but Ophedia had been there and watched the living become these now inhuman creatures, the purple glow in their eyes speaking of some dark magic. Revenants moved in silence, and escaped the confines of the makeshift barriers every day and more often at night.

She came within a block of the barricades. Sentinels and citizens stood along the tops of furniture and rubble set as a makeshift wall. They eyed her with as much suspicion as they eyed the silence beyond. Ophedia stopped for only a moment before continuing.

Farther south, unsettling silence watched another Chalician front. The southern wall held by Deggar had started as a spitting match of braggadocio. Commander Deggar had made threats, holding up his orb of steel, but the Chalicians had given no signs of fear. Within a day, Deggar's position had floundered.

She neared the southern headquarters. The commander had taken over an inn there, and had posted several intimidating Sentinels outside. Two of them played Edi-Foz on top of a barrel.

As she approached, one of them stepped forward, axes in hand.

"Back again to gloat?" he asked. It was Lowden Dakmor, one of Deggar's right-hand men. He bore a cruel scar down his face, and a voice to match.

"Over what?"

"Rumor is you came to town without an axe to your name, and now you're a captain. Don't think we don't know what you had to do to make rank."

Ophedia rolled her eyes. "I've a message for Deggar, from the citadel."

"I'll see if he's accepting messages right now."

"Not sure you get to turn me away," Ophedia said.

"And just what are you gonna do about it, girl?" Lowden said, stepping up to her, puffing his chest out and looking down his nose.

"Probably see if we can't give you a matching scar somewhere else," Ophedia said.

"I'd like to see you try," Lowden sneered.

"What's the trouble," a voice called from the inn door. Ophedia broke her stare and looked past Lowden. The hulking form of the whisker-covered Commander Deggar stood, arms bared, a double-bladed axe strapped across his back. Across his chest hung his new skyfall axe.

"Message from Princep Noss," she said.

He waved her forward. She moved past Lowden, and in response, he shouldered her.

"Down, boy," Deggar said with a chuckle.

Lowden did not turn around.

"What does Noss want now, del Ishé?" he said.

"I'm not privy to the contents," Ophedia said, pulling out a folded envelope from inside her vest and handed it over.

"You going to keep playing messenger? Or are you going to actually get dirty?" he asked.

"Same could be asked of you," Ophedia said.

"Sharp tongue like that is going to get you beat, one day," Deggar said.

"Is that a threat?"

"Friendly warning."

He broke the seal and opened the letter, poring over the contents.

"Not sure what he expects me to do. I can't very well make a first move."

"Am I taking a response back?"

"Make yourself comfortable," Deggar said, turning to enter the inn. "Maybe go arm wrestle Lowden. Or stick a shiv in him. I don't care. Either way, the rest of us will be entertained."

She turned to see the others watching her. She walked over to a barrel of ale set up on the street and poured herself a flagon, then sipped at the watered-down swill with a grimace.

"Can't stand a little grog?" Lowden called.

"If you think this is good," Ophedia said, "I'd have you under a table before I had even begun."

Lowden sneered.

"Hey Dakmor," another Sentinel nearby hissed, pointing up the street.

A figure moved toward them at an awkward gait, like someone walking in a dream. It crossed into a house and disappeared. A few moments later, it reemerged.

"One of 'em got out," Lowden said in a lowered voice.

Ophedia placed the tankard onto the barrel where other spent drinking vessels lay, and walked up next to them.

"Is that what I think it is?" she asked.

"Revenant," Lowden said. "Although we've been calling 'em Indigo Walkers."

"Bigger word than I'd have thought you had room for," Ophedia said.

Lowden chuckled.

They continued to watch the figure move toward them, not showing any indication it even saw them.

"First experience with them?" Lowden asked.

"I was there when they first appeared," Ophedia said.

"It's hard enough to get back to Black Street now," Lowden said. "Deggar is none to happy both of his inns can't be reached."

"Nocc," Lowden swore as three more figures came into view.

Ophedia dropped the tip of her crossbow down, stepped into the stirrup, and pulled back on the string. She hefted it, and drew a bolt from the quiver hanging from her belt. Lowden gave it a glance.

"Weird-looking bolt head."

"Made of skyfall. The same metal as Deggar's axe."

"Better than steel?"

"One way to find out," she said.

She dropped to her knee and aimed. As she touched the trigger, ten more Revenants rounded the corner. Her bolt flung wide.

"Sound the alarm!" Lowden shouted.

The street was suddenly a flurry of activity. Deggar rushed out from the inn, crossbow out.

"Load up, del Ishé!" he said, cranking back on his own, and setting a bolt in the saddle.

Ophedia loaded another bolt. One of the Revenants finally seemed to take notice of the Sentinels there, considered them for a moment, then voicelessly opened his mouth, looking around. Two other Revenants turned and locked eyes with Ophedia. All six eyes blazed a fiery violet, and as one they rushed forward in a frenzy.

"Shoot them!" Deggar roared.

Ophedia followed the command, and let loose with Deggar. Both bolts flew across the space and struck home. Ophedia's hit her target square in the chest and it fell to the ground. Deggar's struck between the eyes and it fell backward, purple light still pouring from its eyes. Two of the Revenants fell. The third rushed at the two closest Sentinels. It took one Sentinel across the face with savage swipes, then shoved the other to the ground and leaped atop him. At this close range, Ophedia saw the Revenant was a woman, her hair savagely torn out in spots; she fought like a wild griffin, clawing at the man in a silent rage.

Deggar walked up to the woman, a new bolt loaded, and with only a few yards between them, loosed it. She fell over and onto the ground, her eyes still burning with purple flame. Deggar turned around with a grim nod, and didn't see from behind him the purple light leap suddenly from the eyes of the Revenant into the mouth of the man she had torn into. At almost the same time, the fire from the first Revenant he had shot leapt to a Sentinel crying out as he held his clawed face.

The two Sentinels screamed in horror, like waking from a horrid dream, then, they went silent. They stood, alert to those around them.

Deggar turned back and saw his Sentinel compatriot standing before him.

"Rov?" Deggar said, as the man suddenly lunged forward.

Deggar leapt back, threw his crossbow to the side, and tore the skyfall axe free from the straps across his chest. He used it to block each savage swipe from the Revenant. Each swing was a full-weight blow, and the Revenant's balance was thrown off more each time.

"Rov!" Deggar said. "Don't make me do this!"

"That's not Rov anymore, commander!" Lowden shouted.

Deggar nodded in resolve, stepped forward, and shoved the Sentinel Revenant backward with his shoulder. He kept pressing the advantage until it fell to the ground. Then, with a single swipe of his axe, he took the man's head off. The violet fire died in its eyes.

The second Sentinel Revenant rushed past Deggar toward Ophedia. She cast her own crossbow away to reach for the long cudgel from her back, but the Revenant was already on top of her, and the heavy stick clattered away as they both toppled to the ground. The purple fire burned in its eyes as it stared down at her. She tried not to let the panic take over as she reached for a knife with one hand, and held the creature's throat with the other.

Suddenly, their eyes locked.

The purple light that bled from the Revenant's eyes was not a light, nor a fire, but a cloud. Beyond that cloud there were no eyes. Those had burned away. Instead, an endless void beckoned from beyond that cloud.

Dream and endless sleep called to her.

Invited her.

And deep, deep within that void, a single pinprick of light stared back.

Just as suddenly the gaze was broken, the Revenant thrown away from atop her as Lowden used her own stout stave to pry him away.

"Get up, girlie!" he shouted.

She gasped for breath and rolled away. With a free hand, she took out an axe and charged. The Revenant wasted no time, and clawed the axe from her hand. She took out a knife but the Revenant once more took hold with a grip no person should have, and wrested it free from her. She reached to her side quiver. All but one of her bolts had fallen free. She took hold of it as the unholy creature tried once more to lock eyes with her.

"Not again," she muttered, and thrust the arrow through the thing's eyes, down through the void, and into the infinitesimal pinpoint of light. While none nearby could attest, she knew she saw the small light explode.

"To me!" Deggar ordered. "We take them all down!"

"I don't want to get infected, commander!" someone shouted.

"I'm not commander anymore!" Deggar said, rushing forward with a roaring laugh. "I'm Magister Guardian of the Axe!"

The other Sentinels rallied, matching his manic laughter, and pressing the eight Revenants back. The Revenants, like kicked ynfalds, finally came to the realization of the situation and retreated back toward the barricades.

Lowden turned to Ophedia.

"You held your own," he said.

"I don't plan on dying any time soon."

"You're savage nasty in a scrap. I see now why people keep you around."

"I'm even meaner when I drink."

"I'd like to see that," he laughed, and held out a hand.

She took his in her own. "Truce, then?"

He nodded. "Now go to the citadel and get more help down here. We can't be expected to hold back those Indigo Walkers as well as the southern wall, while Forenor has only to sing bar shanties at those Cuppies."

"You said two of them didn't rise again?" Aurín asked as they marched down through the city. A chill ran through her spine, and she pulled her cloak closer over her shoulders.

Three of the Paladin Wardens marched behind them, and more were said to be saddling sleipnir, not far behind.

"Three: I shot one, Deggar used his axe to take another down and then I drove a bolt through the eye of a third."

They came to the square, now devoid of anyone.

Aurín looked toward the gate, three blocks away. Two Sentinels stood guard.

Ophedia glanced down the road to the barricades. "I don't see Deggar there either."

One of the Wardens stepped up. He had the swarthy complexion of a Morriegan. In the past several days the Paladins had stopped shaving their heads, and this Warden's thick black hair and mustache were coming in quickly. "If the Chalicians took the wall right now, that would be it."

"I hate wasting time. See that the wall is reinforced. Del Ishé and I will go and find Deggar so he can return to his post."

"I don't take orders from you," the Warden said.

"You're right. You don't. Princep Noss sent me here and ordered you here, after. So for right now, I think my orders hold greater weight. Can you hold things here while I go risk my life against Revenants?"

The Warden pursed his lips and gave a curt nod.

"Let's?" Aurín said with a glance at Ophedia before he took off toward the barricades, leaving the Wardens behind.

"That was something," Ophedia said, falling into step.

"He's going to see a knife goes in my back," Aurín said.

"Then keep moving so he can't find the chance."

They ran down the street and came to the barricades. A single Sentinel sat there on the ground, holding a wounded side.

"Let's see your eyes," Ophedia said.

The man laughed and looked over at them. It was Lowden. He gave them a look and laughed a bloody cough. "You got back faster than I thought, girlie."

"You don't look great."

"I've seen worse, but Deggar told me to hold the barricades from this side."

"I find it hard to believe he went in there."

"Listen," Lowden said, "Deggar is a shunt, for sure, but he's a cunning, brutal one. He'll climb through ranks over piles of dead bodies, but he won't be called a coward."

"Fair enough," Ophedia said. "Now why did they go over?"

"He said if he didn't, they'd keep coming."

"Then let's go pull him back before he becomes one," Ophedia said to Aurín.

She scrambled up the pile, and looked back to Aurín.

He stood considering his route.

"Your little manticör claw giving you trouble?" she smirked.

"It's more like a griffin's claw. And yes."

She reached down with her stave. "Come on," she said.

He took hold and she hoisted him up.

Beyond, the place was a mess. The empty streets were trashed. A few forms lay here or there, with miasmic indigo clouds hanging over them like flies.

"What in Noccitan?" Aurín muttered.

"This'll be fun," Ophedia said, and scrambled down to the street.

"What kind of moron goes charging into a place like this?"

"Besides us?" Ophedia asked.

Aurín chuckled.

"What did Noss say to you about the claw on your hand?"

"He hasn't said much of anything," Aurín said, glancing down side streets they passed. "But everyone keeps eyeing it. I dare not leave it in my room. Oh, and I took the skull to the leather worker."

"What about the other secret you wouldn't tell me about before?"

"I've hidden it, but may have to move it again."

"What is it?"

"A sword."

"Alright. A sword."

"It's a really nice sword. It's just sort of hard to wield with this talon."

"What's so special about it?"

"Well, it's skyfall. So that's something. It's four feet of wickedly curved blade with a two-handed curved handle. At a glance you might think, being skyfall and being such a broad blade, it'd be incredibly heavy, but it's razor-thin. The heft is only because of how long it is. It's scary."

"Probably not so scary as that," Ophedia said, pointing down an alley. At the other end, they could make out a group of five Sentinels running toward them. Behind them, a mob of Revenants dogged their heels.

Deggar emerged from the alley first.

"What are you doing here, del Ishé?" he growled.

"Coming to pull you back."

"We lost three more already. Unless you brought more help, we're in a ship to the Judge."

He turned back toward the alley.

"They're cornered now," he laughed and lunged back into the opening.

"Watch my back," Aurín said, diving forward, the skyfall axe in one hand and talon open like a claw on the other.

The first two Revenants charged out of the alley, and Deggar cut one down, while Aurín's talon shot out, punching five clean holes in the Indigo Walker's chest.

"Best be careful," Deggar laughed. "Only the ones I cut down die."

"Looks like mine do, too," Aurín said with resolve.

One of the other remaining Sentinels was a captain, who readied his crossbow.

"Hold on," Ophedia said, taking out a skyfall bolt and handing it over. "Try one of these."

The man nodded his thanks and loaded it.

"Firing!" Ophedia shouted, and both men out front leapt aside. Two bolts fired and two Revenants fell.

"We can do this all day!" Deggar roared.

A sound up the street pattered in echo off the walls, and Ophedia turned.

"No, Deggar. We can't."

Deggar stopped to look. "Nocc. Nocc!!"

New Revenants walked sleepily toward them, drawn by the sound of their conflict.

"Too many," Ophedia muttered.

"Let's take them with us!" Deggar shouted.

"We're not here to die," Aurín shouted, his claw clamping onto the arm of another Revenant. With a twist, the razor tips flayed flesh. The Revenant pulled back. With a swing of his axe, the thing fell.

"If Death isn't here for us," Deggar said, pointing across the street, "then who is he here for?"

A figure stood there, a black cloak pulled down over his head and frame, with wisps of smoke trailing beneath. Next to him stalked a tiny black shadow. Their first move was sudden, racing across the street to the first Revenant. From the folds of his cloak two black-clad hands appeared, touched the Revenant, and just as suddenly, the Revenant disappeared entirely, as though it hadn't ever existed.

Deggar swore.

Aurín froze.

Ophedia smiled to herself and muttered under her breath, "Hanen."

8

Dreamwyrms

Let writhing lash fall upon he that questions the authority given by the Pantheon. How dare he separate himself from our will. How dare he question the granted purpose by which we have shackled our soul in sacrifice for the people. Have I not suffered enough? Have not the Praetors gone through persecuting flame to bring the truth to all?

—JODDUCE PREVAIN, FIRST PRAEPOSIT OF

THE PRAETORS OF THE CHALICE

"Sleep long enough?" Searn's voice asked loudly in his mind, startling Hanen awake from the desk he was slumped over.

"What?!" Hanen shouted, standing up and knocking over the chair. Whisper started from his spot next to the door where he'd curled up.

Hanen reached up and touched the pair of hoods over his thick and disheveled hair. He ran a hand over the stubble growing in over his face and grimaced.

"You fell asleep reading the journals. I figured you could use a few hours."

Hanen looked around blurry-eyed, undid the clasps and threw both of the cloaks onto the bed. Both journals were out and open on the desk. He reached to shut them and then scrounged around in his bags to find the last ration square from Ymbrys.

"We need food, Whisper," he said, sitting down and taking a

bite. The dried meat and nuts mostly tasted of the honey that glued it all together. It was all he had tasted for eight days.

Whisper slunk closer now that he didn't wear the boneshroud, and nudged at Hanen for a scratch and scrap. Hanen broke off a piece and tossed it to the little creature. He was, unlike most other ynfalds, black from pointed nose to tail, and covered in thumbnail-sized chitinous scales that rustled and rattled. He had sharp little teeth and a tongue that could and often did zip out to taste the air or nab at food. His beady black eyes spoke volumes, and his round little ears laid mostly flat against his skull. His tail was a long, fat affair of scales that clattered against the floor of their own accord to show excitement or wariness. When they walked, Whisper came up to just about Hanen's knee. He was larger than the lapfalds that upper-crust ladies of southern countries often carried around, but minuscule in comparison to some hunting ynfalds Hanen saw on display in Mahndür. He was a loyal companion, and stayed by Hanen even when he wore the cloak of bones now cast on the bed.

Hanen finished the rations and licked his fingers, even if he felt no less hungry than before, and wondered where he'd find anything else to eat. Ymbrys had all but disappeared, so he couldn't go ask him for more. Only once Hanen had spotted Rallia and Dorian moving through the city casually, so he'd followed them from rooftop to rooftop to find where they were staying. Their inn was a fair ways from the Revenant Quarter—as he was calling the places now barricaded to keep the Revenants at bay.

The Revenants.

The Journal appeared intentionally vague on the subject. They were mentioned, but it did not describe how Ollistan Gœrnstadt had made them during the Protectorate Wars. According to history books, they had been under his control. They were why he was called the Necromancer—the only person to ever hold the title. And that was odd. How had he learned to do it, if no one had before?

"What are you thinking about?" Searn said into his mind.

Hanen startled again. He hadn't remembered pulling the cloak on.

"I've got to find some food," Hanen replied.

"That's what you were thinking about?" Searn chuckled.

The bone pin Searn had thrust through his own eye, killing his body, and severing his soul, had since that fateful day been incorporated into the boneshroud. Now, when the cloak was on

Hanen's head, he could hear Searn's voice, instead of reading his words in blood across the bone.

"How did Ollistan command the Revenants?" Hanen asked.

"What do his journals say?"

"You know as much as I," Hanen said. "He made some deal, perhaps with a dark god. I don't know."

"That is not what my master thought."

"What do you mean?"

"Do you recall my mentioning the Heptagrammaton?"

"Yes. It was stolen out of your view," Hanen said.

"I think it is in the Veld now, beyond my ability to ever reach again. I never quite understood it, but there was a deal made with the Veld."

"Not a lot we can do about that now then, is there?"

Hanen and Whisper left the small room they'd been hiding in and descended to an alley by a small set of stairs. The entrance looked out onto the main street leading directly down from the citadel to the southern gate.

"I said once that it wasn't exactly necromancy," Searn said.

"What did you mean?"

"Exactly that. I don't know what it is."

A moment later, two black Sentinels marched quickly past the alley entrance: Ophedia and Aurín.

"Where are they going?" Hanen muttered. He moved forward to peek when a moment later, three Paladins wearing black cloaks marched behind them. "Escorted by Paladins?"

"What is it?" Searn asked.

"Ophedia and Aurín are marching south, with three Paladins wearing black cloaks. They don't appear to be in trouble—just moving with a sense of urgency."

Hanen cut back through the alley and out the other side, then began running down a parallel street. A few windows slammed shutters as he passed. No one went out if they could help it these days. He came to a wider road, not too far from the southern wall, looking west from a prominent inn that one of the commanders had taken over to hold the gate, and to the east, looking toward barricades into the Revenant Quarter. Ophedia and Aurín spoke with the three Paladins, and then took off by themselves toward the barricades. Whisper, a few feet away, saw them and began to shake his tail.

"Down boy. Come on," Hanen muttered, and pulled back up the

DREAD KNIGHT

street and into an alley. Whisper obeyed.

Hanen followed parallel to Ophedia and Aurín, and came out in a street just as a group of Sentinels came pouring out of an alley. The two black cloaked Sentinels were cutting down Revenants coming up from behind them. Aurín had an odd taloned glove on, and in his other hand he now held an axe made of the same metal as the gauntlets Hanen had hidden away. Ophedia shot a crossbow.

"Interesting," Hanen muttered.

"What is?"

"Ophedia made captain. Aurín bears an axe made of the black metal, and on his other hand he wears a claw-like glove."

Searn didn't respond.

Sounds up the street caught Hanen's attention—more Revenants from the north.

Hanen crouched down and opened up his satchel and withdrew two black metal rings made of skyfall. He put each up his wrists and closed his fists; suddenly both hands were encased in skyfall.

He stood, and watched the Sentinels notice the new Revenants arriving on the scene. They walked as someone in a dream—purple fire burning in their eyes.

One of the Sentinels noticed Hanen and pointed at him. Aurín saw him and froze. Hanen took a deep breath and leapt out across the street as the first Revenant came in range, Whisper at his heels. Hanen reached out with both gauntleted hands and slammed the Revenant in the chest, then stumbled forward as it completely disappeared.

"I just don't get it," Hanen said, rushing the next one. He slapped the Revenant upside the head with one gauntlet and nothing happened. It simply lurched sideways.

"What don't you get?" Searn asked.

"When I hit someone with both gauntlets, they merely disappear. But to where?"

"You were able to open a portal into the Veld, to hide the gauntlets away. Why can't that be the solution?"

"It might be," Hanen said.

The same Revenant recovered, spun, and threw its arms around Hanen. Whisper rushed up under the figure and nipped at its heels. Hanen reached up with both gauntleted hands, trying to get a grip anywhere. The figure's purple eyes glared into Hanen's, or tried to. Only, it didn't seem to have eyes. It had only empty sockets bleeding violet light. It didn't seem to see him, only sensed he was there. He got ahold of the man's leg, and then the other gauntlet shot up and took hold of the man's face, mouth open in silent horror, flailing to remove Hanen's hand.

"I can see it," Searn said into his mind.

"See what?"

"The connection. Look deep in there."

Hanen flexed his grip. Suddenly, the purple light went out and the man fell to the ground like a puppet with clipped strings. He lay there, battered, bruised, lying on the street like a sleeper. The empty sockets were no longer there, only closed eyes.

"What in Noccitan?" Hanen said.

"What did you do?"

"Somehow I clipped the connection."

Someone rushed up next to him.

"You going to just stand there and let the others kill you?" Ophedia asked.

Hanen turned and considered her. She held her crossbow up, another bolt nocked. The tip looked like black skyfall metal.

"Captain now?"

"I guess so. Maybe more."

"More?"

"I'll explain later."

Hanen looked over his shoulder. Aurín and the other Sentinels were fleeing back up the street.

"They're not going to stay and help?"

"I think you startled Aurín. He thinks you're Searn."

"Sort of true," Searn muttered in Hanen's mind.

"No," Hanen said, ignoring Searn. "Not Searn. I saw you and Aurín coming this way while I was out looking for food and got mixed up in this."

"So you're not just out here hunting Revenants?"

"No."

"You know not to kill them, right?"

"What do you mean?"

"The flame in their eyes jumps to someone else when they die."

"I don't seem to have that problem."

Another Revenant leapt forward at Hanen. He held both hands up in defense and again, the Revenant merely disappeared.

"That's a great tavern trick," Ophedia said. "What if where they go is worse, though?"

"It's not here," Hanen said. "That's all that matters. If we're not supposed to kill them, why is your crossbow loaded? And with skyfall no less?"

"A gift from the citadel. Apparently striking them with skyfall does the job."

She lifted her crossbow and pointed it at a Revenant. Her shot dropped it, then it gave a little gasp.

"Who is that?" Ophedia asked, pointing up the road.

Far up the street, through the midst of the hundreds of gathering Revenants, a figure walked with his own black cloak over his shoulders. He stumbled forward, lurching as much as the others, yet the Revenants gave him a wide berth, keeping themselves at least twenty feet from him.

"You!" the man shouted, pointing at Hanen.

"It's that Paladin I took these from," he said, holding both gauntlets up. "Slate."

"Time to go, I think," Ophedia said as she pulled the last bolt from the fallen Revenant. "The others are clear, so why stick around?"

They turned to run before Slate could press through the horde when the sound of hooves beat the cobbles. Ten Paladins on sleipnir rushed around the corner. They did not wear gorgets, but wore black cloaks over their backs, and carried large skyfall axes in their hands.

"That's the last thing we need," Ophedia said, grabbing hold of Hanen's cloak and pulling him across the street and into an alley.

"What are you doing?"

"If they see you with me, Noss is going to add my name to the list of people who have some explaining to do."

The Paladins rushed past the alley they'd slunk into and toward the Revenants. One Paladin eyed her as they passed, then returned to driving the Revenants back. Hanen peeked out of the alley, but then immediately covered his ears as a ringing began.

"What is that?!" Searn shouted in his head.

Hanen pulled the cloak from his head, and the ringing stopped screeching in his ears. The gauntlets in his hands grew hot. He made the practiced motion, and the gauntlets disappeared, becoming only rings on his wrist. They clattered to the ground.

"What just happened?" Ophedia asked.

"I don't know," Hanen said. "There was a ringing, and the gloves grew hot."

He moved to the edge of the alley and peeked out again. The Paladins had thrown themselves into the Revenants. One of them held a pole with a large bell swinging from the top.

"The Paladins who are in charge now, they're sort of obsessed with bells," Ophedia said over his shoulder. "Only, the thing is, they aren't Paladins anymore."

"What do you mean?"

"They founded a new Order. They're called Wardens now, and they're absorbing Sentinels into their ranks."

The Wardens rode down several Revenants and came upon Slate, now on his knees before them, begging, and pointing toward the alley Hanen and Ophedia were in.

The Wardens didn't seem to care. One of them leapt down and shackled Slate, the Revenants nearby pressing away from the bell that continued to clang.

The Wardens turned to go back the way they had come.

"Come on," Hanen said. "Let's get out of view entirely."

They moved farther back down the alley and ducked behind a box. The Wardens moved past them, on to the barricades around the corner.

"Alright," Ophedia said. "Let's go."

They walked back out into the street. Revenants lay dead everywhere. They passed one of them that suddenly struggled. Ophedia leapt back with a squeal. The Revenant's leg had been broken, probably shoved to the ground by a sleipnir.

"Come on," Hanen said.

"Wait," Ophedia said, considering the Revenant.

"What?"

"You removed the flame from one of them. I saw it. How?"

"I don't know. I'm not sure I didn't do damage while doing it."

"This man is already as good as dead," Ophedia said. "Why not figure out how to fix him?"

"She has a point," Searn said. Hanen didn't remember pulling the hood back on.

"Alright," Hanen sighed. "We tie him up carefully, and guide him somewhere safe."

Ophedia already had her rope out.

Hanen shoved his way into a random abandoned home, the door rattling in the wind as Ophedia came up the stairs with her prisoner in tow. Whisper sniffed around the back rooms while Hanen riffled through cupboards.

He found a jar, opened the top, and sniffed. He broke the wax on top, and dipped a finger in.

"What is it?" Ophedia asked. She had set the Revenant into a chair and tied him up with her rope.

Hanen pulled out two more jars from the recesses of the cabinet and tossed one to her. "Potted meat."

"No, thank you," she said, wrinkling her nose.

"Not something you favor?"

"I spent an entire summer living off that when I was ten. Potted meat in high summer…terrible."

"Give it to Whisper then. I'll eat these two." He indicated the two jars in his hands. Then he took out his knife and dug the wax off the top, and began shoveling the first jar into his mouth.

"Really been a few days, huh?" Ophedia asked, watching with open disgust.

"Four," Hanen said. "I think."

"Well, finish up. I don't want to stay here too long."

"Bar the door," he said, shoveling down the rest of the contents and wiping his hands off. He placed his satchel on the table, along with the boneshroud, then took out both rings and set them aside.

"What are those?" she asked, coming to stand back across from him.

"The gauntlets," he said.

"Really?"

He took them up and dropped them over his wrists, then clenched his fists. The black gauntlets appeared instantly.

Ophedia's surprise manifested merely as an arched eyebrow. He turned to the figure on the chair eying them both.

"Be careful, Hanen."

"Of course."

"No," Ophedia said, coming around the table. "I mean watch out. If it locks eyes with you…"

"What do you mean?"

"One of them held me down and looked me in the eyes. It beckoned me."

"To what?"

"Let it in," she murmured with a shudder.

Hanen turned back to the table and pulled the boneshroud hood over his head. The silent room grew quieter. He turned back to the Revenant.

"Hold his hair, and make him look at me," Hanen said.

Ophedia did as she was told.

Hanen leaned forward and looked deep into the man's eyes. Beyond the indigo cloud he saw deeper down into black wells, to that infinitesimal pinpoint of light. It moved and squirmed like a tiny wyrm seeking the surface after a rain.

"What are you?" Hanen asked.

He held up his gauntleted hands, and took hold of nothing in front of him, then twisted the gauntlets, tearing open a hole in the air.

"What in Noccitan?!" Ophedia shouted, letting go of the Revenant's head for a moment, before grabbing it again.

"Just hold on, Ophedia," Hanen said, pulling back on the edges of the hole and opening it wider. Beyond the hole sat a world of purple hues. The sky was blanketed by an indigo cloud, and not far off sat mountains, identical to the ones above the city of Haven. There was no city, though. Only a field of oddly-formed grass, each bearing heads, like oats, topped with glowing amethyst grain, ready for harvest.

"Sweet Shepherdess," Ophedia said. "Is that Dream?"

"Yes, I think so," Hanen said.

"Are you going to say hello for me?" Searn asked.

Hanen ignored him.

"Look there," Searn said.

Hanen peered down at the grain that would have been at his feet if he stood on the other side of the door he had opened. From the earth rose a long, white, and eyeless serpent, tangled in a knot around something.

"What do you see?" Hanen asked.

"Nothing but a purple field," Ophedia said.

"A wyrm," Searn said.

"Not a wyrm on the ground?" Hanen asked.

"No."

"Then you must be seeing through the same window but from the other side."

Hanen reached through the hole in the air. As they crossed through, the black gauntlets turned silver. The wyrm began to writhe as his touch came near. From the mass, the eyeless head reared. Its mouth opened slowly, revealing a maw full of short, tiny tentacles, like the creatures that lived in the small tidal pools near Hanen's hometown of Garrou. The tentacles appears to be secreting little bits of slime that if he were not armored, he'd be hesitant to touch. It suddenly struck at the gauntlets, leaving hissing steam across the spot. Nothing happened, and the thing recoiled down into itself.

Hanen reached out and stroked the back of the thing's head. It accepted the movement, and pulled back some of its coils, to show what lay within.

Deep down in the center of the knot of coils sat a form with no figure. Yet it was not a part of it. Smaller tentacles had seemed to form out of the wyrm's underside, and taken hold of the thing within, taking some form of sustenance from it.

"What are you?" Hanen asked.

The wyrm did not respond, but the form in the middle did.

He carefully took hold of the wyrm's body, and tried to pull it away from the form. More folds of the wyrm threw themselves around their little quarry. Then the head lifted slowly, tentatively coiling its way up and around one of Hanen's gauntlets, edging toward the window.

"What is that?!" Ophedia cried out from over Hanen's shoulder, startling him.

"Why aren't you holding him?"

"He stopped struggling. Now what is that?"

"I don't know. I think it's what holds the Revenant in dream."

"I wouldn't let it out," Ophedia said, the head coming near the window.

Hanen reached up with a hand and took a firm hold of the head.

"Why are your gauntlets silver inside Dream?"

"I've no idea why, but they are. Now let me concentrate."

He held the wyrm head in one hand, and with the other, struggled to untangle the form in the middle. Eventually, he was able to hold it in one hand, then lift it gently. The middle of the wyrm came with it, still attached by hundreds of little umbilicals.

He dropped the head of the wyrm, which was thrown off its balance.

Hanen used his free hand to try and pry the tentacles from the form. The man in the chair began to moan.

Hanen took a firmer hold of both as the last and deepest sunk tentacles held on for dear life, and he yanked.

The wyrm screeched, and fell to writhing through the window to the Veld. Hanen could hear screams from all across the field. At the same time, the man in the chair woke from his dream like coming out of a nightmare. Hanen pulled back both gauntlets from the hole, and with a twist, closed the window into Dream.

"Where am I?!" the man in the chair cried out.

"Ophedia, a candle," Hanen said. Evening was falling outside, and it had plunged the place into darkness.

Ophedia fumbled around and lit a candle, while Hanen put the gauntlets and boneshroud out of view.

They all grimaced against the candlelight until their eyes adjusted.

"Welcome back to the land of the living," Ophedia said.

"I…" the man muttered with a voice that had not been used in a long time. "I was in an endless nightmare."

"You're back now," Hanen said.

"How?"

"I don't know," Hanen lied. "We found you."

"Let's get you someplace safe," Ophedia said, and began untying his ropes.

"Food," the man said.

Hanen sighed. He produced the third potted meat and handed it to the man, who dove into it voraciously. Hanen grimaced as he watched the man.

"Why are you disgusted?" Ophedia asked. "That's what you looked like."

"I'm grimacing because I was hoping to eat that myself," Hanen said.

"Then let's get you and this man somewhere safe, and I'll get you some food."

9

Interludes

I am hungry.
"Not a lot I can do about that now, is there," Slate said to the voice in his head. He fiddled with the bone ring hanging from the leather thong on his neck, while the wound in his shoulder where the man who had stolen his gauntlets had shot him throbbed with pain. "They locked us away."
They don't trust you.
"Why should they? I'm from another sect."
And their group?
"They've built some new Order entirely, it seems. They've sent an invitation to me several times, but I don't trust them."
Why not?
"Because I know their origins."
Explain.
"You were once a part of the boneshroud. You know more than you let on."
Explain...
"Searn."
The voice in his head scoffed. *Don't say that name.*
"Don't much care for him?"
He destroyed my body. Made me this.
"Well, regardless, you know that he used the tools I had worked so hard to unlock, and he meant to use those to unify the Moteans, to use them to usurp the Paladins. Now that he's dead, his followers have founded their own order. They want what I have at my command. They'll have me killed as soon as I relinquish it."

Not if I protect you.

"How?"

In life, I was looked down upon, for my looks and for my inability to understand those around me. I feel stronger now, but not whole.

"I feel stupider now that you are in my mind."

Perhaps we share much more than we realize.

"You've taken from me?"

I doubt I can help it. Regardless, I am no longer acting in fear. I am, after all, immortal. I am Deathless, and with that, brings clarity. Let us work together. I think perhaps, through that, we can accomplish much more.

Slate considered for a time.

Well?

"I accept. We work together."

Then put me on.

Slate tore the leather thong from his neck and held up the bone ring. It was small. Almost too small to fit on any finger.

Go on.

He pushed it onto the tip of his index finger. A sensation ran up his arm, and into his mind suddenly. He lost control of his other hand which took hold of the ring, and violently shoved it down over both knuckles, tearing through skin, and causing him to bleed. The ring of bone now sat, bloody, on his finger.

"You shunt!" Slate roared.

"No worse than you," he replied to himself.

The door to the cell opened. Pellian Noss stood outside.

"Shall we go for a walk, Slate?"

"Yes. We would like that," both of them said.

"You have too long walked alone or in the shadows of others, Slate," Pellian Noss said as they walked the walls of the citadel.

Slate walked alongside him twitchily, taking everything in around him.

"We've had our interactions. We've had our differences. But I would hope you see that all I have done has been to convince you of the good we're trying to bring with the Wardens."

"Wardens..." Slate said, glancing at Noss. His face flashed through several conflicting emotions—he sneered, scowled, and then went passive.

"Wardens. The new Order we have founded. I'd like you to join us, and bring what you have under your control to bear."

"What we have to bear?"

Noss stopped and leaned against the parapets. A flock of small, black-feathered gryphs circled overhead on a mid-day updraft. Down below, the Chalician army to the west sat watching the walls. Far to the south, the second front sat just as still.

"I know you have the armor hidden away somewhere. Only this morning with you in your cell, I was finally able to go and retrieve your forge. You'd let it grow cold, making it much easier to take."

"That is ours," Slate said.

"Was," Noss corrected. He took up a book from his side satchel and held it out. "Familiar with this?"

Slate gave a nod. "Shade book."

"Right. But not just a single shade. I've got so many old friends in here now. Several Masters, too. And even…your old master."

Slate gave him a quizzical look. "Old Master?"

"Vanguard."

"He betrayed us all."

"That he did. Got himself thrown into this book as a result. I bet you'd love to hold this book."

Slate eyed it with avarice.

"Yet, you keep back the armor."

"Not much we can do with it now," Slate said.

"Why?"

"Shroud is back. He took both gauntlets and cast that Revenant plague over half the city."

"Shroud?"

"Yes! Aren't you listening?" Shroud returned. "Wearing that cloak. He took them both from us, as he did in Mahn Fulhar. He used them to create the Revenants."

Slate grew quiet, eyeing the gryphs above.

"Now what about the armor?" Noss asked.

"What about it?" Slate replied.

"Will you bring it?"

"We will think about it."

"In the meantime, I won't lock your door. You're a guest. Perhaps I might even convince you to become a Warden, and cast off Pariantür."

"We stopped being a Paladin a long time ago," Slate said.

Noss walked away, and glanced back once. He couldn't quite tell, but thought that with a wave of Slate's mangled index finger the gryphs above were moving at his command.

The forest inn sat atop a knoll with the trees cleared back from its foundations a hundred yards in every direction. For miles past that, the Arbeswald woods rolled. To the east, the oaks stretched to the lake districts and their arable fields. To the west, the oaks turned to pines as they reached the Abei mountains.

The dark roads meandering through the thick roots of the old woods from north to south had proven a slower road than Marn Clouw and Alodda Dülar had hoped. Every stop had offered little hope that a safe road could be found up into the Limaean Plateau, with brigands said to have increased in the past month, and war rumored to hold the capital of Limae under siege. Only the Dead Pass to the north and travel through Castenard offered hope to the two of them, as they raced to reunite with Hanen and Rallia, for they had gone too far south to turn back and make for Haven.

The main room of the Arbwallstave Inn was vaulted on massive oak timbers. Behind the bar, barrels connected to smaller timbers through shiny copper pipes. Men and women stood at the seatless counter, sipping from thick glass drinking vessels. Marn left Alodda at the table by the door, their packs leaning against the wall, and approached the barkeep. They exchanged words for a while before Marn turned back, worry across his brow, the limp in his gait worse off than usual after the steep climb to the inn.

"He only has one room left, and it's not affordable," he said. Twice Alodda's age, his head was now completely shaven, his gray monk robes given to a beggar outside of Birin. Alodda wore a simple lilac-colored smock and a gray travel cloak. Her long blonde hair was braided in a crown around her head. She offered Marn a faint smile.

"The day is young. We can eat and rest for a while and then see if there is good shelter along the road farther south."

Marn shook his head. "He said that outlaws have been proliferating the woods around here lately. If we're to make for Castenard, we'd do better to stay the night, and travel with others."

"Did he say how far to Castenard?"

"A week's travel. The next large inn is a stockyard two days from here."

"How are we to sleep here without a room we can afford?"

DREAD KNIGHT

"It's not ideal, but many just sleep at the tables."

"You're right. That's not ideal."

An older barmaid walked by, hair in disarray, the hem of her dress looking the worse for wear. She set a tray of empty drinking glasses on the bar and the man behind offered her a wan smile.

She turned and looked back at the busy room, then gave a defeated sigh.

"It appears you could use a hand," Alodda said as she walked by.

The woman gave her an exasperated look. "Not a bed to offer, yet the flood of travelers this week is unprecedented."

"This isn't normal?"

The woman shook her head. "Doesn't help both our sons are off with a delivery to the Lake District, and took their wives with them."

"Can I help?" Alodda asked.

"I can't give you a room in trade."

"I understand," Alodda said. "I'm a master seamstress. If you've a spare frock, I can hem that dress of yours in no time."

The woman looked down and scowled. "Not again."

"Let me help," Alodda said.

The woman gave a curt nod and led her to a side door. Within moments she had returned with two frocks, both with the same problem. "My son's wife does the mending, but she has a lot to learn."

"She's used a temporary stitch rather than something more permanent. Give me the afternoon and I'll have all three of your frocks looking like new."

Alodda was true to her word. When she came out to the main room to see the third frock, Marn was behind the bar pouring flagons alongside the owner.

As evening fell, the already crowded room became a din of cheer and camaraderie. The husband and wife's tired faces had transformed into renewed smiles. Alodda had been given five more frocks from travelers who had heard of her deft needlework. Marn held the purse, now full of copper.

During an odd lull, Marn and Alodda approached the woman again. "Mistress Stave," Alodda addressed her.

"Lagaer, please."

"Lagaer. I know earlier you had a room for rent still that many could not afford. Would you take the coin we've earned today in trade for it?"

"I won't hear of it," Lagaer said. "You'll each have a bed in our home. Our sons won't be back for days. You've helped us more than you can know."

Alodda gave her a broad smile in trade. "We cannot thank you enough."

"The thanks to be given is ours," she replied.

"Helping out in whatever kindness we can is the least we can do," Marn said.

"If only there was more kindness such as yours, Kallattai would turn easier."

"It never harms to be kind," Alodda said, and they turned to help offer drinks to the new wave of travelers walking through the door.

Noss sat at his desk and took up the box stashed behind his holy tomes. He opened the lid and took out the *Book of Shades* and set it aside. Under that lay the blue book Aurín had retrieved from the top of the tower. He took up the bone quill next to that, and held it up to consider.

Opening the inkwell, he touched the tip to the red liquid within. The pen lapped it up eagerly. Touching the nib to paper, it began to write with little guidance from him.

Interesting book, the words of Aeger wrote.

"You communicated with them?" Noss glanced at the bind-up.

No. Your new book.

"You read it?"

I did. Afraid of what is in there?

Noss did not reply.

You haven't opened it.

"What is it?"

Do you remember old Brother Gol Vercott?

"Yes. He was insane. Shroud loved speaking with him."

And his apprentice.

"Luva VeGollin?"

The boy never took his vows. Disappeared about the same time as Shroud left Pariantür.

"I wondered about that."

Well, this journal is his. Turns out he helped Shroud fake his death. He was Vercott's secret son. Traveled with Searn for a while, and then became obsessed with skyfall. I think he might have been Skysmith.

"Skysmith? Who invented the dominion coins?"

One and the same.

"His writing is what turned me onto the creation of the bells. Then Aurín came upon his remains…"

Aurín?

"A Black Sentinel and first to join the new cause. I showed him favoritism, and he's repaid me by keeping some of the treasures he found in the Griffin Tower for himself, including a taloned skyfall glove. I'd wager he took it from the remains of Skysmith. He's calling himself Talon."

Fool. We ought to see if we can convince Zoumerik to part with Master Talon's shadebook and give it to this new Talon. He'll have him turned to our side in a matter of days.

"I'll consider that. But back to Skysmith—how did you read his journal?"

He wrote it in blood. His own, I presume.

Noss dropped the pen and grabbed the blue journal from the box and opened it. The pages were blank.

"What did you do?!" Noss roared.

I read the journal.

"You absorbed it all!"

I did. Too bad you didn't get the chance. There were some interesting things in there.

"If you think this is going to convince me to give you anything for this insult, you're sorely mistaken."

You assume I need your approval to do anything.

"You shunt."

No need for name-calling. You may put me away now. Take me back up when you're less angry and maybe I'll tell you a bit more about what I've learned from Skysmith's journal. Searn had more plans in place than any of us realized. I think he ensured Skysmith got himself killed with his obsession so none of us would know.

PART 2

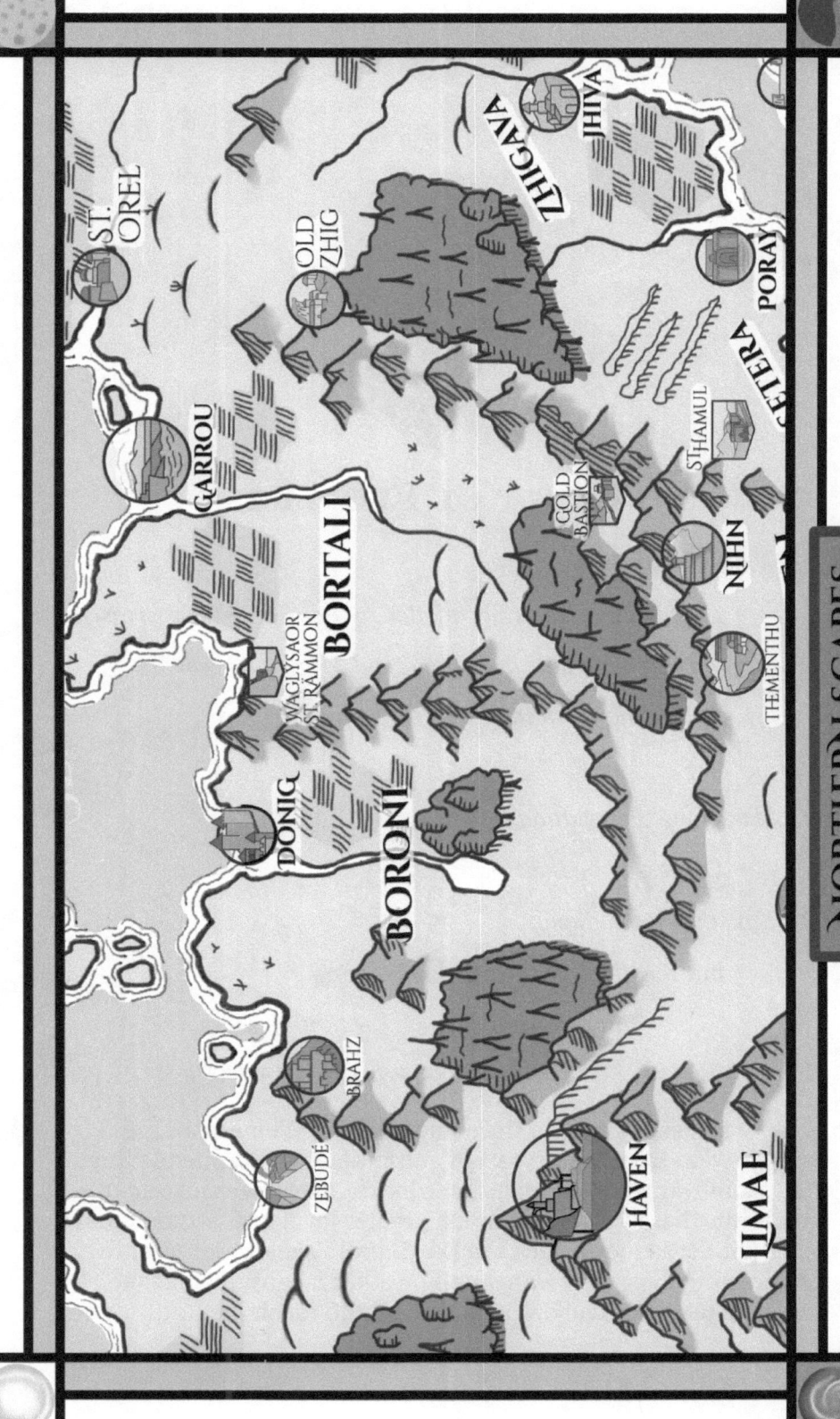

10

Vault of Flowers

Blessings be upon their head,

    Let they who tend the garden, of her delights be praised.

For by the Mother's will shall they tend,

    And bring forth the fruits of the vine.

O, blessed be their hands,

    O, blessed be their names.

Not for their own glory,

    but the glory of the garden blessing,

        they who eat of the trees that blossom.

            —PSALM OF SISTER SEREVIEN

A pleasant joy filled their solemn days. Women came and went from the Crysalas Vault in Garrou, despite the threat of war with Boroni and the locked gates, reminiscent of their time barely a year before. A greater joy flourished in Katiam and Larohz as they healed the Day Blind. Esenath was attentive, redirecting those that were blind by other means. If someone became too over-exuberant, and sought to touch the Rotha, Astrid ensured her safety.

When late evening settled over the city above and curfew insisted most were back abed, Katiam sat in the Sister Superioris's sitting room, hearth blazing, with the Rotha in fresh soil. The Sister Superioris Ermani Wittal was away from the city, visiting a Vault in Zhigava. Katiam had hoped to see her when they arrived, but the escape to a space of their own was even more welcome.

She threw herself down in a comfortable chair. Nearly a quarter century old, she had a rounder figure, even after the year of travel. Her short black bangs were kept up out of her face by a wire crown of silver leaves with a gold rose set in the center. Her blush pink robes hung loose with her belt and traveler robe lying over a nearby chair.

"I don't know how she did it."

"Who?" Astrid Glass asked from the chair next to her. Astrid still had her Paladame regalia on, her short blonde hair framing her face. Bits of white under-robes showed through at the seams of her armor.

"Auntie. When she was Matriarch Superioris. How did she spend day in and day out holding court or conversation with others?"

"I would imagine she set very strict hours," Esenath said, coming over with glasses for the three of them. Esenath was a dark-skinned Sidieratan, who kept her head shaved and wore a brown robe, in observation of her Aspects of Cleanliness and Charity.

"Who eez Auntee?" Larohz hummed, toying with the dirt around her. Her head, if it could be called that, appeared like an immature rosebloom. She bore five leaves, the top three acting as arms, while the newest near the bottom were barely more than vines that gave her stability. The two roots in the dirt were out of sight. She bore no mouth, nor eyes, just the rosebloom. Below that were two thorns that nearly touched, vibrating against one another like insect wings. Small holes near the thorns whistled. With these sounds the Rotha emulated voice.

"My Great Aunt," Katiam answered.

"Graat Aunteee?"

"My...grandfather's sister."

"What eez sisster?" Larohz asked.

Katiam laughed. "I'll explain later."

This seemed to satisfy the Rotha.

"She is learning so much so fast," Astrid said.

"By the day," Esenath said. "She figures out more than she asks about."

"And without eyes nor ears," Astrid said, looking at the little creature.

"Esenath and I think her thorns are both her ears and her voice," Katiam said.

"Speaking of learning," Esenath said. Onelie and Little Maeda have been eating up the attention Narah and Lutea have given them."

"Oh?"Katiam replied.

"Lutea took Onelie off of Toire's hands. The Bronuan princess has been trying to find time for herself, after being all around the city, doing who knows what, and Lutea has already read every book in the Vault. So she's been instructing Onelie on Crysalas Doctrine."

"And Narah?"

"Providing solace and counseling to Little Maeda on the life of a Veiled Sister. I think focusing on that has been helpful."

Both Narah and Lutea had stayed in Bortali when the Matriarch's entourage had been through the year prior, to continue their own missions. Lutea Calimbrise was a larger, stoic woman under the Aspect of Solemnity. She was a scholar with a knack for memory. Her close friend, Narah Wevan, was a Veiled sister, and an extreme one at that, taking on four total vows—Stillness, Sanctity, Solitude, and the dietary Aspect of St. Klare—acting in tandem to voluntarily separate herself from the world. She wore gloves, a wide hood, and a veil over her face. She spoke only in whispers, and none of them had ever seen her face. She bore a sharp wit, and everyone who spent an evening with her in conversation became fast, life-long friends.

"To know they are both in such capable hands is a relief," Katiam said. "Will they be coming with us when we leave?" Katiam asked.

"I should hope so," Astrid said. "If one comes, they both will, and I'd hate to leave them behind."

"Unless their missions here are more important," Esenath said.

"Of course," Astrid said.

"Were the Day-Blind pearls distributed?" Katiam asked.

"Yes," Esenath replied. "The pearls collected from the healings were saved. Half of them will be given out to men around the city who cannot come here to be healed, and half are going to be taken to the Isles of Bronue Jinre along with my notes. Apparently the malady is worse there, which further suggests to me that it comes from even farther north. Shieldmaiden Toire will see to it her father, Rhi Barra, sends scholars to Nasun to help determine if its origins can be identified."

"Can you imagine what we wouldn't know if you had not come from the College at Thementhu?" Katiam asked.

"Katiam. If you had not taken up the Rotha from that desk so many would still be blind, and we'd know nothing."

Astrid rose from her seat and Esenath followed.

"Shall I take the Rotha with me tonight?" Esenath asked, "to give you some rest?"

"No," Katiam said. "Thank you. I'll spend some time with Larohz before bed."

As they left, Katiam lowered herself onto the ground next to the Rotha. The little creature turned its bloom toward her, considering her with a sniff, then held its leafy vines up to be held. Katiam took hold of the lower part of the Rotha's stalk. The original pod shell was now almost completely encased by densely packed roots, fusing as a single brown trunk. Pulling Larohz free from the dirt, the two short root legs came free. The entire Rotha from bloom to root was no longer than eight inches—not much larger than a newborn babe, but hardly comparable. Larohz was nearly as active as some two-year-old girls she had known in the Vaults.

"Shall we try walking again?" Katiam said, lowering Larohz to the rug.

The two stalky legs, only a couple of inches long, got their grip on the rug, and even tighter was the leafy grip on Katiam's finger.

"Try your steps, Little Rose," Katiam said. "You've done it before. You can do it again."

The Rotha threw a foot forward and stepped down. Then the other. Katiam tried to pry her own finger from the leaf bound around it, and the Rotha obliged, focusing solely on walking forward, an inch at a time.

It suddenly toppled over, vines and leaves throwing themselves forward to catch herself to prevent her bloom from bashing itself on the carpet.

It began to purr like a housecör, in little vibrating sobs.

"You are alright," Katiam comforted, stroking the back of the bloom.

"Hurrrt," Larohz said.

"Are you hurt? Or just sad?"

The Rotha considered for a moment. "Saaad."

"Then let's try again. Pick yourself up."

The little creature put its vines down and got one leg under itself, then another, and turned slowly around, then began to walk back across the rug.

"Very good!" Katiam said as it reached the other side, and half fell over once more.

"Verrrry gooood," Larohz repeated. Standing, she turned to Katiam, and proceeded to toddle to her, leafy hands held up to be lifted.

Katiam took up the Rotha in her arms and gave a soft embrace. The Rotha nuzzled into her chest, then looked up.

"Mama Kat," Larohz said.

"Yes, Little Rose?"

"What iz sisster?"

"Sister means from the same mother. From...same plant but different."

"You haz many sisster."

"No," Katiam said. "No sisters."

"You say 'sisster' to all."

"Ah," Katiam said. "That is different."

"How?"

"We are in a sisterhood. Meaning, it is what we call each other to say we are close. We are sisters because we have joined the same group."

"I haz sisster?"

"Yes," Katiam said. "Yes, I believe you do."

"Where?"

"We don't know. We're looking."

"We will find sissterz."

"Yes. I think we will."

Larohz grew quiet, indicating she was tired. She had adopted sleep cycles, and by Esenath's measurements, she grew more when resting than during her active hours. Katiam nestled the Rotha into a provided pot of dirt and took to the bed, the blankets warmed by the nearby dwindling hearth.

She woke to leafy hands touching her face. The Rotha had somehow climbed up onto the bed, and was playing with Katiam's nose.

"Larohz," Katiam said. "What are you doing?"

"Dayyy," it said.

"Alright. But please don't do that while I sleep."

"Why?"

"It is very disturbing."

"Diss. Turb."

"A bother. Something we don't like."

The Rotha considered. "Sorrree."

"That's alright. You didn't know."

A knock came at the door.

"Disturb?" Larohz asked.

"Sometimes necessary," Katiam said, crossing the room to the door.

She opened it and invited Astrid in, who wore her full regalia.

"What is going on?"

"Siobh arrived this morning. Apparently the Paladins arrived at the gates last night and brought news of vül incursions along the coast. Then guess what happened?"

"They were denied entry to the city?"

"Right in one. They set up camp out a ways back from the gate, and Siobh was able to get a message to and from them. They're requesting that we try and get out of the city, join them, and we'll continue on."

"Just us?" Katiam asked.

"Any who will come. Crysalas or Paladin."

"How soon?"

"Tonight."

Katiam turned to the bed to take up the Rotha, but she was nowhere to be seen.

"Larohz?" Katiam called.

Astrid touched Katiam's shoulder and pointed down. The little Rotha stood at Katiam's feet, clinging to her dress.

"My word," Katiam said, lifting her. "You were tripping and stumbling last night, and now you're moving all about."

"We go?" Larohz asked.

"Yes. Let's bundle you in and go help the others."

She took up the Rotha and wrapped it inside her robes. The little creature was used to it now, often helping as she was able, quiet as a sleeping babe and undetectable on Katiam.

She walked out into the Vault's main room to a flurry of activity. Esenath was at the side, sitting with four scribes, scribbling notes as she spoke animatedly. Not far from there, Lutea Calimbrise spoke with one of the local women over a table of books, while Onelie Clemmbäkker watched on. Astrid walked alongside the fiery red-headed Paladame Toire Siobh, and behind them walked both hooded and veiled sisters, Narah Wevan and Little Maeda. They saw Katiam enter the room and approached. Onelie also took the opportunity to break away from Lutea and join them.

"Katiam," Astrid said as they approached. "We're discussing if we need any additional supplies for the trip. By what route will we head south?"

"I had thought we might take the same one, down through Nemen."

"I'd rather not. I fear vül activity. Too few of us are battle-ready."

"What do you suggest?"

"With the coming conflict with Boroni," Toire Siobh said, "Bortali has become paranoid of their other neighbors too, especially Zhigava. There is a well-guarded pass toward Old Zhig that could be used."

"Is it a hard pass?"

"Cold, but well-traveled."

"What is the Crysalas standing in Zhigava?"

"Since they finally broke away from the Ikahalan Protectorship thirty years back," Astrid said, "they don't completely align with the Ikhalans, but I think we can assume a bit of the same coldness."

Narah Wevan cleared her throat and stepped closer to speak in a whisper. "I disagree."

"Why is that, Sister Wevan?" Katiam asked.

"Seterans and Zhigavans have long been associated with the cultures near them. Zhigava is the older of the two. I'd even venture to say that their culture provides origins to much of Ikhalan, Bortalian, and even some Morriegan traditions. They're a quiet people. Reserved. But hardly judgmental. I've spent some time there, and I have never feared for my safety."

"Very well," Katiam said. "Then we agree we go through the Old Zhig pass?"

There was a murmur of acknowledgment.

"The bigger question is supplies," Astrid said. "Old Zhig may have some, but there are only small villages down the river to the coast on maps I've seen."

"There are so few of us," Katiam said. "That shouldn't be a problem." She turned to Narah. "Will you and Lutea be coming with us?"

Sister Wevan nodded.

"So," Astrid said, "by my count: Katiam, Esenath, and myself, Wevan, Calimbrise, Onelie, and Little Maeda."

"Let's not forget the Paladins," Katiam said.

"That is why I'm worried about the villages. The brothers can find their own food, for certain, but it will be a large group of us."

"All we can do is continue our journey," Katiam said, "and pray the pantheon provides."

II

Cornered Rose

It is thought that the Martyrdom of St. Lesset brought about the Golden Century. Indeed the 19th Century saw many great and wonderful things. Ellavon Gavalin is said to have written in this time. His first play, Lesset the Glassblower's Daughter *spun off his career, even if it was arguably his weakest piece. Her death, and its exoneration through that play, single-handedly saw the name Lesset given to one in ten girls for the better part of a century. Her stance against the pogroms in the dead kingdom of Edür initiated the last great shift of borders, the rise in power of the Crysalas Church, and likely the foundation of the Paladames of the Rose as an order.*

—HISTORIES OF GANTHIC

Little Maeda walked arm in arm with Katiam, who had grown used to walking with the old Matriarch Superioris when she was with them. The thinner Crysalas wore cloth over every inch of her body, the insides of which had been plastered with burn ointment. Katiam remembered how young she'd looked, appearing barely of age, yet Katiam had learned later they almost shared a birthday at nearly twenty-four.

"I do wish you would all just leave me," Maeda muttered.

"Why would we do that?" Katiam replied.

"I'm weighing you down. I should have just stayed in Waglÿsaor. Walking this slow is only going to endanger you."

"Every day you get faster," Katiam said, "and your presence is a constant source of joy, for every one of us."

"I fail to understand why."

"It is not out of pity," Katiam replied. "So you can cast that thought far from your mind. You are our friend. We will not leave you behind."

They came to a corner with a young woman selling dried herbs. Katiam pulled Little Maeda with her to the woman's box.

"We should like to purchase some lavender sachets, if you have any," Katiam said.

The woman looked through her box, shook her head, and pointed up another street. "Take that street five more blocks. There is a grocer there. You can see an inn up the street from his stand. The Alewife who runs the establishment is well-known for having a stock of sachets."

"Thank you kindly," Katiam said and turned, Little Maeda hunched over, with her hood giving her the appearance of an old lady. Although the grunts she gave sounded all too real.

"They say that griefdark has been invading from Zhigava into Bortali, in the lower passes especially," Katiam said.

"Oh?" Maeda said. "Why do you mention that?"

"We're far enough into spring now that I would wager we'll find some fresh growth and can harvest it. I think the griefdark ointment you have been using is losing its strength."

"Um..." Little Maeda faltered. "I haven't been using it."

Katiam gasped. "What have you been using?"

"Honey and ointment drawn from a coastal succulent the women here swear by."

"We'll have to consult Esenath," Katiam said.

Maeda pulled up short. "Katiam. If you're going to insist I travel with you, please allow me to choose my own treatment. I do not like the long-term effects that griefdark seems to have on me."

"Such as?"

Little Maeda did not respond, but continued to walk.

"Maeda, I'm a physician. Please tell me."

"My throat and face. That is where I most require ointment. But griefdark relaxes my throat too much. It causes my voice and tongue to drawl and my lips to drool. I am already hideous enough, with everything burned away. To be further reduced is an affront to my dignity. I should like to keep what little I have left."

"I understand," Katiam said. "And I respect that."

They came to the grocer described. Up ahead they could see another pair of women, Esenath and Lutea by the looks of it, entering the inn. They turned to walk up the street when trumpets suddenly sounded from behind. A procession marched up the street, several white sleipnirs at the head, atop which rode gray-clad knights, like Paladins, with blue chalices across their tabards. Rather than gorgets, they wore cylindrical helmets upon their heads, slightly wider at the top. Their beards were trimmed, and they carried aloft long spears with arrowhead-styled tips, the other end bore arrow fletching styled feathers or sleipnir hair. From their belts hung books in red leather and jewel-encrusted chalices.

In their midst rode one who was obviously their leader, seated in a saddle that placed him taller than the others. He had a white mustache and a permanent look of disdain.

At the front of their group rode a younger herald, a scroll out in both hands, repeating his message over and over as they approached.

"Behold, Provost Zehan Otem, second to the Praetor Praeposit Anhouil Chétain. Only the Benefactor Missioner Abithu Omrab, Highest on the Path of Aben holds a higher authority. All kings and their subjects fall under Aben's authority, and shall recognize He Who Reigns in Lomïn as High King. By his divine rule, his Praetors shall be afforded the same respect. For it is by the revealing of his will, through the mysteries of our faith, that his authority is established. Know that by your alms you are invited in. Just as Œron, Redot, Varea, Mahndür, Limae, now shall Bortali be."

Men wearing gray, chalice-less tabards holding up deep chalices appeared on the edge of the crowd that had been pressed to the sides of the street for the procession.

"Salvation is only found by our rule before even thy king. To see they who bear chalice upon chest and in hand is your honor. Your duty is to fill their vessel with silver and with gold. If you fail to do so, know that a mark shall go upon your record. Give only trifles, and you insult your hosts upon this earth."

A man or two finally relented and dropped coins into the chalices.

The orator held a red book aloft; the other Praetors held up their own in response. "Let your eyes turn to the study of the Book of the True Path, by which you shall learn of Aben's will for your life. In three days' time, seek out the Praetors in their newly consecrated Chapel of Aben. There you shall make a donation to the church and in return receive the Book of the True Path. But for your lack of faith and paltry giving to the chalices held to you, know that a silver conta shall be your contribution.

"Follow the Path," he intoned in conclusion.

The others replied in a loud chant, "Follow or despair!"

The Praetors were urging their mounts forward when the white mustached man in the center suddenly called for their halt. He stood up in his stirrups. Rather than a spear, he carried a two-foot arrow-shaped scepter. He took it up and leveled it at the crowd across the street.

"Them," he called.

The crowd parted around two women.

"Oh no," Katiam muttered.

"I cannot see well enough through my veil," Little Maeda said. "Who is it?"

"Astrid and Toire. This was the wrong day to pair them."

"Or the best," Little Maeda said with a giggle.

Neither of the two Paladames had hoods on, and they strode forward to the edge of street.

"What do you want, *le trompeur?*" Astrid called loudly.

The man scoffed and squirmed in his seat.

"I knew by the boyish cut of your hair that you were a Crysalas virago," he chided back. "And by your shrill voice and unclean tongue that you seek to undermine the Paths to Paradise."

Astrid opened her mouth to speak, but the man continued.

"And you," he pointed to the other woman. "I know by your complexion you are the daughter of Rhi Barra, whom I discoursed with not three days prior. The Bortalian king should like to know that his city is infiltrated by seditious spies."

"The only perfidious sedition is yours, radical," Astrid spat.

"Radical? The Church of Œron now has under its care more souls than any other church. We bear the united collection of the West. You've but a few covens, hidden in fear that the light will find you out."

"All flee from a false light," Astrid said, "and find no joy in its glow."

"Foolish words in a city that lives by starblush," Otem said, "and coming from a woman."

"Fine words from an old man who looks down upon the masses, with arrogant hubris. That you must prey upon others attests to your own lack of the one thing all scriptures have called for since pen first found paper."

"And what might that be, degenerate?" he retorted.

"Don't let him press you to rashness, Astrid," Katiam muttered under her breath.

"Compassion," Astrid declared.

"Bah!" Otem sneered. "Further proof of the weakness found in those apart from the road we offer."

He turned and looked at the crowd that had slowly gathered closer to watch the conflict. "It is your duty to your own soul not to offer compassion, but rather a stoic discipline. To follow the orders of your betters. To do your own part in order to look to your own soul, and walk the path offered to you, taking for yourself your salvation. Too long have you dwelt under the presumptuous scriptures that state that thy neighbor's road must be bettered by your labor. Heed not long-held falsehoods, but rather take this path we offer: rules you can gauge and measure against, to see in what ways the robe and crown have failed you. Our goodly High Missioner has been given special revelation time and again, new lanterns by which to travel and to guide."

"That you suggest special revelation comes after millennia of tried and true scripture is presumptuous, pretentious, and pernicious!" Astrid called, stepping up a set of stairs to the door of a home so her voice carried forward all the more. "Cast aside compassion? Cast aside the good of your neighbor? What rotten words! What moldering scripture!" She turned from speaking to the Praetor to instead addressing the crowd. "Have you not heard the scriptures of the Priest of Aben speak of the true and goodly ways? To say from one side of his mouth that you ought not take care of your neighbor's path, ought not assist them along the road with you as fellow travelers, and with the other side of his mouth, past rotten teeth, with foetid air, look to him and his path? He speaks in heresy and sedition. Have the gods been so busy that only now they might spread a new word, overwriting all that once was said centuries later?"

"Yet your witches spew prophecies and doom and change, demanding subservience to fate."

"Our oracles," Astrid said, chin held high, "speak not in new doctrines of rotten flesh, but with self-regulating clarity, given directly by the wife of Aben. To follow the High King in Lomïn, yet deny the authority of his wife, invites a judgment more dire than that of Wyv-Thüm. If I were sentenced to Noccitan for following such evil doctrines, I should ask my sentences doubled, for fear of facing the wrath of Aben."

"Every step we offer, in addition to the Good Old Way, further sweeps clean the dust of the path. It further provides clean tread for thy children to walk an easier road to the Green Green Pastures," Otem said, looking away from his opponent to the crowd. "Would you deny the opportunity to better them? Even if your own journey is already sullied?"

"Therein lies the rub!" Astrid interrupted. "He does not offer you your own salvation. He condemns you to Noccitan. For you do not know the words in his New Scripture book. Indeed, the ink on that text is not even dry, and their own scholars have not completed their generations-long test to see that it is good and right and true. He does not offer you salvation. He offers you slavery to a code that can only position your children to inherit. What mother does not want what is best for her children? What father wishes harm on his son and daughter? Yet this Œronzi man offers a cup of poison, that he would force-feed you to see your children and your children's children under a lash of Œronzi superiority!"

Otem made a hand motion and five of the Chalicians dismounted.

Little Maeda made a move, but Katiam grabbed her arm. The smaller-framed girl groaned in pain and stopped.

"Let me go and help them," Maeda said. "I'm a Paladame. I can fight."

"I know you can," Katiam said, "but please let Astrid and Toire do this, so we can all leave peaceably."

"Five to two is hardly fair."

The five of them, spears in hand, advanced toward the two women at the steps to the home.

Toire took up the lid of a barrel, holding it in one hand underneath, and in her other hand, a short sword came out. Astrid had already drawn her rose-headed mace. The Chalicians stood shoulder to shoulder, and urged one of their number to thrust forward at Toire, standing at the bottom of the stairs. She deflected the spear with her makeshift shield, and the spearhead flew up toward Astrid, who took hold of the end, and pulled the Chalician tumbling forward. Toire swung with a sword-wielding haymaker, the heavy Bronuan-style pommel taking the man across the jaw and laying him out flat.

In response, two of the other Praetors pressed for the advantage

DREAD KNIGHT

and took low swings at Toire. She stepped down between the spears with her long legs, and swung her shield across the face of one of them. The second dropped his spear and threw both arms around her shoulders to try and pin her down.

She twisted and turned her back to him, got her sword arm up behind his own neck, and pulled down. He came bodily off the ground, over her shoulder, then hit the stairs with his back, legs up. He gasped for painful breaths as the wind rushed out of him.

Toire spun, throwing the shield like a disk at Otem's head. The old Praetor blocked it with a gauntleted arm, but his sleipnir startled and reared. Otem barked another command and the other five Praetors dismounted and readied their own spears.

The two remaining Praetors already advancing on Astrid's high-ground position stood between the two women.

"Now it's not looking good," Katiam said.

Toire Siobh held up her sword as the five new Praetors advanced on her.

"Come on down," Otem called to Astrid. "We have proven our position by might. Your coven sister is endangered."

"Eleven against two is hardly fair," Astrid said. "You should have brought more."

"You cocksure fool," Otem said. He dismounted and stepped up to the five Praetors standing over the half-crouched Bronuan Princess, then indicated to three of them. "Arrest that Crysalas virago. We march them before the king as an offering."

"Only just arrived in town and already taking the laws of the land into your own hands," Astrid said, casting aside her overcloak as now five Praetors advanced up the stairs. She wore her full regalia under the cloak, the silver filigree blazing bright as the sun broke through the clouds and cast brilliance upon her.

"Take her down!" Otem roared.

Five spears thrust as one, but Astrid was not there. She leapt high up into the air, her legs whipping up over her head, the mace swinging down and knocking free the helmet of one of them as she tumbled down the ten feet to the cobbles below, back to back with Toire, and behind the five Praetors. She rushed back up into them, her knee rising to meet the shoulders of the man she had already hit with her mace. It drove him face-first down into the stairs. She shoved left and right. Two of the Praetors became a tangled mess, losing their footing and toppling into each other. One Praetor dropped his spear and threw himself at Astrid three steps below him. She ducked and he fell, top-heavy, over her. She lifted and threw him up and over Toire and into the two Praetors next to Otem.

Toire took the opportunity and rushed Otem, who backpedaled away, denying her the advantage of the surprise, but backing him up against his own sleipnir.

The remaining Praetor on the stairs held his spear leveled at Astrid, who had turned to the two tangled Praetors, fighting over one another to rise.

"Look out!" Toire shouted as his spear thrust for Astrid's exposed back.

Astrid glanced, stepped, and took hold of the shaft behind the spearhead and pulled. The man fell the six steps, headfirst, losing his spear, and hitting the cobbles hard.

In the same fluid motion, Astrid spun, spear in hand, and threw it as a javelin at Otem. It impaled him through the right shoulder, and pinned him to a wooden street post.

"Get them!" Otem shouted, now in a rage.

The two women stood back to back surrounded by four addled Praetors with six more unconscious or moaning on the ground.

The crowd stood in silence, then one man barked out a single tension-splitting laugh.

The wave broke and the crowd exploded in uproarious laughter.

"Stop that!" Otem shouted. "Solemnity is a virtue! Mockery of the church is blasphemy!"

"You claimed that victory was the moral high ground," Astrid said to Otem. "Yet now, as the tide has turned, you would try and still claim that victory?"

The four praetors lowered their spears and looked at Otem, shame in their eyes.

Astrid lowered her own weapon and turned to Otem. Blood seeped out of his wound. Astrid took off one metal gauntlet as she approached him and he winced as though she might strike him. Instead, she tore free from her undergarment a piece of white linen and held it to his wound, then yanked the spear free. He dropped to the ground, his hand going up to hold the rag in place.

"You ought to tend to your wounded," Astrid said. "Or would that be looking to someone else's path?"

Astrid turned and walked up the street toward Katiam. Toire fell into stride with her. With one hand, Astrid pushed her own hair out of her face, streaking her cheek with Otem's blood.

She caught sight of Katiam's glance, and smiled.

"Glad you got that out of your system?" Katiam asked as she came up to her.

Astrid nodded. "That felt good."

Toire barked a laugh. "That it did, sister. That it did."

The four of them turned and walked toward the inn. People nearby, men and women alike, gave them congratulatory nods, and laughed with one another, talking about the now embarrassed Chalicians.

"Should we enter the inn, now that we've drawn attention to ourselves?" Little Maeda asked.

From the walls not far to the southeast, a horn suddenly sounded. Everyone froze in their steps to listen. The blast ended, then was followed by eleven short blasts. A horn farther down the wall resounded with eleven of its own.

"What does that mean?" Katiam asked.

"Vül spotted by the wall," Little Maeda said.

"How do you know that?" Astrid asked.

"I'm from here, remember?"

A new horn tone resounded with three long peels.

"And the gates, already closed, are announced as doubly so," Little Maeda said.

"Why?" Katiam asked.

"That means an enemy force has arrived."

"A vül force?" Katiam said.

"A vül army," Little Maeda said. "I think it safe to say that we're not leaving the city tonight."

12

Graysand Siege

Unto thy end give rise,

E'en to thy own demise!

    The sword in hand strikes!

Great enemy despise!

Take from them their prize.

    Impale them with your spikes.

—THE BATTLE OF IPONA

"I'll admit," Commander Bolla Elbay said, "I did not expect Commander Hardin to give up his commission entirely." Noss sat at the head of the table with Aurín and Slate on either side of him. The other Wardens, commanders, and city baronets had closed the door behind them. Half way down the table only Commander Bolla Elbay and Commander Domic remained, Ophedia standing as guard behind the two of them.

"The re-establishment of his old mercenary charter, the Red Banner was a nice touch though," Bolla said as she sipped from her goblet.

Domic nodded her head in agreement.

"What is the Red Banner?" Aurín piped in.

"When Searn founded the Black Sentinels," Commander Elbay said, "he based it off the old mercenary charter, the Red Banner, of which Commander Hardin was the ranking commander. Searn bought the Red Banner charter wholesale, and Hardin came with it."

"It's going to cause tension with the Black Sentinels," Domic muttered. "Two charters in one city?"

"Only for a short while," Noss said. "I intend to offer the Red Banner a contract here in the city while the siege remains. And once we lift it, we'll use them to help us liberate the south."

"He'll take more Sentinels to his Red Banner," Bolla said.

"Yes. And then they'll head east. I'll wager they set up shop in Morriego."

"How does that benefit us?"

"It takes those Sentinels who do not wish to associate with the Wardens as far from us as possible. When the Chalicians continue east, they'll put the same pressure on the Red Banner in Morriego as they are trying to here in Haven. The Red Banner will sow dissension against them ahead of time, and then again when they arrive."

Slate stood from his chair. "We are going to retrieve the tools we spoke of."

"Good," Noss said. "Take who you need to help move them here and we can discuss how best to distribute them."

Slate gave a curt nod and walked out the door.

Noss turned back to the table.

"What is that about?" Bolla asked.

"He's stashed away tools the Wardens have been looking for. I've negotiated for Slate to be given authority at another holding we'll be establishing after the siege."

"You trust him?"

"Not at all." Noss turned to Aurín. "I'd like you to follow him. See that he doesn't do anything drastic."

"I'll take Ophedia, if you don't mind," Aurín said.

"I don't mind," Noss replied, and turned to go.

"Before you leave," Commander Elbay interrupted his movement.

Noss turned back.

"I do not trust Commanders Forenor and Vore. I expect them to betray us."

"Forenor is no longer a Sentinel, but a Warden. You need not worry about him."

"But still, I do," Commander Domic added. "Both Vore and Forenor are close. I suspect they'll act against both the Sentinels and the Wardens."

"And Deggar?"

"A blustering bully," Bolla said. "But true to his word."

"What do you suggest we do?" Noss asked.

"Make me a Warden. Tip the balance of the council to your favor. But on my terms."

"And those terms?"

"I was the first Sentinel to join Searn when he first founded the charter. I want rank befitting that. Hardin became the de facto High Commander when Searn died. I want you to give me high enough authority that I'm effectively the new High Commander of the Sentinels."

Domic stood. "Sounds like I ought to be made a Warden, too."

"You know that our Order is ranked in such a way that no one is the absolute authority over all others," Noss said.

"You outrank all Wardens in Haven," Bolla said.

"Then let's give you a rank and title equal to mine, but in another territory."

"Liberté," Bolla said. "I want Liberté."

"I'll arrange a ceremony in the next several days for you both to join the Wardens. Once the conflict with the Chalicians has concluded, we'll establish you in Liberté." He left the room without another word.

Aurín followed, and turned back to Ophedia. "I'll meet you out on the wall," he said. "Before we go spying on Slate."

Ophedia gave him a nod but stayed with Commanders Elbay and Domic.

"Our joining the Wardens leaves Commander Vore as the sole Sentinel Commander," Domic said after Aurín left.

"Vore will be forced to play his hand with Forenor, or join the Red Banner," Bolla said.

"He may even try and take out his anger out on you," Ophedia said.

"We'll be Wardens, so it won't matter," Domic said. The three of them walked toward the door. "Liberté, huh?"

"It'll be a good opportunity to take some influence for myself," Bolla said.

"Nice town?" Ophedia asked.

"Not as exciting as Haven," Bolla said. "But I suspect many Sentinels wanting to gain authority among the Wardens will journey here to Haven. I should get a good price on my holdings. Liberté will have more affordable estates after the conflict, so I can establish a network of authority there." Bolla turned to Domic. "I'll see to it those you pick to spy on me and the others there will have an easy time of it."

"You know me better than I would like," Domic smirked.

Bolla turned to Ophedia. "I've some new rations at my place. Why don't you come and take some before you go on this not-so-secret mission."

Ophedia held the door open for the two of them as they came out onto the wall. Aurín was waiting there, eying the force outside. The Chalician army did seem more meager than before. The Sentinels guarding the wall stood about, chatting lazily, but with little interest in the army sitting down below.

"This whole thing seems futile," Ophedia said. "I don't understand what they are waiting for, nor why they make no moves."

"It's pretty apparent they want the city for themselves. That we can't even agree if we're at war with them or Œron further complicates everything," Bolla said.

"Vore and Forenor are chatting idly up ahead," Aurín muttered from behind them.

The two commanders stood close in conversation, looking about them furtively. Forenor handed Vore something just as he saw the three of them watching. He turned and marched away. Vore turned and eyed them, then crouched down, his eyes locking with Bolla.

"What is he doing?" Bolla said.

He held a metal sphere in his hand over the stone and dropped it, wincing as it disappeared down into a hole.

Nothing happened.

"Vore!" Bolla shouted, running toward him with Ophedia hot on her heels.

Vore took out a second sphere from his satchel, and from his belt a hammer. He looked up at Bolla and struck the sphere with the hammer as hard as he could manage, and immediately dropped the hammer and took hold of his head. The sphere dropped to the stone and began rolling around of its own volition. The sound it gave off could be felt more than actually heard. Vore screamed in pain, but opened his eyes to see it nearly roll off the top of the wall and down into the street. He panicked and reached for it, picking it back up. His hand melted away. Not by heat, but by vibration. He fell again, stood, and kicked it with his boot into the hole the first sphere had disappeared into.

Bolla stopped where she stood, and there was a moment of brief silence. Then, from the hole, a plume of dust shot up into the air, knocking Vore back. The wall suddenly shifted under Bolla and Vore as the stones became as slack as sand. Ophedia took hold of Bolla to pull her back, the stones under her losing their form. Bolla fought against Ophedia, and shoved her away as the sand collapsed, and the still body of Vore sunk down into it.

The stone-turned-sand collapsed in both directions, out into the stepped space beyond the wall, and backward toward the lane of businesses and homes in the first street. As Ophedia lost her footing and fell toward the street, she had a final glance beyond the wall of a mass of soldiers breaking from the woods and rushing the walls in a battle cry.

Someone was dragging her by her arm across cobbles.
"What? Who?"
"Don't fight me," Aurin said, holding his clawed hand against himself to keep from harming her. She tried to rise to her feet as they both stumbled toward the nearest door. Aurín threw himself bodily through and they struggled past the sand to enter the dark space.
"What happened?" Ophedia croaked through the sand in her mouth.
"You and Commander Elbay rushed forward shouting, and suddenly the entire wall of stone just turned to sand. Did you see what happened?"
"Where is Bolla?"
"She went the other way. Out into the terraces. The Chalicians are right behind us."
"And those on the wall?"

"They just aren't there anymore," he said.

"Then let's hope those at the citadel notice and react soon." She pulled back her cloak and drew both axes. "Did you see my crossbow?"

He shook his head.

Outside the quiet room the roar of soldiers grew.

"Time to prove your worth, Talon," Ophedia said.

He nodded and opened the door.

The street was covered in gray sand. Just over the top of the large new dune in the middle of the wall, the first Chalician soldiers were struggling to crawl their way up and over. Crossbow bolts and arrows flew overhead into the mob and up on the stairs leading down to the citadel. Wardens were already racing down to help.

"Come on!" Ophedia shouted, rushing up through the sand.

"How are you gaining any height?" Aurín cried out, moving hand over foot up the loose slope.

"Macena has sand dunes that outlaws are always hiding in. I tracked one there once. I wasn't successful, but I did learn how to climb a dune and look good doing it."

As she reached the top, a group of soldiers had already taken it from the others. One of them tried to swing his spear around at her head. She dropped to the sand and lashed out with her axe, taking the man across the boots. She stood up into the man's middle and shoved backward. He went flying back down the slope and into the next group of invaders. These had taken the time to wrap their faces with cloth, and had not yet drawn their weapons. Ophedia rushed the next man, two axes crossed to block his sword, then kicked him down on the top of his knee. He screamed as he dropped, and she caught him under the arm with the hooked end of an axe, lifting as she shoved. He cried as the tip bit into soft flesh and threw himself away and down the hill. Aurín stood next to her and unclipped his own skyfall axe from his chest.

They would have to stand alone for these first moments as arrows flew overhead, and the invaders rushed the gray dune. From up the wall at the citadel, a door had burst open and ten Wardens rushed down along the wall, axes in hand. Bells were going off across the city.

"Let's hold on as long as we can," Ophedia said.

"Yes. Let's."

The next group of invaders threw themselves up the hill, a

Chalician Praetor in their midst.

"Do you want the Praetor?" Ophedia asked.

"You're welcome to him," Aurín called over his shoulder as his axe bit through a man's chain mail, links exploding. A second soldier thrust a spear at Aurín, who caught it with his taloned hand, twisted it out of his grip, spun, and ran him through with his own weapon.

Two more soldiers thrust at Aurín. Their tips glanced off the blackened armor on his chest. He laughed and stepped down the hill inside their guards, his axe biting one direction, his talon the other. Both fell clutching at their faces.

The Chalician Praetor was shouting orders, spear held aloft as a banner.

"Hey Cup-skull," Ophedia called down.

The Praetor shot her a look.

"You going to just stand and look nice? Or tread your own path?"

"How dare you!" he shouted, and began marching up the slope.

The man nearest the top of the hill stumbled at the last second, and as he tried to rise to his feet, she smacked the top of his head with the back of her axe. He began to tumble backwards and she shot out with her heavy boot, stomping down on his collarbone and sending him rolling.

"Not much to look at," Ophedia shouted. "Their helmets make them look like pretentious gits."

"Pretentious doesn't begin to describe them," Aurín said.

"Do your helmets double as chamber pots?" Ophedia called down to the Chalician.

"Silence your tongue, heathen!" he shouted up at her. He was halfway up the hill.

"Ophedia," Aurín called, as his axe bit into another man and sent him reeling back down.

"Busy. What?"

"I can see Elbay. She rolled down by the wall."

Ophedia leaned out over the ledge and saw where Aurín indicated. The woman lay half buried and unconscious, if not dead.

The Wardens were almost there to help, and the Praetor had neared the top.

Ophedia roared in courage and dove out, shoulder first into the Praetor before he had a chance to raise his spear. She tackled him, and they went flying in a double-bodied roll down the hill. His spear flew away and his arms went up around her.

"Your city will fall," he roared as his back hit the ground.

"Not by you," Ophedia said, sitting up atop him, holding him by the throat and giving him a hard slap across the face.

He scrambled to grab her wrists and pull her away. She gave him a wicked smile, then smashed her forehead into his nose.

"How dare you strike a Praetor, woman?!" he coughed as blood spluttered across his face.

She laughed. "Hardly the time to discuss nuance of battlefield combat," she said, and repeated the action.

He coughed blood and shoved her away. She threw herself toward her pair of axes as he rolled, wiping his face free of some of the blood and crawling toward his spear. An arrow fell through him and he dropped.

Another wave of soldiers was closing from twenty yards away. Ophedia took hold of her axes, struggled to her feet, and rushed toward the wall to where she saw Bolla.

Atop the wall, the Wardens cut a fine profile alongside Aurín who stood triumphant. Ophedia slid down next to Bolla. Her legs were entirely covered in sand. She set her axes aside, took hold of the woman, and began pulling. Bolla groaned.

"Good. Stay with me," Ophedia said.

The sand shifted and slowly gave up the woman.

"Ophedia!" Aurín shouted down at her.

She looked up and saw him standing in the midst of his Wardens. Noss held in his hand a large hammer, the head made of skyfall. He swung it round and round. The hammer droned with a buzz that filled Ophedia's mind, even from thirty feet below.

The men on the stone terraces rushed at the wall, roaring defiantly.

Noss shouted something unheard over the din and lobbed the hammer out from the wall. It flew fifty feet toward the ground just beyond the gray sand. Ophedia pulled Bolla close, her back against the wall, and braced herself for whatever new skyfall magic would be unfurled.

The men rushing the wall were ten feet from the hammer when it struck the ground. A moment later, the hammer exploded in a pulse. Sand flew backward toward the wall. The men rushing forward were just as suddenly flung backward as boneless rag dolls across the ground a hundred feet, through ranks of men behind them. A few flew up and through the air, and fell dozens of yards away. Their weapons flew back even farther as dangerous shrapnel.

The force struck Ophedia and Bolla, pressing them hard against the wall with a constant, continual force. She tried to scream against the wave of force, but there was no air in her lungs left to do so.

Then there was silence.

The invaders still standing did not move, nor made a sound.

"Ophedia?" Aurín called.

Ophedia gasped for air, "Here!" she cried.

"Bring her," Noss called out from the top of the wall.

Five Wardens leapt down, skidding across the sand to her side, taking Bolla up on their shoulders. Someone threw a rope and together they worked their way back to the top. Ophedia followed with the last Warden, pushing Bolla up from behind.

Finally, she lowered herself by the crenellations, exhausted. A pair of Wardens carried Bolla to the citadel as Noss approached to stand over her.

"Well done, del Ishé," he said, placing a hand on her shoulder.

"You arrived just in time," she said.

"Only because you held the wall. No one else came to your side."

"What are we going to do now?"

"We'll see the people clear this sand, though I'm not sure where it came from."

"Vore. He took a skyfall orb from Forenor and then dropped it down a shaft. He struck a second one with a hammer before dropping it down the shaft onto the other. The entire wall suddenly became sand."

"And Vore?"

"Sunk into the sand. It consumed him."

"Good."

He turned back to the other Wardens. "Bring me more skyfall hammers. I'll stand watch while we reinforce the wall. Then I want you to hunt down Forenor. He'll be brought to justice."

Ophedia tried to rise.

"Where are you going?" he asked.

"Aurín and I still need to go watch Slate as you ordered."

"You're hardly in any condition," Aurín said.

"The city is hardly in any condition to do much of anything,"

Ophedia said. "I'd like to know if he was behind this, as well. Where did Vore get the second orb?"

"That's a good question," Noss said. "Alright. Stop back by the citadel once more and grab another crossbow and bolts, then be off to find him."

Ophedia nodded and began hobbling off toward the door. She glanced out across the field of battle, where Chalicians were dragging the living out of bow's reach to regroup.

"Del Ishé," Noss called.

Ophedia turned.

"If Slate was behind this, put a bolt in him."

13

Dread Cart

Toll once for peasant

Thrice for priest.

Twice for paladin.

None for thief.

Five resound for king enthroned

For dreaming seven ring intoned.

— DIRGE OF THE BRIGAND KING

"That hammer just completely flattened everything," Aurín said.
"Did you feel anything from the top of the wall?" Ophedia asked.
"A wind that nearly threw me off the back side."
"I felt like every muscle was being pressed against the wall. I'm still aching."
"But you're alright?"
"Well enough," Ophedia said.
They came to the Slab. A few people peeked out of the upper windows. A barricade fifty feet from the actual blockade leading into the Revenant Quarter had a handful of guards eyeing them as they walked down the street.

DREAD KNIGHT

Against one wall there was a single merchant stall open for business with a long line leading away from it.

"Ophedia," Aurín said, tapping her shoulder. She followed his taloned finger as he pointed to the stall.

Behind the counter, three older bearded men helped those that approached, handing them small parcels. Behind them all, and a head taller, stood the qavylli spice merchant, Ymbrys Veronia.

"What is he up to now?" Ophedia muttered as they approached the side of the line.

"To the back," someone in line complained as they approached.

"Please, please," Ymbrys replied. "There is always enough for everyone."

He glanced over and saw the two of them and his face split into a smile.

"Ah! My friends!"

He muttered quick instructions to the three older men, then stepped out from behind the booth, taking up his leather-topped staff and approaching.

"Ophedia del Ishé and Aurín Mateau, you both are a sight for weary eyes!"

"Hello, Ymbrys," Ophedia said. "What are you doing here?"

"Do you recall I was making rations? Well, I've about ten different inns helping me make more. It doesn't feed the whole city, but we do what we can."

"Stuck in here with the rest of us, then?" Aurín asked.

"As are we all," Ymbrys said. "Aurín, what do you have on your hand and across your chest?"

Aurín looked down and smiled timidly. "Gifts for joining the new Order."

"I've heard rumors, but nothing official."

"The Paladins of the Hammer have turned their citadel into a new Order, the Order of the Axe. We all carry skyfall weapons now. In fact, we're in the neighborhood looking for one of our Order who may have more tools he's not sharing."

"You must mean Slate."

"You know him?" Aurín asked.

"Of course. He and Commander Vore have been most recently staying at Deggar's old inn on Black Street."

"Should we just stand here and get more answers from you?" Ophedia said. "You know enough."

"More than enough," Ymbrys smiled. "You go there now?"

Ophedia nodded.

"I shall join you," he said. "I'm curious to learn more."

They circled around the southern end of the Slab and into Black Street by Deggar's inn.

"What have Vore and Slate been hiding here?" Ophedia said. "Are they not worried that Deggar will respond?"

Ymbrys shrugged. "They moved in because it has nice stables."

"Why the stables?"

"Dorian and I believe that it is to hide and then move the Dreadplate."

"The what?" Aurín replied. "Dorian?"

"Well, that day when the Revenants appeared, we lost contact with Hanen, but Dorian, Rallia, and I have been moving from inn to inn as able, looking for signs of a rather large suit of armor that Slate is keeping somewhere unknown. Now Slate has stables with a sizable wagon housed there."

"We were sent here to ensure that Slate did as he promised to Noss," Ophedia said.

"Which was?"

"To load up a wagon of skyfall tools and bring them to the citadel."

"And yet," Ymbrys said, indicating to the north and south, "if a cart was taken from these stables, it went south toward the Revenant Quarter. Not toward the citadel."

He took hold of the stable door and pulled it open. The inside was empty.

"Fancy a stroll, Ymbrys?" Ophedia asked.

"Always," the qavyl smiled.

Ophedia dropped to the ground on the other side of the barricade and slunk across the street to look around the corner. Ymbrys landed just as calmly. Aurín scrambled down behind them.

Ophedia made a hand signal and rushed down the street to the next corner, the other two following close behind.

Ophedia turned. "There are ten Revenants in the square," she said.

"What exactly is our course of action?" Ymbrys asked.

"Find Slate, question whether he was behind what just happened at the western wall, then drag him back to the citadel to face charges."

"If he has the Dreadplate?" Ymbrys asked.

DREAD KNIGHT

"Is it important?" Ophedia asked.

There were the sudden echoing cries of several men screaming. The Revenants in the square took off with a lumbering gate.

"Come on," Ophedia said.

They followed the Revenants just out of sight from them.

"I don't understand what they are," Aurín said.

"The Revenants?" Ymbrys replied.

"I think they are connected with the Veld," Ophedia said.

"My dear del Ishé," Ymbrys said. "Whatever gave you that impression?"

"Gut instinct and the purple flame in their eyes."

"You have seen the Dreamlands?"

Ophedia ignored the question and rounded the corner, then backpedaled.

"Stop," she said, holding a hand out. "We found him."

Aurín glanced around the corner with Ymbrys, then back.

Ten men pushed a large wagon. Not far behind them, several bodies lay fallen, including several in the gorget-less Warden armor.

Behind them, Slate strode. He held in each hand a pair of skyfall hammers. He tapped them together like two blacksmith hammers, then swung them round one or two times. The resonant chime that resounded across the quarter seemed to push the men on in their own silence.

"Are they traitors, if they side with Slate now?" Aurín asked.

"Or they always were," Ophedia said. "Probably had them in hiding, and they betrayed the others that came with them?"

"I do not think they're followers of Slate," Ymbrys said. "I think they have little choice."

"What do you mean?" Ophedia said.

One of them glanced their way, bearing purple fire in his eyes.

"Revenants."

"He's somehow driving them on with the hammers in his hands," Aurín said.

"The question remains," Ymbrys said, "how the Wardens are Revenants?"

"When a Revenant is killed," Ophedia explained, "the flame jumps into the nearest person."

"Unless they are killed by skyfall metal," Aurín added.

"That is interesting," Ymbrys said.

"Oh no," Aurín called out, pointing to the top of a nearby

building.

Ophedia could see Hanen standing atop the building's lip.

"A man in a cloak," Ymbrys said.

"No," Aurín replied. "That's Shroud."

"That's not Searn," Ophedia said. "He died."

Aurín glanced around, a panic in his eyes. "We're five blocks from the southern barricades, and Slate is making those Revenants push that cart. I'm going back to the citadel to get reinforcements. I'm not letting him take hold of me again."

Aurín reached under his cloak and pulled out an object in a sack—a heavy bell made of skyfall.

"That's interesting," Ymbrys said.

"Noss says it'll work on Revenants."

He lifted it. Then, with no further warning, struck it with his axe.

The tone that rang from it was deep and deafening. Ymbrys' face twisted. He clutched at the leather-topped staff in his hand. "I do not like that."

Aurín ignored him and walked boldly around the corner.

"That bell more than hurts my sensitive ears," Ymbrys said. "I am going to go south and bring Dorian and Rallia. If the Dreadplate is in that cart, they need to know."

"We could use the help," Ophedia said, but Ymbrys had already walked away without another word.

She shook her head and looked around the corner. The Revenants had dropped their hands from the cart and fallen to their knees. Slate stumbled forward, clutching one hammer to his chest. The ring on his finger had erupted in blood.

"Stop him!" he cried out, pointing his other hammer at Aurín, who proceeded forward, bell held high. The Revenants gave no indication they even heard.

Aurín struck the bell again and continued forward, but gave a furtive look up to the roof where Hanen watched the whole thing in silence.

"What are you doing, Hanen?" Ophedia muttered. "Help him."

Aurín walked up to the first Revenant and struck him down with his axe.

"No!" Slate screamed. "We must not be stopped!"

He stood, overcoming the pain, and held both hammers to the sky.

"We command our lessers!"

DREAD KNIGHT

There were cries and caws from the sky and Ophedia looked up. A black cloud quickly descended from the north. Gryphs. The black creatures came upon the square in a swarm of claws, paws, and beaks. Aurín held his bell up at them in defense, but they hit him hard in a torrent of black feathers, knocking him to the ground. The bell fell free from his talon and it clattered to the cobbles even as his axe flew up to strike at the gryphs.

Something snuffed at Ophedia's hand and she gave a little yelp, looking down to find Whisper's nose nuzzling at her.

Hanen stood not far away.

"Don't do that!" she hissed.

"Sorry," Hanen said, voice darkened by the shroud over his head.

"How is Slate commanding gryphs now?"

"You know as much as I do," Hanen said.

"We need to go help Aurín," Ophedia said.

Hanen nodded and rushed out into the street. Whisper and Ophedia followed close behind.

The gryphs had become a swirling cyclone. The Revenants have taken up their cart once more, heedless of the creatures, and continued down the street.

Slate strode into the cloud of gryphs, hammers raised. He did not notice Hanen, but the gryphs did, and threw themselves away in a violent scramble.

Slate was dropping one of his hammers down onto Aurín's head when Hanen stepped over Aurín and caught the hammer's head in one gauntleted hand.

There was a sudden dull clang as they came together. Slate looked at the cloaked man before him, horror rising in his face.

"You! No! You'll not command us again!"

He brought the second hammer down, this time swinging for Hanen. The other gauntlet shot up and caught that one too.

"Give us back those gloves!" Slate roared, and pressed in, raising a knee to Hanen's chest.

Ophedia rushed in as the gryphs took to the air and began to circle. She took hold of Aurín's cloak and hoisted him out of the fight, pulling him free just as Whisper rushed in and nipped at Slate's heels.

"Go after the cart," Ophedia shouted at Aurín. "I'll fight Slate."

"You can't! You'll become a Revenant!"

"Not if I can help it," she replied.

He held his axe out to her. "Take this for now."
She did.

Slate harried Hanen with both hammers flailing. Hanen backpedaled down the street trying to keep distance between them.

Ophedia placed her axes into their frogs. She was raising the skyfall axe, ready to charge Slate from behind, when Aurín's bell caught her eye. She scrambled over, took up the wooden handle, and lifted.

It was heavier than a steel axe of the same size and shape, and even pulling it up, the scrape of the bricks sent a ripple of resonance through it. She held it out and confidently walked after Slate, who continued to chase Hanen in a blind rage.

The cawing of the gryphs returned. Ophedia looked back over her shoulder. The cloud was descending on them once more. She held the bell out toward them and struck it with the axe, harder than she'd intended. The peal blasted from her hand and she dropped it once more, but not before the wave of sound struck the descending creatures, who fell from the sky, flopping on the cobbles in pain.

"How is he controlling the gryphs?" Ophedia muttered, taking up the bell from the ground again and turning toward Slate. "You'd think he was Ghoré."

Slate had paused from his attack and turned to consider her, his bloodied hand going to his face.

His face turned into an almost inhuman snarl, and he took the first steps of a charge when she struck the bell again. He hesitated.

Hanen rushed up from behind and tore one of Slate's hammers from his hands.

Slate turned around and cried out.

"Stop taking everything from us!" he roared, and went back after Hanen.

Whisper was under heel again. Slate swung wildly at the little ynfald, holding his head against the peel of the bell. Hanen, skyfall hammer in hand, stumbled away like a drunk. Ophedia gritted her teeth against the pain just holding the peeling bell brought to her ears.

"Get at him, Whisper!" she shouted, but she couldn't hear her own voice over the bell.

Slate flailed wildly at the creature at his feet, and finally made contact. Whisper rolled away, his scales clattering. He came to his

DREAD KNIGHT

feet, but looked at Ophedia, scales raised like manticör hackles, watching Ophedia advance.

Slate lifted his hammer in both hands, roaring past the pain, and rushed at Ophedia. She struck the bell again, and he dropped to a knee.

He mouthed protest over the blinding sound. The pain in Ophedia's own head buzzed, but she continued forward and heel-kicked Slate squarely in the chest, knocking him onto his back. She held the bell over him, and raised her axe to bring it down on the bell when a wicked smile broke out over Slate's face.

He looked at his bloody hand, then back and past her, the smile broadening.

She glanced back over her shoulder the moment before the flock of gryphs blindly slammed into her. She turned to brace herself, her other arm going across her face. Through the flapping wings, she could see a horde of Revenants entering the street from every alley entrance. The press of the feathered bodies finally shoved her over onto the ground, the bell flying free from her hand.

The gryphs continued to harass her as she struggled to pull her cloak around her head.

Then Whisper was there, rushing up and over and around her, snipping at gryphs, unperturbed by their beaks and claws. She struggled to her feet and rushed to a house, crashing through the door. She looked back to see the little ynfald still attacking the black gryphs. Several lay dead and most had fled. The Revenants moved down the street, chasing after Slate, now carrying the bell in his hand and going after the cart, only a couple short blocks from the next barricade.

"Why didn't you stop?" Hanen said loudly as he ran from across the street.

"What do you mean?" she yelled back. She could barely hear anything.

"That bell. It's no good. Your ears!"

She reached up to her ears and touched at the sides of her head. Blood.

"Now Slate has it," she said.

"Not a lot of good it will do him. It was harming him, too."

"I expect he won't care if it means he escapes the city with that wagon. Ymbrys thinks it has the Dreadplate in it."

"I'd wager so, too," Hanen said. "Let's stop him."

The fire in the hearth was warm, and the chair Seriah was in was well-cushioned. Rallia sat in the chair opposite hers, playing soft tones on the flute she was trying to learn. She was getting better, but it wasn't what Seriah might yet call music. She could hear the scratch of Dorian's quill on the nearby table.

She settled back into her chair, the mug of ale in her hand. The woman who owned the house could be heard humming in the kitchen. Dorian's coin had bought her hospitality.

The door opened and someone entered.

"Ymbrys!" Rallia stopped playing.

"Leq'y'dis!" Ymbrys said.

"What's so urgent?" Dorian said with a hint of sarcasm in his voice.

"I am," Ymbrys said. "The Dreadplate is making its way to the southern gate."

Dorian scrambled to his feet. "Where?"

"An ex-Paladin of yours, Slate, moves it through the Revenant Quarter in a wagon pushed by Paladin-Wardens-turned-Revenant."

"I don't know what a Warden is," Dorian said.

"The citadel's new Order of ex-Paladins and Sentinels."

"Not something I like the sound of."

"I think, though," Ymbrys said, "that going after the wagon is more important right now."

"Of course. Of course. Rallia?"

"Yes, Dorian?"

"Perhaps you can see our friend somewhere safe?"

"Safer than here?"

"We're poorly situated between the Revenant Quarter and the gate. I'd rather we move somewhere safer."

"Very well," Rallia replied.

"Shall we?" Dorian said, and left the house with Ymbrys.

"Why not just stay right here?" Seriah asked.

In response, there was a sudden roar of people outside. Rallia rushed to the window and opened the shutter.

"Oh no," Rallia groaned.

"What is it?"

"That army to the south has been sitting in complete silence for days, but now I can hear them shouting war cries. They're rushing the walls."

Seriah reached for her satchel, pulled it over her shoulders, and took up her staff.

"What's going on?" the house owner asked, coming out of the back.

"I think the southern gate is being assaulted," Rallia said.

"Nocc," the woman swore. "I should have left earlier."

She disappeared.

"Come on, Seriah," Rallia said, taking her arm and pulling her toward the door.

"Rallia," Seriah said, "why not leave me here and go help Dorian?"

"Because the last time you were stuck between two forces with Dorian, we all almost died in the Rose Convent in Mahn Fulhar. I'll not endanger you if I can help it."

"Why help me?" Seriah said.

"It's the right thing to do."

"Do you always do the right thing?" Seriah asked.

"What kind of question is that?" Rallia replied.

"Listen, Rallia. You're a lovely person, I'm sure, but you followed Searn."

"I did."

"And we know how that turned out."

"Seriah. I have always followed my gut and done what I think is right. It turns out I was wrong to trust Searn. Now I'm doing what I can to make up for that. Can we have a philosophical discussion later? Right now, let's get you someplace in this pantheon-forsaken city that is safe."

Seriah nodded and let Rallia lead her out the door and down the stairs. They came to the street and Rallia hesitated for a moment. Seriah turned her head in both directions. To the left, the roar of those outside the wall grew in clamor. To the right, purple lights were dancing behind the blind over her eyes, and they were growing in number.

"Rallia," Seriah said.

"What is it?"

"The barricades are not far from here?"

"Two blocks north."

"I can't explain how I know, but I can sense Revenants beyond the barricades, pressing up against it in numbers."

"How do you...?" Rallia started. "Never mind. Alright. Then we go west."

The loud crunching sound of the gates being battered began, met by the crash at the Revenant barricades to the north.

"You weren't kidding," Rallia said.

"What is it?"

"Hundreds of Revenants surrounding the cart that Ymbrys described. Come on."

Rallia pulled Seriah across the street and into another alley, then paused.

"What is it?" Seriah asked.

"I thought I saw something," Rallia said, stepping back to peek out into the street.

"Safety?" Seriah urged.

"Yes. Of course," Rallia said, and they ran down the alley.

They came out into the next street. Rallia pulled back on Seriah's arm.

"Stop!" Rallia hissed.

"What?"

"Noccitan. Noccitan!" Rallia swore.

"What is it?!"

"Across the street, twenty Praetors just came out of a house. They must have infiltrated the city. I don't know what we're going to do. We're pressed on both sides."

"You'll be coming with us," a voice said from the entrance to the alley.

"Navien?" Rallia hissed.

"This is fortunate. You can lay down your weapons and come peaceably with me and the Praetors, or you can die fighting."

"Who are you?" Seriah asked.

"Abenard Navien," Rallia answered. "He's a Voktorra of Mahn Fulhar, and he didn't take kindly to my brother and I leaving town without his express permission."

"What do you want with the Clouws?" Seriah asked.

"They owe their service to my king. I'm back in the city with the Praetors to see that they come with me."

"At the cost of bloodshed in the city?"

"We'll not have you speaking up against us, either," another voice said. "Fellow Praetors, take them into custody. Once the gate is open, take them to camp for processing."

"I'll be taking Clouw with me to Mahn Fulhar," Navien spoke up.

"You'll do as you're told, as subject to the church. Now proceed with the day's mission and help at the gate. My men will do with these two what is just and right."

Hands took hold of Seriah and a panicked dread fell over her. Nearby, Rallia struggled against being shackled herself, before they were both dragged away.

14

South Gate

I received a letter from one of my colleagues in the West. Apparently they have discovered the secret of the metal. I've known it long enough, and met enough dangers, that I do not doubt the next letter I receive will concern one of their smiths disappearing.

—JOURNAL OF SEARN VETURRES, ENTRY SIXTY-TWO

Hanen raced ahead, the hammer in his hand made of the same material as the gloves. He ducked into an alley and set it on the pavement, then took his gloves off, opened a door into the Veld, and turned them around. His hands came back encased in silver. He took up the hammer again, and had trouble maintaining his grip on the haft as the hammer tried to jump out of his grip to get away from him.

"What's wrong?" Ophedia asked, coming around the cover to his side.

"Apparently, the Mirror-metal doesn't like skyfall," he said, holding the hammer out for her. "You take it."

"What am I supposed to do with this?"

"Wield it alongside the axe, I don't know, but those Revenants are pressing hard down the street, I lost sight of Slate, and I worry what will happen if that cart makes it to the gate."

Ophedia nodded, and rushed back out into the street just as the horde of Revenants passed, ignoring her entirely as she began to cut them down with axe, or knock them over with hammer. Whisper rushed to her aid and nipped at the heels of those that did

DREAD KNIGHT

give her their attention.

She glanced back at Hanen. "I'm fine! Go!"

Hanen nodded and began climbing a ladder to the rooftops. He raced overhead, leaping from building to building. He came to the corner of the building overlooking the barricades. The cart had been pressed into the backside, and the Revenant Wardens pushing it had left the cart to rush the guards atop.

The horde of Revenants, now in the hundreds, were upon the barricades. Not climbing but pressing against it.

Hanen took hold of a rain chain, and slid down to the ground.

He punched the chest of one Revenant with the gloves, and the man fell backward, dazed but free of the purple fire. Other Revenants suddenly rushed him, trying to overwhelm him with their numbers, while the rest continued to press. Hanen ran up to the top, trying to get out of their reach and immediately regretted it, feeling the makeshift wall begin to buckle. His hood fell from his head, and he stumbled, caught himself, and reached up to pull the boneshroud back down over his face, but not before glancing over to see two figures rush across the street—a Nifaran monk and his sister Rallia. They were ducking into an alley when Rallia glanced over and for a split second, their eyes locked as she considered the silver gauntlets, and bone-colored cloak going up over his head. Then, she was gone.

"Maybe she didn't notice me," he muttered.

Sentinels and Wardens stood atop the city wall, shouting against the tide on the outside. They held makeshift shields up as arrows and then dozens of spears flew into their ranks and overhead. The Warden-Commander Deggar roared his defiance and lifted a round orb in the air. In his other hand he held an axe. He took up the axe and struck the orb, and held his arm back to lob it out over the invaders, when a spear flew over the wall and into his shoulder. The orb fell, and everyone around him shouted in dismay as it dropped, rolled for a moment, then lay still before the gate.

Hanen could see the dust around the orb lift off the ground and then explode in every direction. The gate itself buckled, and the wall shook. Some fell from the wall to the ground below. Then, a stone fell from the wall above, met by the resounding crash of a battering ram outside the gate. It repeated three times, and with each impact, another stone fell. The gate, and wall over it, crumbled, slowly but inevitably.

Under Hanen the barricade shook at the press of Revenants, and the cart began to shift the random bits of wood and rock. He backpedaled, trying to get off the barricades as they moved. Something tugged at his cloaks, and he looked down to Whisper, pulling him backward, and off the side of the stacks of debris. As he fell, both of his cloaks tore free in the little creature's mouth. Looking up at the barricade, a figure rushed up the other side—the old man, Dorian Mür, a paladinial hammer in his hand glowing bright white, and swinging this way and that at Revenants swarming over the pile.

Hanen caught his breath as Dorian looked down at him, a momentary look of astonishment seeing Hanen there, gauntlets on hand, and motioned to him to join.

Hanen shook the embarrassment free, scrambled to his feet, and ran up the pile.

"The cart!" Dorian shouted, striking another Revenant backward.

"But the Revenants," Hanen said.

"I'll drive them back. You stop that cart," Dorian said.

Hanen rushed down the pile and toward the cart as yet another armored figure rushed out from an alley—Slate, his skyfall hammer in his hands.

Hanen threw his gauntleted hands up, catching the hammer in both.

"Give them back to us!" Slate roared. Then his eyes adjusted for a moment and he saw Hanen's face. "It's you!"

The heretic pressed down hard, and forced Hanen to a knee, but he did not relent as he clutched the hammer's head with both hands. He ignored Slate and squeezed.

"You were with that qavyl. And you…" Slate seemed to pause for a moment, as though listening to something. His voice shifted to something unnaturally darker. "You betrayed us. We would have been your king if you had only submitted."

"King?" Hanen replied. The hammer in his hand was beginning to glow a ruddy red between the cracks of the unmeltable metal. The wooden haft burst suddenly into flame, and Slate let go and fell backward with a cry. He got to his feet and rushed at Hanen once more.

It suddenly burst as the metal held between both gloves exploded, as the coins he had held in the Revenant Quarter had, those days ago. Time seemed to slow and the explosion lifted Slate up into the air, pieces of metal fragmenting across his body and face in deep, scarring lacerations. The force threw Hanen in the other direction, and he fought to keep the gauntlets from falling from his hands.

A path cleared through the Revenants as the gate buckled and collapsed. The Revenants rushed toward the gap just as Chalicians rushed in, the press of bodies the only thing preventing the wagon from leaving the city. Ophedia saw Slate leave the wagon and rush at Hanen as the old man, Dorian Mür, appeared at the top of the barricade, a paladinial hammer in his hand, swinging at Revenants who clawed at him to snuff out the light that emanated from him.

Ophedia raced down the street, smacking indigo walkers upside the back of the head with her hammer, putting each out of their misery.

She closed half the distance, and saw atop the wall Lowden Dakmor, one arm bandaged, the other wielding a skyfall axe, single-handedly fighting off Chalicians as they tried to spear him down.

She took off at a hard sprint, past walkers and into the backs of the ten Praetors trying their best to take down the man atop the wall.

Her axe bit metal, and the hammer rang as it struck breastplates.

Dakmor made eye contact with her briefly, then returned to his defense with a new vigor.

"Come to take the fun out of this fight, huh girlie?" he shouted with a maniacal laugh.

"You don't get to have all the fun, Lowden," she called back, dodging the swing of a spear, and bringing the axe up under the breastplate of a Chalician. It split like a knife through cheese and opened his chest. He fell.

She dropped to a knee and brought her hammer around and into the leg of another. She stood as the hammer continued to arc around her, and it struck the feet of a Praetor and he tumbled backward, falling into three more.

"Look out!" Lowden shouted.

Ophedia turned as a new Chalician rushed her. This one she

recognized—Provost Weskar Abrau, the Praetor who held the city of Haven under siege.

He wore a helmet this time, and unlike the other Praetors, larger shoulder pads, framing his head. He thrust with a shorter arrow spear, and she leapt back. He advanced and she threw the head of the hammer in a thrust over the top of his spear as he parried again. She just missed his chest.

He moved with a severe grace, and was met by Ophedia, not normally used to dual-wielding. He swung the spear overhead at her, she dropped back, letting go of the hammer, and bringing her skyfall axe up and shearing the haft of his weapon in two, sending the blade clattering away. He startled, but only for a minute, then brought the short stick in his hand down and rapped her on the head, and then again on each shoulder. The searing pain sent a shock through her arms, and she dropped the axe. He quickly grabbed for the hammer and took it up, and turned as Lowden came flying off the wall with axe held high. Both weapons struck each other metal to metal, and it threw Lowden against the wall in a concussive explosion as Abrau was flattened to the ground.

Ophedia scrambled to her feet just as she watched the wagon clear the opening of the gate, the skyfall bell attached to the back of it in plain sight. Ten yards from there Hanen fought Slate and held a skyfall hammerhead in his gauntleted hands. The metal glowed red hot, vibrating in his hands violently.

"Get d—" she started to shout as all sound went dead and an explosion shot out across the square, flattening everyone to the ground.

As he opened his eyes, two figures stood over him, backlit by the sun high in the sky. He clutched both gauntleted hands to his chest, to keep them from reaching down to take them.

"Rather interesting you went missing this whole week and show back up wearing those," Dorian said.

Hanen squinted.

"And yet," the other said, tall staff in his hand—Ymbrys Veronia, "I am somehow not surprised. The gauntlets of the Dreadplate you've sought, Dorian, missing from the plate, and being used to try and stop the rest of the armor from escaping."

"The Chalicians are pressed back for a moment," Dorian said, "but they're mustering. Let's get into hiding, and figure out a way out of the city as soon as we're able."

"Why?" Hanen asked.

"The cart made it out of the city," Dorian confirmed.

"And Rallia was captured by the Chalicians," Ymbrys added.

"Rallia?!" Hanen retorted.

"Well," Dorian said. "That's a good sign."

"What is?" Ymbrys asked.

"Gauntlets or not, Hanen doesn't seem so far gone he doesn't care for his sister."

"Far gone?" Hanen asked.

"You bear two dark tools used by servants of dark gods, and I watched you use them to destroy a skyfall hammer. So they must have some use, if we're to destroy the Dreadplate. So we can't just rid ourselves of them. Perhaps they do not have a corrupting influence."

"That remains to be known," Ymbrys said, "once we've time to question you on how they came into your possession."

"Once we're on the road," Dorian said. "Right now I want to be far away from this city."

15

Bread and Ale

Pay close attention. I feel a new era of revelations fast approaches.

—FROM THE LAST LETTER OF PRIMUS ALOÍSIAV WEVAN
TO HIS YOUNGER BROTHER ADJUTANT VIAGO WEVAN
DURING THE PROTECTORATE WARS

After being denied access to Garrou, Nichal had ordered a makeshift camp under the stars, filled with a fervent hope that rain did not blow in off the Lupinfang. The twins took shifts standing guard and praying the clouds away.

On the following morning, Loïc nudged them each awake as a nearby farmer and his family arrived to offer Nichal and his entourage a place to stay. By the time they had arrived at the holding, the farmer's family had moved their own things out into the dairy barn to give use of their home to the Paladins. Their farm sat on one of the few hillocks in the valley, and the western gates of Garrou were easily visible from the front porch built around the space.

Jined had seen to a table and chair brought for Nichal, and he sat with Silas and Koel on the porch, taking down copious thoughts and notes. The twins worked with the farmer's family, moving the last of the previous year's hay into the dairy barn, while nearby milk aurochs grazed in a green field alongside a few capricörs.

Jined descended the hill to the farm's well. He lowered the bucket with the crank and then proceeded to pull it up one turn at a time, looking up into the clear sky.

"Grissone and Anka, twin-souled and creator of man," he prayed, "too long you have remained silent. We beseech you to come and deliver us. Hear our prayer and guide our steps."

The bucket came to the top, he took it by the handle, and pulled it to the well's ledge.

"Have I not done so?" a voice said behind Jined.

He startled and turned, knocking the bucket off the ledge. The crank spun as it plunged down into the water far below.

A Paladin stood before Jined, more than a head shorter. The armor the Paladin wore was intricately set with filigree verse. On his belt hung the suggestion of a hammer, yet, nothing was there.

Jined dropped to one knee, both hands coming together as he held them up. "Grissone! My god!"

The god before him smiled and bade him rise.

"Have I not?" Grissone repeated.

"Not what?"

"You beseeched me deliver you and to guide your steps. Have I not?"

"I..." Jined stood dumbfounded.

Grissone circled Jined to the well and began the act of turning the crank.

"I've heard your prayers," Grissone said. "And the Anka has acted plenty of times these past months."

"Then you know all that happened? In Boroni? At St. Rämmon?"

The bucket came to the top and Jined's god set it there. "It saddens me that you would think I did not."

Jined's shoulders sank.

"Did I not say I had things to do, and places to go?"

Jined gave a weak nod.

"Did you not place your trust in me when you took on a third vow? Not only that, but the Vow of Prayer—a promise to be in continual conversation with me."

"And yet I feel a vow-breaker."

"In what way?"

"My mind is constantly plagued by doubts."

"Of?"

"Of my own inadequacy."

"Doubt is no sin," Grissone said.

"But it is a lack of faith."

"Faith without doubt is never reached. That is the point: it is the path to deeper faith. In the seeking, you find the realization that you are always far from reaching it, and yet, you continue to reach for it."

"Is your silence not a sign that I am not worthy of what you have done through me?"

"You are not worthy," Grissone confirmed.

Jined looked up in horror.

"No one is," Grissone said. "That is my point. That you seek to be worthy, knowing you can never reach that status, is faith. That is not, however, why I have remained silent. Indeed, I have not been so silent as you think."

"What do you mean?"

"How many times have I spoken directly to Dorian Mür?"

"I do not know."

"It is not many. And yet, he remains faithful, even to this day, following my promptings. His prayers are made manifest, not only by his faithful request, but as acknowledgment of his actions."

"Then he is safe?"

Grissone laughed. "That you turn your attention to his safety, when faced with your own inadequacy…is why I like you, Jined."

Jined felt the color rise in his cheeks.

"Dorian is never safe, but he is well."

"What must I do to gain your forgiveness for my doubt? To renew my favor in your eyes?"

"Cease believing that very deceit—that you are not favorable in my eyes. Remember all that has transpired. Remember that feeling you held as I empowered you against the bearer of the cloak of bones. Remember those troubles I have guided you into, in order to be a light in that darkness."

Jined touched the hammer at his belt. "Would you have me take another vow right now?"

"Would you?" Grissone replied. "If I asked?"

"I would, although I fear what that would mean."

"In what way?"

"Silence or Pacifism alone remain. There appears to be a coming conflict. If I took either of those, I worry that the vow would be a stumbling block."

"A further portion of my power, and that is the worry? That you might not be heard? That you might not be able to lift your hammer?"

Jined grimaced and shame flushed his cheeks.

"No, I would not have you take a fourth vow right now. It is not the time."

"Then what must I do to cast this feeling away?"

"Ask it of me."

Jined dropped once more to the ground. "Grissone, my god. Please take this doubt from me. Fill me with a courage that drives the doubt away."

Grissone turned to the well, produced a silver ladle, dipped it into the bucket, and came back to Jined.

"I will not take your doubt away," Grissone said. "It is your doubt that shall be a constant reminder that you serve me by your choice. Take this ladle, and with it grant courage to those that drink from it."

He lifted it to Jined's lips and tipped the contents out. It was by no means a large ladle, bearing no more than a mouthful of the water, yet as Grissone tipped its edge, it seemed to pour out endlessly, with a salty sweetness. He drank deeply, and yet more water poured. No amount of water could quench the feeling within him. Soon he could drink no more, and yet the ladle continued to pour, and dribble down his face and armor.

Spluttering, he looked up at Grissone, who continued to pour, a smile across his face.

"Enough?" Grissone asked.

Jined nodded through the deluge.

Grissone stopped pouring and looked up at the sky with a nod.

Jined stood. A feeling of calm settled over him.

Grissone held out the silver ladle.

"Am I to take this?" Jined asked.

"You are. Use it as you need."

"How?"

Grissone gave him a level look. "It's a water ladle."

"So, only water."

"What else would you use it for?" Grissone asked.

"Soup?"

"A holy object, and you would stir soup with it?"

"I...I don't know," Jined said. "If this is to be a holy object given to me, as the oar given to St. Rämmon, I would know what to do with it."

"Trust yourself to do the right thing," Grissone said, placing a hand on Jined's shoulder. "I do."

Grissone turned toward Garrou. A man was riding hard toward them, yet was still a mile off.

Jined checked to see if Grissone had disappeared. He still stood there.

"That rider is important?"

"Anka believes so," Grissone said. "Let us go and be with Nichal when he arrives."

"You would speak with Nichal?"

"No. I shall join you as Brother Hammer."

Jined nodded and turned to walk up the hill, his god at his side.

"Those that drink from the water that comes from the ladle will have confidence restored or strengthened," Grissone explained as they walked. "Water stirred with it shall be made clean. Add to this, upon its filigreed surface sits new scripture I bestow to you. Record it but do not reveal it to others until it is written down in its entirety. Even then, you shall have scribes of worthy note, from each of the six vows, verify and confirm it against all other scriptures, so that there can be no doubt of its veracity."

"All six? But the vow of blindness is no longer practiced."

"It is not practiced at Pariantür, yes."

They came to the top of the hill. Nichal watched them approach, but gave no indication of surprise or curiosity that Jined did not walk alone.

"There is a rider approaching," Jined said. "I am led to believe them important."

Nichal gave a nod.

Jined came and stood behind the table on the porch. The rider neared the bottom of the hill as far off behind them the gates of Garrou opened and a cavalcade rode out in their direction.

The messenger at the bottom of the hill dismounted his sleipnir and walked up the path. As he came to the top, Loïc and Cävian came out from around the house, the latter bearing the Standard of Grissone. They stood on either side of Jined and Brother Hammer.

They both gave a quizzical look then turned their attention back to the guest.

Who's your friend? Cävian signed to Jined.

I was a close friend to Valér Queton, Brother Hammer signed back. We had many a deep conversation. I fully approve of his choice in you, to bear the standard."

Cävian smiled broadly and said no more.

The messenger wore the yellow and green of the city of Garrou, and held a herald's scepter in one arm. He stopped twenty-five paces from the table.

"I come bearing news from Garrou for the Prima Pater of the Paladins of the Hammer."

Nichal gave a wave and allowed him to approach.

The herald moved before the table, gave a curt bow, then stood tall.

"What news?" Nichal said.

"I precede a delegate of riders recently come from the west, who claimed to our king ownership of your city bastion and poorhouse."

"Chalicians?" Nichal asked.

The herald nodded.

"The king allows them to enter and exit your city, but not us?"

"King Vorso expelled them from our city until a decision can be made regarding the bastion. When an agreement is met, the winning entourage shall be allowed access to the city and the bastion."

"So he refuses to make the decision?" Nichal said.

The herald did not reply.

"How long do you give the Chalicians before they arrive?" Nichal asked the group of them.

"They're adopting a slow march," Koel said.

"And our friend herald," Jined said, "rode hard to reach us."

"The Dennigor farm is three miles from the gate," the herald said.

"Will you be staying here to observe the negotiations?" Nichal asked.

"If you will allow it," the man said.

"Then your name, if you please," Brother Silas Merun said, looking up from his parchment.

"Abamar Djer," the herald said, astonishment in his eyes.

"I hope you're not offended that we add your name," Silas said. "We wish to document the proceedings, and it adds an air of posterity and respectability to have within our records all in attendance."

Brother Hammer gave a small smirk.

"Your name will not be on it," Jined whispered.

"In spirit," Grissone muttered back.

Nichal turned. "Brothers, will you please requisition food for all? I make the eight of us, twelve farmers, and if their numbers are the same as they were in Igahli, twenty-one of them. A meal for forty-one people on short notice is nigh impossible."

"May Grissone bless our hands, then," Jined said aloud.

"He surely shall," Brother Hammer said, turning with Jined and the twins as they marched out behind the house to request help from the farmer and his family.

The farmer's sons moved tables, chairs, and buckets for seats to the front lawn, while the women, along with Jined, Didus Koel, and to Jined's surprise, Brother Hammer, took out ceramic jars, hung meats, and wheels of cheese and quickly displayed them on boards.

Brother Hammer moved across the kitchen to stand before a large bowl of dough, his eyes closed and hands held over. The farmer's wife approached and looked down.

"I've never seen a dough rise so fast!"

"Oven is hot," the eldest daughter called from across the room.

"Ball out these loaves," the farmer's wife ordered Grissone, god of man.

Grissone gave a nod and did as he was told. He looked up to the gaping mouth of Jined and gave him a wink.

A ladle of water into the ales, Grissone signed to Jined.

Jined nodded and looked down to the large barrel before him. He took out the ladle from his belt, and from a drinking basin divvied out splashes of water from his ladle into pitchers, then began filling them with ale. He soon had ten pitchers ready to be taken. He eyed the contents.

"Why taste rather than trust," Grissone said with a smile, as he passed by with a tray of dough balls.

Jined gave him a look, but nodded once more.

"Daughters," the farmer's wife announced as she closed the oven. "Stay with me and prepare to take out the bread when we are summoned. Brothers, if you will take ales and boards out now, I am informed they are ready, and the guests approach."

"When you do bring the bread," Jined said, "please sit and join us."

"Rumor is this may be a heated discussion," the woman said. "We shall eat before our family excuses ourselves once more."

"Your amicable presence will be most welcome at the table," Grissone said.

The woman smiled. "You are too kind. Now off with you!"

Jined took up as many pitchers as he could and marched out the door. As he walked around the house he found a circle of tables set out with enough chairs for fifty.

"We've enough food?" Jined muttered to Koel, carrying two trays of cheese and dried meat.

"I should hope so. I heard the farmer's wife declare she would continue to see food readied so long as talk continues."

Jined placed his load down and returned to fetch another. Brother Hammer came around the house with a large basket of bread.

"I've never known bread to bake so fast," Jined said to him. "Did you have a hand in that too?"

"Who can know?" Grissone gave a wink.

"Brother!" Nichal called to them.

Grissone turned. "Yes, Prima Pater?" he replied.

"Place the bread by me, if you will," Nichal ordered.

"If only he knew," Jined said.

"You'll not tell him," Grissone said.

Jined smiled and went back for more ale, to find not four remaining, but ten still.

"At this rate," a farmer's son said, helping him take the ten, "we'll empty our ale barrel."

Another son gave the barrel a shove. "What do you mean by that, Hepmar? Barrel's still full."

Jined offered a silent prayer of thanks, and followed Hepmar out to the tables just as the Chalicians reached the bottom of the hill.

Jined came to sit at Nichal's right hand, and Grissone took the space next to him.

Provost Zehan Otem dismounted from his sleipnir, then the others did as well. He consulted with his book bearer, who then attempted to leaf through the giant book in his possession, but the wind whipped up to prevent him from accomplishing his task.

"Are you doing that?" Jined muttered.

"I am not," Grissone said with a straight face. "The Anka is."

"Oh?"

"He does not like the Chalicians. Never has."

The flustered Chalicians finally gathered themselves and began their march up the path, spears held toward the sky. They came to the top of the hill, and stopped. Not a few of them lost their composure, and gaped at the spread.

"Welcome, Provost Zehan Otem," Nichal said. "We greet you as our guests, and invite you to a table, to break bread together and share a meal."

"For what reason?" Otem asked.

"It is our custom when hosting to eat first, so that any discussion we may have aside from that is tempered."

Otem took a step forward. "I..." He looked around at the table and at the farmer and his family.

Grissone himself took up a pitcher and two tankards, filled them, then handed one to Nichal and circled the tables to give the other to Otem.

"When last we met, we had unkind words," Nichal said.

"I do not doubt," Otem said, "it may happen again."

"Let us put our differences aside long enough to enjoy a meal together," Nichal said, lifting his tankard.

Otem did likewise, and they both drank.

The Praetor lowered his tankard and eyed it with a look of astonishment.

"This ale," Otem said. "I've never had something so incredible."

Nichal smiled. "I was going to say the same thing. Shall we take our seats?"

Otem made a hand motion for the Praetors behind him. They spread out and took their seats. They had added to their numbers and filled the additional nine chairs. More bread came with the women from the kitchen, and soon all were seated.

Nichal stood after everyone had their tankards filled.

"Let us pray for our good health, and success in our discussion," Nichal said.

Everyone lifted their tankards.

"We lift our prayers this day, not only to Grissone and Anka, Twin-Souled and Ever-Watchful, but to Aben, Crysania, and Nifara, those gods that keep a watchful eye over man. Even to the Wyv-Thüm. In their divine providence, we are brought here to this hillock farm to negotiate, to discuss. Before all that, we share what every man ought to do with friend and enemy: the breaking of bread and the sharing of a cup. Continue to bless this day, as you have already done so."

The Paladins said their "amens" while Praetors made the sign of

DREAD KNIGHT

Lantern and Arrow.

Jined lifted his tankard and took a drink.

He recalled the feeling when Grissone had made him his hammer, and they flew from world to world with Nifara. That same sense of elation warmed every inch of him. The flavor of the ale spoke of the green pastures of Lomïn. A sense of permanence in the moment overwhelmed him as the simple flavors at play rolled down his throat. He could not pinpoint that it was anything more than a simple ale, and yet, the taste was indescribable.

Next to Jined, Grissone murmured, "Blessings given."

Grissone took another drink, then as he placed his tankard down, he was no longer there.

16

VISIONS OF FATE

"Ever humanity seeks schism. Why?" the young novice asked St. Nevenhal.

"Listen well, my student. We cannot understand how another thinks. Seek to understand why you might contend with another, and perhaps you will discover why they might contend with you."

"Might I thus prevent such schism?"

"You might. Or you may allow it, because it is what is best for everyone."

—FROM *THE NEVENHAL CONVERSATIONS*

"You know that you cannot stay here in Garrou," Otem said between sips of the ale.

"You've no authority to tell me that," Nichal said. "Acting Prima Pater or fully elected Prima Pater makes no difference. Not only due to my higher ranked authority than you, but by precedence of an older order with established holdings."

"Holdings you abandoned in schism."

"Not true," Nichal said.

"That is what is on record in Mahn Fulhar. Our High Priest declared your church in schism, and your holdings forfeit."

Nichal sighed and sat back, taking a sip himself. It seemed to give him courage and he sat up in his chair. "He declared us in schism and suggested that we ought to put our house in order. To the latter we agreed. We were given the chance to cross the Mahn

Fulhar green to assault the abandoned Rose Convent, to face those who headed the heretical branch, but in doing so we abandoned the bastion located there to your Order. We decided that one bastion was a worthwhile cost to cut off the blight when we could."

"This is what I have said," Otem replied.

"But not the whole of it," Nichal replied. "After this, we sent out messages to those brothers that could leave the western nations and might choose to do so. They were informed that if they chose to leave, that for the time being, they'd not have the support of Pariantür without extensive and hard-wrought communication. It was not an abandonment, but a closing of gates. We are aware that your Order is forcefully removing our brothers from some bastions. If that is so, and it is done peacefully, then so be it. If you have done so with violence, I think that in the long run, you will find us returning in coming years to conduct bitter negotiations."

"Yet you continue east."

"Pariantür is in the east. We move east along the path we traveled last year, to reinforce and consolidate."

"Our Order is strong. We have awaited a moment like this to better establish our control."

"Then," Nichal said, "you freely admit, you follow a course of action that values domination over protection."

"We offer protection under the umbrella of our dictates."

"Which is exactly what I just said," Nichal said calmly.

"It is not!" Otem snapped. "Our Order, isolated as it was for centuries, has developed methods to ensure the redemption of those that follow it. It is the doctrine of the Church of Aben to see people along a path that would lead them to Lomïn. Ours merely takes a proactive approach. The other factions are passive, and suggest the best course in hopes that people might choose to take it. We believe it is not enough. There ought to have been, all along, a stronger directive by the Church of Aben as a whole, to see our flock on the right path. What do you do?"

"Negotiate. Keep people from each other's throats. Deflect attacks that would dishearten. Be an example of faith that invites, rather than forces."

"Example..." Otem replied, his voice dripping. "It is passivity."

"In what way?"

"Your bastions. They are everywhere. Yet you point blame at us for being a presence of dictatorial authority."

"The only complaints ever leveled against us are from

landowners who covet our land. Add to that, those same men find our purchase of the debts of their servants—and through this their servant's loyalty and lives—distasteful, for the loss of forced manpower. We do that only by the request of the indebted, and I've not known a servant of the Hammer who has not paid off their debt and lived their life out in peace and prosperity. What will the Order of the Chalice do when men and women come to your bastions and beg mercy?"

"They shall be afforded opportunity. By their sweat they shall earn a freed soul."

"Their children's freedom. Not their own."

"Do not speak about that which you do not know."

"Nor should you," Nichal said cooly.

They both stopped and eyed their empty tankards. Jined reached over with a pitcher and refilled them. As they lifted their drinks and sipped, they appeared once more to calm down.

"You were sent from the city," Nichal said.

"This entire journey has been rife with walls thrown up. From Bronue Jinre to here."

"Does not your church take that as a sign that they ought to regroup?"

"I have been given holy purpose by Praeposit Anhouil Chétain, to continue in my mission. I cannot stop. Those that do not accept our authority shall be noted, and shall find themselves at odds with our order."

"You would declare war on those that turn you away?"

"They are declared lost. Those who come after me shall face rebuttal."

Nichal shook his head. "You are like speaking to a stone wall."

"Such is my determination," Otem said with a smug smile.

Could you imagine if Dane were here? Cävian signed.

This received chuckles from several Paladins who could see his hands.

"What is so humorous?" Otem asked.

"We've a colleague," Jined spoke up. "He is...difficult. If he were here, I doubt this would be so calm a discussion."

"I invite a passionate debate," Otem replied.

"You prefer a pulpit, where you are the only one speaking," Nichal said.

Otem laughed.

"That's a first, I'm sure," Nichal said.

"A first what?"

"Time you've laughed."

"I laugh plenty," Otem said, offense taken. He looked around the table to the other Praetors to see them confirm. All of them looked away, horror-stricken.

"Did you know that the bastion within Garrou spends more coin on their poorkitchen than any other bastion or fortress in these domains?" Nichal said, changing the subject.

"I cannot tell if you are bragging or not," Otem said.

"I consider it impressive," Nichal said, "and something worth protecting."

"Why protect that?" Otem replied.

"Why protect the care of the downtrodden? Why should we not?"

"When a man comes to a poorkitchen," Otem said, "what questions are asked of him?"

"What questions?"

"Do you inquire why he comes, or what he is doing to better himself?"

"We ask only one question," Nichal said.

Otem took a drink and looked at him intently, awaiting a response.

"We ask him, 'Are you hungry?'"

"That is it?"

"What other question ought we ask?" Nichal replied.

"How can you feed someone who will only begin to lean on you for sustenance, rather than seek to improve their moral status?"

"What does moral status have to do with hunger?"

"It is a sign that they walk the wrong path."

Nichal laughed.

"What is so funny?"

"You came to this farm, and without batting an eye, sat at this table and broke bread with me. Does that insinuate you hunger? Does that not mean you walk the wrong path?"

The look of offense that spread across Otem's face bloomed. "That is not what I mean!"

Nichal sat back. "I know what you mean, Provost, but you do not know what you mean. You would starve the world to prove your point. I would spend every coin at my disposal to first feed the world, then invite them into the fold."

Otem flushed red.

"A person who comes to the Hammer for food shall receive it. While we eat, we read a scripture. We call them to a higher cause, not out of guilt as payment for their bread, but when their belly is full, they can better think for themselves."

"What is your point?"

"I think you have made my point for me," Nichal said. "By questioning the validity of a poorkitchen, I have resolved that we shall not allow you to have the bastion in Garrou."

"We've not even begun to negotiate," Otem said.

"Oh," Nichal said, placing his drink down, "we most certainly are not negotiating. I've already decided I'm not allowing you to have it."

"We have been ordered by the king to negotiate, or else neither of us enter the city again."

"Perhaps I'll send word to my contacts amidst the Crysalas," Nichal said, "and give them the poorkitchen's control. They've plenty of experience helping the downtrodden."

"The Crysalas," Otem sneered.

"I think I finally understand why you and your church hate the Crysalas and Nifarans so very much. You can't stand that they do even more than we do, to grant to any common person a chance at peace and justice."

"I have no respect for those orders. They only enable those who have walked the wrong path."

"Enabling them to adjust their path. You would force people onto a path of your making. A disingenuous path."

"Better a path under our lash than one walking upon the broken glass of false philosophies!" Otem roared. He stood from his chair and began to pace. "At every turn!"

Nichal raised his tankard and found it empty. Jined moved to fill it, but Nichal waved him off.

"First your Prima Pater escapes Mahn Fulhar," Otem roared. "Then at every turn, we're shown the door, harassed for doing the will of the High King in Lomïn. I could write most of that off as persecution, and therefore proof of our truth, but then your beloved Crysalas embarrassed us on those very streets!" He pointed to Garrou. "Now you feed us ashy food, and a bitter cup of mockery!"

Nichal stood abruptly, his hand going to the hammer at his belt.

"You would raise your hammer against us? Declare a holy war?"

Nichal raised his hand slowly, appearing to point at Otem with an accusatory finger, but his gaze cast far in the distance. "It would appear we must cast our differences aside for the time being," Nichal said.

Otem and everyone at the table turned to look past the city of Garrou. A cloud of dust rose beyond the hills, and over the top of the knolls rose a chaotic line. The host of figures marched forward and came to a stop, a handful of miles from the eastern walls of Garrou.

"What in Noccitan is that?" Otem asked.

"Those," Jined announced loudly for the entire hill to hear, "are vül."

17

RISING TENSION

Walked they upon the trodden road,

Another long lost soul.

To gain what fell from their soft grip,

Blown 'bout to and fro.

The paths deep call to know.

— THE TRAVELER

The Abei mountains had grown shorter the farther south Marn and Alodda traveled, but rather than turning to rolling hills they became a series of wildly craggy rocks jutting up into the sky.

Castenard Castle was built on the last one, a giant, pointed slab of granite that looked as if it had been pulled over by a massive titan millennia ago. Under and around the overhang, hundreds of feet below, the city crowded behind tall walls. The entire city was made of the same gray granite as the mountains nearby, so from a distance it appeared as a gray smear in an otherwise green and yellow world of harvested fields. As Marn and Alodda topped the last rise before entering the half-basin, they could see a thick brown smear pressed up against the walls—shanties of refugees come from every direction, seeking admittance to the city.

"That doesn't look good," Marn said. "If what that old man said is true, we have to go through Castenard to get permission to go west."

"Why not circle it then?" Alodda said. "We could be here for weeks if we don't. If we go south we can reach another city."

As though on cue, a patrol of soldiers wearing Castenardi red road out of a stand of trees, beyond which stood an as-yet-unnoticed outpost.

They circled Alodda and Marn, as well as a handful of additional travelers who came up the rise behind them.

"Business?" the man in the lead called out.

"Traveling west," someone replied.

"South," Marn said, putting a protective arm around Alodda's shoulder.

"Well, you're in Castenard lands now. Anyone who trespasses is subject to our rule. You'll need to pay us two royals a piece, or go through Castenard to register."

Marn made a choking sound. "That's extortion," Marn said.

The man reached for the sword at his side and Marn backed down.

"We've only to go down to the city and register?" Alodda asked nicely.

"If you deviate and try to cut away, our riders have orders to treat any who leave the roads with extreme prejudice."

"Let us go down to Castenard," Alodda said to Marn, whose balled fists were whitening at the knuckles. "Even refugees could use a seamstress."

Marn's mouth had tightened to a thin, tight line as Alodda led him away without another word.

The camps of the refugees were not so brown as they'd appeared from far off. The colors of their tents, while weathered, bore the colors of merchants and forest people from the mountains, come to seek the more powerful city's protection. Farther along to the south of the city, a camp of men, women, and children from farther west were in worse straits, wagons full of their belongings, all begging for the opportunity to travel east. Ormachians claimed to have been ousted from their homes by soldiers from Œron, and a handful from Limae were seeking refuge. Beyond them, to the south of the mountains, and just west of the city, battalions of soldiers were positioned in camps facing west—new conscripts digging trenches and refilling them in practice drills.

Over the course of the week, Alodda's seamstress talents paid for meals, and Marn put his net-mending to use to help several refugees better bind their wagons' cargo.

On the sixth day navigating their way to the west, a group of uniformed soldiers came through the lines of wagons and tents. They stopped in front of the circle of people where Marn and Alodda sat. Their leader pulled out a ledger.

"Marn and Alodda Clouw?"

Marn stood and crossed the circle to stand before the man.

"May I help you, captain?"

"Are you Clouw?"

"I am."

"This says you're a monk of Aben, but you do not wear a robe nor tonsure strip."

"I gave my robe to one of the destitute when I set off from Birin with my son's intended in order to find him."

"He abandoned you?"

"He sent us on ahead to Düran, and now with terrible rumors of what is happening in Varea and Limae, we race to seek him out and discover what has happened."

"All of these refugees and merchants and you travel toward the danger?"

"What father would not do so for his son?"

"You're to come with us."

Marn turned to Alodda, who nodded and stood to follow.

The soldiers pushed their way through the shanties toward the city gate, which slammed behind them no sooner than they'd cleared it.

They walked down several side streets and came to a nondescript tavern. The captain entered and after checking the establishment came back out.

"You're to speak with the man by the fire."

As Marn entered, the place was empty, save for the man before the fire sitting in a large cushioned chair. Marn crossed the room with Alodda just behind him. The dark-skinned Sidieratan man held himself with nobility, but did not wear the trappings. He had a short, trimmed black mustache, and his tight, curly hair was oiled and plastered to his head. On a side table a pristine, wide-brimmed brown hat lay next to a crystal goblet of red wine.

"I understand you are a monk, yet do not dress as one, and seek to travel west."

"You do not dress as someone of noble birth, yet you seek us out."

The man gave a false smile, but did not speak.

"I am Brother Marn Clouw. I travel west, yes, seeking my son."

"And daughter," the man corrected.

"Excuse me?"

"Your name is Clouw. An uncommon name, unless you took on the name from a fairytale. If I'm not mistaken, and I never am, the only other notable Clouws on the face of Kallattai run a caravan out of Edi."

"This is true. They did."

"Black Sentinels then are who you seek."

"Also true," Marn said.

"If you're a spy for Edi, you would say less."

"Why should I speak less? I am a monk of Aben and dedicated to the truth."

"Very good. Keep that up."

"Who are you?" Alodda asked.

The man offered an amused smile. "A man of consequence. You may simply refer to me as the Manticör. I've arranged for you to be provided with new, er...worn, monastic robes and a writ of passage for when that does not work, in order for you to travel west."

"At what cost?" Marn asked suspiciously.

"Ah." The man touched the side of his nose. "You'll be traveling south to the port of Boscolón. I've a message and an agent who will be going with you. You're to deliver the message to a man of mine there. Then you're free to do whatever you wish."

"So we're to be couriers and spies."

"Just couriers. You'll be traveling with another courier who has business past Boscolón and I cannot afford to have him seen with the man you're to meet."

"And if we should not agree to go? What you propose adds weeks to our journey."

"If you do not do as I ask, then you won't ever leave Castenard. I'm sure we can find work for you both as camp followers if rumors are established and Castenard goes to war."

Marn and Alodda considered one another.

"I'm offering you the chance to find your son," he said to Marn, then to Alodda he said, "your lover, in exchange for a few weeks' travel, or to be cast to the gutters for the rest of your lives. Either choice is fine by me."

"Will we have time to discuss?" Marn asked.

"You leave right now."

"We've things to gather," Marn said. "My net-mending tools. Her own tools of trade."

The Manticör indicated a pouch on the table. "I do not doubt you'll find the means to replace them."

Marn stepped forward and took up the heavy pouch. He peeked at the gold and message within and sucked down his shock. Alodda balled her fists, but he placed a calming hand on her shoulder. He took up the message from the pouch and read it, nodded, and held it over the candle. The Manticör nodded in satisfaction.

A man stepped out of the shadows. He was heavy-set, built like a fighter. His bald head shone, with sun-tanned skin that implied he came from anywhere outside of the far north. His eyes were nearly black.

"This is Sabell Panza. You're to do as he says, when he says it. With your mission completed, you will be provided with another satchel of coin equal to the first."

"What guarantee do we have?" Marn asked.

Panza laughed, but the Manticör replied. "You have no guarantee. I allow you to leave the city. What more do you need? Now leave. I've others to meet."

Panza turned to the door without a backward glance, expecting Marn and Alodda to follow.

When they came to the street, Panza continued for several hundred feet before turning to them.

"Which direction shall we take?" Marn asked.

Panza held up a hand to silence him. "I wish to make something very clear. I am not your friend. I owe you no explanation for my actions. When we are on the road, I will walk one hundred feet ahead of you at all times and will not converse. In the evenings, the discussions around the campfire are to be only about food. If we come upon other travelers, we will act amiable and say little. When we reach Boscolón, I will put you in contact with the man you deliver your message to."

"And the promised gold?"

Panza had already turned and walked away.

18

INTERLUDES

The landscape of purple hues spread out before him in ever-changing ripples and dunes. A craggy mountain might be there at one moment, and in the next, the mountain might fall away like a smashed child's castle in the sand.

Loth clutched the skull in his arms, holding it facing the way he walked. Yesterday—if there was such a thing as night and day in the Veld—they had come to a vast ocean. At the skull's whisper, a sandbar had risen through the middle and Loth had walked on dry land. It had taken only an hour to cross a sea that appeared to have no other side. Whenever Loth thought himself hungry, a pillar of sandstone would rise, with whatever food he so desired displayed upon it.

He thought at one time he had seen someone crossing the same obsidian flat, perpendicular to him, but they'd disappeared as a gust of sand flew up between them.

Ever on he marched, a thin silver line of light leading from the holes in the forehead of the skull off to the distant horizon.

"Can you sense where we go?" he asked.

I know we go. And I've a vague idea of what I see before me. But all is...confused.

"Then you cannot sense the 'you' we go to?"

Cease with your questions. Only do as I ask.

Loth learned the skull offered little opportunity to speak. Yet, he was drawn to ask more questions. On the fifth day, the desert turned into a scrubland, from which grew crystalline, leafless trees. As he reached to touch one, from the tip of a branch a fruit grew before his eyes, and from that fruit seven more fruit, and from them seven, and so on. He reached up to take the fruit.

You dare not touch it.

Loth pulled his hand back. "Poison?"

Touch it and find out. But should you die, I shall fall here collecting dust.

Loth took back his hand and continued up the rocky hill, avoiding the branches that sought to touch him.

"I have heard that anything can be done here," Loth said.

I would not know. I have never been here. Yet, have you not been fed?

"How do you know that, with no way to see?"

I have fed you.

"How?"

By choosing that it is so.

As they crested the hill, down below a nearly unsurpassable valley of razor rocks opened up before them. Cut through the middle ran a canyon, deep enough the light did not appear to reach the bottom.

You hesitate.

"The only way forward is through a deep and very dark trench."

Then we proceed forward.

"With no means to protect ourselves, it will be dangerous."

Forward, the skull compelled.

Loth sighed and walked down the slope. The dark canyon loomed as a vast maw, prepared to swallow him whole. A prick of light could be seen in the distance. The silvery sheen of the line of light coming from the skull led him on.

One hundred feet in, lights began to shine on the walls of the canyon. They appeared to be mollusks, their slowly opening and closing shells blinking the lights in and out of sight.

What is it? the skull asked.

"Some sort of shellfish, out of water, and glowing. You can see it?"

I can sense it. I control my lessers.

"What does that mean?"

Suddenly, more of them glowed. The glow rippled out, illuminating the way forward as hundreds of the things lit up.

"You are doing that?"

Do not act surprised. The weak-minded always do my bidding.

DREAD KNIGHT

They proceeded for what felt like days in that darkness, the glow of the mollusks upon the walls before and after them. High above, he often heard the sound of skittering. Less often, the purple sky spread as a scar, swallowed soon again by the dark shadows cast by the canyon walls looming overhead.

What is happening? the skull suddenly whispered.

"Nothing is happening," Loth said.

But the silver string of light coming from the skull quavered, then began to imperceptibly shift, as though the other end was moving for the first time.

"I think our destination is changing," Loth said.

Then we must hurry. We must!

The mollusks on the walls burst into glowing light before and after. In that increasing light, he saw up above and clinging to the walls chitinous things, glossy black with tooth-filled maws, many eyes watching them, but daring not approach. Loth felt terror rise in his throat. He held the skull high above his head, and the things shrunk back. He did not lower the skull, but ceaselessly ran through the canyon, daring to hope the other end would be reached soon.

The heavy wagon trundled far ahead on the road. The monk beside her moved with little need for help—the Praetors of the Chalice had been kind enough to let her keep her staff.

"This isn't exactly how I expected to leave Haven," Rallia said. "Certainly not in chains."

"It takes us away from that place," Seriah muttered. "That is enough."

"Why do you detest Haven so much?"

"Have you ever been face to face with a god?"

Rallia did not reply, thinking back to the ocean beach in Mahndür.

"I have," Seriah whispered. "On more than one occasion. Every time was a horror."

"A horror? To be faced with the divine?"

"Twice in Mahn Fulhar. And twice, no, three times, in Haven. I was made to be messenger between them. I was made to see the rise of the Revenants. I almost became one myself."

"That is amazing," Rallia said.

"How?"

"You've been a messenger of the gods. On more than one occasion. That ought to be celebrated."

"Not if you knew which gods made me do so."

"You are a monk of Nifara," Rallia said. "Does she not protect you?"

"Well," Seriah offered, "I think she does now. She pulled me back from the brink after I admonished the others never to speak to me again."

"There you go!" Rallia said, smiling.

"Why does that make you cheerful?"

"Why shouldn't it? You're blessed. I think that's something to cherish. That I am in your company, a chosen of your goddess, means that what happens after this must be by her choice."

"Even being dragged south by those that fly against everything the church of Aben has ever stood for?"

"I shared fish with someone on a beach only a few short months ago. Based on his character, I don't doubt that the Church of Aben—whether Chalician or otherwise—is watched with a scrutinizing eye by their god. I think it'll be a fun adventure to see what comes of these events."

They walked in silence for a time.

"What does sharing a fish have to do with that?" Seriah asked.

"It wasn't a man I ate the fish with. I, too, was made messenger. It was very clear that Aben was who shared with me. Nothing the Chalicians say, though they claim Aben as their god, matches what I felt. Yet nothing they say can ever take from me that feeling."

"I suppose that is also true of my last meeting with my goddess."

"There you go!"

"So what do we do?"

"We let them lead us, and keep an eye on that wagon."

"What about the wagon?"

"That is my true worry. I don't know what is in it, but I have an idea. I'd wager those I came to Haven with will not be far behind us to retrieve it," Rallia said.

"You're speaking in riddles."

"Yes, but that is because we do not need anyone hearing what I think is in that wagon."

"I see. Well..." Seriah touched the blind over her eyes. "I understand, anyway."

Rallia laughed.

The inn above roared with the normal merriment one might expect, while the cellar below sat in a pool of silence. The sisters did not speak as they awaited news. Word was the king might summon Toire Siobh, and Astrid agreed to go with her, if she must, to continue the confrontation she had begun with the Praetors of the Chalice.

The red-headed Bronuan entered the room, and all eyes turned to her. She bore a broad smile upon her face.

"That Praetor," she said, "was just sent from the city, banished until he could meet with Prima Pater Guess, a few miles west of the city, and come to an agreement with Nichal, rather than the king."

"What does that mean for us?"

"It means we proceed with our plans. There is a tunnel leading from this cellar. It lets out south of the city, when the tide is low, and the river has mostly drained. The tide is turning now, so we must go."

"With the tide on our heels," Astrid asked. "Will that not endanger us?"

"If we move this instant, then no. If we hesitate, then yes."

Astrid looked at Katiam, who returned with a nod.

"Then let's go," Astrid said.

Toire nodded and moved past them to a wall, and pressed. It moved out of the way. Others gasped, but Katiam followed through the portal, touching the stone door. It was carved driftwood.

"Clever," she said to Toire, who smiled in response.

The tunnel ran for several hundred feet before it took spiral stairs down into a wet, damp tunnel.

"Continue down this," Toire said, as she pushed to the front of the group. "I'll run on ahead to the end to double-check the water level, but don't hesitate. Move as quickly as you can, but don't run—it's easy to slip and hurt yourself down here."

Katiam nodded and pressed on. The sound of water trickled far off in the distance. The light of their torches was soon replaced by an ambient light and she could hear the sound of the river. Toire stood at the end, the entrance merely a group of large rocks hard to squeeze out of.

"No taking sleipnirs this way," Katiam said.

"And unfortunately, all sleipnirs within any reasonable distance from the city have been requisitioned by the army. So you'll be on foot."

"How far will you continue with us?"

"I'll walk a mile or so before I return, though I cannot go back into the city until the turning of the tide again."

They walked a hundred yards along the trickling riverbed. The sky overhead was clear. The Rotha was strapped against Katiam's chest, but a couple of leaves peeked out and sought the sun.

"Soon we shall have you out in the air," Katiam whispered.

Far behind them, the walls of the city could just be seen over the berm of the riverbed. Bells began to peal.

"Are those for us?" Onelie asked nearby.

"They shouldn't be," Toire said.

She made a signal and she, Astrid, and Esenath all pressed up the side and on to the plain to look.

Esenath gasped.

"What is it?"

"Oh, Katiam," Esenath replied, looking back down.

"What?" Katiam said, holding her hand out for Esenath to pull her up.

The botanist hoisted her up, a dour look on her face.

As she came up over the edge, her heart dropped. Far to the east, an army poured over the hills, miles away, but still as dangerous a sight as she had ever seen. Thousands upon thousands of vül marched on the city of Garrou, no longer a distant threat, but mounting their attack.

"I must return to the city immediately," Toire said, "to secure the exit, so the invading army cannot find an easy way in."

"I understand," Astrid said.

"Will you not all return with me? To the safety of the city?"

Astrid looked at Katiam. "Return? Or flee south."

Katiam turned down the riverbed, where Onelie, Little Maeda, Lutea, and Narah stood. "An army of vül approaches the city walls," Katiam said. "Astrid and I continue south. You may continue with us, flying in the face of danger, or stay behind the walls of the city, and pray the gods deliver you. There is no wrong answer, but you must decide now."

All four looked at each other, then back up with a nod.

"We will go with you," Lutea said. "Let us fly."

Katiam turned back to Astrid. "Perhaps Garrou will distract the vül. There are only a handful of us, but we seven go south."

Astrid turned back to Toire. "Thank you for everything."

"Crysania protect you," Toire said, clasping Astrid's arm.

Esenath, Astrid, Katiam, and Toire dropped back into the riverbed. Toire didn't say another word, but turned and ran back to the secret entrance to the city.

"Let's run up the river as far south as we can," Astrid said, "until the water forces us to the fields above. We're a day's march from the next town. We can tell them of the danger Garrou faces, and hope we do not face any vül scouts ourselves."

They turned as one and began their march through the gravelly river sand, away from Garrou and the invading army.

Pellian Noss had ridden to the south gate the night before to ensure that those that had broken into the city would press no farther than the Revenant Quarter.

It was still a thorn in Aurín's mind, knowing that at any moment he could be surrounded. The people of the city had mustered at the western wall, and houses were being pulled apart for their stone. The gaping sandy breach had been cleared away, spread out in the city or beyond until it was flat. Personal hunting bows, spears, and anything anyone could throw held back the small bands of Chalician soldiers who threw themselves at the wall at regular intervals. Twice they had almost broken through, but Aurín had personally led a group of tradesmen, their tools in hand, out of the gap in the wall to press them back. As both moons slid overhead and campfires were lit in town squares, he tried his best to show courage, and not give into the fear that had gnawed at him for weeks now.

When dawn began to threaten the eastern horizon, Aurín could tell the wall would be more or less secure as the last few stones were put in place by the work crews. How long it would hold, he did not know.

A Sentinel, black cloak over her face, approached from the south.

"Aurín," Ophedia said.

"News?"

"Noss sent me from the south. He is preparing to make a push, to try and force the Chalicians out. The people of the city are rallying there, too. The Chalician force is not nearly so large as we thought, but he needs you to do the same."

"What do you mean?"

"As the sun crests, he wants you to take what force you can out of the gap, and run off the army there."

"That's foolish."

"Why so?"

"Look at those fires," Aurín said. "There have got to be a hundred of them. That's one thousand at least."

"So take two thousand. I'm going with you."

"It's a suicide run."

"Noss doesn't think it is."

"Do we really trust him?" Aurín asked.

"I don't know," Ophedia said. "He's been awake all night, leading men to battle. When he's not, he's plotting."

"Plotting what?"

"He wants to break this siege and begin pressing south. To try and pull the rest of Limae under Haven's banner. To secure the country before the Praetors take half of it for themselves."

"So?"

"So, he told me to tell you he wants to put you in charge of that counter-invasion. But first, you have to break this siege."

Aurín looked her in the eye. "Ophedia. I just want to run."

"I do too," Ophedia said. "But, I watched as a cavalcade of Chalicians moved away from the city, a wagon in their midst, and people in chains. Rallia was one of them."

"Then let's leave and go after them."

"I think Hanen will do that. The best thing we can do is ride this wave. March south. Buy everyone in the world time before the Praetors take any more. I'm much more worried about what empire they will force down the throats of every one of us than anything else. You did commit to becoming a Warden."

"You haven't."

DREAD KNIGHT

"I don't know that my fate will let me not be one. So I'll just keep following along."

"Alright," Aurín said, "but we do this together."

Ophedia nodded, and pulled out a bundle from her cloak.

"What is this?"

"Noss said to take this."

Aurín opened it to reveal a new cloak with slashes like the other Wardens wore, giving the appearance of wings. Across the black surface silver thread embroidered a griffin with one claw a grasping talon and in the other claw an axe.

"Is this supposed to be me?"

Ophedia shrugged. She turned to look down at people working on the wall.

"Who tires of the singing keeping us from our freedom!" she shouted.

There was a general murmur.

"Before we close this gap, let's put out their campfires with blood."

The crowd began to cheer.

Aurín swung the cloak over his shoulders, then stepped up onto a stone, cutting a pose. "You have followed me to repel those that would enter our city. My talon," he held up a clawed hand, "has shed blood this night. But it is still thirsty!"

Men shouted a cry of encouragement.

"Good. Keep going," Ophedia whispered.

"No more shall we repel them," he shouted. "Instead, let us drive them off!"

The sun crested the eastern mountains over the city and struck Aurín, who turned, the silver in his cloak shimmering. He leapt down the stairs to the street. "Let's take the fight to them and cease quivering in our free city!"

He walked to the gap, Ophedia behind him, and stepped out into the stone-terraced slope from the city. He took out his axe, and raised it toward the campfires, a few shadows moving around them as the sun began to cover the entire field in warm yellow light.

"For Haven!" he shouted and began moving forward.

"For the Talon!" the men behind him roared, and as one they charged down the terraced slope toward the waking army of Chalicians.

Part 3

LIMAE AND SURROUNDING

19

A Mutual Understanding

Silence beckons. No companion will it tolerate but darkness.

—*JEALOUS SILENCE*, NEMENESE POEM

Hanen was sitting in the dark inn, the embers in the hearth dying, Whisper curled up under the table, leaning against his leg, when Dorian and Ymbrys found him. The only allowance they made was for him to retrieve his Black Sentinel cloak. He'd ducked into the alley, finding Whisper standing guard over but not touching the two cloaks intertwined in a discarded bundle. He'd rolled up the boneshroud in the cloak, carried both under his arms, and let the old man lead him back to the inn, the gauntlets now in the old man's possession distracting him from even suspecting his other secret.

Hanen spoke little over the rest of that day and the next, as Dorian and Ymbrys took turns seeking ways to leave the city. On the third day, they both returned, exhausted, but determined to pry out of him how he had gotten both gauntlets. He told them how the night they first arrived in town he had wrested the first from Slate, then the night the Revenants appeared he had gone back in and gotten ahold of the second.

Dorian raised the question of why he had not said anything, but Ymbrys motioned for him to let it lie. Hanen's ears burned hot as Dorian concluded with a retort, "What else aren't you telling us?"

On the fourth day, Ymbrys returned to the inn and spoke quietly with Dorian as they both began making preparations. After an hour of this they finally came to Hanen's table.

"There are groups of citizens," Ymbrys began, "who have been leaving the city to march south to raid the Chalicians pillaging the countryside. There is a group of volunteers leaving the city just before dawn, and I've convinced a captain to let me out of the city with two bodyguards at the same time."

"So we're to be your bodyguards?" Hanen asked.

Ymbrys nodded.

"But," Dorian said, turning to Hanen, "we have to know where your loyalty lies."

"What do you mean?" Hanen asked.

"While you've not lied to us, as far as I can tell, you did not share with us, nor your sister, the truth of the gauntlets in your possession. I find that disconcerting. In the past four days, you've done little more than tell us how you got them. I've made allowances for you to share more and you have not."

"I told you, I happened upon opportunities, and I took them. I was endangered each time, and on the second, the appearance of the Revenants made the finding and retrieving of any more of the Dreadplate impossible."

"And yet, Rallia and I could have helped you."

"You went missing after that night, too."

"But not before that, when you had one of them."

"We can't change the past now," Hanen said defensively, "but we can take this opportunity Ymbrys found to go and rescue Rallia."

"If we can even tell where she is going," Ymbrys said.

"Given how easily you always find Rallia and myself, I'm not worried," Hanen said sarcastically.

"You do realize that we also worry about any corrupting influence those gauntlets might have over you," Dorian added.

"Why would that be a worry?" Hanen said.

"Dark tools like the gauntlets, or the still-missing boneshroud, are no doubt gifts of the Mad Gift Giver," Dorian said. "Who can know how the Moteans discovered the use of their skyfall weapons? If I had to guess, I'd surmise that the Black Coterie of gods is behind it."

"That does remain to be seen," Ymbrys said.

"I am not yet convinced. Until then, I'll be keeping them with me."

Hanen opened his mouth to protest, but then thought the better of it.

"Do you have something to say?"

Hanen hesitated and sighed. "What signs have I given you of any sort of corruption?"

"Besides keeping secrets?"

"I would imagine all three of us have secrets, both now and in our past."

"Greed and a desire for power can come to any one of us," Dorian said.

"We have all seen what the gauntlets can do," Hanen said, "both here in Haven, and in Mahn Fulhar. But do I have a legion of enslaved minds at my command?"

Then, Hanen reached into his boot and slapped the gold qavyl gild pound on the table.

"You still have that?" Ymbrys said.

"If I was greedy, do you think I wouldn't have made use of this already, to secure more?"

"We are not saying you are already corrupted," Dorian offered. "It is merely a concern that both of us are wary of."

They settled into awkward silence and sent furtive glances at one another.

"Do you have everything you need to leave the city?" Ymbrys said.

"I would like to go and pack my bag for travel," Hanen said. "If we're headed south, my understanding is the terrain is rough, and hunting will be hard."

"I've prepared rations," Ymbrys said

"And we thank you," Dorian said to the qavyl. "But, no offense, I think Hanen would agree, a little fresh meat is a good idea."

"I won't say no to that either," Ymbrys said, smiling.

Hanen walked up the stairs, Whisper following after him. He locked the door behind him and sat down on the bed. Whisper leaned up against his leg, raising his head to the sky in a demand for scratches. Hanen chuckled and consented.

"I'm not sure what to do, Whisper," he said.

Whisper clattered his tail on the floor.

"Yes, we'll go after Rallia. But after that, honestly, I just want to give the gauntlets to Dorian and walk away."

He had paused in his scratches and Whisper gave him an offended look. Hanen proceeded. "Yes. Maybe we can find where Alodda went, too."

He took a deep breath and rose, folding and placing the

boneshroud deep into his pack, then his spare outfit went over top of that. His bowstrings looked in working order. He took out an oilcloth and wiped it up and down his bow and then across his crossbow. A few of the bolts had not been retrieved over the weeks since he arrived in Haven. He dropped the last five into the bottom of his quiver and pressed it down along the inside of his pack. Then he lifted it onto his back and walked down the stairs.

Ymbrys held his tall staff and wore the thin wooden travel box down the length of his back. Dorian's own pack looked just as meager, but his travel roll looked bulky enough to bear the two gauntlets inside. He wore an older Black Sentinel cloak over his thin frame.

"Let us go and meet with the others," Dorian said and turned for the door without another word. Whisper stayed close to Hanen and Ymbrys followed after.

They arrived at the new inn and the sounds of early drinking and singing gave way to the light and warmth of the fire within. Fifty or so men and women wore not the black cloaks of Sentinels, but red short cloaks that didn't reach the ground. Ymbrys spoke with the leader of their unit, and Hanen quickly turned away, recognizing the woman as Sälla Fife, a Sentinel who'd been a member of the guild in Mahn Fulhar, and disappeared directly after the incident at the Rose Convent.

A few of the others eyed Hanen and his black cloak.

"You still a Sentinel?" one of them asked.

"What else would I be?"

"The lines were drawn. You carry a crossbow. Either you join the Wardens, or you go with those of us leaving under the Red Banner."

"He is under my contract as a bodyguard," Ymbrys said, approaching. "He was granted permission to complete that contract before deciding. Come along, Captain."

Ymbrys turned and bade Hanen follow.

"What was that about?" Hanen asked.

"Not here and now," he replied. "We leave the city with the Red Banner. I've paid their captain to ignore us for leaving when we do."

"Their captain," Hanen replied. "That woman?"

"Yes."

"Then I'm going to stay quiet with hood up."

"Know her?"

Hanen nodded, dropping his hood farther down over his face.

Ymbrys took a corner table and Dorian sat next to him, while Hanen leaned against the wall with Whisper slunk under the table.

As everyone finished their drinks, they began pulling on their packs. Sälla Fife took up a banner and stepped out of the inn onto the street to unfurl it. The banner was merely an unadorned red wool. The others followed after her and fell into a semblance of order.

Ymbrys and his two bodyguards came last, taking up the rear.

"Then the Red Banner truly is back," Dorian muttered with a hint of irritation.

"I do not know who they are," Ymbrys said, "but yes."

"They were a free company of mercenaries," Dorian said. "They formed up before the Protectorate Wars. I thought they disbanded twenty years ago."

"As I understand it," Ymbrys said, "their leader became a Black Sentinel, and brought his Red Banners under the same organization. Now they've disassociated again to re-form his old charter."

"You don't seem to like them," Hanen said.

"They are not much different than a Black Sentinel," Dorian said. "Save that they do not act as individuals, but will follow the coin as companies. I've hired them in the past, but I've also fought against them."

"Not to be trusted?" Ymbrys asked.

"Only until you know who paid their contract," Dorian said. "If they are not against you, they'll not turn on the contract."

The unit of red-cloaked mercenaries began their march to the gate and proceeded past to the road. Sälla had stopped at the gate to speak to a guard, and pointed at Ymbrys as they passed by. Hanen looked up at the worst moment and locked eyes with Sälla. She took up the rear, banner still in hand, and walked up behind Hanen.

"I ought to report who your bodyguard is," she muttered to Ymbrys.

"Oh?" the qavyl replied.

"The Wardens at the citadel have been asking after him. I could make a nice piece of gold right now."

"Yet you'll not?" Ymbrys asked.

"We march for one hour to the lake. At which point, I'll look around and find you've already left. I'll be keeping the gold you paid to feed you for the next three days, as you will have disappeared. Do you understand?"

"Perfectly," Ymbrys said.

Sälla passed them, picked up her pace to march to the front of her company, and left them far behind.

"We do not know if she didn't tell the gate," Dorian said.

"We do not," Ymbrys said.

"It's been far too many years since I have been here to know where and how we'll disappear," Dorian said. "We cannot go east to circle around the lake. We need to head west into the hills, and find our own way down into Varea."

They crested a small rise and the lake stretched out before them. Farms nearby had been burned, and lay smoldering.

"It is no surprise the Chalicians burned crops," Ymbrys said. "It is likely why the Red Banner marches south—to exact revenge."

"They'll be sorely disappointed," Dorian said, "if they hope to find any gold on the Chalicians they come across."

"I forgot about that," Ymbrys said.

"What?" Hanen asked.

"Œron more or less removed coinage from their country. Everything is paid on paper credit."

"How do they trade with other nations?"

"What trade they do, they do with merchant coin," Ymbrys said. "Merchants are given dispensation, but peasants and even the nobility exist entirely off the complex system enforced by the church."

"Limae is not going to react well," Hanen said.

"I think they'll react exactly as the Praetors wish," Dorian said. "Limae will be forced to either submit to the church, or do what they've long considered doing, but haven't acted upon."

"And that is?"

"Declare war on Castenard and the nearby City States of Sidierata."

"Edi nobility are always talking about that fear."

"Does Edi fear Limae?" Ymbrys asked.

"No," Hanen said. "They fear loss of the status quo in trade. If Sidierata unites against Limae, Edi will be left out, since Edi and Sidierata are always at odds."

"Combine that with the war between Hraldor and Temblin," Dorian said, "and Edi is going to be pinched between two conflicts. I almost regret not traveling along the southern states with my entourage instead of via the north."

"Perhaps the pantheon had their hand in that decision," Ymbrys said.

"I would hope so," Dorian said. "I cannot help feeling it was the wrong Pantheon leading me by the nose, though."

They came upon a small forest that grew up the hills.

"Good a time as any," Dorian said, turning off the road.

All three of them ducked into the woods quickly before a single Red Bannerman could turn and see them go.

"Shall we go uphill and see what we can see?" Hanen asked.

"Let us wait for a while," Dorian said. "Until the Red Banner is well out of sight."

"It is my understanding," Ymbrys said, "that there is a road far above us along the tops of the hill. Gossip-mongers in the city called it the Bone Road."

"Bone Road?" Dorian said.

"The various paths, trails, and roads in Limae follow simple naming structures. Just to the south of the lake, the southern road that sits below the hills is the Griffin Road. It's a dangerous road that is victimized by griffins from above. The Bone Road is used more for those assigned by the city to move unseen and is higher still. Not a few youths run it as a challenge for dares, risking threats of sky-born griffin attacks."

"That's what we seek to travel along?" Hanen asked.

"Until we can find a way down into Varea."

"I think we ought not endanger ourselves."

"I will be in no danger," Ymbrys said. "And Dorian is no doubt blessed by his god."

"Then what of me?" Hanen said.

"You've a Black Ynfald," Ymbrys smiled.

"You really believe them so lucky?" Dorian asked.

"Not at all," Ymbrys said, with a broader grin, "but with both you and I on the Bone Road, Hanen has little to worry about."

"You're confident," Dorian said.

"I am a sharp-eyed qavyl. I have no worry of a griffin catching us unawares."

The sun sped past its apex and the Red Banner could be seen fluttering several miles south, when Ymbrys finally turned and said, "Up we go."

"Hopefully this will be no harder than the way up the mountains from the Dead Pass," Hanen said.

"Do not remind me, young man," Dorian said.

Whisper shot up the hill, and began running this way and that, sniffing at bushes and holes.

"Why couldn't the gods have given the thinking peoples the energy of an ynfald?" Dorian huffed.

"The young do," Ymbrys said. "And most outlive the energetic creatures."

"I've never paid much attention," Hanen said, "but how long do ynfalds normally live?"

"I've not made it a study of mine," Ymbrys said.

"My father had an old ynfald that lived to be twenty-five," Dorian said. "My own whelp was given to me when I was only three; he sustained an injury on the farm when I was fifteen and went downhill quickly."

"I seem to recall something of that nature," Ymbrys said. "Unhindered, they live long. Perhaps not so long as a sleipnir, but long enough."

"I've no idea how old Whisper is," Hanen said.

"He's no whelp," Dorian said, "but he doesn't act like an ynfald grown fully into adulthood. Perhaps three or four years?"

Hanen smiled, satisfied that he had more years with him.

Dorian was watching him, and smiled to himself, as though realizing something. Ymbrys had stopped up ahead, waiting for them to catch up. Hanen helped Dorian scramble up the last rise to where Ymbrys stood—on a footpath heading south at an easy rise.

"This is the Bone Road?" Dorian asked.

"I don't think so," Ymbrys said. "Perhaps it is a path leading up to it. We can stop climbing and just stroll to the top now."

"I'd appreciate that."

They continued down that path, trees rising along both sides. They walked at an easy pace for hours until the sun began to cast a twilight between the trees. Whisper trotted ahead of them, then suddenly stopped, his tail flopped down on the road in a single obvious clatter of warning.

"Stop," Hanen hissed.

Ymbrys and Dorian did.

A figure walked along in the opposite direction, wearing only rags, looking tired and weary.

"Revenant," Ymbrys said.

"You can tell from this far away?" Dorian asked.

DREAD KNIGHT

"I can see the imperceptible purple glow of his eyes, yes."

"I know you do not trust me," Hanen said, walking up behind them, "but over the past week, I learned much about the gauntlets, or else I wouldn't have had them on when facing the Revenants."

"What is your point?" Dorian said.

"Give me the gauntlets, and we can stop this Revenant from terrorizing anyone else...perhaps even free him."

"Free him?"

"From his dream."

"That you say 'Dream,'" Ymbrys said, "tells me you know more than you have let on."

Dorian lowered his pack to the ground and took up his bedroll. The Revenant did not appear to have focused on them, but as the gauntlets came into view, it paused and began moving toward them in earnest.

"I shouldn't do this," Dorian said, "but if you've a way to free him, do it." The old man took up the gauntlets, holding them like a venomous drækis before handing them over to Hanen.

He had never donned them without the boneshroud over his head protecting him, and feared that perhaps Dorian and Ymbrys had been right and he could be—if he wasn't already—corrupted.

As he slipped them on, he felt nothing. He stepped forward and held both of the black gauntlets up, and with a twist, opened up a small hole into the Veld. Then, he pressed the gloves through, quickly took out his hands, and reversed the rings. The Revenant rushed at him, closing the distance quickly. His hands emerged, encased now in silver.

Ymbrys and Dorian gasped.

The Revenant charged forward in a shambling sprint. The purple flame blazed in the thing's eyes as it neared to within ten strides. Hanen held both hands up to block the impact. He twisted one wrist and a hole into the Veld was opened. The other gauntlet stopped the Revenant where it stood, and to Dorian and Ymbrys it appeared that Hanen reached into the thing's chest and took hold of his heart. There was a ripping sound and the hole in his chest disappeared, and the man fell to his knees, gasping for breath.

"What just happened?" Dorian asked.

"I don't know exactly," Hanen said. "But from what I've been able to tell, they are asleep. Something from the other side rides their mind—a white wyrm of sorts. The gauntlets, when silver, allow me to reach into the other side and tear that connection away."

Ymbrys crouched down next to the man, and gave him water and food.

"And when they're black?" Dorian asked.

"I saw Slate use them to control the Revenants with one gauntlet, but with two hands, if I strike someone, they disappear entirely. I do not know to where."

Hanen closed the hole and let the gauntlets slip from his hands into Dorian's.

"I want to know more," Dorian said, as he put the gauntlets into his satchel.

"That shall have to wait," Ymrbrys said, pointing up the trail. Ten more Revenants came out of the woods and began lumbering down the trail toward them.

"It appears we will have to leave this trail and go up again," Dorian said.

The man beside them stood on his feet. "Where am I?"

"On a footpath below the Bone Road," Ymbrys said. "Continue down this path, and you should reach Haven soon enough. But do not rest until you are safe. I'd hate for Revenants to once more take you."

The man's eyes filled with terror as he looked up the path and saw the others coming after him.

"No. Not again!" he cried, and fled down the trail without another word.

"Up?" Ymbrys asked.

Dorian nodded, and the four of them pulled themselves up, tree trunk by tree trunk, to safety, and to the danger of the exposed Bone Road.

20

Bone Road

The feather of a griffin has long been sought by hunters and fletchers alike. They are straight, strong, and hold their form for decades. Rot little touches them. Common gryph feathers are fine, but the gravon and griffin will always fetch the greater market price.

—*A TRAPPER'S TREATISE ON TRADE*

It was a fifty-foot scramble to the top. The Revenants had grouped together on the path below and stood staring up at them.

"Why aren't they climbing up after us?" Dorian asked.

"I don't think they can climb," Hanen said. "It's why the barricades in town held them even though those weren't difficult to climb."

"Why not?"

"The wyrms," Hanen said. "Those that control their minds? They are lodged in the ground within the Veld. I wonder at whether the wyrms do not know what to do with themselves when riding the minds of the Revenants."

"Are they truly Revenants, then?" Dorian asked.

"What do you mean?" Ymbrys asked.

"During the Protectorate Wars, the Revenants fought as men fight. They were the dead, turned back from Noccitan, and made to fight on."

"Perhaps," Ymbrys said, "they share much of the same origins, but by different means? That our young colleague here is able to bind them by somehow breaking through to the Veld is only part of that answer."

"Which of course raises another question," Dorian said. "How are these gauntlets able to break through to the Veld?"

"I don't know," Hanen said. "Perhaps it's because they're made of skyfall metal."

"Why do you say that?"

"The Wardens carry skyfall axes," Hanen replied. "When Revenants are struck down, they usually rise again in another person nearby. But killing a person with skyfall seems to end their life and the wyrm within."

"I am disappointed in myself," Dorian said.

"Why is that?" Ymbrys asked.

"I failed to notice that the Warlord's Armor was made of the stuff. Several decades later there was a study that went across my desk requesting funding to study the worthless metal and I denied it. It is never found in great amounts, and unmalleable."

"Or so it seemed at the time," Ymbrys said.

"Yes."

"You need not be too perturbed," Ymbrys said. "The qavylli people have passed it by all of this time as well. Although there have been vast quantities collected over the years, it only collects dust in archives now, unstudied."

Umay rose in the east, and the crescent of Norlock was nearing its setting in the west as they walked along the ridge of the Bone Road all night. Hanen kept his hood back and ears open, listening for anything. Below, Revenants could be heard milling around in the forest. On the other side, in the silvering light, a boulder field tumbled down into the distance. Black creatures bolted across the field, hunting other smaller animals. Whisper stayed close to Hanen's leg, shaking in apparent fear.

"Whisper has a good eye," Ymbrys said, falling into step.

"Oh?"

"The rock gravons are out hunting tonight. I believe they prefer smaller prey, like the rock gnolls that live out there amongst the boulders. Whisper knows he's a target, too."

"I've not seen a rock gravon."

"They're not too large," Ymbrys said, "perhaps twice Whisper's size and black. And they're not known to be too dangerous to travelers who are wary or in groups. They don't have the pointed beaks of the gryphs you see in the city, but shorter beaks, with serrated edges."

Hanen shuddered and put a hand down to Whisper to reassure him.

"Do you think me corruptible?" Hanen said after they had walked another hundred yards.

Dorian walked alone another hundred feet ahead.

"Everything is corruptible," Ymbrys said, "If you give into weaknesses, or rely on your strengths against all odds while not taking the care of others into our considerations, you will be corrupted."

"Then you do suspect it."

"Do you worry?"

"Always. I do not wish to draw attention to myself. I do not want to be any sort of hero."

"Why is that?"

"All heroes fall," Hanen said. "Especially those that seek to be a hero. The gods see to their destruction."

"What do you mean by that? Why do you think the gods would seek to tear down those that might save the world?"

"Why else would each hero fall to his or her own weaknesses?"

"The answer," Ymbrys said, "is in what you just said."

"What do you mean?"

"The liar becomes entwined in his own lies and hangs on his own web. The gloating braggart becomes suspicious of all others who might take from him his glory, and in doing so, foments the same suspicion in others, until the intrigue tears him down. The glory hound seeks ever greater foes until he finally meets his end by one with greater prowess."

"And me?"

"I do not know. That you're not suspicious and furtive is in and of itself a comfort. Let us not forget your family background, too, as that causes me to worry."

Hanen eyed the qavyl as terror rose in him.

"For now, let us take our path forward. Let us retrieve Rallia, and maybe even complete Dorian's mission of capturing and destroying the armor."

Hanen went silent.

"It is perhaps an unspoken temptation that we might try and use the armor for our own means. Does it give into what you fear—the rise of a corrupting power? Who is to say if someone might then recapture and use it for their own means?"

"You read my mind," Hanen joked.

"More so I read my own," Ymbrys said. "But wisdom tells me I ought not to."

The long night continued and eventually, dawn began to light the east. The color of the sticks and branches marking the sides of the road washed out in the twilight. It was apparent as light grew, however, that they were not sticks, but the namesake of the road they walked upon.

"Why so many bones?" Dorian muttered.

"Because of that," Ymbrys said, pointing down the road.

Three rock gravons tore at a carcass. A mountain capricör had made the mistake of following the crest, and the creatures glutted themselves upon the feast. As Ymbrys had described, they were stockier than the scavenging, cawing black gryphs of the city, with powerful legs built for bounding and dull black wings. Their sharp beaks cleaned the carcass quickly.

As they watched, another figure came up onto the road from a side trail. The way she walked, it was apparent she was a Revenant. The gravons quickly noticed her and their hackles raised. The Revenant bore no fear and lurched forward, perhaps smelling the meat and starving. She charged without fear into the mess of them, and the gravons scattered down onto the rocks, then gathered their courage and rushed to take back their kill. They made quick work of the Revenant, bones quickly picked clean. Two of them leapt up into the air to fly away. The third gravon eyed its companions with curiosity, then took an awkward leap before falling back to earth. It looked around for somewhere to skulk to, trying to make sense of its wings. It was then it saw Hanen and the others, three hundred yards away. It began stalking awkwardly forward.

"I don't think that's a gravon anymore," Dorian said.

"Nor I," Ymbrys said. "Hanen, your crossbow."

Hanen nodded and reached into his pack to pull out the bolt quiver. He set a bolt into the crossbow after cranking back on the string.

"Aim well, loose it, then do it again," Dorian instructed calmly. "You might even have time for a third before it reaches us."

The first shot flew wide. He cranked back as the Revenant gravon gained momentum. He dropped to a knee and squeezed. The second bolt struck home in the gravon's shoulder as it closed to within fifty feet. It leapt forward, and Ymbrys suddenly lunged, the butt of his staff taking the gravon under the jaw. The creature looked up at Ymbrys, baleful purple fire in its eye, and clawed at his legs. The qavyl stepped aside, unharmed, his tail flashing side to side as it mesmerized the gravon in distraction.

Dorian tossed the gauntlets to the ground by Hanen's feet and rushed forward, a short sword in his hand. He clipped the gravon's tail and slashed at the creature's wings. It did not roar, but silently screamed its distress.

Hanen dropped his crossbow to the ground, shoved his hands into the gauntlets, and came up in a half crouch as Whisper rushed in, scales rustling, getting up under the creature to nip at its sensitive flesh.

Hanen leapt atop the creature's back, tackling it flat. Whisper rolled away, and Hanen's gauntleted hands took hold of the creature's throat and squeezed.

He fell suddenly to the ground, the gravon nowhere to be seen.

"Where did it go?" Dorian shouted, looking around.

"I don't know. That happens sometimes."

"I saw you do something," Ymbrys said, "when you changed the gauntlets from black to silver. Do it now."

Hanen gave a nod and reached in front of him, twisting his hands and opening a hole in the air before him, a window into the purple Veld. Dorian and Ymbrys moved next to him and looked over his shoulder. The gravon was there, wrestling with a long ropey white thing tangled and struggling around it. The gravon seemed more in control of its faculties, and made quick work of the constricting white wyrm, tearing it to shreds. It tried flying, but the injuries the three of them had made on its body prevented it from taking flight. Finally, it fled away into the distance, without the use of its wings.

"I suppose that answers that question then," Ymbrys said.

"What question?" Hanen asked as he closed the window into the Veld.

"Where those you touch go when you dismiss them. They are not destroyed, but banished to the Veld."

"Only to die," Dorian said.

"It takes grievous wounds to truly kill anything in the Veld," Ymbrys said.

"You seem to know much of it."

"There are schools of study in Hannica," Ymbrys said off-handedly.

"Not among humans," Dorian said. "Perhaps our fear of it is too great."

"Fear of it only makes that fear more powerful."

The sun had come up over the horizon, and the sky was clear. While Dorian and Hanen walked with renewed paranoia, Ymbrys and Whisper no longer seemed to have any fear and strolled alongside one another casually. They made good time across the heights. They could see over the trees leading down to the Limae basin and the roads that crisscrossed the valleys. Smoke from various villages spoke of the Chalician raiders. To the west, the boulder field led far out and away to what appeared to be a drop. Far beyond that, diffused by distance, the Varean countryside spread out to the vast Lake Varea and beyond.

21

Fairness in Darkness

The Deceiver powerless? Hardly. His ancient tongue brings kings to ruin. His webs spin round and round in circles none can fathom. Do not speak to me if you think he has no power. But he has no love. That, he cannot know.

—FROM *KING WISDOM*, APOCRYPHAL PLAY

BY ELLAVON GAVALIN

As the sun began its descent toward the far western horizon the Bone Road began to descend toward a dark forest. Dorian appeared to grow more furtive, eyeing the deep shadows.

"I've little worry of Revenants this far south," Ymbrys said.

"They made their way up to the Bone Road—why not here?"

"It just seems too far south for them to wander. I'm worried about the nocturnal stalking of panticörs."

"Not something I'm familiar with," Hanen said.

"Black manticörs the size of your ynfald," Dorian said. "Forest dwellers. If we sleep close to one another, we'll be alright."

"Or we visit that fire over there," Hanen said, pointing off the path to a campfire over a hundred yards away.

"Do the people of the forest have many clans up here?" Dorian asked.

"Not that I'm aware of," Ymbrys said. "But it never hurts to be considerate."

"My mother was Üterk," Hanen said. "I'll lead."

He walked forward, leaving the two of them behind, Whisper at his heels. The fire had only two figures sitting at it, their backs to him.

"By the dimming light of day, may we share the safety of your fire? We've gold and rations we can share," Hanen said while still twenty yards away.

One of them turned to consider him. "A man and black ynfald. Not a bad bit of luck that."

The second figure started and nudged the first. "And two others. An old man and a traveling qavyl."

"By all means, come. We accept your offer of gold and rations to share our fire and company."

Hanen motioned for Ymbrys and Dorian to follow and proceeded ahead to the light, circled the fire, and froze as he looked across upon two faces he knew well.

Nair and Kash, the traveling storytellers, considered Hanen, with glares that told him they recognized him too.

"Have a seat," Nair said, and Hanen did as he was told.

"Who might you be traveling with now?" Kash asked.

Everything in him told him to flee, to pull on the boneshroud buried deep in his pack. The last time they had seen one another, Kash had all but revealed his true nature to Hanen: the Mad Gift Giver himself, Kos-Yran. Hanen struggled to reach into his side satchel to produce gold coin and a bundle of the rations Ymbrys had made. He tossed them to Nair, who greedily accepted them.

"An interesting situation we find ourselves in," Kash said.

"A paid-for fire," Nair said, nudging his brother.

Dorian came into the light next, and gave the two storytellers a look that flickered with some suspicion, but then settled as he eyed the pot of stew on the fire.

"Gold and rations was the agreed upon deal," Nair said to the old man. Dorian did not hesitate, but reached into his own pack and produced a payment, then sat.

Ymbrys came into the light, then suddenly stopped in his tracks. For the first time, Hanen could see a look of fear in his eyes. He gripped his staff tightly, and seemed to mouth words to himself.

"An interesting companion you have, Sentinel," Kash said, a coldness coming into his voice.

"Gold and rations, I believe I heard," Ymbrys said, ignoring the storyteller's comment.

"We'll not say no to a gift," Kash said.

"A weakness of yours, no doubt," Ymbrys said, matching his air. He took out a small satchel of coin and a few rations, and tossed them to Nair before taking a seat.

Nair stirred the pot, seemingly unaware of the silence around him.

"I feel as though you're all acquainted," Dorian said, "and I am at a loss."

"We first met the young Sentinel here almost a year ago. His caravan escorted us for a time, and we shared a fire every night," Nair said.

"I most recently spoke with him not a few weeks ago in Haven," Kash added, "where we shared a playful riddle and story game."

Ymbrys shot Hanen a furtive look, then turned back to the brothers.

"He got the best of me," Kash said. "A rather unique situation. I gave him a gift."

"What gift did you give our young friend?" Nair asked, genuine surprise coming upon him.

"Nothing more than I am allowed."

Hanen's skin crawled as he thought of what Kash had "gifted" him: The right to choose to follow the Deceiver when he called, or to die.

"Gifts with no stated strings attached to them are always a risky business," Nair said. He stirred the stew a few times. "That reminds me of an old story."

"Storytellers then?" Dorian asked.

Nair nodded.

"I would love to hear one," Dorian said.

"But only," Ymbrys said, "if it comes with the fire we have paid for."

"The sharing of fire implies companionship and a meal," Kash said.

"So long as that is so agreed," Ymbrys said.

Nair produced bowls and filled them with stew from the pot, and doled them out. Dorian took his and lifted it to the sky.

"Grissone, our god," Dorian began praying, unprompted. The storytellers did not close their eyes, but glowered at Dorian and Ymbrys. "Twin-souled Anka, ever watchful, bless these bowls. Let us sleep easily upon it, after this companionship is well-shared. Amen."

He opened his eyes, smiled, and took a bite. Through his mouthfuls he motioned to Nair. "You've a story to tell, why not begin?"

"Very well," Nair said with a dark grin.

The Thirteen-Limbed One, it was decided by the fathers of the pantheon, should be dealt with, though they knew not in what way. Already he had brought Kos-Yran into his council, and Kea'Rinoul may or may not have been scarred, none are sure. The council of Wisdom bade Aben and Wyv stay their hand and consider for a time Achanerüt's actions, as they might, for wisdom's sake, come to some good.

But it was the firstborn of Wyv and Sakharn whose spirit would not be settled to wait. Rionne was, after all, Arbiter and Hand of Justice. When he made a decision, all conceded that it was good and just. He drew his blade, the Judgment Key, and thrust it through his black-metal throne, seated at the top of his Great-City-Which-Now-Lies-Sundered, and at the mighty sound, his four cousins, children of Aben and Crysania, came to sit in council with him.

Rionne's helm sat upon the pommel of the driven sword, and he sat perturbed, chin on fist.

"Why drive your sword into throne unmoving?" Lae'zeq, god of Wisdom, said.

"Why are you perturbed and in such consternation?" Nifara, goddess of Justice, asked.

"Why do you not move but sit in silence?" Grissone, god of Faith, asked.

"What troubles you that you should remove your Crown of Justice?" Kasneterral, the Prince of the Forest asked.

"I am bothered by the events of these many years, in which the Deceiver runs rampant, turning brother against brother, and god against people."

"You speak as though you have a decision made within your brow," Lae'zeq said. "Speak, my closest of friends. For we would know your mind that speaks naught but truth."

"He came from we know not whence," Rionne spake.

"Does he not come from the Veld?" Grissone asked.

"Does he not come from the imagination of his mother?" Nifara asked.

"Was he not birthed by a seed of doubt planted in his mother's mind?" Kasneterral asked.

"Does he not call himself Deceiver?" Lae'zeq asked.

"Yes!" boomed Rionne. "All of these may be true, yet in paradox with one another. What then can we believe?"

"Our fathers have decided that we should do nothing, but first allow time—allowing Deceiver's deceits to entangle him thusly," Lae'zeq said.

"To what destruction? To what end?"

"Let divine justice come," Grissone said. "Let us have faith in our fathers' decision."

Rionne slammed his fist down on his throne, resounding through the entirety of his city. "I cannot wait. Too many now hath died."

He took up his helm and placed it on his head and light poured from his eyes.

> **"Listen well the Judgment meted,**
> **I thusly draw from throne enseated.**
> **Shall it be returned to sheath,**
> **When on the throne sits victory bequeathed."**

He drew then from that throne the blade, flashing white, in preparation for what would then occur.

"Send message that Justice comes," Rionne commanded to his host of winged wrath. "Let Deceiver know that he shall meet his fate upon the Field of Creation. There shall he face the Key of Judgment, and in that moment shall fate be sealed."

And thus began that slow and inevitable march. He could have spoken word and appeared, but instead he marched. For a year and a day he marched. In that time peoples and nations rose to march alongside him, much as they once did to that place, to worship as one tongue. Now they marched to watch the banner of fate unfurl.

Came he then to that place that now lies in wrackéd desolation, far beyond memory and logic. There he stood awaiting his foe. From other direction came the Thirteen-Limbed One. Beside him walked nary but his brother Kos-Yran and mother Sakharn, and in his hand he held a newly forged weapon—a double-headed axe, with zvolder upon its faces, and a long stave of knit web.

"Deceiver!" Rionne called. "I have summoned you to meet your fate."

"My fate was decided by Aben and Wyv, that nothing should befall me until a decision is made," Achanerüt called.

"And thus has a decision been made," Rionne said. "For when I speak, all listen. I have spoken. You shall meet my Judgment Key and let blade decide. For you have wrought great injustices."

"Little do you know," Achanerüt said, "for a greater Destruction comes. It falls in my wake, even as I fell in sundering crash upon the face of Kallattai. I call you my Prophet, and name you god of Destruction."

Rionne scoffed, and took from black sheath the massive white sword, the Judgment Key, and leveled it at Deceiver.

In that moment Aben, Wyv, and Crysania appeared.

"My son and firstborn," Wyv said, "what is this that you do?"

"I fulfill my role as you have done. You Judge on Throne of Noccitan, yet I am Judge of Kallattai."

"And what have you adjudicated?"

"That by admittance of his name, Deceiver must be sundered until he yields."

"No god can be destroyed," Aben spoke.

"Yet can be maimed to the point of death, made powerless and made less than we."

"A great cost will be paid if you do this," Crysania said. "The Future Tapestry has been unfurled."

"A greater debt accrues if we do not." Rionne said, then turned to his mother, who stood with silvered thread bound round her wrists, led to Deceiver's web. "What say you mother?"

"Would you strike down your brother?" said Crysania.

"I would bring him to justice."

"So be it," Achanerüt said with toothy smile across his face.

Rionne marched as he had for the year, and his sword came down clanging across Deceiver's axe. On closer inspection it was obviously built by the hand of Kos-Yran, just as his own Judgment Key had been. Thus came down that Key as hammer on anvil, but neither weapon yielded, neither tired, and neither gave quarter. Oldest fought youngest, and many despaired that this conflict might last until the final days of Kallattai, when clamor arose as Judgment Key gave way, broken in twain. Rionne, Arbiter, did not falter and stepped in to deliver the final blow with severed end. Achanerüt fell upon his back, when voice called out.

"Stand by and wait!" Wisdom spoke. Lae'zeq, god of Qavylli said these words. "Give pause, that in your victory, you have chosen the best of courses."

"Listen to your friend and cousin," Achanerüt said. "For I am defeated, and his words may yet give succor to us both."

"You shall submit to my decision," spake Rionne, "having been defeated."

"There is no deceit in my voice when I say that I shall," Achanerüt said. "Even if you should raise my own axe and with it sever my head from body."

Rionne stood and came to consult with his cousin. He opened his ears to hear what Wisdom would say, for they had long been the closest of companions. Lae'zeq placed hand on Rionne's shoulder. "My boon companion. Listen well. We know not his purpose upon this world, thus our fathers have determined. Should you take this terrible burden, and sunder deity, all shall give nod that you have done so for the betterment of all. Should not we wait? Should not we seek the Will of the Existence who made the All?"

"Are not we given his divine breath?" Rionne said. "Are not we all infused with his will, to give out as we will to others? To mete out his justice?"

"That does not mean that we ought not consider, rather than act blindly."

"I am not blinded by justice," Rionne said. "But I shall not see the world blinded by injustice."

"Then so be it," Lae'zeq said, and touched his forehead to his. "Know that I am with you in this and shall bend Wisdom to your Justice."

Rionne turned, and returned to Achanerüt's side. "I bring about your sundering."

Achenerüt nodded, and eyed the axe that lay close by. Rionne, it is thought, saw the sweet justice it would be, to strike Deceiver down, not with the Judgment Key, but with Deceiver's own axe. Thus he reached for webbéd shaft, and Lae'Zeq felt a pang of doubt enter his mind, and he opened his mouth to speak, but could not, for he had submitted Wisdom to destructive Justice.

As hand touched threads of deceitful webs, they lashed upon Rionne's divine flesh, flaying free divinity, and stripping glory to relic'd bone. Hand thus entwined, the axe took hold of his whole, and wracked Arbiter in a pain unfelt. Turned he then, and unfurled not white but blackened wings of smoldering ash. He turned without a glance to Wisdom, nor to his father, and rose into the sky, corrupted beyond all reason and measure. Not even Nifara could follow as he shot north to his own city, to sunder it himself. Judgment Key was thrust back into throne, and Rionne slayed many a great creature, and in their blood forged an armor that is said shall not be laid to waste until the ending of the world.

Thus began the Wars of Worlds. Rionne himself, no longer Arbiter, but god of Destruction, fell to Deceit, and Wisdom fell to Justice, and that war did not end until the day the True Destruction rained upon the face of the worlds.

As he finished, Hanen noticed that the bowl of stew before Ymbrys sat untouched. Dorian's was empty.

"What is the moral you bring with this story?" Dorian asked.

"Must a story have one?"

"I've not heard this tale told in which Lae'Zeq took such pains," Dorian said.

"Nor would he have it told," the storyteller said. "It reveals him to be as much at fault as Rionne."

"Rionne did nothing wrong," Dorian said. "He was deceived and made a mistake."

"He chose vengeance over justice," the Storyteller said.

"And Wisdom did not," Ymbrys said.

"Did not they both go against their fathers' wishes, and chose instead their own Justice?" the Storyteller asked.

"What right have we to decide whether the gods were right or wrong?" Dorian asked.

"Therein lies the moral," Nair said.

"I fail to see it," Dorian said.

"Perhaps they ought to have merely let fate play out, in the divine chorus of the worlds. For just as mortals cannot fathom the purpose of the divine, neither can the divine fathom the purpose of still greater a purpose?"

Dorian did not reply.

"There comes a time in each path," Kash spoke up, "when a will greater than our will calls for us to act. We always have the choice to submit, or in failing to do so, perish. Is not he who submits even to the Fallen, still doing what is a greater thing?"

"That they are known as Fallen, compromises their rightness," Ymbrys said. "Better to perish and suffer the consequences, than to do evil in the sight of creation."

"Rionne perished that day, even if he continued as pawn," Nair said. "And ever shall his torment be for the mistake he made. Ever shall the Deceiver's glory rise, for having been spared."

"Wisdom stays true to his promise that day," Ymbrys said, "and Wisdom shall forever seek to tug and pull and unravel the webs of Deceit."

"Lae'zeq will fall at the Gates of Noccitan," Nair said.

"Only the Judgment Key can sunder him, and in that sundering, the qavylli prophecy says, shall Wisdom and Justice be reborn as Mercy."

The storytellers merely shrugged together and stood.

"What a pleasant opportunity this has been," Nair said with a toothy smile. "A pleasure to share a meal and story with so important a collection of people. But we've places to be."

"The sun only just set," Dorian said. "Would you travel at night?"

"If they would go, who are we to prevent them?" Ymbrys said.

Nair gave the qavyl a nod, and with his brother beside him, walked into the night.

"That was one of the oddest interactions I've had in a long time," Dorian said.

"Amazing we didn't all end up enthralled—slaves to their wills," Hanen finally spoke.

Ymbrys gave Hanen a look. "You know?" Ymbrys asked.

Hanen nodded.

"I'm missing something, aren't I?" Dorian asked.

"Those two storytellers," Hanen said, "I believe they're the Wandering gods."

"No," Dorian said, and looked at Ymbrys, who nodded. "Truly?"

Ymbrys nodded again.

"I don't know what to say."

"Take solace in the fact that you still live with your will intact," Ymbrys said, but he did not look at Dorian. He stared at Hanen, his fingers tightly gripping his staff.

22

Eccentricities

Humility is better shown than taught.

—PROVERB OF THE LUZORAN HERMITS

Seriah had been set into the back of the cart, huddled up against the large box atop it. They had pressed all night down a long sloping road. Other captives tried to complain, but were quickly silenced by the Chalician soldiers. After day broke, the ground leveled out, and Seriah was made to walk alongside everyone else. They were given a short respite to eat and an hour's repose before they continued their slow and trundling march south.

She was not unused to walking, and accepted water when offered, but did not need the water the other Limaean captives did. As each day began to wind down, the griping began. Men and women complained of their legs, and their demands to know where they were going became an incessant request. The Chalicians paid them no attention.

Dusk cooled to a late spring evening as they were guided off the road and into trees. Fires were lit and the captives were given the opportunity to warm themselves. Seriah sat in silence and listened. The Chalicians ran the camp with military rigidity. Gruel was served, and as the captives finished, several of the louder ones were made to clean the bowls. That didn't prevent them from making their irritation known.

A sleipnir rode into camp, and she was near enough to hear the rider dismount.

"Provost Abrau," one of the Chalician escorts said with a salutary air.

"Praetor Cuyer," the man responded. Seriah recognized his voice. He had not ever addressed her directly, but he had appeared before the Haven Council as the general of the Chalician army, sent to bring the city to heel.

"We've only some gruel left," Cuyer said.

"I've already eaten. Save it for the prisoners," Abrau said. In Haven he'd spoken with terse authority. Now he had a soft voice of care for his soldiers.

"Provost, what news from the front?"

"We hold the western wall of the city hostage, long enough for campaigning to proceed. Although a few units have been allowed to leave the city, I've left several Chamberlains to continue with the siege."

"Why, may I ask, do you come all the way down the pass for us?"

"Word was you found something. I wish to see it and run an inspection at dawn. That will determine whether I'm needed here for the time being."

"Very well, this way."

Both Praetors marched away.

"Water, Holy Nefer?" A familiar voice asked.

"Rallia," Seriah said. "I wondered if they had separated you to go elsewhere."

"No, I've been kept under a watchful eye," Rallia said, offering her a ladle of water. "The same could be said of you."

"Oh?"

"They had two soldiers assigned to watch you all of last night and the march today."

"Am I a threat?" Seriah asked. "I'm blind."

"I think they worry you'll cause sedition. The Church of the Common Chalice does not like Nifarans. If it makes you feel better, they've had four watching me."

"Because you're a Sentinel?"

"Probably. The rest are all Haven townsfolk."

"Have you been able to learn anything?"

"No. But very likely they'll take us somewhere near Aunté the capital of Œron. I overheard one other captive dealing in rumors. They like to take new 'converts' to their faith as deep into their country as possible, to better indoctrinate."

"That doesn't sound good," Seriah said, "but you don't sound discouraged."

"I'm expecting my brother will come after us. Especially given the contents of the wagon."

"What do you mean?"

"That wagon you sat in as we descended to Varea contains something companions of mine have been seeking."

"What is it?"

"A suit of armor made entirely of skyfall metal."

Seriah took a panicked breath.

"Are there any Paladins with us?" Seriah asked.

"The Praetors are the closest thing," Rallia said.

"Good," Seriah said.

"Why?"

"The Paladins of Haven want any skyfall they can get their hands on in order to turn it for their own uses."

"What do you mean?"

"Hey! Sentinel!" a Praetor shouted. "Move along. Water for everyone."

Rallia stood and muttered, "Keep your head cool, and be patient."

The next day they were up before dawn and walking behind the cart again.

They stopped only for water breaks, and even then, it was only enough water to keep them moving. The Praetors rode along the side of the caravan without a word. The following day, the Praetors began reciting scriptures at the captives. The verses spoke of submission to the authority of the church, and of living a basic and common life. Another song sung of earning the opportunity for either freedom or propping up future generations. As prisoners began to grumble, rather than demand they cease the Praetors instead pulled closer and loudly recited scripture, drowning out their captives' complaints.

That evening, Seriah sat at a fire and two prisoners tried to speak with her, to ask for her adjudication over a matter. Several guards came and escorted them away, leaving her alone. Another person came and sat across from her, his wooden spoon clacking on his bowl as he ate. After a long time, the bowl clattered as he set it down.

"This is not the same circumstance as our last meeting when I first presented my plan to the council in Haven," Provost Abrau said.

"And yet, we've spoken to each other as little as then," Seriah said, unsurprised.

"I've been considering you these last two days, and why you allow us to move you south without complaint."

"My goddess has a purpose for me," Seriah said. "Even if I know you do not believe me."

Abrau chuckled. "You might find me a more amicable Praetor than most."

"In what way?"

"I lean more toward a tolerant path than my fellows," Abrau said. "Indeed, if I did not command battles as well as I do, I would never have been allowed my rank—normally reserved for the more pious."

"Why admit this to me?" Seriah asked.

"Because I want you to know that while you will soon be living in Œron, if you comply, you may be allowed to live within the will of your goddess."

"Yet your church would have us all believe that ours are heresies."

"You and I both know that the pantheon exists," Abrau said. "If they choose to call some, it is nearsighted for us to ignore that."

"You ought to be wary," Seriah said.

"Oh?"

"You're sounding a bit heretical yourself."

Abrau laughed. "I follow the tenets of our faith. That is not in question. Although there are those that might wish me to misspeak in a council of our peers in order to entrap me."

"What is it you want of me?" Seriah asked.

"To know that you will not seek to flee."

"I have a blind upon my face. How would I do that?"

"Very well. Then continue as you do, and follow the path we set. I shall leave a word for your good care when I part company. Perhaps they'll even respect my seal and deliver you to the protection of my own household."

"Again, why?"

"Because I noted how little you addressed in the council in Haven before the siege. I got the impression that you were not there of your own volition. I'd like to use you as an example. By treating you well, perhaps you'll become an apologist for me against the heretics in Haven."

"Then you do believe them heretics? Even if you sound a bit like one yourself."

"One can disagree with some of the lesser tenets and not be heretical," Abrau said.

She did not reply.

"I've one more question for you, as you spent so much time with that Paladin, Pellian Noss. Why do they wear bells?"

"A question better left for them."

"You see, when we captured the cart you've been riding in, we also took hold of something else."

There was a muffled ringing as he worked with something in his lap. Seriah knew what he uncovered as the droning peal began to resound. Her hands went to her ears. Abrau had found the bell that had stood in her room at the inn, drowning out the dark gods as they visited.

"Silence it!" she shouted over the din.

He did. As the peal dulled, she could hear others around the camp were shouting in dismay.

"Interesting and discomforting," Abrau said. "What is it?"

"A bell," Seriah said, regaining her composure.

"Similar to the ones that Noss and his people wear."

Seriah nodded timidly. "That is not a thing to be taken lightly."

"No. It does not seem so," Abrau said, standing. "Let us find another time to speak more on this. I've more to do this evening."

The next day's march proved uneventful, although Rallia once more came round with water, and confirmed she was in good spirits.

On the fifth day from Haven, a group of new Chalicians arrived from the west, stopping the caravan for several hours. There were raised voices near the cart, and the air of the caravan changed to a disgruntled silence until they stopped for the evening. Rallia found her way to sit with Seriah.

"What happened earlier?" Seriah asked.

"New Praetors. This one came from the northwest, looking for someone I know."

"Who?"

"You might remember her: Ophedia, she traveled with us to Mahn Fulhar."

"Searn's daughter," Seriah muttered.

"Yes. Her."

"What about her?"

"This new Praetor, he captured her when she was acting as a distraction for us. Apparently he's been tracking her for a while, and finally made it this far. The Provost knows this new Praetor and they do not appear to get along."

"What do you mean?"

"They almost went immediately to blows. This new Praetor, the Curate Yanas Brodier, arrived with five others, and he's a disciple of the Provost sent to Mahn Fulhar, and just as zealous. He immediately assumed that Provost Abrau had left his post in Limae to escort prisoners and a cart. Abrau did not appreciate Brodier's assumption. I was able to make out that Abrau only travels with us another day or two before he intends to cut up another more southern pass to a small force stationed there, to invade the middle of Limae. Brodier didn't bother waiting and asked to either join him or take his place as commander."

"He only just arrived," Seriah said. "Why would he immediately seek to insert himself?"

"Have you ever met someone desperately ambitious?"

"On occasion," Seriah said. "I've adjudicated for them a time or two."

"I think Brodier would do anything to get ahead. Especially if he can be seen successful in the eyes of his mentor."

"The one to the far north in Mahndür?"

"Yes."

"Abrau spoke with me two nights ago," Seriah said. "He may not be so zealous as he appears."

"In the end, that may prove to our advantage," Rallia said. "That they are at odds means we may be able to find the opportunity to escape."

"Hold him!" the voice of Provost Abrau shouted, waking Seriah from her sleep.

"Unhand me!" shouted a self-important voice. "You bear something of obvious heresy and must answer for it!"

"Call off your men, Brodier," Abrau commanded.

"Why should I? You stand endangering your mortal soul."

"Because I willfully bear an enemy object, to be taken back and vaulted for study by the Praetor Librarians?"

"That cart holds within it armor of the black metal used by Limaean heretics."

"You know much for one who has only just arrived," Abrau said.

"You seem to know very little for one who begged for the opportunity to bring the heathens to heel."

"I did not beg," Abrau said.

"You did."

"I spoke with the High Missioner, and it was granted to me. If only to keep your own master's obviously ulterior motives reined in."

"How dare you!"

"I give you two choices," Abrau said. "You may take your men and march back to your assignment in Mahndür, under the new command of Prefect Œnfroi Vechard, who will be there to ensure the mission given is completed. Or, you may continue with me, and see to it that my mission is completed—peacefully escorting these prisoners to Oiquimon, where they can begin their lives as freed members of the Church of the Common Chalice."

"And the black metal armor?"

"Why do you care so much for it?" Abrau asked. "What do you and your master know that I do not?"

"Perhaps if you did not spend so much energy desiring the whole-hearted conversion of Limae, you would know more of the heresies that shall take more time to weed out than you know."

"Often enough, I am the one labeled an eccentric," Abrau muttered. "But I know this: our tenets state our primary purpose, and that is the guidance of the lost, not through force and subjugation. Your ambition—the ambition of your master, the Enquêteur—reveals a much more dangerous future than mine. I'll have no party with it. Make your decision now, Curate. Or I shall make it for you."

The camp around them had grown eerily silent.

"I shall continue south with you," Brodier said through gritted teeth.

"Good," Abrau said, satisfied.

23

The Looming Peal

By Claw and Tooth.

—VÜL BATTLE CRY

The sun peaked over the horizon, driving any chance at getting even a moment's sleep from Jined. He sat up with a groan and looked toward the barn that had been given to house the Praetors. It sat in silence.

Didus stood on the porch, a mug of fresh milk in his hand, and leaned against a wooden post, watching the city and the army beyond. Jined walked up the steps to stand next to him.

"Any change?" Jined asked.

"In the vül? No. Can't say the same for the Praetors though."

"What do you mean? I didn't notice anything."

"You couldn't have, you were snoring so loudly."

"I haven't slept a wink," Jined grumbled.

"You were snoring." He took a sip. "And the Praetors left."

"They what?"

Didus pointed down toward the sea. "They're halfway to the shore, probably hope to arrange for their ship to take them away."

"We're just going to let them go?"

"Nichal was informed. We're confident that they won't get their ship. They may turn west, but then they'll face the stubbornness of

Dane and Boroni beyond."

"And if they roll south," Jined offered, "the vül will chase them down."

"As Nichal said, they must decide if they will stand by Garrou and earn their trust, or abandon them. If the latter, it'll be generations before they can hope to convert a single Bortalian to their religion."

"What do you think of them?" Jined asked.

"The Praetors?"

Jined nodded.

"I've not interacted with them often in my career," Didus said. "But I saw much of the same in the Temblin-Hraldor conflict."

"When you were a boy?"

"And since. I do not doubt if I had not been taken in by the Hammer, I'd be a solider in that prolonged conflict."

"Why does that bring the Chalicians to mind?"

"Zealotry."

"A conflict of beliefs there?"

"Hardly religious," Didus said. "In my opinion, true zealotry is never religious."

"What do you mean?" Jined asked.

"When taken in context, there is rarely a piece of scripture that calls for violence for the sake of hatred. Justice, perhaps, but never blind hatred. And yet, every zealot I've ever known does so out of hatred for all things in conflict with the bearer's belief."

"As Dane does."

"Perhaps. But in what little interaction I've had with Dane there seems to be more of a self-loathing at play."

"Which may also be the same in the zealots you mentioned before," Jined said. "Why do the Tambii hate Hraldor so much?"

"They would say it is because the Tambii are a superior people. That Hraldor has abandoned its roots, even though most Hraldoorish are not from there, but veterans of the Protectorate Wars seeking a peaceful way of life."

"Then again," Jined said, "perhaps it is jealousy."

Didus nodded.

"Have the twins returned?" Jined asked.

"They should be on their way back," Didus said. "Nichal asked them to return after dawn. Silas is still off to the south, taking message to nearby cities for help for Garrou."

"And Nichal?"

"Praying."

Jined nodded. "I'll go and see if there is anything the farmer and family need."

Hourly the city, far off in the distance, peeled the bells, and with each peel the vül army, another mile past the city, stirred. At midday, the twins arrived back, and to the north, Jined could see the Praetors turning back from a side pier.

Nichal had taken a chair on the shaded porch, considering the twins as they rode back up the hill to the farm.

Grissone be with you, Nichal signed, and they both replied back the same.

Didus came out of the house, a pair of mugs in his hands, and handed them down to Loïc and Cävian as they dismounted and gave their reins to a pair of farm boys who had become indispensable.

Loïc began to sign, when Nichal motioned for him to stop.

"Please, drink up, rest, come in out of the sun, and then you can tell us."

They both nodded their thanks and drank deeply. Jined brought a bucket of well water and clean cloths. The twins slumped into two chairs and leaned back, taking wet cloths from Jined and wiping their brows and necks.

"What news?" Nichal finally said, no longer able to wait.

Loïc smiled. *It's quite an army.*

"How many? Who are they led by? What is Garrou doing in reaction?"

We've counted two thousand vül and more arriving all the time.

"In a slow trickle?"

More like the stragglers of raiding parties from the east, Cävian signed. *I'd wager everything from here into the northern Ikhalan hinterland is scraped bare of life.*

"Dorian long suspected word of a vül horde from the north, but the Ikhalans never reported anything of the sort. It has been a long time since the last one."

"The Protectorate Wars did well to cull their numbers for a generation or two," Didus added.

Nichal nodded.

The vül are more or less grouped into three armies, possibly by greater tribe, Cävian continued.

"Do they have a champion?" Nichal asked.

We think there is one, Loïc replied.
That we could see, Cävian added.
"Who is it?"
It's not the Dry-Walker, Loïc said.
Nichal sighed in relief.
The champion stands apart from the others, and no one dares approach him, Cävian said.
"Not one I've heard of yet," Nichal said.
"Perhaps he arose to replace Gold Eater," Jined said.
"It could be. Perhaps they spent the winter preparing for this rebuttal."
Garrou is changing for fresh guards on the hour, Loïc signed. *I think they're training new guards.*
"And their energy?"
Frightened, Cävian replied.
Nichal sat back as he stared off to the east.
What of the surrounding countryside? Jined signed.
The farms have been deserted, Loïc replied.
There are a few patrols scouting around, Cävian added, *but that is all they are doing. The vül have not yet begun to do the same. They're growing restless, though.*
Nichal stood from his seat and walked off the porch.
The others grew silent and watched him stare at the city. After a long while, he turned to consider them.
"I'll not continue from Garrou until I am defeated, or until Garrou asks us to leave. Even if I must stand alone to do so."
Jined nodded and walked down the steps and put out a hand. "We're your entourage," Jined said. "I'll not leave your side."
Nor we, Cävian said, *taking up the standard and coming to stand with Nichal, Loïc just behind.*
Didus grinned broadly. "I was a dead man in Mahn Fulhar. Whether we find victory here or elsewhere, every day is beyond my count. I'm here with you."
"But what about them?" Jined asked, pointing to the north.
The Praetors were riding back toward them, now with another fifty men, all wearing the colors of the city.
"We'll appeal to their better judgment one more time," Nichal said. "If they do not stand with us, they'll have no recourse but to leave the country and return to Œron."
As they came closer, Jined could see the Chalicians numbered fifty. With them rode the herald Abamar Djer, accompanied by

fifty light-armored cavalry. They did not pause at the bottom of the hill, but rode to the top. The farmer and his family came out and huddled on the porch, watching as the soldiers and holy warriors considered each other.

Nichal gave a broad smile in greeting, but Jined could tell it was forced.

"I had wondered where you might have gone this morning, Provost," Nichal said.

The herald pressed his sleipnir forward, holding up a hand for silence from the Praetors.

"The ships belonging to the church of the Common Chalice were found making sail before dawn this morning. Our city has a stringent curfew in place, and ships may not leave mooring without royal decree. We found then a cavalcade of Praetors riding to the coast, despite the declaration that they cease from our walls, with an intention to meet with their ships and flee. The commanders declared an escalation of the Policy of War upon the appearance of the vül army, which places any and all able-bodied men at the beck and call of the king until further notice. Despite protests, the king demands the aid of the Chalician church. Their remaining here will be noted, and their refusal shall be seen as a declaration of war by their church."

"Now you ride here with them, good Herald Djer," Nichal said.

"There was a worry that perhaps you had left, as well."

"We six Paladins of the Hammer stand with Garrou. If you've additional Paladins in the city, who would join us here, we'd welcome them."

"I shall speak with the king."

"What of us?" the farmer called from the porch.

"What of you?" Djer asked. "You are still a farmer. Continue your work and feed our armies."

"But what if the vül should attack?"

"With the crown's permission," Nichal said, "and with the help of the Chalicians, I should like to extend my protection over this farm, in a more permanent arrangement."

Provost Otem barked a wry laugh.

Nichal gave him a glance, but did not reply.

"You six?" Otem continued. "You demand to have my fifty under your command? What safety can you guarantee for this farm?"

"That sounds a bit like a threat," Nichal said.

"In what way?"

"That you might take the farm from us."

"And that is why," Herald Djer said, "I brought this squadron of riders. We should like you to house us as well, so that we may relay messages to surrounding cities."

"I have taken it upon myself to send a message," Nichal said. "My seneschal is away with the news of the vül. I'm sure your king has other heralds on the road now, too. Whether we can house you, we'll have to ask the owner of the farmstead."

"We thank you," he said, and turned to the farmer. "Can you feed the men?"

"For a day or two. Past that we shall have need of more supplies."

"We shall see it done," Djer said.

"What is the king's understanding of the vül?" Nichal asked.

"It is wagered that they'll begin making assaults on the city within the next two nights. You have fought vül often?"

"Twice. And the T'Akai more often than that."

As the next peal from the bells of the city sounded, the herald left the way he'd come. Otem assigned one of his Praetors to act as a go-between with Nichal, no longer on speaking terms. The captain of the squadron of Garrou riders was a curt but amiable man. Nichal negotiated with the farmer to pay him gold for one of his abandoned stone barns. Soon one hundred and twenty people were quick at work disassembling the stones and using it to build barricades and windward walls for guards to stand stationed behind. As evening approached, several squads of scouts with messages ready for relay rode out.

Jined had the final watch, and stood with one Garrou scout and two Praetors who muttered scripture all night long but refused to interact. Jined made small talk with a soldier, obviously made uncomfortable by all the holy warriors around him.

Gray dawn broke under cloudy skies, and Cävian came to relieve Jined, standard in one hand, and pointing his hammer east with the other. Jined followed his hammer, to the vül beyond the city. They had crept closer overnight, but their rear had not diminished.

"Does it look like they doubled?" Jined muttered.

I think so, Cävian replied. *Nichal won't want to stay here.*

"If he commands it, we'll leave."

"You would leave?" a Praetor nearby scoffed.

"More likely, our Prima Pater would ride," Jined said.

"Only you six?"

"And any who would join us."

There was a sudden shift in the vül line in the dusky pre-dawn. The bell sounded, and the black smudge across the horizon suddenly moved. Most surged toward the walls, and the cries of alarm went off over the city.

"Get the Prima Pater," Jined muttered. "Wake the house."

All turned and hollered for everyone to wake. The soldiers leapt from their bedrolls, drawing their arms. Nichal came out onto the porch, bleary-eyed. "Brazstein?"

"The vül attack now."

"Worse," Otem said, coming out of the home himself. He pointed to the horizon. Half of the vül army molded around the city, ignoring the walls, and staying far enough away to remain outside of the threat of arrows.

"I think they're heading for us," Jined muttered.

"I know that it is so," Nichal replied.

"How?"

"A moment before you rose the alarm, a small whisper awakened me and warned me that Kos-Yran sends greetings in the form of a champion."

"Shall we ride and meet them?" Jined asked.

Nichal nodded.

"Saddle up!" Jined called, and the entire farm became a flurry of activity.

A quarter of the circling vül army stopped before the Garrou gates, and upward of five hundred continued to lope across the intervening terrain toward the farm. In the center of the group, a clear circle of the vül stayed far from a singular creature. They quickly ate up the space between the city and the farm.

"We need to ride soon, if we're to keep them at bay," Jined said.

"I know," Nichal said.

Two farm boys approached, the reins of sleipnirs in hand. Jined took hold of the reins of his large black sleipnir, Tyv, and held Nichal's while the Prima Pater mounted. Both twins came from around the house atop their own. Otem was giving half-hearted orders to his Chalicians.

"They mean to take their time," Nichal said. "Shall we pray they pick up their pace?"

"No need," Jined said, taking from his belt the silver ladle

Grissone had given him. "Bring me water," he called to the farmer's wife.

Jined hefted the bucket up, and stirred it with the ladle, then he lifted the ladle to his lips to drink.

"What are you doing, Jined?" Nichal asked.

"Blessing our charge," he said, and handed the ladle to the Prima Pater.

Nichal drank, then smiled.

Jined turned back to the farmer's wife.

"Please serve a sip of water to everyone here. Then we'll ride."

She nodded and proceeded to go about the farm, quickly giving drinks to all. As each took their sip, a sense of urgency rolled over them, even the Chalicians. Otem leapt up into his saddle and almost against his will, urged it forward.

"What is that ladle?" Nichal asked as the farmer's wife brought it back and Jined tucked it in his belt.

"A gift given to me by our god."

"Were you going to share that information?"

"Eventually," Jined said with a wink.

"Do you remember the ride we made against the T'Akian blood priest?"

"The one wearing the red robes? Or the one with the bony growths?"

"I often forget those were two different battles."

"I remember them both, vividly," Jined said.

"The odds were better then."

"I don't know that I agree," Jined said.

"Why is that?"

"You weren't Prima Pater, I wasn't Grissone's champion, and we didn't have Loïc and Cävian then."

"Didn't we?"

"They were scouting to the south for those three months."

"And now Cävian bears the Standard of Grissone."

"I'd say the odds are even, if not very much in our favor."

"Are you both done talking?" Otem hissed. "If we're to charge to our deaths, I'd rather see Aben sooner than later."

Nichal nodded. "Ride with us as battle brothers, Provost Otem. Differences aside."

"Differences aside," Otem agreed, and the Paladins and Praetors pressed forward as one.

24

Mire of Fear

No god more relishes in the giving of blessings than Kos-Yran, and no people more desire the attention of their god than the vül.

—ON THE PEOPLE OF KOS-YRAN

The sleipnirs rode down the hill, the thrill of the charge suffused in each pounding hoof. It ran up Jined's spine, and with the silvered taste of the blessed water in his mouth, he held his hammer aloft as a battle cry escaped his lips. Everyone riding with him hollered in response.

"Onward!" Nichal shouted. "Onward!"

The vül were now not half a mile away, but at an odd sound from the midst of them they suddenly drew up short, not in a ranting, raving line of slavering maws and flashing teeth, but cowering.

Nichal signaled the halt, leaving two hundred yards between the two lines.

The sleipnirs stamped their feet, pawing and huffing, but catching their breaths.

"This is it," Nichal said.

"This is what?" Jined replied.

"Our proving ground. Proof that Grissone believes in us."

"A rather faithless statement," Jined chided.

Nichal gave him a furtive glance.

"Nichal, you were chosen by Dorian, whom we all love and trust. He believed in you. Whether Grissone believes in you or not, we have faith in him."

"You're right."

"And did not Grissone or the Anka wake you this morning?"

"Perhaps that is so."

"You know it is so. Prima Pater or not. You know how to lead men to battle."

Nichal sighed. "You're right. I do."

The vül across the field were as varied as the vül they had faced to the north, or those under the command of Gold Eater the year before. They bore various shades of fur, from black and smoky gray to the patchwork of a piebald sleipnir. Most wore more armor than the scrappers they'd faced in the mountains, bearing clawed gauntlets, or even larger double-bladed cleavers. All eyed the vül to their sides, and none seemed ready to make the first move.

"They were ready to charge us on the farm, so why stop?" Nichal asked.

"Perhaps they fear the strength of our gods over theirs," Otem said.

The line of vül parted in a lurch, making way for a smaller black vül. Every creature pushed and shoved to stay back from the champion. He walked out twenty-five paces and stopped. He wore a black cloak and had upon one wrist three long blades extending another two feet past his hand. His other hand rested on the pommel of a broad-bladed sword. Beyond that, there were no discernible features. Even the black of his fur was not a sleek black, but dull.

"Why do they cower from him in fear?" Nichal muttered.

"Despair!" the black vül shouted. As his words reached them, a wave of fear flooded over Jined, and the large sleipnir under him took a cautionary step back.

"You shall know the fear that rides the shoulders of my vül!" the champion continued.

"Hold!" Nichal shouted, but fear rippled even in his own voice.

"He is only a vül," Jined warned.

"Then why am I suddenly so fearful?" Nichal muttered.

"Encourage others, if not yourself," Jined said.

Nichal pressed his sleipnir out in front of the line, and turned to the Praetors and Paladins.

"Ride we now. Ride we on. Against the fallen, and in defense of the weak.

"We may be few, but we ride.

"We ride with Grissone in whom we have faith.

"We ride with Anka, whose wings give us courage.

"We ride with Aben and his Watchers upon our heels, encouraging us on the true path.

"Ride we on, driving us to the doom of those pitiful, fallen creatures."

He raised his hammer high, and in response the men behind him roared in courage.

"Onward! Onward now! Let our faith carry us, e'en 'gainst so might a foe!"

He kicked heels to flank and his sleipnir took off, Loïc and Cävian hot on his heels and Jined just after. Behind, Jined heard and felt the thunder of the sleipnirs under the Praetors of the Chalice.

"Onward!" Nichal roared.

The vül across the way suffered a command from their leader and began a countercharge. The distance closed faster than Jined felt ready for, and the closer he got, the faster the foreign feeling flooded his veins. It seemed to emanate from the champion, who stood still unmoved, sneering at Jined. The creature mouthed something Jined could not hear over the roar of the two charging groups. They were outnumbered ten-to-one, but Jined prayed under his breath, for courage to surge forward. He felt the golden glow of Grissone supplanting the fear. Tyv, the sleipnir beneath him, galloped and did not slow. Jined charged far ahead of the others and Tyv took a leap into the air, his front hooves coming down on the first vül, pounding him to the earth. Jined swung his hammer down as another vül tried to rise up to slash at Tyv, and Jined's hammer split his skull open.

As he brought his hammer down on another, the other Paladins arrived alongside him. Nichal's sleipnir shoved past the two vül that Loïc and Cävian hewed down, and Nichal's own hammer fell left and right.

"Onward!" Nichal grunted.

Didus Koel was there alongside them too. The five of them pressed deeper and deeper, hymns muttered or mouthed on their lips, speeding their arms and sundering vül who could not gain a scratch upon them. The Chalicians roared their own hymn, their spears driving deep into the vül rank, even as the vül tore one of their number down.

"On to Aben!" Otem cried as the Praetor fell.

"Off to Noccitan," a deep growl surrounded them all in reply.

The sleipnirs nearly stumbled to escape that voice, but so did the vül. Everyone pushed back and away from Otem, and the vül that stood unmoved beside him.

"How?!" Otem cried out, looking down at the vül. The creature smiled wickedly and sunk the metal claws mounted to his wrists deep into the sleipnir under the Praetor. Both man and mount screamed, one in a death throw, the other in utter terror. Otem fell backward off his sleipnir, and scrambled away.

"Enough!" Nichal shouted.

The black vül turned, ignoring the Provost's attempted escape. As the vül eyed each of them, Jined felt a new wave of uncanny fear flow over him.

"Who are you?" the creature said, voice dripping with hatred.

"I ought to ask the same of you," Nichal replied.

"I smell the death of Gold Eater from your midst," the vül said.

"We killed him, yes," Nichal said.

"I should thank you," the vül said, "for removing him from the pack."

"Then you are his replacement?"

"Replacement? No. His superior, for just how cunning I am."

"Cunning, are you?"

"Very," the vül said. "But who are you?"

"I am the Prima Pater Nichal Guess."

"Good," the vül said. "Then the conqueror is finally dead."

"Dorian Mür lives," Nichal said. "You shall not be rid of him so easily, and I am instilled with his authority."

"Are you challenging me? Because I'd rather pit my luck against Grissone's champion." The vül pointed his sword at Jined.

"We shall not rise to a challenge from an unnamed thing."

The vül laughed. "I am Zürok-Tovot, the Fear-Monger. I am empowered by the Cold Fear of the Gift Giver. None can approach me in my terror."

He puffed up his chest and raised both arms to the sky, as though challenging it to fall upon him.

"Sounds lonely," Nichal said.

"What?" Fear-Monger said, snapping to look at Nichal.

"That sounds lonely. None can approach due to fear. You'll

DREAD KNIGHT

never feel the touch of another again."

"It is the price I am to pay for glory."

"An emaciating price," Nichal said.

"Flee me in fear, maggot!" Fear-Monger said.

"No," Nichal shook his head. "But I'll fight you."

"How dare you! Flee!"

"Sounds like you're the one who fears," Nichal said.

"Why do you not flee?!"

Nichal gave his hammer a test swing. "I fear everything. Thus, I fear you no more than anything else. You're just another thing to fear. Another fear to tear down."

"Then you shall know the true face of fear as you die."

One of the vül made a move. Fear-Monger snapped in their own tongue, and the younger, eager vül stopped.

Nichal held a hand up to call for all to hold and then he changed the hand signal to the Silent word for "pray."

The new Prima Pater did not wait for the vül champion to make the first move. He rushed toward the vül, his hammer falling in an arcing swing, then around for another go. Fear-Monger took one step back and raised his clawed arm to take the brunt of the second hit. He pressed forward, his broad-blade slicing across Nichal's breastplate with a shearing sound and sparks flying across his own face.

Nichal fell back a step, holding his hammer haft in both hands, and pressing in on the vül. With each press the vül roared, and another wave of fear washed over the gawking throng.

"Grissone," Jined muttered through the terror rising as bile in his throat. "Offer Nichal strength and courage."

Nichal held up his haft to block another fall of the vül's sword, pressing down upon him with a crushing weight. Then, with a roar, Nichal pushed the creature back and the vül flew up and into the air, and down onto the ground. Nichal took three steps forward, and the vül barely managed to roll away as Nichal's hammer fell where his head had been.

The twins stood nearby signing their own prayer. Protection and speed.

The vül stood again and hit home across Nichal's gorget. A flash of light exploded where the impact was made, and the vül roared his displeasure, blinking away the flash as Nichal pressed again with several attacks Jined could hardly follow. The vül snarled, and started in with a flurry of chaotic attacks. Nichal easily dodged and juked away from each one, but it pressed him backward toward other vül, who themselves pressed back away from their master.

"The vül causes abject fear in his own people," Koel muttered next to Jined.

"We'll see how they react once Nichal finishes this," Jined said. "Just be ready."

Jined began muttering a prayer for Nichal to retain his strength. In response, Nichal took a sudden deep breath, closed his eyes for a moment, nodded, and pressed harder. Fear-Monger cried out in alarm, and turned to run. The twins raised their hands together in prayer, and suddenly Nichal leapt up into the air, his feet several yards off the ground, his hammer high overhead. The vül looked back over his shoulder and paused, seeing nothing there. He only caught sight of Nichal above him at the last moment and tried to bring his arm up. The hammer crashed down with enough force to crack the vül's forearm in two. The three blades flew every which way as the monster cried in pain. Nichal raised his hammer again, and brought it down on the vül a second time, crushing the boot-blacked chest plate he wore.

"Hold!" the vül cried in ragged breaths. "I yield!"

Nichal paused for a moment, considering.

The vül smiled for a split second before his leg kicked out as Nichal's knee.

Nichal roared as he fell, and the vül stood, trying desperately to flee.

"Paladins!" Nichal roared, using his hammer to help himself up. "Raise your hammers!"

Jined did as he was told. Fear-Monger ran south away from Nichal.

"Bring holy wrath upon the enemies of goodness!"

Jined gave into the urge that washed over him from Nichal's prayer. All brought their hammers down at the same time, pounding the ground. The ground shook violently, and Fear-Monger stumbled in a yelp. Nichal strode forward, the ground still shaking, hobbling on his injured leg, and advancing on the vül who was scrambling to regain his footing. Nichal lifted his hammer again and dropped it. The ground lurched under Fear-Monger. Water on the flood plain began to seep up through the ground and the vül began to sink as muddy water rose up around him.

"Again!" Nichal said, and the Paladins once more dropped their hammers. Other vül fell to a knee or began to sink into the muddy ground.

Nichal stood on solid ground over the vül. Covered in the brown mud, arms and legs sunk deep, Fear-Monger looked up at Nichal with fear flashing in his own eyes.

"Mercy!"

"You shall have my mercy," Nichal said. He detached the hammer and chain from his belt, as Fear-Monger raised a hand to block a strike. Instead, Nichal wrapped the chain around Fear-Monger's arm.

"Your gift grants you immortality, I believe," Nichal said. "And so, you shall live. But you'll never be free of your fear, nor this chain, now bound to you for eternity."

"What are you doing?" Fear-Monger cried.

"Granting you mercy, and granting this land a freedom from the fear you bring."

He dropped the hammer onto the earth, but it did not stop. It did not sink slowly into the mud, but fell as a heavy weight in water—suddenly and violently. The chain went taut and pulled the vül down into the mud with it. He disappeared into the mire instantaneously.

The vül nearby renewed their struggle to escape the mud and flee.

"Advance. Advance!" Nichal ordered. The Paladins and the Praetors chased them down, their own steps falling on solid ground, while every step the vül took was a struggle. The light-armored scouts, still mounted, harassed and pressed the vül. The Paladins and Praetors eventually let them continue their chase, while returning to Nichal.

"How is your knee?" Jined asked the panting Nichal.

"Torqued out of joint for a moment, but not broken."

"We should move from this spot," Koel said. "I can still feel Fear-Monger's presence."

"Me too," Jined said. He had Nichal throw his arm over his shoulders and they hobbled together to where their sleipnirs stood, watching them. Another quarter mile beyond the mounts, a single Praetor stood alone, watching them.

"Otem," Jined said, pointing to him.

"Yes," Nichal said. "I know. I almost joined him."

"He's going to lose clout," Jined said.

"Not just with Garrou if the scouts report back all they saw, but with his own Praetors."

Nichal accepted the help from Jined up into his saddle. Jined mounted Tyv next.

"We should press our advantage and continue to the city," Nichal said.

"I agree," Jined said, eyeing Provost Otem, and then to another rider beyond.

"Silas is back," Jined said. "And from the north, too."

"North?" Nichal said, spinning to look.

Otem did not move, just watched them as though it was he they looked at. Behind him Silas rode, holding his hammer high in the air. He was swinging it around and whooping, and indicating behind himself.

"What is that?" Jined said, pointing past the dairy farm to a moving smudge on the horizon.

"Another army?" Nichal replied.

Silas rode right past Otem, who spun in shock.

"What news?" Nichal shouted as he came within hearing distance.

"You'll never guess who rides to the aid of Garrou!"

He pulled up, panting for breath. "There was a Bortalian army making its way north toward Waglÿsaor. They intended to march through the pass to Boroni and start the war. But before I had arrived with the news, they had already been stopped, and turned to march back toward Garrou."

"How?" Nichal asked. "By whom?"

"Dane Marric and his Gospeler church."

25

Ride of the Gospelers

It is rather interesting the lack of sects within the Parianti faith. I have surmised this often, and I believe that the answer lies within their allowance of the philosophies that spring up as often as they die among the Paladins. That they seek faith, and round out their thoughts via many a lonely ride is part of this. But the number of tales of Paladins of great faith gone missing, never to be seen again may also be an as-yet unexplored answer.

—BORAVAN FETRON, NEMENESE PHILOSOPHER

Dane and five other riders took off from the rest of the host at a prayer-infused speed. The rest of the army rode hard to match them, but could not. Over five hundred riders led the host, and behind them another five thousand soldiers moved in a forced march.

"Where did Dane get an army?" Nichal asked Silas.

"I don't know all the details," the younger Paladin said. "When I came upon them, I was riding north with another Paladin who I'd met on the road. He prompted me to ride toward Igahli, and we came upon this army slowly moving east."

"Another Paladin?"

"Yes," Silas said. "Although, now that I think of it, he never told me his name."

Jined smiled to himself.

"And so, you came upon Dane," Nichal pressed.

"With his army."

"They're all followers of his?"

"They are not," Silas said. "A third of the men on foot are from Waglÿsaor, yes, but the rest are the Bortalian army that had made camp twenty miles from Waglÿsaor, awaiting final orders for war."

"They follow the orders of Dane Marric?"

"He rides with a providential purpose," Silas said.

"Truly?" Nichal asked. "No haughty arrogance?"

"Oh, he's still Dane," Silas said with a chuckle.

The five riders out front of the army rode close enough to identify. Dane rode at the center, with Beltran Cautese at his side, as well as three others.

They did not wear Paladinial armor, only brown robes. In the weeks since Jined had left Waglÿsaor, they had ceased shaving, and hair was growing in across their faces and heads, although Dane appeared not to have much of the hair on his head, and what was coming in at the temples was gray, while his beard was a rich black.

Nichal raised a hand in greeting. "Grissone bless you!"

"And the Anka guide!" Dane called as he rode up to them. "Prima Pater," he said, giving a saddle bow, "I have brought an army, just as Grissone led me."

"Did Grissone lead you?" Nichal replied.

"I dreamed so," Dane said. "I saw the host of vül marching west in my dream but eight days ago, and have been mustering what I could and have been riding for Garrou ever since."

"We welcome the help. Six Paladins, a handful of scouts, and fifty Chalician Praetors hardly stand much chance against so many vül. We thought we rode to our doom."

"Chalicians you say?" Dane scowled.

"Yes, they've come to bid for Garrou."

"One of their ambassadors came to Waglÿsaor," Dane said, "not long after you left. His words were not welcome in my city."

"Your city?"

"We have much to speak on," Dane said. "After the battle."

Nichal nodded.

"How would you have us organized?" Dane asked.

"We need riders to circle south, to prevent the vül from going anywhere but back the direction they came."

"It shall be done," Dane said. He took up his hammer from his belt, no longer chained there, and raised it to the sky. The sun flashed off of it, and the riders far off sped up.

As they mustered, Jined looked to the city. The vül worked at the main gates, and past that, groups of them were trying to clamber up the thirty-foot walls. They would still need to make it up the second set of even higher walls, but the way the vül were leaping with the help of others, if they could make it over or through the gate, they'd be able to work on the inner wall with no outside worry.

"Nichal," Jined said, turning to the Prima Pater. "As Dane's cavalry circles, may I lead an assault on the vül attacking the front gate?"

"Who will you take?"

"I'd ride by myself, if that is what I must do."

"Dane circles from the south. We six shall ride for the gate with any Praetors that will go with us."

Jined looked around. Only a few Praetors were near. The majority of them had pulled back from the group, watching as Provost Otem slowly rode back to join them. They made an odd group, giving each other furtive and embarrassed looks. One of the nearby Praetors ignored the far off group and instead gave his full attention to Dane and Nichal.

"Will you ride with us?" Nichal asked him.

The man came out of his thoughts and looked Nichal in the eye.

"I would," he said in a thick Œronzi accent. "And I would know who these brown-robed brethren of yours are."

Dane squeezed out a derisive smile. "A Praetor?"

"Ignore my uniform," the man said. "Never have I so desired to cast this armor and spear away than when watching my own spiritual leader, whom I have followed for so long, turn tail and flee this day."

"I am Dane Marric, Gospeler, and leader of the Simplists of Waglÿsaor. Let us put aside any differences and ride together. Prima Pater? I shall ride with you."

The cavalry arrived, were given their orders, and proceeded south at a canter while forming into groups. Dane turned and gave an order to one of the others in brown, to stay back and lead the army on foot when it arrived. Jined saw who it was for the first time. The Duke of Waglÿsaor.

"Duke Ergis," Nichal said, noticing the same.

"Brother Ergis has pledged his life to the Gospelers," Dane said.

"Disavowed his role as duke?" Nichal said.

"I have committed my life to the study and introspection that Brother Marric and the Gospelers provide," Ergis said.

"More later," Dane said. "Let us ride."

"We drive these vül away," Nichal replied, "for Grissone."

"And the Anka," Dane said, pointing his hammer to the sky as a sigil. It seemed to not just reflect the light of the sun breaking through and upon it, but glow with an inner light.

Jined smiled, touched the ladle on his belt, and then raised his own hammer, following Dane and Nichal as they rode toward the gate, the twins, Didus, Silas, and eight Praetors hot on their heels.

Fourteen riders raced toward the gate, hoping and praying that the army cavalry was getting into place. Dane's hammer glowed brighter and brighter as their destriers' hooves pounded the dirt. One of the vül at the gate finally spotted them, and warned the others. They were two hundred yards from the gate when the vül all turned to brace for their approach. Fifty vül stood against them, outnumbering them three-to-one.

"Grissone, guide my hammer. Guide our hands," Jined muttered. "Grant us the swiftness of the wind, both Paladin and Praetor. Grant us the wind."

There was a sudden rush of wind behind them, and even though hooves continued to pound, Jined felt as though he lifted off the ground. There was a panicked yelp, and next to him rode the Praetor who had volunteered to join them. Jined could almost see through him, and the Praetor appeared to notice the same thing.

"What is happening?" he shouted.

"Our god grants you protection and blessing," Jined laughed.

"Why?"

"Why not?"

"I do not follow your god!"

"But he follows you," Jined said. "Your name?"

"Vathan Ebithai, of Sal-du-Markt," he shouted.

"Then bring the Wind of Œron down upon the enemies of man, Vathan of Sal-du-Markt."

A manic look came into Vathan's eyes. He turned back toward the approaching gate, and shouldered his spear. He laughed and Jined pressed forward with him and they led the charge into the vül, who had foolishly rushed away from the gate to avoid the rocks being throw down at them from the walls.

DREAD KNIGHT

Three vül stood shoulder to shoulder, and Vathan leaned forward, driving his arrow-headed spear into the throat of one of them, as Tyv leapt up under Jined, over the vül's heads. Jined underswung his hammer, taking a second vül in the jaw and laying him out flat. The third slashed with a massive scimitar, more slab of metal than sword, and it went through Vathan's head and Jined's mount, yet, not a drop of blood was shed.

Despite the spear striking the vül, Vathan kept going, and he and his sleipnir rushed through the vül as well, entirely incorporeal. The vül behind the front line fell back in a panic, as Vathan and Jined's attacks struck unprotected backs. The clash of the others meeting the vül resounded. The laughter of battle thrill and the excitement of being untouchable led to the quick demise of most of their enemies, before several broke through and escaped out onto the plains. Vül who hadn't given into their fear rushed at Jined. Some of the strikes met his armor, bruising his flesh beneath. One vül took hold of Tyv's mane, and the black sleipnir tried to rear up, but the vül held him down, and with his open claw reached back to tear at the creature. Nichal's hammer took the vül atop the back of the skull, and it shuddered out a rasping growl as it fell, letting go of Tyv, and just in time. The sleipnir successfully reared and brought both fore-limbs down on the chest and face of another. Jined swung his hammer round, and saw that Dane, backed up to him, was doing the same, his hammer now a brilliant beacon.

The men atop the wall cheered, and archers shot an arcing volley into the fleeing vül beyond. Jined looked out behind the fleeting creatures. The cavalry had arrived in place, and a few of them were rushing to cut them down.

"To the east?" Jined asked of Nichal. The man nodded, and they began riding along the wall, to find the next group of vül to bring low.

The number of Simplists, as Dane called his followers from Waglÿsaor, numbered eight hundred after the battle. The professional soldiers making up the rest of the army marching under his banner had met up with other brigades and continued to chase vül east. Dane had ordered the Simplists to make camp surrounding the farm, and now they worked together, singing a song while they disassembled the make-shift barricades to rebuild the old barn better than it was before. The Chalicians had moved their own camp to the windward side of the milk-stables, and stood watching the Simplists work.

Dane and Beltran walked around the base of the hill with Nichal, while the twins and Jined walked close behind within earshot.

"We found and burned every shade book at St. Rämmon," Beltran said. "In the privacy of Brother Marric's office, of course. Not in some public event."

"We counted twelve of them in total," Dane said. "Possibly only ten. But we found a handful of heretical scriptures, as well."

"We copied down their textual inaccuracies, for our own records, and then burned the originals," Beltran said.

"What of the Paladins?" Nichal asked.

"After you left," Dane said, "ten more disappeared over three days."

"Five others came to us and confessed themselves as Moteans," Beltran added.

"And they recognized the authority we left you with?" Nichal asked.

"There is no need," Dane said. "We're still developing the tenets—the Simple Way has no ranks. We are all equal in the Anka's sight."

"The Anka's sight?" Nichal asked.

"So many prayers are only to Grissone. We pray now always to both Grissone and Anka, and the Anka has been answering."

"How?" Nichal said. "There are no scriptural references to the Anka ever speaking."

"The Anka does not speak," Beltran conceded, "but does reveal things."

Nichal stopped in his tracks. "In what way?"

"I dreamt of the horde of faceless monsters marching west," Dane said. "In response I mustered the city to march. Ergis made his last proclamation as duke that it be so."

"Last one? What do you mean?"

"Lium Ergis committed himself to the Simple Way and denounced his rank."

"Will that not forfeit the city?" Nichal asked. "To the king, I mean."

"It is a risk we decided to take," Dane said, "in the next step in the plan we have developed."

"Developed?"

They all stopped, far enough away from anyone listening.

"Prima Pater," Dane said, "the Simple Way seeks to turn the enshrouded city of Waglÿsaor into a City of Refuge, committed to the Simple Way, and not to any country. Refugees, the religiously persecuted, the downtrodden: all will find safety there."

"Garrou may see that as seditious in nature."

"We shall see," Dane said. "But what are the Chalicians doing here? We've heard some news, and we turned one of their missionaries away at the gate two days after you left."

"They took over the bastion in Mahn Fulhar," Nichal said, "and have continued along the edge of the Lupinfang, trying to establish their hold."

"Have they been successful?"

"The Isles of Bronue Jinre have ousted them, and now, they have been forced to camp here with us, until an agreement can be made on who will control the bastion and poorkitchen in Garrou."

"Then you've only stayed here in order to ensure they do not get it," Dane offered.

Nichal nodded.

"Give it to me," Dane said, "and we shall ensure the Chalicians and their theological despotism does not gain hold here."

"That may be the best solution," Nichal admitted.

The sound of horns from the gate turned their heads, and a large cavalcade issued forth.

"It appears the king may finally be interacting with us," Nichal said.

Dane turned to look up the hill to the farm and bellowed, "Fellows! Make ready for the king of Bortali!"

They moved with semi-chaotic precision, clearing their own tents away. Some women who had followed along began to sweep the path up to the farm porch. Some helped in the kitchen, while others baked bread over fires in designated areas.

"The sun sets in an hour," Dane said to Nichal as they walked up the hill. "That signals the beginning of Velday, and thus it shall be the Day of Bread."

"What do you mean?"

"It means we will feed any and all who will allow us," Beltran said. He turned to Dane. "We could re-purpose the poorkitchen in

Garrou as a House of Bread."

Dane gave a nod. "A good idea."

The king rode at the front of his entourage, pausing at the bottom of the hill to take it all in.

King Abrun Vorso wore a short black beard, with his hair slicked down the back of his neck. He wore the green and gold of the city, and a white fur cape that hung back over his equally white sleipnir. He did not have the look of disdain the others behind him did, but rather, curiosity. He gave his sleipnir heels and pressed up the hill. As he came to the top, three squires on foot rushed to assist him off the saddle.

Nichal had taken his place on the porch. While he had remained silent and avoided everyone for most of the day, Provost Otem stood behind him to his left, no longer pressing to stand as equals to the Prima Pater. Dane stayed at the bottom of the stairs, along with the other Paladins.

"Welcome, King Vorso," Nichal said. He did not bow.

The Simplists eyed Dane to see if they should bow. He did not.

Vorso looked around with a smirk of astonishment.

"Prima Pater Guess," he said, looking up to the porch.

Nichal nodded, stepped down the stairs, and then looked back to the Praetor leader.

"You know Provost Otem, of course, but this brother here is the hero we have to give thanks to." He clasped a hand on Dane's shoulder. "If he had not arrived with the army from the west, I would imagine Garrou would be a vül stronghold now."

"I heard a rumor that a Paladin in nothing but a brown robe rode from Waglÿsaor with my own army to lift the sudden siege."

"It was a god-inspired move on my part," Dane said. "My followers and I came as soon as we were able."

"Of course, now the pass is left entirely unprotected," Vorso said.

"Hardly a concern in the light of current affairs," Nichal said.

"But a concern of mine, nonetheless."

"Shall we find somewhere to sit and speak?" Nichal asked.

The king nodded, and Nichal turned to lead the king up the stairs and into the farmhouse.

The king was given the head of the table, with Herald Djer standing behind him. Nichal took the opposite end, with the twins and Jined behind him. Otem came in unattended and took a seat between the two, and Dane took one across from the Provost.

"You have come to grant my holy order the Garrou bastion," Otem said. It was not a question.

The king did not even glance over at him, but kept a steady gaze on Nichal.

"I owe the men here much," the king said. "I understand a ride of only a few dozen of you charged an army ten times your number, and challenged a vül champion."

"He accepted the challenge and now he lies sundered," Nichal said.

"That should be enough to see me grant a boon," Vorso said. "But then comes an army. My own army. Led by a Paladin who no longer wears his order's armor." He glanced over at Dane. "If my spies are to be believed, the events in Waglÿsaor have been eventful over the past several months, to say the least."

Dane gave no hint of surprise.

"I understand you have, under the Prima Pater's auspices, formed a new off-shoot of the Parianti faith. I hear that even Duke Ergis has not only thrown in his lot with you, but disavowed his rank. That leaves the city of Waglÿsaor in a precarious position."

He turned back to Nichal. "This attack by the vül has given me a clarity I don't think I've felt in years. This imminent war with Boroni wears upon me but I feel I've no way out now."

"Grant us the bastion," Otem said, "and I shall secure peace."

The king ignored Otem and continued. "The vül attack ran through Evzha in northern Zhigava. I fear we shall learn that they have devastated the east. I need to recall my armies to press toward the rising sun, and take some of it back." The king went silent and tapped his fingers on the table.

Nichal did not respond.

Otem opened his mouth to speak. Vorso spoke over him.

"I would be offered a solution by one with more patience than I," he said to Nichal.

"What do you think you ought to do?" Nichal asked, timidly.

"Use this opportunity to drive east. Forget the conflict to the west."

"A contrite heart is the beginning to a clear path," Otem said.

The king turned to Otem finally. "A coward who flees the field is not in a position to offer council."

Otem clamped his mouth shut.

"In the Provost's defense," Nichal offered with a smirk, "the champion gave off an aura of fear."

"Which, as my generals report, did nothing to you. So you laid him low. For that reason I am giving you back the control of your bastion."

"I thank you," Nichal said. "But I would ask you instead give it to Dane Marric and his Simplists."

"Gospelers, I thought they were called," Vorso said, turning to Dane.

"Those of us who commit our lives fully to the Simple Way are Gospelers, but those people who follow our tenets have begun calling themselves Simplists."

"Very well. What will you do with the bastion in the city?"

"It shall be a House of Bread," Dane said. "With it, we shall feed the city."

"Now, what of Waglÿsaor?"

"What of it?" Dane inquired.

"I understand it has practically given itself to you."

"If you would grant me the honor of its spiritual welfare, perhaps we might use that as a means to negotiating peace with Boroni."

"Between myself and the Boronii?"

"Rather," Dane said, "between Waglÿsaor and Boroni. And between Waglÿsaor and Bortali."

"I do not understand."

"As a reward for the deliverance of the city of Garrou, proclaim Waglÿsaor a free city. Free of any crown. A City of Refuge. Peace. Bread."

The king sat back, considering.

"A city with no defined leadership or established spiritual guidance goes against everything the Pantheon stands for," Otem said standing. "It is an anarchic heresy!"

"Sit down, Otem," Nichal said calmly.

"No," Otem hissed. "I've heard enough. A report shall be sent back to Œron, detailing the disrespect we have been shown. See if our countries lose any friendship we once held."

The king barked a laugh. "You think Bortali, or any country on the Lupinfang needs anything outside our own sea? What has Œron ever offered us?"

"We came offering spiritual guidance and you've spat in our face."

"Metaphorically, yes, and I'm fighting the urge to do it in actuality! It is my understanding you'd tried to undermine my own authority in Igahli. Who knows what Praetors you've sent into my hinterlands."

"Missionaries. Nothing more," Otem said through clenched teeth.

"They have one month to leave our borders, but you have two days. You're to report back to your own leaders that the Praetors have no business in Bortali, and shall not set foot here for five years. If they comply with this, I shall only then consider any ambassadors sent."

"How dare you."

"How dare I what?" Vorso asked. "Be a king? Perhaps Œron's king is weak and bows a knee to his lessers, but I do not."

Otem shoved backward, knocking his chair over, and marched out of the room.

A tense silence settled over those who remained.

Nichal suddenly burst out laughing and everyone else followed suit. The twins shuddered in silent laughter, and Dane buried his face in his hands to hold himself back.

After a long while, they settled down. The king held his side, crying in pain.

"Now," he said to Nichal through gasps. "Will you be leaving as well?"

"We shall journey to the southeast, through Zhigava."

"Not through Nemen? Do you not have holdings there and in Setera?"

"The man who mentored me in Waglÿsaor," Dane said, "turned out to be a heretic. He had some considerable power in the Fortress of St. Hamul. I shouldn't wonder if there is more trouble awaiting there."

"Then you go through what may be a vül-infested Zhigava," the king said.

"We must return to Pariantür," Nichal said. "Knowing all roads are dangerous almost makes it easier just to accept that fact, and march on."

"You're a braver man than I," Vorso said. "I pray your god protects you."

"And may Grissone and Anka guide you and Dane's Gospelers here in Bortali," Nichal replied.

26

THE GRIFFIN ROAD REGIMENT

Let only the most courageous carry the banner. For theirs will be a quick and glorious death.

—GENERAL ONFUISTE OF TASHAR

Princeps Noss sat in dark silence at the head of the table, drumming his fingers in thought. Ophedia stood behind the chairs of both Aurín and Bolla Elbay, who now wore a Warden's cloak. She bore the title of Dean and sat at the left hand of Noss. Dean Domic sat after Aurín, and directly across from her sat Deggar, who eyed the city baronets and city guard captains with suspicion. He had ceased trusting them after they had all but refused to help him at the southern wall. The baronets did not return his looks, but bore visages of men held hostage. They no longer had any power on the council, and they knew it. Their six chairs were dwarfed by the eleven Wardens. They had begun bringing their own guards to match the extra Sentinel Wardens at attention alongside the ex-Paladin Wardens.

"And there's been no word from the Red Banner?" Noss finally asked.

"Commander Hardin was reportedly seen in the forests north of Richton," Domic said. "That city is still under our control, but Lor appears to be preparing a trap for any who might choose to take advantage of it—whether that is the bands of Chalician soldiers, or whether Casternard takes advantage of all of this and makes an attempt for Trémont as he did those years ago."

"And no sign of Provost Abrau?" Noss said.

Domic shook her head.

"Why would he leave the field? Unless it is to circle down and take Liberté from the south."

"That is a possibility."

He turned to Aurín. "Are you ready to test your mettle?"

"I thought I had done that at the Battle of Graysand," Aurín chuckled.

"Well, we need to muster an army and march south, doing a sweep of the hinterland, and sending a sign to those in the south. The Wardens I sent down the Dead Pass have secured the pass entirely for Limae. I don't doubt we'll hear from Mahndür on that soon enough. For that reason, I need the old commanders here for negotiations. I want you, and any baronets willing to lend a hand, to form up and march south."

"To what end?" Aurín asked.

"March toward Liberté, but stay eastward of it. I agree with Domic. If what you all say is true about the general animosity with Castenard, the last thing we need is that city-state gaining territory."

"How long do I have?" Aurín asked.

"Let's give you all of today and tomorrow to muster. You leave at dawn the following morning. All in favor of the Talon marching south with a company?"

The Wardens raised their hands. Domic and Elbay joined in, but with more thought than the rest. The baronets eventually joined them.

Aurín stood and gave a respectful bow to the unanimous decision. Then, he turned to Ophedia. "Will you be the first to join me?"

Ophedia had not expected it and looked him in the eyes. "You want me?"

"Of course," Aurín said. "Someone I can trust at my right hand."

Ophedia thought it through and glanced at Bolla, who gave an encouraging nod.

"Alright," Ophedia said in agreement.

The Wardens did most of the heavy lifting, standing on street corners requesting volunteers to join the Talon's army. Young men who had come to the walls were the quickest to join up. A handful of Sentinels were joining, too, when the promise of a stipend was given.

Ophedia walked alongside Aurín, who bore the gait of someone trying to look commanding.

"Why did you ask me along?"

"Exactly why I said. I want someone I trust alongside me. I'll watch your back, and you watch mine."

"Any other reason?"

"I felt like maybe you wanted to get out of the city. This is a good reason."

"What role am I taking? I don't have the tactical mind to lead or plan."

"Then carry my banner."

"Because that's what I want is to draw a target on my back."

Aurín stopped. "Listen. I don't want to do this either. But if you're really too frightened to lend a hand to a friend, keeping me company, then just go right now."

"I didn't say that," Ophedia said with a chuckle. "I'll go."

"Good. I hoped you would say that."

"Baronet Gat is talking about joining us." Ophedia said.

"Why?"

"If I had to guess, I'd say he saw Haven as a lost cause, and wants to put his assets in another city."

"Who should we talk to, to get a better lay of the land?" Aurín asked.

Ophedia stopped before a set of stairs leading up into a private shop. At the top of the stairs sat a hrelgren smoking a pipe held between his green lips. Flashing a smile across his green face, he gave them a wink. "You look like you need something."

"What do you offer?"

"Maps."

He tapped out his pipe and motioned for them to follow inside.

Within the shop, a large map desk sat in the center, the walls lined with map holes and shelves bearing boxes.

"There's been talk about a Sentinel Warden with a claw for a hand. Looks like I'm seeing him for the first time."

Aurín glanced down at the taloned glove and gave a half nod.

"We are looking for a little information," Ophedia said.

"I sell maps, mostly."

"I would imagine you're also a bit of a historian."

"That I am," the hrelgren said, holding out a hand. "Zapas yu Caradadz."

"Ophedia del Ishé," Ophedia said, taking it. "And this is Aurín Mateau."

"A pleasure to meet you both. Tell me what you look for."

"The most detailed map of Limae you can give us."

"I've had a handful of those go in the past several weeks." He turned and began poring over his shelves.

"I wonder who to," Aurín muttered.

The hrelgren came back with a longer map rolled into a scroll, and unfurled it. It detailed Limae in its entirety, as well as the Dead Pass, and continued south to the Kandar Sea.

"This is a map I had the fortune of securing several years ago, made by one of the finest cartographers I've ever seen—Pater Migal Yurlar. He was a Paladin of the Aerie and a zoologist, said to have known where every griffin roosted in the country." As he unfurled the map, he pointed to the bottom corner where the maker's mark read, "Limae and Surrounding Lands, by Migal 'Talon' Yurlar."

Ophedia and Aurín gave each other a glance.

"Talon, huh?" Ophedia said.

Aurín shrugged.

"We are here," Zapas said, drawing their attention back to the map and pointing to Haven. "The Griffin Road stretches fifty miles south through what most Limaeans call the hinterland. It's largely empty. A few holdings sit out there, risking the dangers. Past that, the lower valleys and basins begin. The farther south you go, the less dangerous it becomes."

"But for major cities, there is Haven up here in the north, and Liberté in the south."

"There are a few others. Abdalon and Gryph's Nest specifically. Let's not forget Jerigon's Hold."

"Never heard of it," Ophedia said.

"I have. I passed through there when I left Œron to become a Sentinel," Aurín said. "It's a small pass-through keep, like the border crossing from Düran into Bortali. It controls enough land in Limae to feed the Sentinels that keep watch there."

"Watch for what?"

"Castenard."

"Ah, Castenard," Zapas said.

"What about it?" Ophedia replied, turning to Zapas.

"Perhaps you have noted, at one time or another in your life, that Castenard, while Sidieratan, does not sound as though it shares the same naming convention."

"I hadn't," Ophedia said. "But now that you mention it…"

"Limae established itself over the course of a long century. Castenard was once part of the leagues of bandits that controlled the area. When Limae finally finished its incorporation as a country, Castenard did not take kindly to being made second to Haven. It pressed back for a time and tried to take the southern half of the country for itself. The ruler of Castenard tried leveraging Sidieratan finances for his campaigns, but that ended up only bringing Castenard under Sidieratan control, who would much rather have mercantile peace in the global neighborhood than war."

"How long ago was that?"

"Long enough ago that the Castenardi of today would much rather refocus on taking Limae again. It's a quiet rage they hold. Not like the warmongering Tambii who have been openly eyeing Hraldor and Minor Hrelgreens for centuries."

"Then Castenard is a serious threat," Aurín stated.

"Why didn't the Chalicians ally with Castenard then?" Ophedia asked Aurín. "They might have allied themselves with Castenard, and taken Limae."

"Sidierata," Zapas answered.

"What do you mean?"

"We've still to hear what happened in the south since the siege began, but I would imagine if the Chalicians allied with Castenard, the City States of Sidierata would take that as an Œronzi threat from the west and band together in a League. Taking Haven and threatening the north was a much better move."

Aurín considered the map before him in silence.

Ophedia turned to the hrelgren. "How much for the map?"

"I've only two copies, so I could let this one go for two royals."

Ophedia nearly choked.

Aurín reached under his cloak and came out to place two royals, and five silver coins.

"Tell me what these are for," Zapas pointed to the silver.

"I would like a leather map roll, with cover clips."

Zapas smiled broadly. "You're smart. I like that. I will fetch one."

He turned and left the room.

"We have to step cautiously as we go south," Aurín said.

"What do you mean?"

"I imagine the Chalicians want one of two outcomes. If they truly want control of Limae, it will be by manipulating us to fight both them and Castenard. If we press too hard on Castenard, the Chalicians gain an ally. If Castenard is successful, then the Chalicians can allow Castenard to do so, take them under wing, and use that to impress the rest of the Sidieratans."

"Zapas mentioning the Griffin Road also reminded me, we need to be careful how we move any sleipnirs as we leave the city."

"Oh?"

"The rumor is griffins will target them."

Zapas came out with a large roll of leather and unfurled it. He placed the map atop it, anchoring the corners with leather triangles sewn into it. Then he rolled it up and held it out to Aurín. "May the pantheon grant you the wisdom to succeed."

With respectful bows they left the shop.

"Odd the cartographer was also called 'Talon,'" Ophedia said.

"I wonder if that was not the remains of the man in the tower," Aurín said. "And that Noss knew it and named me so as Talon's Heir."

"Probably worth investigating when we get back to Haven."

"If we ever do."

"What do you mean?"

"Maybe I'll settle down south and never step foot in Haven again. I'm growing tired of watching the commanders...er...deans, dance around each other in political guile."

"You think it'll be any different down south?"

"We won't know until we see it."

Aurín and Ophedia marched out front of the five hundred men and women, keeping a handful of Sentinels they knew by name nearby, and as a buffer to the twenty men leading sleipnirs by rein. Baronet Gat had refused to lead his own, and sat tall, yet wary, after Ophedia made an off-handed remark regarding the possibility of griffin attack. He eyed the skies above, just as the other soldiers now eyed him with their own suspicion. He had arrived at the last possible moment, as the mustered army prepared to leave, bringing with him the twenty cavalry, and another twenty retainers with auroch-drawn carts, bearing tents and additional supplies.

The first night, no tents were raised, but the screeching sound of griffins overhead in the pre-dawn light stole the last hour of sleep from all.

On the second night, Baronet Gat doled out meat and wine from his wagons to those that would help raise tents for the sleipnir and aurochs. The drinking party thrown until well after midnight left everyone as tired as the morning before.

"We all need a true night's sleep," Ophedia murmured.

"We've two more days travel before we clear the Griffin Road," Aurín said.

"Which gives you only two more days to establish who leads this little regiment."

"We also need to retain the regiment," Aurín added. "Gat is already earning their favor."

"Everyone who joined, volunteered," Ophedia said.

"So?"

"So, they chose to join," Ophedia replied. "They want to be here. Show them why."

Aurín nodded and grew pensive.

They came to a fork in the road, offering the opportunity to continue directly south along the road Ophedia had taken up through the scablands where she had left Eunia and Chös. The other choice would cut southeast toward the Abei mountains between Limae and Düran.

"We continue south," Gat declared.

Everyone began to grind into motion as Gat urged his mount forward.

"East," Aurín announced.

The regiment clamored and muttered as they stopped. Gat pulled back on his reins, but did not turn around.

"East?" someone asked.

"We're taking an extra day or two to cut southeast," Aurín said.

"May I ask why?" Gat asked, finally turning around to consider him.

Aurín pushed through the handful of soldiers at the front, and turned to address the regiment. He looked up at Gat.

"To start," he began, "I don't have to give you any reason. This is my regiment. You joined me."

Gat choked on the perceived insult.

Aurín ignored him and looked at the men and women surrounding him. "Secondly, we're not yet a regiment. To the east, a day's march from here, is a plain marked on my map that I'd like to use for a day or two to practice drills."

"The south needs us," someone called. "My sister and her family are down there."

"The south," Aurín said, "doesn't even know we're coming. A day or two won't change that, and I don't need a regiment at my back that breaks and flees at the first sight of a larger force."

"Larger force?"

"Why are you surprised?" Aurín called. "Haven faced a siege for weeks of thousands of followers of the Church of the Common Chalice. How many of those invaders died? Who can know? How many of them now ravage the Limaean countryside? Who can know? You volunteered to join this regiment to bring some relief. You agreed to submit to my leadership."

He turned and looked Gat in the eye. "You came last to us, bringing your squadron of riders. I would have you and your men ready. To scout. To support. To bring glory to your name and to Limae. Are you here to follow me? Or not?"

Gat gave a forced smile. "I came to do as you have said. Bring relief to the south and rid Limae of these Chalicians."

A cheer went up from the army at this.

Aurín gave a nod and signaled Gat and the rest of the regiment to press east.

Ophedia came to stand with him and watch as everyone passed. "Stopping to train?"

"How else are we going to establish a little authority?"

"True."

"And you'll need to start work on your banner."

"My banner?" Ophedia asked.

"I asked you to join me as standard bearer. Make a banner."

"What do you want on the field?"

"I don't care," Aurín said. "You decide."

They watched the last of the regiment pass and turned to follow them, when Aurín stopped to look up at the hills.

"What is it?" Ophedia asked, scanning the rise.

"Looks like we're being followed," Aurín said with a smile.

Ophedia cast her glance up the hill, and her eyes fell on a black form.

"What is it?" she asked.

"Looks smaller than a griffin."

Ophedia nodded. "We'll keep an eye out, in case it's planning on following us."

"And if it is?"

Ophedia shrugged and they turned to follow the rear of the regiment.

A hillock hid the wider field from the road, as well as a small holding built into the backside of the hill. Aurín himself went up to the front door and spoke with the owner, negotiating the purchase of two aurochs ready for taking to Haven for slaughter. Two butcher's sons were a part of the company, and soon they had the meat on the spits of several fires.

Ophedia walked through the haphazard camp. There was no rhyme nor reason to where the fires sat, and the placement of the tents assured her that most had never spent a night in the open air.

One man sat by himself between his tent and a meager fire, staring across the flames to a stand of trees beyond.

"Wary tonight?" she asked.

He looked up, squinting.

"Doesn't look like those trees would conceal more than ten soldiers or spies."

"If that," he said with a gravelly voice she recognized. Lowden Dakmor looked up with a crooked smile, the scar across his face and one side of his mouth preventing all his teeth from shining in the firelight.

"I hadn't realized you'd joined our company," she said.

"I couldn't pass up the chance to hit the road again."

"I never took you for a country boy," Ophedia said.

"Hardly," Lowden said. "But the road always beckons."

"And those trees," she asked.

"Something is moving out there."

"Chalicians?"

"Nope."

She looked down at the bone she held in her hands, half the meat eaten, the rest gristly enough to gnaw at, but her appetite had waned.

She turned from the fire and walked toward the forest.

"What are you doing?"

She didn't answer but walked twenty yards toward the deep shadows and placed the bone on the ground, then backed up to the fire.

"You got a wyloth's foolishness about you," Lowden said.

"You and I have faced Indigo Walkers," she said. "And I've faced worse things myself."

She seated herself upon a stone by the fire. "So, not a fan of the city, not a country boy. Why did you come with us?"

"I joined the Sentinels in Zhigava," he said. "Right after I finished serving on the Ikhalan border."

"Sounds boring."

"Hardly," he said. "Vül love that area. Never a dull moment. But it was join the Sentinels or go back to Old Zhig to make pottery or dig in the mines."

"So now you're here."

"Mountains like Zhigava, but fresher. Newer."

The fire cracked. They sat in long silence.

"It's gone," he said.

"What?"

He pointed over the fire. She peered out toward the trees. The grisly bone was gone.

"Did you see it go?" she asked.

"No. Maybe. Whatever it is, is black as a shadow, and small enough to move."

"Wyloth?"

"Bigger."

Ophedia stood and nodded. "Keep it fed."

"What?"

"Whatever it is," she said. "Keep it fed. It'll be less likely to come into camp and cause trouble. Maybe you'll make a friend."

Aurín moved through camp before the sun had risen, kicking over tent poles or just kicking those under tents poorly raised and collapsed overnight. Shouts of aggravation went up and now a few scrambled out, axes drawn. Aurín came back to the center of camp and stood there while Ophedia fed a fire nearby.

"Don't bother," Aurín said. "No breakfast."

She gave him a look, stood, and kicked dirt into the flames.

Several men pushed their way through others trying to make heads or tails of the dawning morning.

"What in Noccitan are you doing, Mateau?" one man said.

"This camp was a shanty town last night," Aurín barked. "I couldn't believe how poorly you all set your sleeping arrangements. If an army had come across us, we would have all died in our sleep."

"Why the rude awakening then?"

"We can't march if we're not an organized unit, and organization starts in camp."

He turned from the man accosting him to the gathering crowd of men and women.

"I want the camp arranged. We don't drill until the camp is perfect. Camp isn't perfect until I say it is."

He pointed to the ground. We dig a main fire pit here," he said. "From there, I want eight paths for tents between them."

Everyone stared at him.

"What are you waiting for?"

A few men began to move, calling for shovels and starting the work.

After an hour, Aurín took out a long rope, drove a stake in the ground by the central fire, and began walking by tents. He pulled the line taut, and any tents not sitting within an inch of the rope he kicked over. The man working on the tent would holler, look up and see Aurín moving past dispassionately, and start setting his tent up again, taking care to follow the line.

As night came, two sections still hadn't met Aurín's rope line measurements. The other sections eyed the other two with growing irritation. Aurín stood by his fire pit, wood laid, but no fire started.

"You going to make them work in the dark?" Ophedia muttered.

"I am," he said.

"Why are you doing this?"

"I laid awake all of last night," he said, "trying to think of a way to get these soldiers to work together before we even start drills."

"And making yourself their enemy felt like the best way?"

"Getting them to work together, in spite of me."

"Not sure it's working," she said.

"No. It's not. But that's because they haven't realized their error yet."

"Which is?"

"Nothing is stopping those six with straight tent lines from helping the last two. They're just watching them and making enemies, rather than friends."

"You going to tell them?"

"No."

By morning, none had slept, and still the last two groups couldn't draw their tents in a straight line. Aurín ordered everyone to stand in regimented order before him. The two last groups stood in as poor a line as their tents.

"Gat," Aurín called. The baronet stepped forward, looking haggard. Aurín said nothing.

Eventually, Gat raised a tired hand and saluted.

"How many men in your squadron?" Aurín asked with an acknowledging nod.

"Forty," Gat said.

"You and your men are to rearrange your tents and sleipnirs in a circle around the central fire. Your line has been the straightest the longest. Your squadron is now the Black Claws 1st."

He turned to the rest of the regiment and pointed to six men and four women and called them forward. "The ten of you are joining the 1st. You were quick to help any who asked."

He turned to the two groups that had failed to draw straight lines. "The rest of you are to disperse among the rest."

They stood there, a look of confusion on their faces.

"Your idiotic, lazy attitudes will not be tolerated in my regiment. Disperse!"

They began milling into the other lines of soldiers.

"I want the camp rearranged. The 1st in the middle, the rest of you in six groups. Not eight."

Everyone groaned.

"Now," he ordered cooly.

Gat raised his chin. "You heard the commander: Black Claws 1st, circle the fire."

His men and the ten new members rushed to their work, tearing down their tents and walking their sleipnir to the center of camp. The other groups soon fell into their work as well. A few fist fights broke out with those that had been absorbed into their companies, but by nightfall the regiment had met Aurín's requirements.

"Get some food," he ordered from the center of camp. "We start drilling at first light."

There were a couple of groans, but self-appointed leaders swatted at grumblers, and soon the entire camp fell to lighting the fires they had long desired to warm themselves by in the cold mountain air.

27

Battle of Pine Valley

The Banner! The Banner! Look upon the banner!

Follow! Follow! To death or victory!

—SAID TO BE THE LAST WORDS OF GENERAL DOMAT AT THE BATTLE OF MACHEZI

Ophedia came to the break in the low ridge of rocks and crouched low. She hissed, and received a hiss from a bush nearby. She pressed slowly into the bushes and lay prone next to the lookout.

"Anything to report?" she muttered.

"Chalicians," Aurín whispered back, to her surprise.

"I thought you were still at camp."

"I wanted to see it myself. Just below us are three others who came with me. So observe, but don't comment."

She peered off into the darkness, allowing her eyes to adjust. It was the second night she'd taken on midnight recon duty in the week they'd traveled since their training field. The night insects purred and far off behind them, up in the mountains, the yowl of some stalking creature unnerved her. Aurín's purchased musk still lingered in the air despite him no longer applying it while on the road, but he had not quit his vice of the citrus and leather-scented snuff he admitted he had picked up in Haven. The heady mix, with the warming spring mountain night goading resinous pollen from the surrounding trees, made for an odd juxtaposition to the adrenaline that coursed through her veins.

Aurín raised a hand and pointed down to the valley.

The valley floor was a hundred feet below them, but the Black Claw Regiment would move easily down the valley from the north. The tall shrubs, much like the piney bushes of the Griffin Road scrublands, stood a little taller, fuller, and from their vantage point concealed the Chalician regiment camped below from anyone at the same level.

Ophedia tapped Aurín and held her fingers up making a motion to indicate fire. Then she showed him a count of five, four times. He nodded in agreement.

Twenty fires. Besides their main fire, Aurín had demanded his own regiment only keep one fire for every forty people, which worked out to about two fires for each company, and another three fires for the camp followers.

He tapped her shoulder again and pointed to the north. A larger fire sat against the opposing valley wall. The dark shadows of sleipnirs could be seen near there.

Aurín pulled away from the edge and back down to the path, and Ophedia followed.

"Back to camp," Aurín said. "We attack before dawn."

"Oh really?"

"Yes. Let's muster and attack. The officers are over across the valley, farther up valley from the town of Nikcrest. I expect they'll be mounting an assault on the town tomorrow or soon after. Might as well catch them unawares while we can."

They came to the fork in the path and cut up over the higher ridge to the small canyon.

"State your name and business," a guard whispered.

"Aurín Mateau, your Nocc-Given commander."

"I'm sorry, sir," the man said.

Aurín laughed. "I'm only giving you a hard time. Thank you for checking. I'd rather you did, no matter who I might have been. If someone tells you otherwise, you tell me."

"Very good, sir."

"How long would you say we have until dawn?"

"A good three hours, sir."

"Good. Ophedia, muster the 5th, 6th, and 7th companies."

Ophedia gave a mocking salute, and marched off through the

trees to the back of camp.

The 6th Company captain, Enfold, stood at the campfire of the 5th Company's leader, Richtol. Both knew each other from town and got along well.

"Word from the Talon?"

"Muster. We're marching on the Chalicians before dawn."

"About time!" Enfold said.

"Is Dakmor awake?"

"I doubt it. He had watch the night before."

Ophedia excused herself and moved through their camps to the 7th. One of the fires had dwindled to coals, while the other at the back of the canyon blazed, the men around it carousing. They were pointing off into the trees and chucking rocks into the brush with guffaws as they downed dark bottles.

Ophedia pressed up to the fire. "I take it you didn't get the order to keep it down?"

"Hey, look!" the drunkest one slurred. "It's the Talon's pet!"

"Hardly," Ophedia said flatly. "Where is Captain Dakmor?"

"Probably sleeping off his own hangover," one of them said.

"Fetch him," Ophedia said.

One man stepped up to her, almost tripping over a log to get to her. He stood tall and drew in a deep breath. "We don't 'fetch' anyone. Certainly not our commanding officer."

"I don't care what you want to call it. Just get him."

The man placed a hand on her shoulder.

"Wrong move," she muttered.

She dropped to a half crouch, pulling on his hand as her knee rose to meet his chin. He was drunk enough he didn't squeal in pain, but slumped over, out cold. She still held his hand. He was down on the ground face first, his arm behind him. The others hadn't advanced on her.

"Who's going to get Dakmor?" she repeated.

One of them scrambled off as she took out a rope and bound the man on the ground.

The others kept an eye on her while continuing to throw rocks into the brush.

"What are you doing?" Ophedia asked as she finished her rope work.

"There is something out there," one of them offered. "Been haunting our company with its presence every night."

"What is it?"

"Captain says it's a black griffin, maybe a gravon. We don't want no beast messing with our rations."

"Leave it alone," a voice said from the shadows. Lowden Dakmor came into the light.

"Hey Cap..." one of the men said hesitatingly.

"What are you doing with Bronty?" Lowden asked.

"He put a hand on me," Ophedia said, "and tripped."

"I'll see he sobers up."

"I don't know that there will be time."

"Oh?"

"We muster and march," she said. "We're going to take the Chalicians before dawn."

"You heard her!" Dakmor shouted. "Get hoofing!"

The men rushed to their tents and began kicking at others.

"So, the thing we fed?" Ophedia asked.

"Some gravon. Appears to be lame-winged."

Ophedia nodded. "Lamed, huh?"

"Well, at least weak-winged. When I've watched it snag the meat I've left for it, it appears to be slowly rebuilding itself from a starving winter."

"I knocked open a cage of a gravon before I first arrived in Haven. Could be that one."

"Well, Valden and I have been keeping it cared for." He indicated a teenage boy who stumbled out of a tent. He had the same short neck and broad shoulders as Lowden.

"Yours?" Ophedia asked.

"Yeah."

"Why didn't you say?"

"Didn't feel like asking permission. He came into camp with the followers. His mother will flay me alive when we get back to Haven."

The boy approached. "Captain," he saluted.

"No worries, boy. She knows you're mine."

"What are we doing?"

"Marching to battle. Get your sword."

"Did someone feed Shadow?" Valden asked.

"Can't hurt to toss him another meal," Lowden said, and pointed to their company's baggage tent. The boy leapt to and came back out with a whole ham. "He's always had a fondness for animals," Lowden said. "His mother is a laundress though, and she never let him bring any home."

Several new faces pressed up to the fire. "Just a few stragglers left, captain, but we should be ready momentarily."

"Good."

Ophedia excused herself again and made her way back through camp to the command pavilion, which in this little valley was just the fire. The tree canopy didn't allow for the larger tents to be raised. Aurín stood speaking with several captains and Baronet Gat.

"I'll be marching with the 2nd Company," Aurín said. "We march on the command camp here." He pointed to the hastily drawn map, to the opposing canyon wall. "Gat, you're to lead the charge through the camps, with the 3rd through 6th coming after you. The 7th," he said as Lowden came into the light, "you're to take up the rear for the regiment, and net anyone who tries to escape against the tide."

"Yes, commander."

"Permission to position my squadron?" Gat asked.

"Granted. If you've two sleipnirs to spare, del Ishé and I will take them."

Gat nodded, and turned to go with his two adjutants.

"He sure turned a corner," Ophedia said.

"Because I gave him a long enough lead," Aurín said. "He's a man who feels respect through responsibility. I imagine he left the city just to get away from the stifling council. Just as I did."

Ophedia nodded. "I'll get the standard," she said, and turned to enter his tent.

Aurín followed her in and dropped the tent flap behind him.

"What are you doing?" she asked, turning to consider him, cocking an eyebrow.

Aurín gave her a mirrored look and his eyes bugged out in surprise. "Nothing like that," he said. "I need your help putting on my talon, and another surprise as well."

He walked past her to a chair on which his cloak lay and pulled up a pack and put it on the planning table. One claw came out, then another. She circled to his side and after he had laid the claw straps open and put his wrist down into it, she went through the habitual movement of tightening the straps. Lifting his hand, he checked the flexibility and nodded.

He pointed to the other bundle. "Care to open that up?" he asked.

She untied the strings holding the package closed and unfolded the canvas and gasped.

Within lay a griffin's skull. "What?"

"Lift it up," Aurín said.

She did, and found straps underneath.

"I had it outfitted to go over my shoulder above my talon."

"You're really leaning into this," she said.

"I am," he said. "Can you help me into it?"

She gave a nod and came to stand behind him, putting his cloak onto his shoulders first. He turned and she tied the clasps, then lifted the skull onto his shoulder. The straps went across his chest and under his arm.

"You sure you don't want to find a squire for you?" Ophedia said, trying to remain all business.

"Why? Are you not up for this?"

"People are going to talk. They already are. A few drunks called me your pet."

"Anyone who knows you, knows you're nobody's pet," Aurín said.

Ophedia smirked.

"So what if they did?"

"What is that supposed to mean?" she replied, and over-cinched a strap. He gave a wince.

"It means no one makes any unwanted advances."

"You don't need to protect me," Ophedia said. "I can do that myself."

"I understand that, but I also don't need half the camp walking around with a limp."

"Half the camp, huh?"

"Yes," Aurín said flatly.

"How do you know that?" Ophedia asked, finishing the last strap and coming to stand before him. "Are they talking?"

"Because anyone with eyes to see can't help but see it."

"See what?" Ophedia asked.

Aurín locked eyes with hers for a long moment until an awkward flush rose in her cheeks. He averted his eyes before looking back at her, a hardness replacing whatever had just been there. "Never mind," he said. "Prepare your banner."

She gave him a curt nod and turned to take the banner leaning against a tent pole. The leather thong holding the black material to the pole had been bound well. She would have to discuss with Aurín later the idea of hiring the camp follower who had helped her. It would take the woman away from the less reputable tents that had sprung up the day after drills started.

She turned back to Aurín. "Be careful out there, Aurín," she said.

Aurín laughed.

"What's so funny?"

"I was about to say the same to you."

"Well, I'm not worried," she said. "I'm about as lucky as a black ynfald in a scrap."

"My mother used to say that to me," Aurín's said.

"I never would have taken you for a young brat looking for a fight," she said as she pulled open the tent to allow him to exit before her.

"I was the smallest child in town. I was always looking for a scrap to prove myself." As he exited, the men outside saluted. Their smirks dissipated when they saw the griffin skull on his shoulder. Ophedia walked behind him, bound standard in her hands. They came to the central fire, its crackle the only sound.

Aurín turned to two of Gat's men, the reins of sleipnirs in their hands.

"Porwus and Matalind, is it?"

They both saluted with their free hands.

"Please allow me to use your mounts. I'm leaving camp under your command," Aurín said. "No followers leave."

Porwus saluted.

"If we don't return until nightfall," Ophedia said, "there is a black gravon that has been begging for scraps near where the 7th is camped."

"We'll make sure it's run off," Matalind said.

"No. See it fed."

They both looked as her quizzically.

"We don't need the bad luck of it leaving."

This seemed to satisfy them.

Ophedia held the reins for Aurín as he mounted, then leapt up into her own saddle. Porwus handed her the banner pole.

"Lead the way, brave commander," she said mockingly.

Aurín kicked his sleipnir in the sides and they moved down the canyon.

"Feeding that gravon, huh?"

"Lowden and his son have been doing so."

"I didn't know you had such a soft spot for animals. Nor that

Lowden had a son."

"The boy snuck into camp with the followers. He's drawn to animals apparently."

"We'll see him into the 1st, to help with the stables then."

"I think the gravon is the same one I set free. If it followed me and has now attached to the boy, I'm fine with that."

"So long as it doesn't cause any problems."

Where their small canyon met the wider valley there was a large field. Everyone poured out into the space, and ordered into companies. They did so with few words, and soon, the entire regiment stood on array.

The sky was beginning to gray, washing everyone out. Aurín pulled out front. "We march for one mile. Coming round the culver, we'll be quite visible, and have three hundred yards to reach the dense trees. If we don't come across watchmen before that, then that will be the main line. Your captains have their orders. No battle cries until you're in the thickets."

He pulled through the front line of sleipnirs, and circled back in next to Ophedia.

"Care to show them the banner?"

She gave a nod and tugged on the leather strap. It came loose. She gave the pole a good shake, and it unwound itself. It was a plain black wool, but lightly embroidered across its surface was the start of the griffin rampant. Rather than two claws, though, just the one, obviously in the style of Aurín's talon.

A few of the men stifled a cheer upon seeing it.

"Are you ready?" Aurín muttered.

"Are you?" Ophedia laughed.

"I'm never ready to die."

"Then let's disallow them from taking our lives from us."

Aurín held his talon out, as he might a sword, and the sleipnirs moved quickly to a canter.

They ate up the mile across the plain, the few trees slowly increasing in density, the soldiers behind them running in a forced march.

"I hope they don't hear us," Ophedia said.

"It won't matter once we come within view."

They came round the bend as the entire valley opened up. Just as Aurín has stated, it was three hundred yards to the trees.

"Second Company!" Aurín hissed. "Left flank!" The men and women directly behind them rushed off toward the left, just as the sleipnirs kicked into a gallop and rushed at the tree line. Aurín and Ophedia let them ride on, and just before the rest of the regiment came to them, Aurín and Ophedia raced off to the left after the 2nd company.

Aurín kicked his mount into a gallop and ran out through the 2nd, and took the lead.

"Come on!" someone shouted just as several horns sounded from somewhere in the trees. In response, to drown out the sounding horns, the Black Claw Regiment's horns rang, twenty of them in all, and the battle cry went up in response. Aurín disappeared into the trees, his men rushing up behind him. Ophedia took up the rear, and entered the dense, tall bushes. She lost all track of direction, save she could see the canyon wall to her left.

The banner tried to catch on every tree, but somehow she kept it aloft. A few times it dropped out of the saddle spur she had crafted, but she quickly recovered. Men surged around her, vying for a way forward. Aurín could be heard shouting orders ahead. Ophedia then broke out of the tree line and into the open camp space.

Praetors of the Chalice milled about bleary-eyed as their attendants assisted them into their armor.

"Take them prisoner if you can!" Aurín shouted as he drove his sleipnir forward toward the largest tent.

Several Praetors counter-charged toward the line of men breaking out of the pine brush, their short spears held at the ready, but not with the wakefulness the attackers had.

One of the Praetors saw Ophedia on her sleipnir and rushed at her, his spear held low. Ophedia pulled back on the reins, and the steed reared up, his two forehooves flailing wildly at the advancing Praetor. The man backpedaled away, and up from behind three of the men following Ophedia rushed in and fell upon him with axes and short swords.

Aurín was on the ground now, wrestling with a Praetor. Blood covered his talon as the man under him dropped his spear, his face bloody from several lacerations.

Ophedia tried futilely to convince her sleipnir to move toward the command tent and finally gave up fighting against its panic. She leapt off the saddle and rushed up the slope. Two of the Black Claws were pulling a tent into the main campfire. It caught easily.

As Ophedia drew near, Aurín struggled to his feet, and was

hoisting the Praetor to his own. She thought his right arm bloodied by the talon, but she saw now that the blades on Aurín's grip had removed the Praetor's arm at the elbow. She blanched, and looked away, taking a deep breath, then back.

"Call the surrender!" Aurín shouted at his prisoner.

"I cannot!" the man said. "You'll have to kill me!"

"Aurín!" Ophedia yelled. "Don't make him a martyr!"

Aurín's eyes focused on her and gave the man next to him a look.

Aurín threw the man aside and rushed on. Ophedia followed after him, giving the Praetor a single backward glance. Two of his own camp servants had already rushed to his aid even as two Black Claws came to stand over the prisoners.

Ophedia and Aurín moved to the back side of the command camp. Five Praetors, unharmed, were bound and on their knees with ten Black Claws standing over them. A ledge looked out over the valley twenty feet below. The campfires cast shadows in the dawning morning, and through the trees the Chalician army was in full route fleeing southward. Aurín let out a relieved sob next to Ophedia. "We did it!"

Ophedia held her standard aloft and began to wave it back and forth, a cry of victory on her lips met by the men and women in the valley below.

28

Road Between

The violet haze sheaths my vision, and in that darkness are my hopes made manifest.

—ALLER EGAN RHIN, POPULAR POET OF MORRAINE

Seriah was grateful they'd reached better cared-for roads that Rallia told her were signposted to lead south to Sal-du-Markt in northeastern Œron. While there were fewer rocks to trip on during the day, every evening she still fell asleep to the sounds of the grumbling prisoners, unhappy with the plain oat gruel they were given every morning and night.

They walked with no more rest than the sleipnirs were given, even if at an easy pace. The cool spring weather prevented anyone from collapsing in the heat of the day, and Seriah was used to the travel, albeit usually at a more leisurely pace.

Daily, Rallia found the chance to check on her, as well as others nearby. That this Black Sentinel did so, and never a Chalician, was commendable.

The Praetors often could be heard in lively debate with one another, whether nearby or at the far ends of the line of prisoners, named Pilgrims to any passersby. One afternoon, a local Varean magistrate arrived with what sounded like an entire squadron of armed soldiers to discuss their passing. After words and coins were given from Provost Abrau, he left without further issue.

"Taking us from our city is kidnapping," one of the men nearby grumbled to another.

"You have been rescued and delivered, not kidnapped," a Praetor said with a snide superiority. It was Yanas Brodier.

"My family will be wondering where I have gone," the man persisted.

"If you treat your new lives in Œron with respect, you shall be allowed to send letters to those you have left behind. Perhaps they will come and join you."

"We have been taken against our wills," Seriah spoke up, "as prisoners of war. A war that has not been formally declared, and thus, an unjust kidnapping."

"Quiet, monk."

"At least you acknowledge what she is," Rallia added from nearby.

"A Black Sentinel coming to the aid of a Nifaran," Brodier said. "I never thought a heathen would side with the holy, even if heretical."

"Hardly a heathen," Rallia said. "Although I would imagine that considering myself a follower of Grissone is a heretical choice to you, regardless."

"I would. At a minimum, you are a blasphemer."

"I've found that a funny thing," Rallia said aloud, pulling closer to Seriah. "That the newer sect, still in swaddling clothes, would call those that follow centuries-old faiths to be the blasphemers."

"What do you know of it?"

"More than you, apparently," Rallia said. "I was raised in a paladinial poorkitchen. My grandfather often read the holy texts of Grissone, Aben, and Crysania before bedtime."

"Holy words are wasted on children's ears," Brodier scoffed.

"One time," Rallia added, "on a night my brother and I were particularly rowdy, he took out a Nifaran book of codes and read us quickly to sleep."

"I apologize our recorded codes were so boring," Seriah said with a giggle. "Fortunately, with all our eyes bound, no one knows when we're sleeping through the readings ourselves."

Others around the two women laughed.

"This is a serious conversation," Brodier complained.

"A little levity is always a welcomed breath of fresh air," Seriah said. "And you're only going to end this conversation as soon as you lose the upper hand."

"Or you'll just start orating when you feel the time is right," Rallia added.

"I welcome a discussion with those who have decided to walk paths other than the one our church has set," Brodier said. "It provides the opportunity for most to walk themselves further into their sins, exposing themselves for all to see. It provides the opportunity for others to see and learn from those mistakes."

"That's a fast way to force those around you to clam up," Rallia said. "I suppose it's a tactic to provide you more opportunity to talk."

"I'm not the orator many others are, but I do enjoy lifting rocks and seeing bugs and insects scatter when exposed to the light."

"We've quite the life to look forward to in Œron," Rallia replied. "The constant accosting and laying on of guilt is something I'm particularly looking forward to. I'm sorry I missed the opportunity in Mahn Fulhar, but I chose to flee. A mistake, I guess."

"You were in Mahn Fulhar?" Brodier asked. "Who did you escape with?"

"A few friends of mine. I'm sure the old man we freed from the captivity of the crown will be well on his way to Pariantür now."

"You..." Brodier spoke with rising excitement. "You are one of the Sentinels who flees from the Voktorra!"

"Not sure what you mean," Rallia said with a hint of smug satisfaction.

"Did you, by any chance, leave Mahn Fulhar with another Sentinel by the name of Ophedia?"

"The name rings a bell," Rallia offered cooly.

"My luck only continues to improve," Brodier said to himself.

"Isn't declaring luck considered blasphemy to most Abecinians," Rallia offered.

"No more from you," Brodier ordered. "I'm off to speak with Abrau. Say goodbye to any you call friend. You and I will be off to Mahn Fulhar by morning. My master will certainly be pleased that I bring you there myself."

He marched off.

"That was fun," Rallia said.

"What?" Seriah replied. "Antagonizing our captors?"

"We're in for a life of misery, if they get their way. I'm not allowing them to take my spirit."

"You truly consider yourself a Grissoni?"

"I do," Rallia said. "I've often considered whether I ought to have joined the Crysalas, but life had other plans."

"Being a coin-paid bodyguard?"

"It's never pushed holes in my belief. Every trade takes coin for services."

"The holy orders don't."

"What you do is not a trade," Rallia said. "It is a pantheon-ordained calling."

As the cool of night washed over them, a place was found and fires made. Chalician soldiers came around with their bland oats and gave them each a bowl of it. Most ate in silence. Rallia sat next to Seriah and quickly downed her food.

"I'm thinking of disappearing tonight," Rallia said. "Their best guards were watching us today. So tonight we'll be watched by their worst. And those were drowsing in the saddle. Will you go with me?"

"I'm a sight-bound monk. I'd hold you back."

"If any one of us will be made a martyr in Œron, it is you. We should see you safely away."

"To where?"

"There are some mountains nearby. I would guess we're far enough south we could cut across the bottom of Limae and into Sidierata."

"What of those left behind?" Seriah whispered.

"I can't take everyone. I am offering to help you escape."

"I would stay with them. I can offer them succor in our captivity."

"Rallia Clouw?" a Praetor called, arriving at the fire circle.

"What?" Rallia said with irritation in her voice.

"Come with me to the Provost's tent."

"They didn't stop in town," the old man at the bar muttered. "Just trundled on through this morning. Cart at the front." He spoke with another cloak-covered traveler, mud caked at the hem.

Dorian sat with his back to the bar, but Hanen and Ymbrys saw the other man clearly. Slate did not do a good job of hiding who he was. He asked questions with a desperate disregard for his own safety. The word was they were now only a day or two from the border of Œron. They had only just settled into their seats as Slate entered and didn't waste time asking around.

They had first come upon news of a group of Praetors making their way toward Œron with a large wagon, and several dozen men and women led by chains. They had been spoken of in hushed whispers, in fear that their own lives might be taken from them as the prisoners had. Dorian spent most of his time clicking his tongue in disappointment. Ymbrys and Hanen had done the larger share of questioning any town gossip willing to talk.

Whisper kept to Hanen's side, wary of the influx of ynfalds seen in southern Varea. Here they were smaller with scraggly hairs sticking out between their scales, giving Whisper the warning sounds of a beast on guard. There were few cörs here, and even fewer pests. The men who led their ynfalds around had similar appearances, edging for a fight if the chance was given.

"He just up and left," Hanen said as Slate stood and rushed out the door.

"We're not going to get any rest here ourselves, then," Dorian said.

"Oh?"

"He wants that armor back," Dorian said. "He won't stop, knowing he's only a few hours behind them."

"The road to the south of town here bends west," Hanen said. "We could cut across farmland in the dark and beat him there, if he is riding a sleipnir."

"You've been here before?"

"No. But I made plans for my failed caravan to travel to Sal-du-Markt. I recall seeing the name of this town, and considered that bend, and why it was there."

"Why was that?"

"Used to be a dense forest," a man at a table nearby said. "If you gotta cut through Dechard's pastures, better to do it by night, anyway."

"Thank you," Ymbrys said, turning and giving the man a silver.

"You after those Praetors too?" the man asked.

"They have my sister," Hanen said.

"Better get her before they reach Œron," the man added. "Those that get taken to become members of the Church of the Chalice don't come back."

"We'd better get going then," Hanen said, and rose.

Dorian and Ymbrys joined him at the door, just as Slate rode out down the street at a gallop, intently focused on the road ahead of him.

"He'll wear his mount out before he reaches them," Dorian said.

"Let us not assume anything," Ymbrys said. "That he is even here further shows how resourceful he is."

"Then let's go," Dorian said, leading the way to the edge of town.

The three of them traveled as they had these last many days, in helpful silence. Large fallen logs were quickly avoided or climbed over. Whisper moved as a black smear in the red light of Norlok, nearly full, overhead. They came to the large Dechard pastures. The shadows of aurochs lowed to one another in warning, with keener eyes than Hanen and Dorian, and shuffled out of their way as they crossed. At times, the sounds of beating hoofs came across the field and farther away still, firelight made brief appearances through the trees they raced toward.

They came to a small brook running through the field. Ymbrys called for their short pause while they filled drinking vessels and an extra pot. Ymbrys dropped a seed he swore by into each and they caught their breath while they waited for it to work.

Ymbrys took a testing taste, nodded, then handed the pot to Dorian, who drank deeply before handing it to Hanen. He winced past the bitterness the nut imparted. He slipped the pot into his own pack, and they kept going. They reached the forest at the other side of the field. A hundred yards later they came to the road which ran past them before taking another left. The pound of sleipnir hooves thundered from the south and Slate raced past them. In the woods that began again across the road, and far off another several hundred yards, firelights could be seen fed but dwindling in the late evening.

"Quick," Dorian whispered.

"Why bother?" Hanen said as they cross the road.

"What do you mean?"

"Slate is already a part of this now. We can approach, our breath regained, and assess the situation as it plays out."

"The way he rides," Ymbrys said, "he is angry and probably bears a tool or two. Move cautiously. He will not. Our cooler heads, as Hanen said, will win out."

They crept up to the edge of the camp, opposite where the road wound closer to it. Dorian gave a low chuckle and lowered himself to the ground next to a cart.

"What's funny?" Hanen asked.

"This cart," Dorian said. "This is it."

Hanen stood up next to the cart and felt around it. It had a large coffin-like box in its bed.

"Easy enough to reach, sure," Hanen said crouching back down. "But there is no easy way to move this cart away. We can't take it through the forest, and we can't push it through camp."

"Well, this is about as far as I thought through," Dorian said.

"And now," Ymbrys said, "we face that." He pointed past the cart, through the camp, to several Praetors near the largest fire.

"Who goes there?" they asked as a figure rode into camp.

"Slate," Hanen muttered. "Now where is Rallia?"

"Go look for her," Dorian said, and he and Ymbrys continued examining the entirely undefended wagon.

The Praetors stationed around the camp all moved toward Slate, who sat atop his sleipnir awaiting the rousing of whoever led the caravan.

Hanen slipped back out into the darkness and dropped his pack to the ground. He reached deep within, and pulled out the boneshroud. He pulled it over his head, then his Black Sentinel cloak over that. He could suddenly see better through the dark woods. Prisoners around smaller fires were rousing as the Praetors began shouting orders at the man on the sleipnir.

"You have taken what was ours," Slate shouted.

"And you're outnumbered."

"How little you know," Slate said, raising then swinging a hammer about his head.

"Nocc," Hanen muttered, and dropped flat on the ground.

"Get down!" he heard Dorian shout.

Not far from the center of camp, Hanen saw two figures at a dwindling fire watching Slate and the Praetors face off—Rallia and a Nifaran monk.

The hammer flew from Slate's hand, sailing overhead and into the central fire. First, it threw sparks, then a moment later, the pulse of the skyfall metal shuddered through the entire camp. Rallia threw the Nifara monk away as she herself was flung away from the center. The flames in every fire blew out like candles, leaving only ruddy embers for light. Praetors flew in every direction. Men and women screamed. The branches of the forest shuddered with dull, splintering cracks. Hanen held to the ground, face down, as it washed over him. He looked up and through the guidance of the hood he saw people trying to rise to their own feet.

"*Skyfall metal hammer?*" Searn said in his mind.

"Yes. Slate is here for the wagon, just as we are."

"*Who is 'we?' It's been some time.*"

"I've been pursuing Rallia and the Dreadplate, which the Praetors took from the city, along with Ymbrys and Dorian."

"*You're a fool.*"

"I've had little choice, and don't need your opinion right now."

Slate had dismounted from his sleipnir, and marched through the camp with determination. Hanen moved forward in a half crouch, past prisoners of war and fallen Praetors.

Slate stopped, saw the wagon, and visibly sighed in relief. He took up an unlit torch and touched it to embers in a fire pit and stirred. It took the flame and he held it up and walked toward his goal.

"Finally," Slate muttered.

"Yes," Dorian said, stepping up between him and the cart. "Finally."

"Who are you, old man?"

"The man who comes to see you off to Noccitan, for the trouble you've caused."

"But who are you?" Slate said.

"Your Prima Pater, you heretic."

"Ha!" Slate said. "You mean nothing to us." He took from his satchel an object.

Another figure stumbled up into the light of Slate's torch and stood next to Dorian. Rallia, her ears and nose trickling with blood.

Dorian gave her a half smile.

"That you think you can stand against us," Slate said, "is laughable."

Hanen moved slowly up behind him.

Rallia made the first move, rushing forward. The fallen Paladin stumbled backward, surprised by the girl's sudden advance. She tackled him and they both fell in a roll. Rallia rolled over the man and came back to her feet. She spun and fell backward on him with an elbow to the face. He cried out and clawed at her with one hand, taking hold of her arm, throwing her over himself, and getting atop her. He boxed her around the bleeding ear once, then raised his hand to do so again when Dorian took hold of his wrist.

"Enough," Dorian roared, and physically threw the man ten feet with inhuman strength.

Dorian advanced on the addled Slate, leaving Rallia where she was, groaning. Hanen scrambled forward toward Rallia, his hoods dropping off his head.

"Are you alright?" he asked, pulling her over onto her back.

"Hanen?" she muttered, dazed. "Hanen!" she repeated, as she shook her eyes clear. Her ear was bleeding profusely now.

"We have to get you out of here," Hanen said.

"Help Dorian," Rallia said. "That man can't have that cart."

Dorian and Slate flailed at each other, unarmed.

Hanen looked to the cart. Ymbrys was working on moving it, Whisper at his feet.

Hanen ran up to him. "Leave it, Ymbrys," Hanen said.

"Now is our chance," Ymbrys said. "Or it will be hidden within Œron, and it will take years to recover."

"We're surrounded. We can't move this out of camp before the Praetors recover. Let's save ourselves and go."

The qavyl gave him a quizzical look, eyes blank as though he debated with himself. Then, a realization dawned on him. "I see now."

"See what?"

Ymbrys looked around at the camp. Shadows moved toward them.

"It could be taken through to the Veld."

"What?"

"Get the gloves, quickly."

Hanen rushed out into the darkness. He thrust his hands down into Dorian's pack, then came back out with the rings in hand and returned to the cart. Beyond it, Rallia was stumbling toward the cart, now helping someone else through the darkness. The Nifaran.

"I've got the cart moving," Ymbrys said. "But it's heavy."

Hanen came next to him and they took hold of the wagon tongue, pushing it back and forth to get it rolling.

Rallia came alongside them.

"Help Dorian," Hanen ordered.

Rallia nodded and dove into the wrestling match that continued between the old man and heretic.

"What is happening?" Seriah cried.

Hanen ignored her, walked to the front of the cart, crouched, and thrust his hands through the rings. The gloves opened up a tear in the air in front of him. He pulled the hood up over his head.

"I don't know what to do," he whispered.

"What do you mean?" Searn asked.

"We're going to try and push the cart through into the Veld."

"That's a great idea," Searn said.

"The hole is too small."

"So make it bigger."

"I don't know how."

"Just do it."

"Easier said than done."

"Why not?"

"I don't know how!" Hanen shouted.

"The Veld is a realm of possibility. Don't try and overthink anything."

Hanen twisted his hands and the hole opened before him again. Rather than reach through the whole way, he put only his fingers through, took hold of the edges, and pulled back on the tear in the curtain of reality. The portal tore open.

"Yes!" Ymbrys shouted.

Hanen turned and took hold of the cart next to him, and pulled as Ymbrys shoved. The cart budged and rolled halfway through the hole.

"Where will we go?" Seriah cried out.

"Keep hold of the cart," Ymbrys said to her even as he continued to push.

"Who are you?" Seriah said to him.

"A friend."

"A qavyl," Hanen said.

Seriah visibly started at his voice. "I can't. No!"

"Holy Nefer," Ymbrys said, "I ask you to trust me."

"I will not trust him," Seriah said, pointing toward Hanen. "He is evil. Searn lives!"

"Go with us, or go with the Praetors."

"Hanen?" Rallia said, now standing next to Seriah, gawking at her brother. "What are you wearing?"

"I'll explain later," Hanen said. "Can we please go?"

Dorian stood over the addled Slate, groaning from the ground. He looked toward the cart, his eyes puffy, a smile on his face. The smile dropped as he took in the sight: the purple glow of the world beyond the portal, and the hood on Hanen's head.

"What evil is this?!" someone cried. It was a Praetor. He approached with several others behind him.

"Move the cart!" Hanen ordered.

Ymbrys shoved, Hanen pulled, and even Seriah provided leverage, and they got almost all of the cart through. Rallia and Dorian had turned to face the Praetors.

Seriah stepped through onto the purple sand beyond, her hand on the cart, and her head darting blindly around trying to take in her new surroundings.

Through the portal, Hanen continued to pull, the cart having trouble rolling in the soft purple sand, making it even harder to move. A figure rushed toward the cart, and threw himself under it, crawling through into the Veld. It was Slate. Hanen kicked at him and Whisper nipped. The man struggled away, trying to get to his feet.

"Our gloves!" he roared, ignoring the ynfald at his feet and pulling out a dagger, rushing at Hanen in a blind rage.

Hanen backpedaled through the deep sand. Whisper bit at the leg of Slate and he tripped forward as Hanen's gauntleted fist came up and took him in the jaw, knocking him out cold. He fell into Hanen and the two of them dropped in a tangle. Throwing his hand behind him to try and catch himself, one of the gloves fell from Hanen's hand, and the portal closed suddenly.

The tongue of the wagon cracked and disappeared, leaving Dorian, Ymbrys, and Rallia to face the Praetors of the Chalice on the other side. Hanen, Seriah, Whisper, and the now unconscious Slate lay beside the cart laden with the Dreadplate in the despairing silence of the Veld.

29

Interludes

The silver line had grown to a strong glowing thread. It quivered and leapt as though what would be found on the other end moved with intention. It began jerking wildly this way and that, and Loth had to stop relying on the thread and instead move in the general direction it led.

Several days prior he had carried the skull in his arms through a basin in which odd fish swam through the air. He'd slept in the dark shadow of a rock in the center of the basin while a massive form circled about him, curious, but not seeking to harm him. By morning it was gone.

A deep canyon cut across their path now, and he walked up the length of it for a day while the skull in his arms bemoaned how slowly he moved. The crevasse gave no signs of ending. The skull's complaints threatened to drive him mad until he finally gave in and scrambled down into the crack to begin the work of going back up the other side. Rodents with tails thrice their body length peered out from behind rocks, and gave out warning to others. When one peeked out too close for comfort, he saw it bore not two eyes upon its head, but at least a dozen.

At times, the creatures went silent, as a dark shadow stalked through the rocks after them. He only caught sight of the predator once as it moved across the rocks as a flat shadow with rippling edges. He hoped he would not encounter its smothering form while he slept.

The ascent up the other side took three days. The lip of the top taunted him the length of the final day. When he came to an unclimbable cliff edge, he worked his way slowly along it.

"*Up,*" the skull rattled.

"I can't."

"*You must! I am close!*"

"I can't climb up! Stop shouting at me!"

The skull growled. "*Hold me up to see.*"

He did. The empty sockets of the skull stared at the stone wall. Suddenly, there was a vibration moving through Loth's hands, then holes sunk into the stone. In other spots, foot holds jutted out.

"How did you do this?"

"*Anything can be done here,*" the skull said. "*You've only the need.*"

"The need?"

"*Go up.*"

He wrapped up the skull in the cloak over his back and climbed, hand over foot to the edge.

Before him, the form of a silver figure hung, floating in the air. It lay there in repose, four feet off the ground, missing arms at the elbows.

"What is it?"

"*Important,*" the skull said. "*I can feel it.*"

They approached and examined its features. Every surface shone in stunning brilliance. Loth ran his hand along it. Where a helmet might be, it lay open.

"*Show me,*" the skull said, and Loth held it up to see better.

He circled the figure again. Then, he held up the skull to look into the openness at the neck.

"*Closer,*" the skull said.

He pressed it right up to the gap. The silver armor suddenly shuddered. The skull fell from his hands and into the chest plate.

"No!"

The mirrored armor lurched. He tried to reach up and take hold of the skull, but it had lodged into place.

"Come on..." he muttered, trying to pry it out. Then, a hole suddenly appeared in the air by the head. Through it, the dark of night and flames from dwindled campfires could be seen. From the skull, the silver line they had been following led out of that hole into the night.

Loth leapt away, toward a nearby bush, crouching behind it. The silver armor lurched again, then floated into the hole. As it passed through the hole in the air, it turned into a wooden cart.

Two figures came through with the cart: a man wearing a black cloak and a Nifaran monk. Clinging to the bottom of the cart was another, a man he knew well enough: Primus Slate.

"I don't understand," Loth muttered.

When the skull did not reply back, he knew he was free now of its constant muttering and whispers. He was stranded in the Veld.

Rallia leapt down with a splash into the riverbed below, Dorian coming soon after. Ymbrys paused and considered the woods behind them, eyeing the darkness for pursuers.

"Now tell me, where did they go?!" Rallia cried. "What just happened?"

"The Veld," Ymbrys said from above. "And he took that Nifaran friend of yours with him."

"Seriah."

"That was Seriah?" Dorian asked, sipping at water from the stream.

"Yes, why?"

"Who wore the cloak? It looked like the boneshroud," Dorian said.

"It..." Rallia faltered. "It was the boneshroud."

"Seriah is stuck once more at the mercy of he who bears the boneshroud."

"He will not harm her," Rallia said. "I hope."

"What makes you think that?"

"Because of who wears it," Ymbrys said.

"Who wears it?" Dorian asked.

"You know who," Ymbrys said. "He had the gloves on, too."

Dorian did not answer. They stood in dark silence for a long while.

"When did Hanen get the gauntlets?" Rallia asked finally.

"Apparently he took one from Slate the night his people attacked us. Soon after he went for the other," Ymbrys said.

"And the boneshroud?" Dorian asked.

"I fear he has had it since the night that Searn VeTurres died."

The Paladins rode from the city without a backward glance. At the top of the wall, four men watched them go.

"They ride under Grissone's protection," Dikun Polun said.

"Jined Brazstein is blessed by Grissone," Beltran Cautese said. "So long as they follow his prompting, yes, I believe they do."

"On to business," Dane said, turning from the view to look at the three of them. "Dikun, I would ask you to stay here and run the House of Bread. See too if contact can be made with any survivors to the east, and invite them to stay with you."

"If they should prove to be Moteans?"

"If you suspect them to be so, then send them to Waglÿsaor as Paladins. We shall take that as a sign of your suspicion and deal with them as such."

"What of him?" Dikun muttered, indicating the fourth man, standing twenty feet down the wall.

Vathan Ebithai no longer wore the trappings of a Praetor, but the brown robe of a Simplist.

"He will return with Beltran and I, in order to enter into our sect," Dane said.

"And should agents be sent to silence him for his treason against his church?"

"Let us pray his faith in Grissone and Anka flourishes and protects him."

"Let us pray," Beltran added, "he has made the right decision, and his god ordains this change from one faith to another."

"A choice of faith is always honored by the gods," Dane said. "It is we men who forget that and sully our own paths."

Each day, Panza drove them at a grueling pace. He eschewed the use of wagon or sleipnir, and insisted that Alodda and Marn walk as fast as Marn's limp allowed them. Seeing anyone else on the road offered the only respite, as in an effort to remain inconspicuous, he would slow down to a more leisurely pace. His

DREAD KNIGHT

haste had cost them half a day when a bad bit of advice had them on the wrong road, corrected at the next village, and forcing them to take a woodsman path to reconnect with the road they should have taken in the first place. Their evenings only offered them a meager meal paid for by Panza, and a small and uncomfortable bed which had them asleep in moments, only to be roused from a dead sleep at sunrise the next day.

Finally, they crested a rise as the soft, salty tang of sea air breezed above them, revealing the town of Boscolón. When Panza saw it, he merely stated the town's name, and continued on down the hill. Marn stopped and sat on a log left on the roadside for travelers.

"We made it," Alodda said, giving a sob of relief and falling next to Marn.

"So long as Panza keeps his word, we'll be rid of him as soon as we make contact with the man I'm to deliver the message to."

"Do you fear he may not keep to his word?"

"We cannot know. He is a spy, and we know he is. Our lives may be forfeit as soon as he is able to rid himself of us."

"You don't seem worried."

"No matter what happens to me, as hard as life is, I know that I have a protection over me and my family."

"Your faith in the pantheon," Alodda alluded.

"Unfortunately, no."

"What do you mean?"

Marn sighed, looking toward the sea, and glancing down the road to Officer Panza, who'd continued on without a backward glance.

Marn turned to Alodda.

"I've been fearing this conversation for some time now, and every day the weight of it presses upon me."

"Then out with it," Alodda offered with a smile.

"If we're to pursue and find Hanen, you need to know about our family's background. Hanen won't like that I've told you... I'm not sure if Hanen has even told Rallia yet. But it is time they both knew. You ought to know, if you're to tie your fate to ours."

"What is it?" Alodda pressed.

"Do you know about the Protectorate Wars?"

"Of course. My father told many stories of his time serving in it."

"Then you know about the Apostate, the Necromancer."

Alodda shivered. "Yes."

"He had a daughter. She escaped after the wars and went into hiding, fearing that the Deceiver had designs for the Apostate's lineage. A few years later, her own wayward daughter had a son at a very young age. When he was but a babe, a zvolder crept into his crib and bit his leg, laming it. It was taken as a sign that the Deceiver still had designs for the family...and had marked my leg as a reminder."

"You?" Alodda gasped. "You're the grandson of the Necromancer?"

"Great grandson. And Hanen is his great-great grandson. I fear he is just as ill-fated as I am."

"Is that why you became a monk?"

"To pray for all our souls." Marn nodded. "For Hanen's, and now for yours."

"Hanen is a good man," Alodda said. "I will seek him out and we can discuss this news, and decide the best way forward."

"You're not mad at me for not telling you sooner?"

"I wish I had more time to process this, but no, I'm not mad. I understand why you didn't say something."

"Thank you," Marn said. "That's a weight off my chest."

"I'm sure it is." She looked down the hill. "Panza just realized we're not with him. He's going to be irate."

"Let him be. As soon as we've done what we've been sent to do, let's flee from him, and continue on."

"To find Hanen and Rallia," Alodda confirmed.

"Hanen and Rallia," Marn said with a weak smile.

Nikrest was a larger town that might someday easily grow into a city. The relaxed attitude of the citizens told Ophedia that nothing much ever changed, save the ebb and flow of miners who came to the slopes seeking fortunes, and spending those fortunes just as quickly in the local taverns and bawdy inns. Not two days ago, the Chalicians had held a camp outside the town walls, from which they'd berated the inhabitants. Word was that miners had taken turns atop the walls making lewd remarks to the blushing soldiers.

Now, with the Chalicians in full rout from the nearby valleys, a semblance of normalcy had returned. Ophedia walked with a handful of men granted leave to enjoy the sights of town, having taken over the abandoned camp of the Chalicians. Aurín was with the city leaders, negotiating their assistance in the campaign to oust the Chalicians farther south, although Ophedia knew all he really wanted was proffered funds and a few men who knew the nearby mountains to act as scouts. He intended to send the 6th and 7th out on routine patrols and ensure no stragglers from the Chalician army acted as burrs in Limae's saddle.

Lowden and Valden Dakmor walked alongside one another in front of her. The younger man didn't seem much surprised at the sights and sounds of the place, indicating just how jading the city of Haven had been. Ophedia eyed a pair of women leaning out of an upper window with a cowed look in their eyes. Three women in brown robes watched the brothel from across the street, handing out food to several destitute men sitting along the wall.

"Everywhere you go..."

"Did you say something?" Lowden asked over his shoulder.

"Nothing," Ophedia asked. "Just commenting to myself."

They passed through a small market. Hawkers shouted out the sale of tin, silver, and hunting claims in the mountains.

Ophedia passed by without a second glance.

They came to a busy tavern where several men and women from the Black Claw Company stood on the street with drinks in their hands as they talked. Girls moved among them with fresh mugs brimming over onto trays.

"Captain Dakmor!" someone called out.

The Dakmors crossed to the man. Ophedia took longer to cross the street, taking in the rest of the scene and eyeing the street for trouble.

"Yes, Captain, free!" the man was explaining as a girl walked by and put mugs of frothy ale into Lowden and Valden's hands.

"Our company standard-bearer," Valden said, indicating to Ophedia. "Word is she can put away five pints."

"My reputation ran ahead of me, did it?" Ophedia asked.

Valden's eyes popped. "You really can?"

"I can drink any man under the table," she said.

The barmaid eyed Ophedia's frame with an arched eyebrow. "I doubt that," the girl said.

Ophedia gave her a stern look. "Captain Dakmor, anyone here who runs a clean book?"

"Clean book?" Lowden asked. "No. But I run a good book." Ophedia laughed.

"I've been meaning to teach Valden how to do so," Lowden added, as he pulled a book from his chest pocket. Valden was doing the same, giving his father a sheepish look.

"What's that?" Lowden asked.

"I run the book for the street chips game run by the Boys of Bower Street."

Lowden gave him an impressed look. "Alright, son," Lowden said. "3-to-1 on Ophedia to start. We'll modify once we have a taker."

He marched into the inn without another word, Valden and Ophedia following in his wake.

A table was cleared and Ophedia was seated. Five drinks were placed before her, and soon the inn had risen to a fever pitch as men goaded their fellows to join the drink. A large man from the 2nd was pressed through, already looking bleary-eyed. His paunch pressed up against the table, and he reeked of Limaean Strong Ale already.

"4-to-1 on the girl," Lowden called out. "2-to-1 on Braff."

Ophedia smirked and ran her finger around the top of an ale, not taking her eyes off the man.

The bets came to a standstill and the mark was given. Both dropped back their ales. Braff had finished his before she'd made it halfway through the swill. He was working on the second as she placed it down.

"Bring something better than this," she asked the barmaid nearby.

"Finish him and win me coin, and I will," the barmaid winked.

Ophedia nodded and dropped the second one back faster.

Braff gave a loud belch and went for the third. Ophedia had the third half emptied as Braff hit his own limit and lost everything onto the floor. Ophedia finished the third as the cheer went up alongside even more groans.

"Get that fat man outta here!" someone called.

"Pour me some Limaen Strong," Ophedia said to the woman. She looked around. "Anyone got the stomach to go for more?"

A powerfully built Black Claw sat across from her. "I'll take you on, del Ishé."

Ophedia glanced past the man to a group of others who had just pressed into the tavern.

She held up a finger to Lowden nearby. He leaned in.

"What are my odds?"

"I'm giving Ragor 3-to-1. And for you we're paying out 5-to-1."

"Alright. See those five men who just walked in?"

"I do."

"Bring them to the front to watch. By force if necessary, but quietly."

"Yes, ma'am," he said, and disappeared into the crowd.

Ophedia looked at the man across from her and lifted the first of the smaller drinking vessels placed in a line. "You ready to wake up tomorrow?"

He smirked and dropped the first one back.

Ophedia did the same, then dropped two more in quick succession. They kept pace with each other through five drinks when the first wave slammed through Ophedia. She reached for the next with a laugh and lifted it to her seeking lips. Ragor was no longer looked confident, but rather, impressed.

"We still toe-to-toe?" she slurred.

Dakmor put a hand on her shoulder. She looked up to see that Ragor had stopped, staring at her dumbfounded, drinks still untouched. She was two ahead.

A cheer went up, Ragor was dragged away, and another was forced down into the chair across from her.

She tried to clear her eyes to get a good look at the man she had seen walk into the inn. He had a terror in his eyes, his mustache twitching under his nose, as black as his beard. He wasn't in uniform, but dressed as a commoner.

"Three of them got away, but we caught this one and one other," Lowden said. "The other is named Lerot, but this one? I could tell by this one's look that he knew you."

"He does. Probably a spy told to stay in town as the Praetors fled."

The man across from her had a split lip and swelling eye that would be black by morning. The Black Claws pressed in around them at the word "spy."

Ophedia lifted two of the drinks in front of her and held one out to the man across from her. "Care to play a little game, Captain Navien?"

Part 4

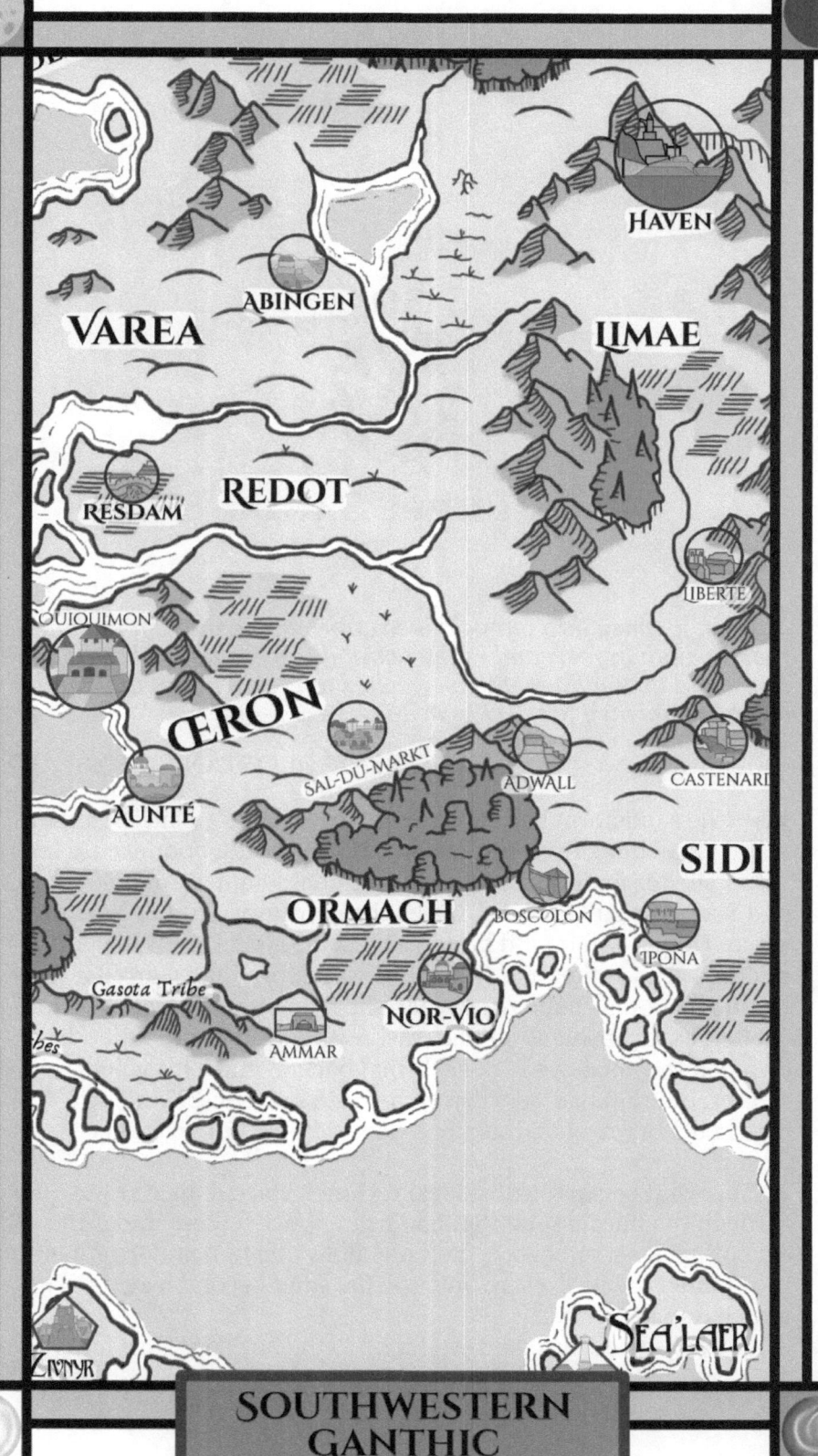

30

Purple Sand

My first journey into the Veld was unprompted and left my mind reeling, both in fear, and in the possibilities. I did not sleep for days, and the madness that scratched at the corner of my mind led me to journey to the Oruche Marches.

—JOURNAL OF OLLISTAN GŒRNSTADT

The sandstorm had raged for hours. Hanen's Black Sentinel cloak hung from one end of the wagon as a poor excuse for shelter underneath. Seriah whimpered quietly at one end, and Slate was still out cold, his hands now buried under the sand where Hanen had bound him to a wheel. Both he and Whisper huddled at the other end. When the windstorm had started it had taken most of his patience to goad the monk under the wagon for shelter, as inconsolable as she was. As the wind grew louder, he'd dropped the hood of the boneshroud back to make his voice clearer, but that had only driven her into hysterics. Now she clutched at a wheel on the other side, sniffing, but no longer crying.

The wind began to subside, and Hanen started digging out through the purple sand that had nearly buried them under the cart. Whisper scratched at the sand alongside him and together they pulled themselves up onto the flat sand beyond leaving Slate and Seriah beneath.

In every direction, sand stretched to the horizons save for one, broken by a black crack into the earth. A handful of shrubs stuck their tops up out of the sand here and there. Another gust of wind kicked up and Hanen pulled the boneshroud up over his head to protect himself.

"We finally made it," Searn's voice said into his head.

"Where are we?" Hanen replied.

"The Veld."

"I know that," Hanen said, looking up at the twilit sky. Stars blinked in and out of view as undulating bands of light moved across the expanse. "But where?"

"Likely in a corresponding space to Kallattai. Try opening another gate and see for yourself."

Hanen took up the rings. He pushed them on and they became gauntlets. Pressing apart the space before him, a hole opened, but not onto the forest he had fled from into the Veld. Instead, he was met by a blast of heavy air smacking him in the face. He braced himself as the wind continued to billow from the other place. Beyond, he could see flecks of dust glowing on what appeared to be cave walls.

He pushed his hand through and the silver of the Mirrorplate appeared.

"Close it," Searn demanded.

Hanen did.

"Was that Noccitan?" Hanen surmised.

"Yes."

"How?"

"Maybe by coming through to the Veld you pushed the Mirror into the next world in a sequence."

"Then can we get back to Kallattai?"

"I don't know," Searn said. "I'm going to think on that."

Searn's voice no longer spoke from inside his head but from beside him. Hanen turned and saw a smudge of darkness next to him. He startled and stumbled backward several steps.

"How?!" Hanen asked. "Searn?"

The shade held up its hand, or the smear of it at least, to consider it.

"That blast from Noccitan. It knocked me from the cloak?" It turned to move, but could not. Hanen looked down at the ground and realized he cast no shadow. He unclasped the cloak, held it out, and dropped it on the ground. Searn's shade stayed attached to the cloak by the form of his legs. Hanen's own shadow now appeared on the sand.

"Interesting," Searn said. "Now pick me up."

"Why should I?" Hanen asked.

"You can't just leave me here," Searn said.

"But I can put you away."

"You really can't risk that now, can you," Searn said. "You're in the Veld now. You have no idea what lurks here."

"What lurks here?"

"I'm not telling you if we can't come to an agreement."

"Later," Hanen said, picking up, but not donning the cloak.

"What are you doing?"

"Going back under the cart to see if I can talk some reason into the monk."

"Good luck with that," Searn said mockingly.

He walked over to the cart, tossed the boneshroud into its bed, and slipped back under the wagon.

"Who's there?" Seriah asked weakly.

"Hanen," he replied, sitting cross-legged at the other end.

Seriah took a quickening breath. "Who were you talking to out there?"

"Talking to?" Hanen asked.

"I heard you out there talking to someone else, but I could only hear you talking."

"No one," Hanen said.

"You're lying," Seriah said. "Tell me the truth. Do you have Searn's boneshroud?"

Hanen thought on his answer.

"Well?" she pressed.

"Yes," he blurted.

"Why?"

"It...was given to me."

"So?" Seriah accosted. "Why wouldn't you wrap it around a stone and drop it in the sea?"

"Because it protects me," Hanen said.

"Protects you?"

"From the dark gods."

Seriah gasped. "What?"

"It shields me," Hanen said. It was a relief to speak it aloud. "Among other things, it makes it so the gods can't see me. It covers me from their view, so they can't make me do things against my will."

"Did it shield Searn from them?"

"I think so," Hanen said.

"Then why did he kill so many good people?"

"Because he wanted to shield all of the world from the gods' influence."

"As though the Black Coterie wouldn't use him to kill all but themselves, and then destroy him in the process."

"He's gone now," Hanen said. "So that leaves it with me."

"To do what?"

"I don't know. But now we have this wagon bearing the black armor, and no way to budge it from the sand. I need to figure out how to move it, so we can hide or destroy it."

"You can't," a voice coughed from between them.

Seriah screamed.

Slate laughed a dusty laugh.

"Who is that?" Seriah asked, turning her head to try and pick out who had spoken.

"He goes by the name of Slate," Hanen said. "He's a Paladin who had the armor in his possession at one point, and he's been trying to get it, just as I and those who traveled with me have."

"You're a fool if you think you can destroy the armor," Slate choked. "Nothing can destroy it. That's the point."

"What do you know about it?"

"Why should I tell you?" Slate asked.

"I've got you tied up with knots the best fisherman can't untie, and if you want me to go and find food, you'd better treat me well."

"I do need water," Slate conceded.

"Seriah, would you like to come out from under the wagon?" Hanen asked.

She gave a nod and awkwardly crawled across the space.

Hanen crawled up out of the hole. Whisper was outside standing guard.

"Are you leaving us here?" Slate croaked.

"Yes," Hanen replied.

Seriah held a hand up and Hanen took it, pulling her free of the sand.

She came to a standing position and dusted herself off with one hand while she propped herself against the wagon.

"Why were you so quick to listen once I said the boneshroud protected me?" Hanen asked.

"Because two weeks ago, if I had been given the chance to use it for the same reason, I'd have done so, but not now."

"Why not now?"

"You wouldn't believe me if I told you. Where are we?"

"The Veld," Hanen said.

"How?"

"I bear gloves that allow me to open up a door into the Veld. Although I'm not sure how to get back now."

"You're not worried I'm going to run off?"

"Blindfolded as you are, you'd fall into a crack in the earth."

He went to place an arm on her, and thought better of it. "I'll leave Whisper here with you."

"Whisper?"

"My ynfald."

With that, Whisper nestled up to her. She laughed in surprise.

"Seriah," Hanen said.

"Yes?"

"I'm sorry."

"For what?" Seriah pressed.

"For what Searn did to you. To everyone."

"Then don't be him."

Hanen walked to the edge of the crevasse and glanced back toward the wagon. Seriah stood leaning against the side, with Whisper next to her. The edge of the crevasse gaped several hundred feet across, a cleft deep enough that he saw only blackness. Looking out past the crack, he could see mountains to the far northeast. He turned back toward the wagon. To the south, the horizon sat as a dark smudge. Wind was starting to pick back up. He walked to the wagon.

"It's empty for miles in every direction."

"The wagon feels buried under all this sand," Seriah said.

"It is," Hanen confirmed and pushed against it. To his surprise, the wagon moved several feet, casting sand away from it. Slate hollered from beneath in protest. Hanen peeked under to see the sand had shifted to fill the hole as Slate kicked his way free. The sand had completely disappeared, leaving only the flat purple ground of packed earth.

"How did that happen?" Hanen asked.

"How did what happen?" Seriah asked.

"It's not loose sand anymore. Just packed earth. Why did it change?"

"Because someone willed it to be so," Searn said, his shade

smudge next to him.

Hanen abruptly pulled his hand back from the wagon, where his hand had fallen on the boneshroud, and Searn disappeared.

The wind licked at Hanen's hair with just enough susurrus to drown out the sounds of Slate and Seriah asleep under the wagon. The black gauntlets on his hands flexed with his moving grip as he considered his next move. He drew a negligent line in the sand with the tip of his armored finger and the line shifted to something perfectly straight. Curious at this, he drew a circle and it came out as perfect as he imagined it. He chuckled, and with a hand wiped the sand clear.

He drew four circles and wrote next to each a name:

Kallattai
Veld
Noccitan
Lomïn

He sat up straight and opened the air before him with his gloves. From within the black hole, a blast of air came from beyond. He pressed a tentative hand through and the gauntlet became silver. He pulled his hands back and closed the gate.

He looked down at his drawing, and saw that the circle he had marked Noccitan had turned black.

He touched the next circle marked Lomïn and considered how he might open up the gate to that place, if it even existed.

"Stupid to think it doesn't," Hanen said. "I've seen Noccitan, so it must."

He held his hand up and touched at nothing, then made a motion like pinching the edge of a corner of a book page, and pulled back. The air opened, but rather than opening to the blackness of Noccitan, or even back to the forest in Kallattai, it revealed a gray place. It took all his strength to pull back further on the edge. Beyond gray walls, around a corner, a soft light glowed, almost greenish. He glanced down to see the circle marked Lomïn begin to turn a shade of green and then back to plain lightly-hued purple sand as the hole before him wrenched free of his hand and slammed shut. His arm ached and he shook it free and turned back to the ground.

"So it's not easy to get to Lomïn, and Noccitan is easy. Why? We came from Kallattai easily enough." He closed his eyes and pictured the forest they had come from, then put both hands up, touched the air, and pulled at nothing. The air before him tore open and through the ragged tear he could see the forest beyond. The bright light of day revealed now long-dead fire pits. There was no one in sight.

The tear fought back against him, but he had a better grip on it and held it open. If he could find a way to keep it open, he could push the cart back through.

Whisper suddenly jumped to his feet, startled by something, and Hanen spun around. The crack in the air slammed shut again.

"Open it back up," Slate said. He stood at the other end of the cart, a knife held at Seriah's throat, his other hand over her mouth.

"What are you doing, Slate?" Hanen asked.

"You're opening that tear back up and we're returning from this godsforsaken place to the real world."

"You don't have the gauntlets. Leave her be or so help me I'll leave you here."

"You don't tell us what to do," Slate said, a wild look in his eyes. "You'll bow before us when we are through."

"What is that supposed to mean?"

"We are king of all those lesser than us!"

"I knew another who said something similar," Hanen said.

"Well you should have remembered," Slate said. "We shall continue to remind you until you bow!"

"Ghoré?" Hanen asked tentatively.

The gleam in Slate's eyes went wild.

"You're Ghoré?"

"We are here," Slate hissed.

"Put the monk down," Hanen said calmly.

"Take off those gloves, or open the gate to Kallattai."

"If you harm her," Hanen said, "imagine what her goddess will do to you." He wasn't sure he believed his own words.

"I care not what this fool does to her," Slate hissed. "I am Deathless!"

"But you don't wish to draw the ire of other gods."

The wild look dissipated and Slate's eyes shone with fear.

"Slate. Let her go."

"I... Give us the armor," Slate said. "We've worked too hard to lose it now."

"Let her go and we can talk about this. Harming her will do nothing to help you. Her goddess will speak ill of you in the afterlife."

Something dawned on Slate as the mad look in his eyes returned.

"Not if she is no longer a sacred member of Nifara's cult," he said with sneering spite.

"What?" Hanen said.

Slate took his hand off Seriah's mouth. She was sobbing, the cloth over her eyes soaked with tears. He reached up and took hold of the blinder.

"No," Seriah cried out. "Please!"

Slate appeared to be debating with himself, his face flashing from a mad look to one of anguish. The man scowled in dark resolution, took a firm hold of the blindfold, and yanked it up and off the girl's head.

Seriah screamed and fell to the ground, her hands going over her face. Slate took hold of her cowl and forcefully pulled back, then took hold of her face.

"Look!" he screamed. "Look injustice in the eye and know that there is nothing good. Nothing true."

Through the tears filling her eyes, Seriah's eyes were forced open, and the purple light of the sky stared down cold and emotionless on her.

She did not speak, only gibbered in terror and shame.

Whisper suddenly darted forward. Hanen shook free any hesitation and followed. The ynfald took hold of Slate's heels. Hanen's gauntleted fist met the man's chin as Slate's hands dropped from Seriah, twisting like claws and grasping at Hanen's gauntlets, almost entirely unaware that he was even there. Avarice took hold of the madman and spittle-flecked his mouth. Hanen took hold of Slate's wrist and saw then the bone ring shoved violently up onto his finger, the skin still angry and unhealed around it.

Slate lashed out, not feeling the pain of Whisper at his heels nor the gauntleted grip Hanen had on his wrist. His other clawing hand scratched at Hanen and his heels kicked at the ynfald. Seriah scrabbled away on hands and knees, crying out in fear, rage, and remorse.

"Give us those gloves!" Slate screeched. He tried to pry into the gauntlets to gain hold of them and the two of them toppled to the ground. Hanen shoved and kicked and got free enough to gain the upper hand.

"You won't get them," Hanen shouted as their roll came to a stop and he tore himself off Slate and stood.

Slate looked at him, unaware of anything around him. With a roar, he rushed at Hanen.

Hanen put his hands up into the air before him and opened the hole in the air to the blackness of Noccitan. Slate rushed into Hanen, his hand outstretched. With one gauntlet, Hanen took hold of the man's wrist and swung him round and through the rent. Slate tripped, and fell through the gap into Noccitan. Hanen opened his left gauntlet and the hole closed suddenly. Slate's hand and wrist fell freely into Hanen's own, severed cleanly. It writhed for a moment, then fell still.

Hanen dropped it into the sand and then fell to his knees, waves of exhaustion rippling through him.

He shot a glance over at Seriah, curled up on the sand and crying. Whisper had circled up next to her, their backs touching to let her know he was there.

Hanen felt sick to his stomach. The clenching, angry hand lying on the sand beckoned him to touch it. Not a drop of blood came from that hand; the bone ring on the finger appeared just as clean, but at the same time screamed of its own filth.

He stood to his feet and lost his balance as whatever blood was left in his head rushed out and he stumbled to the wagon. He took deep breaths as the stars cleared from his eyes and he turned to where Seriah still lay, quietly crying.

"I'm sorry," he muttered.

She did not reply.

"Seriah," Hanen said louder, "I'm sorry."

"Leave me alone," Seriah moaned.

"I'm not leaving you here."

"Leave me alone," Seriah repeated. "Just go."

Hanen thought better of replying and circled the wagon, lowering himself to the ground and dropping the gauntlets off his hands. The claw of a hand lay nearby, desiccating before his eyes.

He reached out and tentatively touched a finger and a flash of blackness washed over his vision. Through the blackness, he saw fanged teeth, the snarling rage of Ghoré.

He tore his hand away, his fingertip blanched white and numb. The color slowly returned.

"I shouldn't do that again without the shroud on," he muttered.

He left the hand where it lay, and stood. As he turned, he could have sworn it looked as though someone, or something, was peeking from the ledge of the canyon. Whoever it was, disappeared. Hanen turned back to the cart, reached into the bed, and touched the boneshroud. Searn's shade appeared next to him, but didn't say anything. It just sat there.

"There appears to be someone watching us from nearby," Hanen said.

Searn didn't respond.

"Slate took the monk's blindfold off her head."

Nothing.

"I shoved Slate through into Noccitan, and he left behind Ghoré."

"Ghoré?" Searn asked.

"So we're talking now?" Hanen muttered.

"What about Ghoré?"

"I think the ring containing Ghoré's shade was shoved onto Slate's finger. Closing the gate to Noccitan severed his hand at the wrist and left it on this side."

"How do you know it's Ghoré."

"Slate said so, and when I touched it, I saw a passing flash of his face."

"Don't do that again without the shroud on," Searn said, "or you'll regret it."

"Looking out for me now, huh?"

"Whatever gave you the impression that I want something bad to happen to you? If something did, I might be stuck here for decades or centuries. I don't love that idea."

"Hanen?" Seriah called.

"I have to go. We'll talk again when the monk is asleep," Hanen said, removing his hand from the boneshroud.

He circled the wagon.

"Nefer?" Hanen said.

She sat up and turned toward him. She looked at him with deep emerald eyes burning red with hot tears.

"I'm no monk of Nifara anymore. My eyes have been unbound."

"That's not true," Hanen said. "You can rebind them. You broke no vow."

"You know nothing," Seriah said flatly. "Nothing about me. Nothing about my order. Nothing about the shame I faced even before this day. Nothing about how the worlds work, or else you would never have taken up those gloves and cloak in the first place. Look what a life of obsession did to... him."

Hanen considered the hand still sitting there.

"Where did he go?" Seriah asked cooly.

"I shoved him into Noccitan."

Seriah gasped, then shuddered and nodded. "Good."

"What happens to him there?"

"If he's lucky, he'll wander for all time. If he isn't, perhaps they'll find him and the Judge will sentence him to a hole from which he'll never come out."

31

Never Death

As final decision of your faith and dedication will you bind your eyes, to show that you are blind to prejudice and favoritism.

—NIFARAN TREATISE ON FINAL VOWS

Hanen awakened to a pleasant breeze. Seriah was nowhere to be seen. He scrambled out from under the wagon and looked around, scanning the endless flat desert around him. He sighed with relief as his eyes fell on her sitting on the canyon edge, Whisper next to her.

He brushed himself off and approached. She had her legs dangling off the ledge, a hand stroking the scales of the ynfald next to her as she took in the landscape.

"It is beautiful."

Hanen glanced up at the star-scattered purple sky. "But is it real?"

"I'm not sure that matters here," she said. "It is beautiful."

"How long has it been since you've seen anything?"

"Five years now."

Hanen leaned over the chasm. If there was a bottom, he could not see it.

"I'm glad you warned me not to wander off," Seriah said. "I'd have fallen in there with my eyes bound."

"May I sit?" Hanen asked.

Seriah didn't look up, but nodded.

Hanen lowered himself down and dangled his legs over the edge. Whisper sat between them, happy to have the attention.

"In Redot, where I grew up," Seriah said, "there were a handful of cautionary tales told of the Veld and of the wondrous things you could do while here."

"What do you mean?"

"Think back to basic cosmological understandings of the worlds. Of creation."

"You mean of the gods and the making of the four worlds?" Hanen asked.

"The wife of Wyv, Sakharn, made this world. She might have had help from the other elder gods, but it was her place. A place to imagine."

"Pretty flat and boring for reflecting a god's imagination," Hanen said with a smile, indicating at the flat desert around them.

Seriah scoffed and gave him a stern look. "Don't."

"I'm sorry," Hanen said, his face going flat.

"She made the Veld as a place where imagination could be made manifest, for any who traversed here."

Seriah took up a handful of sand, and let it pour out into the black void below. Then she took another handful and let it fall into her other hand. It lay there pooled. She lifted her hand and blew. The cloud of dusty sand flew out across the void. Hanen thought he saw the form of a bird in the dust. It faded as a breeze caught and dissipated it.

"How did you do that?" Hanen asked.

"By trying," Seriah said.

Hanen took up sand and threw it out into the air before him. Nothing happened.

"Did I do something wrong?" he asked.

"What were you thinking of?"

"Nothing."

Seriah shrugged. "I was thinking that I'd like to see a bird for the first time in years."

Hanen took up more sand and poured it on his lap, and a cup formed in the sand fall. It wasn't a cup of sand, but an actual goblet.

"Ha! It worked!"

Seriah stood and brushed some of the sand from her robe and walked away. Hanen continued to pour out sand, making one object and then another. As soon as he let an object go, it turned back to sand.

A sound behind him startled Whisper to his feet and the ynfald walked off, his tail wagging behind him. Hanen had formed a fishhook in his hand and turned to the growing sound. The cart was rolling toward him.

"What?" He rushed to his feet and ran toward it as it rolled toward the brink.

Seriah pushed it from the other side. A wave of sand seemed to be rising from behind her, urging the cart forward.

"What are you doing?!" he shouted, rushing to her side and putting his hand on the cart.

Seriah did not speak but continued to push.

"Stop!"

She did not.

He rushed in front of the cart to brake its roll. Seriah was stronger than he thought, and the cart's weight now contributed.

"Seriah! Don't do this! We have to find a way to destroy the armor, not bury it."

The cart pressed up to the edge and Hanen dove out of the way as it rolled to a stop. Seriah leaned on the cart, panting.

"This is how you destroy it," Seriah said. "It must be destroyed, but pushing it across the Veld is only inviting trouble. So would pushing it across Kallattai. No one will find it at the bottom of this crack."

"Why are you doing this?" His voice rose into near panic.

"Because you haven't. Someone has to make the decision."

Hanen took a deep, calming breath, and rushed at Seriah. She gave him a cool, defiant look, and shoved. The cart shifted and Hanen, not yet at her side, could do nothing to stop it. It steadily rolled off the ledge, and time seemed to slow as it tumbled off the brink. The canyon consumed it as the cart toppled over itself, struck a rocky outcropping and began a slow spin into darkness. After a time, an explosive crash sounded up and down the canyon.

Seriah leaned over the edge and nodded to herself.

Hanen dropped to his knees, defeat washing over him.

"I did what you were unwilling to do," she said. "Now no one will find it."

"You don't know that!"

He dropped to his knees, his breath quickening. A roar welled in his throat, but all that came out was a choked sob.

"How in Noccitan can you be remorseful?" Seriah accused. "You're free now."

"My only protection from anything was in that cart."

"I know. I saw the boneshroud lying in the bed. Now it's gone."

"No... No, no, no, no, no..."

Seriah stormed up to him and slapped him soundly across the face. "Stop feeling sorry for yourself. You are free of whatever hold it had over you."

Hanen looked up, eyes red with tears. "You don't understand."

She did not reply, but looked down on him, waiting for an explanation.

"The Deceiver marked me through my family. I am bound to answer him as his servant when he chooses to call in that favor."

"So you wore a dark tool in hopes that he wouldn't use it against you? That's stupid."

"The gods cannot see anyone who wears that cloak. I was more free with it. I am naked and exposed without it."

Her demeanor shifted, and she lowered herself slowly next to him.

"I believe you."

"Why?"

"You have no reason to lie now. Nothing will bring that cloak back now."

"And now nothing can save me."

"Open up a door to Kallattai, and we can go find help together."

Hanen stood and gave one final look down into the crack in the earth, then turned back to her and nodded.

He took out the rings, put them over his wrists, and the gauntlets appeared. Slowly, he turned away from her and took hold of the edges of the gate, then pulled the crack open. The forest appeared.

"You step through first," Hanen said, flatly.

She did and Whisper followed her unquestioningly. The ynfald sat and watched him, tongue lolling out.

"Now you," Seriah said.

"What you did was uncalled for," Hanen said. "You had no right."

"What?"

"I am too far down this road. I have to finish this path, or I'll never know peace."

"Don't do this," Seriah said.

Hanen released the edge of the tear, and it snapped shut, leaving Seriah and Whisper alone in a forest, and Hanen by himself in Dream.

He stood in frozen silence for what felt like hours.

Then, he turned and considered his surroundings. The chasm next to him beckoned, and he considered what work it would take to climb down after the cart. Slate's desiccated hand still lay near where he had thrown the man through into Noccitan. He almost left it, but feared what might happen if someone else stumbled upon it. He took out a hand axe and poked at the hand. Nothing happened.

Taking the Sentinel cloak from his shoulders, he bundled up the hand, careful only to touch it with gauntlets, tied the black sheet into a ball and tucked the knot into his belt. Returning to the canyon, he glanced down the length, and he saw for the first time a small path down into the crack.

"But how far down will it take me?" He walked over to it, and lowered himself the two feet to the ledge.

The path was precarious, and at times he did not trust the purple sandstone under his feet and by his side. By the time he came to the point where the path narrowed too much, he glanced up and saw he was hundreds of feet below the top.

Looking around, it was nearly too dark to see. He turned, back against the wall, and considered his next move.

A clump of the sandstone wall came free in his hand. It almost bore the shape of a stick. As he went to tuck it in his belt, he noticed a small glow on a ledge not far below. He turned to face the wall and lowered himself. The glow came from a small thing that looked like a shellfish. It bore weak tendrils that moved as though underwater. Each tendril glowed faintly.

"What are you?" he asked, and poked at it with the stone rod. It latched on, sinking half its tendrils into the stick. Those left out to flicker in the air glowed a little brighter than before.

"Handy," Hanen said, and held the stick out over the edge.

A series of platforms jutted from the canyon walls, and near the lowermost one, several more of the shellfish-like creatures clung to the walls. Lowering himself ledge by ledge, he came to one near several of the shellfish. The creatures pulled their tendrils into themselves and nearly disappeared. He pried two of them from the rock, and touched them to the stone stick. Nothing happened.

"Come on," he urged.

He dug at the stick with a finger, and some of it gave way to make a small divot. He made a second, then set the stick down, placed the shells onto the divots, and stepped back. After a long moment, they both opened a bit, and attached themselves. Tentacles came from all three and waved at one another, and the two new ones, brighter than the first, appeared at ease. When he picked it up, the three now glowed together, bright enough to see by. Holding it out, he could now see that there was no way to continue descending. A sheer cliff face ran in both directions.

Sighing, he looked back the way he had come, and save for the platforms he had used to descend, it was just as bad.

"I need a way down. If only there was a way to make handholds."

The sound of crumbling sand made him turn as another stone stick dislodged itself from the wall. In curiosity, he reached out and touched it and the stone rod fell into his hand.

Then, he jammed the end into the wall, and it buried itself deeply, firm.

It came out of the wall at will, and the hole he'd pulled it from returned to a flat, solid surface once more, as though nothing had happened.

He looked at the two sticks in his hands, and toyed at the wall with both. He lowered himself down on the edge of the platform and jammed the one without the glowing tendrils into the wall below the level of the edge to test it with his feet. It would hold him. He touched the wall and another rod of stone came out easily. He stuck it back into the wall and hung from it to reach down farther with a toe and kick at the wall. It seemed wherever he willed a rod of stone to form, it would, and where he wanted to kick a foothold into the wall, it came easily, even supporting his weight with little effort.

It was slow going, but in reaching and searching with his foot, the holds would appear, and he made his way bit by bit until weariness began to settle over him.

"I can't be tired right now," he muttered. "I can't afford to be."

A cool breeze moved up the canyon, and as he breathed it in, his weariness left.

"Odd," he considered. "I'm not hungry either. How long have I been here? Days?"

He continued making his way down, not sure how much farther the bottom was, and wished it to come sooner.

"This is Dream, so everything here happens at the whim of the dreamer. If I need a platform..." His foot came down on solid ground—a full ledge that hadn't been there before.

Hanen laughed to himself. "I'm dreaming. It's my dream. It really does answer to me."

He looked at the stick in his hand. "Glow," he said, and breathed on it. The entire stick lit with a soft light. He chuckled giddily to himself.

He held the glowing stick out and willed it to glow even brighter. The light that flashed illuminated everything, revealing he was only a hundred feet from the canyon floor.

He waved his hand and new platforms appeared. He began leaping down step by step, more confident with each leap.

His momentum propelled him, and he almost missed a step and scrambled to catch himself. In his haste, the glowing stick fell from his hand, and the light went out suddenly. He stumbled backward, his head struck the platform he had just come down from, and he spun, stars in his eyes.

Rolling over, he felt the bundle on his belt fall free. He slapped a hand out to grab it, and bile rose in his mouth at the horror of finding his fingers intertwining with the fingers of Slate's hand, exposed from the bundle.

Hello, Hanen, Ghoré's voice sounded in his head. It was not the confident, quiet voice of Searn. It reverberated all around Hanen in a near roar, full of manic eagerness.

"No!" Hanen shouted. He stood as fast as he could, trying to shake the desiccated hand free of his, but it held on tightly. He took hold of the wrist and tried to wrench it free. Then he felt his heel go over the side of the ledge, followed by the rest of his foot, and he began to fall.

32

OLD ZHIG

We do not know the name of that fortress. Only that it was the last stronghold of the vül outside their now cursed forest. But its destruction, and the establishment of Old Zhig, ushered in a new age. The Morrainean barbarians began their migration south, filling the void left by the terror the vül once held. Old Zhig stood against even them.

—HISTORIES OF GANTHIC

A few large, ancient trees grew in gnarled testament to a forest that once spread across the now rocky mountaintop. Astrid stood fifty yards ahead overlooking a crest. Katiam approached with her breath wracked in the thin air. She leaned against the rock opposite Astrid as she caught it. Astrid turned from looking down into the woods thickening below them.

"You can make out an old tower at the other edge of the forest," Astrid said, pointing across the green.

"That is the high tower of Old Zhig," Esenath said as she joined them.

"Will the town accept all of us?" Katiam asked.

She looked back at the train of men and women coming up behind Esenath, the Crysalas interspersed among the refugees that had joined them. Some had followed them after they'd given warning to the town of Bédekvar; others had found them as they'd fled south from the northern Zhigavan towns destroyed by vül, toward their own capital on the Pyracene Sea.

"I doubt we'll be shown much hospitality if we're not spending coin," Esenath said. "If we make it clear we're only passing through, they may oblige in order to see us away faster."

"And when we tell them what may be coming up behind us?" Katiam asked.

"We will warn them," Astrid said, "and assume they'll send the message toward the capital."

"And when more refugees follow us?" Katiam asked.

"I didn't expect those that have joined us to do so," Astrid said. "But any who would follow, unable to defend themselves against the vül, who are we to tell them no?"

"And when Zhigavan soldiers ask us where we take their citizens?" Esenath asked.

Katiam considered her words as she looked at the meager three hundred survivors with them.

"I don't know," Katiam said.

The others reached the top of the rise and crowded behind the three of them. Zhigavans who knew the land began murmuring about the forest and the city just beyond, excited to see the place.

"One of the oldest cities in Ganthic," an old man said. "Most certainly the safest city outside of Pariantür itself."

"What makes you say that?" Astrid asked.

"Never been attacked. Who would?" The old man shrugged and moved past them to go down the hill into the stand of trees.

Astrid gave Katiam and Esenath a look.

"It's a city of craftsmen," Esenath said. "They've long made pottery and such. Perhaps they stay safe because no one would bother?"

Esenath turned and walked down the road with Astrid, gaining speed to lead the train, just as the back end approached Katiam. Onelie and Lutea walked alongside the aurochs that pulled the cart while Little Maeda and Narah rode atop it.

"Did we hear someone mention Old Zhig?" Lutea asked.

"Yes. We're passing through a stretch of woods to the tower," Katiam said.

"Ah," Narah muttered from atop the cart.

"What is it?" Katiam asked.

Narah motioned for Lutea to slow the yoke of aurochs.

Katiam put both hands on the side of the cart. "Have you been to Old Zhig?"

"My father took me here as a little girl," Narah muttered in little more than a whisper through her veil, "to meet some old friends of his father, who served in the wars."

"And?"

"And I would urge us not to stay too long. It is Zhigavan, through and through, but it is also saturated with the forest people."

"Do you have something against them?" Katiam asked.

"Not in particular. While the Üterk in Old Zhig are settled, they maintain ties to their bloodlines. The tribes have allied with vül in the past. Given what we're running from, we would do well to move through quickly."

"Astrid and Esenath are hoping to resupply."

"We may have to," Narah muttered. "But I'd urge us to stay on mission. If we go south, there won't be many villages where we can restock until the coast. If we go east, the same will be true."

Katiam tapped the side of the wagon, and it continued. She walked behind it, taking up the rear, as Little Maeda watched with her feet hanging off the back.

"What is Forest People?" Larohz whistled from her binding as Katiam's breast.

Katiam glanced around to make sure there were no stragglers nearby to hear them talk.

"Are they like me?" Larohz asked.

"No," Katiam said. "They are people who often live in the forest."

"Why?"

"I don't know. Because their ancestors did?"

"I don't know that word."

"Those that came before them. They are called the Üterk."

"Why not call them that?"

"Because... I don't know," Katiam said. "They have cousins called the Riverfolk, and others called the Marcher People. I don't know why we do that. That might not be nice, I suppose."

"Not nice... I am always nice."

"Best not to say that," Katiam said.

"Why?"

"Because it is not nice."

"Am I not nice because I said I am nice?"

Katiam sighed. "You'll understand more later. But it is best not to flaunt it, or always talk of your good qualities. Let others do it. That is the best way to be humble."

"There are so many words," Larohz said.

"Yes."

"When will I learn them all?"

"You won't."

"Am I stupid?"

"Who told you that word?"

"Onelie called herself that while she played her music."

"I'll speak to her. You are not stupid. All of us learn new words all the time. That is part of life."

"I like to learn new words."

"Me too, Little Rose."

The forest was well-cared for, the underbrush trimmed, with few young trees growing between the gnarled old growth. The ground was covered in the leaf-fall from the year before, and life breathed in chitters and warbles of birds and small fauna from the branches. The road was wide and well-lit by the sun, with the first trees a hundred feet back from the edge. Small thorny bushes lined the sides of the road, encouraging everyone to stay on the path. A few of the children in their company risked the thorns and ran amidst the closest trees.

They came out near the tower, nothing but sky seen beyond until they came to the green grassed yard outside the edifice. Below and beyond the tower, the city spread out on the various cliffs and edges that stair-stepped down the valley to a small lake and river pouring out south. A spring-fed pond next to the tower was held back by a wall that dropped away in a tall, thin waterfall.

Astrid was speaking with a pale man with thick black hair, wearing an old style of uniform that reminded her of the traditional Zhigavan clothing she had seen from the ship as they'd harbored in Jhiva the year before.

Another soldier stood with Esenath at the ledge, pointing down into the valley. She had a book in her hands and made notes with charcoal as he spoke.

"What's going on?" Katiam asked Onelie, who stood with the aurochs drinking from the pond.

"Astrid has been speaking with the captain over there," the young girl said. "He's hesitant to allow us all to take the switchbacks down to the city."

"His reasoning?"

"He said there have been a lot of people showing up unannounced in the past week. Several hundred more would not be welcomed."

Astrid stalked over, a dark look on her face.

"He said we can travel through, but we can't stay."

"What is that supposed to mean?"

"It means no one asks for an inn. I am not happy." Astrid turned to the refugees. "Everyone gather round," she announced. It took several long moments, but eventually, they had three hundred sets of eyes and ears paying attention.

"We have been informed that there is nowhere for any of us to stay in Old Zhig."

"Why not?" someone called.

"No room," Astrid said. "So, we're going to travel through, and camp to the south of the city before we continue on. Some of you have expressed knowledge of the city and where we might buy supplies in town. If you need money to buy another cart and yoke for this, please let me know."

"Why go through the city at all if we're not welcome?" someone asked.

"The tower reports that the only way south is down through the city. There are sheer cliffs to the east and west, or you go days out of the way to get south. So this is our only option."

Astrid turned around and walked over the stone bridge that crossed the spring stream, following the cobbles to the top of the switchbacks. Others slowly joined her, with the cart taking up the rear once the aurochs were hitched.

Onelie walked alongside Katiam.

"We ought to keep an eye out for any signs of Crysalas Vault scouts," Katiam said. "We need to send them a warning."

"I'll tell Narah and Lutea that." Onelie dropped back and climbed up into the cart to speak quietly with Narah.

The switchbacks cut past stone-walled brickyards and smoking kiln homes built into the walls of the cliffs. The people working lumberyards and several charcoal pits didn't give them the time of day as they passed.

They came to a square off of which stacks of old stone houses ran into several side streets. Children stopped their playing to watch the refugees walk by.

Esenath cut off into one street, led by the old man who knew the town. The sounds of lowing carried on the wind from a stockyard and stable, along with the scent of manure.

It took hours to trudge past quaint homes that might have been a joy to visit in other circumstances. Shopkeepers stood at their doors, a glazed look in their eyes, unwelcoming, and unwilling to hawk their wares at the slow-moving crowd that constantly filled the street.

They came to the largest square: hundreds of locals had come out to stand along the side of the street. Several men stood around the central fountain, tools in their hands held menacingly to discourage anyone from using the fountain to freshen themselves.

Astrid walked up to the man standing out front as leader.

"What are you doing?" the man asked. "Who are you?"

"Refugees from the north joined our small group of women traveling southeastward," Astrid said. "Vül have been ransacking the north, and these are some of the surviving refugees making their way to Jhiva with that word."

"This is the first we've heard of it," the man said.

"Yes," Astrid confirmed. "That's why I'm telling you."

"The vül have never come through here," the man said. "They don't bother. They've more grief with the north than with us and southern Zhigava."

"That doesn't change the fact that danger looms."

The man rolled his eyes. "Just move along."

Astrid's hand tightened its grip on the handle of her mace.

"Astrid," Katiam said, touching her friend's shoulder. The other woman turned. "Let's leave. We'll go east toward Ikhala and the Protectorate."

"Good luck with that," the man said. "The Jhaga river is in full flood. It washed out several bridges a week ago. There won't be any crossing from here to Jhiva."

"Then we shall have to hope for a miracle," Katiam said, and pulled at Astrid's elbow. As they turned to go, Katiam glanced up at the other woman and saw a smile playing at the corner of her mouth.

"What's so funny?"

"Good job," Astrid said.

"With what?"

"The distraction."

Katiam gave a quick glance around. "I don't understand."

"Good. That means you didn't see it either."

"Did the Vault make contact?"

Astrid gave a slight nod. They came to the edge of Old Zhig, the cold eyes of the townsfolk on their backs and discouragement on their shoulders. Katiam and Astrid stopped and watched the group go by. As Esenath passed, Astrid pulled her aside.

"I believe the river meets the road soon," Astrid said. "Can you take the front, and keep an eye out for somewhere to camp?"

Esenath gave a tired nod and pressed on.

"What will we do in Jhiva?" Katiam asked. "We can't find a ship for three hundred people."

"We don't need to," Astrid said. "Only for those of us going to Pariantür."

"And if everyone wants to go?"

"Let's not dwell on that. We move forward as able. We'll ford that problem when it comes."

Esenath had chosen a field to camp in across the road from the roaring river rushing past in a dangerous torrent. The road split and disappeared into the water.

"I don't think we'll be fording anything," Katiam said.

"I'll arrange for someone to scout ahead," Astrid said, "or go myself."

Katiam nodded and walked toward the river.

"If what they said is true and the bridges are out," Katiam muttered to herself, "finding a ship that will take us is going to prove difficult."

"What is ship?" Larohz asked from its bundle.

"Like a very large wagon that floats on water. We will be on water for many weeks."

"I like walking."

Katiam laughed.

"Why is laugh?"

"I do the walking for you."

"Then I like smell of trees. Do ship smell of trees?"

"No," Katiam said. "Ships don't smell great."

"Then I don't want ship."

"We may not have much of a choice."

"Why not cross river?"

"There are no bridges. We can't cross."

"Can I get down?"

"We'll find time soon."

This seemed to satisfy the Rotha, and Katiam turned back to the camp. Astrid had left her pack and was already marching off to the south on her own.

Everyone had fallen into their normal roles of prepping camp, and as night fell, the central fire blazed. Several pots of food were going around the trench of coals. Despite the quick work, everyone remained quiet. Onelie sat with her lute on her lap, but didn't play.

As Katiam finished her own bowl of soup, two women walked into the firelight. Narah Wevan's hooded figure was easy to recognize, and Lutea stood a head taller. Katiam choked down the last bite as she rose.

"Did the Vault make contact?" she asked as she approached.

Lutea nodded. "They've only one here. They are well-financed via the trades of hind skin gloves and combs." She held in her hands a small strong box. "They gave us a gift, although they've asked us a favor in return."

"Oh?"

"We are not the first to warn Old Zhig of what is happening to the north," Narah said quietly. "Refugees have been coming through for days now, and the Vault has taken them all in as the city denied them."

"You agreed to let them come with us, didn't you?" Katiam asked with a regretful smile.

Narah nodded.

"How many?"

"One hundred and fifty," Lutea said.

Katiam turned back to the camp and sighed. "This may not go over well."

Astrid approached from the camp, a bottle of water in her hands.

"What is going on?" Astrid asked.

"Lutea and Narah bring news, coin, and one hundred and fifty refugees from the Vault in Old Zhig."

Astrid nodded as though this did not surprise her.

"What did you find to the south?"

"There was a bridge, a few miles down. Both ends were washed away recently, leaving just a middle sitting upon two pylons. If we're adding half our number again, I bet that is as far as we make it tomorrow."

Katiam turned back to the other two.

"When will they join us?"

"They're in the dark behind us," Lutea said. "They'll come when we ask."

"We should go and tell the rest of camp then," Katiam said, and the four women turned to give the news to the rest of the refugees.

Another couple dozen men and women came by morning, along

with their children, bringing their numbers to nearly five hundred. A farrier and his family brought two wagons pulled by sleipnirs, as well as two courier coursers. Astrid was given one of them, and the other bore the pregnant wife of a chandler. Their six children walked alongside the sleipnir and their mother.

It was a slow journey to the washed-out bridge, but the slow trudge of past days improved with the children playing around and through the pilgrims.

The water showed no signs of slowing, running full alongside the road, but not threatening to come farther up the bank.

The bridge came into view a long ways off as they topped a rise that descended, along with the river, to the bridge.

"Why did they build a bridge below such a violent descent?" Esenath asked no one in particular from the seat of the wagon.

"The flooding last year was worse," a man nearby said. "There used to be a waterfall right here. Water dropped a hundred feet and pooled before passing the bridge. A damming rock gave way and the flood cut the new drop. This year, the floods renewed and took out the bridge. Jhiva was supposed to levy a tax, but sent word that they'd not be rebuilding the bridge any time soon."

Everyone set about preparing camp without another word.

"At this rate, it'll take us months just to get to Jhiva," Astrid grumbled.

"We were planning on several days in Old Zhig," Katiam offered. "We can afford a bit of time to recuperate. Then we'll see about pushing harder."

Katiam was offered a small shelter against the cart by Narah, and she accepted. She crawled under the blanket and found a pot of fresh soil there. She turned her back to the opening and took the Rotha out and placed her on the top of the dirt. Larohz proceeded to bury herself, contented, and fell still.

"I didn't know you were so tired," Katiam whispered, and lay herself down to rest.

When she opened her eyes, it had grown dark. The glow of a roaring campfire on the other side of the cart caught her attention, along with soft music being plucked by one or two members of the company. Larohz had climbed out of the soil and curled up next to her, stroking her arm with interest.

"Shall we go and see what's happening?" Katiam asked.

"Music," Larohz said.

"Yes, I think so."

"Onelie?" Larohz asked.

"Probably."

"Good."

Katiam crawled out as the Rotha crawled into her robe, and together they circled the wagon. The fire had been built up with dried-out wood from the broken bridge, and everyone gathered around the light and heat. Astrid stood nearby watching everything, keeping an eye out for danger, most likely more worried about the fire catching something than outside threats.

Onelie sat near the fire, her bowl-backed mandolin across her lap. A handful of others had pulled out their own instruments and plucked away as well, though no one had committed to a song, it seemed.

As Katiam neared, she saw that one of the people near Onelie was Narah Wevan, and Katiam smiled to herself.

"Why are you happy?" Larohz buzzed from the folds of her robe.

"How do you know?" Katiam asked.

"I can...smell it."

"You're right. I am happy. I think Narah is going to play."

"What game?"

"Not game. Music. You've not heard her play. I think she's finally giving in."

"Her music iz good?"

"Very."

Narah touched Onelie's arm and Onelie gave a nod and began to strum a rhythmic tune. Another refugee followed along, drawing a bow across his stringed instrument. Another took up a stick to drum, and together the three of them laid out the backbone of a song.

Narah took up a long cloth-wrapped object and unrolled it to reveal her dulcian—a gift from her grandfather, the celebrated Viago Wevan. He'd been a great leader in the Protectorate Wars, and after that, had led the Pariantür Orchestra.

Narah lifted the mouthpiece of the dulcian and brought it into the folds of her veil under her hood. At first, the note she played was imperceptible. It grew in low resonance until it rose above the sound of the other players, and the note struck Katiam with warmth. All grew silent. Narah's fingers began to move, and the rich music flowed from her. It was a haunting song. Katiam had heard it before, when the echoing chapel of Pariantür offered strength to the music. But in this moment, filled with the defeat of the last several days, and the long road behind and ahead, it brought tears streaming from the eyes of any with ears to hear.

It told a story like flowing water, growing from a trickling stream to a river and eventually to the sea. The other musicians followed behind her, almost unable to keep up. Narah was gracious and matched their style, leading them into the night.

As the first song began winding down, Katiam realized that Larohz was buzzing against her. Her whistle matched the tone of the dulcian, albeit many octaves higher.

"You liked that?" Katiam asked.

"Very much. I heard a story."

"Oh?"

"I would like to go to the river."

"Alright," Katiam said, and slipped away toward the sound of the water. They came to the embankment overlooking the roaring water. By the light of Umay far above she could make out the water's hurried movement, and did not dare journey any closer.

"Down please," Larohz said.

Katiam obliged and set the small Rotha on the ground. She was an inch taller than before, easily coming to her knee now.

"When did you grow so big?" Katiam asked.

The Rotha didn't seem to notice the question, and wandered to the edge of a group of bushes. There, Katiam noticed a small white flower she hadn't before, looking like sad bells, in the moonlight.

"What are you doing?" Katiam asked.

"Smelling," Larohz said, and with a leafy hand plucked one of the flowers and turned back to Katiam.

"What is this?" Larohz asked.

Katiam took it from the Rotha and held it up.

"I'm not entirely sure. It looks like yellowbell, but it's white, and the pistil is shaped more like a bell clapper."

"It is a scarknit," Esenath said from nearby. "Though many who don't know its healing properties just call it Waterbell. I apologize if I startled you. I saw you walk this way and followed."

"This flower seemed near the new water's edge," Katiam said. "Why is it called Waterbell?"

"It grows in over-saturated earth. I would wager its roots sat dormant for years. Now that the water is closer, it sent up the flowers."

"What does it do to be called 'scarknit'?"

"Over an open wound, it forces scar tissue to form rapidly. It's not pretty healing, but it does the job as a poultice."

Larohz had gone back and plucked a second one, and held it up to sniff.

"What are you doing, Little Rose?" Katiam asked.

Larohz didn't answer, but shoved it into her flower to consume it.

"Wait!" Katiam said.

"Let her," Esenath said. "It's the leaves used for the poultices. The flowers don't do anything."

The Rotha didn't appear to be affected, but turned back to the riverbank and sat down on the edge.

"What is she doing?" Katiam asked.

"I don't know."

Katiam approached and crouched down on her knees next to the little creature.

"Little Rose?"

Larohz didn't respond, but sat there with her roots dangling over the edge of the water, breathing in the night air.

It grew into an awkward period of time and Katiam thought to stand when she noticed movement in the water.

"What is that?" Esenath asked, seeing it at the same time. "Serpents?"

"Vines," Katiam said, peering closer.

Hundreds of little tiny vines came up out of the surface, inch by inch, seeking out through the water, unperturbed by the rushing currents and taking hold of the pier that stuck up out of the waves.

Katiam and Esenath looked on in silence and wonder as the vines grew up along the sides. They stopped, and the Rotha rose and went to grab another flower, consumed it, then sat on the riverbank once more.

"She's doing that," Katiam muttered.

"Doing what?" Esenath said.

"Healing," the Rotha buzzed.

After three or four scarknit flowers, there was a ropey mass from the bank of the river to the first pier. Katiam and Esenath began gathering the flowers for the Rotha. The little creature began snacking on them incessantly, and the vines exploded in growth. As morning drew near, vines had grown across from one pier to the next.

"Finish," Larohz said, and without another word, began

climbing up the viney mass from the ground to the first pier. It was wide enough the cart might be lead up it.

"Wait!" Katiam called, and moved to climb after her. In the predawn gray, the water rushing past gave her pause.

"Go on, Katiam," Esenath said, handing her a bag of gathered flowers.

Katiam took them, and put a foot on the vines, testing their strength. It had no give whatsoever and she confidently strode up the woody vines to join Larohz, who had crossed to the second pier, leafy hands held up as tendrils grew past her like writhing masses of drækis. By dawn, the vines from the second pier down to the other bank were strong enough for Katiam to cross, and growing stronger with each passing moment.

Katiam took up the Rotha and they both looked back at her work. "Look what you have accomplished!"

"Good?" Larohz asked. "Have I healed?"

"I am so proud of you. I didn't even know you could do this."

"I did not either. Until I did."

Katiam looked at the new bridge in astonishment and awe.

"What else can I do?" Larohz asked.

"I have no idea," Katiam said. "But we'll find out together."

33

Blessing to Curse

There is said to be one great champion of the vül. None outside their peoples know his name, but through tales and whispers he is known. Often called the Devourer or the Hungering One, none know where he lives, but there are times that vül are said to work in tandem. Either their god is more active in their movements than we know, or the Devourer walks where he wills, when he wills.

— A DISCOURSE ON MADNESS AND

THE COLD DEITY OF THE VÜL

"You did not heed their warning?" Nichal was on his feet, pacing the ancient Abecinian chapel that served as a city hall. Jined watched from the side of the stage, as still as Nichal was energetic.

The people of Old Zhig had filed into the place. Some stood outside craning to hear what was spoken.

"Why should we?" asked Lord Gravye, leader of the city.

He sat on the priestly seat wearing his evening robe, looking disgruntled that Nichal had called this meeting just as he was prepared to go to bed. A man of the cloth stood next to him, a tall and timid man who had provided Nichal Guess and the others a place to stay. Silas sat at a makeshift table with the twins. All three acted as scribes for the event.

"Old Zhig has stood for one thousand years," the lord continued. "No man or beast has ever come up against us. Even when Ikhala threatened the north and desired to force Jhiva back under its rule, Old Zhig was not threatened once."

"And if the vül should merely go around you?" Nichal asked. "Will you not stand against them for the sake of anyone else?"

"The only way south is through Old Zhig," Gravye said. "The Cliffs of Torzh to the east and the mountains to our west act together as a funnel. All trade passes through here."

"You thought this was a good thing?" Nichal asked. Jined could tell his cool attitude was fraying at the edges. "You endanger your people."

"Our people are fine. We are blessed by the gods with one thousand years of safety, and our wealth is proof of that."

"Wealth earned through trade, but when the poor and destitute come through, you offer them no hospitality nor a place to stay."

"We'd no way to know if they would not merely stay for good under the pretense of a vül invasion to the north."

"Hundreds of people, Paladames, desperate people fleeing war, and you've the audacity to send them on their way?!" Nichal stood and slammed his hand on the table.

"I don't particularly care for the aggressive air you bring," Gravye said.

"My air?!" Nichal pointed a finger at the man. A group of soldiers surrounding the lord tightened their grip on their spears, but appeared too fearful to be any real threat.

"I bring news," Nichal continued, turning to the room, "knowing full well it's not the first time you've heard it. War comes. It is on your very doorstep. Vül have invaded northern Zhigava and pressed against Garrou. Walls do not scare them, they scale them. These cliffs you think protect the south will pose no threat, if they do not see your wall-less town as a far easier means to the south. That Gar-Talosh, Gold-Eater, did not raze this city to the ground before the Prima Pater struck him down is beyond me. No people with such lack of goodwill should be allowed to strip wealth from people and bask under the same sun. What will you do? Will you continue to stand in ignorance?"

They did not speak. Many lifted their chins in defiance.

"You bring rumors of war," Gravye said, "in pristine armor. You appear unharmed, and small in number. For all we know, you come under pretense, foreign agents seeking to turn us against our own capital."

"What are you talking about?!" Nichal asked, nearly apoplectic.

"We came to give warning, only to find you allowed our sister Paladames to pass by without your help—refugees gone unaided. We warn you of your doom, and you sit cooly thinking that because no one has touched your perfect city for a millennia this means the gods respect any act your ancestors might have done. You think your wealth is a sign of protection. Your wealth is a sign of your deep-rooted rot!"

"How dare you," Gravye said cooly.

"I dare," Nichal spat. "Brazstein, we do not stay in this city another moment. Paladins mount up."

He marched to the door and turned back to the congregation.

"If any would leave with us, they shall leave under my protection. I swear to you all that no stone in this town shall be left in its proper place before this year is out. Perhaps not even a week. Leave with us now, with only what you can carry. If you wait, I will not be responsible for what happens to you."

The Paladins walked to the square outside the chapel, where another Paladin stood with their sleipnirs already saddled. Nichal did not seem surprised; he stepped up into the saddle and began to ride south.

Jined gave a knowing smirk at the Paladin holding the reins of Tyv while he mounted. No one else seemed to give him any mind. Jined took up the rear alongside the new member of their company.

"You would have us leave, Grissone?" Jined asked under his breath as they rode alongside one another. "It is your will?"

"It is," the Paladin said. "For the obvious corruption that sits over this city, and for the vül army that marches south."

Jined sighed. "How large?"

"Three thousand. Under another champion."

"How many champions does he have?"

"I think Kos-Yran usually likes to keep nine across all of his tribes and bloodlines around the world. The Vül-Gour of the north have always been favored, though."

"Why?"

"They stayed the most true to him. The north of Ikhala is all that remains of his people's original homeland, after all."

"Original homeland?"

"Ganthic. The continent was originally the lands of the vül. Now they've only the darkened woods to the northeast of here."

"And now they march for war and for conquest."

"They've been dormant since the Protectorate Wars. So many of them died then, that they've spent the decades rebuilding their tribe."

"And other tribes elsewhere?"

"Never all that strong. Anka thinks they may also have been under a direct command from their god to prepare for something."

"What?"

"The sowing of chaos and dissension."

"Destruction," Jined muttered.

"Destruction is Rionne's domain. Kos-Yran just likes to watch things fall apart. Do you know why Old Zhig is so protected?"

"No."

"A priest of Aben prophesied it one thousand years ago. On this very day. It was taken from one of the last bastions of vül, a champion smote by a simple man. A mighty citadel had stood here and the people tore it down to build Zhig. A kingdom sprang from it and the prophecy stated that it would stand for one thousand years, standing in edifice for the vül that had been destroyed."

"Then what Nichal said... Did you inspire it?"

"I did not. I would imagine those words may have come from one even greater than I."

"The Existence," Jined said.

Grissone made an interesting sign across his chest.

"What was that?"

"What was what?"

"You made a sign, as we might when your name is spoken."

"In respect for He Who Made All."

"I should not have spoken of him so flippantly."

"No," Grissone said.

"I would know more."

"In due time," Grissone said.

"It saddens me to know we ride from a city selected for destruction."

"Imagine how I must feel," Grissone said.

"Will anyone heed the call to join us?"

"The Crysalas Vault saw many on their way. The women who remained may join you, or they may choose to stand in defense of the helpless."

"Should we not?"

"If you remain, you will die. I have other plans for you."

"What?"

"We shall see, won't we?" Grissone offered with a sad smile.

"I don't like that look."

"You'll follow regardless."

"I will."

"Even if I lead you to your death."

"Especially if you lead me to my death."

"Why?"

"To die for you means I will fall for reasons far greater than I could ever hope for."

"Then you follow me for glory?"

"I follow you because I have faith that through my actions the tide of darkness that always scratches at the periphery of my vision will turn, and turn for the betterment of all."

Grissone nodded to himself.

"So, shall we bring warning to Jhiva now?"

"They are receiving messengers with the news now. You are going to come to a bridge that shall defy your understanding. You are to cross it, and when the last refugee from Old Zhig crosses, you are to destroy it so that eastern Zhigava remains free of vül invasion for a little longer."

"Then there will be refugees?" Jined asked.

When Grissone did not answer, he turned to look at his god riding next to him, but the god and sleipnir had disappeared.

Jined put heels to Tyv and pressed to the front.

"We need to move faster," Jined said to Nichal as he came up next to him.

"Oh?"

"There is a bridge ahead. We have to secure it before the refugees arrive."

"Refugees?" Nichal said.

"We're to destroy the bridge after the last refugee crosses."

"Divine inspiration?"

"Divine instruction," Jined corrected.

Nichal gave a curt nod and the six of them all broke into a gallop.

After a time, the roaring river came to meet the road. Dusk was starting and the light was fading. The roar of tumbling rapids on their left gave way to a calmer rush. In the middle of the river, Jined could make out the form of a bridge, and he pressed toward it. Tyv reared up, unwilling to cross. The other sleipnirs took his lead and also refused. Jined leapt down and walked to the slope of the bridge and gasped.

"What is it Jined?" Nichal asked.

"It's made of natural vines," Jined announced.

"Can we cross?"

"It appears sturdy." He pulled on Tyv's reins, walking the sleipnir up the vines, and began to cross. The twins came next, and then Didus Koel stopped in the middle of the bridge and stared up the river.

"By the Pantheon," Didus swore.

Jined turned to follow his gaze. Smoke rose from above the trees underlit by flames.

"Old Zhig is burning," Silas said.

"Did I prophecy that?" Nichal asked.

"You ended a prophecy from one thousand years ago," Jined said. "I'll explain later. Let's get across and assess."

They came to the other side, the sleipnirs glad to be on solid ground after the rush of the river threatening them from below. The twins set about starting a fire.

"Should we do that?" Didus asked. "It will be a beacon to any vül that come later."

Any refugees that make it out of the city will be a beacon themselves, Loïc signed.

And we're hungry, Cävian added. *Who knows when next we'll eat.*

"Alright," Nichal said. "We eat quickly, then prepare for any who will join us."

The twins knew their work and soon had a pot of porridge bubbling. Didus and Silas were double-checking supplies and straps. Nichal had gone back to the middle of the bridge to stand alone, watching the smoke from Old Zhig turn into a glow of destruction as night set in.

Jined crossed the ropey vines to him.

"Should we have stayed?" Nichal asked as Jined approached. "To stand against the vül?"

"No," Jined said. "Grissone said your statement marked the end of a thousand-year prophecy when the vül city that stood there was destroyed and Zhig was built."

"But all of those people!"

"If we had stayed, we would have all died. Grissone has greater plans for us."

"When will the refugees arrive? We rode hard."

"By morning perhaps?"

"Then I will stand watch. Get some sleep, brother."

Jined gave a salute and turned back to the far side of the river.

Tyv had proven not to need a tie, and Jined regretted leaving his saddle on, but left it on to be ready for haste. He found a tree and leaned against it, his hammer in his arms, and needed no prompting to fall asleep.

He started awake at the first cry of alarm coming from Silas who tended the fire. Light had begun to dawn and across the raging river, a man and woman appeared through the trees along the road. The woman limped, leaning on the man's arms.

"Come!" Nichal cried from the middle of the bridge. As they came further into view, they could see the woman's face and hair were caked with dried blood.

"Are you wounded?" Nichal asked as they started up the bridge.

The man shook his head, unable to speak. Didus had water ready as they came to the other side and the twins took the woman from the man and carried her to someplace comfortable to sit.

"The blood?" Didus asked the man as he finished drinking.

"Her husband's," he croaked.

"Then you are?"

"His brother. He stood against the vül as we escaped."

"Are there others?"

"I don't know. Maybe. She sprained her ankle rushing out of the city, and we've not looked back even to watch the flames rise and light our way."

"Five more!" Nichal shouted from the bridge.

The twins rushed over and goaded the man running with four women. As they came to the bridge Loïc turned to Nichal. *I see more women, Crysalas by the look ofs it. They've children.*

Down the road, a flood of forty children ran ahead of four women in pink and white robes.

"Run!" the women urged, and the children fled forward even faster.

Three hundred yards behind them came twenty vül.

"Jined!" Nichal shouted, and strode back to the other side of the river.

Jined needed no prompting and rushed up the bridge as the children ran past him. One almost lost her footing, but he caught her arm and pulled her back to the middle. The last child crossed as the first Crysalas sisters began their crossing.

"How many more?" he urged, taking hold of the arm of the first woman.

"This is it," she said. "Five sisters, one was a Paladame, but she stayed to hold them back."

"How many?"

"Countless," she said. "What hope is left?"

Jined pointed at the children now on the other bank. "There is your hope."

Her lips tightened to a thin line and she nodded.

Jined rushed to the other side where Nichal and the twins stood. One last survivor fled before the slavering vül coming down the road, who were stumbling over one another to get at the old man in the gray robes of a priest of Aben.

"Loïc and Cävian, take him to safety," Nichal muttered, and began walking forward, his hammer held high.

The twins rushed forward, their hammers held low, and Jined marched behind them, muttering a prayer of protection. The vül slowed their advance, but they did not seem to fear. Rather, they parted to allow the largest of their number through. The fear in the priest's eyes grew and he fled all the faster and collapsed into the twins' arms. The three of them turned and rushed back to the bridge.

Nichal stopped and cut a defensive stance.

"That is a lot of vül," Jined said. "Are you sure you want to take them on?"

"I won't keep them all for myself. You can have some, too."

Jined laughed, and together they prepared for the assault. The vül stopped fifty yards from them. The largest vül wore plate armor that looked like a forge grate, complete with glowing red embers within.

"What in Noccitan..." Nichal said.

The creature walked five strides toward them.

"Turn back," Nichal called out.

The creature laughed and from the center of his chest flames spurted.

"How many champions must we put in the ground?" Nichal taunted.

The monster looked back to those behind it and signaled them forward.

"It doesn't appear he's one for small talk," Jined muttered.

The vül rushing forward leapt with gauntleted claws. Jined

sidestepped one and Nichal cut it down with a hammer upon his skull. Jined spun and took the next one across the face, then continued to spin, bringing the hammer onto the shoulder of the next.

"Let them press us to the bridge," Nichal said. Jined agreed and they fell back ten paces as the next wave came. One made contact and smashed Nichal across the chest, sending him back in a roll. Nichal came to his feet, as surprised that he stood as the vül that had tried to knock him down.

"Did you?" was all he had time to say as the vül pressed the advantage. Nichal thrust his hammer forward and took him in the chest.

Jined fell back to Nichal and smote the knocked over vül as they retreated back to the bridge. Loïc and Cävian stood atop the bridge signing prayers. Loïc stopped and pointed behind them. The vül with a furnace in his chest rushed at them like an iron carriage, roaring like an auroch bull.

"Brace!" Jined shouted.

Nichal turned just in time and held up his hammer. The vül smashed into both of them, sending Nichal flying up along the bridge. Jined dug his feet in and bore the brunt.

The flames spouting from the monster's chest licked at Jined.

"Back!" he shouted, and the vül pressed back a step.

"Grissone, help!"

Light flashed from Jined's outstretched hand, but the vül did not seem affected.

The other vül stopped twenty feet from the bridge. The vül pressed up to Jined, and put a hand on his chest.

"Try and stop me," the vül finally said. "The hate that burns in my chest cannot be quenched by blood or the deaths I bring to the world."

Jined could not press back against him, and he retreated step by step up the bridge. A quick glance behind him informed him that the others had crossed. The survivors from Old Zhig watched in horror as the vül horde pressed up slowly onto the bridge, eyeing Jined as their next meal.

"You shall know my name," the vül said, "so you may tell the champions who failed, those in Noccitan, that one greater than they has bested the champion of Grissone."

"Grissone," Jined called.

"My name is—"

"Silence him!" Jined interrupted.

Suddenly all fell to utter quiet around them. The wind still moved and the river still rushed, but there was no sound. The vül champion continued to speak, no doubt detailing his exploits. Jined did not hear him. There was nothing. He opened his own mouth to speak another prayer, but he had no words either.

Grissone give me strength, he mouthed, voicelessly, but nothing seemed to happen.

Light, he signed with his free hand, and the hand began to glow.

At that, he let out a silent laugh.

The vül stopped and looked at the glowing hand.

Jined held his hammer down to his side and let it drop to the bridge. With the now freed hand, he signed to those behind him. *Close eyes!*

A verse came to him from the Book of Canticles. Then he held both hands up and signed,

> *Your wings, they are a shelter,*
> *Bring them round my shoulders.*
> > *Bright feathers full of might,*
> > *I am want for nothing.*

Jined felt a peaceful weight settle upon his shoulders and a bright light shown all about him from whatever had settled on his back. The vül before him took a step backward. Others scrambled over one another to get away. Two vül fell into the water and tumbled down through dangerous rapids.

> *Lift me up in your strength,*
> *My enemies shall know fear.*
> > *Send them far from me,*
> > *Truly send them to the ends of the earth.*

Other vül turned tail and ran back toward Old Zhig, leaving the furnace-chested vül alone on the bridge.

> *By your holy light, I am led.*
> *By your power alone do I draw breath.*

Jined took a deep breath, closing his eyes to draw in more than he knew he could.

> *Bring mighty gales upon the wicked.*
> *That they shall no longer draw their own breath.*

A mighty wind began to swirl around him. The furnace vül fell to his knees and gripped the vines of the bridge, but only for a moment, as the vines began to shred away in the gale. The bridge's sinews exploded in flaying greenery and the vül was thrown up into the air. The flame in his chest guttered and then went out. He looked into Jined's eyes in abject horror as his eyes went glassy, and his grip failed. He flew through the air, down the stream and fell into the turbid waters, swallowed whole. He did not resurface.

> *It is for your delight that I serve,*
> *And I am content that you would use me.*
> *Your will would be done without me.*
> *I am at peace. For you have made me so.*

Jined looked down. He floated three feet over an empty pier. The viney bridge had been utterly destroyed. Sound rushed back to his ears, and cheering washed over him.

He turned to look at the people on the other bank and laughed at his situation, fifty feet from shore.

"Grissone?" he muttered. "Lift me."

He took a flying leap, and made the length, landing solidly on the ground.

"You destroyed the bridge and the vül?" Nichal asked.

"You tell me," Jined said.

"We had our eyes closed. Even then, the bright light beyond my eyelids has me seeing stars."

Jined looked around at the smiling faces, and saw a young boy standing by the shore, staring vacantly out at the river.

"You are safe now," Jined said, walking up to him. The boy turned to look at Jined, but didn't seem to see him. His pupils were white.

"I saw a bright ælerne eagle come down on the Paladin's shoulders. It protected him and destroyed the monsters."

"You watched?" Jined asked.

"It was so beautiful," the boy said with a smile. "I can see it now. I hope it never goes away from my vision."

The Anka came down? Loïc asked, as he and his brother came to stand next to Jined.

And blinded the boy, it appears, Cävian added.

What I wouldn't give to see nothing else but the Anka for the rest of my life.

34

Sky Grazer

Graceful severity, sleek and slim.

The sword is death, severs life at whim.

—SWORD OF KALLIDON

Neither Ophedia nor Aurín wore their Sentinel cloaks. Aurín appeared as carefree as he had ever been, ever since they had first met in Edi City, having donned an armless long tunic and short boots, an Œronzi peasant outfit. Ophedia wore a simple peasant frock, her shoulders glad to be free in the bright summer sun. They made a pair, looking like peasant merchants on a journey.

"I had not realized how high all of Limae was," Ophedia said.

"What do you mean?" Aurín asked, his eyes on the two sleipnirs pulling the cart.

"We've been descending since Haven," she said. "And since we left Adwall it's been a continual slope from there to the sea, but not so steep that it kept farmers from doing what they do. The land is long and wide enough from east to west that I can see why Limae has never made a play for it."

Aurín nodded. "Castenard and the rest of the Sidieratans would never allow it. If Ormach truly is falling to Œron, I'd imagine the City States will make a bid or deal."

"Then why are we looking at Boscolón? Besides resupply, I mean."

"As I understand it, Adwall used to be a fortified city. It has been burned to the ground in every conflict with Castenard for the past two hundred years."

"Again," Ophedia said, "what does that have to do with Boscolón?"

"Adwall is on its own: too far south to be defended by Haven. Liberté is large enough to hold off Castenard, but not strong enough to offer any help to Adwall. If Limae had control over a major port on the Kandar Sea, like, say, Boscolón?"

"We could just as easily have sent someone else," Ophedia said.

"We could have," Aurín said, "but I needed to get away for a bit. This provides an opportunity for me to bring back supplies to give to the soldiers from their own leader's hand. And lastly, I just don't trust anyone else with knowledge of my plans."

"You don't worry Haven will see this as a sign of sedition?"

"The commanders who didn't think of it themselves will," Aurín said. "The Wardens certainly won't. If we're successful, we establish a very powerful standing in the world arena."

They came over a rise and looked down over the basin leading to Boscolón. It was not an overly large city, but it had two walls: one around an older original city that ran against the sea and one side of the harbor, and one around the rest of the city. There did not appear to be any recent growth, but rather, several sections built upward. It reminded Ophedia of Edi City and a few Macenan towns she had seen out east.

"Walled," Aurín said, "but not easily defended."

"Nor was Adwall," Ophedia offered. "If you plan to defend either, you'll have to play for both."

"That is my intention."

"I understand. But if you don't have the rest of Limae helping, we'll be crushed. Castenard will cut both off from the north and Œron will come for Boscolón. Isn't it Ormachi?"

"I believe so. Though given the number of Sidieratan flags flying from ships in the harbor, Sidierata will bid for it, too."

"I don't see how you can do it. Limae has no allies."

Aurín did not respond, but grew quiet as they rode down into town, the sun beginning its descent in the west.

The inn they found was a quiet one. Ophedia played the peasant wife and brought Aurín a drink, over-dramatizing how she placed it before him and then took a seat across from him.

"Do you want me to cut your bread for you too, my husband?" she asked, voice dripping with sarcasm.

"Oh stop," he said, rolling his eyes. "We're in the city now, and I didn't see a single Praetor from the gate to this inn."

"Well, regardless, no reason to draw attention to ourselves," Ophedia replied.

"You draw attention wherever we go."

"I can't help my looks," Ophedia said.

"That's what I meant."

"How do we want to break up the work tomorrow?" she changed the subject.

"Are you more comfortable eyeing the pier? Or looking through the Old City?"

"If the Ormachi aren't keen on Œronzi occupation, your accent may earn you sour looks on the pier. They won't have much of a choice but to cater to you in the Old City."

"Especially if the city leaders are positioning themselves," Aurín conceded.

"It's decided then. I'll start on the pier, looking for Sentinel ships, supplies, anything."

"And trouble."

"You want me to look for trouble?" she asked, arching an eyebrow.

"I do. Trouble makers. Anyone dissatisfied with the present circumstances."

"Sounds like fun," she said, and downed her drink.

The harbor was a busy one. Several large warehouse offices stood against the stone ledge and agent stalls sat against those, with keen-eyed men eyeing the ships as they unloaded product. Easily a third of the buildings were stuccoed hrelgren offices, though not all of the ships at their own piers were hrelgren. At one hrelgren pier, she stopped to eye a larger ship with the name "Rising Dawn" across the side. Others gawked at its unique design and its two rows of cannon ports. Ophedia continued down the pier. Three or four of the thirty-or-so ships were qavylli merchants, and were the first qavylli ships Ophedia had ever seen up close. Poking out from one side of their ships, outriggers settled down in the water. The one on the pier side had been levered out of the water, long keel-like blades being cleaned of barnacles.

Groups of qavyl worked on their own projects, from cleaning and repainting the hull, to moving boxes from the deck to the office. Their tails flipped like a cör's, providing them balance as they moved, and when they stood with a crate in their arms, their double-jointed legs lifted with ease. They did not have to speak, but rather gave little whistles and clicks to each other, while two of them sang a worker song unlike anything Ophedia had ever heard. One of them wore a hat that ran down its back to its waist, and kept track of the other's actions with a ledger.

She reached the end of the piers and turned round to consider her next direction.

"You look like you're searching for something," a man nearby said. She turned and found she stood before a man in a red cloak. "You look familiar, too."

"You're Red Banner," Ophedia said.

"That you know what Red Banner is tells me my gut was right. You're a Sentinel. Or perhaps no longer."

"Not sure it's your business, if you left the Black Sentinels yourself."

He pulled back the side of his cloak to show a sword strapped there. "It is my business if we're looking for new recruits."

Ophedia laughed. "I'm the wrong person to go press-ganging," she said.

"Oh? You think anyone will miss you?" he snapped his finger and four men came out of an alley. "A pretty recruit at that."

She reached for her belt and sighed, forgetting she had only one club, the rest left in Adwall.

She turned and bolted, drawing her club as she fled.

But the men expected it and took off in pursuit. She swung the club wildly to her right, taking the first man across the chin. Another took hold of her left arm and she swung back in the other direction and he laughed as it hit his arm.

Another grabbed her other arm, and they pulled her to a sitting position on the cobbles. Sailors nearby stopped what they were doing, watching, but did nothing.

The first man came and stood over her.

"You have fight," he said. "I like that."

"And friends," someone called from nearby.

The man looked up with a quickly dissolving sneer.

Ophedia struggled to turn and see who spoke.

"She's one of yours?"

The woman came around into view and Ophedia smiled. "What are you doing here, Eunia?"

She'd not heard from the woman since they had parted ways on the Griffin Road, Eunia and her husband going south to warn others, while Ophedia had delivered the news of the Chalcian invasion to Haven.

The press-gangers pulled Ophedia into a standing position and she shook her hands off and dusted her dress.

Eunia turned to the Red Banner leader. "Anything else you want to say?"

"I'm sorry," he said, and turned to walk away, his men behind him.

"I'd say I'm getting tired of rescuing you," Eunia said, "but I'm not."

"Me, either."

Eunia turned and began walking away with a backward glance to make sure Ophedia was coming.

"You going to take me to your bakery to be accosted by a Chalician?"

Eunia laughed. "No. Not this time."

They walked past a warehouse and up to the door of a smaller building. Two men stood outside, armed, but not cloaked. Inside, men and women stood at various tables with maps and papers.

"What is this?"

"The Southern Resistance," Eunia said.

"Quick answer."

"We've been watching you and Aurín since Nikrest."

"Really?"

She indicated to a table across the room. Aurín stood there with three others, including Chös and Avarr, the capricör shepherd from the Griffin Road.

"What are you doing here?" Ophedia asked Aurín as they approached.

He looked up and gave a smile. "Chös found me this morning after we parted. We had people trying to catch up with you ever since."

"Would you mind filling me in?" Ophedia asked.

"We traveled south after we split up on the Griffin Road," Eunia said. "In short, the south was willing to work against the Chalicians. Castenard has always been interested in taking portions of southern Limae, but he hasn't made a move yet. When the Chalicians began marching south from Haven, all of the small disparate resistance fighters left only a spy or two in every city and fell back, then down here to Boscolón."

"Apparently, the goal was to fight an underground war before conflict even erupted," Aurín said.

"We've been watching for Castenard to make a move," Avarr said. "When he does, our forces planned to take Boscolón, and circle up behind Castenard and cut off his supply."

"What if we experience Chalician or Sidieratan rebuttal?" Ophedia asked.

"That is more a worry if done under Limaean flag, but not if Boscolón declares itself independent. Sidierata will be more likely to side with us."

"But not the Chalicians who want all of Ormach."

"Not so much," Eunia said. "No."

"I've been trying to convince our friends here," Aurín said, "that we escalate and unite causes. Boscolón would be a welcome addition to Limae."

"What's to be negotiated?" Ophedia asked, looking at the table. Others perked up and turned. "We have an army in Adwall," she said raising her voice for everyone to hear. "No doubt Castenard has spies both here and there. He knows Boscolón has plans and likely has counter plans of his own. That Adwall is occupied not by Chalicians but by Limaeans? He's going to move. So let's move faster." She leaned over the map. "How many days travel from Castenard?"

"Four days forced march," Eunia said.

"We can have the Black Claws down here in Boscolón by tomorrow morning. If the Red Banner is already here, they take both gates and the Black Claws will take over the city by force if we must."

Eunia gave Ophedia an awkward glance.

"What is it?"

Eunia shot a look to the third man at the table.

"I take it you're important?" Ophedia said, pushing pretense aside.

"I am," the older man said. "Probably more important than you."

"I'm the daughter of the founder of the Black Sentinels. You can do better?"

"Perát de Bosco. I am lord of this city until Œron takes full control of Ormach in four months."

"And yet you're here in a seditious cell."

"I have zero desire to see my city taken from me. I will see Boscolón free of any rule."

"You'll be under someone," Ophedia said. "Castenard would probably love a port as much as Limae. If you think you'll become an accepted city-state of Sidierata, you're sorely mistaken. You'll be subsumed by Castenard in a heartbeat, if all I've heard of them is true."

"I do hate that idea almost as much," Perát said.

"Then side with Limae and make everything as easy as possible."

"What does Limae offer?"

"A bastion of liberty as friend and ally, and a chance to stick it to Castenard. What more excuse do you need?"

The man looked down at the map.

"You've all been dancing around me, courting me and my help, for a week now. You bring a woman with the forceful nature of her father, who I never called friend, but respected immensely, and she tells me what I've been asking of you within moments of entering." He turned to Aurín. "Bring your soldiers. We're fighting with Limae."

Aurín held out a hand and they shook. Then he turned to Ophedia. "I was going to ask you to use a bit more tact, but I'd have been wrong to do so."

Ophedia gave a nod. "I'll bring back the Black Claws?"

"Ride hard. I want you back before sunset tomorrow."

"We'll be here sooner. See some barrels of ale ready for when we arrive."

"Expecting your men to be thirsty?" Perát asked.

"Our men and women are always thirsty," Ophedia said with a flippant wave of her hand. Then she touched her chest and innocently said, "I want the barrels ready just for me."

DREAD KNIGHT

Ophedia had the 1st riding out front of the rest of company. They neared the gate in silence, and Ophedia worried perhaps she had made a grievous error. Only two soldiers stood atop the wall, the gates open wide. Eunia appeared next to the gate and gave a nod. Ophedia sighed in relief.

The Black Claws marched into the gates to people standing on both sides. One man began to clap. Then another. Soon the applause roared, urging the company forward.

They moved, street by street; the entire city had gathered to cheer their entrance. Ophedia stopped at a square, to let the other groups 1st through 6th pass, until the wagons in the rear came up with the 7th guarding them. Ophedia began moving again, black banner held high, as she followed. Navien sat shackled in the last wagon, along with five other prisoners.

The company neared the gates to the inner city. At the top of the wall, she could see Aurín standing next to Perát de Bosco, waving to the crowd and company.

It happened very quickly. Someone threw handfuls of silver coins into the air and people rushed forward to grab for them. Ten men rushed out of the crowd with staves in their arms. They shoved the poles into the wheels of the prisoner cart, locking it in place. Others took hold of soldiers' arms and Ophedia's reins. A man with a massive sledge smashed at the side of the wagon where the prisoners's chains were attached. The men who'd lodged poles into the wheel spokes took hold of the prisoners on the wagon and manhandled them away into the crowd.

It happened so quickly Ophedia had no time to react. As fast as they had appeared, the gang disappeared, taking the prisoners with them. The people rushing to grab at the silver had faded back into the crowd as well, likely avoiding anyone who might ask for it back. Ophedia glanced up at the wall to where Aurín stood, a look of embarrassment across his face.

"How did that just happen?" Dakmor asked.

"I don't know," Ophedia said. "But I'm sure de Bosco will have something to say about it."

"None of us expected that."

"I know. They did it in full sight of the city leadership, when our guard was entirely down. Navien slipped through my fingers again."

"You've quite the history with him, don't you?"

"I do. I probably ought to go after him."

"If you need anyone to join you, I'll volunteer myself and Valden."

"Thank you. I'll keep that in mind."

When she next saw Aurín, he was seated next to Perát de Bosco at a table not unlike the Sentinel council at Haven in a much nicer war room than the one in the warehouse. They looked up as she walked in, and Aurín gave her a sheepish look. Eunia approached from a group nearby.

"What happened?" Eunia asked. "Everyone got really quiet before you all entered the inner city."

"Not now," Ophedia said, and crossed the room.

Perát opened his mouth to speak, but Ophedia interrupted him.

"I am aware of the embarrassment I caused with the prisoners we brought from Adwall escaping. I should like to go after them and save face."

Perát gave her a smile and instead stood and circled Aurín, pulling out a chair and indicating she take a seat.

"Please, del Ishé, join us."

Aurín gave her a nod and she did as she was asked. A servant brought a large tankard and set it before her as Perát took his own seat again.

"We did not expect anyone to make the move they did, though I am not surprised, given who you had as prisoner."

"Who? Navien?"

"I was unaware of who this Navien is, although Commander Mateau explained that you have a history with him. No. I'm referring to the prisoner you didn't know you had."

"I don't understand."

"One of the prisoners, whom Aurín says revealed his name to be Lerot Mendon, was under a pseudonym."

"I suppose he was important?"

Perát nodded. "My brother: a Chalician fanatic and spy."

"And now he, along with Navien, is in the wind," Aurín said. "I hope this doesn't change your opinion of us."

"Not at all," Perát said. "As I said, I am not surprised this happened. In fact, I plan to use this to try and drive his cell out of the city. We're going to leave the western gates less protected, and begin a routine search. If we're lucky, they'll take this as an opportunity to fall back to Nor-Vio, where the Chalician hold is stronger, which should free us up to prepare for a Chalician and Castenard rebuttal."

"We're just going to let them go?" Ophedia said.

"Why not?" Aurín said.

"Navien is only going to continue to be a burr under everyone's saddle. I want to go after him."

Perát tapped his fingers on the table in thought. "We do need an agent willing to go deeper into Chalician territory."

"Let me go," Ophedia said.

"You could end up captured and behind enemy lines with nothing but Chalicians around you," Perát offered.

"I think I'll be alright."

Perát glanced at Aurín, who nodded.

"Very well. You leave the day after tomorrow."

Ophedia spent the rest of that day and the next preparing, and as morning came Aurín walked her to the gate.

"Why are you actually going?"

"I don't know," Ophedia said. "If Rallia was captured, if Hanen hasn't gotten to her, perhaps I can?"

"If Navien finds you, that's it. You'll either be taken back to Mahn Fulhar in chains, or put under lock and key in Œron."

Ophedia shrugged.

"I'd rather neither happened to you," Aurín said.

"Why did you leave Œron in the first place?"

"A girl."

"Left because of her? Or left for her?"

"She had an affair with another man. I decided I'd rather not see them every day for the rest of my life, so I left. I considered joining the church but heard I could make money standing around as a Sentinel, and thought that was a better idea."

"With what happened in Mahn Fulhar, do you think you made the right decision?"

"I met you," Aurín said.

"What's that supposed to mean?"

"I think it's pretty clear," Aurín said.

"I'd rather you not make this into something it's not."

"Is it not?" Aurín asked.

"You've had your share of flings. I saw you once or twice at an inn with one woman or another up in Mahn Fulhar."

"But since then?" Aurín asked.

"No. I suppose you haven't."

Aurín reached over his back, took up a long, large bundle, and held it out.

"What is this?"

"A gift."

"Aurín...I'm not sure I can accept this. I don't want you to get any ideas."

"I'm giving this to you regardless. You may need it. And I'd regret not giving it to you if something were to happen."

"Knowing we may never see each other again," Ophedia added.

"I understand. And I understand you might not return my feelings, but I've said it now."

She took the heavy object and sat down on a bench by the gate to unwrap it. A long handle curved to reveal a hand guard from which rose skyfall metal for a handsbreadth before beginning a long rounded curve of three feet. Rather than coming to a point, it terminated in a flat two-inch chisel. She hefted it. For skyfall, it was lighter than expected, but then, it was also incredibly thin. The ripples in the metal were defined, and the dark folds almost appeared red in the pre-dawn light.

"I found it driven through the griffin skeleton's rib cage. I think it struck a killing blow against its master and he got his revenge before dying."

"This sword seems so old. It's not from any culture I've ever seen."

"Yet still made of skyfall. I thought forging of the metal was a new discovery, but this sword tells me it may be more of a rediscovery."

"Have you named the sword yet?"

"Have you named your stout stick?" Aurín said in rebuttal.

She smiled. "No, I have not."

"I hadn't settled on one yet."

"But you have thought about it."

Aurín gave her a sheepish look. "Something like Graze or Grace."

"Naming it after me, huh?"

He smiled.

She held it out and flicked it. Then took it in two hands and swung in a chop.

She looked back at Aurín with a smile. "Sky Grazer."

35

Spies and Subterfuge

Serving bread unto his friends,

They broke their fast together.

And secrets shared bought trust and love,

Through sun and rainy weather,

Their friendship bound by tether.

—*THE TRAVELER*

The innkeeper's wife approached with a platter of rough ends cut off the roast and several tough bread heels.

Marn accepted the platter with thanks.

"I'm sorry it's not more," she muttered. "I tried."

"You are doing as you are told," Marn said. "I understand."

"I slopped some of the drippings into the platter. It'll soak into the crusts, I hope."

"I welcome it," Alodda said, quickly reaching for a piece of the soggy bread and shoving it into her mouth before someone came to take it away.

They had been stuck in the common room of the inn for three days. Panza had come and gone, a look of murder on his face every time he glanced at them. They had heard a rumor of the man they sought, Lerot Mendon, at this inn, only to discover he had been in the north, on the south end of Limae and captured by a Limaean battalion.

The inn was directly across the street from the city barracks, and Panza had come and gone, his own mission forfeit, as he fretted over how to assist those loyal to Lerot Mendon. He'd given Marn and Alodda little attention, but members of the cells Panza had contacted kept vigil over them. Word had come that Lerot was being brought to Boscolón as prisoner. Panza and the other agents moved quickly, leaving the inn under the supervision of two guards of less consequence.

Marn pushed the largest piece of meat toward Alodda, the red not charred completely away, and took nibbles of some of the tougher pieces as the woman left their side.

"Eat quickly," he muttered. "We can make for the door soon after."

"Right now?" Alodda asked.

"Panza and the others are gone, and we don't know for how long."

"There is no one standing outside the barracks though. No one to see us fleeing to them and give us aid," Alodda said.

"We have to try. I fear they'll try to get my message from me through you."

"Why is it so important?"

"I can't say. But I know that even Lerot does not want to know it. I don't know who he is in the grand scheme of things, but perhaps he can keep you and me alive, so long as Lerot does not find out. I trust Panza less and less every day."

"I've eaten enough," Alodda said. "Let's go."

Marn nodded and stood, platter in his hands, and limped toward the bar.

One of the two guards at the table by the door stood. "What are you doing?"

"Tidying up," Marn said. "Allow me this little pleasure."

The guard rolled his eyes. Marn placed the wooden platter on the counter and awaited the innkeeper's wife to appear. She was a long time coming, and the second guard finally got fed up and came behind the counter to take it from Marn.

Marn turned and gave Alodda a wink, then swung the platter just past the man's face and into the row of mugs above the barrels.

The man ducked, Alodda rose to rush the door, and Marn turned to go after her, when twenty men and women poured into the bar, Panza at the head.

Marn, Alodda, and the guards froze, and for that split second Panza took the room in with a glance.

"Tie them up and get a cart ready," he ordered. "Place them by the hearth."

The others sat down five men already tied in ropes, and set them free from their bindings, including a blonde man the others seemed to defer to.

Panza whispered to the blonde man, who looked at Marn now trussed up and seated before the fire. The man nodded and crossed to them.

"I understand you've a message for me?" the man asked. He rubbed at his scruffy face.

"I don't know you," Marn said.

"I'm Lerot Mendon. Word is you bear a message from Castenard for me."

"Again," Marn said, "how do I know I can trust you? I don't know you."

"But I know them," a voice from behind said.

The blonde man turned to consider another one of the prisoners brought in.

Alodda sunk deeper into her chair, wishing she could bury her face in her bound hands.

"And who would that be, Abenard?" the first man said.

"Signore Mendon," Captain Navien said, "I was in pursuit of this man and woman, among others, when I entered Limae. While they are not my true quarry, they are a good second."

"Just like that Sentinel who captured us in the first place?"

"I would not trust any message they bring," Navien said. "They are traitors turned against Mahndür. They are no friend of the Abecinian Church."

"I am a monk of Aben," Marn said.

"Are you now?" Mendon asked.

"Turned traitor for not joining with the Chalicians when they came to Mahn Fulhar," Navien stated.

"Traitor to the Chalicians. Perhaps we ought to just kill them now and be done with it," Panza said, coming to stand with them. "Their message from the Manticör may now be compromised."

Panic rose in Alodda's chest.

The murderous look in Mendon's eyes was cold and calculating.

"Well?" Mendon said. "Out with it."

"I ought to leave the room," Panza said. "The Manticor was

quite clear that I not hear the message. He thought only you ought to know."

"He still doesn't trust you after that time you stuck a knife in him?"

Panza gave Mendon a wicked smile.

"Take them with us," Navien said as Mendon opened his mouth.

"Excuse me?"

"Take them to Nor-Vio. They can deliver their message there."

"Why not have it from them now, kill them, and be done with it?"

"The message will be better delivered away from Boscolón," Marn said. "Where you can act upon it quickly, and without worry of recapture."

"I can use them as bait," Navien added, "to draw my quarry to me."

"And if I decide to kill them anyway?" Mendon asked.

"I've given you my meals as we sat rotting in Limaean shackles," Navien said. "You practically begged for them under extreme hunger, but you promised me favors in return."

"You would take the lives of these two in trade?"

Marn lowered his head in humility as Mendon made eye contact.

"Very well, into the cart," he conceded. Then he turned to the Voktorra. "But Navien, the first sign they try and flee, we cut their throats and leave them in a ditch."

Navien nodded and stepped forward, taking hold of Marn and Alodda's shoulders.

"Why are you doing this?" Marn asked as Navien pressed them out the door to the cart waiting for them.

"Traitor or not, I'll not kill a priest or monk. I want your son and daughter in chains and taken back to Mahn Fulhar. This girl is the key."

"Why are we in such a hurry?"

"Your friend, del Ishé? She'll be in pursuit soon I think. I want as many miles between us and this city as possible, before she catches up."

"Afraid of a girl?" Marn mocked.

"I do not fear her, but I'll not risk suffering embarrassment by her a third time."

"And my message for Mendon?"

"Keep it to yourself. The longer you hold it, the longer you live. Or at least it'll take longer for him to grow impatient and torture it out of you."

Nor-Vio, capital of Ormach, bore the largest harbor Alodda had ever seen. Marn's disinterest suggested there were larger harbors somewhere in the world, but the lattice of stone piers that filled the bay, with hundreds of ships awaiting loading and unloading into and out of the sprawling city, left her gawking. It was a relatively flat city that bore short walls and spread out into the surrounding hillside.

The hills beyond the city were covered in crops and the valleys between stood pregnant with orchards awaiting the harvest at the end of the summer. The streets appeared at first to be filled with vendors, but as they drew nearer, no hawkers' calls met them, instead an eerie silence.

"Refugees," Navien said from a sleipnir beside the wagon.

"What do you mean?" Marn asked.

Navien had been more cordial than Alodda had expected. He did not seem to bear them disdain, but had maintained a conversational professionalism for the five days it had taken to reach Nor-Vio.

"Of all the lands the Chalicians have brought under their god-given guidance, no country is more important to them than the salvation of Ormach. The people were given one year to either stay or leave. Those you see are those finally willing to leave their homes, flooding the city to buy passage elsewhere."

"Why Ormach?" Alodda asked.

"Ormach was established centuries ago as a breadbasket. Under the guidance of the fallen Order of the Hammer, it was at first a boon. The land was taken from warring nations and made a place that would quickly feed those that needed it."

"How is that a problem?" Marn asked.

"The Paladins leveraged that food," Navien said. "If a country capitulated to the demands of the Paladins, they would be fed in times of blight and famine."

"Again, I do not understand the problem."

"Œron is not arable enough to feed itself and its growing

control," Lerot Mendon said from nearby. "Ormach is hardly controlled by the Paladins anymore. Our cities flourish, while surrounding nations starve."

"And these starving people flee?" Alodda asked at they neared the gate.

"They've had almost a year to leave," Lerot said. "Leave, or stay under Chalician rule."

"Under Œronzi rule," Marn said.

"No. Ormach will remain separate from Œron. The Fortress of Ammar is to be under Chalician rule and is to become the new capital of Ormach. Each city of Ormach will swear subservience to the Church of the Common Chalice as their sovereign."

"A theocratic hegemony," Marn said.

"You're more educated than I give you credit for, priest," Mendon said. "I thought you were a net mender."

"A net mender can understand the world around him better than a high-born prince observing the starving from his tower."

Mendon scoffed, and rode away.

"Touched a nerve?" Marn said.

"His brother is lord of Boscolón," Navien said.

"Ah. Then he's no freedom fighter. He's the traitor inviting the griffin into the capricör barn."

"You would do wise to keep that tongue behind your teeth," Navien said with an amused smile.

"Why should I?" Marn said. "As soon as you reveal your hand, either Lerot kills the lot of us, or the Chalicians take us to Œron to live out the rest of our days as slaves under their regime. I have zero hope that we will see anyone we know ever again. I'll certainly make sure you never find my son nor daughter."

"You're frightening your charge," Navien said, then kicked his own sleipnir in the sides and rode on ahead.

"Am I?" Marn said, giving Alodda a sheepish look.

"No," she replied. "But why are you antagonizing them?"

"I think Navien is turning," Marn said. "At least, I pray for such, with every word sent to Lomïn."

"What do you mean?"

"He left Mahn Fulhar with the goal of taking us back. Now he's forced to act as an agent for a church that has no one's best interests in mind but their own."

"Then why egg him on?"

"Because he may be the ally we need."

They reached the gate, and Lerot negotiated with the guard captain stationed there. After gold changed hands, Lerot came to the cart.

"Navien, you're to see the cart and your prisoners through the city to the inn where we'll be staying. Have you been in the Nor-Vio before?"

Navien shook his head.

"Then pay one of the captain's guards and he'll escort you. Did you see the Red Tower as we approached?"

"I did," Navien said. "Round, tall, and near the western edge."

"Near that is a sizable inn. The Draft. It'll have a sign with two sleipnirs pulling a barrel. You'll meet us there. Fail to do so, and I'll see you beaten."

"You've no need to threaten me," Navien said. "We all serve the same cause."

"Good."

Lerot turned to his men and Panza, and they moved into the city.

"What happens now?" Marn asked.

"We traverse the city, and attempt to reach Lerot in time to avoid his wrath."

"He hopes to be granted Bosocolón, doesn't he?" Marn asked.

"Given his brother appears to be siding with Limae, I doubt he'll get that wish. From what I've learned of Lerot, he's a vindictive man and would like to see his brother bleed. I expect he'll position himself to swear allegiance to the Praetor sent to bring Ormach under heel."

As they entered the city, the atmosphere shifted again. Despite the low, spacious homes, wide streets, and clean blue sky overhead, tents and bedding sat against every open wall. Coughing and misery hovered in a palpable miasma, far worse than the frantic desperation of Castenard.

They broke off the first street and entered a square. Guards had been stationed by the fountain to keep people from defiling it, but they could hardly hold back the hundreds of refugees, awaiting the chance to leave.

"How long until the Chalicians fully take control?" Marn asked.

"In three weeks the first crop of harvests begin in earnest. Lerot says those who haven't made it to ships will be forced to work the fields."

"One might ask why they don't just leave east on foot, but I know why," Marn said.

"Oh?"

"Castenard is forcing people to pay fines to pass through their control. I suspect they plan to press refugees into the armed service."

"Then Limae can burn under its folly for not making all of this easier."

"How can you say that?" Marn asked. "Limae stands against the tyrannical forces brought against them. By your logic, you would just have everyone submit to the Chalicians without a single question as to their right to do this—-merely because they orate and demand. You're a Mahndürian, for Pantheon's sake. Where is your sense of freedom? You're a guild member."

"A Voktorra," Alodda corrected.

"What is that supposed to mean?" Navien snapped.

"Your guild maintains authority and power. That's your job. I'm not sure you truly understand what the guilds stand for, or else you would have stood against the Chalicians when they first entered our city."

Navien turned away from them to focus on the road.

They passed through another square. Marn sat upright, looking behind them.

"What is it?" Alodda asked.

Marn placed a finger to his lips, then pointed through the square as they left, to three figures cautiously following after them.

Alodda threw her hands to her mouth to keep from gasping.

The tallest of the three was a qavyl with a walking staff, followed by a smaller old man with a brown hood over his head, and walking confidently with her own staff, Rallia Clouw.

"What do we do?" Alodda asked.

"We wait," Marn said. "At the rate we're going, we won't reach the inn until well after dark. Let them decide how to make their move."

"But they did see us?"

"Yes," Marn said. "Dorian saw us first, and pointed us out to my daughter."

Alodda grew quiet, her heart racing in her chest, and tried not to look behind them. She could not help but steal glances now and again.

The qavyl followed them, staying a street behind, but Rallia and Dorian soon disappeared from view.

They came to another large square, this one cleared of refugees and made into a lackluster market with threadbare stalls. Sailors stood at a few tables hawking passage for prices no man could afford, and a few desperate people tried, without success to haggle them down.

"How can they stand here and offer paid passage if they have it to give?" Alodda asked.

"Because of the demand. They can afford to wait."

"No man in his right mind would buy passage from any one of these," Navien said from the cart seat, his irritation growing.

"Why is that?"

"Half of these sailors are Œronzi. They'll take people to Œron or the penal islands. The other half may be pirates, for all we know."

"I've heard not a few of these sailors are taking these refugees to drop them off on the shores of Hannica," a new voice said.

Navien turned to the qavyl walking alongside him.

"There are no human countries in Hannica," Navien said. "What would your people say to so many refugees dumped off on your coast?"

"It would be an interesting situation, I do not doubt."

"Do I recognize you?" Navien asked.

"You might," the qavyl said. "You're accent speaks of Mahndürian descent. I was in the north over the winter."

Navien gave the qavyl a suspicious glare.

"I think you will more likely recognize my companion," the qavyl indicated toward Navien, who looked to his right.

The Voktorra turned just as Rallia thrust the tip of a stout staff between his eyes, laying him out flat. Rallia quickly stepped over Navien, tied him up, and lugged him into the cart as Dorian appeared out of the crowd and hopped into the driver's seat.

"Let us get off the main streets," Dorian said over his shoulder.

Rallia leapt into the bed of the cart and cut the ropes from their wrists.

"Sorry we didn't act sooner," Rallia said as her father pulled her into a deep hug.

"We saw you coming and patiently waited, "Marn said. "We need somewhere no one will find us."

The qavyl kept out front of the cart, and they moved down a side street before coming to a smaller square, full of the stale smell of refugees. This one did not seem so full of despair, the other side of the square sporting the face of a poorkitchen of the Paladins of the Hammer.

"Paladins are still here?" Rallia asked.

"Some will stay here as long as they can," Dorian said. "I'd imagine they're working in tandem with the Crysalas."

Dorian hopped off the cart and walked across the square to the door and knocked. No one came.

"There isn't no one there," a beggar nearby said.

Dorian turned to the beggar. He had a shroud over his eyes.

"When hearts despair, solace is easily found, but hard gained," Dorian said.

"Quatrodox 3, 75:6," the beggar said, and dropped back his hood to reveal a bald head, although he kept the burlap veil over his eyes.

"Ah," Dorian said. "Closed up, but not gone."

The beggar turned and indicated they follow to another door.

"What is your name and rank?" Dorian asked.

"I would ask you first," the man said. "If I did not recognize your voice."

Alodda and Rallia followed the two Paladins into the dark torchlit hall.

"Of course, I don't expect you to recognize me," the Paladin said to Dorian. "I'm Pater Minoris Evral Polun."

"Dikun's brother!" Dorian exclaimed. "What providence to find you here, a beggar on the streets of Nor-Vio, rather than in Ammar where I sent you."

"It has been an interesting year," Evral said.

"You have no idea," Dorian said.

"Given you are here and not in the north where your missives said you would be is both surprising and not. We've much to speak of."

"There is a man bound in the wagon," Dorian said. "If you wouldn't mind sequestering him away for a bit until we decide what to do with him..."

"Yes, Prima Pater," Evral said.

He disappeared down a hall.

"Can we trust him?" Marn asked.

"We trust as we can, but stay wary. That he is still here in Ormach may indicate he stands against the Chalicians."

"That doesn't mean he's not a Motean," Rallia said.

"I'm confused," said Marn.

DREAD KNIGHT

"We've much to speak on," Dorian said. "I'd imagine we will have to wait to speak, though, if you'll trust me to guide us along."

"Of course we trust you," Marn said, putting a friendly hand on Dorian's shoulder.

The old man smiled back.

36

Nor-Vio

Several countries have foundation histories via interactions with the Holy Orders. Redot was once tied to the Nifarans, and Nemen holds strong ties with the Crysalas. But Ormach is without a doubt the most successful endeavor made by any order. Our country has never known famine nor blight, and our foodstores have cut off the lifeblood of many a war. Never shall our country fall, for all know better than to curse the hand that wields the plowshare.

—DIGIJAN HOLLWAN OF ORMACH, 2176

The stick she had found provided her some comfort, but every traveler passing the other way filled Seriah with a new fear, despite the little black ynfald that kept to her side, bristling or shivering a warning before even Seriah noticed travelers coming upon her. Before, her staff and robe offered her confidence and protection. Now, the light of the sun upon her shoulders and the color of the world in her eyes distracted her from her goal: reach a coast and sail as far away as possible.

A blind farmer and his wife had taken her in three nights before, offering her cheese and dried meat enough to last her several more days, but the hungry and destitute passed her by, eyeing the sack tied to her belt, and she worried they might accost her. As she bore no eye covering, no Nifaran staff, and a coarse head of unshaven hair, they might think her sickly. She found ash in a dead fire ring near a stream and she used it to further that appearance, wiping her face with the stinking stuff. Few eyed her as a potential companion now. So she walked, lonely but not desiring nor trusting any company save Whisper the ynfald.

The salty tang of the sea wafted through the trees, and she found she walked faster now, hoping to come upon further signs. The sea did not make an appearance, but a long inn at a crossroads did.

It appeared smaller than it was, a small cottage on the roadside, with a covered walkway going back into the forest toward the form of a larger common room in the shadows.

She came to the door and knocked. A woman opened the top half of the door, and took a step back as she saw the forlorn traveler there.

"What do you want?"

"Room and board, if you'll have me."

"Not if you're sickly. Not if you don't have coin."

"I am not sickly. While I do not have coin, I've a wheel of cheese, given me by a farmer from three days back up that road."

"I'm not one for charity in these trying times," the woman said, and went to shut the door.

"Please," Seriah said, placing her hand on the door. "I don't need much. I just need to know how far from the sea we are?"

"The sea?"

"I need passage elsewhere."

"Good luck with that," the woman scoffed. "Nor-Vio and Boscolón are down different directions on this road, and neither will have you easily away. Nor-Vio is the worse of the two, if rumors are true."

"Then I'll go to Boscolón," Seriah said.

"Not tonight you won't," the woman said with a sigh, and opened the door. "Night is falling fast, and no one but the foolish travel from here to Boscolón in the dark."

"Dangerous road?" Seriah asked.

"Dangerous men," she said. "But under my roof, you'll be safe."

"Thank you. I'll do anything you ask, if you'll provide shelter."

"Oh, I'll put you to work, alright," she said and guided her down through the hallway to the covered walk. Before they stepped outside the woman stopped. "Cheese?"

Seriah nodded and took out the second wheel and handed it to her.

"Ah, this is Krida's work. Good." She put it onto a shelf in a pantry, then took up a basket and shoved it into Seriah's hands.

"Go on into the main room and gather up any bread ends people are leaving untouched and bring them back here. They'll go in the pottage for tomorrow."

Seriah gave the woman a timid nod and walked toward the main hall, Whisper slinking along in her shadow as she entered. It wasn't anything special to look at: dark, with too few windows, and everyone packed in closely. It stunk of sweat and stale beer, men and women shoulder-to-shoulder, bearing an additional stink of sailors.

Most had hard ends of bread left untouched on their platters, and Seriah took them into the basket. She almost considered taking a bite off one, but it felt rock hard in her hand, and she decided the better for it.

Near the small hearth, a table of men sat around a black-haired, beautiful young woman in a leather vest and trousers. She had a heavy quarterstaff and an oddly shaped sword leaning against the wall next to her.

"You can't seriously expect us to believe the dead walked," one man was saying.

Seriah froze, her hand reaching for an end piece.

"It's true. I almost became one myself when the air was filled with black ash. Those that sucked it in died and came back."

Seriah recognized the voice.

"I call false," the man said.

"May I choke on this beer if I'm lying," the girl said, then lifted her tankard and drained it. She did not choke. She slammed the tankard down and belched and then locked eyes with Seriah. "What are you looking at, woman? Don't believe my story?"

"I do," Seriah murmured. "I was there."

The woman's face dropped, and she glared at Seriah, taking her in.

Seriah lifted a hand and covered her eyes for a moment, then looked at the other woman again.

"How?" The woman stood.

"You leave the table, you leave the winnings," one man said.

"You take my winnings I break your fingers."

The man gave a shifty glance at the others around the table, and sunk down in his seat.

Whisper nudged at the dark-haired woman's hand, and she looked down and laughed, crouching down and giving the little ynfald a scratch. She stood, took her staff and sword off the wall and circled the table.

"Nefer?"

"Hello, Ophedia," Seriah said.

"You get those bread ends?" the innkeeper called from across the room.

Seriah turned with the basket, and Ophedia followed.

The woman took the basket. "She with you, Ophedia?"

"Uh," Ophedia said, eyeing Seriah in confusion.

"I've come looking for room," Seriah said.

"You can stay with me," Ophedia said.

"You know her?" the innkeeper repeated.

"We go back a ways," Ophedia said.

The innkeeper gave her a nod and walked away without another word.

"Friend of yours?" Seriah asked.

"I paid her quite a bit of money when I arrived. She'll stay out of our way."

"I don't understand," Seriah said.

"Let's go somewhere private to talk."

Ophedia turned down a side hall and they walked to a private room. She opened the door and showed Seriah and Whisper through before following.

Seriah took a seat on one of the two beds, and looked up at Ophedia.

"Why are you this far south?" Seriah asked.

"I was going to ask you the same thing," Ophedia replied as she scratched the ynfald. "But I'd rather know why you're not blindfolded as a Nefer?"

"It was taken from me."

"Chalicians?"

"Slate."

"Figures. Were you taken from Haven?"

"Along with others, including Rallia Clouw."

"Where is she now?"

"I couldn't say. Now why are you here?"

"Haven sent me along with others to the south on campaign against the Chalicians. I'm pursuing a Voktorra who has it out for all of us."

"So, it's fate," Seriah said.

"I don't believe in that," Ophedia said flippantly.

"You sound like your father," Seriah said.

"I am not Searn," Ophedia muttered.

"Prove it," Seriah said.

"I'm here pursuing the man holding a firebrand to our feet every step of the way."

"So?"

"If I can lay hands on Navien, I can keep him from going after us. Keep him off the trail of Rallia or Hanen."

"I know where Hanen is," Seriah said, "and no one will like it."

"Go with me to Nor-Vio," Ophedia offered.

"Deeper into Chalician-controlled territory?" Seriah asked.

"Maybe we'll find you a ship there and they can take you wherever you want."

Seriah sighed. "I'm not sure a ship will be enough."

Ophedia paused as Seriah stopped in the middle of the road, Whisper sniffed at her hand.

"What is it?" Ophedia asked from farther up the road.

"There is nothing good to see in that city," Seriah said.

Ophedia glanced at the walls of the city of Nor-Vio, a few hundred yards away, took a whiff, and shrugged. "I smell a little hearth smoke. Low tide. Not much more."

Seriah shook her head. "It reminds me of Temblin."

"I never liked that country," Ophedia said. "Everyone there was sad and angry."

"That's what I smell."

"You smell sadness?"

"Despair."

Ophedia walked behind Seriah now, letting the woman move slowly through the street. She walked with no confidence, but rather, took in the face of every person settled in along the side, as twilight crept over the sky and stars blinked into view.

Every so often Seriah gave a little sob and wrenched on the staff Ophedia had given her. Ophedia didn't share the feeling, but understood. It was no different than the streets she had slept on as a young girl in Morriego and Setera, and then even a few nights in Macena. The scale of the despair was what nearly pushed Ophedia into her own fugue state. Every street, no matter what turns they took, was filled with people sleeping and living, and pursuing a false hope. Every one of them sought passage away. Seriah could not possibly hope to find a single ship willing to take her. If she'd still been sightbound as a Nifaran, she might. But she refused to talk about what had happened, and shut down each attempt at conversation if Ophedia brought it up.

Inns still had rooms available, as so many of the refugees could not afford to part with money intended for passage. Still, in every inn that Ophedia looked into, when she returned to the street, Seriah had already continued on, taking in the depressing sights with eyes that had not seen light in many years.

They came to another street crammed with people. Seriah walked into the space, looking left and right. Those sitting there gave her a glance, and looked away, or back to conversations with those nearby. Ophedia eyed the glow from windows and closed doors. One door opened and the silhouette of someone filled the space. Above the door hung a sign of a cup topped with froth.

Whisper took off from Ophedia's side toward that door and Ophedia sighed. "What now?"

She crossed toward the door as the figure knelt down to pet the ynfald. She looked up as Ophedia came near, and Ophedia smiled as she locked eyes with Rallia Clouw.

"He always finds us," Rallia said with a smile. "How does he do that?"

"I'm starting to think that fate is involved, but I don't believe in fate."

Rallia leaned in and gave Ophedia a warm embrace.

"Fate, huh?"

"More than you know," Ophedia said. "I've someone with me."

She turned back to the square. Seriah stood unmoved in the middle of it.

"Someone we know?" Rallia asked.

"Hard to recognize her without the blindfold on her eyes."

Rallia gasped. "Seriah?"

Ophedia nodded. "She found me in an inn as I made my way here. I brought her here to find passage away."

"But where is her blindfold?"

"She hasn't told me. I think something happened."

"Why don't you come in—I'll bring Seriah."

Ophedia gave a backward glance to Seriah and then walked into the inn.

It was fairly full, but her attention immediately went to a table not far from the hearth.

The qavyl Ymbrys sat with three others. When he saw her, he smiled, and the others turned in response. Dorian Mür, Marn Clouw, and Alodda Dülar gave her their own smiles as she crossed the room, Whisper at her side, weariness pressing down on her.

"Ophedia!" Alodda threw her arms around her.

"Not someone I expected to see here," Dorian said.

"Nor I, you," Ophedia replied.

"What brings you to this desolate city?" Ymbrys asked. "Looking for us?"

"I wish that were true," Ophedia said.

"You have found what you were after, though," Marn said. "If you're looking for Captain Navien."

"How do you know that? You were in Boscolón?"

"Yes," Marn said. "Sent from Castenard with a message for a man trying to usurp the city ruler."

"You're a spy now?" Ophedia arced an eyebrow.

"Forced to be, yes," Alodda added.

"What was the message?" Ophedia asked the older man.

Marn chuckled. "A message better left on my tongue as long as possible. The Manticör, an agent of the Doge of Castenard sent message of when the Casternardi army would be arriving at Boscolón. That we're long past that city made my message obsolete. I knew I'd be a dead man as soon as the message left my mouth."

Alodda gasped.

"Further, the reason we were told not to give the message with Panza nearby, is that the Manticör requested that Mendon take care of Panza, who'd outlived his usefulness and is a suspected traitor."

"But with no message delivered..." Alodda muttered.

"They'll probably spend time here in the city backstabbing each other," Marn said.

"And what of Navien?" Ophedia asked.

"When we came upon Marn and Alodda," Dorian said, "Abenard had them tied up in the back of a cart. We liberated them, and now Navien is in our...care."

"He's here?!"

"Bound and gagged in a room upstairs."

"The innkeeper hasn't cared?"

"Our host is a Paladin in hiding," Dorian said. "So, no. He

hasn't questioned my choice."

Ophedia took a seat.

"Did you see Rallia?" Marn asked.

"Yes. She's coming in with Seriah."

"Seriah?" Dorian replied in astonishment.

"She came to town with me. I thought perhaps we could find her passage away."

Dorian stood to move toward the door, then stopped in his tracks.

"Oh no," he said, the first hint of defeat in his voice Ophedia had ever heard. "By Nifara and Grissone, what have they done to her?"

Someone touched Seriah's shoulder, and she flinched, turning to look at the woman.

She had two shoulder-length braids that ended in silver caps. Her eyes were a dark shade of blue, and they welled with tears as they locked eyes. She did not have the sinking despair of those on the street, but of someone who bore a deep sadness for Seriah.

"Do I know you?" Seriah asked flatly.

"Oh, Seriah," the other woman said, and threw her arms around the smaller framed woman. "What did they do to you?" A quiet sob escaped her. Even through the woman's tears, Seriah recognized Rallia's voice.

Seriah returned the embrace, a soft whimper escaping her as she fought back the tears. Rallia's own sob broke like a dam and they held each other in mourning loss.

After a time, their tears subsided to slow, deep breaths.

"Where is Hanen?" Rallia whispered, fear in her voice.

"Still in Dream," Seriah said flatly.

Rallia took hold of her shoulders and pressed her back, looking her in the eyes. "Did he do this to you?"

Seriah shook her head sheepishly.

"Is he alright?"

"I don't know that anyone in his circumstance would be alright."

"Because he's in the Veld?"

"That," Seriah said, "and—"

"Because he bears the boneshroud," Rallia said matter-of-factly.

"You knew?"

Rallia shook her head. "I learned after you escaped into the Veld."

"I believe you," Seriah said. "Why are you here?"

"Dorian, Ymbrys, and I have been trying to head east to find safe haven, but it turns out the gods have had plans for us this whole time. Two days ago we found my father and Alodda Dülar, Hanen's intended."

"Does she know?"

"I think it's time we told her. Come on."

Rallia turned Seriah toward the inn, arms on her shoulders, and guided her into the door.

Across the room, a table of figures stood. While she did not recognize them, she knew each of them.

The qavyl, Ymbrys Veronia, wore long red robes of silk. Next to him stood a blonde girl in blue, Alodda, and an older man, Marn, who bore every resemblance to Rallia, save he bore a great burden in his eyes and a healthy belly. Ophedia stood with a tankard in her hand, not looking at Seriah. Lastly, the small old man, Dorian Mür, lifted a hand to cover his mouth.

"Come and rest, Holy Nefer," Ymbrys said, circling the table and pulling out a chair.

"I am no Nefer," Seriah murmured. "Please, call me Seriah."

She stood at the seat, but did not take it.

"How did you and Whisper escape the Veld?"

"The Veld?" Marn asked in astonishment.

"That is where Hanen is," Rallia said. "When Dorian, Ymbrys, and Hanen came to our rescue, he went into the Veld, taking Seriah and Whisper there. The opening closed before any of us could go after him."

Seriah looked around the table to eyes that did not show surprise.

"What are you Clouws?" Seriah asked, looking Marn, Rallia, and Alodda in the eyes.

"What do you mean?" Dorian asked.

Marn turned to Dorian. "The Clouws are touched by gods," Marn said.

"How did you know?" Rallia asked.

"What do you know?" Marn asked.

"I've told no one," Rallia said, "but I was given a message and blessing by a god in Mahndür."

"Who?" Seriah asked, coldly.

"Aben, father of the White Pantheon," Ymbrys said. "Just as you, Seriah, are touched by your own goddess."

Seriah gave Ymbrys a furtive look.

Alodda took a seat and the large loaf of bread from the middle of the table and held it in two hands. The others gave her a glance, and saw her stern look.

"What is it?" Marn asked the young woman.

"Everyone sit," she ordered.

They did.

"We've all been on the road with one another for months now, in one form or another. Holy Nefer, Seriah, just like the rest of us, we've all been found in the same locations around the world at various times over this past year, and it seems fortuitous, yet, not everything has been said. I think it is time we all clear the air. If the gods would continually put us in the same place, we do this together."

Seriah crossed her arms.

"I don't mind sharing," Ophedia offered. "If it'll clear the air."

Alodda tore a piece of bread off the loaf and handed it to Ophedia. The woman took the offering, bit, chewed, and swallowed.

"Well, for anyone who didn't already know, I'm the daughter of Searn VeTurres. My mother, another Sentinel Commander, left me an orphan. Searn found me, took me on, and that's kind of it. I'm technically a Black Warden now, but I'm not really sure if anyone knows what that means yet. I'm here now, trying to make sense of all this."

"Not shy about admitting who your father is," Seriah stated.

"As pretty much everyone in Mahn Fulhar and Haven knows, and chooses to mention it to me every time I'm in a room? No, not really."

"It doesn't bother you?"

"We can't choose our parents. Both of mine abandoned me as a baby. I am not a VeTurres, nor an Elbay. I'm Ophedia del Ishé."

"Dorian?" Alodda indicated, handing him a torn-off piece of bread.

The old man took it, but did not eat.

"You don't want ninety-eight years of history right now," he said. "I was a hero in the Protectorate Wars. I struck down the Deceiver's chosen champion Ollistan Gœrnstadt. While I'm no longer Prima Pater, I am hunting down a cursed armor I ought to have sought and destroyed decades ago. It would seem it is lost in another world entirely, now."

Alodda handed Marn a piece.

"My grandfather was the childhood friend of Dorian Mür. His wife, my grandmother, was the daughter of Ollistan Gœrnstadt."

Rallia gasped.

"I'm sorry this is how you found out, Rallia," he said. "The Deceiver sent a zvölder to me as a baby, and its bite crippled my leg and gave me my limp. Our family was marked by the Black Coterie with a curse, perhaps for failing him in the Protectorate Wars."

"I believe this may be true," Ymbrys said. "It is why I've been following your family, Rallia. I've been seeking out the long history of the Clouws, Unteels, and even," he indicated toward Ophedia, "the VeTurres."

"Why is that?" Ophedia asked, arching an eyebrow.

Alodda tore off a piece of bread and handed it to the qavyl, who took it and placed it down with a smile.

"I am a scholar of sorts," Ymbrys said. "I sought answers to two genealogies. The line of the Necromancer has been answered. Marn and his offspring are the answer to that. At first only a hobby, I also sought the lines of two older families: the Turrians and Untellians."

"I know the tale," Marn said. "Storytellers up north like to elaborate on it from the old epic, but what exactly are you saying?"

"I believe that your grandfather, Nethendel Unteel, is descended from the Untellians. And you, Ophedia, are descended from the Turrians. Hence your father's name, VeTurres. It likely came from the Turrian name."

"What does it matter?" Ophedia asked.

"Untellians and Turrians came from the same family, the Tellian family. Two brothers journeyed together and founded a kingdom. The brother who became known as Untellian was chosen by the White Pantheon, while his younger brother, Brase Turrian, was courted by the Black Coterie. It sundered their family and their kingdom. Turrian and his line were blessed with good fortune amidst bad luck, and Untellians in opposition were given blessings in humility. I believe this is why it would appear that everything you touch, Ophedia, seems to prosper. So long as you do not cross the dark gods, that blessing holds."

"And we Untellians?" Rallia asked.

"You prosper, but never rise to more than humble ends."

"Throw in the curse of the Deceiver..." Dorian added.

Ymbrys nodded. "I do not know the extent of that effect yet."

"Wouldn't Aben blessing me be a sign against that?" Rallia asked.

"I believe it might," Ymbrys said.

"Separate from all of this," Seriah said, "I bear my own curse."

Everyone turned to her, and Alodda held a piece of bread out to her.

"In Mahn Fulhar, I became an unwitting pawn. I was made messenger of the Deceiver to my goddess. In my message, I ushered in a new era."

"What do you mean?" Dorian asked, while Ymbrys nodded solemnly to himself, his grip tightening on the staff in his hands.

"I mean I delivered words from a fallen god to my holy goddess, and apparently when she received those words, it marked the beginning of a new era. One that would lead to a great imbalance."

"Something happened in Haven as well," Ymbrys said.

"I don't know how you know this," Seriah said, "but yes."

She gathered herself, and spoke. "Revenants rose in Haven when men and women breathed in a black mote of ash. I breathed one in and I was set to die. My goddess came to collect me and others, and I begged she take me. Instead, she marked me and took that blackness from me. It gave me a sight I did not have before."

"Sight?" Ymbrys asked.

"I can see the purple flames of the Veld-touched."

This seemed to satisfy him.

"Not much later and the Chalicians invaded Haven. I was captured, alongside Rallia, and taken south. I thought myself safe and protected by Nifara. Instead, when Hanen, Ymbrys, and Dorian came to my rescue, I was thrust into the Veld, alongside the heretic Slate. In a bid to take control of the contents of the wagon, Slate tore my blind from me. Hanen shoved him through a new gate into Noccitan, and then, on my own demand, sent me and Whisper through to Kallattai. Now we are here."

"How did Hanen open doors to other worlds?" Alodda asked.

"Hanen has in his possession a pair of gauntlets, from that

armor I told you that I pursued," Dorian said.

"They belong to the Dreadplate, yes," Seriah said. "But now no one has the armor."

"What do you mean?" Dorian asked.

"I pushed it off a cliff, into an endless chasm, that no one can reach the bottom of, along with the cloak."

"Cloak?" Alodda asked.

"Boneshroud," Rallia said. "Hanen also has the cloak that Searn VeTurres used at the Convent."

"Oh, no," Marn groaned.

"But," Dorian said, putting a hand on Marn's arm, "I do not fully fear that Hanen is so far gone that the cloak has somehow corrupted him."

"I don't think so, either," Ophedia said.

"You knew?" Rallia asked.

"I was first to know. I guessed it was so in Haven," she added with a smile.

"Corrupting?" Alodda asked.

"Yes. It is a cloak made of chain links," Dorian said. "Each link is made from bone. It would seem it holds the shades of those that died to make it."

Alodda sighed, her shoulders drooping.

"Questioning your choice of beau?" Ophedia asked.

"That's cruel," Seriah said to her, and turned to Alodda, whose face had grown grave. "But it is a question I have myself."

"Marn shared some if this with me," Alodda said, "as we journeyed to find Hanen and Rallia. This is very dark news, but I'll not cast judgment until I have looked Hanen in the eyes and asked him myself."

Alodda took the last piece of bread and broke it in two, giving one half to Whisper. "What of you, little ynfald? What part do you have to play in all of this?"

The animal looked up, swallowing the piece of bread greedily, then lolled his tongue at her.

"Dorian," Ymbrys said, "may I speak with you?"

Dorian rose and they both walked halfway across the room. Seriah's keen ears picked out pieces as they muttered.

"I understand, but I am going to speak with the Khamntyr," said Ymbrys in a low voice. "They may be difficult to find, without journeying all the way into the Oruche Marches, but I think I must consult with them."

"I've not dealt with their people since the Protectorate Wars," Dorian said.

"And even then," Ymbrys said, "not with the tribe I seek."

"You're still being very mysterious," Dorian said.

"I always am," Ymbrys said. "When next we meet, I will explain more. But you must keep these Untellians, Turrians, and the Nifaran protected. I fear they are important to the success of the White Pantheon's plans."

"And the Black Coterie's," Dorian said.

"Less than you think, actually," Ymbrys said.

A long moment later, Dorian came back to the table.

"Where did Ymbrys go off to?" Rallia asked.

"He had an errand to run out of the city. We shall see him again, I do not doubt."

"I would have liked to have said goodbye," Rallia said, her face downcast.

Marn placed a comforting hand on his daughter's shoulder.

The rest of the evening went on in relative silence as each at the table became mostly introspective. The only happy face was Whisper's, as each negligently scratched behind his ears.

37

KOA GAHN

Bellows rise and bellows fall, forging metal and iron awl.

Terror brings the hammer down, on peasant head and golden crown.

—*ALL THE CROWNS BEFALLEN*, BY ELLAVON GAVALIN

Stars fell away in streaks as the interminable fall went on for ages. Hanen would have screamed if he had voice, but it took all of his effort to keep back the sound of Ghoré's laughter. The flutter of wyloth wings brushed his face, and he swiped at the feeling with his free hand, worried that if he touched his head with the desiccated claw entwined with his other hand, then Ghoré would enter his mind.

Why fight me? Ghoré taunted. We are friends, are we not? This dream could be ours.

"Leave me!" Hanen croaked. "End this falling!"

Falling? Ghoré chided.

Hanen reached behind himself and felt the packed earth under him. The roaring of his own heartbeat in his ears stopped suddenly as he leapt to his feet. Far above, the purple sky was only visible as a crack in the blackness.

"When did we land?" he muttered to himself. "Where am I?"

The claw in his hand suddenly began to glow. He held it back, startled, and then looked closer. The sand and dust on the skin illuminated everything nearby.

"How did you..."

DREAD KNIGHT

You really aren't smart, are you, boy?

Hanen ignored him and held up the glowing thing to look around. The bottom of the canyon was only a couple meters across. A flat, sandy path cut around corners. Along the walls rose vertical streaks of light. He approached one to find it was some sort of mollusk climbing up the walls with a silvery trail of slime streaking behind it.

He reached out to touch the shell. Its seven tendril-like stalks retracted into the shell, and from pores in the chitin a burst of silver dust puffed out. Hanen sneezed as it hit his nose, and the black world suddenly reversed to a silvery one. The silver streaks turned black, but far above the purple sky remained. The walls contorted around him in wavering shifts. The sides of the canyon started to collapse down over him and the violet crack closed.

"No!" he shouted, and held up the dead hand glowing black.

Silver walls morphed and pulled back away from him. A portion of the sky broke away from the rest and probed down over Hanen. He shoved against the wall as the form moved over him. A maw opened and a barbed tongue licked at the wall, consuming the silver mollusks with a swipe.

Hanen fought back a panicked breath as the thing moved down the canyon in search of more food. Hanen stood and fled the other way, the silver world slowly fading to blackness. The silver lines of the mollusks had been washed clean, and the glow from the hand faded.

"More light?"

Do it yourself, Ghoré said. *If you need it so badly.*

"We're stuck with each other," Hanen said. "The least you can do is help."

The least you can do is give in and give up.

"No."

There was a rumble and scrape on the walls above. Hanen pressed down against the wall again, and looked up at the purple sky as something moved across the backdrop. Not a sinewy thing, but heavy, with legs that shoved their way along the hard sandstone walls. Its massive form gave off the smell of a rancid tree nut. Its foreshortened neck belied a heavy head, and after its stalky form passed by, an incredibly long and whip-like tail continued on for meters.

Let me in, Ghoré roared in his mind, and slammed against his thoughts with several heavy punches.

Hanen visualized pushing back against the Wyloth King's attack, and suddenly he could see Ghoré before him, the weird and elongated fingers of the freakish man locked with his. Ghoré's other arm flailed about, the taut membranes of his wings causing wind to surround them.

"Stop this!" Hanen hissed. "You'll draw it back."

A lesser mind to be commanded. Give me your mind and body!

"I will not."

You will. You'll not leave this place until you have.

"When you take over and kill me, you mean. I will not give you that pleasure."

Then die, and I'll take you anyway.

The ground began to shudder and the walls of the canyon pushed away as shards of stone rose up, making a maze of the once-straight path.

Hanen stepped left and right, dodging the rising juts of stones, fleeing down the path as the hand entwined with his tried to run him through.

A silence suddenly washed over him and the stones stopped as he came to a wider spot in the canyon floor. The destroyed remains of the cart stood before him.

"Given up trying?" Hanen said.

Tell me what that is, Ghoré demanded.

"The cart."

I don't know what that means.

Hanen ignored the voice in his head and approached. Within the shattered wood, the Dreadplate lay like a fallen body. Hanen reached within the pile and pulled out pieces of wood, his hand brushing over the bone links. For half a second, Ghoré screamed as Searn's voice entered Hanen's mind.

Hello, Hanen.

Don't touch that again, Ghoré said, his voice quivering in fear.

"What are you worried about?" Hanen chuckled.

I'll not go back in there.

Hanen shoved his hand back into the debris and took hold of the boneshroud, despite the roaring scream that Ghoré let out into his mind in a torrent of expletives and curses.

"What is he doing here?" Searn asked, his shade form appearing next to Hanen.

"His grip on my hand can't be removed. I think I'm stuck with him now."

"Nonsense," Searn said.

His shade took hold of the claw that held Hanen's. It shuddered, cringed away, slipped off, and fell to the ground. It continued to shudder and shrivel into a fist as Hanen watched Searn's ephemeral form try to pry the ring from the finger.

Searn chortled to himself. "I think you don't have to worry about him now. You can take the hand up by the wrist, if you'd like."

Hanen did not. Instead, he pulled the boneshroud free from the cart and pulled it over his shoulders.

"Does that feel better?" Searn asked.

"Safer," Hanen said, eying the hand on the sandy floor.

"So, where are we?" Searn said. His shade form had no features, but it looked around, taking in the space.

"At the bottom of a crevasse in the Veld."

"Why is the cart destroyed?"

"Seriah pushed it off the edge, along with the boneshroud."

"Where is she now?"

"I sent her back to Kallattai."

"Then you still have the gauntlets?"

"I do," Hanen said.

"Then let's work out how to move this armor without further interruption."

Searn's shade moved up to the pile of wood and took hold. It would not move. He looked around at the sand and motioned with his hands, and the sand began to shift in little whorls.

"You do that so easily," Hanen said.

"Because it is," Searn said. "Everything in the Veld responds to the mind."

"But you have no mind. You are shade only."

"I am no different than those that have escaped into the Veld to avoid death."

"What do you mean?"

"My mentors taught me that many escape death by casting themselves into the Veld at their moment of physical death, thus avoiding the Judge. It is part of the theory we used in the crafting of the boneshroud."

"I don't understand."

"Just because you cannot understand how I can have no body but have a mind does not mean it isn't true."

"Well, then show me how you're moving the sand."

"I can move the sand, called oneirion, because that is its purpose. The Veld was made by the Judge's Wife for the purpose of creativity. A place where thoughts and dreams manifest. The sand is responsive to the mind because it is made of mind."

Searn crouched down and Hanen joined him. He took up sand in his hand.

"You don't need to hold it. Tell it what to be."

Hanen dropped the sand and pictured the Aerie in Haven.

"Now, command the oneirion."

When he opened his eyes, a miniature in-scale version of the citadel sat in the sand.

"Good!" Searn said. "Pick it up."

He reached under the citadel, the sand shifted to stay in form as he lifted it. Hanen blew at the tower. It turned to dust and billowed into Searn's face.

"Sorry!" Hanen exclaimed.

Searn didn't appear offended, and the sand stuck to his face for a bit, giving form to his features.

"Why the look?" Searn asked.

"I have an idea. May I try something?"

Searn gave a nod.

Hanen took up handfuls of oneirion and poured it over Searn's shade, willing it to stick. Once he had completely covered him, he touched the sandy form. Searn now bore most of his features, including clothes.

"Interesting," Searn said. "Good thought."

Hanen gave a nod of satisfaction, and turned to the woody mess. He took up more sand, and poured it from his hands, but the sand fell into ridge lines. Breaking off one of the lines as a stick, he handed it to Searn, who held it in his hands as Hanen took another and began to use the pole as leverage to move wood away.

"Come on," Hanen said, "let's clear this away."

They worked together for some time. After a while, the silver streaks of the wall mollusks blinked into view again and began their climb.

"What are those?" Searn asked.

"Some sort of shelled snail. If you touch them, they puff out a cloud that makes you see everything in reverse color."

"Interesting. Did they go away, only to return?"

"A bigger creature came by and ate those that were out."

DREAD KNIGHT

"There are bigger creatures here."

"At least in this canyon," Hanen said. "I didn't see any when up above."

"Imagine the exploration that could be done here," Searn said.

"Is that what you would do? If you had the time?"

"Well, I do. Have the time, I mean. I am immortal now."

"I'm not," Hanen said. "I'd like to figure out how to get out of this canyon. It's not safe."

"Fair enough," Searn said, and turned back to the work. Soon, all of the wood had been cleared, leaving the black suit of armor lying on the sandy canyon floor.

"What now?" Hanen asked.

"We make the armor move."

"How?"

"You know how," Searn chided.

"What do you mean?"

"Don't act clever. You move skyfall metal with the Gloves of Eons—they're made of skyfall."

"The what?"

"The gauntlets. You have been too focused on other things. They are called the Gloves of Eons."

Hanen took out the rings and dropped them over his wrists and the Gloves of Eons appeared.

He turned to the pile of armor, and held out his hands. He felt no push nor pull.

"Nothing is happening."

"No patience?" Searn asked.

Hanen sighed, and held the gauntlets up again. He twisted them around, as he had when drawing coins to him, but nothing pulled back.

A dark shadow moved overhead. Hanen and Searn both shot looks up at the violet sky. It was the creature with the long, whip-like tail again.

"What was that?" Searn asked.

"I don't know," Hanen said. "It went over me earlier."

"Then let's get this armor moving. The sooner we are out of here the better."

Hanen walked up to the armor and touched the chest plate with the gauntlets. Pulling them back, there was a little pull as the plate stuck to his hands slightly. He touched it again and imagined the plate armor standing up, then lifted.

The entire suit lurched, then fell back to the sand again.

"That's something!" Searn said.

"But only when I touch it."

"Then touch it," Searn said. "That thing is coming back."

Hanen glanced over his shoulder to see the dark form moving back up the canyon, and growing as it lowered.

"Make some light," Hanen grunted as he put the gauntlet to the armor's shoulders and lifted. It shambled to its feet like a street show marionette. It provided some of its own support, but Hanen was forced to move it as though lifting a body.

He shifted it around to put it between himself and the thing descending toward them. Searn stood next to him, having taken up Ghoré hand, the sand covering it beginning to glow.

"It's spotted us," Searn said, holding the glowing light up higher.

"Of course it has," Hanen said. "It lives here and we're moving a giant suit of black armor!"

The scrambling of its legs on the walls ground to a halt, then it tucked its fat legs together and dropped to the canyon floor, half into the light shining from Searn's hands.

Its head bore a resemblance to a scaled bovine, but with a mouth full of heavy, sharp teeth. Its torso was thick with stalky legs, and covered with bony plates. Along its shoulder ridge, spines ran with membranous skin taut between them. It wasn't a tall sail, nor wings that might allow it to glide, but the spines seemed to move involuntarily. The tail was five times as long as its body and it snapped like a whip in the darkness. It groaned with a hissing grunt, "Kooaa gongggg..."

"What am I supposed to do?!" Hanen asked, trying to keep the Dreadplate between him and the creature.

"Use the armor on the...Koa Gahn!" Searn said.

"Koa Gahn?"

"It's what it said! I don't know!"

Hanen pushed the armor toward the creature as it advanced on the towering armor. He braced himself, expecting the thing to impact with its full weight. Instead, it hit the armor like a solid, unmoving wall.

Hanen laughed in surprise.

"What?"

"It didn't move me at all."

"There isn't much that can move skyfall. Hit it back."

Hanen closed his eyes and imagined the suit throwing a swing. While it bore no hands, the arms of the skyfall metal suit swung forward and smashed the Koa Gahn in the side of the face. It shook its head in surprise and shoved forward, angry at the suit, not seeing the man behind it. The long whip-tail lashed out and around the suit. It was not prehensile, but swung over and over again. It struck Hanen with its weight, but not the tip, covered in calcifications.

"Watch that tail," Searn said.

"I'm trying," Hanen grunted, pressing the armor forward again.

"It's not smart, but it is angry now," Searn said.

"All I can do is pummel it," Hanen said. "We drive it off or beat it to a pulp."

"Then do it!" Searn ordered.

Hanen shifted the weight of the armor and pushed the creature up against the wall. Hanen lost his balance and tripped, losing his grip on the armor. It stumbled toward and into the creature, but didn't collapse.

"You're still driving it?" Searn said.

"Not as well, but yes!"

He moved his gauntleted hands as though he wore the armor and began swinging with controlled punches at the creature's head. It roared out with a lowing, "Gaaaang—gaaahng!"

Its tail moved with less muster as it cowered down into the wall, the form of the armor over it. Hanen shoved and the armor fell and toppled on the creature. It could not move against the weight, but its tail lashed about trying to do something.

"What do I do now?" Hanen muttered. "It's still alive."

"Make a sword and kill it."

"Make? Oh."

He took up some sand and let it fall to the ground, solidifying as it did. A thin sword hung from his hand.

"I don't want to do this," Hanen said.

"Then it'll hunt us from here to Noccitan."

Hanen pursed his lips in resolve and raised the sword over the struggling creature, then drove it down through its eye and jaw. It slumped over, still and dead.

"Let's get out of here," Searn said, looking up at the cliffs and purple sky above.

38

THE ARBORIST

Dream not. Fear not.

—COMMON PROVERB

Hanen tried to drive the armor onward with one hand and move oneirion with the other. From the side of the cliff, he willed stair steps to appear, wide enough for the Dreadplate to traverse. Hanen was unsure how many hours they had been at it, but while they'd proceeded up the cliffs, the glowing mollusks had disappeared and reappeared again. Silver stripes were a poor timekeeper, but it was something. Twice the armor had almost fallen off a ledge, and twice Hanen had saved them from starting over. Searn found he could not go farther than twenty-five feet from Hanen, anchored still to the cloak on Hanen's frame.

As the silver slime trails dissipated once more they were nearing the lip of the canyon. Hanen sat down, panting.

"You're not actually tired," Searn said.

"What?"

"You're panting for breath as though you're tired. No one is ever tired here. You only think you're exhausted."

Hanen dropped a gauntlet off his hand and touched his throat. His heart wasn't pounding.

"I don't understand."

"This is not a physical place, as physical as you may be. This is a place of thought."

"What is not possible here then?"

"You're only limited by your imagination."

Hanen eyed the ledge twenty feet above them, then crouched down to the ground and touched the solid sandstone, and closed his eyes. The ground began to rumble and moments later, the ledge they stood on was level with the top. Hanen opened his eyes and looked around. It was not the scrubland that had been there before, but a forest of short, gnarled trees fifty yards away.

"Well done," Searn said.

"Thanks. Wish I'd thought of it sooner. Who is that?"

Standing at the edge of the forest, two figures watched them. One wore a long black robe, lined with an amethyst-like purple. From the folds of his robe, a silver chain ran to the other man, who was on his knees, a short scruff of hair on his head and face, staring at the ground.

"Be careful," Searn said.

"Why?"

"That one of them has the other in chains ought to be enough. I can tell by the purple lining of his black cloak, he's a mage: a Somnumancer of the Veld."

"And?"

"You just started figuring out how to use the oneirion. This man will have full mastery of it. My mentor, Zephyr, was a highly skilled Somnumancer. There are many levels of greatness among them. Be wary, is all I'm saying."

Hanen touched the armor and it stood a bit taller. With a thought, the sand that covered Searn fell from his form and he was only a shade again. Hanen walked forward, the armor shambling alongside him.

"Assume that the mage can't see me," Searn said. "Until you know otherwise."

Hanen came to within twenty-five feet of the mage and stopped.

"You and your armored companion are a stranger in these parts," the man in the black robe said.

"We journey where my path takes me," Hanen replied. "Have I entered a place I ought not to have?"

"To have come out of a crevice is of interest. That you trespass within my demesne is, I hope, only a misstep."

"If I have misstepped," Hanen said, "I should hope you will accept an apology as recompense."

"Üterk diplomacy," Searn muttered in Hanen's ear. "Good. See how he responds."

"You have upon your shoulders an intriguing cloak, and your guardian who looms beside you is reminiscent of legends."

"My companion and I should like to better understand how we can quickly leave you be. If you will point the way from your demesne, I shall take leave."

"What makes you think I would like you to leave without first experiencing my hospitality?"

"Standing in ominous silence as I approach, with slave upon your chain, I should wonder and fear at your power."

"This little thing?" the mage said, motioning to the man on his knees. "He is no pet. He pays my fee."

"Fee?"

"I came upon him but a few days ago. He told me wondrous stories, and in return, I showed him still more wondrous things. When he has come through, he shall call me friend and master. Not as slave, but as companion."

"Then he experiences a dream within this dream?"

"Truly, it is no dream he experiences," the mage said, "but nightmare."

He turned to the forest and waved his hand and the trees stepped aside, revealing a path.

"Will you join me? I've a feast beyond compare prepared. We can all eat."

"Follow," Searn said. "But offer nothing without being asked. Everything is in trade, but he will not tell you the value of his own answers."

"An Üterk Dinner Feast," Hanen muttered under his breath.

"What did you say?" the mage asked back over his shoulder.

"I wondered in awe at this forest," Hanen said. "It is a vibrant creation."

"I am rather proud of it," the mage said.

After a long while the forest thinned out and they crested a hill to the view of a crater. Within that crater, a tall tower as twisted as the branches of the trees they had passed lay waiting. A single door sat closed thirty feet above the ground.

The mage, tugging on the silver chain, walked to the base and then circled the tower on blocks that pressed out of the side and disappeared as easily.

"The first test," Searn said. "Move quickly."

Hanen touched the side of the tower and five blocks shot out of the side, providing stairs for himself and the Dreadplate. They followed after the mage, circling until they came to the door. The mage had disappeared within. Despite how thin the tower was, the door let into a large hall, terminating in a huge door at the other end. Hanen crossed, and by the time he had reached the door, it was as tall as himself. He pulled on the ring, and walked in.

The room beyond held a giant table, with little room to move around it; piled high on every surface, plates and platters of exquisite food lay in spreads. At the other end, the mage sat on a throne, a chain running from him to his "pet," watching and considering Hanen as he took in the sight.

"Well?" the mage asked. "What do you think?"

"An impressive array," Hanen said.

"Will you not taste?"

"It would be insulting of me to take food that has not been explicitly offered in friendship."

"You bear Üterk blood, do you not?" the mage asked.

"My mother was from the forest."

"Of course. How silly of me to think I could outsmart a Dreamer. Please, eat, my friend."

"I must still refrain," Hanen said.

"And why is that?"

"You may call me friend. It is your right. But how can our friendship grow if I do not know your name?"

"A wise choice of words. I am Gvelindar the Arborist."

"Use the title Magi," Searn whispered.

"A fascinating title, Magi Gvelindar."

Gvelindar smiled. "Respectful, I appreciate that, but I hold the rank of Magus."

"I shall not misstep again, Magus."

"I take no offense," Gvelindar said. "Please. Eat."

Hanen took a seat, pulling the Dreadplate to stand behind him. He eyed the food before him, considered the steak dripping with fat, dried meats, and a small plate of humble poultry. He reached for the latter, and took a bite. The smell and taste was there, but as he swallowed it, he understood. It was all oneirion sand. He swallowed, and placed the rest down on his plate."

"Is that all you will have?" Gvelindar asked.

"I am satisfied," Hanen said.

"Our friend here," Gvelindar said, "gorged himself, having not eaten for many weeks. Is not that interesting?"

"How one can be in the Veld for any amount of time and not discover they need no food? That is interesting. What did he do to fall under your chain?"

"He told me an unbelievable story when first we met, and I have punished him for lying."

"It must have been quite the tale," Hanen said.

"He swore he had walked for weeks at the command of a skull. He explained that the skull led him through the same crevasse you arose from. He said he found a silver suit of armor and that it was sucked into Noccitan, and then a suit of armor—not unlike yours—emerged."

Hanen's heart began to skip.

"He has been charged with journeying through nightmare. If he can emerge, so be it. If he does not, then he shall join my grove."

"Your grove."

"I am the Arborist. I have a grove of trees. Each contains the shattered mind of those that have failed."

"A sad fate, I do not doubt."

"Now. Tell me of your journey. Where do you hail from, and where do you go?"

"I would be most willing to tell you this tale, if you would but spell out the consequences of the telling."

"If you lie, your fate lies within my forest," Gvelindar said. "If you tell a truthful tale, I shall allow you to pass from my forest, with my blessing."

"This I cannot do," Hanen said, "for a tale requires elaboration. Therefore, all tales are lies, even if they speak truth."

"Well said."

"I shall tell you a story," Hanen said. "In return, you shall tell one to me. We can both walk away friends, having learned something from the other."

"I am not Meresmand the Tollkeeper," Gvelindar said. "I can enjoy a story without needing another tree for my garden. I accept."

The table disappeared and all that remained was an open hearth pit burning with violet fire between them. The man on the other end of Gvelindar's chain heaved a heavy sigh, revealing his face. Hanen recognized the man. Loth. The man Rallia and he had turned back over to Pater Minoris Averin at the Green Bastion.

Hanen looked back to the man in the robe, face still obscured by his hood.

"I am reminded of the tale of Corwan the Horner and his journey."

"I believe I recall the tale," Gvelindar said, "but I question how that tale will tell me of yours."

"Mine is a boring story, but through his I might tell a more interesting one."

Gvelindar gave a wave of his hand.

Corwan Horner lived in a land that is no more. He was said to travel north and south and back again, making and selling his wares carved of bone and horn. No matter his luck, he never knew wealth, and desire grew within his heart. He did not seek to die a king, but perhaps more than a peddler upon the road.

And so, he took up his tools and the large family lyre—strings set on a yoke of massive horns—and took a road not oft-traveled. Passing homes and villages that never saw a traveler he plied the carving of lanterns and drinking vessels, and by evening fire he played bright songs upon his lyre.

One night, Corwan met a traveler. The crooked storyteller spoke of a mountain, and upon that mountain an ancient city. They who dwelt there were said to speak gold into the pockets of foolish men and make princes cast aside their crowns.

He followed the storyteller's instructions and journeyed north, and there he found that mountain. It had no top, for the clouds had consumed it, and upon the slopes there lived a people. From those people, winged and savage, he traded horn for a companion—a scaled ynfald that was said to be hewn from the mountains there. Small and wily, it made for a silent companion, but faithful, made as it was by the same god who made the winged peoples there.

Up the mountains they trekked, and there they saw, as all the stories tell, a mighty castle, built by ten but housing only five denizens, with gate arch standing a hundred feet high.

Despite it standing open, he stood at the door and awaited admittance. For days he stood in the cold, too polite to enter.

A form climbed the mountain and approached the door—three times the size of the man, and Corwan's scaled companion rattled at the monster's approach. Through the snow it trudged, and his figure took form.

As was said, he stood three times the height of Corwan, or taller. His heavy head with drooping cheeks, and long tusks that crossed over his chest with each other, were supported by a neck as thick as a spruce. His shoulders, covered in furs of unknown beasts, hunched against the cold. On his back, he bore a slab of metal that might have trussed a bridge before acting as his sword. Behind him, he dragged a sleigh, upon which the carcass of an animal as massive as he lay.

"How long have you waited here, human?" the monster grumbled.

"Long enough to await hospitality."

"Why did you not knock, inquiring if none would greet you?"

"I saw no knocker, and did not wish to impose."

"Impose, you have. We cannot have one of the thinking people dying at our gates. Come."

Into the gate they walked, and Corwan followed behind the sleigh. He was taken to a large building, and there the giant placed the body before a massive fire to thaw.

"What is the purpose of your visit?"

"I carve horn for those that would purchase my skill. I've been told by those who live in valleys below that wisdom and riches can be made here."

The giant laughed. "We've no riches, we five who still live here, but we know how best to live. For we have lived the longest."

"What is the secret to your longevity?" Corwan asked.

"A simple life. Beyond that, I've no wisdom to share. What need have I for a horner?"

"To bring pleasure to a simple life. I see the massive tusks upon the beast by the fire. What will you do with it?"

"Little."

"Why not make from it a lyre like my own?" Corwan produced his instrument and played an old song.

"How would I make such a thing?"

"Why, if I gave this lyre in trade for food and shelter, and some wisdom, then you could copy it to make your own, that befits your size."

"Your much smaller hands shall be deft with sinews. Help me with the carcass, and give me your lyre, and I shall lead you to wisdom."

And so they set about to work together. By Corwan's skilled

knifework, the giant, who spoke little, gave up his name: Ämma-Tor. Skin removed, Ämma-Tor prepared the meat they unveiled—some to hang for salting and storing, other bits into a great pot over the fire.

"Go now across the courtyard to a great tower. Act as my messenger, and tell the brothers you find there that a feast will be held this night."

The courtyard that he crossed was deep with snow and miles to traverse, and just as he thought he would not find the building mentioned, it coalesced from the blinding blizzard.

If it was a flat wall or round tower, he could not tell, for its width was beyond understanding. He did not hesitate to knock, rapping hammer upon the wood, and after what seemed like hours, the door opened and Corwan stood looking at the legs of another giant.

This one bore a form that Corwan could not comprehend, and it peered down upon him, thinking perhaps, the same.

"What are you?" the rich voice asked.

"A horner of humble origins, come with a message from Ämma-Tor."

"Come in out of the cold," the giant said, "and be warmed."

The giant led the way into a drafty room, and took a seat by a roaring fire, where another sat, with a massive goblet in his hand.

"Greetings, little one," the second giant said. This one was taller and thinner.

"Greetings. I bear a message from across the courtyard. A feast is to be held this day."

"We have awaited the return of the Hunter for so long. It will be good to eat once more."

The first giant motioned toward the second. "My brother, Lu-Koritü, is always hungry, even if hunger will not bring us low."

"We think so much clearer on a full stomach," Lu-Koritü said. "Then I can better discuss the wonders of the world made by our Creator and in turn, his Creator."

"Do you not eat as often as we smaller beings?" Corwan asked.

"Only when food is at hand," Lu-Koritü said. "And that is rarely."

"We smaller beings perish without it."

"I wonder if that will one day happen to me," Lu-Koritü said.

"I do not worry," the other said.

"My brother Po-Tumigal worries about little, save for keeping me from harm. Older brothers are like that."

"Hardly older," Po-Tumigal said. "Mere moments."

"Then you are twins?" Corwan asked.

"In a way, all ten of the Gigantes are brothers," Lu-Koritü said. "But none so close as we two. Practically twins, as you say."

"Have you never been to the sea?" Corwan said.

"Why change the subject?" Lu-Koritü asked.

"I do not. But rather, the sea is full of bounty and food. I know fishers there who cast nets and bring in food to feed a hall of men."

"I should like to see this," Lu-Koritü said.

"Not without the blessing of our Eldest Brother," Po-Tumigal said.

"Bah. I am hungry. If I choose to leave, I shall leave."

"We thank you for your message. Perhaps you can journey down the hallway from here into the Hall of Mysteries, and tell the Sage that it will be so. For he would continue in his studies and ignore the food entirely, if we did not warn him."

Corwan bowed in reverence and took to the hallway, long and deep.

It seemed to stretch for miles, and darkness surrounded him, with torches smoldering high above yet far from each other. Finally, he came to the Hall aforementioned, and there, a great table sat, upon which mountains of books hid from full view the Sage sitting there.

Circling the table, Corwan looked at the scholar. He bore the resemblance to a griffin, in many ways, if a giant took that form for himself. And he was lost in thought.

Corwan cleared his throat, and finally, the Sage made a motion with his hand, and finished the page he read, turning to consider the man beside him.

"A horner by trade," the Sage surmised, "and covered in the gore of Ämma-Tor's trade, by the looks of it? He has returned with food?"

"Indeed, he has. Lu-Koritü and Po-Tumigal have sent me further, to give you news of the upcoming feast."

"Very well. I shall come when the time is right. But tell me, why are you here?"

"I seek to rise above my station."

"Does not every one of your people?"

"Most do. Most seek fortunes. I seek only to be more than I am."

"Why?"

"Why do you not appear as the others, but rather, bear the looks of a griffin in many ways?"

"Do you think it because I sought to better myself?"

"I do not know."

"It is true. I was once a seeker of betterment, like yourself. In my wayward seeking, I was brought low. I laid there, as one dead, but as one alive, for we Gigantes cannot truly die, until a carrion gryph chanced upon my carcass. I became as that gryph. I am now Zerax-Ti—the ravenous Sage, for now I hunger only for more knowledge."

He glanced down at the patient ynfald beside Corwan. "What I would not give to have been found by one so loyal and happy with his circumstance."

"Would you give me wisdom, by which I can make myself the sage that you are among my people, I would trade for that this loyal mongrel at my feet."

Zerax-Ti considered, then gave a solemn nod. The ynfald approached, his scaled tail flapping upon the stones. The giant reached down and gave him a pat, then turned back to Corwan.

"I can give only knowledge. Not wisdom. Therefore, I urge you to ascend to the room above, where the leader of the Gigantes, Ogir-Thalla resides. Never has he perished, but remains as he has always been. If any can share the wisdom of his satisfaction it is he."

And so, Corwan climbed stairs that his own legs could not stride. Up he climbed, until air seemed to flee the place. Finally, he came to an open doorway leading into a great hall, with stone and wooden frames far above in the darkness. Across the floor he walked, until he reached the great chair there. Upon it sat Ogir-Thalla, cross-legged and considering the approaching man. He was larger than the others, and bore a long face, eyes deep with consideration. He had no clothing, but long fur kept him modest. The only adornment upon him was a third eye painted upon his forehead.

Before the throne there sat four braziers, and Corwan lowered himself before the Gigantes ruler. For hours it seemed they sat, and no word was spoken. Finally, Corwan could bear it no longer.

"I've come in search of wisdom."

Ogir-Thalla did not speak.

"I waited without until Ämma-Tor appeared, and together we prepared the carcass he now cooks for a feast for you and the others. I gave him a lyre—my only means of entertainment."

Ogir-Thalla did not speak.

"I met the brothers, Tu-Koritü and Po-Tumigal, and learned of the prior's hunger. I shared with him the knowledge that might sate his hunger."

Ogir-Thalla did not speak.

"Zerax-Ti took in trade for my closest companion, a promise that you would offer me wisdom, not for riches, but to better myself, to rise above the horner I am, into something greater."

Ogir-Thalla did not speak.

"I have traversed lands and cold mountains, waited in patience, and been left starving. Your brothers offered me food, warmth, rest, knowledge. In return, I have given my time, my companion, and secrets to those who needed answers. Perhaps I am to learn that to understand wisdom, I must give everything up?"

Ogir-Thalla did not speak.

"Zerax-Ti indicated that you of all the Gigantes are most satisfied with life, and want for nothing, and remain unchanged. He further said that you have perhaps the greatest wisdom to offer. What wisdom would you give me? How can I improve myself?"

But Ogir-Thalla said nothing.

Lesson conveyed, Corwan Horner left with nothing.

39

Moral of the Story

Lies and deceit go hand in hand.

By magic in dream your soul's command.

—FROM THIS THE COMMON PHRASE

"LIES AND DECEIT" IS PARAPHRASED

"**A**n interesting choice," Gvelindar said. "What lessons do you think this taught Corwan Horner?"
"He sought wisdom. Wisdom can only be imparted to those that seek it. But it is never reached," Hanen concluded.
"Yet Ogir-Thalla is satisfied."
"Is he?" Hanen retorted. "He never spoke."
"But he did," Gvelindar said. "Corwan Horner tells the tale differently when you ask him."
"You know Corwan?"
"The first among the Somnumancers. After he left that throne room, he descended once more. Zerax-Ti he studied with and asked questions Zerax-Ti could not answer. It is said that is why he left to find answers elsewhere. Corwan returned to the brothers but they had gone. Lu-Koritu had left to find the sea, and his brother went after him. They are now the Mad One and the Beach Bound Thinker in the Kandar Sea. When the feast was held for the

three that remained, there was no food. Obsessed with the creation of a lyre for himself, Ämma-Tor burned the food in negligence, and was sent away in exile. The arrival of Corwan Horner destroyed the five Gigantes left in that city. There are tales of his seeking out and bringing the others to ruin as well, before he finally settled in the Veld."

"Why?" Hanen asked.

"Because of the words that Ogir-Thalla spoke."

Hanen leaned back in his chair as Gvelindar dropped back his hood to reveal his face.

He didn't appear much older than Hanen. His hair was thick, but kept short, and grew in across his face in a tight and curly beard. His eyes bore a slight purple glow. Behind his ears, he bore intricate tattoos seen on some of the Üterk storytellers that often made their way to the taverns of Bortali.

"Corwan asked him to speak. Demanded it, in fact, and Ogir-Thalla spoke.

"'You petty creatures, obsessed with greatness, and fearful of death. Listen now to the lessons you have been taught before you arrived. The stripping of what you have does nothing, but it does provide the opportunity for you to learn the two greatest lessons. The first is the lesson I tried to teach you by example. Silence. It is there much is learned.'

"'And the second?' Corwan asked.

"'Patience. Of which you have none. Had you been patient in your life as horner, you would have found greatness merely by being who you are. Something you shall now never be again.'"

"Patience and Silence, and without that he turned to evil?" Hanen asked.

"With that, he realized wisdom was something no mortal would ever possess. That is to say, until he found his way to the Veld, where time means nothing, and patience can be sought in the immortality of the space. With that, he established balance and perfection in the horrors to be crafted here. A balance had been struck. Until your arrival."

"My arrival?"

"Your arrival into the Veld, as well as that witch in the north who tears a pathway eastward, bringing change to our perfectly balanced dreams. That cannot be tolerated."

Hanen sat back in his chair and took a calming breath.

"He's going to make a move," Searn muttered.

Hanen gave a small nod and stood. "I am going to leave now."

"Oh no. We're beyond that," Gvelindar said. "I've already prepared an exquisite nightmare for you. I'm sure you can already feel the tendrils of its pull crawling up your legs."

"I feel nothing," Hanen said with a smug smile.

"You will. When you are fed to the plague that grows, made by Corwan himself, to the south and west."

"What plague?"

"As terrible as the one that comes from the north."

"Day Blind?"

Gvelindar gave a solemn yet wicked nod.

"This new plague within the Veld. It is a plague of wyrms, is it not?"

Gvelindar gave Hanen a dark look. "I do not care for how much you know, a stranger in these lands, who walks unperturbed. The council would give much to understand you."

He rose from his chair, and continued to rise into the air on tendrils of oneirion as he floated toward Hanen.

Hanen struck out, his gauntleted left hand taking hold of Gvelindar's wrist, and with a twist, he dropped the man to his knees. He let go of the Magus' wrist for a moment and with both gauntlets Hanen opened the space before Gvelindar and a blast of air shot out of the black world of Noccitan.

"What is that?" the Magus muttered.

"The place you most fear, and why I do not doubt you left your forest home so long ago, so that you could stay as far from its black reach as possible."

"Noccitan," Gvelindar swore.

"Correct."

"Why show me this?"

"I am no Judge, but beyond that portal lies the Judge's domain. Given the arboretum that lies outside of this tower, you, of all men, deserve the horrors found in there."

"Please," the Magus begged, "do not do this."

"Free your forest of the damned."

"It is not that simple."

"Then make it simple."

Gvelindar snapped his finger and across the room, Loth looked up, his eyes clear, but full of horror. He began to scream.

"The haunted cries of them all being freed at once will shatter this part of the Veld. The backlash of that would be catastrophic."

"I don't care," Hanen said.

"Have you never done something so wicked that you could not take it back?"

"Haven't we all?" Hanen replied.

"Then how can you judge me for my actions?"

"Because I do not repeat those wrongs I have committed—I learn from them."

Gvelindar moved with a sudden burst of speed, turned in a twist, and reached for Hanen's face. Hanen shoved his gauntleted palm into Gvelindar's chest, and the Magus was repulsed back and through the hole in the air instantaneously. He barely landed on his feet and looked Hanen in the eyes before he rushed at the portal. With a thought, Hanen closed it, leaving the Magus in Noccitan on the other side.

The ground beneath Hanen lurched, newly forming sand coming up to his shin. The Dreadplate behind him was slowly sinking backwards.

"The oneirion is giving way," Searn said calmly.

"I figured that out," Hanen said, rushing toward the door. His steps grew heavier as he trudged through the sand. Behind him, Loth fought on hands and knees to crawl through the room. Even as he did, his cries of terror continued. Hanen came to the door, which collapsed like a castle in the sand as he touched it. He was swimming in the stuff now and struggling. He closed his eyes, imagining the sand around him bending to his mind. Instead, a heavy black weight scooped him up in its arms, then trudged forward.

As the tower gave a final lurch, Hanen took hold of the arms of the armor and closed his eyes. He tumbled in a long roll down the dune the tower had become and slid to a rest.

He coughed sand from his mouth as he stood. The armor was half buried. All around him, the sounds of fear of those waking from their long nightmares filled his ears. Hundreds of people all struggled toward the dune of purple sand. Hanen stood and wiped himself clean, and lifted his hands, trying to make the armor wrench itself free. It moved and struggled, and finally rolled out of the sand and down to solid ground.

"We have to get out of here," Hanen said to himself. He took hold of the air and tore open a new hole, this time to Kallattai. Sunlight streamed through. He goaded the armor toward the portal, but it would not fit through the small hole.

DREAD KNIGHT

He rushed in front of it and stepped through, taking hold of the wrist of the armor. He pulled on it, when the hole in the air snapped closed, leaving him on one side, the Dreadplate on the other.

He looked down at the knee-deep water in which he stood. Reeds grew around him.

"Out of one dream, and now hungry and lost who knows where."

Up out of the water, tall creatures with lanky arms and legs emerged. Their faces were long, with short, straight tusks jutting from their mouths, curved horns atop their brows, and a short bony horn on the ridge of their noses. Without another word they took hold of him with thick fingers, tearing the gauntlets from his hands and the cloak from his back. Something struck him from behind, and all went black.

40

Interludes

The fugue state dissipated after what felt like days. Many of the men and women in the hills made their way to the pile of sand now marking where the tower once stood. Eralt Loth did not speak to anyone, but spent hours staring at the star-filled, twilit sky above, or circling the sandy dune, only to return to where he'd started to stare at the suit of black armor, identical to the silver one he had dropped the skull of the deathless beast into.

It did not move. It only stood there. Twice he had tentatively touched it, caressing the black surface and the waves of beaten metal that made up its form. It bore no hands, but everything else sat locked in place. The gauntlets that would normally grace its wrists, he knew, were in the possession of that Sentinel. If ever he could find a way through to the real world, he would seek the man out, and kill him.

When he grew agitated enough, he circled the dune again, returning to the Dreadplate once more.

After repeating this countless times, others began to join him in silence. Some whimpered a shed tear, to wash away whatever nightmare the Arborist had put them through. With each circuit, they came back to the black metal form. Few dared to touch it. Others fell and bowed to it as savior that had delivered them from the evil that haunted their memories still.

Soon hundreds of people were making a silent, vigilant circling of the fallen tower of the Arborist, in open worship of the black god-like form of the Dreadplate.

DREAD KNIGHT

"With high summer harvest coming to a close across the country, more men and women have arrived to give their support," Bolla Elbay said. She wore the boot-blackened armor of a Warden now, and stood at relaxed attention by her seat.

"How many?" Dean Noss asked.

"Three hundred today," Bolla said. "Not as many as four days ago, but close."

"By my reckoning," Domic said, "that makes for seven hundred recruits unassigned to battalions."

"Bolla, who will you assign to the forming of a new battalion?" Noss asked.

"This brings me to my next point," Bolla said. "I believe we will need to decide on three leaders."

"Three?"

"Seven hundred means we'll be ready to start another unit soon after. We may even split those seven hundred in two, to form a core, and then slot newer recruits in when they come."

"Very well," Noss agreed. "And the third?"

"Captain Demaro has requested a transfer."

"Has he? Does the leadership of a battalion not suit him?"

"Demaro has asked to be transferred to you."

"Me? He is no Warden."

"He would like to discuss that with you. I believe he expressed interest in becoming your assistant, or squire."

"Interesting. Very well." Noss rose from his seat. "Well, I think I leave the citadel in good hands."

"How far will you travel?"

"The call for help in the south is urgent. I hope to reach Liberté in seven days time. I'll have whoever hasn't moved their rears south whipping up dust. I'll not have us lose ground to Castenard."

Noss made his polite leave, and disappeared. Others soon excused themselves, leaving only Elbay and Domic. The two women sat in silence for some time, listening for any eavesdroppers.

Bolla finally took a sip of her wine before speaking. "How many Wardens leave with Noss?"

"Thirty. He left several trusted ex-Paladins to continue training of the new Wardens."

"Do you have a reason to not trust any of them?"

"I don't trust anyone," Domic said.

"I'd be hurt, if I was surprised."

"Did you note Noss's reaction to the news from the Northern Scapes?"

"He did not seem surprised that the Chalicians are failing there, too."

"But he did seem agitated that his 'friends' there have also been ousted," Domic said.

"He changed in that moment, though. He seemed resolute to secure Limae permanently. He is not the scholar who showed up in this council hall desiring only to secure the library and leave."

"No. He seems more now to be a prince come into his tentative inheritance."

"Well said," Bolla replied. "Did you sneak anyone into the battalion traveling south with Noss?"

"Even if I did, I wouldn't tell you. You'll know if I learn anything we ought to know."

"And if you hear any word of del Ishé."

"Of course." Domic stood and excused herself, leaving Bolla Elbay in silence.

To call the blackness palpable was no metaphor. For days, if time could be counted, Slate had lain still, hoping and waiting for something to change. Waiting for the weight to lift. But it never came. Every breath was a chore and hunger gnawed at him. He expected he would grow thirsty, but the moist air seemed to feed that need. After a time, even the hunger did not seem to be all that pressing.

Eventually, he found the will to move and began to stumble through the darkness. Smears of light from flat lichen that grew upon some walls provided not enough light to see by, but enough to cast long and eerie shadows that moved. How they moved, when nothing seemed to live in this dark place, he did not know.

Some unknown call pulled at him, and he wandered ever onward into the darkness. It pulled harder than the small voice in his mind that told him to come and be judged. That he was not dead could be the only reason he had the strength to withstand that call.

At long last, he found what he had sought. Strewn across stalagmites lay armor, identical to the black Dreadplate he had spent so many years studying, but rather than black, this one was made of perfectly reflective silver. It appeared dropped from a great height. When he touched it, it was cold. Cooler than the muggy darkness around him. He threw himself upon it, just to feel something. Anything. Then, after letting the choking sobs leave him, he felt every inch of it with the fingers on his remaining hand. Inside the chest plate he found an odd thing, not cold, but like bone.

You know me, a voice said into his mind.

He recoiled. He knew that voice. Although this one held a different air about it.

Tentatively, he touched the thing within the cavity again.

You know me, it repeated.

"How do you know this?" Slate muttered, not breaking contact with the thing.

You held my other half, the voice said, *upon the hand that you have lost.*

He pulled the object up out of the armor. It was an inhuman-looking skull, resembling wyloth or savern more than man. The teeth were heavily fanged and the brow heavy. Above the brow, an anti-crown of holes had been neatly punched in the bone in a row from temple to temple.

"I did," Slate replied. "You are Deathless."

And did I command you?

"We had come to an arrangement."

And now?

"It cost me my hand and I ended up here."

Then you can move me.

Slate laughed.

Why do you laugh?

"Nothing can move you."

Put me on, and see.

"Put you on? You're not the armor."

Why not.

The armor suddenly lurched.

You have moved me.

"That isn't me!"

The armor stood and threw itself about like a puppet. Slate

watched in amazement as it suddenly began to walk, but seemingly on nothing, as it stepped up into the air.

He took hold of the armor and was lifted into the sky, quickly, too far up to dare let go.

"What do I do?" he asked.

Get in.

Slate considered how he might. The hole at the top was wide enough, if barely, for the thick throat of a vül if a beast of that size were to wear it. He struggled to climb up the armor, the skull gripped in his remaining hand, fingers sunk into the row of holes.

It took all of his weakened strength. The Mirrorplate continued to rise in the air, and neared the ceiling. He would fall hundreds of feet, or be crushed. He put a foot down into the hole, and then fell down into the armor feet first. His thin frame fit into the space, feet sliding naturally into the legs of the armor, then his torso and head down into the breastplate. His wrists, held above his head, jammed violently into the neck, forced above his head. The skull of Deathless was still held with his remaining hand over the top, and his handless wrist jammed up into the hole at the bottom.

The tight confines lodged both hands over his head, the freakishly inhuman skull now sealing him in. The voice of Deathless surrounded him in an evil laugh.

I can feel my other half near!

The suit smashed against the ceiling of the cavern, and kept going, up through the rock as though it was sand. Slate, for the first time in his life, felt powerful.

After a time, it stopped rising. Now in some other cavern, it began to walk. Another rise, and then, stillness.

Long hours went by.

Ghoré said nothing.

A door suddenly stood before Slate back into the Veld. He cried out in relief and fought to move, but the armor did not obey his, nor Ghoré's command. Then, a figure was thrown through the gate. A man in a black and purple robe. All at once, the portal closed, leaving Slate within the armor in darkness, and a quivering man at his feet.

"What?" the man said, looking up. "What is this?"

Tell him what we are, Ghoré said. *Speak with my voice.*

"We..." Slate said. "We are Deathless."

Aurín had not left his post the night before, but stood on watch as the line of torches filtered out of the trees. How many were field-tested soldiers, he did not know. If the spies were to be believed, the other City States had contributed units to Castenard's campaign. If Sidierata had sent any ships to blockade the port, they hadn't appeared yet. Regardless, de Bosco assured him that help may yet come from Edi and Hraldor, if the hrelgren ships they had contracted made it past the Sidieratan opposition.

Word had come down from Adwall of a meager Castenardi army sent to hold back those still within the walls from helping Aurín in Boscolón. The bigger worry was rumor of winds changing, drawing air toward the walled mountain city. If that occurred, it wouldn't take long for the small army at their walls to light the young surrounding forests and put Adwall once more to flame.

"What are our orders?" Dakmor asked, eyeing the now encircling army in the early morning light.

"Nothing. We await their action. We await word from Castenard to myself and Lord de Bosco, detailing their intentions."

"Some of the men are restless."

"Then tell them to continue work on the sewers and walls."

"Is that an order, sir?"

Aurín looked at the man next to him with irritation.

"I'll issue the order."

Aurín turned back to the army without and prayed to any god that would listen, hoping the message to Haven had arrived in time for help to come.

The three Praetors sat in silence. The room had been stripped of Parianti decor and cleaned. In a few weeks time, new furnishings would arrive to turn the entire Ammar Citadel into a Chalician haven.

Provost Weskar Abrau looked about to the two men across from him. The young and haughty Yanas Brodier, acolyte of Provost Otem, kept his back pole-straight, his face a mask hiding the fears of youth. He had spent far too much time since their arrival ingratiating himself to the other man at the table, Provost Romab Voglain, known as the Grand Sacristan. He had been posted at the citadel since the Paladins had been ousted. His rigidity was genuine. He had spent the intervening months recording the contents of the round building, determining which books were to go to which library controlled by the Praetors. He bore a head of thick white hair, but had no more than ten years over Weskar.

"I'm quite interested to hear what the Mareschal has to say," Brodier said to break the awkward silence.

"Mmm," was all he received from Voglain. He preferred his long silences, except when he was speaking. The tension between Brodier and Weskar had not abated since the attack on the camp, and the escape of the monk and Sentinel. Abrau had made the choice to change courses, taking the prisoners of war here to Ammar, rather than on to the capital. Brodier fought against his command the whole way, sowing dissension, unsuccessfully, as he suggested he take command of the prisoners and continue on to Aunté. But, as soon as they had arrived at Ammar, and word had come that the Mareschal, Provost Waquelon Dâjeaux, was on his way, Brodier had changed his tune.

Where Abrau dreaded the sight of the blustering and forceful Mareschal, Brodier had not stopped extolling his virtues, desiring nothing more than to ingratiate himself with the man as soon as he arrived.

The door opened, and Brodier stood a bit too fast. Weskar only rose after Voglain slowly raised himself from his own throne-like chair.

The Provost who entered strode in like a ship's captain. The spurs on his heels rang like bells, and the blue cape on his back was bound by the hands he held there.

Waquelon Dâjeaux did not wear a helmet, but kept his short black hair slicked on his head and a small mustache on his upper lip. Attendants filed in behind him carrying his personal accoutrements, including a standard, a large chalice, his helmet, and a broadsword, the sign of the War Provosts. Long ago Abrau had envied the role of War Provost, but he had been given orders equal enough to satisfy that itch. The additional responsibilities he had taken on as Catechist in Ouiquimon provided him with more political clout than most War Provosts could muster.

Dâjeaux came to the final seat at the table, but did not sit.

He looked to his host, Voglain, who had closed his eyes and held hands up to the sky in supplication.

"High King in Heaven, you hath bestowed upon our fellow

protector of the faith a safe journey. Restore unto him that which he lost upon the road, and recall unto him the words he has been sent to deliver. By the path you have set before us."

"By the Path," the other three intoned.

"I've little time to waste with pleasantries," the Mareschal said.

"I would never have expected you to," Voglain said. "You have always treated your conversations as you have your opponents in the ring. Decisively."

Dâjeaux nodded and took a deep breath. He turned to the other two. "Why are you here, Abrau, and not in Limae?"

"I do not answer to you," Abrau said. "I am here out of necessity. Things have changed in Limae, and I am reassessing the situation from here."

"It had been my intention to continue on to Limae to give you the changing orders from the Praeposit, so this is fortuitous. I have no doubt that Chetaîn would like to know you are here."

He turned to Brodier. "Why are you not in northern Varea?"

"I have had to change my own course, to pursue an escaped prisoner. My path has led me here."

"Then no doubt you've recent word from Otem in Mahndür?"

"Last I heard he planned an expedition across the Lupinfang. Mahndür is entirely under our sway. Bortali and Boroni are next."

"This is what news was received before I was sent this way."

"Then it appears everything goes to plan," Voglain said. "I shall have the keys to all of Ormach officially in my hands by the end of the month."

"Save for Boscolón," Dâjeaux corrected.

Voglain blanched.

"There is little we do not know," Dâjeaux said. "What plans are being made to bring Boscolón back under heel?"

"I would suppose you come to provide that information yourself," Weskar said. "After all, Voglain is no soldier."

"But you are," Dâjeaux said. "Your failure in Haven allowed the Limaeans to secure their south, and set off a war with Castenard."

"Conflict with Castenard was always a possibility," Weskar said. "While the loss of Haven, for the time being, is something I will have to answer for, Castenard and Limae smashing heads against one another, like a pair of rutting capricör, provides us all the chance to secure everything else."

"It is for this reason only that Praeposit Chetaîn has not recalled you to answer to him in Oiquimon. The Northern Scapes will be, by now, under Otem's guidance. I have been sent to negotiate cooperation from the other City States of Sidierata. This will provide all the leverage we need to snap our jaws shut over the Luzoran Hermits and the Morriegan Church, unifying the church of Aben utterly."

"And Castenard?"

"Anhouil has expressed his disdain for the city. They're nearly as godless as the Limaeans. You are to use Castenard as a bargaining chip to ensure that Limae stays out of our way."

"The other City States may not agree to letting Castenard go," Abrau said.

"I have it on good authority that Sidierata will do anything, if it means us backing their end goal of razing Edi City to the ground."

"You mean to allow that?"

"Nothing is more precious than keeping the trade lanes open. Nothing opens the path to Lomïn better than seeing control over every path. On land, and on sea."

"Trading a single land-locked Sidieratan city for a promise to help them destroy their own enemies," Weskar replied, "seems in opposition to our mission."

"You gave no question to taking control of Limae. You did not speak up against Otem going north."

"Everyone knows better than to speak up against Otem," Weskar said. "Especially when in relation to anything he and Chetaîn have planned."

"Be careful, Abrau," Brodier said cooly.

"That's Provost Abrau," Weskar corrected. "I thought I could convert Limae with little bloodshed, but there were unknown forces at play. As you have surmised, the best bet for us right now is to pull back from that mission field, and instead parlay for a tentative peace with them."

"Is there a word for my next step?" Brodier asked.

Dâjeaux gave the younger Praetor a confused look. "I'm not even sure why you're in this meeting."

"Young Curate Brodier has expressed great desire to serve the faith here in Ormach," Voglain said. "Given we've three Provosts in the room, I had wondered if we might put it to a triumvirate vote, to place him under my command. I have use for one of such righteous zeal. If only to do the things I find distasteful."

"Fine," Dâjeaux said, raising a hand. "I really could not care less."

DREAD KNIGHT

"But..." Brodier said in protest.

"Silence, Curate," Weskar said with a smug smile. "I think the responsibility and firm hand of Voglain would do you well. It would be hard for you to rise to the rank of Provost without such administrative experience under your belt." He raised his hand. "I also agree."

"Good," Voglain said in finality. "Brodier, your first assignment is to prepare an inventory of sleipnir in Ormach. You have my permission to requisition any and all unchurched attendants as are needed to perform this task."

Brodier opened his mouth to speak, and then gave a weak salute before leaving, tail between his legs.

"He is still loyal to Otem," Weskar said as Brodier closed the door.

"I do not care," Voglain said. "He is an able body, with enough vim and vigor to do that job. None of the scholars I brought with me has it in them to go out and do it. If he does not succeed in a timely manner, I'm sure I can find years of work for him to do."

"I am off to Nor-Vio," Dâjeaux said. "Where I'll be taking a ship to Sidierata to begin negotiations. Abrau?"

"Well, it appears, I am no longer needed here. I'll go to Boscolón and see if I can't make something of the Limaean mess. I'll send word to you with news."

Dâjeaux rose with a nod.

"Will you allow us to feed you and provide at least one night's sleep?" Voglain asked.

"I prefer the field," Dâjeaux said, "and the Path to Lomïn found upon the road."

The Mareschal left the room with as much finality as he had entered with.

"He will cause enough of a mess himself," Weskar said.

"You seem to think that I care," Voglain said. "All I care about are my books, and numbers. If you care so much, and worry it will somehow cause trouble for the church, then perhaps you've a path to walk."

"But is it ordained?" Abrau muttered.

The older man put a hand on his shoulder, but he did not smile. "The only way to find out if the destination lies upon the path, is to walk it."

The tent had been prepared by Captain Demaro himself. Noss could tell. Everything was in its proper place, and spartan. His locked chest sat atop the table, alongside the unfurled map. He ran a finger over the parchment. They were a short day's ride to Liberté, and Noss had demanded all be rested and fresh for the march in the morning. If the scout's rumors were to be believed, Gryvio Castenard himself had besieged the second largest city in Limae. His full estimated might had not been brought to bear, which meant the recently arrived message from Aurín and his army farther south needed Noss's relief just as badly.

He took out a key and unlocked the chest, then lifted the lid. He chuckled to himself. Within lay a single book, and tied to it, a pen. Both sat in rumpled-up parchment and paper, all blank. When he had put them in, all had writing across it. He reached under and took up the book, placed it down on the map, and touched the pen.

Bawdy poetry? The voice of Aeger said directly into his mind.

"It looks like you still consumed all of the writing, regardless of the content, and better than you ruining another good book of mine," Noss said. "I certainly can't have you growing hungry and consuming the shadebook."

You know I wouldn't do that, Aeger said.

"No. I don't."

Don't you trust me? Aeger asked.

"Once again, no."

Where are we?

"Not far from Liberté. Rumor is at least half of the Castenardi army is outside the city there."

Why not let it burn?

"We need its wealth. It ought to be the capital of Limae. The country has often wanted such, but the Hammer has long kept it from its goal. So we'll relieve it. Add to that, I do not wish for its library to be burned."

Library? Aeger said with interest.

"A sizable one. Rumor is they've a few hidden treasures that you and I would like to get ahold of."

Tell me more.

"Mostly journals by Ruíd Palore. His study of the older peoples may come in handy."

I'm not familiar with his work.

"Recording histories and stories of the Oruche, Üterk, and their kin, as well as the Tambii, and even the Morraineans."

What has that got to do with any of us?

"Your prejudice against anyone not of paladinial scholarship is showing," Noss said wryly. "Palore's work has been far too often overlooked, save by the Morriegans. They hail his work as exemplary. Well, what little that has survived. I would like to find out if Limae has been holding out. I know a few in the Morriegan nobility who would quickly ally themselves with us, if we could provide older texts they've long sought."

And how do you know what they do not?

"Because I've been seeing them on wild egg hunts elsewhere for ten years to keep that knowledge to myself."

Ever the miser.

"Ever the shrewd."

Perhaps. So, the siege?

"Yes. I'd appreciate us setting aside our differences and discussing tactics."

Have you considered your General Azermo?

"I figured that was where we'd start."

ANDREW D MEREDITH

Part 5

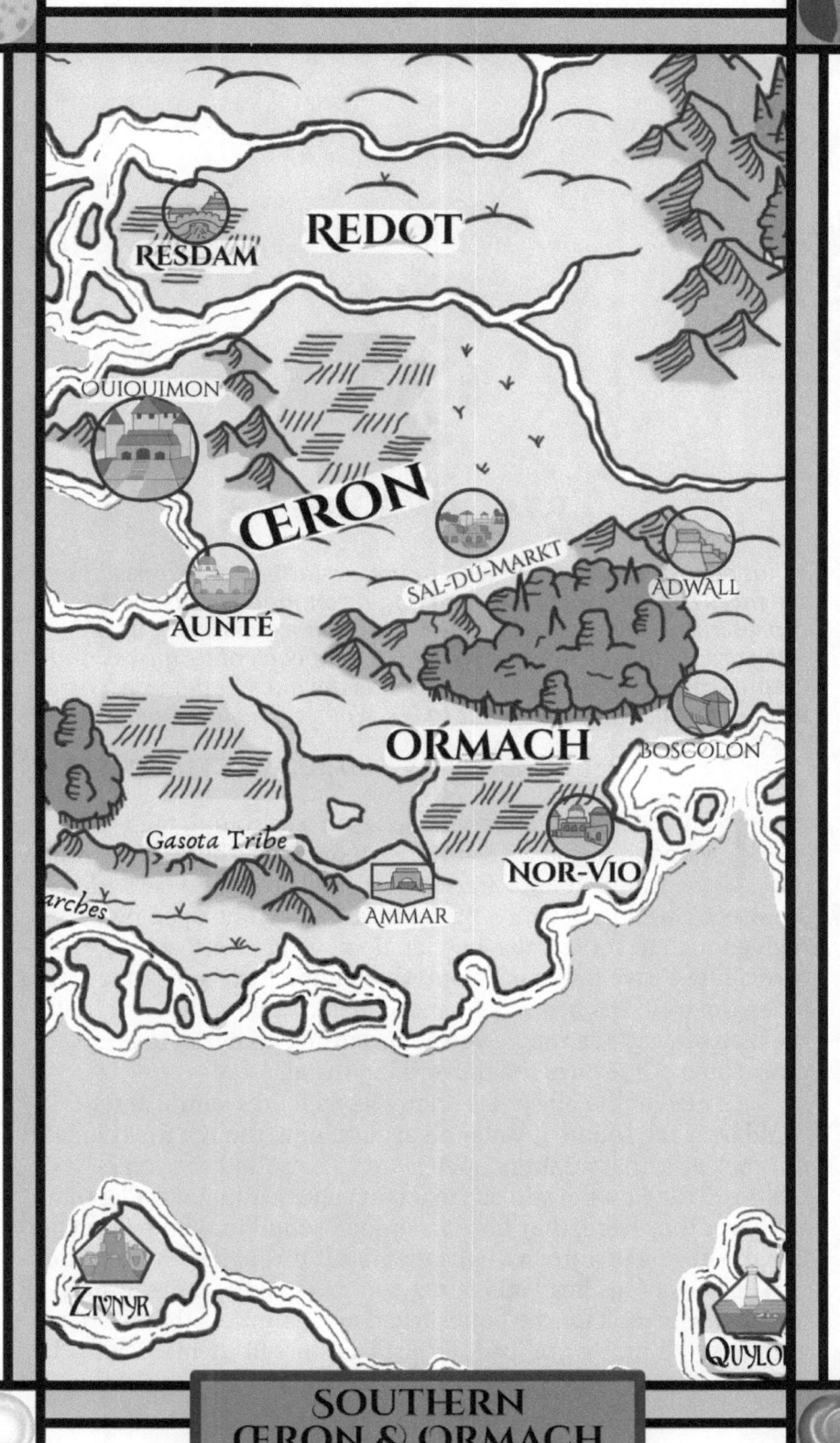

41

Trial of Elders

What beautiful artistry is seen in the variations of peoples upon the faces of Kallattai. That each god wrought a people, best representing their contribution is an allegory in and of itself. They created just as they were made, and each of us makes and creates and discovers and wonders as the gods wonder. All of those point upward. All point to He Who Is. Too often we forget.

—MUSINGS OF AN OLD MAN, BY VIAGO WEVAN

Hanen came to. The room he lay in was round, made of a wooden frame with either skin or canvas hung taut around the frame. It appeared to be a single room house with a stone cooking corner set on one side, a small stone open pit set high enough to stay off the wooden floor. There were no furnishings, save for a rack from which hung tools and some cloth along the wall. His bed was no more than a mat on the floor, and the blanket was of a rough-hewn, burlap-like material to keep away some of the bugs that hovered in the air.

The smell of the place was damp, like a fetid swamp, and he could hear the sound of water all around him, though the room did not rock as a boat might in open water. The sound of people talking drifted on the still air, in a language he did not understand. Whoever they were, they bore a rounded sound to their speech, like the lowing of aurochs, consonants cut through with staccato.

The back of his head still stung, and hurt all the more as he sat up quickly to look for the boneshroud and gauntlets that had been taken from him. He grabbed his head as stars lit up his vision. He wore nothing but his trousers. Bug bites littered his skin. He pulled the blanket over his shoulders and tried slowly to stand, hoping he could find water for his parched mouth.

Next to the cold hearth, a jar of water sat with a tight lid over it to keep the bugs out. He opened it, sniffed at the contents, and drank deeply of the cool water.

Behind him, the slats shook as someone untied a flap-like door from the outside, their tall frame casting dull shadows on the skins.

The door opened and Hanen stumbled back against the opposite wall, away from the figure that stepped in, right out of a nightmare.

It bore a tall, thin frame of corded muscles, easily head and shoulders taller than Hanen. Above double-jointed legs ending in hooves, it wore only a loin cloth over its thin groin. The taut muscles on its chest seemed more akin to a powerfully built man than the massive muscles of a vül, although the thick, long neck holding up its heavy head was more vülish. It bore a long face that almost reminded Hanen of a sleipnir or auroch, but there the resemblance ended. From its mouth jutted short but straight tusks. Its long nose had a ridge of short bony growths that implied being a part of a single horn. Its brow bore the weight of two black horns that curled up above its head. Along the back of its neck, a short but thick mane of coarse black hair ran down its spine. The arms were long and sinewy, terminating in four thick fingers. In one arm it held a jar covered in a blanket. It looked first to Hanen's bed, and then adjusted its eyes to see Hanen almost cowering against the wall.

"I see you are awake," the creature said. It enunciated around its tusks, showing all of its flat, bovine teeth in a semblance of a smile.

Hanen did not reply. The creature crossed the room to the hearth, and in response, Hanen circled the room back toward his bed.

"You are probably quite hungry," the creature said. "Our hunters say they saw you come through from the Veld. You may not need food there, but it catches up with you quickly when you come back to the world."

"Then," Hanen said tentatively, "this is not the Veld?"

"Oh, certainly not," the creature said with a smile.

"What are you?"

DREAD KNIGHT

"By your tone, I take it you are not from Œron or Ormach."

"Bortali," Hanen said, "and Edi."

"I'm not much acquainted with human lands. None of our tribes live among your people, so I am not surprised. I am your first Khamntyr?"

Hanen gave a weak nod.

"Then I say, '*Romuru.*'"

"Ro-Mu-Ru?" Hanen replied.

"Yes!" the Khamntyr said. "It is a sort of greeting among the Gasota people."

"Gasota?" Hanen asked.

"Do you think there is only one tribe of Khamntyr?"

"My head hurts," Hanen said. "This is all very new to me."

"Ah yes," the Khamntyr said, and took the lid off the jar, releasing the fragrant scent of heavily spiced food. He took up a spoon and wooden bowl from beside the hearth, then pulled out a helping of greens from the jar. From below the hearth, he drew out a thick, white, pasty chunk, and put that over the top. He crossed the room slowly, holding the bowl out. "Please. Take."

Hanen took the offering and held it as the creature served out his own bowl before coming to sit in the middle of the room, crossing his legs. The creature took a large bite of the white, thick stuff, folded the greens into it with another finger, and shoved the whole wad into his mouth. As he chewed, he indicated that Hanen do the same.

Hanen put his hand into the stiff white, took up some of the greens, and put the bite in his mouth. The white stuff was flavorless, but the greens bore a wild assortment of spice, though not hot on the tongue. The explosion of flavor washed over his hunger and he began eating voraciously. The Khamntyr snorted in a sort of laugh.

When the bowl was clean, he looked up to see the Khamntyr still ruminating on his first bite.

"I...I apologize for my lack of manners."

"Nonsense," the Khamntyr said. "To eat with such gusto is a sign of respect in our culture."

"Then we are in a village of yours?"

"Hardly a village. This is one of our largest settlements. You shall be allowed to go about it once we determine who you are and why you are here."

"I am a prisoner then?"

"Only as a precaution."

"You're my jailer?"

"I do not like that term. I am a member of the council. My wives and I are known to enforce the laws within the boundaries of Barador."

"Coming from the east and north," Hanen said, "we only know of the Khamntyr through myths and legends. I had never given thought to you actually existing."

"My friend, we exist! Both here and across the entire world. I am not surprised at your ignorance, though. We remain a small people. The Œronzi barely acknowledge we exist, although the Oruche trade with us often. You bear the look of an Oruche."

"My mother is Üterk. They are tribes that are closely related to the Oruche."

"I see."

"My name is Hanen Clouw."

"It is good to meet you, Hanen Clouw. I am Guyyan Fifth-from-Kowavi, of the Barad-Gasota."

"Fifth-from-Kowavi?" Hanen asked.

"Four generations past, my ancestor Kowavi was a mighty Khamntyr."

"I see. Thank you for your hospitality, Guyyan," Hanen said, bowing his head.

"I will take my leave from you now that you have eaten," Guyyan said. "I must present what I have discovered of you to the council."

"Then this was a questioning?"

"More than you know," Guyyan said.

Hanen opened his mouth to speak, but Guyyan interrupted him.

"There is more of the meal in the jar. It will stay warm for some time. It is best eaten warm. Cold is not so good, so do not leave it open. The biting flies will swarm. If enough of them swarm, it'll draw furies."

Without another word, he left the hut.

Hanen stood after a while and refilled his bowl with more of the white meal and greens. He waved away the flies from the container, replaced the lid, and quickly ate the contents of his bowl to keep the pests away.

The entire place grew increasingly warm as the day continued, but that passed as the end of the day approached. The flap opened abruptly, revealing the full sun as it began its final descent.

"Oh! It is warm in here!" Guyyan said.

"It will cool with evening, I would hope," Hanen said.

"No breeze is foretold at this time," Guyyan said. "Tonight will be a hot and moist one."

He turned to the door and made a motion. Another figure stepped in, almost as tall as Hanen, and all knobby joints—a young Khamntyr, bearing tusks that were only just beginning to show. The ridge upon its nose was covered in skin, and the black horns on its brow were short, not yet long enough to begin curling.

"*Romuru*," Hanen said in greeting.

The younger Khamntyr startled and took a step back.

Guyyan gave a low, moaning chuckle.

"It speaks," the younger Khamntyr said.

"Of course he does, my son." Guyyan turned to Hanen. "This is my youngest son, Bouyan. Give your greetings, Bou."

"*Romuru*," Bouyan said with a curt bow. He brought out another jar and handed it to his father.

With little explanation, Guyyan walked around the room, took sticks from sconces, and dipped them into the jar. As they came out, the tips were smeared with a white paste. "Dwov-glow," Guyyan said as he finished and turned to the confused look on Hanen's face. "As it grows dark, the glow will increase. It is not fire, but we will not entrust you to fire until the council has decided."

"What is it they must decide?" Hanen asked.

"Whether you are to be trusted, naturally. We must consult the auguries, and determine if your actions have been for good or for evil."

"Auguries? Like telling the future?"

"No!" Bouyan said. "We Gasota do not deal in Past and Future, but read what the world speaks!"

"My son," Guyyan said, placing a hand on the younger Khamntyr's shoulder. "Calm your water."

Bouyan lowered his head.

"After we have determined your case, I shall explain more. Until then, please rest."

The two Khamntyri turned and left. The father chided his son in low tones Hanen could not understand.

As Guyyan predicted, the night was hot and uncomfortable, and Hanen tossed and turned in his sleep.

After dawn broke, the door opened, and Bouyan entered. He had wrapped his chest in a cloth of zigzagging reds and beiges. He looked at Hanen, who rose groggily from the mat.

"Romuru," Bouyan said.

"Good morning, Bouyan," Hanen replied.

"I am to escort you to the elders." He turned and walked out of the door.

"Am I to follow y...? Alright," Hanen said, rising to his feet and going to the door.

He was surprised to find the room he'd been kept in was twenty feet off the ground, although to call it ground was incorrect. Every building was built standing on heavy stilts over open still water. Tall rushes grew in places where farmers tended them in waist-deep mire. Most of the homes were similar to the one Hanen had been inside, with walkways running between them. It was as much a city as any other. Khamntyr made up the vast majority of the people in the city, although Hanen caught sight of a handful of men trading with the larger creatures. The female Khamntyr were of a lighter hue, from buff to white. They wore colorful skirts over more ample lower halves, and they adorned their shorter horns and ears with gold.

Bouyan walked down sturdy stairs to the walkways below, then waited for Hanen to come to his level.

"This way," Bouyan said.

"I see rushes and box gardens," Hanen said, making small talk. "Do your people keep livestock?"

"Livestock?"

"Animals."

"We eat no meat as you humans."

"You wear leather and cloth, though."

"Most is made from reed fibers," Bouyan said.

"What about the hides on the houses?"

Bouyan gave Hanen a sideways glance.

"They come from the selkhines."

"Selkhines?"

Bouyan pointed to an open space of water. Within, figures moved, with fins for hands, and long tails rather than legs.

"What are they?"

"They eat pests and fish in the water, which helps in keeping our crops healthy. When they die, we use their skin and bones, but never their meat. It is burned in some of the auguries. The elders say..." Bouyan stopped talking. "I have said too much. Come."

As they moved through the city, some noted their passage, but most ignored them.

"Humans are not an uncommon sight here," said Hanen.

"Of course not," Bouyan said. "We've many friends. The men of the Marches come here to trade with us. Hrelgrens and qavyl do, as well."

They came around a run of ten houses all bearing red lintels. Outside one of the small houses, a female Khamntyr stood watching their approach.

"Bouyan," the female said.

"Abaya, mumu," Bouyan said.

"Your father forgot his staff when he left. He's been too busy to return for it."

She held out an ornate staff of office as tall as Guyyan, topped with an old lacquered horn. Bouyan took it, and the female turned and entered her home.

"Your mother?"

"Yes," Bouyan said. "My father's seventh wife."

"You've many brothers and sisters then?"

"Six older brothers and twice as many sisters."

"You're the youngest?"

"For now. My father's first wife is with child. If it is a son, I will finally be free."

"Free?"

"'The youngest son is a cherished thing,' the saying goes. So I am doomed to a life that never leaves the city. If another son is born, I'll be allowed more freedom."

"You've been waiting many years for this?"

"Yes. I'm four years old," Bouyan said with pride. "Nearly an adult."

Hanen stifled a laughed and was glad the Khamntyr walked in front of him.

They made another turn and came to what must have been a town square. A lattice of walkways crisscrossed around vines and reeds that grew up out of the water. Dwovs hovered lazily everywhere, unperturbed by the people that conversed with each other. Across the square sat a larger building not much taller than most. It was built up on a foundation of stone that appeared to be from ages past.

At the door to the place stood Guyyan. Bouyan approached his father and handed him the staff.

"Thank you, son," Guyyan said taking it. "I see you have not lost your charge."

Bouyan looked back to Hanen. "He is still here."

Guyyan waved with his hand to Hanen. "You're to come with me. We'll be presenting you to the elders in a moment."

"What am I to say?"

"You will enter the elders' circle. You are to stand in the center. Turn to whoever asks you a question, give a bow, and say 'by the Truth,' and then answer their question, in truth only. Lies are dealt with severely here."

He turned to his son. "Bou, you will lead the way."

Bouyan leapt forward toward the door, his head held a little higher.

"The High Elder of our tribe is an ancient Kam-Nasur of the First Tribe. If he asks you any questions, give as respectful a bow as you know. In all things, his opinion overrules all others."

"How will I know when it is he that speaks?"

"You will know."

The hallway was lined with more hide and canvas, and through it, Hanen could hear clear voices speaking in a tongue he did not know, but was distinctly Khamntyri. They came to a T in the hall and Bouyan took another corner, wafting smoke circling over his shoulders.

"*Mouran doe gofirag,*" one voice in the adjacent room said.

"*Egilla Hanen Colouw,*" Bouyan replied.

"Bring him forward," the voice boomed in the common tongue.

"Go on," Guyyan said from behind.

Hanen walked forward and turned the corner.

The room beyond was large in circumference but the edges were enshrouded in shadow and smoke. A shaft of light cut down through the smoke from the hole in the peaked center of the roof.

Around the room several Khamntyr sat cross-legged, their faces unseen in the darkness. Guyyan moved to a final spot and sat down on the ground. At the head of the eight elders there sat a ninth upon a throne further shrouded in smoke. Hanen could only make out the feet of the one who sat there. The hooves were much more massive than the other members of the Gasota people: the Kam-Nasur.

Bouyan stood by the wall, and when Hanen glanced at him, the young Khamntyr indicated he take the center.

The sweet-smelling smoke thinned as he walked forward and into the shaft of light.

"Hanen Clouw, walker of Veld," Guyyan said calmly, "you are brought before the Elders to give testimony of your actions and to confess the purpose of the objects taken from you. Let us bear witness to what you have to say, and determine if the truths you speak are good or ill omen."

Hanen turned to where Guyyan sat, and gave a slow, but short bow. "By the Truth," Hanen began. "My name is Hanen Clouw, and I have spent many days in Dream, brought here by your hunters when I left the Veld."

"We found upon your person gauntlets made of motah efuil...the stars which have fallen," another elder said. His voice cracked with age. "Upon your back there sat a grotesque mantle made of bone. By what means is motah efuil forged? By what means is bone carved to resemble mail?"

"By the Truth, I did not make the skyfall gauntlets. Nor did I make the boneshroud you found upon my shoulders. The latter I was given. The gauntlets I took from a man who sought its secrets, intending ill upon the world with them."

"What are they, though?" another asked.

"By the Truth, they are a part of a larger suit of black armor. The rest is trapped within the Veld. I was not able to bring it back through."

"What do you intend to do with it?"

"By the Truth, I do not know yet," Hanen said. "I was separated from those I traveled with. They intended to seek its destruction."

"And the 'boneshroud,' as you call it?" the older voice asked.

"Made by a dead man," Hanen said and added, "by the Truth."

"But how?"

"By the Truth, I know how," Hanen said, "but I will not share it, for I would not have someone else try and replicate it."

"Do you think us capable of such monstrous things?" another asked.

"I have only just met the Khamntyr," Hanen said. "By the Truth, how would I know what you are capable of?"

There was a loud murmur, then several broke into the low Khamntyri language to speak amongst themselves.

"Tell us of the Veld. Tell us what you saw there," Guyyan said.

"By the Truth," Hanen began, "I was stranded there when I opened a portal into that place using the skyfall gauntlets. There I held prisoner the man I took them from and with me journeyed a Nifaran. He attempted to escape, threatened our lives, and took the blindfold from the monk."

This produced a gasp from several of the Elders.

"In response, I sent him to Noccitan."

"You killed him?" another asked.

"By the Truth, no," Hanen said. "I opened a portal to Noccitan and pushed him through."

"The gauntlets open portals to all the worlds?" someone hissed.

"What happened next?" Guyyan asked, bringing the story back to the present.

"By the Truth, I sent the Nifaran back to Kallattai and then went after the armor, which had been pushed into a crack in the earth. After I accomplished this, I was confronted by a Magus: the Arborist."

"Yet you live?" the oldest Khamntyr replied.

"By the Truth, I did. He, too, has been cast to Noccitan. His tower collapsed to sand. In order to escape, I fled into Kallattai, but the armor was left there. I was unable to goad it through, as the portal I made to flee through was too small."

"The Arborist is gone?" someone muttered. "We must send scouts to see."

There was a susurrus of whispers near the Kam-Nasur's seat. The large creature who sat there replied in a low voice with whomever counseled it. The conversation subsided, and there was a deep booming as the Kam-Nasur cracked a heavy pole on the wooden floor. All fell silent.

The creature leaned forward on the throne, which creaked under it, but no light fell on its form.

"Ha-nen Cloo," it said in the deepest voice Hanen had ever heard. He felt the vibration of that low and ancient voice in his chest. "Tell us your ancestry."

"By the Truth, I am the firstborn son of Marn Clouw, son of Thanessa and an unknown man. My grandmother is the daughter of Nethendel Unteel and Aella, daughter of Ollistan Gœrnstadt. By the Truth."

"What you speak is a truth?" the Kam-Nasur asked.

"By the Truth," Hanen nodded.

"Aella's mother, Belivah, was my friend," the Kam-Nasur said. "I advised her against following that man."

"What assurance does this council have," a new voice piped in from near the throne, "that you bear no ill will? That you are not under the thrall of the Deceiver?"

"By the Truth, that my great-grandfather was the Apostate and instigator of the greatest war in recent history puts my testimony into question, I know," Hanen said. "But I have also received an assurance that I am not enthralled unwillingly."

"Explain," the Kam-Nasur demanded.

"By the Truth, I have recently come from the Limaean city of Haven. There, while I wore the boneshroud upon my frame, which grants me invisibility to the gods, I came upon the god Kos-Yran, in hidden mortal form. He challenged me to a test of sorts. I won. He granted me a boon."

"If you have been blessed by Kos-Yran, then you are doubly cursed," the old Gasota Elder said from the other side of the room.

"This may be true, by the Truth," Hanen said, "but he told me that when the Deceiver demands my fealty, I will have complete choice in the matter. I will be given free will to either follow or die."

"In what way is this an assurance?"

"It means I have a choice."

The elders muttered to each other again.

"By the Truth, who can know the heart of any breathing being?" Hanen asked. "We can infer and guess but we cannot know. I have spoken with dark gods. I have even faced the third eye of Wyv-Thüm, and lived. In fact, I have watched as the full might of Grissone himself came down upon the man who made the boneshroud. He did not die that day. His body was only destroyed when he thrust a pin of bone into his own eye. Yet, he did not die. He lives on in the boneshroud—proven to me when I was in the Veld, as his shade manifested next to me there.

"I have always felt fully in control of my will. It will take much convincing for me to turn to the Deceiver. I have ensured this is so, by sending my loved ones far from me. If I could destroy the cloak I would, but I need it. I need to remain invisible to the dark gods if I am to retrieve the armor, and find a way to destroy it."

"Then you do mean to destroy it?" the thin, reedy voice by the throne asked. "Even after discovering so much?"

"What good would armor like that do for me? Besides make for me countless enemies who envy it for themselves?"

"Then," the thin voice said, "great and wise Kam-Nasur Tolvan, you have heard my own testimony this past night. Will you give the care of this man unto me?"

"Having heard his testimony, you still wish to ask for this?" the Kam-Nasur asked.

"I do. I believe there is hope to be had in this descendant of the Untellian line."

"So it is done," the Kam-Nasur said.

From beside the throne, a figure stepped out into the light, a long, leather-topped staff in his hand. "It appears I arrived among the Gasota just in time," Ymbrys Veronia said.

42

Dread Cult

Kasne et Terral was first to trust his people with their own well-being. I am not convinced that his gardened sanctum confines him, but instead provides a means by which he touches the forests of the world—of every world—and through that he still speaks to his Khamntyr.

—PEVROD *IH* BARROMOTH, HRELGREN SCHOLAR

"Why did you come here, of all places?" Hanen asked.

"The Khamntyr were the first I visited when I left Hannica," Ymbrys said.

They walked side by side through the town. Bouyan walked several paces behind them. The three of them drew more eyes now—or at least to Hanen it seemed more watched them this time through the community.

"I spent a year here among them," Ymbrys continued, "and to the south of here with the Oruche people. I learned more than I thought I would, but most important of all, I learned of Ollistan and Belivah's early life, after he came to the Oruche Marches to learn of the Veld."

"But why are you here now?"

"To find you."

"Why?"

"After you escaped with the cart into the Veld, I traveled with Dorian and Rallia to the southeast, to the Ormachian coast, and the Ormach capital city of Nor-Vio. After that, providence would have us run first into Marn and Alodda, and then Ophedia and

Seriah."

Hanen stopped in place. "Alodda?"

"Yes," Ymbrys said. "Alodda and your father left Düran in search of you. World events in Sidierata saw them skirting the bottom of Limae, seeking a way north to find you."

"World events? Are they safe?"

"As safe as they can be. Nor-Vio is a city of refugees seeking to escape Chalician rule. I believe Dorian and Rallia will keep them safe for the time being."

Hanen began walking again.

"What happened with you and Seriah in the Veld?" Ymbrys asked. "What didn't you tell the Elders?"

"What do you mean?"

"You know what I mean, Hanen."

Hanen sighed. "After I shoved Slate into Noccitan," Hanen said, "Seriah tried to rid us both of the cart and the boneshroud. She pushed it off the ledge into the crevasse herself."

"Why did you send her to Kallattai alone? Why didn't you go with her?"

"I was angry."

"Why?"

"She had taken that choice upon herself. She had taken it away from me."

"And now?"

"And now what?"

"Are you still angry?"

"I don't think so, no. I went after it because I feared that someone would find it anyway. My fears were confirmed when I met the Arborist."

"Who was he?"

"A mage. A dangerous one, too: he ensnared people into nightmares, as trees in his arboretum."

"Ah, then a literal title, it seems."

"I saved my skin through a sharing of stories, and in the end, he attacked me. I opened up a portal to Noccitan."

"So you said."

"Now I fear that the armor left unattended on the other side will be found."

"But without the gauntlets, it's unusable."

"That may be true, save for the fact that I also lost another object I did not mention to the Elders."

"Oh?"

"Slate had upon his hand a ring of bone."

"This ring was important?"

"It was the ring that contained the shade of Ghoré Dziony."

"Ah..." Ymbrys mused. "That is rather problematic."

"When I shoved Slate into Noccitan, he had hold of Seriah. I shut the gate, and it cut his hand off cleanly. The ring consumed what life was left in the hand, and it became a desiccated thing. I was able to handle it safely until I took a tumble. Ghoré invaded my mind and tried to drive me mad. I found the cart at the bottom of the canyon, and retrieving the boneshroud allowed Searn to drive Ghoré out of my head and restore me."

"Where is this hand and ring now?"

"I dropped it when the Arborist's tower collapsed."

"Perhaps it is also buried, and no one will find it. Now, why do you think that you could not bring the armor back with you?"

"I tried," Hanen said, "but when I open portals between the worlds, it is harder to do if I go in the wrong direction. They move in sequence. So from Kallattai, Veld is easiest. From there, Noccitan. I cannot go through Noccitan."

"Because of fear?"

"Because the Judge told me I could only appear before him dead, or bearing the skull of a fallen god."

Ymbrys wrung his hands on his staff.

"So I don't know what we will do with the armor, even if we go through to retrieve it."

"I have an idea I'm formulating," Ymbrys said.

Hanen pursed his lips in consternation.

"What are you thinking?" Ymbrys asked.

"The Arborist's last victim was Eralt Loth."

"Not a name I'm familiar with."

"He's a Motean that Dorian left imprisoned at the Green Bastion. Yet somehow he was in the Veld. He's a vindictive man. If he survived the tower's collapse, then the armor and ring are with him. If he finds either, or worse, both..."

"Perhaps we ought to discuss this with the Elders. They may allow us both to go into the Veld to ensure they are safe."

"Do the qavyl know much of the Veld?" Hanen asked.

"We are perhaps more knowledgeable than most humans. Not as much as the Oruche, and certainly not as much as the Khamntyr, but even they handle the Veld in a very different manner."

"What do you mean?"

"The Khamntyr are an interesting people. They have tribes across the world, and each makes a study of Past, Present, or Future."

"A study of them?"

"Yes. They have various means of reading each of them. The Gasota here make a special study of the Present. They study the movement of water, wind, leaves falling... In this they are able to understand what is occurring, here and across the world. They believe the four worlds breathe and spell out what happens as it occurs. Being so near the Oruche Marches, this tribe especially likes to study the Veld, and keep an observant eye on those who cause problems there."

"They knew of the Arborist, but did not interfere with him? Despite his cruelty?"

"They do nothing in the Veld that would affect anything. They merely observe."

"What good does that do?"

"I'm not sure it does good, nor ill."

They returned to the Elders' hall, but the backside this time.

Bouyan stepped up alongside them. "My father informed me that you may enter the Hall of Observances. He is there now, awaiting you."

Ymbrys gave the young Khamntyr a nod and entered, Hanen close behind.

Guyyan stood outside another door. "The Kam-Nasur has decided you may take the objects into your possession, Wisdom-Bearer."

"Thank you, Guyyan. Will you join us in there?" Ymbrys asked.

Guyyan gave a nod, and he and his son entered the next room first.

The small room within was a gallery of sorts. Along the wall, various objects from different cultures sat on display.

In the center of the room sat an interesting sculpture that looked like a metal vine with copper leaves. It reached to the ceiling, and went out a hole there.

"What is the purpose of that?" Ymbrys asked.

"This is our weather vine," Guyyan said. "Wind that strikes the leaves out in the air resonates to tell us from which direction it comes from, and with what intensity. When rain strikes it and falls from leaf to leaf, sages can determine much of the world at large."

He walked to a pool of water, in the center of which sat a basin made of crystal upon a pillar, filled to the brim with water. A single drop fell from the bowl into the water, sending ripples out from where it struck.

"And this?" Ymbrys asked.

"The water augury," Guyyan said. "When more than single droplets fall, we begin a watch to read what it may mean."

"How can you read the movements of water to read the world?" Hanen asked.

"The wing flutter of a dwov can cause subtle whisperings of trees, falling leaves, and even the tumble of water over rocks. From that shift, if one has the eyes to see, you can read the state of the world."

Hanen watched another droplet fall.

"It is why our hunters found you as you came out of the Veld. You sent out ripples from the Veld into Kallattai in abundance."

He turned to another plinth on which lay both the folded boneshroud and atop that the gauntlets.

"Do you see anything when you touch them?" Ymbrys asked the Khamntyr.

Guyyan shook his head.

"Then, if you will, please put them both into a satchel and give them to me."

"You will not touch them yourself?" Guyyan asked the qavyl.

"That would not be wise."

Guyyan took up a satchel of rough material. He folded the gauntlets into the boneshroud, placed it into the satchel, and handed it to Ymbrys.

"Where will you go now?"

"I mean to enter the Veld myself," Ymbrys said. "Hanen and I have unfinished business there."

"Allow me to go with you," Guyyan said.

"We will not spiritwalk," Ymbrys said, "but enter as we do. It will be much less safe than how your people travel."

"I understand," Guyyan said.

"Very well," Ymbrys said. "We will need to journey back to where Hanen was found."

"I will make the arrangements," Guyyan said, and left, his son following close behind.

"Where exactly are we?" Hanen asked.

"What do you mean?"

"I mean on Kallattai. I assume we're near the Oruche Marches."

"We are just north of the Oruche Marches, which sit between the Sevelaad marshes and the Oruche Marchlands."

"Sevelaad marshes?"

"Do you know Sevelaad Lake?"

"The large inland lake, almost sea, in Ormach?"

"The marsh makes up the southwestern edge. It's large enough the Gasota tribe can remain in place for some time, although I think they may migrate back over to the Oruche side soon. They've not for fifty years."

"We're much farther south than I thought."

"How so?"

"The fissure I crawled out of was located one hundred yards from where I entered the Veld. When the Arborist took me to his tower, it was not but a couple hours south. Now we're at least a week south?"

"The Veld does not exactly correlate to Kallattai."

"What do you mean?"

"As I understand it, the Veld is larger and more expansive when nearer to large gatherings of people."

"So the distance is shorter because of how few live between where I entered and where I left?"

"Exactly."

"The seas must be much smaller then," Hanen said.

"I would think so," Ymbrys said.

The sun began its descent as Guyyan returned.

"Will Bouyan be joining us?" Ymbrys asked.

"He is my youngest son. He is not allowed to leave the city."

Guyyan stepped down off the walkway and into the water to forge ahead. Ymbrys did the same, showing no trouble entering the water. Hanen dropped down into the waist-deep water, taking up the rear.

"Follow my wake," Ymbrys said. "Guyyan will not step in muck he cannot move in and I will follow him. Step off our wakes, and you'll likely find mud not easy to escape from."

The sun dropped under the horizon just as Norlok rose full in the east. There was a brief moment when both sunk below the water's surface and in a burst of orange in the west and red in the east, the entire marsh suddenly glowed. The shadows of fish and the chubby forms of Selkhines moved through the water. It was an eerie and magical moment that froze Hanen in place.

"It is moments like this," Guyyan said aloud, "that our people and the Oruche say the four worlds are closest to one another. Here in the Sevelaad, Kallattai and Veld are close to one another at all times. Especially if you enter the open water of the lake."

"Why is that?" Ymbrys asked.

"Because of the island that sits in the center. The Kam-Nasur believes that the full moon of Umay set to come a week from now will be an even greater moment."

"What lies in the center of the lake?" Hanen asked.

"A tower and an entry into the Veld."

"An entry?"

Guyyan said no more. As the glow in the water faded, and Norlok fully emerged from the horizon, he turned and continued north.

Several times Hanen stumbled, and after an hour he was soaked through. Any other time of the year, his teeth would have been chattering. The only true irritation to be felt came from the bugs that swarmed around them. The other two seemed unperturbed. Ymbrys moved easily in the water, and at times turned to warn Hanen of a muddy sinkhole.

As Norlok came to its zenith, Guyyan stopped and looked around.

Ymbrys considered the Khamntyr.

"It is here," Guyyan said. "Or near here."

Ymbrys gave a nod and held out the satchel to Hanen. "Take out the gauntlets, but quickly. If what you said was true, and Searn appears when you touch the cloak, I should like to enter the Veld without his interference."

Hanen nodded his compliance, and thrust a hand down into the sack.

"What's going on, Hanen?" Searn asked in his mind.

Hanen ignored him and took hold of one gauntlet, then the next, and pulled them free. Searn dissipated again.

"Now what do we do?" Guyyan asked.

"Just watch," Ymbrys said as Hanen slipped the gauntlets on.

He took hold of the air before him, and pulled open a rift. The Khamntyr gasped.

Ymbrys came to look over Hanen's shoulder and they peered through the hole that viewed into the purple Veld.

"It is more beautiful than I imagined," Guyyan said.

"There," Ymbrys said, pointing down the long slope of a hill in the Veld. In the bowl-like valley below stood a pile of sand. Near the edge, a small encampment had formed, with all tents facing toward a tall object of black.

"Who are they?" Ymbrys asked.

"When I was there, the entire area around where the Dreadplate stands was a forest of gnarled trees. With that gone, I think those may be the survivors."

"Those enslaved by the Arborist?" Guyyan asked.

"I think so," Hanen said.

"Well, shall we go and see if we can talk to them?" Ymbrys asked, and stepped through the portal. He looked back and motioned for Guyyan to follow. The tall Khamntyr stepped through and looked all around him in awe. Hanen stepped through himself. His foot hooked the edge and he tripped into the other two as his foot left the water behind and stepped onto solid ground. They all fell into a roll down the sandy slope. As Hanen struggled to his feet, he looked up at the closing hole in the air to see another coming in after them as it closed behind.

43

Visions of Hate

"I leave now to find those tribes. They may know by what path the prophet Morrig and ancient men traveled, and where our origin may be found."

—LAST WORDS OF IGGON VEMORT BEFORE

TRAVELING EASTWARD, PAST THE BORDERS OF

THE PROTECTORATE OF THE HAMMER

"Bouyan?" Hanen muttered.

"What did you say?" Guyyan asked, and looked back up the hill. "Oh, no."

The young Khamntyr looked up at the purple sky above, hugging his arms in protection. His father ran up the hill with a low moan. "How could you follow us?!" he shouted. "Do you know what this will bring down upon us?!"

"I don't understand," Hanen said. "I thought it was merely a tradition of a protective father."

"I think it is a strong superstition," Ymbrys muttered to him. "They believe in doing as little as possible to affect the world around them, so they can better read their auguries. That means following tradition to the letter. Bouyan is perhaps too young a Khamntyr to understand."

"He is only four," Hanen confirmed.

"Almost an adult in their culture, yet still so very young to us."

Ymbrys turned back down the hill. "It appears whoever leads those survivors is coming, with his followers behind him."

"Loth, do you think?" Hanen asked.

"Likely. Perhaps he will be reasonable, but probably not. You had best leave the Gloves of Eons on."

"How do you know their name?"

"How do you?"

Hanen looked away. "Searn told me."

"Interesting... I wonder how he came to know their true name..."

"I would be better protected with the boneshroud on, too."

"Why?"

"In case Loth has Ghoré's ring."

"And if he doesn't?"

"Then we ought to find it."

"Why?"

"Better we find and destroy it, than anyone else."

"Very well. If Loth appears to have it, then I'll give you the cloak."

Hanen agreed to this. The two Khamntyr came to stand next to them.

"My son has followed us into the Veld," Guyyan said.

Bouyan said nothing and kept his head bowed.

"I take responsibility for him, and apologize for any trouble this may cause."

"There is no need to fret," Ymbrys said.

"There is if his actions have causality to the mission."

"Then," Ymbrys said, "let us hope it is for the good intended by the gods."

Guyyan made a solemn nod and signed himself in an odd way. Hanen pulled his gauntleted hands behind his back, then they all turned to face the people walking up the hill. At the head of the group walked Loth. He wore a purple cloak over his shoulders that terminated in a ceaseless fall of sand.

"He has discovered how to manipulate the Veld," Hanen muttered.

"Can you?" Ymbrys asked.

Hanen nodded. He turned and knelt down, taking up some sand in the gauntlets. By his mind he formed a plain mask with only eye slits. He lifted the piece to his face, and it stuck fast.

Loth came to a stop fifty feet away. His followers kept their distance, another fifty feet behind. "What manner of travelers are you? Have you come to make offering to the Dread Knight?"

Hanen stepped forward, hands held still behind his back and nodded.

"What do you bring in offering for so great an honor?" Loth asked loudly, so those behind could hear.

"I brought freedom," Hanen said. "What more do you need?"

"What do you mean?" Loth asked. "We were freed by the Dread Knight. For when we awakened, the nightmare collapsed and all that was left standing was the knight."

"Take me to the Dread Knight," Hanen said, in as hollow a voice as he could muster, "and I will show you how you were freed."

Loth eyed them suspiciously, then turned and began to walk down the hill. Hanen followed.

"What are you going to do?" Ymbrys asked.

"I have no idea, but we need to undermine his authority. If I can touch the armor, I can regain control of it."

The four of them walked down after Loth. The crowd of people parted and folded in behind them. They wore on their faces either looks of horror or passivity. Hanen was thankful he'd thought to pull the mask on over his face, so they could not see the sadness he felt for them. Sorrow seemed to emanate from them in a cloud. Bouyan gave a low, mournful sigh himself in response to that feeling.

They came to the bottom of the hill and Loth crossed the flat to where the black armor stood, just as Hanen had left it. Following him closer, the others stopped, leaving distance between themselves and the towering figure.

"What creature could wear that armor?" Guyyan asked.

"It is almost too large for even your frame," Ymbrys agreed.

Loth stood beside the armor as an attendant serving a king, and considered the four of them.

"Hail the Dread Knight. Monumental deity."

The cultists all around dropped as one onto their knees.

"What god do you think you worship?" Ymbrys asked. "Only one god appeared in armored form, and he is far to the east."

"The Dread Knight is a new god. Ascendant. It shall rise and march across the worlds and lay waste."

"It cannot move without knowledge of what it is," Hanen said.

"What would you know?"

Hanen revealed his gauntleted hands. With a subtle move, the armor shifted ever so slightly. The cultists gasped. Loth eyed Hanen cooly, unsurprised.

Loth knew. In Hanen's heart, he could tell that Loth knew who he was—likely had known him since the moment they came through from Kallattai.

The people around him turned as one. Their eyes glowed indigo like Revenants, but they seemed not to be dead. Within their gaping mouths a coin sat on their tongue like a wafer.

Hanen noticed too late that the sand under his feet was going slack, as spikes of sand shot up around his arms, suspending them in place. A tendril of the stuff covered and consumed the gauntlets surrounding his hands before he could begin to manipulate them.

Loth held his hands out toward the four of them and began throwing them wildly. With each action, sand burst and froze in various ensnaring forms. One lashed out and struck Ymbrys in the head, knocking him sideways. Another set of long lines flew across Bouyan's feet, and the young Khamntyr tripped and fell. The people nearby fell on him, and he began to holler in a panic. Others rushed to hold Hanen in place.

Only Guyyan kept his composure. Despite his size, he deftly dodged rising lances of hard sand which would have impaled a slower victim. Loth threw up walls of sand and the Khamntyr punched his way through. It forced Loth into a panicked backpedaling up the sandy hill, unable to do much more than the same.

The fallen Paladin roared out a command for help and others raced up after the Khamntyr advancing on their leader. A few grabbed at his legs, but fell back, either kicked away, or by rising sand spikes. All crawling up the hill ground to a slow advance. Guyyan reached for Loth, his heavy hand taking hold of the man's robes. Loth sneered and the robe dissipated into sand falling from his emaciated frame.

Bouyan appeared next to his father and struck Loth with a fist. At his son's actions, Guyyan dropped Loth to the sand and pushed the boy away as a large spike rose between them, barely missing Bouyan. The young Khamntyr scrambled away as more spikes rose. Guyyan turned to look at Loth, who threw his hands up one after the other, trying to impale them both. Guyyan advanced on the man on the sand.

"Look out!" Bouyan cried.

Guyyan hesitated for one moment at that cry.

DREAD KNIGHT

He did not move fast enough as three spikes shot up from three different angles, impaling him through the torso and crisscrossing, locking him in place.

He roared against the hold, but Loth was faster, rising from the sand, an object pulled from the ground.

"Father!" Bouyan cried out in alarm.

With a flick of his wrist, Loth lifted what he had pulled from the sand and touched Guyyan's forehead with the desiccated hand bearing the ring of Ghoré. Guyyan gasped, and all of his muscles went ridged.

Loth took something from a pouch at his side, and placed it into Guyyan's mouth. Then, after a few long moments, Loth dispelled the spike holding the Khamntyr in place. Guyyan fell, then slowly struggled to his feet, despite the mortal wound in his chest.

Loth and Guyyan walked down the hill to stand before Hanen.

Loth considered the dying creature beside him. "I'd have used you, Sentinel, but this will work and look so much better."

He took hold of Hanen's wrists through the sand entrapping him and yanked, taking the gauntlets from him. He shook them free of sand, and turned them over in contemplation. He held the desiccated hand up and considered whatever words Ghoré was telling him, then nodded. He turned, Guyyan following him to the armor. Loth made a motion, and the Khamntyr put his back to the breastplate. Loth shoved the Ghoré hand into a sandy sash around his waist and then dropped the gauntlets onto his own hands. He touched Guyyan's chest, took a smear of blood, and touched the armor. With a two-handed motion, the front of the armor flayed open. Guyyan weakly stepped backward into the armor, and with another wave of Loth's hands, the armor closed on itself, leaving only Guyyan's head exposed.

Loth turned around toward Hanen and Bouyan. Not far from them, Ymbrys lay still.

"This is quite the trouble you've gotten yourself into," Loth said. "I suppose this will be better. Leaving you here to rot in the Veld."

"Where will you go?"

"I'll just open a hole into Kallattai and take my new pet with me."

He held his hands out and made a motion.

The air ripped open, and into the Veld spilled ten Khamntyr hunters, at their head, a majestic leader almost twice the size of the others.

"Tolvan!" Bouyan said in a hushed tone.

The Kam-Nasur's brow was not a pair of horns, but rather a large and boney frill that rose like a bowl, with several horny nobs at the top. It grew down his nose as well, giving him the appearance of a creature two feet taller than the Gasota, as though wearing the skull of a great beast upon his face like a mask. He wore robes tied to his frame by exotic sashes, and held in his hand a slab of metal like a five-foot cleaver, moving it with the ease of brandishing a butter knife.

Despite outweighing two Gasota combined, Tolvan rushed forward, his weight barely an inconvenience.

Loth fell back behind Guyyan in the armor. The armored Khamntyr's head lolled about with little strength left, eyes tired, but terror-filled. By Loth's guidance, the Dread Knight lifted its arms in defense, absorbing the attack from Tolvan.

The hunters wasted no time charging into Loth's followers before they could react.

They moved with a brutally elegant speed, some with longer two-handed weapons, others with short cleavers in each hand. Every weapon was long and rectangular, edged on all three sides, like wood chisels the size of swords no human would wield. In the purple light of the Veld, the weapons moved in spinning arcs. The mindless cultists threw themselves at the Gasota warriors, unflinching as the weapons cut through them, armed with daggers of indigo glass in their hands. The Gasota roared as they were struck, but pressed through the pain. A cultist was the first to fall still, lying there with gaps in his flesh, yet not bleeding, but looking as someone asleep. Then, another cultist fell. Then five more, before the first Gasota hunter succumbed to his wounds and fell in the same sleepy repose as the cultists around him.

The Gasota were outnumbered, but the tide shifted as they pressed their way up to the cultist leader.

Tolvan fought against the Dread Knight, blocking blows, and side-stepping ham-fisted attacks, his own massive sword making no dent in the armor. Loth tried throwing up his lancing spikes of sand, but Tolvan's moves broke his concentration, and he was unable to gain any proper advantage.

Finally, the armor lost footing on the sand, and in a cry of surprise, Loth was pinned under the armor falling on him.

Tolvan wasted no time and leapt over and around the armor. He took hold of both gauntlets and tore them from Loth's hands,

DREAD KNIGHT

tossing them to another Gasota. Then he began moving his hands in rapid motions. The sand around him formed up, and pulled the inert armor of black metal into a standing position. Loth tried to crawl through the sand to get away. With a free hand, the Kam-Nasur took hold of him, and sand formed up and hardened around Loth.

Bouyan rushed up the hill to the Kam-Nasur and fell to his knees before the Dread Knight. His father's face drooped, bloody and weak. He looked down at his son.

"Father?" Bouyyan said. "I'm sorry."

"And yet," Guyyan replied, "you are old enough to face the consequences of your actions. Follow the journey the Kam-Nasur sets for you, and you will see me at the end."

Tolvan came to stand next to the Dreadplate, almost as large as the metal form, and looked Guyyan in the eye.

"You have served your tribe well, but even in the Veld, there are times to pass on to Noccitan."

Guyyan gave a weak nod, and then his head slumped and lay still. His flesh became suddenly taut, and then fell off as sand poured from Tolvan's hand, taking away any semblance of life from him, and leaving only the Khamntyr's lifeless skull.

"He is returned to his fathers before him, to the pasture of our god," Tolvan stated solemnly.

Bouyan lowed a mournful cry to the sky and the hunters nearby gave a similar voice to match his.

44

Visions of Fate

There is a darkness in my soul, that dream doth feed and nightmare empower. I fear it will be the destruction of my mind, or its liberator.

—UNKNOWN

Within the hour, the Kam-Nasur had built an Elder Hall of oneirion sand. Loth had not moved, but rather, the hall had been built up and around both he and the armor. Ymbrys, recovered from the blow to his head, sat with Hanen to one side, while the hunters who had accompanied their leader into the Veld formed a tribunal.

Bouyyan lay prostrate in genuflection, his face buried in the sand before the Kam-Nasur's throne.

"Thus you are banished from the tribe," Tolvan decreed, "for the dishonor you brought to your father and clan."

"How may I find absolution?" Bouyan said.

"That you ask this," Tolvan said with the hint of a smile, "shows you are on your way. This shall be determined."

He turned to Loth. "Eralt Loth."

Loth did not respond.

"I understand you once held a Hammer of Pariantür. Therefore, I cannot pass judgment on you."

"Kam-Nasur," Ymbrys said, bowing to the ground, "his Prima Pater is not far from here. He could be made to journey to the

Prima Pater for judgment."

"This shall be considered," Tolvan said. "By what way will you journey back to the world of Kallattai?"

"We cannot return by way of a mere portal opening in the air," Ymbrys said. "It appears that the armor must go one direction, when traveling that way. Therefore, it would have to traverse through Noccitan, to Lomïn, and finally to Kallattai. As I understand it, we are not far from a gate to Kallattai. If you shall allow it, I shall journey with the armor in that direction, to discover a way back through. From there, I believe the best course of action is to steal it away to Hannica, where the qavylli can determine the best means of destroying it, if it is possible."

Loth scoffed.

"What words would you speak?" Tolvan asked.

"That you would even think you can destroy it is folly," Loth said. "Even the gods cannot touch it."

"And mortals," Tolvan said, "should not speak of that which they do not understand."

With a wave of Tolvan's hand, sand creeped up and covered Loth's mouth. The Kam-Nasur turned back to Ymbrys. "If you are to journey to the gate, then the exile shall join you, as jailer of the heretic, Loth." He turned to Bouyan. "Thus you are stripped of your family name, and shall be merely Bou. See the heretic Loth delivered to his Prima Pater. When that goal is fulfilled, you shall follow the guidance of the qavyl, Ymbrys Veronia. When he determines you are ready to return to the Gasota tribe, then you shall be redeemed."

Bou lowered his face even farther, a sob escaping him.

Tolvan turned to the congregation. "Now, I've words to speak with Ymbrys and the human Ha-nen, alone."

The sand collapsed from around Loth, save for a hard coating binding his arms. Bou took hold of him, and led the way out with sunken shoulders, the other hunters on his heels.

Tolvan approached Ymbrys and Hanen and knelt next to them. The walls closed in behind them, giving them quiet privacy.

"You have grown in power in the Veld," Ymbrys said.

"I have not waxed nor waned. I merely have not taken the time to flex these muscles of the mind for some time. My friend, do you recall the words we spoke when you first journeyed from our tribe to seek out the descendants of the Necromancer?"

"You told me that you had been granted a series of visions, but that you were unwilling to share them."

"Indeed. You advised me to keep them in my heart, and to consult wisdom as to the right time."

"Those words were true."

"No truer than now," Tolvan said. "For the time came to pass when I saw the face of Hanen Clouw before the Elder Council."

"Me?" Hanen said. "I don't understand?"

"But you shall," Tolvan said. "And regardless of what I reveal and say, you will listen. For Wisdom dictates it."

"What do you mean?"

"I shall show you."

He waved a hand over the sand, and forms rose from the dirt, like the Kam-Nasur in miniature.

"The Kam-Nasur were the first made by Kasnetyr. From our tribe the others rose, and over time, our tribe waned, and took up positions of leadership and council among all the tribes. Our god taught us the means of visions and augury, to study the past, present, and future by reading the ripples of the world."

At a mere movement, trees rose and leaves fell and gravestones came up from the earth and the leaves blew between the graves in whorling patterns.

"The first tribe knew all three, but our children, those of the various tribes across the world, grew in specific expertise. The Gasota, for example, more than all the other tribes, have come to understand the Veld. By reading the actions within, they can understand much of what occurs across the whole of the Veld. I came to be their leader three hundred years ago, to sit in judgment, but just as much so, to learn from them. I learned long ago how to consult the dead in service to the Judge, and even to read the future in the ripples of the threads of reality, although in that I am weakest.

"Not but a year ago, I journeyed in Dream as I slept, as the qavyl Ymbrys stayed with us as guest. In that dream, I was cast on the tides of the four worlds, and given a vision—I saw past, present, and future. I saw the formation of the World Rose, far off in a land most distant, from a council of seed pods, from which others would be born and carried in their dormancy to the utter reaches of the four worlds to await their birth. I saw one such seed placed upon a desk. Then I saw the death of the World Rose. This is what I did not share with you, Ymbrys, for I did not feel it my place."

"Alas, what you have seen has come to pass."

"That is what I have come to understand. But even with the World Rose having died, hope was born. Within the Veld, a new power has arisen, and she marches to the doom of those that have long held sway here."

He turned to Hanen.

"Not but a few months ago, I was haunted by another set of dreams. It is these that I must share with you, whatever the cost."

A chill ran up and down Hanen's spine, but he did not speak.

"The whispers of the grave spoke to me. They sung upon the wind, and showed me a horror of horrors: souls locked within their own bones, and hewn together into a cloak of menacing evil. No sooner had I seen this, broken out in a cold sweat, than I saw a familiar place. The halls of the dead, in which are recorded all the souls, and a figure wearing that cloak spoke unto a god who once knew me by name and let me leave those hallowed halls. The Judge let that figure leave as easily as I after a century of service to him. Then I saw that same figure, once more enrobed, and he commanded the dead to be imbued with the unholy light of the Veld. In that instant, I saw his face and I knew his eyes, and they, Ha-Nen, were yours."

"Are these all true?" Ymbrys asked.

Hanen gave a glance to Ymbrys.

"Hanen," Ymbrys said, "did you make the Bone Shroud?"

"I did not," Hanen said. "But I have repaired it."

"With what?"

"With blood shed from a bolt shot through my shoulder. I did not intend to."

"Hanen Clouw," Ymbrys continued, "have you visited the Judge?"

"He riffled through my mind and soul with his third eye." Hanen's voice quavered, unable to stop himself from admitting it. "And he let me walk free."

"Hanen Clouw," Ymbrys pressed, "did you create the Revenants in Haven?"

"In my attempt to destroy the skyfall coins I had taken from those enslaved by it, I accidentally exploded them across the city, and those that inhaled it became Revenants."

"What are these 'Revenants?'" Tolvan asked.

Ymbrys turned back to the Kam-Nasur. "Different than those unfettered souls that took hold of hosts in the Protectorate Wars."

"They are controlled by a parasitic wyrm from the Veld," Hanen said.

Tolvan nodded. "This is not good. For it confirms that my third vision is also true and shall come to pass."

"What vision?" Ymbrys asked.

"One I had the night you arrived two nights ago, my friend."

"I think you had best tell us."

"There is another Magus not far from here. He cultivated a garden of grotesque things to the west of the Oruche Marches. Our friends among those tribes say that he was found dead two years ago, murdered in Kallattai by a dark figure who fled in a cloak not of any world. Because of his death, his creations broke free of their confines, and have begun to bleed across the Veld. I saw in my third vision his murder by the man in the bone cloak. In shifting vision, I saw the present, two days ago, as a new infestation of mind wyrms were let loose in a human city nearby: in Nor-Vio."

At this, Ymbrys gasped.

"And lastly, I saw those wyrms move toward the same gate you seek. I think they mean to enter the world as a blight upon the land."

"Why do you gasp?" Hanen asked.

"That is where I left our friends."

"Alodda? Rallia?"

"And Marn."

"Your friends?" Tolvan asked.

"My sister, my betrothed, and my father."

"The strike on the city was swift and fierce. Few live."

"Can we know if they live?"

"I...might be able to see," Tolvan said, "by showing you my vision through my eyes. But, you cannot change what has happened."

"I have to know," Hanen said.

Tolvan nodded, took up sand in his hand, and blew it into Hanen's face without warning.

He was standing next to Tolvan in a city. People ran in every direction with chaos at their heels. Soldiers ran roughshod, hacking at each other and at commoners. Some had a purple glow in their eyes, and others just the crazed look of madness. Down the slope of the city to the sea, Hanen could see the ships burning, while others fought to clear their mooring and escape.

"We must go that way," Tolvan said. "That is where my vision took me."

"Why can we not explore?"

"There is some play," Tolvan said. "But we must stay close to the path set for us, or we may find ourselves lost in madness."

Hanen followed the lumbering Kam-Nasur through the streets. People ran past and even through the two of them with little effect. As more ran from one location, it was easy to follow the danger to the source.

"This event was present. Thus, it took place as I saw it," Tolvan said. "Past events are easier to traverse and walk amidst, because their after-effects are heavier and established. I believe some great evil was unleashed. What we must see is what happened after."

They had come to a square, and in the center stood a Chalician Praetor—not one that Hanen recognized, though he reminded him of the one in Mahn Fulhar, albeit much younger. He was shouting orders, though no sound could be heard. Other Chalicians finished cutting another Praetor down. The purple light in his eyes flared out, and then exploded into the mouth of another Praetor. He convulsed for a second before he turned on his comrades and attacked.

The leader roared his defiance, and turned in surprise to a group of people rushing into the square, Ophedia del Ishé at the lead, a massive black sword in her hand. Behind her ran Dorian and Marn, wooden staves in their hands, Rallia rushing alongside them, and even Whisper and Seriah. There came just behind them two others: Alodda, and finally, the most surprising, Abenard Navien.

The Praetors, those cursed with Veldic flame and not, turned on the newcomers and attacked.

In the chaos, the Praetor leader raised above his head an orb of black metal and threw it into the fight, directly at the feet of Alodda and Marn Clouw, and then there was a dull black shadow that washed over the square in an explosion.

Hanen awakened from the vision in a gasp.

"What happened next?!" Hanen asked. "Show me!"

"I do not know," Tolvan said. "With the explosion of black I was forced into the vision of the future."

"I must know!"

"What did you see?" Ymbrys asked.

"A... a Praetor threw a skyfall orb and it..."

"It fell to the feet of his love and his father. I do not know how any could survive."

"Then," Ymbrys said, "we must get through the gate, and journey to Nor-Vio."

"I can take the gauntlets and go myself to find out," Hanen said. "Let Nocc take this mission."

"You will not do that," Ymbrys said.

"What?"

"I said you will not do this. It is time I took responsibility. We journey to the gate. There you will cross over and assist me with moving the armor toward Hannica. We will find out what occurred in Nor-Vio. I promise."

Hanen slammed the ground with his fist in frustration.

"No matter what happened," Ymbrys said, "You can't change it."

"I could have abandoned this whole thing and passed into Düran with Alodda."

"But you did not," Ymbrys said. "Now you'll face the consequences of your actions, and help me."

Hanen took a deep breath and looked into the qavyl's eyes. "Very well. Tell me what to do, but do not expect me to act friendly."

"I agree to this," Ymbrys said, with a sad tone in his voice.

Tolvan waved his hand and the entire building of sand collapsed. Bou stood alongside the black armor. Ymbrys took the gauntlets from Tolvan and handed them to Hanen.

"Open a portal to Kallattai, Hanen, for the Gasota."

Hanen did as he was told and placed the gauntlets on his hands, then with a quick twist, a hole stood in the air. Tolvan clasped Ymbrys' shoulder.

"I trust you and what you must do," Tolvan said. "Let Wisdom guide you."

"Wisdom," Ymbrys said, "guides us all."

Hanen wore the gauntlets, moving the armor in a slow march. The lifeless skull of Guyyan topped the armor. Alongside him, Bou trudged, unwilling to look up. He held in one hand a chain leading back to Loth, and in his other hand, a bundle containing the desiccated hand of Slate. Behind them all, Ymbrys walked, humming a tune to himself. They topped a rise, and Hanen gave one backward glance. Across the valley below and up the other side of the slope he could see a smear of blackness.

It imperceptibly moved down the side of the hill, and had already moved around the side of the bowl. As they came up over the lip of the edge, he could make out the smear running along the near horizon parallel to them. After several hours of walking, they had drawn closer to the smear. Topping another short knoll revealed it cut across their path. It sat on the ground like a pall, yet, it was no cloud, nor swarm of gnats, but something else.

"What is that?" Bou asked.

"In our path," Ymbrys said matter-of-factly. "Onward, and we'll examine it."

They drew nearer and Hanen's heart sunk further in his chest. It stood like a river of ash. It was hundreds of yards wide, and was formed by small cones of displaced earth. From a few of the mounds ghostly pale things pressed up to consider their surroundings, or to toss small bits of black dirt away. A sibilance of small piercing screeches filled the air, discordant with the wind that had picked up in the past hour.

"What are those?" Bou asked.

"Dreamwyrms," Hanen muttered.

Ymbrys approached the edge, not daring to actually come within five feet of a wyrm's hill. He took a pouch from his staff, and tossed it out across the black dirt twenty feet. Before it had even impacted, several white tendrils lashed out with lightning speed, fighting for dominance to examine what had fallen amidst them. The screeching grew louder, and just as quickly as it had started, ceased.

"I'd not want to be that satchel," Ymbrys said. "Let us follow the path they carve for a time, and see if we can go around."

He indicated for the others to precede him, and they began to walk once more.

The path the dreamwyrms had carved continued, and at times sat even wider and unsurpassable. They came to a break in the land, with rocks tumbling down to another valley floor a hundred feet below. The small wyrm hills took the easy routes, splitting around jutting rocks, and at the valley floor split into two paths, running north and east. Far off to the east from their vantage point, the tendrils appeared to break into a multitude, spreading out across the horizon. One tendril running northerly shot in an incredibly straight line.

"We need to follow that one," Ymbrys said.

"But how can we cross?" Bou asked.

"I cannot guide the armor to step from stone to stone," Hanen said. "There is not that much finesse."

Ymbrys stared vacantly toward the horizon, his hands wringing the staff. He gasped.

"There is a skyfall coin clamped in Guyyan's mouth," he said. "Retrieve it."

Bou looked away as Hanen reached up and into the skull that topped the armor. Between two teeth he found a small item and took it out, handing Ymbrys the coin of black metal.

Without another word, the qavyl tossed it out into the colony. Again, the creatures screeched and writhed from their holes to fight for the chance to examine it. Then they recoiled, flailing to pull back from where the coin had landed.

"Good," Ymbrys said. "Alright. Let's cross."

"What do you mean?" Hanen asked.

"Stay close to the Dreadplate, all of you, but we can cross unperturbed."

Ymbrys indicated toward the black earth, and Hanen put the gauntlets back on and guided the armor forward. As it stepped into the first part of the black earth, wyrms shot up to consider. The first that touched the metal shrank back with an ear-piercing screech. All across the blackness, the wyrms flailed at the sky, undulating in anger. The Dread Knight walked unperturbed. No tendril would rise within ten feet of it, and so they all stayed close and followed behind as the black metal figure walked stiltedly across the colony and to the other side.

As they came to purple sand once more, the screeching subsided, and all fell still around them. Now with the black path on their right, they proceeded northward.

"That was not so bad as I thought it might be," Ymbrys said.

"If we should have misstepped?" Bou asked.

"Then I should imagine us lost for all time."

"Would they consume us?" Bou pressed.

"Perhaps oblivion is given," Ymbrys said. "Or perhaps they enslave your mind here in nightmare."

As they came over the next hill, they saw before them a vast lake, and in the center a rocky island. The black earth dreamwyrm colony made its way over a narrow causeway toward the center.

"That is where we journey," Ymbrys said, and began walking down the hill to the edge of the water.

Bou cried out as Loth rushed forward and yanked the bundle from Bou's hand, before rushing out into the black earth. Without thinking, Bou rushed after him.

"No, Bou! Grab the chain instead!" Hanen shouted.

Bou looked back all too late to realize where he stood. Pale wyrms rose from the ground around their feet, locking Bou and Loth in place, the latter laughing maniacally.

"What are you doing?" Ymbrys asked calmly.

"You fools! These wyrms respond to stronger minds!" Loth shouted, holding the revealed hand of Ghoré over his head. With a wave, the wyrms moved like mesmerized drækis before a charmer. Bou struggled against the wyrms.

"You see? They need only be commanded."

Ymbrys sighed. "They do not follow his command, but his movements, in preparation to str…"

Hundreds of the wyrms lunged up, encasing Loth instantly, dragging him down to the ground, and into it. The chain pulled at Bou and he let it go in an attempt to free himself. Hanen kneeled to reach out over the ground, attempting not to touch the wyrms himself. Bou trudged forward, trying to get back to the makeshift road, but sunk, slowly, into the earth. His eyes locked with Hanen's, full of fear in the final moment before he disappeared entirely.

Silence reigned.

"Come," Ymbrys said.

Hanen rose from the ground where he had dropped to his knees. "We just leave? What about Bou? Loth?"

"Loth has been delivered to his judgment, I hope. And Bou? We cannot know if he still lives, although little dies in the Veld. There are fates worse than death here."

"Then even Loth may still return."

"He may. Or perhaps locked in a nightmare of his own making for all time."

"And the hand of Ghoré?" Hanen asked.

"A disappointing loss," Ymbrys said.

Hanen guided the Dreadplate forward, an eye over his shoulder toward where Loth and the young Khamntyr had fallen, hoping he might see movement from the exile, and worried he would instead see Loth emerge.

45

Plains of Ikhala

River our mother; the Saints, our surrogate lords.

By water and by faith, doth we raise our swords.

—IKHALAN VOW

At the last village, Jined and Nichal were barely able to speak with the people, who knew only Ikhalan and had little to no knowledge of the common tongue. From what they had gathered, the river left the fish locks, and a couple of leagues later let out into a wide open basin. The Crysalas who had come with them from Old Zhig walked alongside the single cart they had requisitioned; the old sleipnir pulling it was goaded along by the Abecinian priest, Father Chirtab. Next to him rode the small blind boy, Brin, who spent most of his time staring at the sky "watching the Anka." He had become a mascot for the group of men, women, and children now under the escort of the Paladins, as they passed from Zhigava into Ikhala, and down along the Forest Road.

"The trees are growing thicker," Didus said.

With each bend in the river, Loïc agreed.

Are you sure you understood them right? Cävian asked. *Your Ikhalan is really no good, Jined.*

"I never said it was," Jined replied. "Chirtab assured me that he understood. Zhigavan and Ikhalan are similar."

"The river appears to be widening and slowing down," Nichal said. "If we come to a good place to stop and water the sleipnirs we'll set up camp and continue in the morning. We seem to be traveling south. So that's something."

Silas gave the Prima Pater a nod and rode on ahead. Loïc joined him and the hoofbeats of their mounts faded into the distance.

"I negotiated for some food," Didus said. "Although I think they took more silver than it was worth."

"What did they give you?" Nichal asked.

"Some dried porridge peas, oats, and some sort of dried meat powder."

Fish, Cävian signed.

"How do you know?" Didus asked taking out a jar from the sack across his lap.

I can smell it from here.

"Every village and town we've come across has given us fish," Jined grumbled. "I'm getting tired of it."

"Ikhalans are a people of river and wood," Nichal said. "Their livestock is lean and wooly, but not much for meat."

"You would think," Jined said, "that after the Peace Accords of St. Kien twenty years ago they would use that time to make use of the lands Dorian ceded to them."

"Dorian only gave them the land back after they had completed paying off the war debt. I understand they did so with the last of their coffers, and had nothing by which to purchase livestock to begin the repasturing of the Midlands."

"Hardly seems fair. Could Dorian not have helped?" Didus asked.

"He wanted to," Nichal said. "But as soon as the accords were struck, they asked all Paladins to vacate their lands, and have kept sentries and guards at our borders to keep us out. The only time we are welcome is by request, or by what the Crysalas tell us via news from their Vaults. Now we're tramping through Ikhala, without permission, and likely to face trouble if any one of authority finds us."

"With woods this thick," Didus said, "that seems unlikely."

They came around a corner to find Silas and Loïc dragging branches across the road to a small clearing while their sleipnirs stood ankle-deep in the river drinking thirstily. The other sleipnirs picked up their pace to head toward the water, the wagon sleipnir much slower.

The four Paladins dismounted and let their mounts follow the other two. Sister Tomiza Cirilav and the three other Crysalas took care of the cart, unhitching the old nag and seeing it to the water. The others helped the Paladins gather wood from near the water's edge. Didus set about with Silas to make a fire and start water to boil, while the twins pulled down some evergreen bows to prepare some shelter as the clouds darkened overhead.

Jined and Nichal walked down the road side by side.

"I'm worried we're taking too long," Nichal said. "I'm not even sure we're following the refugees with Astrid and the others."

"I hope that once we reach the Chorvon river, we'll cross and be in a much better situation. The rolling hills of the Protectorates will be a welcome sight."

"We've the Protectorate of Saints to cross after the Chorvon. Hardly the rolling hills of the Protectorate of the Hammer."

Jined sighed. "I forgot."

"I have, a time or two. I'm eager for home."

"So are we all," Jined said.

A cool breeze came up the road from ahead. The trees broke, and nearby the sound of falling water grew louder. The road ended abruptly ahead, cutting to the right, away from the water. A berm of rocks in front of them blocked their view.

Jined stepped up to the rocks with the Prima Pater just behind him. The rocks stood as an overlook. A hundred yards below, and stretching far off to the horizon, the woods had ended. The waterfall next to them fell down to the continuation of the river below, cutting a ribbon across the land.

Far off in the distance Jined could see a large train of travelers circling up to make their own bed.

"Astrid and Katiam you think?" Nichal asked.

"I would guess so," Jined said. "Perhaps one or two days lead on us."

"Good. Let's get some food and rest. We'll catch up with them before they reach the Chorvon."

As they came back to camp, the water was already boiling away in two separate pots. Didus sprinkled powder from the jar he had purchased. As they sat around the fire, the sleipnirs quietly grazed in the shadows around them. Loïc and Cävian broke out their instruments and plucked at the strings they had tuned. The Crysalas, along with the priest, muttered quiet prayers to themselves, while the other men and women sat in the silence like they did every night. The forty children tossed twigs into the fires, but stayed as quiet as the adults.

The twins set their instruments aside as Didus finished his work over the pot and passed around wooden bowls of the oat, pea, and fish gruel. It could have been much worse. The salt and spices Didus had used helped mask much of the fishy smell and taste. The twins gulped their food down and went to the stream to wash their bowls and hands before returning, taking up their instruments once more.

Loïc drew the bow across the three-staved lyre held upright on his knee, while his brother held the bowl-bodied mandolin across his chest and plucked at the strings with his fingers. Together, the song they played verged on both a jig and mournful ballad. It was a song they had been developing over the intervening nights since Garrou. They'd not put words to it yet, but often Jined caught Nichal muttering to himself along with the tune. He'd been known to sing at times, but rarely alone, and never to work on his own song.

It was a peaceful night that ended with the embers dying down and each man finding sleep easily.

Jined awakened to Loïc kicking at his side. He rolled to his knees, leaping up.

"What is it?"

Come.

They both set off at a jog down the road to where Cävian and Nichal stood looking out over the expanse.

"What is it?" Jined asked from below.

"More trouble than we could imagine," Nichal answered back.

Cävian had offered his hammer down to Loïc and then Jined, pulling them up to join.

The sun had fully risen, and the smoke from the refugee camp on the horizon was not much, but enough to spot. Along the floor of the rolling hills below, and farther east of them, a camp was set up at the edge of the woods, two miles away. There was no mistaking the camp was full of vül.

"We have to move quickly," Jined said.

"The vül aren't all," Nichal said, and pointed much farther east to the other horizon. Dust was being kicked up by some advancing army.

"Who is it?"

"Given how carelessly the vül act, I doubt it is another vül party."

I'm wagering Ikhalan, Cävian signed.

"And you, Nichal?" Jined asked.

"I fear worse. Possibly T'Akai. But they're moving in this direction. If they spot the fires from the refugees there could be trouble."

Jined nodded. "I'll ask Sister Cirilav to watch from here, and only come down to the plains below when all is safe."

"We'll see if we can at least get the vül moving to where the Ikhalans will drive them out," Nichal said.

Jined dropped back down to the path and sprinted to camp. Didus was working the fire up to boil water.

"We move," Jined said in a commanding voice.

Didus did not bat an eye, but stood and kicked his meager fire to dust, and rushed to the water to clean the pot. Silas was coming out of the woods adjusting his armor.

"Sleipnirs," Jined said. "Quickly."

Silas gave a low yip and Jined clicked his tongue; from the woods, the sleipnirs came out from their grazing. They all worked to get the sleipnirs saddled and their straps tightened, then walked them down the road to the turn.

Sister Cirilav took command of tearing down the camp, and sent the two Zhigavan men and the priest to act as lookout over the plains, while the Crysalas and women rounded up the children and prepared for their flight or joining of the Paladins when the all-safe was called.

The Paladins adjusted the straps once more, and mounted. Cävian had broken the standard of Grissone down and hung the master-fashioned piece from the sleipnir's haunch while the pole was strapped to his side in two lengths.

The road from the overlook descended quickly, but not so steeply that the mounts needed caution.

The first double switchback left them in trees, but as they came to the next break overlooking the waterfall and pool below, they had a good view of the woods to the west and the vül now beginning to move. Far to the west, Jined could now make out the army kicking up dust.

"Definitely mounted," Nichal muttered.

The road's course ran a mile away before turning back toward the river. If the vül had fully broken camp, Jined could not see beyond the hills with which they now rode level.

DREAD KNIGHT

"We ride south with the road," Nichal said. "It will be the easiest ground, and hopefully the fastest route to the Crysalas."

"Hope and prayer is all we can seek," Didus said.

"Well said," Nichal replied, and put heels to the flanks of his mount.

Jined did the same to Tyv, and the six of them rode hard, prayers on their breaths and the twins' hands speeding them along.

The road and the hills fought for height and view. At times Jined caught view of hulking figures marching southward parallel with them, albeit far off. Other times he caught sight of the dust billowing above the army to the east.

Nichal drove his own mount the fastest, eventually keeping a hundred yards ahead of the rest of them.

He suddenly pulled up short, and stopped at the top of a rise. Jined slowed to a canter and then a trot as they approached. He looked back to find that they had covered miles of ground in a short while. Tyv walked up to Nichal, and Jined's shoulders sank. Across the river, calm, but wide, an army of well over a hundred vül marched.

From the hill they could make out the advancing army from the east. Fifty Ikhalans rode. They appeared to have wings sprouting from their backs at that distance.

"Ikhalans then?" Jined asked.

"Vityaz Errants, I think," Nichal said.

"Knights?"

"Yes. Sons of the landowners wishing to make a name for themselves. A scrap with vül would do that, but so would fighting us and ousting us from Ikhala, alive or dead."

"Probably best we don't give them a reason to kill us then," Jined said.

"That may prove difficult," Didus said as he came up next to them.

"Why?" Nichal asked.

Didus was looking west. Nichal smiled.

Fifty Paladins rode hard across the plains, making their presence known with a loud hymn sung. At their head rode Jurgon Upona. He spotted them and the entire squadron turned and rode toward their vantage point.

The hymn broke off and turned instead to welcome laughter and camaraderie. Jurgon dismounted and dropped to a knee before Nichal.

"Prima Pater," he said. The other Paladins still mounted gave a solemn bow of their head and saluted.

"What are you doing here?" Nichal asked.

"Following divine guidance," Jurgon said. "I've come from St. Hamul with help. Others rode north into Zhigava. I took a ship from Poray to St. Dantil, and we've been riding east, in hopes to find you."

"The Ikhalans allowed you to ride up the Chorvon?"

"We didn't ask. None have followed us from St. Dantil since we left last night."

"Regardless," Nichal said, "I am glad you are here."

Jurgon nodded. "There is more to be said. For now, we've vül to ride against."

"The numbers are much better now. If we ride with the Ikhalans, we may have near-even numbers."

"We've a river to cross," Didus said, pointing back to the water separating them from the vül a mile off.

Jined rode Tyv down into the river. It was not deep. He pressed forward, praying quietly for safety. Fifty yards later and he passed up the other side. The five who had traveled with him, along with Jurgon, did not hesitate but followed, the other fifty soon after.

The vül moved in groups of twenty. The western-most group saw the Paladins riding toward them and turned to spread out and prepare for the hammer-wielding riders.

Cävian had the poles off the side of his saddle up, and screwed into the bottom of the standard, and then raised the icon high.

Didus broke into the song "The Ride of the Broken," and everyone else immediately joined. The song sung of ten Paladins, each mortally wounded, riding against enemies of every type, fighting until the last brother fell, the final enemy's severed head in his hand.

Jined felt energy course through him. Loïc was not far from his brother, his hands signing prayers emphatically. Other silent brothers fell in alongside him, their words infusing those around them.

The vül were within a hundred yards and closing. Far off to the other side of the vül force, the Ikhalans were charging into the other flank of the monstrous vül .

Jined leaned forward, pointing his hammer at the closest vül, a black-coated creature with steel bracers and a pair of axes in its hands. Tyv leaped up and over the vül entirely, his middle set of legs caving the monster's skull in. They came down and Jined brought his hammer on the next vül. Tyv reared up and kicked at a third.

"Grissone! Give succor and light!" Jined cried.

The Standard of Grissone in Cävian's hand suddenly flared gold as a ray from the sun shot upon it. It should have blinded Jined. It did blind the vül. They lost their momentum, some reacting violently by covering their eyes.

As Tyv came back down to the earth, Jined urged him forward through the vül being cut down left and right and pressed on toward the main body of the vül force.

They had stopped their loping advance across the rolling plain to face him. He did not know if he rode alone, but he pressed on at the urging in his heart.

Forty vül stood in a tight line. Jined roared his defiance as some with slings began lobbing skull-sized rocks at him. One sailed directly at him in an arc that would no doubt strike Tyv in the chest. It turned suddenly down and into the ground.

He closed to fifty yards, and the center of the line collapsed and turned to run, just as arrow shafts struck, and the lances of the lead Ikhalan Vityaz Errants struck deep.

They wore four wings off their backs, giving them the appearance of some avenging aelerne. Most of the men bore large mustaches under sharp noses. On their heads they wore sleipnir-hair-plumed helmets covering their eyes, a single slit from ear to ear giving them view of their quarry. Jined laughed victoriously and fell into the remaining vül in front of him. His hammer swung left and right, tearing heads from necks, and puncturing steel plates on vül chests. He struck one vül as one of the Ikhalan Vityaz rammed a spear down the vül's throat.

"I shall count this one as my trophy," the man said in stilted common tongue. He had a bushy black mustache that climbed up the sides of his face.

"If you will allow us Paladins to fight alongside you, you may have all of my kills," Jined replied.

The man gave a broad smile. "After this fight, we shall break open casks together, either here or in the Green Lands."

Jined gave a salute and turned right. Tyv's front hoof stamping down on the knee of another vül as Jined struck the creature atop the head.

The other Paladins had only just arrived. He had ridden alone. The vül fell back toward the woods they had come from, and the Paladins and vityaz did what they could to race after them, while rounding up and killing the vül that remained. Each refused surrender, and gnashed at their enemies as they fell. Soon the roar of vül had subsided, leaving only the tension of two different groups interspersed around the battlefield, and eyeing each other suspiciously.

The twins had come next to Nichal and consulted with him as Jined rode toward them.

They give us murderous looks, he saw Loïc sign.

Or at least they desire us to turn and leave their lands, Cävian replied.

One of the vityaz left the forming Ikhalan line. It was the heavily mustachioed rider. Jined turned and rode out to him, meeting him in the middle of the field.

"My friend," the Ikhalan said.

"Primus Jined Brazstein," Jined said.

"Bogatyr Guorth Veltyar. I lead this company of vityaz. You Paladins break the treaty?"

"We only break the treaty out of necessity," Jined said. "For this we apologize. If you will allow us an explanation, you will perhaps give us permission to leave."

"Be quick, leader of Paladins."

"I am subservient to the Prima Pater, who sits atop that sleipnir by our standard, with the red slashed cape," Jined said. "We have ridden from Zhigava, following friends who went before us, pursued by the vül who invaded the Northern Scapes. We would have taken a ship home, if the refugees who preceded us toward the Protectorates had."

"Then the trail of people to the south are yours?"

"They are friends, and we take responsibility for them, yes. Have there been problems?"

"No, my friend. Our company of riders was sent to ascertain their purpose, and we might have reached them this day or next, if these vül had not been seen, nor your company."

"Our Prima Pater apologizes that we have not gone through all of the diplomatic steps to enter your country," Jined said. "But as protectors of those who have fealty to us, it was more important we kept them safe from Kos-Yran's people."

"That you hold their safety over your own is commendable. I

am, of course, required to determine if we must take hostages back to St. Nevenhal."

"These vül we faced this day, they will come back."

"Indeed they will."

"What if we offered our help in preparing a camp for you and your vityaz. Will our labor pay for your permission to pass south?"

"A hastily raised camp is a sight best not seen by any."

"Then let us work side by side and raise it together. So that you and your men can reside in comfort."

"I accept your offer, in return for our friendship," Guorth said.

Jined gave a salute, and they both rode away from one another. Jined came to Nichal. "I've purchased our freedom," Jined said.

"Freedom?" Nichal replied.

"Their leader, Bogatyr Veltyar, ought to take a handful of us to their capital for trial, for breaking the accords. He would rather we break open a cask together. I asked him to allow us to help him build a permanent camp nearby, for the vityaz to prepare for more vül. In recompense, he'll allow us to travel south to the Protectorates, unmolested."

Nichal turned to Jurgon who now stood nearby. "How many pacifists came with you?"

"Ten. They're leading the baggage southward."

"See that half of it comes this direction. Have the other half go south toward the refugees under Astrid and Katiam's leadership, along with the refugees who travel with us. Loïc, go and fetch the Crysalas and those they watch."

Loïc saluted and rode back toward the switchbacks they had descended from.

"Katiam?" Jurgon pressed.

"Yes. That is why we are here. We're in pursuit of them."

"I shall see them safely to the Protectorates."

Nichal gave a nod. "We may be here for some time preparing this camp. Although I'd rather get home."

"We all would," Jined said, "but think of the friendship we can establish here now."

"With the vül acting up, and who knows what the T'Akai have been up to since we left, friends would be good to have."

Jurgon turned with a salute and rode west toward his baggage train.

"Now," Nichal said to Jined, "shall we go and meet your new friend?"

Katiam awakened next to the fire. Larohz was playing with a small wooden toy Katiam had been given at the last village. The Ikhalans were a suspicious, but hospitable people. They were quick to disappear when the refugee train came through their towns, but just as quick to send someone to speak with Astrid or Lutea, who had a working knowledge of their language. They were quickly asked their purpose, and what it would take to keep them moving along. It had been a quick and repeatable discourse. They made it clear they traveled south, with little desire to stay more than a night. Supplies were often given with little or no coin exchanging hands, and often as they left, blessings in the form of small gifts were given them by children or the elderly. Foreign signs of blessings and wards were made.

They had left the last great stretch of the forest after traveling down switchbacks, and they were three days slowly crossing the plains, with word that they would reach the Chorvon River soon. If they could find passage over that, they'd be only a three or four day walk across a narrow portion of the Ikhalan-patrolled Protectorate of the Saints before they reached the Protectorate of the Hammer.

Astrid sat across the fire, poking at the embers.

"I had always thought the Ikhalans lived only close to the main rivers."

"It's true," Astrid said.

"Yet we're crossing open and unpastured land," Katiam said.

"It's very rocky here and we're nowhere near a big city. The forest comes too close, and we're not all that far from the Pyracene, so that comes as no surprise to me. That last village was full of signs of forestry and fishing."

"That may be true," Katiam said. "It is just surprising to me that no one has accosted us."

"I have kept an eye out for that, too," Astrid said.

"The villages have let us go without question."

"But not unnoticed," Astrid said.

"What do you mean?"

"I suspect they've sent plenty of messengers to larger settlements, or ahead of us. None of them want us around, but the

Ikhalans believe that hospitality is the highest form of blessing one can use to ward off a curse."

"The Crysalas do not curse."

"But the dark forest does," Astrid said.

Within the hour, they had broken camp and begun their road south. The midday sun came and passed when they finally topped a rise to a sight they'd long waited to see. The slope down to the Chorvon was a welcome sight. Villages and towns dotted both sides of the bank, and fishers were out in the wider river pulling in their hauls. They were only a couple of hours walk to the nearest riverside village.

Esenath came up alongside them, and touched Astrid's shoulder, indicating behind them.

They all turned to see a caravan of three wagons coming up behind, the bald pate of a Paladin sitting in the driver's seat of each, and a small train of a handful of men and women, as well as forty or so children.

"Esenath, why don't you and Katiam take the refugees down to the nearest town and begin the negotiations," Astrid said. "I'll wait here for the Paladins. Perhaps they can help us with the trip across the river."

Katiam and Esenath pressed on down the road, the refugees behind them.

The town they'd arrived at was called Sturgeon Mud. The women of the city were more gregarious than those of the woods, but they still eyed the refugees with suspicion, guiding them toward the pier. They found an inn with a large warehouse, empty of product, and quickly negotiated shelter for far too much gold.

Esenath disappeared after a time and came back with two men rolling a barrel of ale. With help from others they had it propped up and tapped, and poured flagons for the people who hadn't known more than boiled water and oats for weeks.

Soon the barrel was empty, but not before one of the quieter men who had traveled from Zhigava had spoken with the inn's owner, and passed more coin to him—though the same refugee had spent the past several weeks denying he had any.

Another barrel appeared, then a third. Soon the refugees began dancing. Instruments long left cold were warmed up, and joy flowed in the room.

Astrid appeared at the door and waited for Katiam to notice her.

Katiam crossed. In the quiet of the doorway, she could finally hear Larohz whistling along with the music.

"You need to come with me to meet them," Astrid said.

"The Paladins?" Katiam asked.

"Yes."

She turned and walked across the street to another tavern. This one was much nicer, and the innkeeper wore the suit of a sailor. Paladins sat near the fire and Astrid approached them from the back.

"Brother?" Astrid said, touching the shoulder of the closest. He turned, and his face lit up.

"Katiam!" Jurgon Upona said.

"What are you doing here?" Katiam asked, throwing her arms around him in a welcome embrace.

"I've a lot to tell you," he said. "But first I must know if you have been well."

"Yes. Very."

"Nichal and Jined have been following you from the north. They're only a day behind you."

"Then why are you here?"

"Because the Prima Pater is not the only thing pursuing you."

"What do you mean?"

"The vül have been forming a warpath south. Jined, and the Paladins who came with me from St. Hamul, and a large squadron of Ikhalan knights have kept them at bay. He asked I come ahead of them to see you continue your path safely south."

"We only just arrived. Tomorrow we're going to negotiate a way across the river."

"I've already assigned two brothers to spend tonight doing so. You'll leave at dawn. But please allow us to go with you, as well as the fifty refugees Nichal has been escorting."

"With us?" Astrid said. "I mean, of course, but why?"

"I have completed all I have been asked to do. Now I must find a way to reach my wife."

"Ah," Katiam said. "I'm not sure how we can find our way to the Veld."

"I do," Jurgon said. "She visited me in a dream. We must go to the Oracle above Pariantür."

"We had planned to go there anyway," Astrid said, "before we go down to the Hammer."

"Then let me escort you there," Jurgon said.

"We would be honored," Katiam said.

48

AUTHORITY AND CHOICE

Fear is voracious, and hope requires little sustenance.

– VIAGO WEVAN

Rallia blew softly on the pipe in her hands, harmoniously matching the musician playing a bowed lyre by the fire. Whisper lay at her feet. Ophedia and Marn mulled over a makeshift Edi-Fo'z board. Alodda sat next to Seriah, her mug of ale and bread untouched.

"Are you going to eat that?" Seriah asked.

Alodda took a deep breath and turned to look at her, eyes half vacant. "No," she finally said.

Seriah rose and took hold of both. "I'm going to take them to Navien."

Alodda nodded. "Shall I go with you?"

Seriah shook her head. "I'll be fine."

She walked to the stairs and reached the top. She startled as Whisper whipped past her and walked to the door ahead of her, his tail flapping on the wooden floorboards as he sat, considering her as she approached with his tongue lolling out.

She precariously took the mug and plate in a single hand and opened the door.

It was a comfortable room. The fire in the hearth still burned.

Abenard Navien lay on the bed, one wrist shackled to the wall by an iron chain attached at the other end to the mortar of a stone wall. He held in both of his hands a small book. Finishing where he was, he sat up on the bed and placed a strip of paper between the pages, then closed it.

Seriah placed the plate and mug down on the side table and crossed to the fire, putting new wood on the embers.

"I thought perhaps some fresh bread and ale might do you good," Seriah said.

"I've not been starving," Navien said, "but thank you."

Seriah sat on the stool next to the fire and considered the man.

He was not tall, but stocky. His black beard might normally have been kept well-trimmed, but it had grown scraggly in the past few days. He took up the ale and drank it carefully, then picked at the bread with the practiced movements of a higher-born man.

"I understand Dorian is away."

"How have you discerned that?" Seriah asked.

"He told me."

"Ah."

"How do you feel about my being kidnapped and taken prisoner to who knows where?"

The heat rose in Seriah's ears at the accusation. As the roaring subsided, she looked him in the eyes. "That an authority higher than a king has chosen that, it's hardly kidnapping."

"That you assume all kings above morality is an interesting philosophy. More so, given your background."

"My background?"

"I know you're a Nefer. Or once were."

"Again with unlikely inference. Has someone told you this?"

"You've lighter skin around the eyes, as though the sun has never touched it."

"I was," Seriah said quietly.

"I did not know a Nifaran could cease being so."

"My blindfold was taken from me," Seriah said. "It broke my vow."

"I am not in Mahn Fulhar right now," Navien replied. "But that does not mean I am no longer a Voktorra."

"My vows as a Nifaran are different, answering a higher calling."

"While I am a religious man, and I confess I agree that taking the cloth is a higher calling, please do not belittle other callings. It is beneath you."

Again, the blood roared in Seriah's ears.

"Now, to repeat my question: as a Nifaran, or an ex-monk, how can you be alright with my being kidnapped and taken elsewhere against my will?"

"You held Alodda and Marn in captivity as a means to leverage the capture of the Sentinels. How are your actions any better?"

"While distasteful," Navien said, "I am under orders from my king to bring back my quarry by whatever means. He remains king, while the authority you're acting under has surrendered his. That you say you are no longer a monk while Dorian is still Prima Pater in your eyes is a contradiction."

"I came up here to do a good deed and bring you some bread and ale, not to debate you."

"You came up here for more than just bread and ale," Navien replied. "You want to justify Dorian's actions as much as I want you to."

Seriah rose. "Finish your drink."

Navien lifted the mug and drained it, then handed the empty vessel to her. He took the bread and handed her the plate as well. She turned to go.

"Holy Nefer," he said calmly.

She stopped at the door, but did not turn. "I am no longer a Nefer."

"Regardless," Navien said, "I'm sorry."

"For what?"

"For whatever happened to you. Whoever took that away from you."

"It was not just one, but many."

"What do you mean?"

She turned and looked him in the eye. "My choice and will have been subverted by the fallen, both mortal and immortal. That you and those of the west have so quickly adopted the tyranny of the Chalice, and that so many Paladins have run into the arms of a heresy that forsakes all gods has me reeling, as it should you."

"What do you mean?"

"You ran unquestioningly to the Chalicians," Seriah said. "I do not doubt you will say that it was because the High Priest in Mahn Fulhar so quickly joined. You no doubt believe that he is a high moral authority, and this justifies his actions, and through that, yours."

"I do."

"Yet you are quick to assume an old man with nearly a century of faithfulness to his god to be in error and fallen from the faith."

"So it would appear."

"Therefore a holy man can be wrong. Noccitan, nearly half the gods have fallen. How can you so willingly accept the actions of your High Priest, without examining the doctrines of this new branch almost violently overtaking all others? The actions of one man should not dictate the paths of all. Nor your path."

"The same should be asked by you," Navien said.

Seriah turned without another word and left.

Dorian had returned, and stood with the innkeeper, a Paladin who had gone into hiding after the Chalicians announced their order null and void. The others had gathered nearby, save for Rallia, who was about to ascend the stairs.

"I was just coming to find you," Rallia said.

"I was offering Navien bread and ale. He just finished."

Rallia examined her face, and offered a kind smile before turning to precede her down the stairs. "Dorian has returned with news."

Seriah followed, placing the mug and plate on the bar.

"Please take a seat, Seriah," Dorian said.

The innkeeper placed a flagon in front of her, retaining his own in his hand.

"Brother Narris and I just returned from the pier. We've found a ship that has agreed to take us, along with other members of the Grissoni church, east. Likely we'll have stops along the way, and if members of our company wish to part ways before we reach the Protectorates, so be it."

"When do we leave?" Ophedia asked.

"At dawn."

"What of Navien?" Seriah asked.

"We will be taking him as well, yes. We can't have him dogging our steps."

"Especially since I will not be going," Rallia said. "I mean to find Hanen."

"You can't stay without us," Alodda said.

"I can," Rallia replied. "I wish to complete what Hanen would have wished, and see you somewhere safe. You'll go to Edi and our offices, and we'll meet you there once I've found him."

"How?"

"I'm not sure," Rallia said. "If Ymbrys went west, I'll track him down and we'll find Hanen together."

"Then this is goodbye," Ophedia said.

"I'll see you all to the ship to ensure Navien doesn't find a way to follow me, and then I'll head west."

"I wish you would come with us," Marn said. "But if anyone is best equipped to find Hanen, it's you."

"Thank you, Father," Rallia said.

"I'll go see to Navien," Ophedia said. "I'd at least like to get him back to Boscolón, but farther would be best."

She disappeared up the stairs.

"What did you and Navien talk about?" Dorian asked Seriah.

"Authority. Why you giving up your title to another Prima Pater is no loss of authority, and that his High Priest doing it at the drop of a hat is questionable."

"Similar to you saying you're not a Nifaran anymore because someone else took a piece of cloth from your eyes?"

Seriah did not respond, and welcomed the interruption of Ophedia coming back down the stairs with Navien in tow, both hands now shackled.

"We'll be on foot," Dorian said. "But let's not walk as a mob. I will lead the way with Seriah. Ophedia and Rallia, why don't you take Navien next, and Alodda and Marn after. Brother Narris, will you and any others you send take up the rear, and keep an eye out?"

The innkeeper gave a nod. Dorian offered Seriah an arm and led the way out onto the street. The sun was beginning to set and lamplighters navigated through the people settling themselves against the walls.

When they came to the first corner, Dorian paused to look back to the others, gave an approving nod, then turned back to the task.

They walked in awkward silence for some time before Dorian broke the tension.

"You didn't answer my question earlier."

"Hm?" Seriah replied.

"You defending my choice to no longer be Prima Pater yet consider myself to have not given up any authority. Presumably this was in regards to the justification of keeping Navien prisoner."

"And that his acts of imprisonment against Alodda and Marn were unjustified as a means to get at the person he is really after: Hanen."

"I'd add to that, he doesn't have authority for even that," Dorian said. "But that is neither here nor there. My question to you was why do you consider yourself no longer a Nifaran, simply because your blind was removed?"

"Because...because it goes further than that," she blurted out. "I feel as though I've not been a Nifaran since I stopped believing that the goddess had favor in me."

"Do all Nifarans have specific favor?"

"What do you mean?"

"Are you all visited by her and called to become monks?"

"Well, no."

"Good. I was worried. Because Grissone never visited and called me, either. Yet I became a Paladin and eventually the Prima Pater. That might have been problematic." Dorian had a twinkle in his eye as he glanced at Seriah.

"Still," she continued, "that a dark god used me against her might indicate that I was their tool, and not hers."

"A man who builds a house and finds out later it was made for the explicit purpose of a brothel is not culpable," Dorian said. "Furthermore, when you were in Haven, did she not visit you?"

"Yes," Seriah said.

"Then you were chosen," Dorian said.

She mumbled in an affirmative.

"How does one terrible person removing a piece of cloth hammer a final nail in the coffin of your vow?"

"He took that from me. Our vows declare that the placing of the cloth is a final sign of our devotion to justice."

"Ah. There you go."

"What?"

"You've convoluted the sign for the actuality."

"What do you mean?"

"You seem to be under the impression that the cloth is the devotion, and that by removing the cloth you are no longer in service of Justice."

He turned a corner to a main thoroughfare that led straight down to the water a mile away.

"You know that the Crysalas take Aspects of Purity."

"Yes."

"If a sister unknowingly partakes of meat when she has taken the Aspect of Preservation, she may go through purity rights to re-enter that aspect in good conscience. In fact, we do not even seek to determine whether she did it willfully or not. We take her at her word. The guilty conscience is hers if that is the case. If someone willfully gave her the meat, she can seek justice against the person who did so. Still, she may choose to re-enter that aspect."

"I suppose I see what you mean."

"That being said, did you willfully take the cloth off?"

"It was taken from me."

"Then you are still committed to Justice? To the calling your goddess has placed upon you?"

"I suppose I am."

"Suppose all you want," Dorian said. "The decision is yours. We all must choose, each and every day, to continue forward. Myself included."

Seriah glanced at him with concern.

"Do you think I haven't considered hermitage? To disappear from the annals of history, ever since the day my wife died? I have. But I know I would find regret if I did so. To be alive at two of the greatest moments in modern history astounds me."

"Two?"

"The Protectorate Wars, and now whatever this is. Imagine if tomorrow the world ended, and I knew I had a part to play but refused. I would march to the gates of Noccitan if I knew the way, and stand there in defiance of whatever the Black Coterie mustered against me."

"Because it would see you quickly to Lomïn and your wife?"

"Admittedly, that is true. But no," he said, stopping, "you know why."

"Because it is the right thing to do."

Dorian nodded.

They walked another hundred yards.

"I still see things," Seriah murmured. "Since that day she met me and healed me."

"What do you mean?"

"There are purple flames at the edge of my vision all the time. Like the flames I saw surrounding me in Haven."

"Even here?"

"Yes. Especially here. It has been growing for days. To the east, the entire horizon blinks with purple that I can only just see when I try."

"What do you feel it means?"

"I think the Veld wants to come through."

They had crossed a square. From another side street, a group of sleipnir entered. Dorian sighed.

"What is it?" Seriah asked.

"Praetors."

Seriah looked back toward Rallia and Ophedia, Navien between them. She made a motion to Rallia, but the Sentinel didn't see her. Navien was giving both of the women next to him trouble. Ophedia had a hand over his mouth and Rallia shoved him from behind.

Navien tore his head back from Ophedia's hand and shouted, "Praetors!"

Everyone in the streets parted out of fear or deference.

"You!" the lead Praetor called, pointing a half-spear at Navien.

Seriah recognized the voice. "That's the troublesome Praetor who arrived late to our prisoner-of-war train," Seriah muttered.

"Provost Abrau?"

"No. Abrau was kind, in his own way. This is Brodier."

The Praetors rode across the square. Navien refused to move, and dropped to a knee to prevent them going any farther.

"What is this?" Brodier asked.

"They're Sentinels!" Navien cried. "I'm a servant of the church. There! The Prima Pater of the Church of Grissone precedes me!"

Brodier shot a suspicious look around the square, then back to the three of them.

"Spout no lies, Mahndürian!"

"It is true!" Navien declared. "I came south at the behest of Provost Otem, to seek out these two Sentinels, and they turned the tables on me!"

The Praetor looked at the Sentinels. Seriah could see Ophedia keeping her face from him.

"I know you, don't I?" he said, touching her with the tassel end of his short spear.

Dorian leaned into Seriah. "Either Ophedia will make the first move, or Rallia will hopefully leave Navien and the two of them will make a break for it."

"Is there not another way?" Seriah said. "I wonder if Navien can be brought to our side."

"Not brought to justice?" Dorian goaded.

"Justice would be the Praetors collapsing under their own bloated weight."

Dorian chortled and closed his eyes. A moment later, a light flared overhead.

Everyone in the square looked to the sky, but Seriah and Dorian watched Marn rush up with several of the hidden Paladins to grab Navien before bolting toward Dorian and Seriah with Rallia and Ophedia just behind them.

"Go!" Alodda shouted from next to them, emerging from the crowd, Whisper at her side.

Dorian and Seriah turned and ran down the street. A moment later the sound of hooves on cobbles resounded off the walls of houses. The Chalicians tried to ride them down, save for the crowd that made movement almost impossible.

"Stop them!" Brodier shouted.

On they raced, out into another less-dense square. It gave the Chalicians all the room they needed and they rode to cut them off from their flight. Brodier's light sleipnir reared next to Seriah and she threw herself backward as Rallia rushed up under the mount and smacked it across the jaw with her club.

The sleipnir stumbled and Brodier fell from the saddle to the cobbles with a crunch of metal.

"This way!" Dorian called.

Rallia scrambled to her feet, taking Navien's arm and pulling him toward Dorian.

"Stop right there, Dorian Mür!" Brodier shouted.

Dorian gave him a glance and stopped.

"Come on, Dorian!" Rallia shouted, turning to him.

Seriah turned and looked back into the square. The other Chalicians near him had pulled up behind. Brodier had cast his spear aside and had taken out a bundle from his satchel. Unfolding it, he revealed a large bell of skyfall metal.

"Oh no," Seriah said.

"By the judgment of Noccitan and the hope of a green dawn in Lomïn," Brodier shouted, "let sunder all who oppose the Church of Aben and its protectors, the Praetors of the Chalice!"

He struck the bell with a hammer he had produced, made of the same metal. Both began to reverberate across the place, and everyone near him fell to their knees holding their heads.

"Dorian," Seriah said, pulling close to his ear.

"What is it?"

"The purple glow is sprouting up everywhere. Like the vibration is calling through to the Veld."

"Then we need to stop him," Dorian said and rushed Brodier

when the hammer suddenly exploded in the Praetor's hand, the shockwave throwing Brodier fifty feet into a wall. Dorian and Seriah were knocked flat. She struggled to her feet as smoke and dust settled over the silence that pervaded.

Black motes of ash floated in the air. Dorian coughed next to her. She rolled toward him and spoke in his ear. "Cover your mouth," she said.

He did.

"Rallia, Ophedia," she called. "Everyone! Cover your mouths!"

There were groans and light coughs. Someone in the smoke, made more blinding by the twilight quickly settling, went from coughing to a gasping choke, and then fell silent. Seriah was on her feet and walking toward the sound. In the white smoke, a pair of indigo eyes suddenly appeared.

"No," Seriah hissed.

Other sets of eyes flared around her. She gasped and a black mote shot into her mouth. She spat and coughed, and tried to fight the returning feeling of evil coursing through her windpipe and settling in her chest. A flash of vision placed her in the Veld for only a moment before the purple light in her chest snuffed out and she was back in Kallattai.

A breeze moved down the street and toward the ocean below, taking most of the black motes with it.

"No," Seriah said. "Please Nifara, no."

The smoke cleared. Dorian held a cloth over his mouth.

Rallia had tied a gag over Navien's, while she and Ophedia had pulled their cloaks around their faces. Alodda and Marn had pulled their hoods over their heads and mouths as though preparing to cross a dusty plain.

Motes still clung to the air, moving precariously as though with a mind of their own. Seriah reached out to touch one.

"Stop!" Dorian called, reaching out to stop her.

She pulled away from him and touched it anyway. The mote shuddered away from her touch. She took a deep breath and pulled it into her lungs, and the purple Veld snapped into her vision. Dreamwyrms were everywhere. Some stood rigid, a small violet light held at the tip. The wyrm trying to fight for her mind shriveled and died.

She was in Kallattai again.

"What happened?" Dorian said, his hands on her shoulders. "Your eyes blared purple."

DREAD KNIGHT

"I'm immune, it would seem," Seriah said. "When I inhale them, I see into the Veld for a moment, and then the wyrm dies through our connection. I could destroy them all, but I saw how many there are."

"You can't breathe them all in," Dorian said. "It would be like trying to catch every snowflake on your tongue." He turned to the others and signaled for them to continue toward the water. "How many did you see?"

"Let me try and look again," she said as a mote drifted past her. She sucked it into her mouth and looked around as the Veld flared into vision before disappearing again.

"That cannot be good for your health," Dorian said.

From an alley, the light of three Revenants bloomed and they came rushing out of the darkness toward the group of them. Rallia shoved one to the ground and his head struck the flagstone and the light went out. A purple flame shot across the street into someone's mouth and they lurched suddenly to their feet.

"They will not die," Ophedia said, "unless struck down with skyfall. Marn, take Navien's arm."

Navien tried to give them only dead weight to work with, but Marn did not seem to mind as he dragged him bodily down the street.

Ophedia took a wrapped object off her back and began unraveling it. Within, the massive black sword of skyfall metal did not gleam, but stood as a sooty smear on the air. She took the lead and Revenants rushed toward her. The blade moved in a spinning arc through the first man, slicing him cleanly in two. Alodda gasped in horror as the two halves fell near her feet. Two more Revenants rushed at Ophedia and she smashed the first in the face with the pommel, and brought the blade down through the shoulder of the next. The massive, curved blade was sharper than a chef's knife, and cut deeper than the tongue of a politician. Ophedia moved with violent grace through the Revenants rushing them as they moved through the streets. Rallia swung at the others who made it by, laying them out flat.

"Halt!"

Seriah and the others spun to see Brodier advancing toward them, cloth over his own face. He held the bell in his hand, and produced an orb of skyfall.

Both began to ring. He lobbed the orb high into the air, up and over the nearest roofs, and it exploded over the city. Seriah could see the blackness spread out from the exploded orb, catch the wind, and shoot toward the bay.

"This will be a horrific night," Dorian said with a deep sigh.

"We can't keep running," Rallia said. "He'll only chase us to the water, and destroy our ship."

"Now do you see, Navien?" Seriah said, taking the arm of their captive. "The Chalicians do not believe in the shepherding of people to Lomïn. They would destroy as the Moteans do. As all who seek power do."

Navien shot her only furtive looks, and she saw defeat enter his cold eyes. He moved to wipe tears from them with his wrist, and in that moment the cloth over his mouth dropped, and a mote of black slunk in and down into his lungs. Purple fire erupted from his eyes, burning away any tears that sat there.

47

Examples Made

Blackened metal, sharper than the stars that pierce the sky,

Hast sundered thus the strongest built,

    and from body sunders life,

        from e'en they that call themselves immortal.

—FROM *ALL THE CROWNS BEFALLEN*,

BY ELLAVON GAVALIN

Ophedia smashed the hilt of Sky Grazer against the face of one Revenant, addling the woman, and sending her stepping backward. In a spinning arc, the blade carved through another man and he fell into two pieces.

"Abenard!" Seriah shouted.

Ophedia turned to see the Voktorra on the ground, his eyes now ablaze with purple fire. Ophedia stepped toward him, blade raised.

Rallia let go of Navien's arm.

"You hold him down!" Seriah ordered.

Rallia's grip tightened again. She and her father held Navien down as he began to flail.

"What are you going to do?" Dorian asked.

"I don't know," Seriah said. "Ophedia, keep the Revenants away."

Alodda was pressed up against the wall, fear clearly in her eyes.

Ophedia took out a crossbow bolt from her quiver and handed

it to Alodda. "If any Revenant comes at you, stick them with this."

"I can't do that!" Alodda said.

"You can. Or you become one."

Seriah had her hands on Navien's chest, her eyes closed. She was the only one without cloth on her face. She took a deep breath and several motes flew into her mouth. Violet light behind her eyelids strobed. Navien thrashed on the ground against Marn and Rallia, his legs almost kicking Seriah in the head.

"Ophedia!" Dorian shouted.

Ophedia startled and raised her sword just in time to block the grasping hands of a Revenant with the flat back of the severely curved blade. She flung him back and stepped up as he spun, smashing him over the back of the head. He fell to the ground unconscious.

"They can be knocked out!" she said triumphantly.

No one listened, their attention on Navien. Ophedia cut another Revenant down.

When they came one at a time, the Dreamwyrms not yet accustomed to their bodies, they were easy to deal with. She turned up the street to where Brodier stood. He had his own hands full as Revenants flailed at him.

The flames in Navien's eyes suddenly bloomed from his mouth in an arc of light that curved into Seriah's mouth. Her face shot to the sky, eyes burning purple for one more moment before going out.

Navien had fallen back to the ground, still.

"Now help Ophedia," Seriah said to Rallia.

The other Sentinel leapt up and took her heavy staff in hand and came to Ophedia's side.

"To the pier?"

"No," Ophedia said. "To Brodier. Or we'll never be rid of him."

Rallia nodded in resolve.

"Be careful. When you kill them without skyfall metal, the flame passes to the nearest victim, and they rise again."

"Then I'll just have to lay them out," Rallia said.

They rushed toward another Revenant trying to rise to her feet. Rallia swung her staff up under her chin and she fell to the earth.

"I would hate to be them when they come to," Ophedia said. "If they come to."

"Let's try not to think about it. We take out Brodier."

Brodier had fought his way down the street toward them, five

Chalicians at his heels, their spears flashing in and out of Revenants.

"You can't kill them!" Ophedia shouted, as flames erupted from the fallen and into others.

A clattering sound came from an inn and the door exploded off its hinges as twenty Revenants poured out into the street between the Sentinels and Praetors.

Ophedia's blade fell on two of them in succession, and Rallia spun her staff in wide arcs. Brodier fell back toward the square with his men.

Dorian and Marn were suddenly there, makeshift staves of broken wood. Together they forced back or sundered the Revenants from the tavern, and made space for them to regroup.

Alodda appeared next to them, her hands shaking, holding the bolt shaft in her hand. It dripped with blood.

"I killed him..." she said softly.

"He was already dead," Dorian comforted her.

Navien had a piece of wood in his hand, his mouth covered once more as he walked alongside Seriah.

"We need to get to Brodier, and do something about the bell in his hand," Dorian said.

"Give me something better to fight with," Navien said, a cool darkness in his eyes.

"No," Ophedia said. "You'll stab us in the back."

"I will not."

"You might. Or betray us again to Brodier."

"Wouldn't you have called to friends?" Navien asked.

"I still don't trust you," Ophedia said.

"I've died and been brought back," Navien said. "Let me prove my worth."

"Ophedia," Rallia said. "We need more blades."

She looked at Dorian and Marn.

The older man gave her a nod. "Give him a crossbow."

"So he can shoot us in the back?"

"I'm a good shot. All Voktorra are," Navien said. "I swear on my life I will not harm you."

"I'll hold the bolts," Alodda said. "If he tries to shoot any of you, I'll just stick him with this." She menaced the bolt in her hand with a nervous laugh.

Ophedia sighed and took her crossbow from her back and handed it to Dorian, who in turn gave it to Navien.

"Alodda," Rallia said, "keep an eye behind us. Whisper, guard Alodda."

The little ynfald shook its tail, tongue lolling out.

Ophedia and Rallia rushed out into the square. A bolt flew over her shoulder and into the eye of a Revenant, felling the thing.

"Watch it!" she shouted over her back and brought Sky Grazer down through the clavicle of another, pear-cutting the man with violet, hungry flames in his eyes.

Rallia pulled the bolt from the fallen Revenant and spun, jamming it into the chest of another, her staff sailing overhead and in a reversal, thrust into the forehead of the next.

The Revenants in the square had stopped paying attention to them and turned instead to the Chalicians.

Brodier's spear sundered Revenant after Revenant as he held the ringing bell toward them, and they did not rise. Blood dribbled from his ears. The Chalicians around him killed with their spears. Ophedia and Rallia carved their way across the square toward Brodier as he was quickly outnumbered by his own men, possessed by the Dreamwyrms.

Ophedia cut the nearest Praetor down, her blade shearing through the metal of his armor and deeply across his chest. He fell silently.

"Back!" Brodier shouted. He reached to the satchel at his side, taking up another orb. Rallia and Ophedia froze. The two remaining living Praetors behind Brodier pressed against the Revenants as their leader held the orb aloft.

"Drop the orb and give yourself up, Brodier!" Dorian shouted.

But the Praetor had a mad glint in his eyes. He struck the orb with his hammer and tossed it in a long arc toward the street they had emerged from. Ophedia gasped as it struck the flagstone and rolled to a stop before Alodda's feet.

Marn leapt toward the girl, shoving her backwards onto the flagstones, and fell atop the orb. He looked up for a short moment at Rallia, then tightened his lips in resolve and ducked his head down, completely covering the black orb.

The explosion pulsed out, but did not spread black motes everywhere. Revenants fell to the ground, then struggled to rise once more. Marn was nowhere to be seen. Alodda sat there where she had fallen, tears streaming down her dust-covered face.

Brodier pointed his hammer at Ophedia. "You're next!"

Rallia stepped in front of her. "No. You fight me."

"Attached to the old man?"

"My father," Rallia replied. She held her staff to Ophedia.

"You can't fight him barehanded," Ophedia muttered, taking it.

"Give me the sword."

Ophedia didn't hesitate.

Rallia held the sword out to consider its heft.

"Back!" Brodier called to the two Praetors next to him.

They did as they were told. Ophedia glanced at the others. Navien was helping Alodda to her feet. Dorian came next to Ophedia.

"We don't know Brodier's skill," he muttered.

"If what Rallia said is true," Ophedia said, "and she is blessed by Aben, then who better to take him down?"

"That is a very good point," Dorian said.

Rallia and Brodier circled each other for a time. Brodier readjusted his hold several times, while Rallia switched stances regularly. Brodier made the first move, lunging forward with a spear thrust, which Rallia deftly sidestepped. The Praetor spun the bell in a wide follow-through and Rallia leapt back, the curved blade in her hand crossing herself, and clanging against the bell. A low reverberation sounded.

"He is no Paladin of the Hammer," Dorian muttered.

Rallia took the advantage as Brodier tensed for another swing and rushed toward him. Brodier lifted the bell defensively across himself to block the thrust, catching the back curve and pressing down, but not fast enough to prevent the tip from sinking through the armor in his thigh as though it was cloth. It was not a deep cut, but enough to cause him to cry out. He punched out with the pommel of the spear, taking Rallia across the top of the nose. She tumbled backward and performed a roll, her feet coming up in a kick to prevent the Praetor from coming any closer.

Brodier advanced on her slowly, and yanked a Praetor spear from a corpse, locking it along his left wrist, the bell back behind.

Rallia stood in place, low, with one foot pointed toward her opponent. Sky Grazer was held out behind her. Both stood locked in consideration of the other.

"Your path ends today," Brodier said. "You will stand before the Judge, and he will give you a sentence befitting of one who opposes one blessed by his brother god."

"You think your actions will see you dining with your god?" Rallia said.

"I am promised a manor full of those who will thank me for the salvation I have given them."

"You gave no one anything but guilt in this life," Rallia said. "You'll serve a better example to those still living."

"Ha! An example?"

"Aben said to Gulliben that a one-armed man has a better chance to serve than a rich man lavishing money upon his friends."

"Do not speak holy words at me," Brodier spat, and rushed at Rallia, spear thrusting forward.

Rallia spun and stepped within the reach of the thrust. Brodier gave his own spin, and brought the bell around. Rallia stepped under the spear and around the back of Brodier. The Praetor twisted around, the bell curving into an arc directly toward Rallia's head. With a quick flick of her wrist, she caught the bell with the blade, cutting it cleanly in two. Sky Grazer continued through Brodier's right hand, wrist, and upper arm, splitting it as though made of butter. Rallia kept pressing, and as she reached his shoulder, she gave another twist, and the blade cut up and through the socket, shearing his arm entirely from his body. His cry became a scream, but it was not as shrill as the two halves of the bell that struck the flagstone. Where it had split, it glowed red hot.

Brodier fell to the ground just as the metal of the bell exploded, sundering the square into silence once more.

Ophedia got to her feet, coughing against the smoke. As the dust cleared, Brodier was gone. The other Praetors had fallen dead. She helped Rallia to her feet, and the Clouw woman put Sky Grazer back into her hands.

"What did you mean?" Ophedia said, helping her across the square to somewhere she could catch her breath.

"About what?"

"A one-armed man being a better example?"

"A one-armed man is an example of folly, or an example of faith through adversity. It will be up to Brodier to decide which it is."

"You think he lives?"

"I don't see him anywhere."

Ophedia shrugged.

"Let's get to the ship now," Rallia said.

"That won't happen," Dorian said, standing near the street leading down to the bay.

Ophedia and Rallia came to stand with him, as well as Navien and Alodda. The entire bay was full of ships either sailing away at full speed into the water, or entirely engulfed in flames.

"Noccitan," Ophedia cursed.

48

Interludes

The Castenardi army had courage, but their resolve meant nothing in the face of the Wardens. Thirty men had countercharged Noss and the five Wardens who rode with him. The skyfall hammer in Jerund's hand sent one man flying up and over his compatriots, and the newer, larger bell carried as standard by Pendür rang so loudly it almost set Noss's own ears to bleeding.

They had flown through the thirty brave Castenardi with ease, half of them falling to their knees, clutching their bleeding ears. The soldiers' eyes grew in terror as his riders rode ahead of him, their long-shafted axes of skyfall slashing at the air. These were no Paladins of the Hammer, set against hordes of slavering monsters. No. The men realized they were vengeance made manifest, bearing their bloodletting blades against the men the Paladins of the Hammer were meant to protect. That fear dawned in their eyes, and their weapons faltered. The Limaean army come to relieve the city of Liberté roared a battle cry, and charged the field behind Noss and his Warden riders.

The other ten Wardens among the irregulars urged the line on.

Arrows rained from the walls of Liberté on the back of the Castenardi army, buckling the flank trying its best to muster against Noss.

He did not relish battle, but the feeling of a quick victory was exhilarating.

A gap opened up as the opposing force folded, and a lane appeared for the elite guard surrounding Doge Gryvio Castenard.

He was a haughty man, heavy set, and wearing light armor. He held a mace over his shoulder, and barked orders with face raging red. Noss pulled up short, reached into his satchel, and took out a skyfall orb and a mallet.

The Doge gave his men the order to stand their ground as Noss tapped the orb and tossed it in an arc into their midst.

"Too easy," Noss muttered to himself. "But I've no time to draw this out."

The orb burst, and the Doge and his dreams of dominion over Limae died.

The other man had introduced himself as Magus Gvelindar. That he had fallen through from the Veld and into that darkened realm was a conversation piece that drew them together. Neither trusted the other. The mage of the Veld held contempt for Slate and his uncomfortable position in the Mirrorplate. Slate could not help but feel the other man was trying to manipulate him with every word. The other voice in his mind, pouring from the skull he held in his hand, told him that Gvelindar was not to be trusted. That was enough for Slate.

The mage walked alongside the plate as it moved, not of Slate's volition, but moved from somewhere else.

"Like the blackened plate, your armor bears no arms," Gvelindar said.

Slate had found through the days they had stood there unmoving and now the time spent marching through the black caves of Noccitan, that silence was best. The mage often revealed his thoughts through self-admiring introspection.

"Are they the same?" Gvelindar continued. "Is the mirrored silver of this armor metaphor given life?"

The mage had gone quiet.

"He expects you to speak," the skull said.

"We've made a study of the black metal," Slate said. "But the mirrored metal is not something our scholarship has found."

"Perhaps it is time to begin," Gvelindar said.

"By what means?" Slate asked. "Slinking around in Noccitan we shall discover nothing."

"Then, perhaps we will find answers there," Gvelindar said.

"I can see nothing from within this armor," Slate said.

"We've entered a wide bowl. The ceiling is miles above. Rising from the middle of the bowl is a white pillar. If I didn't know better, I'd say it was made of clouds."

"A tower of clouds?" Slate asked, curious.

"This is something you know?"

"There is a poem about four towers. One black, one white, one empty, one of might," Slate said. "The Morraineans have a penchant for poetry."

"Yes, we do," Gvelindar replied.

"You are Morrainean?"

"Something I assume we have in common," the mage said, "although I left behind my life there long ago."

"As did I," Slate said. "I hated it there in that wind-swept and desolate place. I was a prince."

The Mirrorplate marched down the bowl toward the white tower as the two of them, the naked mage, and the entrapped, skull-bearing ex-prince of Morraine, told each other stories of their homeland to keep the madness of Noccitan at bay.

Trumpets sounded from the distant hills, jarring Aurín awake. He had his talon on his hand as quickly as possible, and kicked the mat of the squire sleeping by the door.

"Sir?"

"Bring my armor to the wall," he said, pulling his cloak over his shoulders and rushing out the door.

He took the stairs to his right, rushing up to the top of the wall, then sighed in relief. The Castnardi army still sat a quarter mile from the city, unmoved. They were still assembling the catapults, but work had ceased as the camped army turned to face the hills behind them.

Down the main road from Adwall, a tendril advanced. What army it was, Aurín could not tell from this distance. But the reaction of the army below gave him hope.

A few of the smaller battalions still eyed the wall. De Bosco's spies had identified one of those as a Tashar unit. That they had not contributed more than forty men did not surprise Aurín's advisors. Tashar meddled in plenty of Sidieratan affairs. It was surmised that helping Castenard with Boscolón would ensure their help if they ever succeeded in attacking Edi.

As the hours wore on, others came to the wall, watching the army march from the hills. Soon a second arm circling from the west formed.

"I suspect whoever they are will arrive by nightfall," someone said.

"Frankly, I'm surprised Castenard doesn't just attack us," Aurín replied.

"They can't," Perát de Bosco said. "If they were to make it into the city, they'd have no way to reinforce it before that army arrived."

"Then we wait."

"As we planned to do," Perát responded. "If the Castenardi army just leaves, we'll let them. If they fight and break, then I've already arranged for several squadrons to give chase."

"It would be best if we drove them entirely out of your lands."

"I agree. If they are persuaded to leave, then diplomacy will prevail."

An hour before sunset, most of the people of the city had gathered at the walls. Soldiers leaned on crenellations, their spears bristling. Townspeople waited down in the street listening for news.

The new army that had appeared flew black banners of Limae. That alone sent a buzz through the city. From the army, a second, smaller group had broken away and circled to the west as a threatening flank. This army bore several red flags of The Red Bannermen. They all stopped within three hundred yards of the Castenardi army, and from the main group, five sleipnirs rode out to meet opposing riders from Castenard. Aurín caught himself holding his breath again.

"Who rides to meet with Castenard?" Perát asked.

"I don't know," Aurín said. "At least four of them are dressed as Wardens."

The ten sleipnirs and their riders stood near one another and spoke for some time. Soon the Castenardi delegates turned and rode back to the camp, one rider rode harder, and then down the line. The entire camp folded and began breaking camp immediately.

The five riders from the new army rode slowly down and through, unmolested, to the gate.

At their lead rode Dean Pellian Noss of the Wardens.

Aurín made his way to the gate, and ordered it open as Noss arrived. He stood there stoically, and as Noss approached, he gave a flourishing bow. "Dean Noss!"

"Warden Mateau," Noss said in reply.

"You convinced Castenard to break the siege?"

"I did. Can we speak somewhere privately? With the leader of the city?"

"Of course," Aurín said. "I already ordered Perát de Bosco to return to his keep to prepare for your arrival."

"Ordered?" Noss asked.

"Strong word. He has obliged," Aurín said, now walking alongside Noss's sleipnir. "He was on the verge of losing his city to Œronzi rule when we arrived. His brother has been conspiring with both Castenard and agents in Ormach to take the city from Perát. I offered him Limaean protection if he joined the country. I'd say Castenard took that as an act of war, but he arrived sooner than that, marching on both Adwall and Boscolón before ink had dried."

When they arrived at Old City, Perát stood at the gate with a dozen servants.

"My lord Noss," de Bosco said with a deep bow. "Welcome to my city. Your city."

"Not my city," Noss said. "If what Warden Mateau says is true, you will join our brotherhood of leaders. But that is then."

"And this is now," de Bosco said. "I have baths being prepared for you and your men."

"I shall allow my men to partake, but I think it important to give you the news I have as quickly as possible. Immediate actions will be necessary."

The servants led the other Wardens away, and Noss and Aurín followed de Bosco to his private chambers. Noss took a seat as Perát handed him a large goblet of rich red wine. He poured a glass for Aurín and himself, and they sat.

"What did you tell Castenard?"

"Well, the good news is, you don't have Doge Gryvio Castenard himself out there in that army."

"We received missives."

"Yes. From Gryvio's brother, Nercutio. Gryvio is dead."

"Dead!?" Perát replied, spluttering wine.

"He was personally trying to lay siege to Liberté. My army

arrived from the north and Gryvio fell to my own hand. His army fell back to Castenard, with his wife at the lead. The Adwall siege was lifted at the same time. I told Nercutio that he had best start marching, because Boscolón was now under Limaean control, and that if he wanted to secure the throne of Castenard for himself, he'd need to get back soon. I added that the Wardens and Red Banner would hunt down and kill any soldiers in his army who remain once dawn rises."

Perát sighed and slumped in his chair in relief.

"Now we only need to worry about the Chalicians," Aurín said.

"Yes," Noss said. "That is the greater problem, of course. Until then, let us celebrate this victory for all of us."

For two days he had walked. Sleep had not come, as pain became his constant companion. The wrapping he had pulled across his upper torso was wet. Whether it was the roughly applied balm, or his wound oozing through the bandages, he did not know. He did not care. The pain from the shards of black metal that had scathed half his face left him feeling nothing but pain, the sliver-like shards were, he could feel, stuck in his bones.

He had wandered out of the city and along a road. He did not know in which direction he journeyed. The sky above was a confusing assortment that gave no direction. He did not know if it was day, night, or nightmare.

All avoided him as he neared them. At least he thought that was so. He did not recall if he had seen a soul upon the road. The writhing garden that grew along the road had beckoned him several times. But when he had fallen into the ghostly pale tendrils and they had covered his body, it had been to no avail. He still lived, with pain screaming through his body to match the wails of the things that sought his mind. The metal shards lodged in his skull and ribs were anathema to the writhing things, and kept them from entering his mind fully. Instead, they only brushed at his subconscious.

He came to notice companions walking alongside him—a pair who seemed to walk both in day and night, hunched over by burdens greater than he bore. They spoke in hushed tones with each other, but he did not understand the words. A third figure came to walk on his other side. She led a flock of odd creatures behind her, who grazed upon the horrific tendrils. They bore a horn on their face like a crescent moon, with ends pointing outward. The pair did not seem to notice her, and she did not give them any attention.

"Where do you wander?" she asked.

"To the ending of this pain," he replied.

"He speaks," one of the figures on his left said.

"Yes, but how?" the other replied.

"You seem to answer someone's question, but we did not ask," the first man said.

"She demands a respect I cannot fathom," Wounded-Man said.

"She?"

The woman at his side touched his right shoulder, the only remaining one, and the two others at his side gave a small gasp.

"What is this? You leave your Pasture?" one of them said.

Wounded-Man stopped and finally considered those around him with his one remaining eye.

The Shepherdess stood with a comforting hand on Wounded-Man's shoulder, letting her flock graze nearby.

The other two bore similarities that told him that they were brothers. One had a large jaw and bald head. Night shone on him and gave the appearance of a multitude of eyes across his face like a Zvolder. He bore a permanent smile. No. His teeth were so large they were affixed in a grimace of pain to match that which coursed through the Wounded-Man.

Grimacing-Zvolder's brother bore a full beard and head of hair, all standing up on end. His forearms were larger than any blacksmith's Wounded-Man had ever seem. No. He wore gauntlets like paws, as much a part of his arms as the slivers of metal scratching at Wounded-Man's skull. Like the large shard that had replaced his left eye.

The Shepherdess had not yet answered the question. The two brothers waited.

"I go where I wish within my realm," she finally said.

"Do you not still serve sentence beside the Black Throne?" the Hairy-One asked.

"My body does," the Shepherdess said. "But my mind will always be free, and be mine."

"Once it did not," the Grimacing-Zvolder said. "Once you and your servants served me."

"The Magi serve themselves," she said. "I serve you no longer. A queen does not serve her sons. She commands them in her realm."

"It is a good thing we do not stand in your realm," Grimacing-Zvolder said.

"Do not provoke her," Hairy-One said. "She might ensnare us in her realm, and what good would that do us?"

Grimacing-Zvolder gave a curt nod.

"How is it," Wounded-Man croaked past parched lips, "that I stand in both?"

The three of them turned to consider him.

"That question drew us to you," Hairy-One said.

"The same is said of me," Shepherdess said. "The wounds by which you suffer appear to bristle with an unknown power."

"Ah…to have a servant who walks both worlds at once," Grimacing-Zvolder said, longingly.

"We near the Imbalance," Shepherdess said, "and you have both chosen your Scale-Weight, I am told."

"A king may have many servants."

"And a queen admirers," the Shepherdess said.

"Do you still pursue Vanity as Consort?" Grimacing-Zvolder asked.

"Stop," Hairy-One said. "Do not provoke her."

"You've no need to defend him nor I," the Shepherdess said.

"While curiosity beckons me," Grimacing-Zvolder said, "I grow bored. The metal that bristles his skin is abhorrent. I have a Scale-Weight." He turned to go.

"Wait," Hairy-Man said. "My own curiosity is piqued. Do you court this man?"

"We have only just met," the Shepherdess said. "But curiosity tends to each of us. Let it play the judge for this crossroads chat."

"What purpose lies there?" Wounded-Man spoke.

"We stand at a crossroads," the Shepherdess said. "The worlds are thinnest at places like this. You seem to walk in two worlds, by what means we do not know. That you walk in Veld may be the only reason you still live, for I know no man who can suffer such wounds as you have and not succumb to the pain alone."

Wounded-Man noticed the pain again. It was stronger when he looked at the two odd men next to him.

"What is your name?" Hairy-Man asked.

"I was a Praetor of Aben, Yanas Br…"

"No," Grimacing-Zvolder said. "He did not ask you what you

are called. Not what your title is. What. Is. Your. Name."

He fought past the pain screaming in his mind and realized it was the same pain he had always lived with. The pain of seeking acceptance. Of being seen by his superiors. Of covering up his pain with the anguish of others. Of revenge for being taken from his mother at an early age.

"I do not remember the name I was given at birth. It was replaced. But word is that as I was pulled from my mother's arms, she cried out 'Mevsdar.' That word haunted me for years. I did not know its meaning. It is an Old Tongue word."

"'Revenge' in Oruche," Hairy-One said.

"But in the oldest tongue," the Shepherdess said, "it means 'Appeal to Justice.' It is your true name. Mevsdar. Yet, you have forsaken your name."

"I have not served Justice," Mevsdar said, falling to his knees. "Instead, I have sought to bring my pain to all who would oppose me. What must I do to bring myself to justice?"

"Men and woman come to me," the Shepherdess said. "Each comes with desires for power. For control. What do you come with?"

"I come with the pain that once gnawed at my mind, now manifested."

"You would have me take that pain from you?"

"No," Mevsdar said. "I would take Pain as my boon companion. I would take agony as my allotment. I would suffer for my actions."

"To what end?"

"To heal the wounds I have caused and sunder the curses the Deceiver has wrought upon the world."

"Do you renounce him?"

"I have no need," Mevsdar said. "I renounce the actions of my fellow mortals, who through deceit have become the greater curse on the worlds."

"I name thee my Scale-Weight," the Shepherdess said.

A gong across creation pealed.

Grimacing-Zvolder and Hairy-One were gone.

"They left?" Mevsdar asked.

"They fled," the Shepherdess said. "They no longer had any chance at power over you."

"Where do I go now?"

"You shall follow me and I shall teach you how to act as my servant."

"What shall I call you?"

"In the Veld, I am Zanghard. But I answer to Shepherdess."

"Then I shall call you that, my Shepherdess. Please lead me where I must go."

"First we shall go to my pasture, where you shall sleep. I've need of you, but not until you have your strength again."

She took a step off the crossroads and into a field of purple grass, and Mevsdar, the Wounded-Man, followed her to his rest.

Noss and Aurín arrived outside the warehouse that had acted as the underground when Aurín had first arrived. Eunia and Chös stood at the door and crossed to them.

"He is inside. Unarmed and alone."

"Has he given any indication why he came?"

"No. But there have been people watching him since he arrived. He was direct and asked for you, Aurín, immediately. I don't think he knows you're here just yet, Dean Noss."

"Then let's go meet our friend," Noss said sarcastically.

Entering the warehouse, men and women moved about around tables covered in maps. In the center, sheets of canvas had been hung to keep whoever was within from viewing the rest of the place. Eunia led them up to the sheets, and pulled them apart to allow Noss and Aurín to enter from behind the man seated at the table. Over on a side table sat a Chalician's helmet, spear, and book. The man at the table had not been stripped, but quietly waited. Aurín came around the table, and Provost Abrau gave him a forced, but friendly smile. When he saw Noss come around into view, the smile turned genuine.

"When last we saw each other, you had threats, which you made good on," Noss said.

"And in response," Abrau said, "you sent my army packing. Since then you've done the same to the armies of Castenard."

"Why then are you here?" Noss cut to the heart of the matter.

"Because you have my deepest respect. I should like to align some of our goals in the future. I said it when I first came to Limae, and I say it now: I asked for the opportunity to bring Limae under Chalician heel, for its own good. Others will react poorly to your defeating our army. I wish to prevent that."

"Why should we trust you?" Aurín asked.

Abrau laughed. "You shouldn't! But I come bearing news, and I would like to hope that you will use it to your advantage."

Noss pulled out both chairs opposite Abrau and sat in one. "Go on."

"I do not know what knowledge you have of our church's actions across the continent, but Limae was not our only goal. One of the chief agents of the Chalice journeyed north to Mahndür."

"Provost Otem," Noss said. "We have received news."

"Very well. Now that he has taken Mahndür under wing, he journeys to the Northern Scapes to bring them to heel. Once this is accomplished, and it will be, then Otem will have means to bring his arm down over Düran, and the church's goal of Morriego, crushed between the pincers of our armies from the north and south. We had hoped to have Limae as a primary headquarters to enact the waves, but you ensured that did not happen. In fact, I suspect that I will be replaced, perhaps violently, by someone who will be less understanding, and they'll still come for Limae anyway."

"What of the south?"

"That is the even more dire situation for you, I'm afraid. The church has sent Mareschal Waquelon Dâjeaux to Sidierata."

"He is someone I ought to know?" Noss asked.

"An understatement. He is the chief War Provost. He will 'negotiate'—which is merely a euphemism for the gauntlet he will bring upon them—with the City States, and turn them whichever direction he would like them to face."

"Such as Limae."

"I do not know. But you know they are City States and not a unified country for a reason."

"They were united enough to try for Boscolón."

"I disagree," Abrau said. "They allowed Castenard to try for portions of Limae, but they would not have allowed him to take Boscolón for himself."

"I agree," Noss said. "Ipona would never allow Castenard to have a port. They might have accepted Boscolón as a City State, even a puppet of Castenard, but not direct control. No one likes Castenard. Keeping them landlocked is a primary concern of a third of the City States."

"Now that you've defeated them, Castenard may raise Noccitan to ensure they have this defeat avenged."

"So it may behoove the other dukes to offer help just to silence them," Noss said.

"Thus, Limae may continue to be at war. Especially if Otem gets word, and he chooses to march first to Limae before going down to Düran."

"Then I think we're in a better position than you realize," Noss said.

"Why is that?"

"Because we know something you do not."

Abrau cocked an eyebrow.

"Otem was ousted from the Northern Scapes. He's fleeing back toward Mahndür to lick his wounds."

"Oh my," Abrau said, his face quirking into a wry smile. "That changes everything."

"How so?"

"Otem does not lick wounds. He retaliates. If he doesn't work to bring all of the Chalician Church to bear against the Northern Scapes in response, I will give up my spear and become a fisher."

"Interesting," Noss said.

"The Northern Scapes may have just saved your country," Abrau said.

"Then we need only worry about Sidierata," Aurín said.

"And Ormach," Noss said. "Given the change of hands at Castenard, we may be able to make the most of this entire situation."

"Change of hands?"

"I killed Gryvio Castenard. His brother is rushing home to take power before Gryvio's wife does."

"Another interesting turn," Abrau said.

"Now, why exactly are you here?" Noss asked. "What are you hoping to gain out of your defeat at my hands?"

"A friend," Abrau said. "I want Limaean liberty. But you know I also want a Chalician foothold."

"Then what are you proposing?"

"A negotiation for Chalician presence, but with some subterfuge involved."

"Please continue."

"Allow me to take control of the bastion here in town as a Chalician chapel. From there, allow me to place certain select Chalicians in other bastions in the country. You'll make a statement that the bastion here in Boscolón is the only way any

Chalician may enter the country. I'll vet them and ensure that no agents who would seek trouble will enter."

"To what means?"

"To avoid being recalled to Ouiquimon. I fear for my life, for the failure of not taking Haven."

"Then you place your life in my hands," Noss said.

"It already is. You can imprison me now, and turn me over as a bargaining chip to be left alone by the Church of the Common Chalice. Or, you can take my hand, and we make something even stronger, without the hot breath of my order sending uncomfortable shivers down your spine at every turn."

Abrau held out his hand.

Noss considered it for a long moment. He finally took the hand offered and they shook.

Part 6

PYRACENE & THE EASTERN PARIANT

49

DREAD KNIGHT

From whence came the falling sky, none know but the gods. And even they say little.

—QAVYLLI POET, JEGUA DENAI

The beach of the island was rocky, with patches of oneirion everywhere. A path cut around the circumference, and Hanen guided the armor up to the lip, Ymbrys following behind.

The rocks that jutted toward the sky were taller than the Dreadplate, and made of a sand-blasted black glass. As the path led up and past them, Hanen stopped abruptly, almost slipping down into the bowl beyond. The entire island was a massive crater of black, almost purple, obsidian. Age-old cracks and fissures broke up the surface that ran down the long slope. In the very center, a lip appeared to sit over another gaping hole in the ground.

Ymbrys stood next to Hanen, both hands wringing his staff. "Not what I expected to find," he said.

"What did you expect?" Hanen asked.

"I'm not sure. But not this." Ymbrys knelt down and touched the surface. "Pure oneirion. Fused to glass."

Hanen guided the armor along the bowl toward a precarious

pathway encircling the whole of it.

Some fissures led up from the beach, and in them the Dreamwyrm colonies had found their grip to move up and into the bowl.

They came to the top of the path to find steps that had been carved down through the glass.

"Shall we?" Hanen asked.

"Yes," Ymbrys said.

Hanen noticed glows and ephemeral movement in the glass, and at places it was clear and deep.

"What can cause a formation like this?" Hanen asked.

"I would imagine something very heavy dropped into the center with such force that heat was generated. That heat fused the sand into this glass."

"Is the gate that heavy?" Hanen asked.

"It may be. Or the gate was formed atop it. It reminds me of the capital of the Qavylli Republic. It sits in a large bowl atop a mountain. It is not so lifeless. The Great Library is built in the very heart of it. That's where my own adventure began."

"Where you stole whatever it was you took?"

Ymbrys nodded, his hands tightening on the staff.

They came finally to the bottom of the stairs. More obsidian stones stood upright, clawing for the sky. These were not sandblasted, but circled the rim of another hole, this one sheer and vertical, several hundred feet across, and leading down into the blackness. On two sides, stairs were carved once more, this time circling down the walls of the hole. Both sets of stairs helixed down. The other set was covered in a writhing mass of Dreamwyrms attached directly to the stairs, using the sand that covered it for grip.

Descending into the darkness, they found a black monolith in the center of the flat, violet floor of the anti-tower.

The stairs leveled out three hundred feet below the top. Black oneirion covered the ground, Dreamwyrms writhed all around them. They both stayed close to the armor as the wyrms squealed and retracted from the armor's presence.

They walked to the center of the sand, the dark monolith's form and function made apparent as they approached.

Obsidian blocks had been stacked in a square arch over a metal grate standing upright, but at a weird angle. Tendrils of the Dreamwyrm colony moved through gaping, pitted holes in the surface and into the space beyond. Through other holes gray sky shone through.

"That is the gate?" Hanen asked.

"So it appears," Ymbrys said. "The wyrms don't seem to want to touchs it. Is it the same metal as the armor?"

"They are finding a way through, though," Hanen said.

"But not touching it," Ymbrys confirmed.

"No more than a wyloth could fit through there. How are we to go through?"

"By opening it," Ymbrys said. "Then we'll close it after us."

Hanen approached and touched it with the flat of a gauntleted palm. There was a thrumming vibration, as though the armor and gate welcomed each other, sharing a memory.

Hanen made a gripping motion, as he did when he gathered skyfall coins, and the gate shuddered, but did not budge.

He repeated the action, taking hold of the vibration that seemed to connect the metal, then pulling back on the nothing. His legs ached with the pain of the gate pulling against him, and he relented.

"What is wrong?" Ymbrys asked.

"The gauntlets. They can take hold of the gate, but it puts weight on me. I don't have the strength."

"What if you press on the gate at the same time as you press with the armor itself?"

Hanen nodded and guided the armor up against the gate and with one hand pressed it forward, while with the other hand reached out for the gate. The vibrations that coursed through the gate, armor, and gloves, rose in a harmonic crescendo. The grate moved an inch.

"You're doing it!" Ymbrys shouted.

Hanen pushed harder, and gray light streamed out through the growing gap.

The Dreamwyrms began to sprout from the ground, screaming in a discordant cacophony to the harmonics of the skyfall metal.

They grew up around them in a sickly forest, gathering together in a mass, pulling away from the gate, and rising into a ten foot pillar of white ghostly tendons. Then, the fleshy serpent opened up, and from it walked a figure out of a nightmare. Wyrms hung from him like a robe, leading back to the mass like a horrific umbilicus. In the mass, a chain led from the figure down into the ground.

"What in Noccitan is that?" Hanen asked.

"As I said before," the figure rasped, "they've only awaited a greater mind to command them."

"Loth?" Hanen responded.

The wyrm-robed thing pointed the desiccated hand of Slate at them as a scepter, and the ground erupted with wyrms. They were hesitant to rise near the armor, but with urging from their new master, they suddenly exploded under Hanen's feet, and began wrapping up the legs of the Dreadplate. Ymbrys had stepped away to avoid being touched, but to Hanen's perception they did not come near Ymbrys, or at least writhed away as his staff came down on the sand.

The armor suddenly lurched, and Hanen fought to right it. The lower half of the armor was encased in the wyrms now, and they fought to move it with their bodies, all the while their screams rising to a fever pitch. They quivered in pain at the touch of the skyfall, but still continued to climb up its height.

Loth tugged at the chain behind him, and up out of the ground, covered in wyrms, and eyes full of terror, Bou emerged.

"At them, child!" Loth shouted. Bou was forced forward, thrown at Hanen bodily, arms bound by white tendrils.

Hanen dodged Bou and moved the armor toward Loth.

Another heap of wyrms began to mound up between them, and at Loth's tug, Bou was pulled back toward Hanen from behind. As Hanen willed the armor to move, it fought back against him. It strained Hanen's muscles and agonized him as the final inch of the armor disappeared under ghostly white flesh.

The wyrm's screams shifted in tone. At first discordant to the armor and the gate's vibration, then matching. The entire pit rang with the frequency. Hanen turned to see the gate now shaking in its place.

Hanen rushed out through the wyrms to get away from it, and threw himself to the sand that surrounded them.

He turned in time to see the mass pushing up against the gate. Loth walked up and pressed his hands against it.

The resonance rose sharply and for the smallest of seconds went silent.

Then exploded.

The gate blew outward, disintegrating the wyrms across the face of the armor, and out through the other side of the gate. The armor turned as new wyrms rose up to cover the spaces where the

DREAD KNIGHT

first had died.

"We can't have you following us," Loth said, and pointed a hand toward Hanen. The wyrms lurched toward him.

"Take back control!" Ymbrys shouted.

"I can't!" Hanen said. "It's too strong!"

"Then find a way to cut the wyrms away!"

Hanen touched the sand and threw up spikes as Loth had done to them. Wyrms wrapped up each and constricted until they exploded into sand.

Bou had fallen to his knees, trying to cover his ears from the screams of the wyrms around him.

Hanen picked up sand and threw it toward Loth and the armor to form walls. Nothing worked. They advanced on him in a slow, implacable march.

"Cut them!" Ymbrys shouted.

"With what?"

"Anything you can imagine."

Hanen shoved his armored hands down into the sand, imagined what he needed, and pulled his hands free, now holding in his gauntlets a sandy axe, the long blade guarding his hands. With one swing he severed the chain from Bou to Loth, freeing the young Khamntyr, then charged at the armor, shearing wyrms from its frame, only to have more replace those that fell. It moved slowly, but implacably, swinging heavily with its arms. He blocked the attacks, and the wyrms killed themselves on his blade. With each strike, dust fell from the sword, and its integrity waned.

In a rush, Hanen circled around to where Ymbrys and Bou stood, close to each other and stomping at wyrms that rose.

He handed the axe to Bou, who took it tentatively. "Fight back!" Hanen said. He turned to Ymbrys.

"Give me the boneshroud," Hanen said. "I'll be able to focus and take control of the armor with it."

Ymbrys eyed him, hands wringing the staff, and then he nodded and handed him the satchel. The three of them split up as the armor clambered through where they stood, Loth just behind, hissing maniacally.

Hanen ran around the wyrm-covered circumference of the gate, pulled the boneshroud out of the satchel, and threw it over his head.

Searn appeared before him, and sudden calm fell.

"Where are we?" Searn asked quietly.

"The Veld. At the gate leading to Kallattai. Loth has control of the Dreadplate."

"Why did you give him the gloves?"

"I didn't," Hanen said, holding up his arms. "He is using Dreamwyrms to manhandle it into place, I think with the help of Ghoré."

"Why did you take so long?"

"I can't explain right now. I need the shroud to focus. To take control of the..."

The armor crashed into him from behind, and wyrms grabbed at him and the cloak, pulling on it. Hanen tried to wrench free, but the wyrms individually took hold of links in the shroud. Hanen felt a tear as he wrenched free, scrambling away. He regained his footing, and looked around, Searn was gone.

Searn's bone pin hung from the boneshroud where links had exploded from the frame. He reached down and took hold of the pin, and Searn bloomed back into view next to him.

"Why can I no longer feel the shroud?" he asked.

"It broke."

"That was foolish," Searn said.

The way to the gate was clear.

"Through!" Hanen shouted.

Ymbrys nodded to him and rushed toward the gate. Hanen rushed after him, but Bou was too slow and the armor scrambled after Hanen under Loth's goading, locking Bou on the other side.

"The child!" Ymbrys called out futilely.

Searn's shade next to Hanen dissipated as they came through to Kallattai.

The ground on the other side was covered in a black blight, from which smaller wyrms rose groping for their boots, but none were larger than two inches. The blackness spread from across the top of the platform they appeared to be on. Hanen scrambled away as the armor crashed into the entry and froze in place in a flash of blinding light. Hanen blinked his eyes clear. The half of the armor that had come through, apparently suspended in place, had wyrms across its surface, but they were as small as the ones on the ground. Behind, larger wyrms in the Veld would not dare press through, and the face of Loth peaked through gaps the armor did not fill. The armor was not black, but rather a spiraling twist of black and silver metal. Being stuck between both worlds, the Dreadplate and Mirrorplate stood as one, immobile yet threatening to break through at any moment. Guyyan's head atop the armor also appeared to be a wyloth-like skull with a black anti-crown of holes. Ghoré's skull.

"Do you have control?" Ymbrys asked, coming to stand next to Hanen.

"It's stuck. I cannot move it, nor can Loth."

"Bou!" Ymbrys called through. "Fight as you can. Do not give up!"

"Tell me what's happened," Searn said in his ear. "I can help."

Hanen ignored him for the time being and turned back to Ymbrys. "The wyrms are spreading."

"They're minuscule," Ymbrys said. "Perhaps they can be destroyed by something like fire."

"They coil and scream at the touch of skyfall," Hanen said. "If the armor was completely in control of someone, perhaps it could repel them, and drive them back to the Veld."

"No one can put the armor on," Ymbrys said. "Not with wyrms covering it."

"Is that a Khamntyr skull?" Searn asked.

"We must bring it through entirely, if we are to destroy it," Ymbrys said.

"Destroy the armor?" Searn said. "That's stupid. It's a tool to be used."

"Skyfall has caused enough damage," Hanen muttered to him. "A skyfall orb killed Alodda."

"In the wrong hands, innocents die," Searn said. "It should not fall into the control of a zealot like Loth."

"Do you know Loth?" Hanen asked.

"I've not interacted him more than our time in the Veld," Ymbrys said.

"He thinks you're talking to him," Searn said. "I knew Loth, yes, though, he did not know me—a man full of rage and hate. When focused in the right direction, he turned many to the Motean philosophy."

"He would see the whole world infested," Hanen said.

"He would. More of those you love will die," Searn said.

Hanen stared at the twisted armor.

"How would you take control?" Hanen muttered.

"Stick my pin into that Khamntyr skull."

"What?"

"I can use the skull to wrest what control Loth has over it. You can use the gauntlets on this half, and together, we'll force him back into the Veld."

"And if it doesn't work?'

"I'm willing to bet my shade on it," Searn said.

Hanen walked forward toward the gate.

"What are you doing, Hanen?" Ymbrys asked.

"Taking a gambit."

Loth's face shoved in where it could, to consider Hanen as he approached. "Give us control of the armor!" Loth rasped. "We'll spare you."

"No," Hanen said. "You wouldn't."

He reached up with Searn's pin in his gauntleted hand, and touched it to the forehead of Guyyan's skull. He pulled his hand away, only to find the gauntlet stuck in place, and his hand came free. The left arm of the armor rose, and shoved itself into the gauntlet, which dropped from the skull. Searn's pin stuck, fused to the forehead. The gauntleted arm shot out and grabbed Hanen by the wrist, and lifted him up.

Trying to escape, Hanen let go of the other gauntlet, and he slipped out and fell to the ground. The Dreadplate's other arm slipped into the second gauntlet, completing the armor. Hanen scrambled backward as the armor fell from its confines of the gate and into Kallattai, becoming fully black once more.

The Khamntyr-skulled Dreadplate turned and considered the gate, like staring in a mirror at the silver Mirrorplate that now stood on the other side, wyloth-skulled. Loth fell to his knees, wyrms scrambling from him, bowing respectfully to the silver armor.

Not to the armor. To another figure. The magus Hanen had condemned to Noccitan, who stepped down from behind the Mirrorplate.

The Magus looked through the portal to the Dreadplate, gave a respectful nod, and turned as Bou charged him, sand axe in hand. The Arborist waved and the sand in Bou's hand collapsed and reformed as chains that whipped around the Khamntyr, pulling him to his knees.

The Dreadplate turned back to Hanen. The sockets of the Khamntyr skull were not hollow, but filled with deep pits of blackness.

It moved toward Hanen, not in a lurch, but as someone accustomed to armor. Hanen tried to get to his feet to rush away,

DREAD KNIGHT

but it took hold of his shoulders and forced him back down into a kneeling position. Then the Dread Knight pulled the boneshroud from Hanen's back as a parent removing a hat from a child and shoved him aside.

It took the mantle of bone and draped it reverently over the skull, shoving it down into the plate as a hood.

Hanen crawled away to the edge of the platform where Ymbrys stood. They were atop a tower, as far off the ground as the pit had been deep. An island surrounded them, and a lake beyond that. Black veiny tendrils were going out over the green hill of the island. He could see no way down.

"What did you do, Hanen?" Ymbrys whispered.

"Searn. He thought he could control Loth's half of the armor. But as soon as I touched him to Guyyan's skull, it stuck fast, and forced me from the gauntlets. You saw the rest."

"You stupid man," Ymbrys said with a sigh.

Hanen turned on him. "Who cares?" Hanen shouted. "You've done nothing but follow, and observe, and whiffle. You have no care but for yourself and that stupid staff that you hold like its some precious thing. Like it's talking to you. Is that why nothing I do surprises you? Because you are under the same curse? What is under that leather, Ymbrys? More skyfall? Shades of qavyl you've killed?"

"No," Ymbrys said with a weak smile. "But you're not far off."

From the gate, sand began pouring out. The Arborist stepped through, and from the ground sand began to form up. He spotted the two of them and raised his hands, sandy tendrils shooting toward them, but they collapsed as they passed the edge of the sand.

The Dread Knight turned and waved for him to stop. Then, it indicated Hanen step forward.

Hanen approached.

The armor motioned for him to bow. Hanen hesitated, but dropped to a knee, his hand touching the sand.

The Dread Knight put a gauntleted hand down on top of his head.

"Hanen," Searn's voice reverberated from the entirety of the armor.

Hanen started, but could not move, the armor pinning him in place.

"You have done well. You betrayed me in Mahn Fulhar.

Otherwise, you've done everything I needed you to do. Look at me now—an immortal and unkillable Dread Knight."

"What do you want?"

"Your friendship."

"And if I say no?"

"I hold your skull in my hand. It would take nothing for me to kill you. No. I want you to watch now. See what you could have done if you had put the armor on yourself. You've earned your life. Your punishment is to observe as I establish myself, and know that you could have truly been my heir. Now you'll simply suffer as I establish a kingdom. An empire."

"You made the boneshroud to make yourself invisible to the gods."

"I made the shroud so they could not interfere."

Sand piled up behind the armor at the Arborist's command, into a throne. More oneirion piled around Hanen as it had Loth when the Kam-Nasur ensnared him. Searn let Hanen go and sat in the throne that had formed before the gate. Still more sand poured through, turning the entire platform purple, under a dark gray sky.

Obsidian Tower

How many ancient tales have gone unsaid?

By what means do legends come into being?

—THE RAVINGS, LINE 137-138

N avien and Ophedia pulled at the oars, while Dorian and Rallia worked at the ropes and tack for the single lateen sail. The man at the dock who had sold them the rig had laughed as they got in. Rallia had quickly taken command, having been out on ships in the Lupinfang with her father. The calm lake, large as it was, was easy to sail upon, and the wind was in their favor.

Seriah sat in the bow, and acted as navigator, the tendrils of purple she could see under them along the bottom of the lake leading them toward the center. To the northwest there was a bright beacon to her eyes, open or closed. As night fell, Rallia and Dorian took turns at the oars. The wind stilled to a whisper, so Ophedia and Navien could rest. At the second watch, they switched again.

Seriah did not sleep, the purple glow of the Dreamwyrms threatening to haunt her dreams. The breeze licked at her head. It no longer tickled the short hair coming in slowly. She ran one hand over the top, as her other hand scratched Whisper behind the ear.

As morning began slowly dawning, a square monolith rose from the horizon miles away. Rallia came and sat next to her, but did not speak, her hand resting on the ynfald's shoulder.

"What will we find there?" Rallia finally asked.

"I don't know, but it is important. What do you hope to find there?"

"Closure."

"For what?"

"Why Hanen kept secrets from me. We have done everything together. I've followed every plan and scheme he's ever had. I trusted him." She looked over at Alodda, asleep in the stern. "Why is she still here?"

"Alodda?" Seriah asked. "I suspect she is just as confused as you are, and wondering if there is more to it."

"And if there is not?" Rallia asked.

"Then it is her choice in what to do next."

"You seem calmer than in Nor-Vio," Rallia said.

"Because I'm resolved to my fate."

"Then you believe in fate?"

"Poor choice of words, I suppose. I am following the path set before me."

"I suppose I am, too. I just hope that the gods know what they are doing, choosing you and I."

"I rather hate that hope has two meanings."

"What do you mean?" Rallia asked.

"You said you 'hope' the gods know what they're doing. That is a very different word than when Dorian says something about having 'hope' in Grissone to guide him."

"That is more a trust, I suppose. I meant that I have more of an 'aimless, feeling about in the dark.'"

"Trust is a good word. I think it's more than that, though."

"Confidence," Navien said from nearby.

Both women turned to him glancing back over his shoulder to them.

"I followed my king's order with a confidence that he knew what he asked. It is tied to duty, but also led by my experience. Erdthal has been king for six years. I was often assigned duty over him when he was prince. He never showed the usual signs of corruption. He is never drunk. He spent dutiful time at the cathedral. He did not womanize. He was, to all appearance, a good man, and a good king. But now I've spent time examining his actions and mine, I come to wonder what you all seemed to see without years of intimate interactions with him. Why is he so obsessed with the capture and gaining of the boneshroud? Why did he give in so quickly to the Chalicians who came to Mahn Fulhar?"

"Perhaps you did not see corruption because it came from the High Priest?" Seriah asked.

"Perhaps. But why then did Erdthal give up his authority so easily? He never does anything without thinking long and hard about something. I need to know why. I worry that I will not like the answer."

"So, why did you come with us?"

"To understand whether the boneshroud truly has a corrupting influence, or if it is just another form of power by which already corrupt men grow worse."

"And you think not?" Rallia asked.

"Look at Ophedia," Navien said. "Daughter of Searn VeTurres, but she does not seek power. She holds a blade made of skyfall, but she does not lord it over us. Nor does Aurín."

"What about him?"

"He is similarly armed, but he was never cruel to me. Either of them could have seen me dead in a heartbeat. Searn would have."

"What then do you surmise?" Dorian asked, finally butting into the conversation.

Navien and the others looked at the old man.

They had stopped rowing.

"Power has a corrupting influence," Navien said. "Whether it brings a mortal low cannot be known unless you know the man."

"All can be corrupted," Dorian agreed. "But no one who has strayed is without hope."

"That," Navien said with a determined look, "is what I hold onto."

The base of the black obelisk on the horizon finally joined the ground, and a steep hill rose up out of the water. The sun peeked to shine on both, revealing it to be a tall gray tower, rising from the green hill below. Clouds gathered in a swirl over the top of it.

Alodda and Ophedia had awakened from their light slumber, and came to the bow.

"Is that it?" Ophedia asked.

Seriah nodded. "The entire tower glows purple to me."

"Well," said Dorian, "there is no better time than now."

"It appears we're not the only ones traveling that way," Navien said, pointing west. Three other ships had the lead on them heading toward the island. Blue pennants flew from them.

"Chalicians?" Alodda asked.

"I think so," Rallia said.

"Then give me one of your axes, Rallia," Alodda said, holding out her hand.

Rallia took an axe off her belt and handed it over.

Alodda gave it a few test swings, and gave Rallia an embarrassed look.

The Chalician ships disappeared around the back side of the island.

"Which way?" Rallia asked.

"Let's land directly ahead and gamble going the other direction," Dorian said.

Rallia gave a nod and pulled on a rope. The sail caught wind, and the ship pulled ahead. With her hand on the tiller, the bow cut right toward the shore.

The pebbly beach sloped up out of the water, and Rallia ran the ship aground. Ophedia and Navien leapt off the bow, took hold of a rope thrown to them, and pulled it farther onto shore. Whisper came next unbidden. Alodda and Seriah followed, and Dorian tossed packs ashore before lowering himself down.

They drank the last of their water and Rallia handed out biscuits to each to give them something for their stomachs. The wind sheared past them and up the tower toward the swirling clouds above. Flashes formed in the gray. The top of the tower appeared to have black tendrils slowly creeping down the side.

"Is everyone ready?" Dorian asked.

"As we'll ever be," Ophedia said, Sky Grazer strapped to her back. "What's the plan?"

"Up to the tower," Dorian said, "to look for an entrance."

Rallia gave a nod and began walking up the hill without another word.

Tufts of grass provided handholds where the slope was steepest, and Whisper quickly found easy paths where others could follow. The tower appeared to be made from black stones. Arriving at its base, they saw it to be obsidian, once smooth, the years having blasted its surface. A few of the stones bore signs of shattering, perhaps from the weight of the tower.

"Who built this?" Navien asked.

"I don't know," Dorian said. "It reminds me, in some ways, of the inside of the Oracles of the Crysalas, although they were built inside of craters."

"It slopes more than most towers should," Navien said. "As though it is built up against something."

"Like a crater?" Dorian said.

"Or a reverse crater?" Ophedia jested.

"How would that be possible?" Navien asked, but no one answered.

They circled farther and came upon an outcropping of stones against the side. Rallia crept ahead to look past the stones, then stepped out confidently, motioning for the others to approach.

The open doorway entered the wall and turned to the right, the same direction they had gone.

Navien reached into a satchel and took out a grease torch and entered, crouching down to strike flint, and soon had a flame.

"There are stairs," he called back.

"Then we go up," Dorian said.

A second torch was lit, and Rallia once more led the way. Ophedia and Dorian followed after, then Alodda and Seriah. Navien took up the rear with his torch backlighting them.

"What awaits us?" Alodda murmured.

"I don't know," Seriah said.

"Do you see anything?"

"Purple. Everywhere above. But I don't know what it means."

"Do not dwell on it," Navien said from below. "We press on, and face what we find together."

They traveled up endless steps of obsidian, the walls on either side of the same material. Despite their upward climb, they each had the odd sensation of traveling downward in an endless spiral up the black tower.

51

Riders Raising White

The savage bloodthirstiness of the people across the mountains. Who can fathom? We can surmise, and we can discuss, but we can never understand.

—PATER JIARNGARLO

Bogatyr Guorth Veltyar rode alongside Nichal. The rest of the vityaz had left them at the border between the two Protectorates. In the five days spent raising the camp, Nichal and Guorth had become fast friends. Though from what Jined gathered, Guorth made fast friends with everyone.

Upon stepping off the ferry, and into the Protectorate of the Hammer, Jined was awash with a sense of relief, and he breathed deeply of the air that rushed over the rolling green hills.

"One of the vityaz said that their people were named after Ikhail," Silas said to Didus. "If they follow Grissone, why are they not a part of our church?"

"Because they hold different beliefs than we do. It has been a source of religious contention for centuries."

"Then they are followers of Grissone?"

"They prefer the worship of his prophets over him."

"Why?"

"It may be worth your investigation at the Library at Pariantür," Didus said. "We'll need scholars of their beliefs and peoples in the coming days, if they truly are interested in a discourse with us."

"Perhaps the Bogatyr can answer questions," Silas said.

"He may," Didus said. "Remember that two days ago he said he is no scholar, nor an Exemplar, but ranked high enough to come as the first of many diplomats the Ikhalans will send. Seek to understand our own faith in Grissone. Study well that you may defend your own faith."

Three miles away, the first signal tower came into view as they topped the rise.

"Brother Cävian, the standard, if you will," Nichal ordered.

Cävian pressed past the Prima Pater and lifted the standard high. Loïc stood just behind him. A break in the swiftly moving clouds overhead opened and a ray of light struck the metal. The company remained silent.

After a long while, the light at the top of the tower began to strobe. Didus had out a ledger and charcoal, writing down the tower's message. He handed it to Nichal.

"Welcome Prima Pater," he muttered as he read. "Proceed south to Massif Tower before Pariantür. Signal will precede you."

A cheer went up from the company of Paladins.

Nichal looked up at Jined. "Lead the way, Jined."

Onward they rode. Hymns were sung, and they barely slowed as evening fell. They stayed westward of the line of signal towers that stood every few leagues, and after three days, the top of the Parianti Massif came into view. They followed the road that soon appeared, running from Fozobaça on the coast. Signs of recent travel greeted them, with camps set up in crescent-shaped bowls, where the refugees had stayed each night and cleaned up after themselves. Soon villages belonging to those owing allegiance to the Hammer sprouted up, and news of the passage of refugees only a day or two ahead spread. Hope once more spurred them on. Their road was coming to an end.

They crossed a river, and took the long slope to the rise south of it, atop which stood the Yellow Clay signal tower. From there a better message would go to Massif Tower, and Pariantür not much farther along. A small bastion sat at its base, and a Paladin tending his garden watched them at they came to the top. He was one of the oldest Paladins Jined had ever seen in the Protectorates outside of Pariantür itself. His eyes were gray with blindness—an even odder sight at a watchtower.

"In the name of Grissone, welcome," he said, wiping dirt off his hands, and standing by the gate. He did not seem so blind as his eyes appeared.

"Greeting, Primus," Nichal said, noting the cordons hanging from the old man's robes.

"Who might I say is calling?" the old man asked.

"Acting Prima Pater," Silas announced.

"Ah! Dorian!" the old man replied, a smile forming on his lips. "My old friend!"

"I am afraid not," Nichal said, dismounting and approaching the gate. "Nichal Guess, *Acting* Prima Pater."

"Then Dorian is…" the man said with defeat in his voice.

"He has given me his title and sent me home to Pariantür."

"That brings me more sadness than I can say. I served with him in the Protectorate Wars, you know."

"That was long ago," Nichal said, and took a deep breath, his chin stiffening. "May we send a signal ahead of us?"

"Surely," the old man said, and turned to lead the way to the tower entrance.

Nichal followed, Silas after him, and Jined last. As he came to the door, the old man's hand shot out and grabbed his arm.

"You are touched by Grissone," he said mysteriously.

"I…am," Jined confirmed.

"I can see it."

"But you're blind," Jined said in surprise.

"I was blinded when Grissone showed himself to me in all his glory. Now I only see what is lit by his holiness."

Jined lowered his head. "I believe you."

"You've a road ahead of you, my son," the old man said. "When next you speak to Grissone, ask him when he will visit me again."

"I will," Jined said.

The old man pushed him through the door and shut it behind him.

"What was that about?" Nichal asked as Jined came into the main hall.

"The old man is touched by Grissone, he says. He noticed the same in me."

Nichal cocked an eyebrow, but then turned as a side door opened and another Paladin entered, and gave a salute.

"Pater Segundus," he said.

"Acting Prima Pater now, Primus Gellun," Nichal said, recognizing the man.

"I see," Gellun said stoically. "Yes. I received a message from the towers to the north. Shall we go up to the top of the tower to prepare a signal?"

"Please."

They climbed a spiraling set of stairs to the top. A man sat at a desk, an eye at a spyglass, jotting ticks and dots down on a slate with chalk furiously.

"We shall wait," the Primus said in a quiet voice. "Brother Poledan is receiving."

They waited. The man in the chair turned around, his face ghostly pale.

"Poledan?"

"Primus," he said shakily.

"This is the Acting Prima Pater," Primus Gellun said.

"Oh, thank Grissone," he said, crossing the room and handing Gellun the slate.

"What is it?"

Poledan just motioned to the slate.

Gellun stared for a long moment. "Oh no."

"Primus?" Nichal asked.

Gellun looked at Nichal. "The day that we receive back our castellan...no better hope could be had."

"What is it?" Nichal asked.

"T'Akai. A large force. They entered from the north, apparently traveling by night. They're a day's ride from here and race into the Protectorate directly toward the Massif."

"What?!" Nichal exclaimed. "Why?"

"I am merely the messenger."

"The refugees," Silas hissed.

"You know of them?" Gellun asked.

"We've been trailing them for months now."

"They will reach the Massif by nightfall, I believe."

"Jined. Prepare the company. We ride to intercept."

Jined turned and flew down the stairs, and burst out into the garden.

"We ride!" Jined shouted. "Now!"

Some Paladins had their sleipnirs at the trough, while others awaited their turn.

Jined mounted Tyv next to Bogatyr Guorth.

"What is happening?"

Loïc and Cävian pulled up next to them.

"T'Akai. They entered through the Protectorates and have been advancing by night. They were spotted a day from here. We ride to intercept them."

How many? Loïc asked.

"Enough. They ride toward the refugees."

It has been a long time since we last fought T'Akai, Cävian signed.

"Well, we ride against them again now."

The company rode south, a war hymn driving them on. Nichal caught up within the hour, after giving his message to the signal tower. They topped rise after rise, hoping to gain some sight of invading force or refugee, to no avail, until two hours from setting sun. They topped the final hill leading down into the plains surrounding the Massif.

To the south, the Massif stood as mound upon mound of tree-covered earth, all rising to a row of brown peaks. The refugees moved toward the base, once more within reach. If they could circle the Massif and arrive at the shores of Lago Crysan, then ships to Hamulon would no doubt be on their way across to pick them up and deliver them to the protection of Pariantür.

To the east, across the bowl, a black stain rushed as gnats upon a carcass, moving in a loose line, spread out and crawling across the surface of the plains.

"T'Akai," Nichal said.

"What should we expect?" Didus said.

"Never faced the hordes?" Jined asked.

"No."

"Where vül are cunning, but brutal," Nichal said, "the T'Akai are severe and skilled. Every move is made with calculated intent. They will not toy with you. They will kill you without a thought."

"Their mounts are just as problematic," Jined said.

Didus gave him a look.

"Imagine vül if they had no mind. The crocotta they ride are just so."

"Then let us buy time for the Crysalas with our lives."

The Paladins turned as one and rode hard to intercept the T'Akai. The far edge of the opposing battleline, easily a mile past the closest T'Akian raider, pulled far ahead, with uncanny speed.

The massif was only a few short miles away now, rising far above them in the distance. The line of T'Akai was as far from the mountains as they were.

Jined rode out front, Didus at his side.

"I count three hundred," Nichal shouted from behind them.

Jined made a hand signal confirming understanding, and leaned forward.

"This may be it!" Didus shouted.

"It may," Jined said. "They ride in our land. Pariantür must already know and will send help."

"We cannot count on that," Didus said.

"But we can count on faith."

Didus drove his mount ahead.

"Grissone," Jined muttered, "do not forsake us. Bring help. Bring relief."

On they rode.

They came within a mile of the T'Akai, who now rode directly at them. A handful rode straight for the Massif. One rider in particular did not pay them any attention, but rode far ahead and by themselves toward the mountains.

"Shall I?" Jined asked.

"No!" Nichal said. "We must trust the Paladames to defend themselves."

Half the distance was closed.

Then half that, leaving only a quarter mile. Jined could see and hear them.

They bore green flesh, like hrelgrens, but a darker green akin to evergreen trees. Their mouths too, were similar to hrelgrens, but with sharper beak-like upper lips. They also bore a pair of opposable thumbs like hrelgrens, but it was there the similarities ended. They stood a head taller than most men, and that was not considering the tall black horns that rose sharply off the top of their skulls. Their eyebrows were bony knots, and from their cheeks a pair of gnarled horns curved down before curling forward. Their feet ended in black hooves the same color keratin as their black horns.

They held in one hand long-handled axes, as utilitarian as they were exquisitely crafted. Their other hand rested on the shoulders of their mounts.

The crocotta bore short and powerful hind legs and long forelegs. Their powerful heads sat lower on their chests, on a stout neck. Their slavering, foreshortened face ended in a bar of gnashing teeth, fused in a line. From their heads, a ridge of short hair ran down their spine, terminating in a muscled, but short tail, covered in the same bristly hairs.

The riders lay upon their mounts' back, their chests upon the shoulder ridge of the creature underneath.

With the clamoring rumble of the crocottas calling to one another, the T'Akai hissed and gnashed orders at each other in their unknowable speech.

Two hundred yards away, Cävian rode out ahead, Standard of Grissone held high.

"Paladins of the Hammer!" Nichal announced. "Hymn of Deliverance!"

As one, they raised their voices high, and the T'Akai across from them suddenly halted, dropped from their mounts, and dropped to their knees, laying their axes before them, and bowing their heads to the ground.

The paladinial line faltered then; a hundred yards away from the T'Akai, the charge collapsed, and they stopped.

Nichal pulled up short next to Cävian, and held a hand up for silence.

Only the wind made a sound. The T'Akai did not move. Jined watched Nichal and Cävian consult. But they did not advance.

One T'Akah finally raised his head, but did not rise. He looked down the line of his fellow warriors, nodded to himself, and looked Nichal in the eye. He motioned to his mount. All of the crocotta were well-behaved, and had dropped to their own haunches, following their masters' guidance. The one T'Akah rose finally and walked to his mount, and took from its side a white wooden signal and raised it respectfully to Nichal. Then, with his other hand, he took hold of his shirt and removed it along with a bandolier of knives. Having bared his chest, he took three ceremonial steps forward. He waited for just as long before taking three more. He came to within fifty yards and did not move again.

Nichal stepped down from his sleipnir, and Cävian joined him.

The Prima Pater looked back at Jined, then turned to cross to the T'Akah.

"Interesting turn of events," someone said next to him.

Jined looked to his left and smiled.

"Brother Hammer," Jined said cautiously.

Didus and Loïc were on Jined's other side. Brother Hammer

had appeared between Jined and Guorth.

"I should like to know what they're saying," Guorth said, offhandedly.

"Do you now?" Hammer asked.

"Would it be too much trouble?" Jined asked.

"Not at all."

Suddenly, despite the distance and wind, they could hear Nichal muttering to Cävian as they walked stoically across the field.

"They raised the banner in good faith," Nichal muttered. "Let us be respectful, but very much on our guard."

Silence. If Cävian signed anything, no one knew.

"I do not know," Nichal replied. "I know of no time they've ever parlayed for negotiation."

Silence.

They came to stand within a few short paces of the T'Akah.

"By Grissone, god of faith and man, you have raised a white flag, and we respect it so long as you explain," Nichal said.

"We come in good faith," the T'Akah rasped, speaking words practiced but unfamiliar to him. "On dire mission, blessed by the priests of Ki Rin Yu and Krisnya."

Nichal paused, then started, "Ah! Kea'Rinoul and Crysania. Thank you, Cävian."

"Yes," the T'Akah said. "As you say." He bowed at the waist. "I am Emissary Gahn zar'Tlain, escort to high priestess Vuduin eb'Gatha."

"I am Prima Pater Nichal Guess of Pariantür."

"We must apologize for this sudden invasion of your lands," Emissary zar'Tlain said.

"Apologize?" Nichal said. "T'Akai raiding within our lands is nothing new."

"From the Iroche peoples, yes," zar'Tlain said. "I do not come from that savage stock."

"I do not understand?"

"Beyond the mountains to the east there are many lands. Many peoples as well."

"Why after all of these years do you finally seek a discourse?" Nichal asked.

"The Iroche assured me that they have been in continual conversation with your people."

Nichal did not reply.

"They have assured the empire that it has been in continual discourse over the past two centuries."

"Centuries?" Nichal replied. "Then you acknowledge and approve of their involvement in the Wars seventy years ago? In their continual raids and bloodshed since then?"

"I assure you, I know of no war seven decades ago. The Iroche rode against your people in this?"

"Our order has stood against the T'Akai and your raids for a millennia. It is a constant strife that knows no end."

"Then we have trespassed to great risk to our lives."

"You crossed our plains, by night, without that knowledge? I doubt that."

"Your Eastern Council advised us on our mission to do so."

"Eastern Council?" Nichal replied.

"In Kalidon. The Order of the Rod tells us that for Priestess eb'Gatha to reach your oracle we should traverse by night, and even then, we would be risking death. You are known as a violent order."

Nichal scoffed. "We defend all men with our hammers, against those that would shed blood mercilessly."

"The Iroche are a bloodthirsty people, indeed. That they have lied to our empire disturbs me. It shall cost them dearly in the council of Tak and Kah. Yet, it is not surprising. Our people are a people of blood. To die in battle is so very great an honor, regardless of our bloodline."

"I should ask you then to state your purpose for traveling here. If you've a further desire for discourse, you will be quarantined until our Order can determine what to do."

"I humbly thank you," zar'Tlain said. "But our mission has been successful to the best of our capabilities now."

"How so?"

"My kin behind me, all my own descendants, have risked their lives for the honor of escorting the Priestess to the Oracle. Even now, she has reached her destination. With your permission, I shall retreat, and leave back for our lands."

"That you have come this far," Nichal said, "I cannot let you just leave. You and your brethren have seen more of our lands than any T'Akai in the present day."

"What would you have us do, to spare our lives?"

"You will submit to be escorted to a bastion. You will be provided for, but you will be our prisoners until we can decide what to do with you."

"On behalf of my clan, I accept."

"Good," Brother Hammer muttered.

"That they agree?" Jined muttered.

"That Nichal did not just order their deaths."

"What did he mean the Eastern Council?"

"Do you think Pariantür my only followers?"

"Did he mean the Ikhalans?" Jined said.

"We've not interacted with T'Akai," Guorth said.

"Then who is the emissary talking about?" Jined asked.

Grissone merely winked at him.

Nichal had turned back and ridden toward them, leaving the T'Akah where he stood.

He pulled up to Jined.

"Apparently, this entire T'Akian force comes from an entirely different faction than the ones we often exchange blows with, and they are a distraction for a single priestess to go to the Oracle. Loïc and Cävian, I want you to ride to the Oracle Bastion. You're to see that the Crysalas are safe, and then return to us. When you have returned, we shall proceed to Pariantür."

The twins nodded.

"Pater Koel, I'm going to ask you to take twenty Paladins as escort to the Old Kiln Bastion. Do you know it?"

"I believe so."

"Good. You'll sequester the T'Akai there as guests and await orders. You may interact, and begin building a diplomatic relationship with them."

"Yes, Prima Pater."

"The rest of you, we ride to catch up with the refugees. We'll see that they are provided for on the Lago Crysan at Hamulon, so they can be integrated into Parianti lands. Fall out."

Pater Koel selected his men, then dismounted and walked out to speak with the emissary. Nichal turned to Jined. Brother Hammer was gone again.

"Before you feel a need to repeat what you learned," Jined said, "we all heard it."

"Oh?"

"Grissone showed up, and obliged when I asked."

"I see. What do you think?"

"I think we've entered an interesting time," Jined said.

"That T'Akai would seek to speak with us is odd enough,"

Nichal said. "To learn that they have their own factions is astonishing, but not surprising."

"I agree."

"Now what trouble waits for us at Pariantür?"

"As we face our own factions and problems?"

"I'd also like to figure out what Eastern Faction we didn't know about."

"And of course, the Ikhalans."

"Yes. I suspect we've entered a new era," Nichal said. "I just hope that we can survive the flood of changes these new times bring."

52

Symbolic Life

The sap of life that binds the sisters from all cultures is strong. That you do not see that gives me pause.

—SISTER REVA DONNIS

The refugees had broken into song as they came around the base of the Massif and into view of Lago Crysan beyond. Fisher's Island blocked the view to the Port of Hamulon and Pariantür beyond, but Katiam knew it was there, within reach.

"Rosston is just down that road," Lutea Calimbrise said.

"The caravan will precede us, and begin the crossing of the Lago, if they can requisition boats," Astrid said.

"They deserve the rest and will welcome it," Lutea said.

Astrid nodded. "Katiam and I go to the Oracle."

"As do I," Jurgon said.

Esenath had taken her satchel from her sleipnir. "You did not think you would leave us here," she said.

"We have reached our destination, and do not know where it takes us after this," Katiam said.

Behind Esenath, both Onelie and Little Maeda stood shoulder to shoulder.

"Katiam," Astrid said, "I think they all mean to come with us."

"We do not," Lutea said from atop the wagon, Narah next to

her. "Our journey with you ends here. Someone needs to see the refugees to Pariantür, and both Narah and I have studies to get back to."

Narah stepped to Little Maeda and placed a gloved hand on her. The girl turned and gave her a warm embrace. They whispered something to each other, and then parted.

The others said their farewells to Lutea and Narah, and then turned toward the path, cutting up into the mountain.

It was a short canyon, only a hundred yards long, which came out to an echoing courtyard outside a paladinial bastion. It appeared derelict, the door entering the stone building shut and locked.

Jurgon pulled on a cord and a bell somewhere deep within resounded. After a long while, he pulled it again.

On the third try, someone called out from inside for them to be patient.

Finally, the bar on the other side of the door slid, and the door cracked open, revealing the face of an old man. "Hello?"

"Greetings in the name of Grissone," Jurgon said. "And by Crysania and her purity."

"What do you want?" the old man asked. He was not rude, but appeared genuinely confused.

"We have journeyed from the west to visit the Oracle."

"It is closed. It has been for some time."

"We still must visit the shrine," Jurgon said.

"I can't allow that. The Crysalas forbid it."

Katiam stepped forward. "I am Katiam Borreau, great niece of the Matriarch Superioris. She is no longer with us, but in a vision instructed me to journey eastward. I must visit the Oracle."

"We really ought to consult with Pariantür," the old man said, considering. "It is deemed dangerous to go to the Oracle now. Women have died. Disappeared."

"I was one of them," Katiam said. "But I returned."

"Well, I really shouldn't."

"Brother," Jurgon said, "perhaps you recognize me? I am Jurgon Upona, the Prima Pater's Seneschal. I remember you. You were honored two years ago as a veteran of the Protectorate Wars: Primus Gevelib."

The old man smiled at Jurgon remembering his name. "Of course I remember that. I'm old, not forgetful. If the Prima Pater has sent you, then of course you may proceed."

DREAD KNIGHT

Sound shot up the canyon from whence they came.

They turned as one as into the canyon came a beast, teeth bared and slavering. Atop it sat a veiled figure, the forehead obviously topped with a pair of horns.

Jurgon stepped out in front of the others, hammer at the ready. Astrid, Esenath, and Little Maeda took out their maces and came to stand with him.

"Back!" Jurgon shouted as the beast pulled up short.

The figure atop it dismounted, ignoring their threats. The figure turned to the mount, whispered something in the creature's ear, and patted its shoulder. It turned, gave a hesitant glance at its rider, then shot back down the canyon.

The veiled figured turned back to them.

"I said stay back, T'Akah!" Jurgon roared.

The old man from the bastion came to stand next to him, hammer used like a cane.

"You need not do this," Jurgon said to Gevelib.

"Nonsense, young fool. I am sworn to protect this bastion from all trouble."

The veiled figure stood only thirty feet from them. They finished adjusting a satchel across their form, held up a hand in a sign of peace, and reached up to take the veil from their face.

"No sudden moves," Astrid said.

"What is a T'Akah doing here of all places?" Jurgon asked no one in particular.

The veil came away and revealed a face Katiam knew. She stepped through the Paladames and cut the distance in half.

"Vuduin?" Katiam asked.

"Sister," the T'Akah said in perfect common tongue.

Katiam crossed to stand directly in front of the T'Akah now. The others murmured behind her.

"I have followed the commands we were given by the Mother," Vuduin said. "I have found you."

"I do not know what a proper greeting is between a human and T'Akah, but will you allow me to embrace you?"

Vuduin gave a solemn nod.

Katiam put her arms around the creature, choking down the fear that ran through her body. The Rotha strapped across her breast quivered.

"Is your Iwarat safe?" Vuduin asked.

"So long as you swear to its safety, then yes."

"I swear it," Vuduin whispered, then turned to the rest of them. "I swear to the safety of the Iwarat! I, High Priestess of Krisnya, Vuduin eb'Gatha come in peace, not in war. I swear my life to this Paladame and the precious treasure she carries."

"This is a rather unprecedented moment," the old Primus said. "I'm not entirely sure what to do."

The sound of hooves resounded once more up the canyon, and two riders came into view—Loïc and Cävian, the latter bearing the standard of Grissone.

The old Paladin wrung his hands at the sight. "The standard!"

The twins pulled up short as their eyes fell on Vuduin.

"It's alright," Katiam said, holding up a hand in peace.

You are safe? Loïc signed.

Yes, Astrid signed back. *Be at peace.*

They dismounted and crossed the space.

Peace has been made with the T'Akai who escorted the priestess, Cävian said.

"We're to journey to the Oracle," Katiam said.

Nichal sent us to ensure you are safe, and your journey blessed, Loïc said.

"It is blessed," Katiam said. "But please see to the refugees who head to Lago Crysan."

Of course, Loïc replied. He turned to Astrid. *We have been trailing you all of this time.*

Jurgon told us, Astrid signed.

The twins turned to notice Jurgon for the first time.

"I'll continue journeying with them," Jurgon said.

You'll keep them safe? Loïc asked.

Jurgon nodded.

Loïc turned back to Astrid. *Be safe.*

I shall, Astrid said.

And I shall pray for your health and safety every day.

Astrid put a friendly hand on his shoulder. He touched her shoulder, turned, and walked back to his mount.

Cävian approached Katiam and Astrid.

"Cävian," Astrid said in a low tone, "I'm not sure we'll see you and Loïc again."

I know, Cävian signed. *I'm not sure Brother would willingly admit that, though. He still cares for you.*

"I know," Astrid muttered. "He needs to forget me."

I doubt he ever will, Cävian said.

"Then please see he moves on. As best you can."

Cävian said nothing, his hands wringing the Standard of Grissone. *Why did you never tell him yourself? You knew, but you did not tell him to find someone else?*

"Because I was selfish. I've meant to, ever since Mahn Fulhar. There just never seemed to be a right time."

Nor would there ever be. I am not happy with this.

"Nor I. I'm sorry. But let us allow him to stay in his ignorance. He doesn't need to know that I have always known."

This is a heavier burden than the standard.

"I know. I am sorry for that."

Cävian turned to Katiam.

Goodbye, Katiam. I shall ask the Crysalas to pray for you, wherever it is you go.

"Thank you, Cävian," Katiam said, and gave him a warm embrace.

He returned to his mount and Loïc held the standard as his brother climbed up. They gave a quick wave, and rode back up the canyon.

The old Paladin now had the door open, Jurgon next to him. The women entered and made their way through halls and up stairs, and finally came out to an overlook on a cliff atop the bastion, looking out over the plain. Two miles away, a line of T'Akai parted from a group of Paladins and slowly began to ride away, a handful of sleipnirs leading them to the north.

"I think that's Nichal," Astrid said, pointing.

The twins could be seen crossing the plain toward the Paladins assembled there, the Standard of Grissone glinting in the sun.

"None have fallen," Vuduin said. "This pleases me."

"Why is that?"

"We came in peace. The Tlain clan offered themselves in sacrifice to see me here."

"Why did you come?" Katiam asked.

"I left the Iwarat in my care, and intended to travel through the Veld itself, from another Oracle near our temple. There is much within that realm that would have prevented my passage. I could not be sure of my safe arrival. Now that we are here, we can journey along that path together."

"Within the Veld?" Katiam asked.

Jurgon approached to listen, but did not come too close, the sight of the T'Akah still giving him pause. "You've a way to go into the Veld?"

"We shall consult at the Oracle above," Vuduin said. "If there is any way into the Veld, it will be here at the Oracle."

"Then let us begin our ascent," Astrid said. "We will, of course, follow the Path as it is laid before us."

"Then this Oracle, too, has a Prescribed path?" Vuduin asked.

"Of course," Astrid said. "Just as the Oracle to the west, and the one in Hannica."

"This is not my Oracle," Vuduin said. "I shall follow your guidance."

They walked to the arch in the stone. The old Paladin had gone back to his bastion, leaving those journeying to the top alone.

Onelie and Little Maeda dug through packs and took out travel tack at Esenath's instructions, and began doling them out.

"Night will fall soon," Esenath said, handing food to the T'Akah. "Even if we do not rest and press through, we will not reach the top until tomorrow evening. We must eat."

The Priestess nodded and took a bite of the dry tack. She did not show a sign of displeasure, but eyed Katiam.

"May I see the Iwarat?"

Katiam smiled. "Yes."

She unbundled the Rotha from her chest. The vines unfurled from Larohz's form. The T'Akah held her hands to her own chest, wringing in pleasure.

"She appears healthy," Vuduin said.

"I have seen to that," Esenath said. "I am a botanist."

"What are you?" Larohz asked.

"It speaks?!" Vuduin said.

"Yes. Does not yours?" Katiam asked.

"No. She has her demands, but not through words."

"Loosetongue Tea is what opened up her ability to speak," Astrid said.

"I do not know this word," Vuduin said.

"It is a flower," Esenath said. "I shall show it to you when there is time."

"We've plenty of time on our journey," Vuduin said. "I look forward to comparing our discoveries."

"As do I," Esenath said, "and to meeting your Rotha."

"You know other Rotha?" Larohz said. "Sisters?"

"I do," Vuduin said. "The Iwarat shall be most pleased to meet you."

"Has Sister a name?"

"Only Iwarat," Vuduin said.

"I would like to meet Iwarat," Larohz said.

"Then let us begin our long journey to meet her together," Katiam said, turning back to the stone archway.

"Have you made this journey before?" Vuduin asked Katiam.

"Several times, with the Matriarch Superioris."

"Am I to make journey?" Larohz asked.

"Yes," Katiam said kneeling down to the small creature. "You will walk in front of me. You may ask for help, but it is important that while you journey, you think upon the journey."

"I do not understand."

"We are Crysalas. In our aspects and life, we emulate and observe purity. It draws us closer to Crysania, and gives us a glimpse of her character. We begin a journey up a Fated Path. The three stages are meant to show three aspects of Purity. These three tell a very specific story. That of life and death, and the victory that they lead to in a life given to purity and holiness."

"I do not know Crysania," Larohz whistled.

"Crysania created you," Vuduin said, kneeling down next to her.

"Made me?"

"The gods each made people. Crysania made all of the flowers."

"Then I am only a flower?"

"You are not only a flower. The Iwarat are the First Flowers."

"Did she make you? And Mama?"

"No. The T'Akai were made by their god—Ki Rin Yu. He made the grenaoral, from which came the T'Akai, the hrelgrens, and the accursed gheronarl."

"And Mama?"

"Grissone made men and women," Katiam said.

"Then why follow Crysania?"

"I follow Crysania," Vuduin said. "She calls many females of all peoples."

"Then I will journey up Fated Path to follow her."

The little Rotha turned toward the archway and led them through.

The first stage, the Solitude, led through a tight canyon, with high, sheer walls. Every few steps it turned again, winding its way along, isolating each person to their own thoughts.

"What am I to think?" Larohz asked Katiam, who helped her up the steps the Rotha could not climb.

"This portion of the path represents the Path of Life we each walk. No matter who we meet, our Path is our own, and we walk it alone."

"But we are not alone," Larohz said.

"You're right. We walk together."

"I mean life," the little creature said matter-of-factly.

"Oh?"

"Life is all around us. Everywhere. I smell it."

Katiam breathed deeply and began to notice the green smell. The Rotha was right. It was everywhere.

They walked for hours, and Katiam started to notice the sound of birds on the wind and small insects crawling on the walls, barely taking note of her. Before she knew it, the path had come to an end, and they all stood before the next portal, one that led into darkness.

"We can stop and rest," Astrid said, "or we continue. The second stage, the Judgment, is all within the dark cave ahead. Time will be meaningless, but it is not a long Stage, even if it will feel like it."

"The sooner we reach the top, the better," Esenath said.

"I don't like the looks of this one," Onelie said, eyeing the darkness.

"This is my least favorite as well," Katiam said. "But it must be done."

"What does this Judgment represent?" Vuduin asked.

"Death," Astrid said, "and the journey through Noccitan to be Judged."

"Come," Little Maeda said to Onelie, taking her hand. "Let us journey there together."

They went first. Esenath and Jurgon followed with Vuduin close behind. Katiam walked toward the portal with the Rotha and turned to see Astrid standing there.

"Astrid?"

The Paladame stood unmoved. Katiam came back to stand with her. "Is something wrong?"

"I've made the journey up this Fated Path many times. I've never been bothered by the Judgment. It seemed so far away and unreal, that I never let it touch me. But now?"

Katiam remained silent.

"After Killian died. After that monster held my life in his hands, I've felt the tentative call of Noccitan. I've cried myself to sleep in terror of it many times. I've often wanted Noccitan. I've wanted to get lost in its tunnels, and never see another soul for all of time."

"And now?"

"Now I have purpose," Astrid said, glancing to the Rotha with a faint smile. "I want to see her grow. I want to protect her precious life and her innocence. Her purity."

"And Loïc?" Katiam asked.

"A constant friend," Astrid said, a flush rising across her face.

Katiam waited.

"I was foolish for not releasing him years ago. I lied to myself, thinking he was merely a friend who wished well of me. Now, as we leave, I'm faced with the fact that we'll never see each other again. I regret the damage I've done. But I also fear that if we did return to Pariantür, I might give into a relationship with him that I would never truly be a part of."

"And so our leaving," Katiam pried, "is this you running away?"

"No," Astrid said, with a bitter smile. "This is not running. Full of regrets as it may be, this is following a calling—to revile the death I desired, and see the Rotha to her destination."

"Then let's journey together," Katiam said. "Even through Noccitan, if we must."

Astrid gave a nod and strode forward into the darkness.

The cave at times ascended and descended, through winding tunnels and wide open caverns. Esenath and Little Maeda held torches leading them through. The shadows that scratched at the corners of Katiam's vision gave her several startles, and one time Onelie screamed at a cast shadow jumping when Little Maeda tripped. Both fell to laughter. After many, many hours in the cool of the earth, they came out into the next opening of the sky, the stars far above vivid in the night.

"Well?" Katiam asked Astrid.

"Honestly, I was bored."

Katiam laughed. "I can't say the same."

"Well, I much prefer your company in the light, than walking alone in that darkness."

"Me, too," Katiam said.

"And me," the Rotha said, coming and touching Astrid's calf with a leafy hand.

Astrid knelt down and stroked the little creature's head and back.

"Come on, Little Rose. This next stage is my favorite."

She picked up Larohz and strode forward into the next stage, the Glory, without hesitation.

Katiam followed, and the others soon after.

It was a simple canyon that rose gently, switching back every few hundred feet. After one switchback, Esenath raised her voice in a song to the stars. It was a wordless song, but her voice began to reverberate off the walls, not just in an echo, but in a pitched resonance that struck the sandstone walls like a bell.

Astrid and Katiam joined in with harmonies. Onelie almost took her lute out, but Little Maeda stopped her. It was tradition that only voices be raised. For hours they walked, singing with each other. The Rotha provided her own whistle, and Jurgon a rich baritone. Vuduin sang with a shrill, nasally voice that provided a thrumming accent to everyone else. They arrived at a large bowl-like section, each totally given in to the song, and all around them the song rose in crescendo as the sun peeked up over the horizon, through the canyon, and struck with such brilliance that each faltered, the echoes dying, not in an ending, but in awe.

The sun shown against crystalline rocks in the walls, and they walked the last hour in silence, coming out to the top, and entrance to the Oracle itself, satisfied in the journey they had taken.

The door to the Oracle was unlocked, and Astrid pulled it open, entering first.

Despite it being so near to Pariantür, it was not as large of a monastery as the one in Mahndür. At the top sat a simple bastion dormitory and kitchen. The spiraling set of stairs led down to the hole set in the bottom, and Astrid led the way down to its frame.

A tight set of stairs spiraled into the hole, and came out on a short tunnel terminating in an iron grate, a chain and lock across it.

Jurgon walked to the lock and took out a key.

"How do you have a key?" Katiam asked.

"Seneschal to Dorian Mür, remember? I hold one of the skeleton keys that opens nearly every lock under Parianti control."

With a click, it opened, and the chain came free.

The women entered a nearly identical cavern as the Oracle in the west. Alcoves with small crystal rosebuds, many now missing, circled a basin, in which sat black sand. This Dweol too, had died.

"What do we do now?" Astrid asked.

Katiam placed a finger to her lips and pointed to Larohz, who knelt beside the edge of the pit and appeared to be crying, a pitiful whimpering whistle sobbing from her.

53

MANIFESTED DREAMS

Whether sleepless or in Veld, on and on, the night goes on.

I lay with thoughts tormenting me, I cannot find the morning dawn.

— ESSTANTÉ VE LA DÓR, POET OF MORRIEGO

The Dread Knight moved as Searn had in life. He did not stalk, but moved about with a casual air of curiosity. He moved from the gate to the edge several times, looking down the height without any fear. He often considered his new body, and the gauntlets on his arms. He gave no attention to Hanen watching him, curled up, half way from the gate to the opposte edge.

Hanen brushed aside small black tendrils that rose from the violet-hued sand that poured out of the gate as they reached up to touch him. Across the top of the tower Ymbrys stood against an edge unperturbed by the height.

Loth could be seen through the gate, still entirely enshrouded in wyrms. Gvelindar had Bou encased in sand and forced him to move the stuff like an auroch, pushing and pulling piles of oneirion through the gate. So much had been forced through that it piled up and poured off the tower on all sides, and down its edge.

Hanen peeked out over the edge and saw for the first time a set of stairs leading up the side, made visible by the sand washing over its surface. On those stairs, figures moved up the side—Praetors of the Chalice, weapons at the ready.

Hanen turned back to Searn, his Khamntyr skull draped with the boneshroud giving him a nightmarish appearance. From the depths of the shadows in his eye sockets a darker blackness lay. That piercing black finally fell on Hanen, after hours of ignoring him.

The Dread Knight stalked over to Hanen, who stood barely at chest height, and looked down.

"I should thank you," Searn said, his voice as dark and hollow as it was at the Rose Convent when he had last truly lived. "But you did owe this to me."

"Owed you?" Hanen asked.

"You betrayed me. You used flames to keep the shades from me, and it resulted in my death. You could have walked away, though. You could have let that be it, and who knows who might have carried my shade, or how many years it would have taken for this to play out. Yet here we are."

"If you aren't going to thank me or spare me, kill me now and be done with it."

"Oh, no. Why would I do that? You're going to follow me—act as my witness, and be a bait for the dark gods that seem so fascinated with you. I will see everything burned down, and after you see the gods dead at my feet, I'll kill you."

"To what end?"

"Because I can," Searn said nonchalantly. "Men of the past sought power and to rise above their station. I have been given it. Those born into power need not rise to it, they need only do what they please, and use it to their means. I've no physical desires. Certainly not in this impenetrable body. The only desire I have is to see the gods beg for mercy, and die."

Hanen stared at Searn, emptiness consuming him.

"There is no fear in your eyes," Searn said.

"What do I have to fear? You promise me death after my world is gone. What difference is there between now and then? That cursed black metal has already killed those I love. I just don't care if you burn the rest of the world down. Especially if there is no hope."

Searn laughed. "Exactly! Hope died when the last link in the chain of the boneshroud was completed. This is no deceit of

Achanerüt. This is not even the madness of Kos-Yran, for something even he could not fathom was made by a mere mortal. The gods were dealt a crippling blow that they will never recover from. I am no pawn of theirs. Only despair made manifest. A dread despair. It would fill me with a glee to match this rising elation, if I didn't feel as hollowed out as you do now."

"Lord Dread," Gvelindar said, crossing the sand to Searn's side. He indicated across the tower to where ten Praetors crawled up over the edge, weapons in hand.

Searn turned fully toward them, and stood up to full height. The Praetors crowded together upon seeing him, and set their weapons to ready.

Searn lifted a gauntlet, and black tendrils rose from the sand, up the boots of one unassuming Praetor. The others backed away, and then seemed to realize how high they were, and pressed forward, away from the edge. The tendrils sunk into the man's ankles and he cried out in sudden gasping pain, then fell to his knees with a scream that cut off in silence. His eyes burned purple, and he rose, a new fire in his eyes. He turned, weapon fallen, and took hold of the nearest comrade, and threw him across the sand. Tendrils whipped up over that man's body and soon he too rose, purple fire in his eyes.

The others screamed and retreated toward the stairs, but Gvelindar lifted his own hands and the sand itself rose in the forms of men who shambled toward two Praetors who had been forced from the others.

One Chalician thrust his spear through the advancing sandy figure. Purple exploded from its back but did not slow its advance. They cried out as arms enclosed them, holding them in place as additional black tendrils rose and took their minds from them as well.

The final Chalician dropped to his knees, purple fire burning in his eyes.

Searn turned back to Hanen.

"You see? I could do the same to you. Lock you in a nightmare, in a half-life, and force you to participate. I like the idea of having you watch, fully aware."

He looked across the tower to Ymbrys. "That qavyl, however."

Searn stalked toward Ymbrys and stopped halfway across from him, hesitating.

"What trick do you have up your sleeve, qavyl?"

"Trick?" Ymbrys asked. "Why trick what can't be fooled?"

"Don't bother with flattery," Searn said. "You've been twisting my words, trying to change my opinions since the day we first met, and I've grown tired of talking to you."

He raised his gauntleted hands, and the purple sand began to bend to his will.

Suddenly, up over the lip of the tower came the first glimmer of hope Hanen had felt in what seemed like an eternity of darkness.

The Rotha continued its low, moaning whimper, knelt on its knees, with leafy hands clasped as though in prayer. It swayed ever so slightly.

"She has been like that for hours now," Astrid said.

"And she may yet, for hours still," Katiam said. "I think she mourns the death of the Dweol."

"She mourns a mother she was never destined to know," Vuduin said.

"Her mother?"

"The Rotha, they are the seeds of the Dweol itself. Of several Dweol, but Dweol nonetheless."

"How do you know this?"

"We've plenty of scholarship backing it up," Vuduin said. "Nearly all of it was confirmed when the Dweol at my Oracle shattered, and the Rotha in my possession awakened."

"Where is she?"

"She is currently in the care of my sister."

Jurgon and Esenath came from the other side of the room.

"We've searched every alcove," Esenath said, holding up a wooden bowl. "Two smaller Dweol buds remained."

"I hope it shall be enough," Vuduin said.

Larohz stopped her mourning hum suddenly and turned to Katiam. "Why did she die?"

"So that you could finally live," Vuduin answered.

"But why?"

"That is something we shall seek to answer together, Little Rose," Katiam said.

"Iwarat," Vuduin addressed the little flower child, "do you

understand what the four worlds are?"

"Four worlds?"

"Kallattai, Veld, Lomïn, and Noccitan," Onelie said.

"Noccitan? Like the cave?"

"It represented Noccitan, yes," Astrid said.

"There are four worlds," Vuduin explained. "Four places separate from each other, yet, close. In places such as this oracle, they are closer. The Dweol had vines connecting the Veld here, and in other oracles, to the other worlds. You have journeyed here because we have need to travel through the Veld."

"Why?" Larohz asked.

"So we may pass beyond the lands we live in, into ones unknown," Katiam said. "To find others like you."

"I should like that."

"We need you to open up the portal for us," Vuduin said.

"How would I do that?"

"By using some of the power your Mother left you. Until you are able to make that power for yourself," Vuduin said, placing the bowl down next to the Rotha. "Esenath, have you prepared the concoction as I instructed?"

"What is this?" Katiam asked.

"Moonglow flowers," Esenath said. "I've prepared a bitter tea. It is supposed to help us."

"Is it safe?"

"Moonglow is not toxic. Harmless." Esenath offered the vessel to the T'Akah.

Vuduin took a sip. "It shall help those who have not journeyed in Veld before to do so safely."

Esenath moved from person to person and gave them a drink from the bottle she had prepared. She had cut it with mead, and the bittersweet drink puckered Katiam's mouth as she drank.

Vuduin took a petal of moonglow and gave it to the Rotha. "Consume this. Then take a crystal from the bowl."

Larohz did as she was told and the white petal disappeared into her bloom. She did not say anything, but reached into the bowl and took up a crystal. It disappeared as well. The bloom head was thrown back and pink light shot in a beam to the ceiling. The Rotha's whistles rose in crescendo. Along the wall, unseen crystals exploded in pink light.

"Quickly," Esenath said to Jurgon and the younger women. "Gather what you can!"

They rushed to the points of light and gathered more of the crystal blooms.

"What is happening?" Katiam shouted.

"She is using the power of the Dweol," Vuduin said.

The Rotha curled over and the beam tore down through the black sand in the basin, blowing it out of the way in a parting path. At the bottom of the basin a hole was unveiled. Beyond that hole, a purple sky.

The glowing pink light pouring from Larohz snuffed out.

"Now," Vuduin said, "Let us journey together into the Veld."

The last boat came across the water and shoremen took hold of the rope the boat's owner threw to them. Loïc and Cävian began helping those in the boat up to join the others along the pier. Across the square, Nichal stood speaking with two men wearing the garb of the carter's guild. They sent a pair of boys next to them off in another direction, and followed at their own pace after.

Nichal crossed to Jined.

"They've enough carts to carry all of the men and women out of Hamulon to Minuvol for establishment."

"How long will they remain refugees there?"

"That will depend on them," Nichal said. "Some may leave from there to go elsewhere in the world. Others may swear fealty to the Hammer and come here to Hamulon, or elsewhere."

The echoing sound of shod hooves rang from up a street.

"It would seem Pariantür finally sent someone to greet us."

The other Paladins quickly gathered, and Cävian set the Standard into his stirrup as they waited.

From over the cobbled rise several squadrons of Paladins appeared, with a single Paladin riding out front that Jined, Nichal, and the twins recognized—the stern Chaplain of Pariantür, Hiram van Höllebon, whom the Prima Pater had sent back from the journey early with the disgraced Pater Gui in tow.

The Paladins stopped at the edge of the square, filling the street behind them by the hundreds, their hammers at attention.

Another Paladin appeared next to Hiram. He was almost as tall as Jined, and built like an auroch.

"Primus Bevril de Gorm," Nichal said, "who I assigned my duties as castellan when we left."

"Paladins!" Bevril roared. "Salute!"

"Hammer! Hammer! Hammer!" The entire company roared and lifted their hammers in the air toward Nichal. Then, with a snap, their hammers returned to attention.

Hiram dismounted and crossed the square on his own. He gave a salute and then a curt bow to Nichal.

"Welcome back, Pater Segundus," Hiram said.

"Chaplain Höllebon," Nichal said.

"Nichal Guess has been given authority by Dorian Mür to be Acting Prima Pater until a general election can be taken," Jined said.

"Of course. But if the Prima Pater has passed, then all Pater Segundii enter pillory until the election can determine which shall be made the new Prima Pater. Out of respect for Pater Segundus Athmor, Pîr, and Emiro, what would you have us call you?"

"Pater Segundus Pír is no longer with us," Nichal said.

"Then we've multiple promotions to fill," Hiram said casually. "Shall we see you off to Pariantür?"

"There is much to speak of," Nichal said. "We spoke to a delegate of the T'Akai that must be answered by our diplomats. That will need to be arranged by nightfall."

"T'Akai?" Hiram asked. "We received a message that there were some spotted. I know that Bevril was preparing to go and meet them with steel, but then the news of your arrival came."

Nichal turned to Bevril. "We can convene and I'll give you details before you act."

"I shall see it arranged," Hiram said.

"As castellan of Pariantür and Pater Segundus, I will," Nichal said more firmly.

"Respectfully," Hiram said, "Parianti law would have you making few decisions while you're on trial."

"Trial?"

"In the investigation of the passing of authority," Hiram said.

"Are you arresting me?" Nichal asked.

"Pater Segundus," Hiram chided, "that would not be an appropriate way to look at this. You are, by tradition, on pillory, as are the other Pater Segundii, until all has been determined."

Nichal looked to Jined.

Jined shrugged.

Hiram had turned on his sleipnir already and begun riding back to the collected Paladins. Bevril gave the command and the company turned in place in a parade form, to begin going back up the street.

The company ahead parted for them, and Nichal, Jined, and the twins passed through to the front, leaving Silas behind to administrate the refugees.

"I had hoped merely to come home," Nichal said. "But it appears that returning to a normal life will not come anytime soon."

"We will take this one day at a time, together, "Jined said.

Nichal glanced at the twins and made a motion for them to move out front of him. As they passed, Loïc glanced back over his shoulder to Nichal.

We will stand with you, too.

Navien had moved to the lead, his torch out front as they ascended the stairs. They came to the end of the long curve and into a large room, with four doors in it. Across from the one they came out of another set of stairs descended back into blackness. Rallia crept over and listened at it. The other two doors led out into the sky beyond. A trickle of sand fell across the door, splattering on the lip outside. Dorian walked to one of them and peeked out, and ducked his head back in.

"How are you all with heights?"

Alodda gave a nervous laugh and walked to the edge, and quickly came back in, shaking her head.

"There are steps up along the outside of the tower," Dorian said, "finishing the ascent to the top."

"I don't know if I can," Alodda said.

"We'll be around you," Ophedia said, coming to stand next to her.

"We can't stay here," Rallia said, coming to the middle of the room. "I hear voices. Far off, but far below, coming up the second set of stairs."

"The Chalicians?" Navien asked.

"I suspect so," Rallia said.

"This is the only way forward," Dorian said. "I'll lead."

"No," Ophedia said. "Let me. You can encourage from the rear."

She walked to the portal, and balked at the drop below. They were now hundreds of feet in the air. To her left, stairs jutted against the slight slope of the tower. Sand fell from thirty feet above, hitting the stairs, and making them more visible, albeit slippery with sand.

She moved up the first few steps, almost crawling, to maintain her traction. A quick glance behind showed Rallia, then Seriah behind her. Rallia moved confidently, Seriah, not as much. Whisper kept against the wall, showing the first sign of fear she had ever seen in him. Abenard came next, with Alodda following behind with a hand on his belt, while Dorian came up last, his eyes closed as he walked confidently, his mouth muttering a prayer. Upward they climbed, until she came to within ten feet of the top, and saw a welcome surprise: Ymbrys Veronia. The qavyl had not spotted Ophedia yet. She looked back down the line of people behind her, sitting on the precarious step, the massive sword on her back awkwardly clattering on the stone. The others paused, and Dorian opened his eyes and locked with hers.

"Ymbrys," she mouthed.

He gave a nod, closed his eyes, and dropped down along the stairs to climb the stairs like rocks to get around the others, as though he was a child climbing a pile of wood. He came to her side and pulled himself up.

"I had to stifle a laugh of surprise," she whispered.

"There is much you can do with faith and prayer," he said. "Let us go and speak with Ymbrys."

Dorian preceded her to the top edge, and kept low, below the lip. He hissed until the qavyl glanced down at him, surprise followed by relief upon his face.

Ymbrys turned away, moving his hands behind his back, glancing back at Dorian as he replied

We have just lost control of the armor, Ymbrys signed. *Just as we were about to make it through the portal up here, we were attacked. I think in a desperate move, Hanen put Searn into the armor, who is now fully in control.*

Dorian turned back to the others with a sigh.

"What is it?" Rallia asked.

"Hanen lost control of the armor by putting Searn's shade into it."

"NO!" Rallia hissed.

Dorian gave a sad nod.

"The armor is skyfall, isn't it?" Ophedia asked.

"Yes," Dorian confirmed.

"Then I can sunder it," Ophedia said, and began unstrapping the sword from her back.

Dorian turned back to Ymbrys. *Anything else?*

Searn has the boneshroud, too.

Dorian swore.

Who else is with you? Ymbrys asked.

Rallia, Ophedia, Seriah, a Voktorra turned to our help, and Alodda.

Alodda? Ymbrys gave Dorian a look of surprise.

Dorian nodded back.

Then hope remains for Hanen.

Ophedia pressed up next to Dorian. "Let me lead," Ophedia said. "Rallia and Navien will start with their crossbows. You do your light tricks and try and do better than that lug of a Paladin did in Mahn Fulhar."

"Light tricks?" Dorian responded with a smirk.

"You know what I mean," Ophedia rolled her eyes.

"Those were not tricks. Jined is champion of a god, and his 'light tricks' were a full infusion of faith-based miracles."

Ophedia shrugged. "Do that. Back me up. I need to get close to the armor and cut it to ribbons."

"Supposedly your father also wears the boneshroud. Miracles will have no effect."

Ophedia looked Dorian sternly in the eyes. "He is not my father. He may have had a hand in my birth, but I am my own woman."

"Fair enough," Dorian said.

"So, what are we supposed to do then?"

"I'm not saying your idea isn't the only option we have, besides just leaving and letting the world burn. But that's not an option, is it?"

Ophedia shook her head.

A commotion came from above. Dorian turned back to Ymbrys.

Ten Chalicians, Ymbrys signed. *They're being taken control of by means of Dream.*

Dream?

"Are we going up?" Rallia whispered from behind.

Dorian gave a nod, and Ophedia moved to shoot up the stairs, but Dorian's hand fell on her shoulder.

"What?"

"First," Dorian said. "We pray."

Dorian closed his eyes. "Grissone, Twin-Soul to Anka, your words fill our hearts with hope. Your wings are a protection to us in the twilight of our years. Bless us with your light and strength. Infuse us with your hope. Let us make no misstep as we walk in the darkness, but deliver us from the ravages our enemies rain upon us."

His hand reached out toward Rallia and Navien. "May their bolts fly true. May Aben's blessing be upon their shoulders."

He turned, eyes closed, toward Seriah. "Her goddess so chose her. Ask your sister to shower her blessings upon her chosen woman. May you remember Alodda, daughter of Abgenas Dülar, servant of the Hammer. Suffuse her with the spirit of hope. Call your brothers here to watch over their servants. To the qavyl, Ymbrys, call Lae'zeq. To the Khamntyr, the Prince of the Forest. May the Pantheon shine as one, to sunder they who have forsaken the gods."

Finally, his hand rested on Ophedia's shoulder. "And may the sword of this fine young woman sheer metal as paper, that she bring wrath upon Searn VeTurres. May her sword be the judgment of Wyv-Thüm, ushering that fallen monster before the throne of the Judge. Amen."

The others muttered their "amens."

"So," Ophedia said, "can we go now?"

Dorian nodded and followed her up and over the edge.

54

Trailing Darkness, Abundant Light

TURRIAN: Vanity, my brother? What know you of vanity?

With your humble means, and self-sacrifice.

All you do, you do for others, a cobble to be trod upon.

I would see you pulled from the street and your name lifted as mine own.

I would see an edifice raised to both our names.

I would see those that dared to tread upon you made as you once were.

UNTELLIAN: Still, you do not understand. I am not trod upon in shame.

Nay, I am paving the path that leads others to glory.

I am not trod upon, my brother.

If that is my fate, I accept it. If it is not, then I seek it.

TURRIAN: Then we must part. For this impasse leaves us at odds.

— FROM *BRASE TURRIAN, PRINCE OF WOE,*

DREAD KNIGHT

ELLAVON GAVALIN

First, Hanen watched Ophedia confidently stride over the lip. In her hands she held a massive, curved sword of skyfall metal. Behind her, Dorian Mür emerged. As his hands brushed the sand and he rose to his feet, the sand stuck to the form of an invisible hammer in one hand. Behind him, Seriah Yaldedít came up with staff in hand, and next to her the ynfald, Whisper. Then to Hanen's surprise, the Voktorra, Abenard Navien came up over the edge, and to Hanen's greater relief, his sister, Rallia. Both bore crossbows and dropped to their knees, letting loose bolts into two Chalicians, who dropped flat onto their backs, and did not rise again. Lastly, Hanen's heart took a leap as Alodda Dülar came up over the lip, the wild fear in her eyes softening as they fell on Hanen's, and then took several turns through a deep sadness, and finally, resolve.

Searn had his back turned to them, and slowly came around to consider the attackers. Despite the lifeless skull that topped his armor, Hanen swore he saw a smile.

He waved his hand, and the remaining Revenant Chalicians rushed forward. Dorian moved like a bolt of light, his ephemeral hammer striking the first Praetor down. Three others dove atop him, pressing him to the ground, and black tendrils began to rise from the sand that carpeted everything now.

Up out of the sand, the form of Loth appeared, covered in the writhing wyrms, and he stood over Dorian, his face emerging to leer down at the old man.

Hanen waited no longer and touched the sand below him, concentrating. A spear formed, and he raised it toward Loth. He threw it in an awkward toss, which struck Loth ineffectively. The heretic turned his attention to him, and surged across the space toward Hanen, his wyrm-covered hand taking hold of Hanen's throat before he could bring another sandy spear up, pressing him toward the edge of the tower.

"You have been a thorn in our side for long enough," he hissed. The wyrms covering him offering sibilant whispers.

"Better a thorn than a disgusting abomination," Hanen croaked out.

"Abomination?" Loth replied. "We are transcendent!"

"For one," Rallia said, the axe in her hand coming down through Loth's arm, Hanen dropped to his knees to catch his breath. "These wyrms are disgusting."

Her foot swung around as she dropped low to the ground herself, sweeping Loth from his footing. As he hit the sand, he smiled and dissolved.

Hanen and Rallia locked eyes. Hanen reacted to the form of Loth rising behind Rallia, who spun in response, the axe cleaving wyrms from his chest. "Two, you're slow."

It appeared Loth had anticipated her move, and wyrms on the sand locked her feet to the ground. He advanced on her with a wicked smile plastered across his face. She struggled as the wyrms began to encase her leg.

"And three?" Hanen asked.

"Those who forsake the gods are forsaken by all."

Light broke through the clouds, a ray shining down upon Rallia. The wyrms screamed in response, and the hesitation was all she needed. She spun away, the staff coming off her back in a wide arc. Loth stumbled backward, and his foot went over the edge. He dropped the desiccated hand of Slate in surprise, and grasped for the end of Rallia's staff, fear plastered over his face. Rallia let go of her staff, and he disappeared over the edge.

Alodda rushed across, Whisper at her heels, nipping at wyrms now retreating back through the gate.

"Hanen!" Alodda threw her arms around him.

"What are you doing here?" Hanen said. "I thought you died."

"Died?"

"I saw a vision of a black orb exploding."

"Hanen," Alodda said. "Your father…"

"Father threw himself on the orb," Rallia said. "He saved us."

The pit in Hanen's stomach deepened.

"You can't be here," Hanen said to the two of them.

"Well, we are now," Rallia said.

"Searn can't be stopped. Not by any force, physical or otherwise."

"You put too much faith in his invincibility."

"He can't be killed," Hanen doubled down.

"No one is deathless," Rallia said.

Hanen gasped and looked around, his eyes falling on the hand of Slate.

"What?"

"I have an idea."

Across the tower, Ophedia tried to break through to Dorian, pinned to the ground by three of the Revenant Chalicians. The remaining soldiers, purple fire in their eyes, stood in the way. The wyrms at their feet flailed and grasped, and sought to trip her with every step. The distraction at her feet became nearly unbearable when Navien stepped up next to her, a Chalician spear in his hand. Whisper appeared at her other side, nipping at the wyrms.

Confidence restored, she cleaved one of the men in two. As he fell, wyrms rose and filled the gaps in his flesh, and he stood back up. She spun and took off one of his arms. Again, wyrms rose to reattach it.

"Why won't they die?" she shouted, then spun, cutting two of them in half. Navien ran a third through and leveraged the Revenant around toward the edge of the tower. The man rasped then shoved himself up the spear shaft.

Navien almost let go, but Whisper took hold of the man's heel, and Navien pushed against his opponent's chest, sending him spinning off the edge, spear and all.

Stuck between two Revenants, Ophedia hacked and slashed, every wound healed by wyrms in an endless frustration. From behind one, Seriah smacked him on the head with her staff. The indigo-walker turned as she slammed him in the chest and a purple flame rushed from his eyes and mouth and into Seriah's before going out.

The last three Revenants pulled backward toward Dorian and those atop him, as the magus, Gvelindar, strode through the gate, pulling on the chain bringing Bou with him.

"We need to free that Khamntyr," Hanen said.

"A what?" Rallia asked.

"I'll tell you later. He's barely a child, and held against his will."

Hanen advanced, Rallia and Alodda behind him. Whisper rushed over and slunk around Hanen's feet, nipping at wyrms that dared to peek up through the sand.

"Ah, storyteller," Gvelindar said.

"Let the Khamntyr go," Hanen shouted.

"Why? He makes a fine trophy."

"He's no trophy," Hanen said.

"We shall see," Gvelindar said. He dropped the chain in his hand, and it lifted itself like a snake and pulled Bou toward them, his arms bound to his side. Like a puppet on a string he was tossed through the three of them, easily sidestepped.

"He's toying with us," Alodda said. "Like dangling a ball of yarn before a housecör."

As though he knew what she had said, the chain, at the Arborist's command, suddenly yanked Bou toward the edge to throw him off.

Hanen leapt and grabbed for the chain just as Bou went over the edge. Bou lowed in terror.

The chain went taut as Hanen hit the floor, and the heavy weight of the Khamntyr pulled at him. Nothing held Bou but a chain made of mind-sand that could be dispelled at any moment.

"And so you see your predicament," Gvelindar called. "I could let him go without regret. Or you swear fealty to me."

Hanen ignored the magus and reached out to try and get hold of anything.

Gvelindar cried out in alarm as Whisper was up under him, nipping at his heels. The chain began to dissolve. Hanen let go of the chain as sand poured off the side and through his fingers. With a thought, the sand solidified as it cascaded over Bou and stuck him in place like mortar. Hanen took a deep breath and willed the sand to rise, bringing the Khamntyr with it.

Bou's arms flung up over the edge and he clamored up and collapsed in exhaustion.

They both turned, tired, and saw Rallia and Whisper attacking the Arborist, who tried throwing up spikes of sand, but with little effect. The ynfald was unperturbed, and Rallia moved with determination.

Alodda dropped to Hanen's side, holding out two water skins. Hanen took them and handed one to Bou. "Bou, drink. Then we attack."

Ymbrys came alongside them. "Hanen, we must move against Searn. Dorian is being crushed by the Revenants holding him."

"Why does the armor just sit there?" Alodda asked. "Why doesn't he just kill us all?"

"He wants witnesses to his greatness. We appeal to that. We work up his pride."

DREAD KNIGHT

Gvelindar had retreated from Rallia and Whisper and looked to be ready to flee back through the gate.

"Searn!" Rallia shouted, walking out front of the Dread Knight.

Searn turned and regarded her. He made a motion with his hand, and the magus next to him lifted his own, and a new throne of purple sand formed behind the knight.

"You're done, Searn," Rallia said.

Searn laughed, lounging on his sandy throne like a king watching court performers. "You think this is over? You stupid girl. I should have had you killed in Mahn Fulhar."

"I don't need to fight you," Rallia said. "She does."

Rallia pointed to Searn's right and he turned as Ophedia brought the massive Sky Grazer down on his wrist, shearing metal with a scream that ripped through reality.

Searn looked at the fallen hand curiously. The missing hand did not stop the rest of his arm from shooting out and striking Ophedia, throwing her ten feet across the top of the tower, sword clattering to the ground next to her.

Searn rose and held his other hand down to the fallen gauntlet. It levitated up and reattached itself.

Ophedia struggled to her knees and reached out for Sky Grazer, but as she did, it scraped across the ground toward Searn. Ophedia threw herself after it, trying to make a grab for it, but it shot into the air and into the Dread Knight's awaiting gauntlet.

"You brought me a gift, daughter. A sword worthy of the armor."

He drove the point down into the stone of the tower, burying a foot of the black metal.

"Now," he said, looking around, unperturbed that they had attacked. "Let us have you all swear fealty."

The three Revenants holding Dorian brought him before Searn, holding him down on his knees. With a wave of the Arborist's fingers, sandy hands came up out of the ground, and took hold of each of their shoulders, pressing them forward in a line. Ymbrys side-stepped the tendrils and walked to him of his own volition.

"You each continue to be a nuisance," Searn said. "I'm debating which of you I will kill, and which I'll make watch."

"You could give me the Khamntyr, and the brother and sister," Gvelindar said. "He took my collection from me, after all."

"No," Searn said. "Your days of toying with mortals is over. You serve me now, Gvelindar. Your century of hiding from the others is done." Searn turned back. "Now. Which of you will give me your loyalty? Who will die?"

Seriah rose to her feet defiantly.

"Dodged death enough times, monk?"

"Death holds no fear for me," Seriah said. "But it shall constantly nag at you, for what few moments you have left in this world."

She reached into her tunic and pulled out a stick.

"Put that paltry thing away," Searn said.

"Searn VeTurres, I judge you fallen and apostate."

"Silence," Searn grumbled.

"I deem you chastised by the gods, and when you stand before the Judge, none shall stand to give defense. Your actions are abominable and you are fallen!" She broke the stick in two.

"Silence!" he said, rising from his throne and smashing a gauntlet across her face. She fell to the ground, skidding several yards across the sand. Alodda threw herself toward the girl. Navien rushed toward the throne in a frantic play. Searn's gauntlet shot up and held him by the throat, then cast him aside. He hit the ground hard, landing on his arm.

"That is enough, anathema," Ymbrys said, taking a step forward.

"Qavyl," Searn said, considering the languid figure.

"More than that."

"I know," Searn said. "I would see you fall first. Unsheath your staff, and see what you are truly made of."

"That is not Wisdom's will."

"Then why are you even here?" Searn said.

"As witness to a new era."

"Foolish. That's what you are."

Searn took a tentative step forward.

"He is fearful of Ymbrys," Rallia muttered.

"But why?" Hanen replied.

Ymbrys had not moved.

Searn walked up to stand over the qavyl. "Will you stop me?"

"The Bane of War unsheathed, shall sunder brother and friend," Ymbrys said.

Searn turned back toward the throne, his hand reaching for Sky Grazer and pulling it from the ground. He spun the sword around and it arced across the middle, toward Ymbrys.

A flash of light shot up from the ground where Dorian had

been, and the old man stood between the Dread Knight and the qavyl. His hands slammed together, catching the sword between them. With another twist, Searn was forced back two steps, sword thrown back behind him. Dorian stood firm. White light poured from his mouth, words muttered under his breath.

"Back, you foolish old man!" Searn roared.

Dorian dropped the cloak from his shoulders. He did not wear armor, but light formed around him as such, covering him in a blinding glow, wings of pure light across his back. He rushed toward the Dread Knight. Searn had no time to get his sword up in front of him before Dorian slapped both of his hands on Searn's chest. The impact flashed in an explosion that sent Searn stepping backward, stumbling through the throne, crumbling it as sand on the beach.

Dorian pressed the advantage, and Searn scrambled to get the sword up in front of him, but Dorian slapped the sword aside. In his hand, the ephemeral hammer formed and he brought it down on Searn's wrist.

"This is not my first time fighting this armor," Dorian said.

"You faced Polgrawn when you were a young man. He was a moron," Searn said. "I am not."

Searn pressed forward now, both hands on the sword. It sliced violently through the air, and Dorian deftly side-stepped each swing.

Alodda leapt to help Ophedia up while Navien pulled Seriah from harm's way.

Searn spun as his footing took him to the edge and he paused to consider Dorian.

"That was an impressive attempt. You won't find me falling."

"It was worth the try," Dorian shrugged.

Searn thrust forward, and Dorian leapt backward, the wind catching the wings of light behind him, and he blew away and landed near the gate. He kicked off the edge and spun as his hammer shot out across the space. Searn stepped aside and Dorian flew off over the edge, to the gasp of the others. A gust of wind lifted him up in the air, and he flew up over the tower, hovering out of reach.

Searn leveled Sky Grazer at him. "Come down, old bird."

Dorian slowly lowered to the ground and landed, a hand touching the ground, eyes closed.

They opened, and pure white light poured from them. He

moved toward the black knight in a single streak of light, hammer held forward, and it struck Searn's chest like a bell. Searn fell to the ground and Dorian stood over him, raining blows down upon him. His other hand grabbed for the boneshroud around Searn's Khamntyr skull to pull it free. Searn's gauntleted hands scrambled to stop him and took hold of Dorian's wrist, and with the other, pulled the boneshroud from his head, and just as quickly bound Dorian up in it like the jacket for a madman. The light around Dorian snuffed out, leaving only an old man on the ground, bound and powerless.

The skull atop Searn's armor looked at each of them, then fell on the form of the Khamntyr, crouching in fear.

"Are you next? Will you face me as I wear your father's skull as a trophy?"

Ymbrys stepped up and on the way, his leather-topped staff cracked on the flagstone. Searn stopped and looked down at the qavyl.

"Are you ready to face your fate, Luck Thief?" Searn scoffed.

"This is the end," Ymbrys said. "You will find I am too quick for you to ever catch me."

Searn stalked forward, and Ymbrys stayed well out of reach, stepping deftly away. Ymbrys never made a move toward Searn, only moving from one side of the tower to the other.

Rallia moved toward Dorian, but Searn stopped and pointed his sword at her. "You. Stay."

Rallia halted in shock at the command.

Searn chucked the sword at the qavyl in a spinning arc and Ymbrys stood tall and defiant, stepping out of the way. The sword spun off past the edge of the tower. Ymbrys rushed forward at that moment, his staff flashing as he tried to find purchase somewhere in the armor, some chink.

The sound of the whirling sword came back, and Seriah cried out. Ymbrys turned to see the sword flying toward Searn's outstretched hand. He closed his eyes, resolve washing over him as the blade straightened out and flew toward him and Searn.

Dorian rushed in front of Ymbrys and Sky Grazer's curved blade pierced him through, slicing through the boneshroud, casting it down like a limp rag. Dorian hung, suspended from the sword stuck again in the stone, eyes on the sky.

"Prima Pater!" Rallia shouted.

Hanen took hold of her arm to stop her from moving forward as

Searn dropped to his knees, the hulking armor lifting the shattered boneshroud like a child clutching at a blanket.

"Let go of me!" Rallia cried.

Hanen pulled her away and stepped between her and Dorian.

The Prima Pater looked, his eyes focusing through the pain. He gave a wan smile. "Here is your chink in his armor," he spluttered.

Hanen thrust his hand down into the satchel at his side. His fingers brushed the hand that he had put there when Loth had fallen from the tower.

Give, Ghoré's voice said.

Hanen closed his eyes and grasped the hand. Time stopped and suddenly he was somewhere between death, life, and dream.

Ghoré hung in the air as a black smudge. His head hung like a skull, purple-hued. His arms flapped, keeping him aloft.

"Come to give yourself to me?" Ghoré hissed.

"No. I want to give you something better."

"Go on."

"I know you resent me," Hanen said, "but there is someone you hate more."

"VeTurres."

"Follow my lead, and you can ravage his mind as much as you wish."

"I want that."

"I thought you might."

The world snapped into view, and Hanen held the lifeless, desiccated hand in his. No moment had passed. Hanen leapt atop Searn as he tried to pull what remained of the boneshroud up and over his head, his skull mouth opened in a roar. Hanen's hand fell on the bone pin stuck in the skull, and a vision of Searn flashed in his mind. The skull's mouth roared in rage. Searn pressed to take hold of Hanen's mind, as Ghoré had. Hanen thrust the desiccated hand in his other grip down into the open mouth of Searn. Through the connection, Hanen felt Ghoré invade the inside of the skull. He was not just there in the ring of bone on the hand shoved down Searn's bony throat, but elsewhere too, as an inhuman skull in the Mirrorplate still locked in the Veld. The soul of the Deathless Beast, cleft in two when Searn stole the ring for his boneshroud, was once more made whole. Searn did not have a boneshroud over his head to protect him from the spiritual assault.

The Dread Knight rose, gauntleted hands held to the skull as the voice of Searn and Ghoré screamed from within, lost in their battle of wills. A hand went up to lean on the portal, and in a spasm, he shoved and the gate rocked. The armor lost a step, and he fell toward the gate. The Arborist threw up bracers of sand to keep the armor from crashing through the gate, but the weight was too much, and it crashed through the sand, pushing the Arborist through before him.

The Dread Knight fell through the portal itself, and the silvered Mirrorplate stumbled out, the skull of Ghoré replacing Guyyan's skull. In confusion, the Mirror Knight spun and rushed back through, and the black emerged. The two sides of the Knight's will fought for dominance over the singular mind of Searn, and they rushed back and forth through the portal in confusion, until in a moment, both once more stood in the portal in a mottled blend of Dread and Mirror.

Pressing against both sides of the portal for balance, the foundation shook as the black Dread Knight emerged once more onto the top of the black tower. Ghoré's voice was screaming, as Searn's was entirely snuffed out. The stones around the portal suddenly collapsed, leaving the gateway to Veld a tear in reality.

The air exploded in a wild vortex of sand, and the hollow rasping voice of the Deathless Beast cried out—the vortex lifting him high into the air, black armor donning violet wings of sand. Searn's voice broke through in a final cry of desperation, and the armor looked skyward and shot up into the air, sand trailing behind it like an evil black and purple comet.

Hanen turned to the others, gathered around Dorian in a half circle. Rallia and Seriah knelt down to their knees, the latter with hands folded in prayer.

He was no longer bigger than life, but seemed small. Yet, even as he hung there, suspended on that massive sword, he looked at peace.

"Do not mourn me, girl," Dorian said to Rallia with a weak smile. "I died to this world long ago. I go now, my goal reached. My wife awaits me with her brother."

Rallia let out a sob.

"Does she come?" he said to Seriah.

The girl looked up, tears streaming down her face. She glanced over her shoulder and she nodded.

He turned and looked at Hanen. "Now that you have come back to the proper path, walk it to its end."

"What awaits me?" Hanen asked.

Alodda slipped her hand into his and gave it a squeeze.

"That is only for you to discover," Dorian said.

"We need to get off this tower," Ymbrys said.

"I'll be going by another way," Dorian said with a weak laugh. His eyes looked up into the sky, surprise and relief washing over his face. "I am forged anew by the Pariantür, lifted by the wings of the Anka, and into the arms of Grissone."

Hanen realized in that moment, Dorian bore a soft glow. As it grew brighter, Dorian became more ephemeral, until his nothingness matched the light in a single bright flash, leaving only the sword where it stood.

Hanen looked to the purple tear into the Veld, and the black streak that continued to rise into the air above them. Ophedia took hold of Sky Grazer and wrested it free from the stone, following the others to the stairs to begin a wild descent. The silence was only broken by the rumble of the tower rocking on its foundation.

"Down!" Rallia shouted, helping Seriah.

Navien and Bou supported each other, while Hanen and Alodda came behind them. Ophedia and Ymbrys took up the rear. The little ynfald rushed through their legs and down the tower, turning often to ensure everyone followed him.

They flew down the stairs as fast as they could, the threat of the tower collapsing on itself rumbling beneath their very feet. They came to the base and rushed down the hill toward the shore.

Hanen glanced back into the sky. The black, purple-tailed comet rose, the clouds parting in an angry spiral, and disappeared.

Then, the clouds flashed like fire, and down through the sky hurdled the Dread Knight, striking the top of the tower and continuing down and through, stones exploding out and away, finally striking the earth with such a violent impact that the ground underneath them gave way, and a shockwave blew out and over them, laying Hanen flat atop Alodda. Bou flew through the air, landing hard on an arm. Navien pulled Seriah behind a standing stone. Ophedia stood tall and watched the entire thing. Ymbrys, just as unperturbed, leaned on his staff, Whisper casually sitting next to him.

Stones of the tower fell for minutes, then silence reigned. A new crater lay before them, scattered with piles of black stones, the Dread Knight buried far beneath.

55

Aftermath

The path it draws the traveler on,
To the unknown shore.
Toward that distant horizon,
Away from closed door,
Toward future, ever forward.

The long road, ahead and straight
Its eddies as the sea
The road winds like wind and rain
The lands a tapestry.
Take now your life, be free.

—*THE TRAVELER*

Jined passed under the gate of Hamulon, the lively sounds of New District fading as he strode to the top of the final knoll. He saw the tallest dome first, atop the great chapel, then others popped up into view, and finally all of the valley of Pariantür opened up before him.

The Fortress Monastery, the Father Citadel of the Order of the

Hammer, lay like a massive sledgehammer in a field, head pointed to the east. A mile away lay the entrance, at the pommel of the "haft." The haft, a long building of seven levels, housed stables and the living quarters of the Paladins—enough to house ten thousand. At the other end of the haft sat the Hammer's Head. The blocky lower levels themselves stood twice the height of the haft, and atop that, the twenty-two domes. The northern "head" of the hammer was the cloistered headquarters of the Crysalas, housing their living quarters and offices. The rest of the head was shared, or administrated by the Paladins.

After more than a year away, it beckoned him—though he expected to find his room musty and needing a good airing out. If he was even allowed to return to it as he was now a brother bearing the Vow of Poverty. The Paladins around him pressed off down the hill, Nichal, Loïc, and Cävian at the head, being escorted to who knew what fate.

"What happens now?" Jined muttered.

"Trust in your friends," Grissone said, appearing to ride next to him. "Have faith in me."

"And if corruption has sunk its claws into Pariantür?"

"Then rely on those that have not fallen. Pray for those who have. Let their own path reveal their loyalties."

"By your will," Jined conceded.

Grissone was gone.

The scent of porumarias blooming orange across the hill filled him with a sense of home as he rode down toward Pariantür.

The Veld held a still silence. Even as the wind moved, there was an echoing that could only be described as thoughts in the minds of those who walked the purple sand in a line.

Larohz turned this way and that, as though her imagination ran rampant, and while sightless, she seemed to see. She walked alongside Katiam, often scampering between rocky outcroppings by the road they made with their feet. Ahead of the two of them, the rest of the dreamwalkers marched.

Vuduin led the way, staying ahead of the others by several yards.

Behind the T'Akah, Jurgon, Esenath, and Astrid walked, weapons held at the ready.

Little Maeda and Onelie followed behind them, Onelie walking with her lute strapped across her front. When conversation lulled, she plucked at the strings.

Katiam lost track of time, and wondered if they hadn't walked for days. When she turned back to look where they had come from, she could still see the rocks of the Massif, no more than a few hours behind them. Wind whipped across the path that they had tread, obscuring their passage, yet she could see what she thought was a figure following in their wake.

She stopped to get a better look, and noticed it whipped up its own dust cloud. Whoever it was, was moving fast.

"Astrid," she called over her shoulder.

"What is it?" her friend said, coming next to her.

"Something is coming."

Astrid peered. "They're riding a sleigh of some sort," Astrid said.

Vuduin and the others came to stand next to the two women.

"What is it?" Onelie asked.

"I don't know," Vuduin said.

Jurgon stepped out front of them, the figure on the sleigh with more discernible features now. "I know who that is," he said, his stern sadness melting.

He took off at a run.

The sleigh curved sideways, revealing the creature that pulled it was the small capricör-like beast with crescent moon-shaped horn—the reyem Katiam had met when she had visited the Veld: Derioth.

Katiam looked from Derioth to rider with a smile, and saw the tear-streaked face of Sabine Upona throw herself off the back of the sleigh and close the distance to her husband. The two of them collided and fell to the sand in an embrace, kissing each other's tears away and trying to see each other through their own.

Astrid threw an arm over Katiam's shoulder, while the Rotha's leafy hand sought Katiam's other hand, and the three of them stood watching. The others watched with various levels of fascination and embarrassment. After long minutes, the two of them rose, and returned to the others. Derioth trundled toward them with the sleigh cart behind him.

Sabine would not let go of Jurgon, nor let him take his hands

DREAD KNIGHT

off her waist. But she reached out with one hand and took Katiam's own and squeezed. "You made it."

"Ahead of you, it would seem," Katiam jested.

"I had much to do, to ensure that things were left in good stead. I fear even that was not enough."

"What do you mean?"

"I've made a name for myself among the magi," Sabine said. "Now I can do more."

She glanced down and saw the Rotha holding Katiam's hand. "What is this?"

"I am Larohz," the Rotha whistled.

"It speaks," Sabine said.

"Among other things," Jurgon said.

Sabine looked up and saw the T'Akah, but didn't seem surprised.

"I am Vuduin eb'Gatha."

"Of course!" Sabine said, smiling immediately and giving a deep bow. "I am Sabine Upona. My voice often spoke with you in communications from the Matriarch Superioris."

"I have cherished our conversations," Vuduin said.

She looked to Esenath and gave a smile, then her eyes fell on Onelie and Little Maeda.

"I recognize you," Sabine said. "Onelie Clemmbäkker, if I'm not mistaken."

Onelie gave a curtsy.

"A veiled sister," Sabine said, giving a solemn nod of her head.

"Maeda Salna," the young Paladame said.

"You have taken on new aspects," Sabine replied.

"Yes."

"We should continue on," Vuduin said, "and find ourselves shelter, so we may discuss our path."

"Where do you travel?" Sabine asked.

"Eastward. By command of our goddess," Katiam said. "To find other Rotha, and fulfill a great calling given by Crysania."

"I can't wait to hear about it," Sabine said. "Nor to tell you of the wake of destruction I've left out west, dismantling covens of magi."

"You've been busy," Katiam said.

"So have you," Sabine replied.

The nine of them turned and continued their journey east, across purple sands and matching sky.

Loïc stood halfway up the aisle and watched his brother at the front of the chapel. The pole of the standard slid into place, dropping down through the brass and striking the stone underneath with a clang.

Cävian adjusted how it faced, and turned back up the chapel, eyeing its placement to be seen from the door, then knelt down and slipped the small bolt through the base, locking it.

He straightened his pleated leather as he stood, adjusted his armor, and walked up the aisle, face rigid and focused. As his eyes met Loïc's, he broke into a smile.

I was lost in thought again, wasn't I? Cävian asked.
No more than usual, Loïc replied.
Have I been distant?
No more than usual.
Are you hungry?

Loïc lifted his hands to speak, and Cävian held a finger up to silence him.

No more than usual? His brother asked with a wry smile.
I suppose we've both had a lot on our minds.
This is true.

They came out of the chapel and looked around.

It appears the garden door is closed, Cävian said. *We could speak privately there.*

Loïc nodded and they walked over to the door leading out onto a terrace, raised gardens filling most of the space. Dwovs hovered over flowers, gathering summer nectar.

This road has been a long one, Loïc said. *You were given the standard, which you take quite seriously.*
I do.
It's left me wondering what my purpose is.
Worried I'm going to leave you behind?
Possibly.

Brother, Cävian took his twin's shoulders in his hands and looked him squarely in the eyes. No words were spoken. They just looked intently at one another. Then, they both nodded.

They walked together in silence, sniffing at flowers, looking out over the lands surrounding Pariantür, pointing at birds circling far above. Everything seemed to have returned to normal.

Nichal and Jined will need us, Cävian said.

More than even they know, Loïc replied.

Especially if friends are lost through the trials that come.

Such as Nichal's trial for the position of Prima Pater?

Cävian shook his head. *When Moteans start revealing their hands.*

It is a good thing I have you by my side, brother.

It is a good thing we have Grissone at our side, brother.

The Roan Grass Inn awakened lazily. Navien stoked the fire, and glanced up at Seriah as she roused in the chair next to the hearth.

"I meant to go back up to the room," she said.

"Probably best you didn't. I could hear Ophedia snoring through the wall. Did that wake you?"

"No," Seriah said. "Another dream."

"Dreamwyrms? Do you still see them?"

Seriah nodded. "Both when I am awake and asleep, whether my eyes are open or closed."

Navien nodded and turned back to the fire, losing himself in the flames.

"Last night the innkeeper mentioned we're not far from Boscolón," Seriah said, breaking the tension.

"Only a few hours' ride," Navien confirmed, his attention coming back to her.

"Have you noticed Ophedia getting more nervous the past two days?"

Navien gave a brief chuckle, one hand raising to toy negligently with his beard. "Yes."

"Do you know something I don't?"

"I think she is nervous about seeing Aurín."

"Aren't you?"

Navien nodded solemnly. "For entirely different reasons."

Ophedia did not appear for another hour but came down as put together as Seriah had ever seen her. She had her black Sentinel cloak back on, and her hair combed out, lying over the cloak. Her black vest over a white, airy blouse was flattering, but not immodest. Sky Grazer was strapped across her back once more.

"You look the soldier and bounty hunter," Navien said.

"Good," Ophedia said, glancing down at herself. "And the sleipnirs?"

"Ready."

They rode at an easy trot, and by mid-morning came within view of Boscolón. The fields outside the city still bore the damage of a camping army, but otherwise, that it had ever been under attack was a distant memory.

Flags flew atop the walls, not just of Boscolón but Limae, and above them all, a tall black banner. Ophedia stopped her mount, and Navien pointed to the banner flying there.

"I don't know that banner," Seriah said.

"It is hers," Navien said. "She bore that banner under Aurín's command."

They rode down to the western gate. When Ophedia's name was announced, a runner was sent off ahead as the gates boomed open for the three of them.

Riding through the city, no one gave them much attention. A black-clad Sentinel in the city was apparently not an odd sight.

At the gate of Old City they were led through with little trouble, and at the manor keep, their sleipnirs were taken from them.

Ophedia followed a valet up through the main halls and down a long, carpeted corridor to a fine dining room, in which sat two men, who rose as they entered. Perát de Bosco sat at the head, the colors of the city now framing him in finer clothing than he had worn when last they had met. To his left, Aurín Mateau stood, a smile across his face. He did not wear armor nor talon, but had on a black doublet, his mustache as well-kept as usual. Ophedia came to the far end of the table and stopped.

"Lord de Bosco. Captain Mateau, I have returned from the west."

"No need for rigidity," de Bosco said. "It is good to see you returned. Although odd you walk so casually with a known spy."

"Our arrival precedes us?" Ophedia pressed.

Perát nodded.

"Abenard Navien has proven his worth in the past weeks. I would ask you show leniency to him. If the flags atop the city are to be believed, that Boscolón is now Limaean, then I ask that Limaean liberty be granted to the man."

"Your word alone is enough to offer him our goodwill," Perát said.

Navien stepped forward and dropped to a knee.

"Lenience offered or not, I would offer my services as an apology. I've extensive experience as guard and would act as butler or valet. I would cherish the opportunity to see my talents put to use."

"I've little use for a manservant," Perát said. "Aurín?"

"I'm sure we can find use for him. If not here, then in Adwall."

Perát nodded. "Come, sit and join us. We'll eat, and you can tell us of your adventures."

The three of them rounded the table and sat in the plush chairs. Servants brought more food and they ate to their hearts' content.

The garden was not large, but lavish. Aurín more than once brushed Ophedia's shoulder with his own as they walked alongside each other, and she did not pull away when he did so.

Navien walked with Perát's valet, who expounded extensively to him about roles and propriety. Seriah sat silently on a bench along a wall, watching birds and flowers, hands folded in her lap.

"Adwall, huh?" Ophedia said.

"Noss has given the city to me," Aurín said. "Perát wants to work with me to make the keep as nice as this one."

"As a show of loyalty?"

"Yes," Aurín said. "Because he genuinely cares. We've quickly become close friends."

"And Noss?"

"I think Noss does what he wants. He's a scholar first."

"I worry about him," Ophedia said.

"What about?"

"I mentioned him once, and Seriah visibly paled. I worry he is not so good as he makes himself out to be."

"Few men of power and authority are good."

"But some are," Ophedia said.

Aurín chuckled.

"What's so funny?"

"The Ophedia of a year ago, still practically a girl, was far more cynical."

"And you?"

"Have you ever known me to be cynical? Truly?"

"No," Ophedia said. "It's part of what I like about you."

"Then you do like me."

Ophedia swung to hit him in the arm, and he dodged away. She gave him an offended look and swung again. He let her hit him this time.

"I may be an optimist," Aurín said with a wince. "But I am not naive."

They completed another circle of the garden.

"Why did you agree to take Navien on as your valet?" Ophedia asked.

"Because, as I said, I am not naive. I do not yet trust him, and I'd like to keep him close."

"Enemies closer and all that?"

Aurín nodded.

They walked a little farther.

"Where will you go?" Aurín asked.

"I'm not sure," Ophedia said.

"I've set aside rooms at Adwall for you. If you need a place to keep things."

"In Adwall, eh?"

"The keep is more like the manor here. There are several private apartments. You've certainly earned your keep."

"Oh, have I now?"

"Noss offered to give you an inn in Haven. I told him you may prefer Adwall or Boscolón."

"Very assuming of you, to think I want to settle down."

"If you don't want them, I understand."

Ophedia stopped, then slowly turned to face him. "I think I'd like that. But only if you also provide a place for Seriah, too. She deserves somewhere quiet."

"There is a garden there, as well. We can make sure she has all the peace she needs."

"I'd rather that Noss not know about her," Ophedia said.

"Then we'll make sure he doesn't know she's there."

"Aurín," Ophedia said.

"Hm?"

"I hope you don't think my coming to stay at Adwall is anything more than leaning on a friend."

"You mean in regards to what I said before you left to go

journey west?"

"Yes."

"I understand," he said flatly.

"That doesn't mean I'm opposed to our friendship blooming into something more, though, of course."

Ophedia walked away, and Aurín's smile grew into a dumb grin.

Hanen leaned on the deck railing as they neared the city. Eleven hills, half of them visible from the water, rose up into the sky, each with piers and docks. At the top of each hill an estate sat, overlooking the other hills with greedy disdain.

"This is Edi City?" Alodda asked. She wore a loose blouse, and held a cloth in her hand for wiping the sweat from her brow. Her hair was braided up in a crown around her head to keep it off her sweating neck.

"Our office and apartment are over there to the right, on Aritelo Hill."

Rallia came to stand next to them at the railing, a smile on her face. Whisper threw his front paws over the railing and the four of them watched the first pier grow closer.

"The captain has made arrangements with the Seritue docks," Rallia informed them. "The other refugees from Nor-Vio will be processed there."

"And us?"

"We'll put our Black Sentinels cloaks on, and shouldn't have a problem," Rallia said. "But the walk through the city will take most of the day."

The tap of Ymbrys's staff on the deck hailed his approach. Hanen's heart sunk inside, as it did every time the qavyl came near. Ymbrys appeared next to them, Bou standing just behind him, now draped in a loose robe of red silk tied with a sash around his torso.

"Do we have everything together for the disembarkation?" he asked.

"Yes," Rallia said, looking at the other two.

The crowd of travelers from Ormach pressed up to watch the

sailors bring them to port as orders began to sound and ropes were untied, and sails put away. Dock workers accepted lines thrown down to them.

The people on deck grew restless and pressed at the gangplank when it was finally lowered. Ymbrys had earned the respect of passenger and sailor alike, and they parted for him and the Clouws. The captain stood at the top and Ymbrys pressed a coin into his hand in thanks and they exited. Coming down to solid ground, the soldiers who stood there to process the others ignored Hanen, Rallia, and Alodda at the signal of the captain, and they began their walk through the city. Most paid them little attention, although the Khamntyr following close behind turned a few heads.

"Is it always this hot?" Alodda asked, sun reflecting off the plain yellow stone at the base of the buildings nearby.

"At midday in summer it can be," Rallia said. "Eastern houses benefit from the shade in the afternoon, so most people stay indoors at midday, and do their business before and after."

"I shall get used to it," she said determinedly.

They came to a large square, from which a switchbacked street led up to the elaborately carved gates of the Seritue Estate. Ymbrys stopped and turned to the three of them.

"Have you everything you need?" he asked.

"So long as nothing problematic has happened at the office," Rallia said, "I'm sure we'll be fine."

Ymbrys gave Alodda and Rallia a quaint smile. "May I speak with Hanen a moment?"

The two of them stepped several feet away and Rallia pointed out features of the gate above.

Ymbrys turned to Hanen and held out a hand. Hanen tentatively took it from the qavyl, and a wide medallion of gold dropped into his palm.

"I gave this to you when this adventure started. Take it again, and with it start again. Make a better life for yourself than you had." Ymbrys glanced over Hanen's shoulder to Alodda. "She has followed you to the literal ends of the earth, to the brink of endless dream and destruction, and yet still she stands here."

"And if greater destruction looms?" Hanen asked.

"Oh, I am certain that it does," Ymbrys admitted. "Who knows what lies buried under that mountain of rocks where the Dread Knight fell back to earth? Who knows what happens north, south, east, and west of us? Your misadventure is not the only goings on in this world."

"Then why subject Alodda to that? If I am a pawn of Achanerüt, meant to be called, what hope is there for her?"

"Hanen. That you ask that question is the seed of hope. A seed, lying dormant, still holds the potential for growth. Hope is never gone. That it can die is the greatest deceit the Deceiver ever crafted."

Hanen looked over toward Alodda, his sister, and the little ynfald sitting next to them.

"I've made grave mistakes," Hanen said. "I've closed off the people I love from my life in the selfish pursuit of protection, and lost all of that."

"Just because you closed doors to them, does not mean they have left you."

"How do I move forward, now that they know all of that?"

"They do," Ymbrys said. "Yet they are still here. Isn't that enough?"

Hanen let out the breath he felt he had held for weeks. "Thank you, Ymbrys."

"For?"

"Being here. I don't truly understand why. You have always been here, not guiding, but urging me on, even if I did not listen."

"It felt like the wise thing to do."

"You use that word a lot."

"Which?"

"Wise. Wisdom. Why? Is that a qavylli thing?"

"A story for another time, perhaps."

Hanen nodded, and walked over to Alodda.

"Rallia," Ymbrys called. The younger Clouw sibling turned. "Would you walk with me? We can catch up with your brother and Alodda later."

Rallia gave a whistle and the ynfald followed her, Ymbrys, and Bou as they walked away together down another street.

"Where are they off to?" Alodda asked.

"Probably looking to give you and I some time to talk without someone else listening."

"Oh?"

"We've not really had time alone since the tower."

"No," Alodda said. "I suppose we haven't. You've been overly quiet these past couple weeks."

"I have. I've had a lot to think about."

"We all have," Alodda said.

Hanen stopped and she turned to consider him.

"Alodda," Hanen said, "I'm sorry."

"For?"

"For leaving you at the border and continuing on with Dorian. For not telling you everything sooner. For even taking up the boneshroud in the first place. I knew it was wrong, but I did it anyway."

"It was not a good decision," Alodda said. "But then again, if you had not, and everything had not happened as it did, would you have been there to think to use that creepy hand on the Dread Knight, to drive it mad?"

"Possibly."

"All of those things occurring just as they did... I've wondered these past few weeks if it was fate or destiny."

"Perhaps," Hanen said.

"In which case, does anyone have any control of what will happen?"

"We always have choice," Hanen said.

"How do you know that?"

"Because a god told me."

Alodda's eyes opened wider in astonishment.

"Not a good one. But in it I was promised that it was true."

"You truly have spoken to gods?"

Hanen nodded.

"Will you tell me the whole story?"

"It will take time."

"We have time, Hanen Clouw."

She slipped her arm into his and they continued to walk.

"Then you forgive me?" Hanen asked.

"If you ask me."

"Alodda?"

"Yes?"

"Will you forgive me?"

"I did the moment I saw your face atop that black tower."

Hanen smiled.

Whisper tramped from place to place, taking in the new sights and sounds. A startled cör in an alley chased him off a time or two, but his spirit never wavered. One aggressive pack of street ynfalds made to rough up the little black one, but scuttled off when Whisper cowered by Bou's legs.

Ymbrys walked with confidence, his staff a constant rhythm. Rallia's own stout staff, a new one she had crafted from a beam she took from the ship's carpenter, struck flagstone more often.

"What is so important about the staff you walk with?" Rallia asked.

Ymbrys's grip tightened, and he closed his eyes for a moment, considering. "That is a very important question to ask," Ymbrys said. "And why I left my homeland continent of Hannica."

"Oh?"

"Our god, Lae'zeq, god of Wisdom, has marble statues of himself carved and placed in various places around our continent. From time to time, he was said to inhabit the marble, and speak from them. As time passed, he spoke less and less. Our high priests have speculated based on the wisdom he has given, that he has left the qavylli to their own wisdom and devices."

"And the staff?"

"A spear that was held by the statue in our capitol. I stole it."

"Stole it?"

"I was led to, by what I believe was the spirit of Lae'Zeq. I have spent these past few years trying to reconcile what I did, and whether I was right to do so."

"You worry whether the voice that spoke to you was Lae'Zeq?"

"I have wondered," Ymbrys said. "But I have not questioned the voice that speaks to me now."

"Speaks to you now?"

"Yes."

"The message Aben told me to give you. It was not meant for you, but for who you carry?"

"You see to the heart of it."

"Then the staff..."

"A spear, actually. War Bane, it is called."

Ymbrys held out the staff.

Rallia looked at him quizzically.

"I am not offering it to you, but you may touch, Wisdom says."

Rallia touched the staff with a finger. The smell of parchment and old paper washed over her. A tall figure stood in that place, with pages of a book for wings, covered in black ink scrawlings, each word dripping with truth and wisdom. The figure did not turn around, but his long, bushy tail twitched on the ground.

"Hello, Rallia," the figure said, voice high-pitched and scholarly.

Rallia's soul dropped to its knees, head bowed.

"I'll not keep you long. The change it might bring upon you would be too much for you to comprehend. Suffice it to say, I have longed to meet you. Ymbrys speaks highly of you."

"What must I do to grow wiser?" Rallia asked.

"Seek it out."

"There is nothing I want more."

"Would you take up this spear, if it was given?"

"Yes."

"Why?"

"To be the truth that sheds light upon deceit."

"A worthy path," Wisdom said.

Epilogue

One of the Wardens called and Noss approached the workers drawn from peasants begging for his sponsorship, so they could leave Ormach, now that the Chalicians had taken full ownership of the country. Whatever it was that had happened in Nor-Vio provided all the cover Noss needed to travel, by night mostly, to the lake, and then to the island in the center.

"What is it?" he asked.

"We found someone."

"Alive?"

"Yes."

He looked over the ledge to the scree-field below. A man lay, his bottom half pinned under the rubble. Despite the bruises and lacerations across his flesh and face, Noss knew him.

"Place skyfall shackles on him," Noss said.

"Who is he?" a Warden nearby asked.

"His name is Eralt Loth. A zealot from Haven. But he may have answers about what happened here. Now, see him shackled, and a bell placed in his cell."

"Yes, Dean Noss. It will be done."

Another cry went out, and Noss turned, a pile of black stones falling away as several of the workers ran down the mountain of black rubble in a panic.

Noss pressed up the hill toward the place they had fled.

A hole had been uncovered, bottomless and black.

Noss stared down into the depths.

A resonant peal of a bell rang up and out of the hole. A man next to him grabbed his bleeding ears. Noss was not affected, the bells hanging from his ears in discord to the deep peal down the abyss.

Still, the drone of the sound filled his ears, and in that sound a single word formed.

"Deathlesssssssss."

THE END

TO BE CONTINUED IN

VOLUME FIVE OF THE

KALLATTIAN SAGA

DREAD KNIGHT

GLOSSARY 1

DRAMATIS PERSONAE

HANEN CLOUW (*Ha-NEHN Khl-OW*) — A Black Sentinel mercenary and organizer of the Clouw Sentinel Merchant Detail. Hanen is a 1st Lieutenant in the Black Sentinels, and thus has earned his second hand axe.

RALLIA CLOUW (*Rah-LEEAH Khl-OW*) — Like her older brother Hanen, Rallia is a 1st Lieutenant in the Black Sentinels, though she prefers to carry a staff she had built with both of her clubs mounted on the ends. Rallia is also deft with a razor, and often shaves the heads and faces of fellow Black Sentinels.

JINED BRAZSTEIN (*Jih-NED BRADJ-steen*) — Rank of Brother Excelsior. Vow of Chastity. Son of Jarl Jaegür von Brazstein of Brazh, Jined left home to avoid execution for murdering a fellow prince of Boroni. Jined joined the Paladins of the Hammer as a Penitent, committing his life to Grissone, the god of Faith.

KATIAM BORREAU (*Kah-TEE-um Burr-OH*) — A Paladame of the Rose. Personal physician to the Matriarch Superioris and Prima Pater. Aspects of Peace, St. Klare, and Dignity.

SERIAH YALEDÍT (*Sur-EYE-uh Yah-leh-DEET*) — Monk of Nifara. She is known for often establishing orphanages in towns that have none.

ABAMAR DJER *(ABB-ah-MAR ZHAIR)* — Royal Herald of King Abrun Vorso of Bortali.
ABENARD NAVIEN *(Abb-ih-NARD NAY-vee-EN)* — A ranking member of the Voktorra guard guild in Mahn Fulhar.
ABITHU OMRAB *(Ab-ee-THU Om-RAB)* — Benefactor Missioner of the Church of the Common Chalice.
ABRUN VORSO *(AB-roon VOR-so)* — King of Bortali.
AEGER *(A-gur)* — Cup. Deceased Paladin of the Hammer. Rank of Brother Primus. Vow of Silence. Shade-bound in a pen.
AELASAEV *(AY-lah-save)* — Alewife of the Ighali District of Bortali. Owner of the Stone Cask Inn.
ALODDA DÜLAR *(Uh-LAW-thuh Doo-LARR)* — A seamstress and daughter of Abgenas Dülar.
ANHOUIL CHÉTAIN *(An-WEE Che-TANE)* — Praeposit of the Praetors of the Chalice.
ASTRID GLASS *(AH-strid Glass)* — Paladame of the Rose. Aspects of Discretion, Compassion, and Honor.
AURÍN MATEAU *(AW-reen Ma-TOE)* — A Black Sentinel from Œron. The Talon of the Wardens.
AVERIN *(AV-er-in)* — Pater Minoris of the Green Bastion.
BARRA SIOBH *(Bar-ah Shee-ov)* Rhi (King) of Bronue Jinre.
BELL *(Bell)* — A mysterious Paladin, member of the Motean sect.
BELTRAN CAUTESE *(BELL-tran CAW-tease)* — Primus. Co-Founder of the Simplists Sect.
BOLLA ELBAY *(BO-lah ELL-bay)* — Black Sentinel Commander. Warden of the Axe.
BENEVEN *(BEN-ah-venn)* — Owner of the Stone Cask Inn in the Ighali District of Bortali.
BOUYAN *(BOW-yun)* — son of Guyyan, a four year old Khamntyr of the Barad-Gasota.
BROTHERS HAMMER *(Bruther HAMM-err)* — A mysterious Paladin who quotes scripture. Revealed to be the god of Faith, Grissone, in physical form.
CÄVIAN *(CAVE-ee-an)* — Paladin of the Hammer. Rank of Brother Excelsior. Vow of Silence. Twin of Loïc.
CHÖS TELMAR *(CHAHSS TEL-mar)* — A Black Sentinel.
DANE MARRIC *(DAEN MARE-ik)* — Gospeler of Grissone-Anka. Founder of the Simplists Sect.
DEGGAR *(DAY-gar)* — A Black Sentinel Commander.

DIKUN POLUN *(DIE-kunn POLE-un)* — Purser of Dorian Mür's Entourage.
DIDUS KOEL *(DIE-duss COAL)* — Pater Minoris of the Paladins of the Hammer. Vow of Prayer.
DORIAN MÜR *(DOOR-ee-an MEWR)* — Prima Pater of the Paladins of the Hammer. Head of the Church of Grissone. Vow of Prayer. Became the youngest Prima Pater in history, elected almost unanimously during the Protectorate Wars. He still holds the title, seventy-five years later, at the ripe age of 95.
EIMEÉ DÜLAR *(AY-MEE Doo-LARR)* — Seamstress. Wife of Abgenas Dülar.
ERALT LOTH *(Err-ALT LAW-th)* — Paladin of the Hammer. Rank of Primus. A Motean.
ESENATH CHLOÏS *(AH-sen-oth Khloh-EES)* — Paladame of the Rose. Botanist. Sidieratan. Aspects of Cleanliness and Charity.
EUNIA HALLA *(YOU-nee-ah HA-lah)* — A Black Sentinel from southern Mahndür.
FEDELMINA BARBA *(FE-dell-MEEN-ah BAR-bah)* — Paladame of the Rose. Aspects of Clarity and Peace.
GAT *(GHAT)* — Baronet of Haven in Limae, and Commander of the Black Claws 1st.
GAHN ZAR'TLAIN *(GON zar tl-AYN)* — A T'Akah, head of clan Tlain.
GEVELIB *(Gev-el-EEB)* — Primus, Protectorate War Veteran. Blinded by seeing Grissone.
GOREG VON THOMMÜS *(GOR-eg von TOE-moos)* — Jarl of Thom in Boroni.
GRYVIO CASTENARD *(GRY-vee-oh CAST-en-ard)* Doge (Duke) of Castenard.
GUARIN *(GOO-ar-in)* — A monk of Aben.
GRUZ FORENOR *(GROOS FOR-an-ur)* — A Black Sentinel Commander.
GRAVYE *(Gah-vee-ay)* — Lord of Old Zhig.
GUORTH VELTYAR *(GOO-orth Velt-YARR)* — Bogatyr (Middle Ranked Knight) of the Vityaz (Knight) Errants of Ikhala.
GUYYAN *(GY-ahn)* — Fifth-from-Kowavi, Khmantyr of the Barad-Gasota.
GVELINDAR *(GV-ehl-en-DARR)* — The Arborist. A Magus of the Veld.
JURGON UPONA *(YOOR-gahn Oo-POH-na)* — Paladin of the Hammer. Rank of Primus. The Prima Pater's Seneschal.

Husband of Sabine Upona. Vow of Prayer.
KASH *(CASH)* — A storyteller.
LAROHZ *(LAH-rose)* — The Rotha.
LEROT MENDON *(Lehr-ott Men-DAHN)* — A Spy. Brother of Perát de Bosco.
LOÏC *(Low-EEK)* — Paladin of the Hammer. Rank of Brother Excelsior. Vow of Silence. Twin of Cävian. From Setera.
LOR HARDIN *(LORE HAR-din)* — A Black Sentinel Commander.
LUPHINI GOLLIN *(Loo-FEE-NEE GO-lin)* — Saint of Nifara.
LOWDEN DAKMOR *(LOW-den DAHK-more)* — A Sentinel Captain, now an entry level Warden, from Haven Limae.
LUTEA CALIMBRISE *(loo-TEE-ah Kal-ihm-BREE-SAY)* — Paladame of the Rose. Aspects of Charity and Solemnity.
MAEDA SALNA *(MAY-dah SAHL-nah)* — Paladame of the Rose, "Little Maeda," Aspects of Virginity and Honor.
MARN CLOUW *(MARN Khl-OW)* — Father of Hanen and Rallia Clouw. A monk of Aben.
THE MANTICŒR *(The MAN-tee-core)* — Spymaster of Castenard.
NAIR *(NAY-er)* — A storyteller.
NARAH WEVAN *(NA-rah WAY-vahn)* — Paladame of the Rose, Veiled Sister, Aspects of Silence, Sanctity, Solitude, and St. Klare.
NICHAL GUESS *(Nih-KAHL GESS)* — Pater Segundus of the Paladins of the Hammer. Castellan of Pariantür. Vow of Poverty.
NIDIAN *(NID-ee-an)* — A monk of Aben.
NERCUTIO CASTENARD *(Nerr-cyoo-she-oh CAST-en-ard)* — Brother of the Doge of Castenard.
ODITTE FOI *(Oh-DIE-tt Foo-AH)* — Abbess Superioris of the Crysalas Convent in Mahn Fulhar.
OLLISTAN GŒRNSTADT *(Oh-lih-stan Gehrn-statt)* — The Necromancer of the Protectorate Wars.
ONELIE CLEMMBÄKKER *(OH-Neh-lee CLEM-bah-ker)* — Daughter of the Jarl of Clehm.
OPHEDIA DEL ISHÉ *(Oh-FEE-DEE-ah del EE-shay)* — A new Black Sentinel and apprentice to Searn VeTurres.
PELLIAN NOSS *(PELL-ee-an NAH-ss)* — Paladin of the Hammer. Pater Minoris of the Piedala Fortress. Vow of Prayer. Dean Pellian Noss, Princep of this citadel.

PERRAH *(PEAR-ah)* — a Rancher.
PERÁT DE BOSCO *(Pear-att dee BOSS-co)* — Lord of the City of Boscólon.
ROMAB VOGLAIN *(Rome-abb Voeg-layn)* — Chalician Provost, the Grand Sacristan.
ROGVAN *(Roeg-vann)* — Duke of Ighali in Bortali.
SABELL PANZA *(Sabb-ell PAN-zah)* — Spy of Castenard.
SABINE UPONA *(sah-BEEN oo-POH-nah)* — Paladame of the Rose. Assistant to the Matriarch Superioris. Aspects of Humility and Discretion.
SÄLLA FYFE *(SAW-luh FIE-ff)* — A Black Sentinel.
SEARN VETURRES *(SURN Veh-TOOR-ez)* — Captain of the Black Sentinels.
SILAS MERUN *(SIGH-luss MARE-un)* — Paladin of the Hammer. Rank of Brother Paladin. Nichal Guess' Senechal.
SLATE *(SLATE)* — Paladin of the Hammer. Rank of Primus. Vow of Silence. Motean. Real name Yngver Morrin
STEVAN FILIP *(Ste-VAN FILL-ip)* — A Paladin almoner.
TERMIA DOMIC *(TER-mee-ah DAH-mic)* — A Black Sentinel Commander Domic, Black Knife of the Wardens.
TOIRE SIOBH *(tw-AHR shee-OHV)* — Shieldmaidens. Daughter of the Rhi of Bronue Jinre.
TOLVAN *(Toll-vahn)* — the Kam-Nasur residing over the Barad-Gasota.
TOMIZA CIRILAV *(Toe-EE-zah Seer-ih-lahv)* — a Crysalas from Old Zhig.
TYV *(Tivv)* — A Sleipnir purchased from a farmer. Suspected to have noble steed blood.
VALDEN DAKMOR *(Vaul-denn DAK-more)* — Son of Lowden Dakmor.
VATHAN EBITHAI *(Vah-thh-an Eb-ee-thy)* — Chalician from Sal-du-Markt.
VORE *(Vor)* — Sentinel Commander.
VUDUIN EB'GATHA *(Voo-doo-in eb GATH-ah)* — T'Akah. High Priestess of Crysania.
WAQUELON DÂJEAUX *(Wah-kell-on Dah-Jee-oh)* — the Mareschal, Provost of the Chalice.
WESKAR ABRAU *(WESS-kar AB-raoo)* — Provost of the Praetors of the Chalice. Known as the Catechist.
WHISPER *(WHISPER)* — A smaller black ynfald.
YANAS BRODIER *(YANN-ass BRO-dee-ehr)* — A Curate of

the Praetors of the Chalice.

YMBRYS VERONIA *(IM-brees Ver-OH-nee-ah)* — A qavyl spice merchant.

YULAN VORE *(YOO-lan VORR)* — A Black Sentinel Commander.

ZAPAS yu CARADADZ *(ZAH-PASS yoo CAR-ah-DAJ)* — A hrelgren map merchant.

ZEHAN OTEM *(ZAY-han OH-tem)* — Provost of the Order of the Chalice. Known also as the Enquêteur.

ZÜROK-TOVOT *(Zoo-rock TOE-Vott)* Champion of Kos-Yran. The Fear-Monger.

GLOSSARY 2

PANTHEON OF KALLATTAI

The Existence — *Maker of All* and *He That Is*. The world of Kallattai came into being at his word: BEGIN. He made first the two brother gods, and then the two sisters as their wives. Power was granted to them, and through them all was created, and the Existence was worshiped.

ABEN (*A-benn*) — *High King in Lomïn, the Ever-Day*. Made from a white star. His way is the Path. His Gray Watchers hold lanterns to guide those that seek the Path. His tenets are an Arrow, pointing the way to the green fields of Lomïn. The Chalice raised symbolizes his first domain, the sea. And from those depths the Ancient Ones sing.

WYV-THÜM (*WIHV THOOM*) — *The Three-Eyed Judge in Noccitan, the Ever-Night*. Brother to Aben, and formed by the Existence from the well of a black star. When he descended to his Realm of Noccitan he donned the title Thüm, or Judge.

CRYSANIA (*Cri-SAH-nee-ah*) — *Life Mother, Purity Resplendent, and Seamstress of the Future Tapestry* is wife to Aben. Only she can untangle the knots caused by time and see what the future holds. Her people are those that seek to protect the Dweol, the World-Roses that speak directly to her and one another, providing the Crysalas Integritas a chance to glance, ever briefly, at the Future.

SAKHARN (*Sa-KAHRN*) — *Wife to Wyv, Shepherdess of the Veld*—the Dreamscape from which the impossible is dreamed and made fact. She is the goddess of the Improbable, for she impossibly birthed the Deceiver without her husband to sire him.

THE CHILDREN OF ABEN AND CRYSANIA

LAE'ZEQ (*Lay-ZEK*) — *Firstborn of Aben, god of Wisdom, Curious One*. His people, the qavylli, follow his path into the depths of knowledge, for upon his own pages he wrote the secrets of life. Long has he now sojourned, seeking an answer to the prophecy that ties his fate to the death of his closest friend.

GRISSONE-ANKA (*Gri-ZOHN AHN-kha*) — *Twin-Souled, god of Faith*. As Grissone came of age his soul was two. The Anka, who soars above all and sees all, is joined to him. He was the creator of man, who abandoned Grissone to worship many. Now his loyal followers are few: the Paladins who seek protection of the people who no longer follow their god.

NIFARA (*NEE-FA-rah*) — *The Virgin of Justice, Soul Messenger, Once-Betrothed, Future Healer*. She learned to step between worlds from her once-betrothed, Kos-Yran, before he fell. She bears now the responsibility of that now-mad god, escorting souls between worlds they were never meant to set foot upon. Justice is her only concern, as she attempts to balance the scales perfectly.

KASNE et TERRAL (*Kaz-NEH et Teh-RAHL*) — *Prince of the Forest, Toucher of Souls*, Youngest of Aben and Crysania, Kasne strode from the forests that he had created, his people, the Minotyr on his heels. And yet it was he who agreed to leave his own people to take the enslaving Gren under his command, and from them came the Hrelgrens, touched by his hand, and blessed with a command of peace.

Andrew D Meredith
THE CHILDREN OF WYV AND SAKHARN

RIONNE (*Rye-OWN*) — *Firstborn of Wyv and Sakharn, Creator of Civilization, the Arbiter, The Fallen Warrior*—fallen to ruin when he was deceived by Achanerüt. Driven mad, he slew his greatest creations, and turned his own people into a scourge of the sky.

KEA'RINOUL (*Kee-AH-rih-NOOL*) — *The Scarred One, He-Who-Was-Beautiful.* Kea'Rinoul abandoned his own people, the Goranc, for he had been a god of beauty, marred by his fallen brothers. It is said he is a god who bathes in the blood of his followers, the T'Akai, wracked with torment by his own visage.

KOS-YRAN (*KOSS-EE-RAHN*) — *The Mad Gift-Giver, Once-Walker-Between-Worlds, Kashir Two-Gloves, the Walker.* Yet now he is banished to wander, gifting curses to those that seek him out. His own people, the vül, though small in number, are an infestation upon the civilized, sowing mayhem and destruction wherever they call home.

ACHANERÜT (*AH-ken-er-OOT*) — *The Deceiver, The Weaver, The Thirteen-Limbed One, Fatherless.* His thirteen limbs sow lies and weave dissension. His eyes see far, and bring kings to their knees. All that is in ruin is his attribute. All that is built up fears that he shall tear it down. The machinations of his web cannot be understood, even by the gods.

GLOSSARY 3

BLACK SENTINELS

The Black Sentinels are a mercenary organization in which each individual seeks out their own bodyguard contracts, and pays dues back to the organization, thus allowing them to wear their trademark black, peak-hooded cloak. They carry various weapons to denote their rank, which equates to their pay grade, hidden under their cloaks to keep their ability concealed.

BANDED CLUB — Initiate to the Black Sentinels carry a single club.

BLACK CLOAK — Officially marks their entry in the organization.

2ND CLUB — Sergeant rank. Common rate for their service is a full silver Baro a day in the northern nations.

HAND AXE — Lieutenants can negotiate a higher pay, armed with a more lethal weapon.

2ND AXE — 1st Lieutenants have several clients willing to give them a good reference.

CROSSBOW — Only by being promoted by the upper echelons can a Black Sentinel become a Captain.

BATTLE AXE — Commanders are rarely seen away from the Black Sentinels headquarters in Limae.

GLOSSARY 4

PALADINS OF THE HAMMER

The Paladins are the followers of Grissone, god of Faith. Each Paladin takes on one of the five active Vows. (The sixth vow, Introspection, or Blindness, is no longer taken.) The Paladins were founded in the Hrelgren Imperial Year 1111, the same year the T'Akai first appeared, launching attacks into what is now the Protectorate of Pariantür, (simultaneously against the Hrelgren Empire and Qavylli Republic.) Heeding Grissone's call, the seven apostles founded the Order, and peoples from every nation came to help them build Pariantür to defend against the T'Akai incursion. Many of the men who survived the war stayed on at Pariantür, joining the Order.

VOWS OF THE PALADINS

VOW OF PRAYER — Those that adopt this Vow ground themselves in the memorization of scripture, making the conscious effort to speak their inner thoughts directly to their god.

VOW OF POVERTY — Paladins are supported via family stipend or by their own trade. Paladins who take this vow perform additional duty to pay for their room and board and they may not keep personal items.

VOW OF CHASTITY — Those that take this Vow are forbidden from marrying. Many avoid contact with members of the opposite sex entirely.

VOW OF PACIFISM — Paladins who take this Vow never raise their hammer against another, seeking peace by any other means.

DREAD KNIGHT

VOW OF SILENCE — Brothers who take this Vow do not speak another word for the rest of their lives, instead communicating through their hands. These brothers also give up their surnames as their founder, Sternovis did.

VOW OF BLINDNESS — This Vow is no longer taken. Those that did bound their eyes away from the world.

HOLDINGS OF THE HAMMER

The Paladins live in communities of two or more brothers and their monasteries are scattered across the world, having different sizes and designations.

BASTIONS
A least two Paladins stationed at a bastion at any given time. Can be as high as twenty-five. Most major cities and towns have a bastion and many are raised at intervals along long stretches of road between cities.

FORTRESSES
Commanding local bastons, a fortress houses upward of one hundred Paladins.

CITADELS
There are four Citadels. Each commands a network of Fortresses and Bastions.

PARIANTÜR — Pariantür is the head of the entire order and acts as guardian over the eastern lands known as the Protectorate of the Hammer. Over half of the entire order is stationed there— over seven thousand Paladins. There is enough space to house over ten thousand Paladins if necessary. The Paladames have over three-thousand sisters stationed at Pariantür.

ST. HAMUL — This citadel holds sway over the Order in the eastern nations of Ganthic. Nearly five hundred brothers are stationed there.

THE AERIE — Located in the country of Limae, the Aerie has nearly four hundred brothers stationed there. Commands Northwestern Ganthic fortresses and bastions.

AMMAR — Located in Ormach, Ammar Citadel has over one thousand Paladins stationed there. While this citadel controls the fewest Fortresses and Bastions, it boasts one of the greatest human libraries outside of Pariantür.

ANDREW D MEREDITH

RANKS OF THE HAMMER

Those seeking admittance to the Order of the Hammer begin as either:

ACOLYTE — Individual who seeks out Pariantür to become a Paladin.

PENITENT — Individual who has chosen servitude over imprisonment or worse.

These lower level Acolytes and Penitents are grouped together and don brown robes and shaving their heads. They act as servants to the Hammer at Pariantür while learning to live as a Paladin.

ESTUDIATE — Having learned the Rule of St. Ikhail, Estudiates lives a life of routine and constant change as they are tested in various occupations over the course of a year. During this time they will review each Vow, and come to a decision regarding which Vow they will take. This decision marks their graduation to Neophyte.

NEOPHYTE — Having taken on a vow, the Neophyte begins study under a master in their chosen or assigned trade. They are given their hammer, which is chained to their belt by the twenty-two links, and they are given the Vow-Bead which will hang from their belt until they receive cordons.

Vow of Chastity — Haloed Hammer
Vow of Poverty — Stylized Pattern
Vow of Silence — Tower
Vow of Pacifism — Shield
Vow of Prayer — Anka's Wing
Vow of Blindness — Simple Band

PALADIN — When the Neophyte is given their armor, they are officially called a Paladin, but in name only. It is only if they proceed past this level that they will be considered a true Paladin by the Brotherhood. They have a single year to test as a Journeyman in their field if they wish to proceed. If they do not master their chosen profession, they will wait anywhere from five to ten years before being allowed to test once more.

DREAD KNIGHT

BROTHER PALADIN — If deemed worthy, a Paladin is given the red cordons, marking them both a Master in their trade, and a Brother Paladin. Full member of the Brotherhood with full rights to vote on all matters. If leadership requires they move to a new trade, they will learn from and proceed through the same lessons and trials, however, nothing can take their rank of Brother Paladin from them.

BROTHER EXCELSIOR — Brother Excelsiors are the equivalent to a lieutenant, commanding brothers of lower rank, marked by green cordons. Quite often they are true experts or specialists in their assigned trade. A Brother Excelsior in the Smithy might be an expert at metal inlays. A baker might specialize in selecting and negotiating superior ingredients.

BROTHER ADJUTANT — Marked by white cordons, there is rarely more than a single Brother Adjutant in any occupation at a single location. They often fill vacant leadership roles when a higher rank is not present. This rank is also considered the first "true" leadership rank.

BROTHER PRIMUS — Leaders and masters, the black-cordoned Primus commands respect and authority. Primuses often hold the highest rank at Fortresses.

PATER MINORIS — A Paladin will rarely rise to this rank without there being a vacancy. Each Citadel is led by one, and many fortresses have a Pater Minoris stationed there as leader. There is a Pater Minoris representing each Vow stationed at Pariantür. Besides wearing gold cordons, their armor is also often adorned with symbology reflective of the long traditions of a Citadel. The five Pater Minorii stationed at Pariantür fill very important roles in the community.
- Pater Minoris of Prayer Hiram van Höllebon, Chaplain to Pariantür
- Pater Minoris of Poverty Mason Diggle, Keeper of Fealty
- Pater Minoris of Chastity Pol Dunkirk, Hospitaler
- Pater Minoris of Silence Daveth, Grandmaster Smith
- Pater Minoris of Pacifism Klous Girard, Groundskeeper

PATER SEGUNDUS — Under the Prima Pater rules a council of four Pater Segundii, each representing a different Vow. They are marked by blue cordons and their words hold nearly as much authority as the Prima Pater himself.
- Pater Segundus of Poverty Nichal Guess, Pariantür's Castellan
- Pater Segundus of Pacifism Gallahan Pír, Master Scribe
- Pater Segundus of Silence Athmor, Master Cellarer
- Pater Segundus of Chastity Agapius Emiro, Sacrist

PRIMA PATER — There is only one Prima Pater. A Prima Pater's armor is crafted to match the motifs and symbols of the founding saint of their Vow. When a Prima Pater's rank is passed on, one of the Pater Segundii under him will take on the role, donning armor of their own figurehead saint, thus ensuring that another Vow takes the helm.

GLOSSARY 5

THE CRYSALAS SOCIETAS

Followers of Crysania are known collectively as the Members of the Crysalas Societas. This includes women of the secret Vaults, known as the Crysalas Integritas, Paladames of the Rose known officially as the Crysalas Honoris, the Shieldmaidens of Boroni and Bronte, and several smaller factions of female qavylli and hrelgrens who have chosen to follow Crysania. All of these Societas meet in secret Vaults across the world of Kallattai, guarding prophecies gathered from the Dweol and each other.

Centuries ago, the Church of Aben long ago and went further into hiding. The majority of the Crysalas fled to Pariantür, where they formed the Crysalas Honoris, known as Paladame. This formation tricked down over time to changing the nature of the Crysalas Vaults to guarding women from predatory men and political leveraging.

ASPECTS OF PURITY

Across the entire organization members of the Crysalas take on Aspects of purity, rather than Vows as Paladins do. Some of these have been around since the foundation while others have developed over time. Most sisters take on an average of three Aspects, though some take on more. They are noted publicly by adornments, which creates a general customized look among the sisters who otherwise wear only white robes and headdresses. These Aspects fall into four categories:

BLOSSOM — Purity of Form
THORN — Purity of Choice
LEAF — Purity of Service
ROOT — Purity of Function

ASPECTS OF THE BLOSSOM

ASPECT OF CLEANLINESS — *(Shaven Head)* This Aspect focuses on a ritualistic and meticulous cleaning regimen.

ASPECT OF SILENCE — *(Veil)* Wears a veil over their face so they cannot be seen. They are not completely silent, talking in quiet whispers. Sisters of this aspect experience an aloneness that others naturally give them.

ASPECT OF VIRGINITY — *(Gilded Rose)* Women who select this Aspect are forbidden to marry. While most Crysalas do not marry, they are not forbidden from doing so as these sisters are.

ASPECT OF PEACE — *(Wooden Mace)* Sisters who take this Aspect vow to cause no harm to another.

ASPECT OF STRICTNESS — *(Solid Plate on Shoulder)* — Sisters who take this Aspect have no choice over their diet. They must eat what they are served, and may not leave any of it untouched, nor ask for more when the meal is concluded.

ASPECTS OF THE THORN

(It is often frowned upon that any sister take more than one Thorn Aspect, as each is known to be stringent and difficult.)

ASPECT OF SANCTITY — *(Gloves)* Sisters who take on the Aspect of Sanctity do not feel the touch of another save through their gloves.

ASPECT OF SOLITUDE — *(Fetter Hat)* The fetter hat is a very recognizable adornment. It forces the wearer to look towards their feet at all times.

ASPECT OF SOLEMNITY — *(Black Circlet)* One of the harder Aspects to master, the Aspect of Solemnity allows no outward emotion.

ASPECT OF PRESERVATION — *(Leaves—no roses on uniform)* Those who take this Aspect may not eat any meat.

ASPECT OF ST. KLARE — *(Thorn Necklace)* This Aspect was developed when members of the Aspect of Preservation employed a work-around for abstinence from meat via excess drink. St. Klare developed a variant that was ascetic, allowing eating only breads, insects, water, and some fruits and vegetables.

DREAD KNIGHT

ASPECTS OF THE LEAF

ASPECT OF DISCRETION — (*Rose Earrings*) This Aspect requires a sister to listen intently to others without interrupting.

ASPECT OF CHARITY — (*Brown Robe*) The Charitable Sisters are very often found matched with the Paladins who take on the Vow of Poverty.

ASPECT OF COMPASSION — (*Dwov Elbow Guards*) These sisters are required to serve those with needs that can be met.

ASPECT OF OBEDIENCE — (*Bell Earrings*) The Aspect of Obedience is not a slaving Aspect, but one that allows one to be congenial, and helpful as requested.

ASPECT OF DIGNITY — (*Bound Sleeves*) — Those sisters who practice this Aspect seek to restore the dignity of those that are ailing or are elderly.

ASPECTS OF THE ROOT

ASPECT OF HUMILITY — (*Heavy Boots*) — The menial, janitorial tasks of a sister of the Aspect of Humility keep the order continuing as they do what no one else wants.

ASPECT OF CLARITY — (*Scroll Front Cloth*) Those sisters with a knack for memory, or wish to develop such a gift take on this Aspect. They are constantly testing one another with the recitation of verse.

ASPECT OF HONOR — (*Thorn Spiked Mace*) Of all the Aspects, this is the most practiced among the Paladames at Pariantür. While they do not go out on patrol against the T'Akai, they act as guards at all the hidden Vaults across Ganthic.

ASPECT OF FORM — (*Plain Bracers*) The Aspect of Form practiced hand to hand techniques, to grapple and contain opponents.

ASPECT OF FUNCTION — (*Utility Belt*) Those that seek to master an art or craft will take on this Aspect and delve as deeply as they can into their art.

GLOSSARY 6

MONKS OF NIFARA

The Monastic Order of the Staff, or the Monks of Nifara as they are more commonly known, are perhaps the oldest religious organization on Kallattai, and make up the sole followers of Nifara. While the largest community of monks are humans, Nifarans can be found in every race on Kallattai. Their purpose is to offer judgment between two arguing parties. They rule fairly, impartially, and quickly. Some deem their judgments too harsh, but this is tempered by their consistency. When a monk of Nifara is addressed, the correct honorific in the lands of man is Nefer. This is said to be a very old title, dating back to an older name for Nifara, Nefereh. When a judgment is made, a stick is broken, and given to each side of the argument, in memoriam. Nine times a judgment has been made that was deemed world-shifting. When that occurred, the monk broke not a stick, but their staff. These nine are honored above all others, with statuary made in their likeness at the Templum of Nifara in Birin. While there are many myths surrounding the Nine Saints, the most interesting fact is that none of their tales reference how they died.

GLOSSARY 7

PRAETORS OF THE CHALICE

Until recently, the Church of the Common Chalice has remained an isolationist branch of the Abecinian Church, remaining in nearly total isolation in Œron.

The military arm of the church is known as the Praetors of the Chalice, and bear some similarities to the Order of the Hammer, in that they built their organizational ranks loosely off their Eastern rivals. The learned class is open to all members of the Church of the Common Chalice who purchase a seat at the university, however, anyone not of Œronzi heritage will rarely rise to rank of Praetor. Exceptions have been made.

Those seeking admittance to the Order of the Chalice begin as an:

ACOLYTE — When sufficient training has occurred to indoctrinate the Acolyte, they rise to the role of level of Etudiant.

ETUDIANT — The Etudiant lives a life of routine and constant change as they are tested on various subjects. This is generally a ten year training.

PRAETOR – To be a Praetor is equivalent to a Paladin Excelsior. This provides them with a graduating rank above that of most Paladins.

CHAMBERLAIN – Equivalent of the Brother Adjutant, but considered first among the Lay.

CURATE – Equivalent of a Primus. Considered the first of the Leadership ranks. Generally those of Curate rank hold lands. Assigned holdings are treated as owing allegiance to the church, and not the country in which they are located.

PREFECT – Equivalent of a Pater Minoris. It is believed that there are three to five Prefects serving each Provost.

PROVOST – Equivalent of a Pater Segundus. There are an unknown number of Provosts. A Praetor can only be made Provost by agreement between Praeposit and Benefactor. And it is from the Provosts that the Benefactor chooses replacements for Praeposit.

PRAEPOSIT – Equivalent of the Prima Pater of the Hammer.

BENEFACTOR – Head of the Church of the Common Chalice. Considered a living prophet.

GLOSSARY 8

WARDENS OF THE AXE

Recently established in the City of Haven, the Wardens of the Axe are made up primarily of Paladins of the Hammer who have cast aside their faith in Grissone, and sought instead to establish a secular order. Most if not all of them adopt the Motean Philosophy, that believes that the gods who grant power to mortals gift them a mote of power that can be harnessed and used in perpetuity.

The Moteans conducted studies under three Brotherhoods: the Feather, the Bell, and the Gauntlet. Harnessing use of skyfall metal, the Feather discovered that one could lock a portion of their soul, or shade, into a quill and then with blood, a book, preventing them from ever truly dying. The Bell discovered that resonant bells of skyfall allow focus, and a cutting off of the rest of the world. Through that they also developed hammers and orbs. When struck by other skyfall, their resonance rises to the point of explosion. The Gauntlet studied older skyfall relics such as axes (sharp axe edges mounted into normal steel) that hold razor's edges that never dull. They also made a study of the Dreadplate armor, but only unlocked a single gauntlet's ability, to control those under the influence of skyfall-minted coins worn or consumed.

The Wardens are now a unified Motean sect, having absorbed the Black Sentinel organization.

WARDEN TIERS

SENTINEL — These still follow the old Sentinel ranks, save that when you reach Captain, a Sentinel must stay a Captain in perpetuity, being given skyfall crossbowbolts, or join the Wardens.

VIGILANT — Vigilants are the primary Warden tier. Anyone who becomes a Warden (the first rank of Vigilant) and those above, are all collectively referred to as Wardens (as all Paladins are referred to as Paladins).

    WARDEN — When a Sentinel becomes a Warden, they are given their skyfall Black Axe. (The steel of the axe is boot-blackened to match the skyfall edge.)

    CENTURION — The Warden leadership's goal is to have only one Centurion to every one hundred Wardens. Currently most former Paladins of Excelsior or Adjutant Rank hold this rank. They're given a skyfall orb.

GUARDIAN — The Leadership/Officer Class of Warden generally regard each other as equals. A Guardian's domain is their kingdom. A higher ranking Warden who comes as guest to any Guardian's domain is considered subservient in rank to the domain ruler.

    MAGISTER — Former Paladins of Primus took this rank. These are the de-facto leaders over lower-ranked Wardens. This rank unlocks access to skyfall tools.

    DEAN — Warden Deans are considered equal to one another. When they gather, they stand on equal footing for decisions made by democratic council.

OTHER TITLES

    PRINCEPS — A Princep is the local Warden ruler of a domain or fortress. Dean Pellian Noss is the Princep of Haven, so all Wardens in Haven answer to him in questions of rule.

    PERSONAL TITLES – Wardens have also started to take on descriptive titles, in the tradition of Moteans calling themselves names such as Cup or Talon. They bear no authority with the title, but it may give a glimpse into their personality.

Afterword

When I began writing *Dread Knight* I had a general idea where I'd be starting and where it might end, but not entirely sure how the threads would come together in a way that satisfied myself and would satisfy you, the reader. I'm pleasantly surprised with the resolution. It ends, interestingly enough, similarly to the way the original version of this story did: on a high tower. Some tropes you can't break free of. I might not be a massive fan of dragons, but a battle with a wizard (or three) at the top of a tower with nothing but the horizon to see in every direction is stuck in my psyche. So here we are. The end of an era, as it were. *Dread Knight* closes up all the loops I wanted, and left some threads for the upcoming stories I plan to tell.

Thank you for sticking with me this far. There is more to tell, and I can't wait to revisit the world of Kallattai in the coming years.

If you're able to spread the word to others, please do, both in reviews and over coffee with your reader friends. That's really the best way for anyone to find my books. I can holler out until I'm hoarse. But you, you are how friends and family find me.

—Andrew D Meredith

ANDREW D MEREDITH

And to all those that contributed to the Kickstarter bringing this book and hard covers for all four of the Kallattian Saga books to life, thank you!

Alex Fergus — Alexandra Corrsin — Andrew Mattocks
Ben Nichols — Ben White — Benjamin Kahn — Bill Adams
Catie Rizzo — Cat Mckinney — Chase McGlinchey — Chris
Chris Cousino — Craig Meredith — Daniel Hardez
David Holzborn — Deborah Torrance — Derek Bailey
Derek Gorny — Dewey Conway — Diane Meredith-Gordon
EJ B — Elizabeth Illyia-Noelle Allen — Elzabeth Sayed Ahmad
Emma Adams — Heather Cooper — Hugo Essink — Irinel Finco
Jan Berčič — Jared Leys — Jeff McIntyre — Jessica
Jennifer 'Bidlingmeyer' Osterman —Jessie Rizzo
John McMasters — Josefine Fouarge — Kayla Yetman
Lee Schenkel — Lydia Pierce — Major Havoc — Mark Meredith
Matej Michňák — Mathias Blikstad — Michael Dubost
Michael Hunter — Michael Sugarman — Michael
Nick Chamillard — Nicolas Lobotsky — Niko Salazzo
Orangutank — Paul Hijmans — Pete Wagar — Phil Wallace
Quinn Giguiere — Rebecca Writz — Renae Meredith
Richard Nimmons — Rocco Levitas — Ross O'Dell
Ross Watson — Ryan Hacala — Sara Lawson — Scotte Meredith
Scott A. Widener — Sean — Sean Robinson — SongOfInsanity
Starcy — steve — Sue Rizzo — Susanne Daniels — Teague Tozier
Thomas K. Carpenter — Thomas Sanchez — Timothy Wolff
Todd Harris — Tori Tecken — Varsha Ganesh
Z. R. McCormick — Z.S. Diamanti

To the Long Road Ahead and Straight!

—Andrew D Meredith

ABOUT THE AUTHOR

Andrew D Meredith's journey has taken him to many fantastical places. From selling books in the wilds of western Washington to designing and publishing board games for *Fantasy Flight Games/Asmodee*. He's now committed to the quest he was called to so long ago: the telling of fantastical tales, and bringing to life underestimated characters willing to take on the responsibilities no one else will.

AndrewDMeredith.com

@AndrewDMth

Andrew D Meredith

DREAD KNIGHT

600

www.ingramcontent.com/pod-product-compliance
Lightning Source LLC
LaVergne TN
LVHW041736060526
838201LV00046B/827